Quatermain

Quatermain

The Complete Adventures: 3

Child of Storm

★

Allan and the Holy Flower

H. Rider Haggard

Quatermain : the Complete Adventures: 3—
Child of Storm & Allan and the Holy Flower
by H. Rider Haggard

Leonaur is an imprint of Oakpast Ltd

ISBN: 978-1-84677-596-3 (hardcover)
ISBN: 978-1-84677-595-6 (softcover)

http://www.leonaur.com

Publisher's Notes

The views expressed in this book are not necessarily those of the publisher.

Publisher's Note

Suggested reading sequence for the Allan Quatermain stories:

1 Marie
2 Child of Storm
3 Allans Wife
4 A Tale of Three Lions
5 Maiwas Revenge
6 Hunter Quartermains Story
7 Long Odds
8 Allan and the Holy Flower
9 Heu Heu or the Monster
10 She and Allan
11 Treasure of the Lake
12 The Ivory Child
13 Finished
14 Magepa the Buck
15 King Solomon's Mines
16 The Ancient Allan
17 Allan and the Ice Gods
18 Allan Quartermain

Contents

Child of Storm 7

Allan and the Holy Flower 217

Child of Storm

Dedication

Dear Mr. Stuart,

For twenty years, I believe I am right in saying, you, as Assistant Secretary for Native Affairs in Natal, and in other offices, have been intimately acquainted with the Zulu people. Moreover, you are one of the few living men who have made a deep and scientific study of their language, their customs and their history. So I confess that I was the more pleased after you were so good as to read this tale—the second book of the epic of the vengeance of Zikali, *the Thing-that-should-never-have-been-born*, and of the fall of the House of Senzangakona—when you wrote to me that it was animated by the true Zulu spirit.

I must admit that my acquaintance with this people dates from a period which closed almost before your day. What I know of them I gathered at the time when Cetewayo, of whom my volume tells, was in his glory, previous to the evil hour in which he found himself driven by the clamour of his regiments, cut off, as they were, through the annexation of the Transvaal, from their hereditary trade of war, to match himself against the British strength. I learned it all by personal observation in the 'seventies, or from the lips of the great Shepstone, my chief and friend, and from my colleagues Osborn, Fynney, Clarke and others, every one of them long since "gone down."

Perhaps it may be as well that this is so, at any rate in the case of one who desires to write of the Zulus as a reigning nation, which now they have ceased to be, and to try to show them as they were, in all their superstitious madness and bloodstained grandeur.

Yet then they had virtues as well as vices. To serve their Country in arms, to die for it and for the King; such was their primitive ideal. If they were fierce they were loyal, and feared neither wounds nor doom; if they listened to the dark *redes* of the witch-doctor, the trumpet-call of duty sounded still louder in their ears; if, chanting their terrible

Ingoma, at the King's bidding they went forth to slay unsparingly, at least they were not mean or vulgar. From those who continually must face the last great issues of life or death meanness and vulgarity are far removed. These qualities belong to the safe and crowded haunts of civilised men, not to the *kraals* of Bantu savages, where, at any rate of old, they might be sought in vain.

Now everything is changed, or so I hear, and doubtless in the balance this is best. Still we may wonder what are the thoughts that pass through the mind of some ancient warrior of Chaka's or Dingaan's time, as he suns himself crouched on the ground, for example, where once stood the royal *kraal*, Duguza, and watches men and women of the Zulu blood passing homeward from the cities or the mines, bemused, some of them, with the white man's smuggled liquor, grotesque with the white man's cast-off garments, hiding, perhaps, in their blankets examples of the white man's doubtful photographs—and then shuts his sunken eyes and remembers the plumed and kilted regiments making that same ground shake as, with a thunder of salute, line upon line, company upon company, they rushed out to battle.

Well, because the latter does not attract me, it is of this former time that I have tried to write—the time of the *Impis* and the witch-finders and the rival princes of the royal House—as I am glad to learn from you, not quite in vain. Therefore, since you, so great an expert, approve of my labours in the seldom-travelled field of Zulu story, I ask you to allow me to set your name upon this page and subscribe myself,

Gratefully and sincerely yours,

H. Rider Haggard
Ditchingham
12th October, 1912

To James Stuart, Esq.
Late Assistant Secretary for Native Affairs, Natal.

Author's Note

Mr. Allan Quatermain's story of the wicked and fascinating Mameena, a kind of Zulu Helen, has, it should be stated, a broad foundation in historical fact. Leaving Mameena and her wiles on one side, the tale of the struggle between the Princes Cetewayo and Umbelazi for succession to the throne of Zululand is true.

When the differences between these sons of his became intolerable, because of the tumult which they were causing in his country, King Panda, their father, the son of Senzangakona, and the brother of the great Chaka and of Dingaan, who had ruled before him, did say that "when two young bulls quarrel they had better fight it out." So, at least, I was told by the late Mr. F. B. Fynney, my colleague at the time of the annexation of the Transvaal in 1877, who, as Zulu Border Agent, with the exceptions of the late Sir Theophilus Shepstone and the late Sir Melmoth Osborn, perhaps knew more of that land and people than anyone else of his period.

As a result of this hint given by a maddened king, the great battle of the Tugela was fought at Endondakusuka in December, 1856, between the Usutu party, commanded by Cetewayo, and the adherents of Umbelazi the Handsome, his brother, who was known among the Zulus as Indhlovu-ene-Sihlonti, or the Elephant with the tuft of hair, from a little lock of hair which grew low down upon his back.

My friend, Sir Melmoth Osborn, who died in or about the year 1897, was present at this battle, although not as a combatant. Well do I remember his thrilling story, told to me over thirty years ago, of the events of that awful day.

Early in the morning, or during the previous night, I forget which, he swam his horse across the Tugela and hid with it in a bush-clad kopje, blindfolding the animal with his coat lest it should betray him. As it chanced, the great fight of the day, that of the regiment of veterans, which Sir Melmoth informed me Panda had sent down at the last moment to the assistance of Umbelazi, his favourite son, took place almost at the foot of this kopje. Mr. Quatermain, in his narrative, calls this regiment the Amawombe, but my recollection is that the name Sir Melmoth Osborn gave them was the Greys or *Upunga*.

Whatever their exact title may have been, however, they made a great stand. At least, he told me that when Umbelazi's *impi*, or army, began to give before the Usutu onslaught, these Greys moved forward above 3,000 strong, drawn up in a triple line, and were charged by one of Cetewayo's regiments. The opposing forces met, and the noise of their clashing shields, said Sir Melmoth, was like the roll of heavy thunder. Then, while he watched, the veteran Greys passed over the opposing regiment "as a wave passes over a rock"—these were his exact words—and, leaving about a third of their number dead or wounded among the bodies of the annihilated foe, charged on to meet a second regiment sent against them by Cetewayo. With these the struggle was repeated, but again the Greys conquered. Only now there were not more than five or six hundred of them left upon their feet.

These survivors ran to a mound, round which they formed a ring, and here for a long while withstood the attack of a third regiment, until at length they perished almost to a man, buried beneath heaps of their slain assailants, the Usutu. Truly they made a noble end fighting thus against tremendous odds! As for the number who fell at this battle of Endondakusuka, Mr. Fynney, in a pamphlet which he wrote, says that six of Umbelazi's brothers died, "whilst it is estimated that upwards of 100,000 of the people—men, women and children—were slain"—a high and indeed an impossible estimate.

That curious personage named John Dunn, an Englishman who became a Zulu chief, and who actually fought in this battle, as narrated by Mr. Quatermain, however, puts the number much lower. What the true total was will never be known; but Sir Melmoth Osborn told me that when he swam his horse back across the Tugela that night it was black with bodies; and Sir Theophilus Shepstone also told me that when he visited the scene a day or two later the banks of the river were strewn with multitudes of them, male and female.

It was from Mr. Fynney that I heard the story of the execution by Cetewayo of the man who appeared before him with the ornaments of Umbelazi, announcing that he had killed the prince with his own hand. Of course, this tale, as Mr. Quatermain points out, bears a striking resemblance to that recorded in the Old Testament in connection with the death of King Saul.

It by no means follows, however, that it is therefore apocryphal; indeed, Mr. Fynney assured me that it was quite true, although, if he gave me his authorities, I cannot remember them after a lapse of more than thirty years.

The exact circumstances of Umbelazi's death are unknown, but the general report was that he died, not by the *assegais* of the Usutu, but of a broken heart. Another story declares that he was drowned. His body was never found, and it is therefore probable that it sank in the Tugela, as is suggested in the following pages.

I have only to add that it is quite in accordance with Zulu beliefs that a man should be haunted by the ghost of one whom he has murdered or betrayed, or, to be more accurate, that the spirit (*umoya*) should enter into the slayer and drive him mad. Or, in such a case, that spirit might bring misfortune upon him, his family, or his tribe.

H. Rider Haggard

Chapter 1

Allan Quatermain Hears of Mameena

We white people think that we know everything. For instance, we think that we understand human nature. And so we do, as human nature appears to us, with all its trappings and accessories seen dimly through the glass of our conventions, leaving out those aspects of it which we have forgotten or do not think it polite to mention. But I, Allan Quatermain, reflecting upon these matters in my ignorant and uneducated fashion, have always held that no one really understands human nature who has not studied it in the rough. Well, that is the aspect of it with which I have been best acquainted.

For most of the years of my life I have handled the raw material, the virgin ore, not the finished ornament that is smelted out of it—if, indeed, it is finished yet, which I greatly doubt. I dare say that a time may come when the perfected generations—if Civilisation, as we understand it, really has a future and any such should be allowed to enjoy their hour on the World—will look back to us as crude, half-developed creatures whose only merit was that we handed on the flame of life.

Maybe, maybe, for everything goes by comparison; and at one end of the ladder is the ape-man, and at the other, as we hope, the angel. No, not the angel; he belongs to a different sphere, but that last expression of humanity upon which I will not speculate. While man is man—that is, before he suffers the magical death-change into spirit, if such should be his destiny—well, he will remain man. I mean that the same passions will sway him; he will aim at the same ambitions; he will know the same joys and be oppressed by the same fears, whether he lives in a *Kafir* hut or in a golden palace; whether he walks upon his two feet or, as for aught I know he may do one day, flies through the air. This is certain: that in the flesh he can never escape from our atmosphere, and while he breathes it, in the main with some variations prescribed by climate, local law and religion, he will do much as his forefathers did for countless ages.

That is why I have always found the savage so interesting, for in him, nakedly and forcibly expressed, we see those eternal principles which direct our human destiny.

To descend from these generalities, that is why also I, who hate writing, have thought it worth while, at the cost of some labour to myself, to occupy my leisure in what to me is a strange land—for although I was born in England, it is not my country—in setting down various experiences of my life that do, in my opinion, interpret this our universal nature. I dare say that no one will ever read them; still, perhaps they are worthy of record, and who knows? In days to come they may fall into the hands of others and prove of value. At any rate, they are true stories of interesting peoples, who, if they should survive in the savage competition of the nations, probably are doomed to undergo great changes. Therefore I tell of them before they began to change.

Now, although I take it out of its strict chronological order, the first of these histories that I wish to preserve is in the main that of an extremely beautiful woman—with the exception of a certain Nada, called the Lily, of whom I hope to speak some day, I think the most beautiful that ever lived among the Zulus. Also she was, I think, the most able, the most wicked, and the most ambitious. Her attractive name—for it was very attractive as the Zulus said it, especially those of them who were in love with her—was Mameena, daughter of Umbezi. Her other name was Child of Storm (Ingane-ye-Sipepo, or, more freely and shortly, O-we-Zulu), but the word *Ma-meena* had its origin in the sound of the wind that wailed about the hut when she was born.[1]

Since I have been settled in England I have read—of course in a translation—the story of Helen of Troy, as told by the Greek poet, Homer. Well, Mameena reminds me very much of Helen, or, rather, Helen reminds me of Mameena. At any rate, there was this in common between them, although one of them was black, or, rather, copper-coloured, and the other white—they both were lovely; moreover, they both were faithless, and brought men by hundreds to their deaths. There, perhaps, the resemblance ends, since Mameena had much more fire and grit than Helen could boast, who, unless Homer misrepresents her, must have been but a poor thing after all. Beauty Itself, which those old rascals of Greek gods made use of to bait their snares set for the lives and honour of men, such was Helen, no more; that is, as I understand her, who have not had the advantage of a classical edu-

1. The Zulu word "Meena"—or more correctly "Mina"—means "Come here," and would therefore be a name not unsuitable to one of the heroine's proclivities; but Mr. Quatermain does not seem to accept this interpretation.—*Editor*

cation. Now, Mameena, although she was superstitious—a common weakness of great minds—acknowledging no gods in particular, as we understand them, set her own snares, with varying success but a very definite object, namely, that of becoming the first woman in the world as she knew it—the stormy, bloodstained world of the Zulus.

But the reader shall judge for himself, if ever such a person should chance to cast his eye upon this history.

It was in the year 1854 that I first met Mameena, and my acquaintance with her continued off and on until 1856, when it came to an end in a fashion that shall be told after the fearful battle of the Tugela in which Umbelazi, Panda's son and Cetewayo's brother—who, to his sorrow, had also met Mameena—lost his life. I was still a youngish man in those days, although I had already buried my second wife, as I have told elsewhere, after our brief but happy time of marriage.

Leaving my boy in charge of some kind people in Durban, I started into "the Zulu"—a land with which I had already become well acquainted as a youth, there to carry on my wild life of trading and hunting.

For the trading I never cared much, as may be guessed from the little that ever I made out of it, the art of traffic being in truth repugnant to me. But hunting was always the breath of my nostrils—not that I am fond of killing creatures, for any humane man soon wearies of slaughter. No, it is the excitement of sport, which, before breechloaders came in, was acute enough, I can assure you; the lonely existence in wild places, often with only the sun and the stars for companions; the continual adventures; the strange tribes with whom I came in contact; in short, the change, the danger, the hope always of finding something great and new, that attracted and still attracts me, even now when I *have* found the great and the new. There, I must not go on writing like this, or I shall throw down my pen and book a passage for Africa, and incidentally to the next world, no doubt—that world of the great and new!

It was, I think, in the month of May in the year 1854 that I went hunting in rough country between the White and Black Umvolosi Rivers, by permission of Panda—whom the Boers had made king of Zululand after the defeat and death of Dingaan his brother. The district was very feverish, and for this reason I had entered it in the winter months. There was so much bush that, in the total absence of roads, I thought it wise not to attempt to bring my wagons down, and as no horses would live in that *veld* I went on foot. My principal companions were a *Kafir* of mixed origin, called Sikauli, commonly abbreviated into Scowl, the Zulu chief Saduko, and a headman of the

Undwandwe blood named Umbezi, at whose *kraal* on the high land about thirty miles away I left my wagon and certain of my men in charge of the goods and some ivory that I had traded.

This Umbezi was a stout and genial-mannered man of about sixty years of age, and, what is rare among these people, one who loved sport for its own sake. Being aware of his tastes, also that he knew the country and was skilled in finding game, I had promised him a gun if he would accompany me and bring a few hunters. It was a particularly bad gun that had seen much service, and one which had an unpleasing habit of going off at half-cock; but even after he had seen it, and I in my honesty had explained its weaknesses, he jumped at the offer.

"O Macumazana" (that is my native name, often abbreviated into Macumazahn, which means *one who stands out*, or as many interpret it, I don't know how, *watcher-by-night*)—"a gun that goes off sometimes when you do not expect it is much better than no gun at all, and you are a chief with a great heart to promise it to me, for when I own the White Man's weapon I shall be looked up to and feared by everyone between the two rivers."

Now, while he was speaking he handled the gun, that was loaded, observing which I moved behind him. Off it went in due course, its recoil knocking him backwards—for that gun was a devil to kick—and its bullet cutting the top off the ear of one of his wives. The lady fled screaming, leaving a little bit of her ear upon the ground.

"What does it matter?" said Umbezi, as he picked himself up, rubbing his shoulder with a rueful look. "Would that the evil spirit in the gun had cut off her tongue and not her ear! It is the Worn-out-Old-Cow's own fault; she is always peeping into everything like a monkey. Now she will have something to chatter about and leave my things alone for awhile. I thank my ancestral Spirit it was not Mameena, for then her looks would have been spoiled."

"Who is Mameena?" I asked. "Your last wife?"

"No, no, Macumazahn; I wish she were, for then I should have the most beautiful wife in the land. She is my daughter, though not that of the Worn-out-Old-Cow; her mother died when she was born, on the night of the Great Storm. You should ask Saduko there who Mameena is," he added with a broad grin, lifting his head from the gun, which he was examining gingerly, as though he thought it might go off again while unloaded, and nodding towards someone who stood behind him.

I turned, and for the first time saw Saduko, whom I recognised at once as a person quite out of the ordinary run of natives.

He was a tall and magnificently formed young man, who, although his breast was scarred with *assegai* wounds, showing that he was a warrior, had not yet attained to the honour of the "ring" of polished wax laid over strips of rush bound round with sinew and sewn to the hair, the *isicoco* which at a certain age or dignity, determined by the king, Zulus are allowed to assume. But his face struck me more even than his grace, strength and stature. Undoubtedly it was a very fine face, with little or nothing of the negroid type about it; indeed, he might have been a rather dark-coloured Arab, to which stock he probably threw back. The eyes, too, were large and rather melancholy, and in his reserved, dignified air there was something that showed him to be no common fellow, but one of breeding and intellect.

"*Siyakubona*" (that is, "we see you," *anglice* "good morrow") "Saduko," I said, eyeing him curiously. "Tell me, who is Mameena?"

"*Inkoosi*," he answered in his deep voice, lifting his delicately shaped hand in salutation, a courtesy that pleased me who, after all, was nothing but a white hunter, "*Inkoosi*, has not her father said that she is his daughter?"

"Aye," answered the jolly old Umbezi, "but what her father has not said is that Saduko is her lover, or, rather, would like to be. Wow! Saduko," he went on, shaking his fat finger at him, "are you mad, man, that you think a girl like that is for you? Give me a hundred cattle, not one less, and I will begin to think of it. Why, you have not ten, and Mameena is my eldest daughter, and must marry a rich man."

"She loves me, O Umbezi," answered Saduko, looking down, "and that is more than cattle."

"For you, perhaps, Saduko, but not for me who am poor and want cows. Also," he added, glancing at him shrewdly, "are you so sure that Mameena loves you though you be such a fine man? Now, I should have thought that whatever her eyes may say, her heart loves no one but herself, and that in the end she will follow her heart and not her eyes. Mameena the beautiful does not seek to be a poor man's wife and do all the hoeing. But bring me the hundred cattle and we will see, for, speaking truth from my heart, if you were a big chief there is no one I should like better as a son-in-law, unless it were Macumazahn here," he said, digging me in the ribs with his elbow, "who would lift up my House on his white back."

Now, at this speech Saduko shifted his feet uneasily; it seemed to me as though he felt there was truth in Umbezi's estimate of his daughter's character. But he only said:

"Cattle can be acquired."

"Or stolen," suggested Umbezi.

"Or taken in war," corrected Saduko. "When I have a hundred head I will hold you to your word, O father of Mameena."

"And then what would you live on, fool, if you gave all your beasts to me? There, there, cease talking wind. Before you have a hundred head of cattle Mameena will have six children who will not call *you* father. Ah, don't you like that? Are you going away?"

"Yes, I am going," he answered, with a flash of his quiet eyes; "only then let the man whom they do call father beware of Saduko."

"Beware of how you talk, young man," said Umbezi in a grave voice. "Would you travel your father's road? I hope not, for I like you well; but such words are apt to be remembered."

Saduko walked away as though he did not hear.

"Who is he?" I asked.

"One of high blood," answered Umbezi shortly. "He might be a chief to-day had not his father been a plotter and a wizard. Dingaan smelt him out"—and he made a sideways motion with his hand that among the Zulus means much. "Yes, they were killed, almost every one; the chief, his wives, his children and his headmen—every one except Chosa his brother and his son Saduko, whom Zikali the dwarf, the *smeller-out-of-evil-doers*, the *ancient*, who was old before Senzangakona became a father of kings, hid him. There, that is an evil tale to talk of," and he shivered. "Come, White Man, and doctor that old cow of mine, or she will give me no peace for months."

So I went to see the Worn-out-Old-Cow—not because I had any particular interest in her, for, to tell the truth, she was a very disagreeable and antique person, the cast-off wife of some chief whom at an unknown date in the past the astute Umbezi had married from motives of policy—but because I hoped to hear more of Miss Mameena, in whom I had become interested.

Entering a large hut, I found the lady so impolitely named the Old Cow in a parlous state. There she lay upon the floor, an unpleasant object because of the blood that had escaped from her wound, surrounded by a crowd of other women and of children. At regular intervals she announced that she was dying, and emitted a fearful yell, whereupon all the audience yelled also; in short, the place was a perfect pandemonium.

Telling Umbezi to get the hut cleared, I said that I would go to fetch my medicines. Meanwhile I ordered my servant, Scowl, a humorous-looking fellow, light yellow in hue, for he had a strong dash of Hottentot in his composition, to cleanse the wound. When I returned from the wagon ten minutes later the screams were more terrible than before, although the chorus now stood without the hut. Nor was this altogether wonderful, for on entering the place I found Scowl trimming up the Old Cow's ear with a pair of blunt nail-scissors.

"O Macumazana," said Umbezi in a hoarse whisper, "might it not perhaps be as well to leave her alone? If she bled to death, at any rate she would be quieter."

"Are you a man or a hyena?" I answered sternly, and set about the job, Scowl holding the poor woman's head between his knees.

It was over at length; a simple operation in which I exhibited—I believe that is the medical term—a strong solution of caustic applied with a feather.

"There, Mother," I said, for now we were alone in the hut, whence Scowl had fled, badly bitten in the calf, "you won't die now."

"No, you vile white man," she sobbed. "I shan't die, but how about my beauty?"

"It will be greater than ever," I answered; "no one else will have an ear with such a curve in it. But, talking of beauty, where is Mameena?"

"I don't know where she is," she replied with fury, "but I very well know where she would be if I had my way. That peeled willow-wand of a girl"—here she added certain descriptive epithets I will not repeat—"has brought this misfortune upon me. We had a slight quarrel yesterday, White Man, and, being a witch as she is, she prophesied evil. Yes, when by accident I scratched her ear, she said that before long mine should burn, and surely burn it does." (This, no doubt, was true, for the caustic had begun to bite.)

"O devil of a white man," she went on, "you have bewitched me; you have filled my head with fire."

Then she seized an earthenware pot and hurled it at me, saying, "Take that for your doctor-fee. Go, crawl after Mameena like the others and get her to doctor you."

By this time I was half through the bee-hole of the hut, my movements being hastened by a vessel of hot water which landed on me behind.

"What is the matter, Macumazahn?" asked old Umbezi, who was waiting outside.

"Nothing at all, friend," I answered with a sweet smile, "except that your wife wants to see you at once. She is in pain, and wishes you to soothe her. Go in; do not hesitate."

After a moment's pause he went in—that is, half of him went in. Then came a fearful crash, and he emerged again with the rim of a pot about his neck and his countenance veiled in a coating of what I took to be honey.

"Where is Mameena?" I asked him as he sat up spluttering.

"Where I wish I was," he answered in a thick voice; "at a *kraal* five hours' journey away."

Well, that was the first I heard of Mameena.

That night as I sat smoking my pipe under the flap lean-to attached to the wagon, laughing to myself over the adventure of the Old Cow, falsely described as worn out, and wondering whether Umbezi had got the honey out of his hair, the canvas was lifted, and a *Kafir* wrapped in a *kaross* crept in and squatted before me.

"Who are you?" I asked, for it was too dark to see the man's face.

"*Inkoosi*," answered a deep voice, "I am Saduko."

"You are welcome," I answered, handing him a little gourd of snuff in token of hospitality. Then I waited while he poured some of the snuff into the palm of his hand and took it in the usual fashion.

"*Inkoosi*," he said, when he had scraped away the tears produced by the snuff, "I have come to ask you a favour. You heard Umbezi say today that he will not give me his daughter, Mameena, unless I give him a hundred head of cows. Now, I have not got the cattle, and I cannot earn them by work in many years. Therefore I must take them from a certain tribe I know which is at war with the Zulus. But this I cannot do unless I have a gun. If I had a good gun, *Inkoosi*—one that only goes off when it is asked, and not of its own fancy, I who have some name could persuade a number of men whom I know, who once were servants of my father, or their sons, to be my companions in this venture."

"Do I understand that you wish me to give you one of my good guns with two mouths to it (i.e. double-barrelled), a gun worth at least twelve oxen, for nothing, O Saduko?" I asked in a cold and scandalised voice.

"Not so, O Watcher-by-Night," he answered; "not so, O He-who-sleeps-with-one-eye-open" (another free and difficult rendering of my native name, Macumazahn, or more correctly, Macumazana)—"I should never dream of offering such an insult to your high-born intelligence." He paused and took another pinch of snuff, then went on in a meditative voice: "Where I propose to get those hundred cattle there are many more; I am told not less than a thousand head in all. Now, *Inkoosi*," he added, looking at me sideways, "suppose you gave me the gun I ask for, and suppose you accompanied me with your own gun and your armed hunters, it would be fair that you should have half the cattle, would it not?"

"That's cool," I said. "So, young man, you want to turn me into a cow-thief and get my throat cut by Panda for breaking the peace of his country?"

"Neither, Macumazahn, for these are my own cattle. Listen, now, and I will tell you a story. You have heard of Matiwane, the chief of the Amangwane?"

"Yes," I answered. "His tribe lived near the head of the Umzinyati, did they not? Then they were beaten by the Boers or the English, and Matiwane came under the Zulus. But afterwards Dingaan wiped him out, with his House, and now his people are killed or scattered."

"Yes, his people are killed and scattered, but his House still lives. Macumazahn, I am his House, I, the only son of his chief wife, for Zikali the Wise Little One, the Ancient, who is of the Amangwane blood, and who hated Chaka and Dingaan—yes, and Senzangakona their father before them, but whom none of them could kill because he is so great and has such mighty spirits for his servants, saved and sheltered me."

"If he is so great, why, then, did he not save your father also, Saduko?" I asked, as though I knew nothing of this Zikali.

"I cannot say, Macumazahn. Perhaps the spirits plant a tree for themselves, and to do so cut down many other trees. At least, so it happened. It happened thus: Bangu, chief of the Amakoba, whispered into Dingaan's ear that Matiwane, my father, was a wizard; also that he was very rich. Dingaan listened because he thought a sickness that he had came from Matiwane's witchcraft. He said: 'Go, Bangu, and take a company with you and pay Matiwane a visit of honour, and in the night, O in the night! Afterwards, Bangu, we will divide the cattle, for Matiwane is strong and clever, and you shall not risk your life for nothing.'"

Saduko paused and looked down at the ground, brooding heavily.

"Macumazahn, it was done," he said presently. "They ate my father's meat, they drank his beer; they gave him a present from the king, they praised him with high names; yes, Bangu took snuff with him and called him brother. Then in the night, O in the night—!

"My father was in the hut with my mother, and I, so big only"—and he held his hand at the height of a boy of ten—"was with them. The cry arose, the flames began to eat; my father looked out and saw. 'Break through the fence and away, woman,' he said; 'away with Saduko, that he may live to avenge me. Begone while I hold the gate! Begone to Zikali, for whose witchcrafts I pay with my blood.'

"Then he kissed me on the brow, saying but one word, 'Remember,' and thrust us from the hut.

"My mother broke a way through the fence; yes, she tore at it with her nails and teeth like a hyena. I looked back out of the shadow of the hut and saw Matiwane my father fighting like a buffalo. Men went down before him, one, two, three, although he had no shield: only his spear. Then Bangu crept behind him and stabbed him in the back and he threw up his arms and fell. I saw no more, for by now we were through the fence. We ran, but they perceived us. They hunted us as wild dogs hunt a buck. They killed my mother with a throwing *assegai*; it entered at her back and came out at her heart. I went mad, I drew it from her body, I ran at them. I dived beneath the shield of the first, a very tall man, and held the spear, so, in both my little hands. His weight came upon its point and it went through him as though he were but a bowl of buttermilk. Yes, he rolled over, quite dead, and the handle of the spear broke upon the ground. Now the others stopped astonished, for never had they seen such a thing. That a child should kill a tall warrior, oh! that tale had not been told. Some of them would have let me go, but just then Bangu came up and saw the dead man, who was his brother.

"'Wow!' he said when he knew how the man had died. 'This lion's cub is a wizard also, for how else could he have killed a soldier who has known war? Hold out his arms that I may finish him slowly.'

"So two of them held out my arms, and Bangu came up with his spear."

Saduko ceased speaking, not that his tale was done, but because his voice choked in his throat. Indeed, seldom have I seen a man so moved. He breathed in great gasps, the sweat poured from him, and his muscles worked convulsively. I gave him a pannikin of water and he drank, then he went on:

"Already the spear had begun to prick—look, here is the mark of it"—and opening his *kaross* he pointed to a little white line just below the breast-bone—"when a strange shadow thrown by the fire of the burning huts came between Bangu and me, a shadow as that of a toad standing on its hind legs. I looked round and saw that it was the shadow of Zikali, whom I had seen once or twice. There he stood, though whence he came I know not, wagging his great white head that sits on the top of his body like a pumpkin on an ant-heap, rolling his big eyes and laughing loudly.

"'A merry sight,' he cried in his deep voice that sounded like water in a hollow cave. 'A merry sight, O Bangu, Chief of the Amakoba! Blood, blood, plenty of blood! Fire, fire, plenty of fire! Wizards dead here, there, and everywhere! Oh, a merry sight! I have seen many such; one at the *kraal* of your grandmother, for instance—your grandmother the great *Inkosikazi*, when myself I escaped with my life because I was so old; but never do I remember a merrier than that which this moon shines on,' and he pointed to the White Lady who just then broke through the clouds. 'But, great Chief Bangu, lord loved by the son of Senzangakona, brother of the Black One (Chaka) who has ridden hence on the *assegai*, what is the meaning of *this* play?' and he pointed to me and to the two soldiers who held out my little arms.

"'I kill the wizard's cub, Zikali, that is all,' answered Bangu.

"'I see, I see,' laughed Zikali. 'A gallant deed! You have butchered the father and the mother, and now you would butcher the child who has slain one of your grown warriors in fair fight. A very gallant deed, well worthy of the chief of the Amakoba! Well, loose his spirit—only—' He stopped and took a pinch of snuff from a box which he drew from a slit in the lobe of his great ear.

"'Only what?' asked Bangu, hesitating.

"'Only I wonder, Bangu, what you will think of the world in which you will find yourself before to-morrow's moon arises. Come back thence and tell me, Bangu, for there are so many worlds beyond the sun, and I would learn for certain which of them such a one as you inhabits: a man who for hatred and for gain murders the father and the mother and then butchers the child—the child that could slay a warrior who has seen war—with the spear hot from his mother's heart.'

"'Do you mean that I shall die if I kill this lad?' shouted Bangu in a great voice.

"'What else?' answered Zikali, taking another pinch of snuff.

"'This, Wizard; that we will go together.'

"'Good, good!' laughed the dwarf. 'Let us go together. Long have I wished to die, and what better companion could I find than Bangu, Chief of the Amakoba, Slayer of Children, to guard me on a dark and terrible road. Come, brave Bangu, come; kill me if you can,' and again he laughed at him.

"Now, Macumazahn, the people of Bangu fell back muttering, for they found this business horrible. Yes, even those who held my arms let go of them.

"'What will happen to me, Wizard, if I spare the boy?' asked Bangu.

"Zikali stretched out his hand and touched the scratch that the *assegai* had made in me here. Then he held up his finger red with my blood, and looked at it in the light of the moon; yes, and tasted it with his tongue.

"'I think this will happen to you, Bangu,' he said. 'If you spare this boy he will grow into a man who will kill you and many others one day. But if you do not spare him I think that his spirit, working as spirits can do, will kill you to-morrow. Therefore the question is, will you live a while or will you die at once, taking me with you as your companion? For you must not leave me behind, brother Bangu.'

"Now Bangu turned and walked away, stepping over the body of my mother, and all his people walked away after him, so that presently Zikali the Wise and Little and I were left alone.

"'What! have they gone?' said Zikali, lifting up his eyes from the ground. 'Then we had better be going also, Son of Matiwane, lest he should change his mind and come back. Live on, Son of Matiwane, that you may avenge Matiwane.'"

"A nice tale," I said. "But what happened afterwards?"

"Zikali took me away and nurtured me at his *kraal* in the Black Kloof, where he lived alone save for his servants, for in that *kraal* he would suffer no woman to set foot, Macumazahn. He taught me much wisdom and many secret things, and would have made a great doctor of me had I so willed. But I willed it not who find spirits ill company, and there are many of them about the Black Kloof, Macumazahn. So in the end he said: 'Go where your heart calls, and be a warrior, Saduko. But know this: You have opened a door that can never be shut again, and across the threshold of that door spirits will pass in and out for all your life, whether you seek them or seek them not.'

"'It was you who opened the door, Zikali,' I answered angrily.

"'Mayhap,' said Zikali, laughing after his fashion, 'for I open when I must and shut when I must. Indeed, in my youth, before the Zulus were a people, they named me Opener of Doors; and now, looking through one of those doors, I see something about you, O Son of Matiwane.'

"'What do you see, my father?' I asked.

"'I see two roads, Saduko: the Road of Medicine, that is the spirit road, and the Road of Spears, that is the blood road. I see you travelling on the Road of Medicine, that is my own road, Saduko, and growing wise and great, till at last, far, far away, you vanish over the precipice to which it leads, full of years and honour and wealth, feared yet beloved by all men, white and black. Only that road you must travel alone, since such wisdom may have no friends, and, above all, no woman to share its secrets. Then I look at the Road of Spears and see you, Saduko, travelling on that road, and your feet are red with blood, and women wind their arms about your neck, and one by one your enemies go down before you. You love much, and sin much for the sake of the love, and she for whom you sin comes and goes and comes again. And the road is short, Saduko, and near the end of it are many spirits; and though you shut your eyes you see them, and though you fill your ears with clay you hear them, for they are the ghosts of your slain. But the end of your journeying I see not. Now choose which road you will, Son of Matiwane, and choose swiftly, for I speak no more of this matter.'

"Then, Macumazahn, I thought a while of the safe and lonely path of wisdom, also of the blood-red path of spears where I should find love and war, and my youth rose up in me and—I chose the path of spears and the love and the sin and the unknown death."

"A foolish choice, Saduko, supposing that there is any truth in this tale of roads, which there is not."

"Nay, a wise one, Macumazahn, for since then I have seen Mameena and know why I chose that path."

"Ah!" I said. "Mameena—I forgot her. Well, after all, perhaps there is some truth in your tale of roads. When *I* have seen Mameena I will tell you what I think."

"When you have seen Mameena, Macumazahn, you will say that the choice was very wise. Well, Zikali, Opener of Doors, laughed loudly when he heard it. 'The ox seeks the fat pasture, but the young bull the rough mountainside where the heifers graze,' he said; 'and after all, a bull is better than an ox. Now begin to travel your own road, Son of Matiwane, and from time to time return to the Black Kloof and tell me how it fares with you. I will promise you not to die before I know the end of it.'

"Now, Macumazahn, I have told you things that hitherto have lived in my own heart only. And, Macumazahn, Bangu is in ill favour with Panda, whom he defies in his mountain, and I have a promise—never mind how—that he who kills him will be called to no account and may keep his cattle. Will you come with me and share those cattle, O Watcher-by-Night?"

"Get thee behind me, Satan," I said in English, then added in Zulu: "I don't know. If your story is true I should have no objection to helping to kill Bangu; but I must learn lots more about this business first. Meanwhile I am going on a shooting trip to-morrow with Umbezi the Fat, and I like you, O Chooser of the Road of Spears and Blood. Will you be my companion and earn the gun with two mouths in payment?"

"*Inkoosi*," he said, lifting his hand in salute with a flash of his dark eyes, "you are generous, you honour me. What is there that I should love better? Yet," he added, and his face fell, "first I must ask Zikali the Little, Zikali my foster-father."

"Oh!" I said, "so you are still tied to the Wizard's girdle, are you?"

"Not so, Macumazahn; but I promised him not long ago that I would undertake no enterprise, save that you know of, until I had spoken with him."

"How far off does Zikali live?" I asked Saduko.

"One day's journeying. Starting at sunrise I can be there by sunset."

"Good! Then I will put off the shooting for three days and come with you if you think that this wonderful old dwarf will receive me."

"I believe that he will, Macumazahn, for this reason—he told me that I should meet you and love you, and that you would be mixed up in my fortunes."

"Then he poured moonshine into your gourd instead of beer," I answered. "Would you keep me here till midnight listening to such foolishness when we must start at dawn? Begone now and let me sleep."

"I go," he answered with a little smile. "But if this is so, O Macumazana, why do you also wish to drink of the moonshine of Zikali?" and he went.

Yet I did not sleep very well that night, for Saduko and his strange and terrible story had taken a hold of my imagination. Also, for reasons of my own, I greatly wished to see this Zikali, of whom I had heard a great deal in past years. I wished further to find out if he was a common humbug, like so many witch-doctors, this dwarf who announced that my fortunes were mixed up with those of his foster-son, and who at least could tell me something true or false about the history and position of Bangu, a person for whom I had conceived a strong dislike, possibly quite unjustified by the facts. But more than all did I wish to see Mameena, whose beauty or talents produced so much impression upon the native mind. Perhaps if I went to see Zikali she would be back at her father's *kraal* before we started on our shooting trip.

Thus it was then that fate wove me and my doings into the web of some very strange events; terrible, tragic and complete indeed as those of a Greek play, as it has often done both before and since those days.

Chapter 2

The Moonshine of Zikali

On the following morning I awoke, as a good hunter always should do, just at that time when, on looking out of the wagon, nothing can be seen but a little grey glint of light which he knows is reflected from the horns of the cattle tied to the trek-tow. Presently, however, I saw another glint of light which I guessed came from the spear of Saduko, who was seated by the ashes of the cooking fire wrapped in his *kaross* of wildcat skins. Slipping from the *voorkisse*, or driving-box, I came behind him softly and touched him on the shoulder. He leapt up with a start which revealed his nervous nature, then recognising me through the soft grey gloom, said: "You are early, Macumazahn."

"Of course," I answered; "am I not named Watcher-by-Night? Now let us go to Umbezi and tell him that I shall be ready to start on our hunting trip on the third morning from to-day."

So we went, to find that Umbezi was in a hut with his last wife and asleep. Fortunately enough, however, as under the circumstances I did not wish to disturb him, outside the hut we found the Old Cow, whose sore ear had kept her very wide awake, who, for purposes of her own, although etiquette did not allow her to enter the hut, was waiting for her husband to emerge. Having examined her wound and rubbed some ointment on it, with her I left my message. Next I woke up my servant Scowl, and told him that I was going on a short journey, and that he must guard all things until my return; and while I did so, took a nip of raw rum and made ready a bag of *biltong*, that is sun-dried flesh, and biscuits.

Then, taking with me a single-barrelled gun, that same little Purdey rifle with which I shot the vultures on the Hill of Slaughter at Dingaan's *Kraal*,[1] we started on foot, for I would not risk my only horse on such a journey.

1. For the story of this shooting of the vultures by Allan Quatermain, see the book called *Marie*.—*Editor*

A rough journey it proved to be indeed, over a series of bush-clad hills that at their crests were covered with rugged stones among which no horse could have travelled. Up and down these hills we went, and across the valleys that divided them, following some path which I could not see, for all that live-long day. I have always been held a good walker, being by nature very light and active; but I am bound to say that my companion taxed my powers to the utmost, for on he marched for hour after hour, striding ahead of me at such a rate that at times I was forced to break into a run to keep up with him. Although my pride would not suffer me to complain, since as a matter of principle I would never admit to a *Kafir* that he was my master at anything, glad enough was I when, towards evening, Saduko sat himself down on a stone at the top of a hill and said:

"Behold the Black Kloof, Macumazahn," which were almost the first words he had uttered since we started.

Truly the spot was well named, for there, cut out by water from the heart of a mountain in some primeval age, lay one of the most gloomy places that ever I had beheld. It was a vast cleft in which granite boulders were piled up fantastically, perched one upon another in great columns, and upon its sides grew dark trees set sparsely among the rocks. It faced towards the west, but the light of the sinking sun that flowed up it served only to accentuate its vast loneliness, for it was a big cleft, the best part of a mile wide at its mouth.

Up this dreary gorge we marched, mocked at by chattering baboons and following a little path not a foot wide that led us at length to a large hut and several smaller ones set within a reed fence and overhung by a gigantic mass of rock that looked as though it might fall at any moment. At the gate of the fence two natives of I know not what tribe, men of fierce and forbidding appearance, suddenly sprang out and thrust their spears towards my breast.

"Whom bring you here, Saduko?" asked one of them sternly.

"A white man that I vouch for," he answered. "Tell Zikali that we wait on him."

"What need to tell Zikali that which he knows already?" said the sentry. "Your food and that of your companion is already cooked in yonder hut. Enter, Saduko, with him for whom you vouch."

So we went into the hut and ate, also I washed myself, for it was a beautifully clean hut, and the stools, wooden bowls, etc., were finely carved out of red ivory wood, this work, Saduko informed me, being done by Zikali's own hand. Just as we were finishing our meal a messenger came to tell us that Zikali waited our presence. We followed him across an open space to a kind of door in the tall reed fence, passing which I set eyes for the first time upon the famous old witch-doctor of whom so many tales were told.

Certainly he was a curious sight in those strange surroundings, for they were very strange, and I think their complete simplicity added to the effect. In front of us was a kind of courtyard with a black floor made of polished ant-heap earth and cow-dung, two-thirds of which at least was practically roofed in by the huge over-hanging mass of rock whereof I have spoken, its arch bending above at a height of not less than sixty or seventy feet from the ground. Into this great, precipice-backed cavity poured the fierce light of the setting sun, turning it and all within it, even the large straw hut in the background, to the deep hue of blood. Seeing the wonderful effect of the sunset in that dark and forbidding place, it occurred to me at once that the old wizard must have chosen this moment to receive us because of its impressiveness.

Then I forgot these scenic accessories in the sight of the man himself. There he sat on a stool in front of his hut, quite unattended, and wearing only a cloak of leopard skins open in front, for he was unadorned with the usual hideous trappings of a witch-doctor, such as snake-skins, human bones, bladders full of unholy compounds, and so forth.

What a man he was, if indeed he could be called quite human. His stature, though stout, was only that of a child; his head was enormous, and from it plaited white hair fell down on to his shoulders. His eyes were deep and sunken, his face was broad and very stern. Except for this snow-white hair, however, he did not look ancient, for his flesh was firm and plump, and the skin on his cheeks and neck unwrinkled, which suggested to me that the story of his great antiquity was false. A man who was over a hundred years old, for instance, surely could not boast such a beautiful set of teeth, for even at that distance I could see them gleaming. On the other hand, evidently middle age was far behind him; indeed, from his appearance it was quite impossible to guess even approximately the number of his years. There he sat, red in the red light, perfectly still, and staring without a blink of his eyes at the furious ball of the setting sun, as an eagle is said to be able to do.

Saduko advanced, and I walked after him. My stature is not great, and I have never considered myself an imposing person, but somehow I do not think that I ever felt more insignificant than on this occasion. The tall and splendid native beside, or rather behind whom I walked, the gloomy magnificence of the place, the blood-red light in which it was bathed, and the solemn, solitary, little figure with wisdom stamped upon its face before me, all tended to induce humility in a man not naturally vain. I felt myself growing smaller and smaller, both in a moral and a physical sense; I wished that my curiosity had not prompted me to seek an interview with yonder uncanny being.

Well, it was too late to retreat; indeed, Saduko was already standing before the dwarf and lifting his right arm above his head as he gave him the salute of *Makosi*,[2] whereon, feeling that something was expected of me, I took off my shabby cloth hat and bowed, then, remembering my white man's pride, replaced it on my head.

The wizard suddenly seemed to become aware of our presence, for, ceasing his contemplation of the sinking sun, he scanned us both with his slow, thoughtful eyes, which somehow reminded me of those of a chameleon, although they were not prominent, but, as I have said, sunken.

"Greeting, son Saduko!" he said in a deep, rumbling voice. "Why are you back here so soon, and why do you bring this flea of a white man with you?"

Now this was more than I could bear, so without waiting for my companion's answer I broke in:

"You give me a poor name, O Zikali. What would you think of me if I called you a beetle of a wizard?"

"I should think you clever," he answered after reflection, "for after all I must look something like a beetle with a white head. But why should you mind being compared to a flea? A flea works by night and so do you, Macumazahn; a flea is active and so are you; a flea is very hard to catch and kill and so are you; and lastly a flea drinks its fill of that which it desires, the blood of man and beast, and so you have done, do, and will, Macumazahn," and he broke into a great laugh that rolled and echoed about the rocky roof above.

Once, long years before, I had heard that laugh, when I was a prisoner in Dingaan's *kraal*, after the massacre of Retief and his company, and I recognised it again.

While I was searching for some answer in the same vein, and not finding it, though I thought of plenty afterwards, ceasing of a sudden from his unseemly mirth, he went on:

"Do not let us waste time in jests, for it is a precious thing, and there is but little of it left for any one of us. Your business, son Saduko?"

"Baba!" (that is the Zulu for father), said Saduko, "this white *Inkoosi*, for, as you know well enough, he is a chief by nature, a man of a great heart and doubtless of high blood (this, I believe, is true, for I

2. *Makosi*, the plural of *Inkoosi*, is the salute given to Zulu wizards, because they are not one but many, since in them (as in the possessed demoniac in the Bible) dwell an unnumbered horde of spirits.—*Editor*

have been told that my ancestors were more or less distinguished, although, if this is so, their talents did not lie in the direction of money-making), has offered to take me upon a shooting expedition and to give me a good gun with two mouths in payment of my services. But I told him I could not engage in any fresh venture without your leave, and—he is come to see whether you will grant it, my father."

"Indeed," answered the dwarf, nodding his great head. "This clever white man has taken the trouble of a long walk in the sun to come here to ask me whether he may be allowed the privilege of presenting you with a weapon of great value in return for a service that any man of your years in Zululand would love to give for nothing in such company?

"Son Saduko, because my eye-holes are hollow, do you think it your part to try to fill them up with dust? Nay, the white man has come because he desires to see him who is named Opener-of-Roads, of whom he heard a great deal when he was but a lad, and to judge whether in truth he has wisdom, or is but a common cheat. And you have come to learn whether or no your friendship with him will be fortunate; whether or no he will aid you in a certain enterprise that you have in your mind."

"True, O Zikali," I said. "That is so far as I am concerned."

But Saduko answered nothing.

"Well," went on the dwarf, "since I am in the mood I will try to answer both your questions, for I should be a poor *Nyanga*" (that is doctor) "if I did not when you have travelled so far to ask them. Moreover, O Macumazana, be happy, for I seek no fee who, having made such fortune as I need long ago, before your father was born across the Black Water, Macumazahn, no longer work for a reward—unless it be from the hand of one of the House of Senzangakona—and therefore, as you may guess, work but seldom."

Then he clapped his hands, and a servant appeared from somewhere behind the hut, one of those fierce-looking men who had stopped us at the gate. He saluted the dwarf and stood before him in silence and with bowed head.

"Make two fires," said Zikali, "and give me my medicine."

The man fetched wood, which he built into two little piles in front of Zikali. These piles he fired with a brand brought from behind the hut. Then he handed his master a cat-skin bag.

"Withdraw," said Zikali, "and return no more till I summon you, for I am about to prophesy. If, however, I should seem to die, bury me to-morrow in the place you know of and give this white man a safe-conduct from my *kraal*."

The man saluted again and went without a word.

When he had gone the dwarf drew from the bag a bundle of twisted roots, also some pebbles, from which he selected two, one white and the other black.

"Into this stone," he said, holding up the white pebble so that the light from the fire shone on it—since, save for the lingering red glow, it was now growing dark—"into this stone I am about to draw your spirit, O Macumazana; and into this one"—and he held up the black pebble—"yours, O Son of Matiwane. Why do you look frightened, O brave White Man, who keep saying in your heart, 'He is nothing but an ugly old *Kafir* cheat'? If I am a cheat, why do you look frightened? Is your spirit already in your throat, and does it choke you, as this little stone might do if you tried to swallow it?" and he burst into one of his great, uncanny laughs.

I tried to protest that I was not in the least frightened, but failed, for, in fact, I suppose my nerves were acted on by his suggestion, and I did feel exactly as though that stone were in my throat, only coming upwards, not going downwards. "Hysteria," thought I to myself, "the result of being overtired," and as I could not speak, sat still as though I treated his gibes with silent contempt.

"Now," went on the dwarf, "perhaps I shall seem to die; and if so do not touch me lest you should really die. Wait till I wake up again and tell you what your spirits have told me. Or if I do not wake up—for a time must come when I shall go on sleeping—well—for as long as I have lived—after the fires are quite out, not before, lay your hands upon my breast; and if you find me turning cold, get you gone to some other *Nyanga* as fast as the spirits of this place will let you, O ye who would peep into the future."

As he spoke he threw a big handful of the roots that I have mentioned on to each of the fires, whereon tall flames leapt up from them, very unholy-looking flames which were followed by columns of dense, white smoke that emitted a most powerful and choking odour quite unlike anything that I had ever smelt before. It seemed to penetrate all through me, and that accursed stone in my throat grew as large as an apple and felt as though someone were poking it upwards with a stick.

Next he threw the white pebble into the right-hand fire, that which was opposite to me, saying:

"Enter, Macumazahn, and look," and the black pebble he threw into the left-hand fire saying: "Enter, Son of Matiwane, and look. Then come back both of you and make report to me, your master."

Now it is a fact that as he said these words I experienced a sensation as though a stone had come out of my throat; so readily do our nerves deceive us that I even thought it grated against my teeth as I opened my mouth to give it passage. At any rate the choking was gone, only now I felt as though I were quite empty and floating on air, as though I were not I, in short, but a mere shell of a thing, all of which doubtless was caused by the stench of those burning roots. Still I could look and take note, for I distinctly saw Zikali thrust his huge head, first into the smoke of what I will call my fire, next into that of Saduko's fire, and then lean back, blowing the stuff in clouds from his mouth and nostrils. Afterwards I saw him roll over on to his side and lie quite still with his arms outstretched; indeed, I noticed that one of his fingers seemed to be in the left-hand fire and reflected that it would be burnt off. In this, however, I must have been mistaken, since I observed subsequently that it was not even scorched.

Thus Zikali lay for a long while till I began to wonder whether he were not really dead. Dead enough he seemed to be, for no corpse could have stayed more stirless. But that night I could not keep my thoughts fixed on Zikali or anything. I merely noted these circumstances in a mechanical way, as might one with whom they had nothing whatsoever to do. They did not interest me at all, for there appeared to be nothing in me to be interested, as I gathered according to Zikali, because I was not there, but in a warmer place than I hope ever to occupy, namely, in the stone in that unpleasant-looking, little right-hand fire.

So matters went as they might in a dream. The sun had sunk completely, not even an after-glow was left. The only light remaining was that from the smouldering fires, which just sufficed to illumine the bulk of Zikali, lying on his side, his squat shape looking like that of a dead hippopotamus calf. What was left of my consciousness grew heartily sick of the whole affair; I was tired of being so empty.

At length the dwarf stirred. He sat up, yawned, sneezed, shook himself, and began to rake among the burning embers of my fire with his naked hand. Presently he found the white stone, which was now red-hot—at any rate it glowed as though it were—and after examining it for a moment finally popped it into his mouth! Then he hunted in the other fire for the black stone, which he treated in a similar fashion. The next thing I remember was that the fires, which had died away almost to nothing, were burning very brightly again, I suppose because someone had put fuel on them, and Zikali was speaking.

"Come here, O Macumazana and O Son of Matiwane," he said, "and I will repeat to you what your spirits have been telling me."

We drew near into the light of the fires, which for some reason or other was extremely vivid. Then he spat the white stone from his mouth into his big hand, and I saw that now it was covered with lines and patches like a bird's egg.

"You cannot read the signs?" he said, holding it towards me; and when I shook my head went on: "Well, I can, as you white men read a book. All your history is written here, Macumazahn; but there is no need to tell you that, since you know it, as I do well enough, having learned it in other days, the days of Dingaan, Macumazahn. All your future, also, a very strange future," and he scanned the stone with interest. "Yes, yes; a wonderful life, and a noble death far away. But of these matters you have not asked me, and therefore I may not tell them even if I wished, nor would you believe if I did. It is of your hunting trip that you have asked me, and my answer is that if you seek your own comfort you will do well not to go. A pool in a dry river-bed; a buffalo bull with the tip of one horn shattered. Yourself and the bull in the pool. Saduko, yonder, also in the pool, and a little half-bred man with a gun jumping about upon the bank. Then a litter made of boughs and you in it, and the father of Mameena walking lamely at your side. Then a hut and you in it, and the maiden called Mameena sitting at your side.

"Macumazahn, your spirit has written on this stone that you should beware of Mameena, since she is more dangerous than any buffalo. If you are wise you will not go out hunting with Umbezi, although it is true that hunt will not cost you your life. There, away, Stone, and take your writings with you!" and as he spoke he jerked his arm and I heard something whiz past my face.

Next he spat out the black stone and examined it in similar fashion.

"Your expedition will be successful, Son of Matiwane," he said. "Together with Macumazahn you will win many cattle at the cost of sundry lives. But for the rest—well, you did not ask me of it, did you? Also, I have told you something of that story before to-day. Away, Stone!" and the black pebble followed the white out into the surrounding gloom.

We sat quite still until the dwarf broke the deep silence with one of his great laughs.

"My witchcraft is done," he said. "A poor tale, was it not? Well, hunt for those stones to-morrow and read the rest of it if you can. Why did you not ask me to tell you everything while I was about it, White Man? It would have interested you more, but now it has all gone from me back into your spirit with the stones. Saduko, get you to sleep. Macumazahn, you who are a Watcher-by-Night, come and sit with me awhile in my hut, and we will talk of other things. All this business of the stones is nothing more than a *Kafir* trick, is it, Macumazahn? When you meet the buffalo with the split horn in the pool of a dried river, remember it is but a cheating trick, and now come into my hut and drink a *kamba* (bowl) of beer and let us talk of other things more interesting."

So he took me into the hut, which was a fine one, very well lighted by a fire in its centre, and gave me *Kafir* beer to drink, that I swallowed gratefully, for my throat was dry and still felt as though it had been scraped.

"Who are you, Father?" I asked point-blank when I had taken my seat upon a low stool, with my back resting against the wall of the hut, and lit my pipe.

He lifted his big head from the pile of *karosses* on which he was lying and peered at me across the fire.

"My name is Zikali, which means 'weapons,' White Man. You know as much as that, don't you?" he answered. "My father 'went down' so long ago that his does not matter. I am a dwarf, very ugly, with some learning, as we of the Black House understand it, and very old. Is there anything else you would like to learn?"

"Yes, Zikali; how old?"

"There, there, Macumazahn, as you know, we poor *Kafirs* cannot count very well. How old? Well, when I was young I came down towards the coast from the Great River, you call it the Zambesi, I think, with Undwandwe, who lived in the north in those days. They have forgotten it now because it is some time ago, and if I could write I would set down the history of that march, for we fought some great battles with the people who used to live in this country. Afterwards I was the friend of the Father of the Zulus, he whom they still call *Inkoosi* Umkulu—the mighty chief—you may have heard tell of him. I carved that stool on which you sit for him and he left it back to me when he died."

"*Inkoosi* Umkulu!" I exclaimed. "Why, they say he lived hundreds of years ago."

"Do they, Macumazahn? If so, have I not told you that we black people cannot count as well as you do? Really it was only the other day. Anyhow, after his death the Zulus began to maltreat us Undwandwe and the Quabies and the Tetwas with us—you may remember that they called us the *Amatefula*, making a mock of us. So I quarrelled with the Zulus and especially with Chaka, he whom they named Uhlanya (the Mad One). You see, Macumazahn, it pleased him to laugh at me because I am not as other men are. He gave me a name which means 'The-thing-which-should-never-have-been-born.' I will not speak that name, it is secret to me, it may not pass my lips. Yet at times he sought my wisdom, and I paid him back for his names, for I gave him very ill counsel, and he took it, and I brought him to his death, although none ever saw my finger in that business. But when he was dead at the hands of his brothers Dingaan and Umhlangana and of Umbopa, Umbopa who also had a score to settle with him, and his body was cast out of the *kraal* like that of an evil-doer, why I, who because I was a dwarf was not sent with the *men* against Sotshangana, went and sat on it at night and laughed thus," and he broke into one of his hideous peals of merriment.

"I laughed thrice: once for my wives whom he had taken; once for my children whom he had slain; and once for the mocking name that he had given me. Then I became the counsellor of Dingaan, whom I hated worse than I had hated Chaka, for he was Chaka again without his greatness, and you know the end of Dingaan, for you had a share in that war, and of Umhlangana, his brother and fellow-murderer, whom I counselled Dingaan to slay. This I did through the lips of the old Princess Menkabayi, Jama's daughter, Senzangakona's sister, the Oracle before whom all men bowed, causing her to say that 'This land of the Zulus cannot be ruled by a crimson *assegai*.' For, Macumazahn, it was Umhlangana who first struck Chaka with the spear. Now Panda reigns, the last of the sons of Senzangakona, my enemy, Panda the Fool, and I hold my hand from Panda because he tried to save the life of a child of mine whom Chaka slew. But Panda has sons who are as Chaka was, and against them I work as I worked against those who went before them."

"Why?" I asked.

"Why? Oh! if I were to tell you *all* my story you would understand why, Macumazahn. Well, perhaps I will one day." (Here I may state that as a matter of fact he did, and a very wonderful tale it is, but as it has nothing to do with this history I will not write it here.)

"I dare say," I answered. "Chaka and Dingaan and Umhlangana and the others were not nice people. But another question. Why do you tell me all this, O Zikali, seeing that were I but to repeat it to a talking-bird you would be smelt out and a single moon would not die before you do?"

"Oh! I should be smelt out and killed before one moon dies, should I? Then I wonder that this has not happened during all the moons that are gone. Well, I tell the story to you, Macumazahn, who have had so much to do with the tale of the Zulus since the days of Dingaan, because I wish that someone should know it and perhaps write it down when everything is finished. Because, too, I have just been reading your spirit and see that it is still a white spirit, and that you will not whisper it to a 'talking-bird.'"

Now I leant forward and looked at him.

"What is the end at which you aim, O Zikali?" I asked. "You are not one who beats the air with a stick; on whom do you wish the stick to fall at last?"

"On whom?" he answered in a new voice, a low, hissing voice. "Why, on these proud Zulus, this little family of men who call themselves the 'People of Heaven,' and swallow other tribes as the great tree-snake swallows kids and small bucks, and when it is fat with them cries to the world, 'See how big I am! Everything is inside of me.' I am a Ndwande, one of those peoples whom it pleases the Zulus to call *Amatefula*—poor hangers-on who talk with an accent, nothing but bush swine. Therefore I would see the swine tusk the hunter. Or, if that may not be, I would see the black hunter laid low by the rhinoceros, the white rhinoceros of your race, Macumazahn, yes, even if it sets its foot upon the Ndwande boar as well. There, I have told you, and this is the reason that I live so long, for I will not die until these things have come to pass, as come to pass they will. What did Chaka, Senzangakona's son, say when the little red *assegai*, the *assegai* with which he slew his mother, aye and others, some of whom were near to me, was in his liver? What did he say to Mbopa and the princes? Did he not say that he heard the feet of a great white people running, of a people who should stamp the Zulus flat? Well, I, 'The-thing-who-should-not-have-been-born,' live on until that day comes, and when it comes I think that you and I, Macumazahn, shall not be far apart, and that is why I have opened out my heart to you, I who have knowledge of the future. There, I speak no more of these things that are to be, who perchance have already said too much of them. Yet do not forget my words. Or forget them if you will, for I shall remind you of them, Macumazahn, when the feet of your people have avenged the Ndwandes and others whom it pleases the Zulus to treat as dirt."

Now, this strange man, who had sat up in his excitement, shook his long white hair which, after the fashion of wizards, he wore plaited into thin ropes, till it hung like a veil about him, hiding his broad face and deep eyes. Presently he spoke again through this veil of hair, saying:

"You are wondering, Macumazahn, what Saduko has to do with

all these great events that are to be. I answer that he must play his part in them; not a very great part, but still a part, and it is for this purpose that I saved him as a child from Bangu, Dingaan's man, and reared him up to be a warrior, although, since I cannot lie, I warned him that he would do well to leave spears alone and follow after wisdom. Well, he will slay Bangu, who now has quarrelled with Panda, and a woman will come into the story, one Mameena, and that woman will bring about war between the sons of Panda, and from this war shall spring the ruin of the Zulus, for he who wins will be an evil king to them and bring down on them the wrath of a mightier race. And so 'The-thing-that-should-not-have-been-born' and the Ndwandes and the Quabies and Twetwas, whom it has pleased the conquering Zulus to name '*Amatefula*,' shall be avenged. Yes, yes, my Spirit tells me all these things, and they are true."

"And what of Saduko, my friend and your fosterling?"

"Saduko, your friend and my fosterling, will take his appointed road, Macumazahn, as I shall and you will. What more could he desire, seeing it is that which he has chosen? He will take his road and he will play the part which the Great-Great has prepared for him. Seek not to know more. Why should you, since Time will tell you the story? And now go to rest, Macumazahn, as I must who am old and feeble. And when it pleases you to visit me again, we will talk further. Meanwhile, remember always that I am nothing but an old *Kafir* cheat who pretends to a knowledge that belongs to no man. Remember it especially, Macumazahn, when you meet a buffalo with a split horn in the pool of a dried-up river, and afterwards, when a woman named Mameena makes a certain offer to you, which you may be tempted to accept. Good night to you, Watcher-by-Night with the white heart and the strange destiny, good night to you, and try not to think too hardly of the old *Kafir* cheat who just now is called 'Opener-of-Roads.' My servant waits without to lead you to your hut, and if you wish to be back at Umbezi's *kraal* by nightfall to-morrow, you will do well to start ere sunrise, since, as you found in coming, Saduko, although he may be a fool, is a very good walker, and you do not like to be left behind, Macumazahn, do you?"

So I rose to go, but as I went some impulse seemed to take him and he called me back and made me sit down again.

"Macumazahn," he said, "I would add a word. When you were quite a lad you came into this country with Retief, did you not?"

"Yes," I answered slowly, for this matter of the massacre of Retief is one of which I have seldom cared to speak, for sundry reasons, although I have made a record of it in writing.[3] Even my friends Sir Henry Curtis and Captain Good have heard little of the part I played in that tragedy. "But what do you know of that business, Zikali?"

"All that there is to know, I think, Macumazahn, seeing that I was at the bottom of it, and that Dingaan killed those Boers on my advice—just as he killed Chaka and Umhlangana."

"You cold-blooded old murderer—" I began, but he interrupted me at once.

"Why do you throw evil names at me, Macumazahn, as I threw the stone of your fate at you just now? Why am I a murderer because I brought about the death of some white men that chanced to be your friends, who had come here to cheat us black folk of our country?"

"Was it for *this* reason that you brought about their deaths, Zikali?" I asked, staring him in the face, for I felt that he was lying to me.

"Not altogether, Macumazahn," he answered, letting his eyes, those strange eyes that could look at the sun without blinking, fall before my gaze. "Have I not told you that I hate the House of Senzangakona? And when Retief and his companions were killed, did not the spilling of their blood mean war to the end between the Zulus and the White Men? Did it not mean the death of Dingaan and of thousands of his people, which is but a beginning of deaths? Now do you understand?"

"I understand that you are a very wicked man," I answered with indignation.

"At least *you* should not say so, Macumazahn," he replied in a new voice, one with the ring of truth in it.

"Why not?"

"Because I saved your life on that day. You escaped alone of the White Men, did you not? And you never could understand why, could you?"

"No, I could not, Zikali. I put it down to what you would call 'the spirits.'"

"Well, I will tell you. Those spirits of yours wore my *kaross*," and he laughed. "I saw you with the Boers, and saw, too, that you were of another people—the people of the English. You may have heard at the time that I was doctoring at the Great Place, although I kept out of the way and we did not meet, or at least you never knew that we met, for you were—asleep. Also I pitied your youth, for, although you do not believe it, I had a little bit of heart left in those days. Also I knew that we should come together again in the after years, as you see we have done to-day and shall often do until the end. So I told

---

3. Published under the title of *Marie.—Editor*

Dingaan that whoever died you must be spared, or he would bring up the 'people of George' (*i.e.* the English) to avenge you, and your ghost would enter into him and pour out a curse upon him. He believed me who did not understand that already so many curses were gathered about his head that one more or less made no matter. So you see you were spared, Macumazahn, and afterwards you helped to pour out a curse upon Dingaan without becoming a ghost, which is the reason why Panda likes you so well to-day, Panda, the enemy of Dingaan, his brother. You remember the woman who helped you? Well, I made her do so. How did it go with you afterwards, Macumazahn, with you and the Boer maiden across the Buffalo River, to whom you were making love in those days?"

"Never mind how it went," I replied, springing up, for the old wizard's talk had stirred sad and bitter memories in my heart. "That time is dead, Zikali."

"Is it, Macumazahn? Now, from the look upon your face I should have said that it was still very much alive, as things that happened in our youth have a way of keeping alive. But doubtless I am mistaken, and it is all as dead as Dingaan, and as Retief, and as the others, your companions. At least, although you do not believe it, I saved your life on that red day, for my own purposes, of course, not because one white life was anything among so many in my count. And now go to rest, Macumazahn, go to rest, for although your heart has been awakened by memories this evening, I promise that you shall sleep well to-night," and throwing the long hair back off his eyes he looked at me keenly, wagging his big head to and fro, and burst into another of his great laughs.

So I went. But, ah! as I went I wept.

Anyone who knew all that story would understand why. But this is not the place to tell it, that tale of my first love and of the terrible events which befell us in the time of Dingaan. Still, as I say, I have written it down, and perhaps one day it will be read.

Chapter 3

The Buffalo With the Cleft Horn

I slept very well that night, I suppose because I was so dog-tired I could not help it; but next day, on our long walk back to Umbezi's *kraal*, I thought a great deal.

Without doubt I had seen and heard very strange things, both of the past and the present—things that I could not in the least understand. Moreover, they were mixed up with all sorts of questions of high Zulu policy, and threw a new light upon events that happened to me and others in my youth.

Now, in the clear sunlight, was the time to analyse these things, and this I did in the most logical fashion I could command, although without the slightest assistance from Saduko, who, when I asked him questions, merely shrugged his shoulders.

These questions, he said, did not interest him; I had wished to see the magic of Zikali, and Zikali had been pleased to show me some very good magic, quite of his best indeed. Also he had conversed alone with me afterwards, doubtless on high matters—so high that he, Saduko, was not admitted to share the conversation—which was an honour he accorded to very few. I could form my own conclusions in the light of the white man's wisdom, which everyone knew was great.

I replied shortly that I could, for Saduko's tone irritated me. Of course, the truth was that he felt aggrieved at being sent off to bed like a little boy while his foster-father, the old dwarf, made confidences to me. One of Saduko's faults was that he had always a very good opinion of himself. Also he was by nature terribly jealous, even in little things, as the readers of his history, if any, will learn.

We trudged on for several hours in silence, broken at length by my companion.

"Do you still mean to go on a shooting expedition with Umbezi, *Inkoosi*?" he asked, "or are you afraid?"

"Of what should I be afraid?" I answered tartly.

"Of the buffalo with the split horn, of which Zikali told you. What else?"

Now, I fear I used strong language about the buffalo with the split horn, a beast in which I declared I had no belief whatsoever, either with or without its accessories of dried river-beds and water-holes.

"If all this old woman's talk has made *you* afraid, however," I added, "you can stop at the *kraal* with Mameena."

"Why should the talk make me afraid, Macumazahn? Zikali did not say that this evil spirit of a buffalo would hurt *me*. If I fear, it is for you, seeing that if you are hurt you may not be able to go with me to look for Bangu's cattle."

"Oh!" I replied sarcastically; "it seems that you are somewhat selfish, friend Saduko, since it is of your welfare and not of my safety that you are thinking."

"If I were as selfish as you seem to believe, *Inkoosi*, should I advise you to stop with your wagons, and thereby lose the good gun with two mouths that you have promised me? Still, it is true that I should like well enough to stay at Umbezi's *kraal* with Mameena, especially if Umbezi were away."

Now, as there is nothing more uninteresting than to listen to other people's love affairs, and as I saw that with the slightest encouragement Saduko was ready to tell me all the history of his courtship over again, I did not continue the argument. So we finished our journey in silence, and arrived at Umbezi's *kraal* a little after sundown, to find, to the disappointment of both of us, that Mameena was still away.

Upon the following morning we started on our shooting expedition, the party consisting of myself, my servant Scowl, who, as I think I said, hailed from the Cape and was half a Hottentot; Saduko; the merry old Zulu, Umbezi, and a number of his men to serve as bearers and beaters. It proved a very successful trip—that is, until the end of it—for in those days the game in this part of the country was extremely plentiful. Before the end of the second week I killed four elephants, two of them with large tusks, while Saduko, who soon developed into a very fair shot, bagged another with the double-barrelled gun that I had promised him. Also, Umbezi—how, I have never discovered, for the thing partook of the nature of a miracle—managed to slay an elephant cow with fair ivories, using the old rifle that went off at half-cock.

Never have I seen a man, black or white, so delighted as was that vainglorious *Kafir*. For whole hours he danced and sang and took snuff and saluted with his hand, telling me the story of his deed over and over again, no single version of which tale agreed with the other. He took a new title also, that meant Eater-up-of-Elephants; he allowed one of his men to *bonga*—that is, praise—him all through the night, preventing us from getting a wink of sleep, until at last the poor fellow dropped in a kind of fit from exhaustion, and so forth. It really was very amusing until it became a bore.

Besides the elephants we killed lots of other things, including two lions, which I got almost with a right and left, and three white rhinoceroses, that now, alas! are nearly extinct. At last, towards the end of the third week, we had as much as our men could carry in the shape of ivory, rhinoceros horns, skins and sun-dried buck flesh, or *biltong*, and determined to start back for Umbezi's *kraal* next day. Indeed, this could not be long delayed, as our powder and lead were running low; for in those days, it will be remembered, breechloaders had not come in, and ammunition, therefore, had to be carried in bulk.

To tell the truth, I was very glad that our trip had come to such a satisfactory conclusion, for, although I would not admit it even to myself, I could not get rid of a kind of sneaking dread lest after all there might be something in the old dwarf's prophecy about a disagreeable adventure with a buffalo which was in store for me. Well, as it chanced, we had not so much as seen a buffalo, and as the road which we were going to take back to the *kraal* ran over high, bare country that these animals did not frequent, there was now little prospect of our doing so—all of which, of course, showed what I already knew, that only weak-headed superstitious idiots would put the slightest faith in the drivelling nonsense of deceiving or self-deceived *Kafir* medicine-men. These things, indeed, I pointed out with much vigour to Saduko before we turned in on the last night of the hunt.

Saduko listened in silence and said nothing at all, except that he would not keep me up any longer, as I must be tired.

Now, whatever may be the reason for it, my experience in life is that it is never wise to brag about anything. At any rate, on a hunting trip, to come to a particular instance, wait until you are safe at home till you begin to do so. Of the truth of this ancient adage I was now destined to experience a particularly fine and concrete example.

The place where we had camped was in scattered bush overlooking a great extent of dry reeds, that in the wet season was doubtless a swamp fed by a small river which ran into it on the side opposite to our camp. During the night I woke up, thinking that I heard some big beasts moving in these reeds; but as no further sounds reached my ears I went to sleep again.

Shortly after dawn I was awakened by a voice calling me, which in a hazy fashion I recognised as that of Umbezi.

"Macumazahn," said the voice in a hoarse whisper, "the reeds below us are full of buffalo. Get up. Get up at once."

"What for?" I answered. "If the buffalo came into the reeds they will go out of them. We do not want meat."

"No, Macumazahn; but I want their hides. Panda, the King, has demanded fifty shields of me, and without killing oxen that I can ill spare I have not the skins whereof to make them. Now, these buffalo are in a trap. This swamp is like a dish with one mouth. They cannot get out at the sides of the dish, and the mouth by which they came in is very narrow. If we station ourselves at either side of it we can kill many of them."

By this time I was thoroughly awake and had arisen from my blankets. Throwing a *kaross* over my shoulders, I left the hut, made of boughs, in which I was sleeping and walked a few paces to the crest of a rocky ridge, whence I could see the dry *vlei* below. Here the mists of dawn still clung, but from it rose sounds of grunts, bellows and tramplings which I, an old hunter, could not mistake. Evidently a herd of buffalo, one or two hundred of them, had established themselves in those reeds.

Just then my bastard servant, Scowl, and Saduko joined us, both of them full of excitement.

It appeared that Scowl, who never seemed to sleep at any natural time, had seen the buffalo entering the reeds, and estimated their number at two or three hundred. Saduko had examined the cleft through which they passed, and reported it to be so narrow that we could kill any number of them as they rushed out to escape.

"Quite so. I understand," I said. "Well, my opinion is that we had better let them escape. Only four of us, counting Umbezi, are armed with guns, and *assegais* are not of much use against buffalo. Let them go, I say."

Umbezi, thinking of a cheap raw material for the shields which had been requisitioned by the King, who would surely be pleased if they were made of such a rare and tough hide as that of buffalo, protested violently, and Saduko, either to please one whom he hoped might be his father-in-law or from sheer love of sport, for which he always had a positive passion, backed him up. Only Scowl—whose dash of Hottentot blood made him cunning and cautious—took my side, pointing out that we were very short of powder and that buffalo "ate up much lead." At last Saduko said:

"The lord Macumazana is our captain; we must obey him, although it is a pity. But doubtless the prophesying of Zikali weighs upon his mind, so there is nothing to be done."

"Zikali!" exclaimed Umbezi. "What has the old dwarf to do with this matter?"

"Never mind what he has or has not to do with it," I broke in, for although I do not think that he meant them as a taunt, but merely as a statement of fact, Saduko's words stung me to the quick, especially as my conscience told me that they were not altogether without foundation.

"We will try to kill some of these buffalo," I went on, "although, unless the herd should get bogged, which is not likely, as the swamp is very dry, I do not think that we can hope for more than eight or ten at the most, which won't be of much use for shields. Come, let us make a plan. We have no time to lose, for I think they will begin to move again before the sun is well up."

Half an hour later the four of us who were armed with guns were posted behind rocks on either side of the steep, natural roadway cut by water, which led down to the *vlei*, and with us some of Umbezi's men. That chief himself was at my side—a post of honour which he had insisted upon taking. To tell the truth, I did not dissuade him, for I thought that I should be safer so than if he were opposite to me, since, even if the old rifle did not go off of its own accord, Umbezi, when excited, was a most uncertain shot. The herd of buffalo appeared to have lain down in the reeds, so, being careful to post ourselves first, we sent three of the native bearers to the farther side of the *vlei*, with instructions to rouse the beasts by shouting. The remainder of the Zulus—there were ten or a dozen of them armed with stabbing spears—we kept with us.

But what did these scoundrels do? Instead of disturbing the herd by making a noise, as we told them, for some reason best known to themselves—I expect it was because they were afraid to go into the *vlei*, where they might meet the horn of a buffalo at any moment—they fired the dry reeds in three or four places at once, and this, if you please, with a strong wind blowing from them to us. In a minute or two the farther side of the swamp was a sheet of crackling flame that gave off clouds of dense white smoke. Then pandemonium began.

The sleeping buffalo leapt to their feet, and, after a few moments of indecision, crashed towards us, the whole huge herd of them, snorting and bellowing like mad things. Seeing what was about to happen, I nipped behind a big boulder, while Scowl shinned up a mimosa with the swiftness of a cat and, heedless of its thorns, sat himself in an eagle's nest at the top. The Zulus with the spears bolted to take cover where they could. What became of Saduko I did not see, but old Umbezi, bewildered with excitement, jumped into the exact middle of the roadway, shouting: "They come! They come! Charge, buffalo folk, if you will. The Eater-up-of-Elephants awaits you!"

"You *etcetera*d old fool!" I shouted, but got no farther, for just at this moment the first of the buffalo, which I could see was an enormous bull, probably the leader of the herd, accepted Umbezi's invitation and came, with its nose stuck straight out in front of it. Umbezi's gun went off, and next instant he went up. Through the smoke I saw his black bulk in the air, and then heard it alight with a thud on the top of the rock behind which I was crouching.

"Exit Umbezi," I said to myself, and by way of a requiem let the bull which had hoisted him, as I thought to heaven, have an ounce of lead in the ribs as it passed me. After that I did not fire any more, for it occurred to me that it was as well not to further advertise my presence.

In all my hunting experience I cannot remember ever seeing such a sight as that which followed. Out of the *vlei* rushed the buffalo by dozens, every one of them making remarks in its own language as it came. They jammed in the narrow roadway, they leapt on to each other's backs. They squealed, they kicked, they bellowed. They charged my friendly rock till I felt it shake. They knocked over Scowl's mimosa thorn, and would have shot him out of his eagle's nest had not its flat top fortunately caught in that of another and less accessible tree. And with them came clouds of pungent smoke, mixed with bits of burning reed and puffs of hot air.

It was over at last. With the exception of some calves, which had been trampled to death in the rush, the herd had gone. Now, like the Roman emperor—I think he was an emperor—I began to wonder what had become of my legions.

"Umbezi," I shouted, or, rather, sneezed through the smoke, "are you dead, Umbezi?"

"Yes, yes, Macumazahn," replied a choking and melancholy voice from the top of the rock, "I am dead, quite dead. That evil spirit of a *silwana* (i.e. wild beast) has killed me. Oh! why did I think I was a hunter; why did I not stop at my *kraal* and count my cattle?"

"I am sure I don't know, you old lunatic," I answered, as I scrambled up the rock to bid him good-bye.

It was a rock with a razor top like the ridge of a house, and there, hanging across this ridge like a pair of nether garments on a clothesline, I found the "Eater-up-of-Elephants."

"Where did he get you, Umbezi?" I asked, for I could not see his wounds because of the smoke.

"Behind, Macumazahn, behind!" he groaned, "for I had turned to fly, but, alas! too late."

"On the contrary," I replied, "for one so heavy you flew very well; like a bird, Umbezi, like a bird."

"Look and see what the evil beast has done to me, Macumazahn. It will be easy, for my *moocha* has gone."

So I looked, examining Umbezi's ample proportions with care, but could discover nothing except a large smudge of black mud, as though he had sat down in a half-dried puddle. Then I guessed the truth. The buffalo's horns had missed him. He had been struck only with its muddy nose, which, being almost as broad as that portion of Umbezi with which it came in contact, had inflicted nothing worse than a bruise. When I was sure he had received no serious injury, my temper, already sorely tried, gave out, and I administered to him the soundest smacking—his position being very convenient—that he had ever received since he was a little boy.

"Get up, you idiot!" I shouted, "and let us look for the others. This is the end of your folly in making me attack a herd of buffalo in reeds. Get up. Am I to stop here till I choke?"

"Do you mean to tell me that I have no mortal wound, Macumazahn?" he asked, with a return of cheerfulness, accepting the castigation in good part, for he was not one who bore malice. "Oh, I am glad to hear it, for now I shall live to make those cowards who fired the reeds sorry that they are not dead; also to finish off that wild beast, for I hit him, Macumazahn, I hit him."

"I don't know whether you hit him; I know he hit you," I replied, as I shoved him off the rock and ran towards the tilted tree where I had last seen Scowl.

Here I beheld another strange sight. Scowl was still seated in the eagle's nest that he shared with two nearly fledged young birds, one of which, having been injured, was uttering piteous cries. Nor did it cry in vain, for its parents, which were of that great variety of kite that the Boers call *lammefange*, or lamb-lifters, had just arrived to its assistance, and were giving their new nestling, Scowl, the best doing that man ever received at the beak and claws of feathered kind. Seen through those rushing smoke wreaths, the combat looked perfectly titanic; also it was one of the noisiest to which I ever listened, for I don't know which shrieked the more loudly, the infuriated eagles or their victim.

Seeing how things stood, I burst into a roar of laughter, and just then Scowl grabbed the leg of the male bird, that was planted in his breast while it removed tufts of his wool with its hooked beak, and leapt boldly from the nest, which had become too hot to hold him. The eagle's outspread wings broke his fall, for they acted as a parachute; and so did Umbezi, upon whom he chanced to land. Springing from the prostrate shape of the chief, who now had a bruise in front to match that behind, Scowl, covered with pecks and scratches, ran like a lamp-lighter, leaving me to collect my second gun, which he had dropped at the bottom of the tree, but fortunately without injuring it. The *Kafirs* gave him another name after that encounter, which meant "He-who-fights-birds-and-gets-the-worst-of-it."

Well, we escaped from the line of the smoke, a dishevelled trio—indeed, Umbezi had nothing left on him except his head ring—and shouted for the others, if perchance they had not been trodden to death in the rush. The first to arrive was Saduko, who looked quite calm and untroubled, but stared at us in astonishment, and asked coolly what we had been doing to get in such a state. I replied in appropriate language, and asked in turn how he had managed to remain so nicely dressed.

He did not answer, but I believe the truth was that he had crept into a large ant-bear's hole—small blame to him, to be frank. Then the remainder of our party turned up one by one, some of them looking very blown, as though they had run a long way. None were missing, except those who had fired the reeds, and they thought it well to keep clear for a good many hours. I believe that afterwards they regretted not having taken a longer leave of absence; but when they finally did arrive I was in no condition to note what passed between them and their outraged chief.

Being collected, the question arose what we should do. Of course, I wished to return to camp and get out of this ill-omened place as soon as possible. But I had reckoned without the vanity of Umbezi. Umbezi stretched over the edge of a sharp rock, whither he had been hoisted by the nose of a buffalo, and imagining himself to be mortally wounded, was one thing; but Umbezi in a borrowed *moocha*, although, because of his bruises, he supported his person with one hand in front and with the other behind, knowing his injuries to be purely superficial, was quite another.

"I am a hunter," he said; "I am named 'Eater-up-of-Elephants';" and he rolled his eyes, looking about for someone to contradict him, which nobody did. Indeed, his praiser, a thin, tired-looking person, whose voice was worn out with his previous exertions, repeated in a feeble way:

"Yes, Black One, 'Eater-up-of-Elephants' is your name; 'Lifted-up-by-Buffalo' is your name."

"Be silent, idiot," roared Umbezi. "As I said, I am a hunter; I have wounded the wild beast that subsequently dared to assault me. (As a matter of fact, it was I, Allan Quatermain, who had wounded it.) I would make it bite the dust, for it cannot be far away. Let us follow it."

He glared round him, whereon his obsequious people, or one of them, echoed:

"Yes, by all means let us follow it, 'Eater-up-of-Elephants.' Macumazahn, the clever white man, will show us how, for where is the buffalo that he fears!"

Of course, after this there was nothing else to be done, so, having summoned the scratched Scowl, who seemed to have no heart in the business, we started on the spoor of the herd, which was as easy to track as a wagon road.

"Never mind, Baas," said Scowl, "they are two hours' march off by now."

"I hope so," I answered; but, as it happened, luck was against me, for before we had covered half a mile some over-zealous fellow struck a blood spoor.

I marched on that spoor for twenty minutes or so, till we came to a patch of bush that sloped downwards to a river-bed. Right to this river I followed it, till I reached the edge of a big pool that was still full of water, although the river itself had gone dry. Here I stood looking at the spoor and consulting with Saduko as to whether the beast could have swum the pool, for the tracks that went to its very verge had become confused and uncertain. Suddenly our doubts were ended, since out of a patch of dense bush which we had passed—for it had played the common trick of doubling back on its own spoor—appeared the buffalo, a huge bull, that halted on three legs, my bullet having broken one of its thighs. As to its identity there was no doubt, since on, or rather from, its right horn, which was cleft apart at the top, hung the remains of Umbezi's *moocha.*

"Oh, beware, *Inkoosi,*" cried Saduko in a frightened voice. *"It is the buffalo with the cleft horn!"*

I heard him; I saw. All the scene in the hut of Zikali rose before me—the old dwarf, his words, everything. I lifted my rifle and fired at the charging beast, but knew that the bullet glanced from its skull. I threw down the gun—for the buffalo was right on me—and tried to jump aside.

Almost I did so, but that cleft horn, to which hung the remains of

Umbezi's *moocha*, scooped me up and hurled me off the river bank backwards and sideways into the deep pool below. As I departed thither I saw Saduko spring forward and heard a shot fired that caused the bull to collapse for a moment. Then with a slow, sliding motion it followed me into the pool.

Now we were together, and there was no room for both, so after a certain amount of dodging I went under, as the lighter dog always does in a fight. That buffalo seemed to do everything to me which a buffalo could do under the circumstances. It tried to horn me, and partially succeeded, although I ducked at each swoop. Then it struck me with its nose and drove me to the bottom of the pool, although I got hold of its lip and twisted it. Then it calmly knelt on me and sank me deeper and deeper into the mud. I remember kicking it in the stomach. After this I remember no more, except a kind of wild dream in which I rehearsed all the scene in the dwarf's hut, and his request that when I met the buffalo with the cleft horn in the pool of a dried river, I should remember that he was nothing but a "poor old *Kafir* cheat."

After this I saw my mother bending over a little child in my bed in the old house in Oxfordshire where I was born, and then—blackness!

I came to myself again and saw, instead of my mother, the stately figure of Saduko bending over me upon one side, and on the other that of Scowl, the half-bred Hottentot, who was weeping, for his hot tears fell upon my face.

"He is gone," said poor Scowl; "that bewitched beast with the split horn has killed him. He is gone who was the best white man in all South Africa, whom I loved better than my father and all my relatives."

"That you might easily do, Bastard," answered Saduko, "seeing that you do not know who they are. But he is not gone, for the 'Opener-of-Roads' said that he would live; also I got my spear into the heart of that buffalo before he had kneaded the life out of him, as fortunately the mud was soft. Yet I fear that his ribs are broken"; and he poked me with his finger on the breast.

"Take your clumsy hand off me," I gasped.

"There!" said Saduko, "I have made him feel. Did I not tell you that he would live?"

After this I remember little more, except some confused dreams, till I found myself lying in a great hut, which I discovered subsequently was Umbezi's own, the same, indeed, wherein I had doctored the ear of that wife of his who was called Worn-out-old-Cow.

Chapter 4
Mameena

For a while I contemplated the roof and sides of the hut by the light which entered it through the smoke-vent and the door-hole, wondering whose it might be and how I came there.

Then I tried to sit up, and instantly was seized with agony in the region of the ribs, which I found were bound about with broad strips of soft tanned hide. Clearly they, or some of them, were broken.

What had broken them? I asked myself, and in a flash everything came back to me. So I had escaped with my life, as the old dwarf, Opener-of-Roads, had told me that I should. Certainly he was an excellent prophet; and if he spoke truth in this matter, why not in others? What was I to make of it all? How could a black savage, however ancient, foresee the future? By induction from the past, I supposed; and yet what amount of induction would suffice to show him the details of a forthcoming accident that was to happen to me through the agency of a wild beast with a peculiarly shaped horn? I gave it up, as before and since that day I have found it necessary to do in the case of many other events in life. Indeed, the question is one that I often have had cause to ask where *Kafir witch-doctors* or prophets are concerned, notably in the instance of a certain Mavovo, of whom I hope to tell one day, whose predictions saved my life and those of my companions.

Just then I heard the sound of someone creeping through the bee-hole of the hut, and half-closed my eyes, as I did not feel inclined for conversation. The person came and stood over me, and somehow—by instinct, I suppose—I became aware that my visitor was a woman. Very slowly I lifted my eyelids, just enough to enable me to see her.

There, standing in a beam of golden light that, passing through the smoke-hole, pierced the soft gloom of the hut, stood the most beautiful creature that I had ever seen—that is, if it be admitted that a person who is black, or rather copper-coloured, can be beautiful.

She was a little above the medium height, not more, with a figure that, so far as I am a judge of such matters, was absolutely perfect—that of a Greek statue indeed. On this point I had an opportunity of forming an opinion, since, except for her little bead apron and a single string of large blue beads about her throat, her costume was—well, that of a Greek statue. Her features showed no trace of the negro type; on the contrary, they were singularly well cut, the nose being straight and fine and the pouting mouth that just showed the ivory teeth between, very small. Then the eyes, large, dark and liquid, like those of a buck, set beneath a smooth, broad forehead on which the curling, but not woolly, hair grew low. This hair, by the way, was not dressed up in any of the eccentric native fashions, but simply parted in the middle and tied in a big knot over the nape of the neck, the little ears peeping out through its tresses. The hands, like the feet, were very small and delicate, and the curves of the bust soft and full without being coarse, or even showing the promise of coarseness.

A lovely woman, truly; and yet there was something not quite pleasing about that beautiful face; something, notwithstanding its childlike outline, which reminded me of a flower breaking into bloom, that one does not associate with youth and innocence. I tried to analyse what this might be, and came to the conclusion that without being hard, it was too clever and, in a sense, too reflective. I felt even then that the brain within the shapely head was keen and bright as polished steel; that this woman was one made to rule, not to be man's toy, or even his loving companion, but to use him for her ends.

She dropped her chin till it hid the little, dimple-like depression below her throat, which was one of her charms, and began not to look at, but to study me, seeing which I shut my eyes tight and waited. Evidently she thought that I was still in my swoon, for now she spoke to herself in a low voice that was soft and sweet as honey.

"A small man," she said; "Saduko would make two of him, and the other"—who was he, I wondered—"three. His hair, too, is ugly; he cuts it short and it sticks up like that on a cat's back. *Iya!*" (*i.e. Piff!*), and she moved her hand contemptuously, "a feather of a man. But white—white, one of those who rule. Why, they all of them know that he is their master. They call him He-who-never-Sleeps. They say that he has the courage of a lioness with young—he who got away when Dingaan killed Piti (Retief) and the Boers; they say that he is quick and cunning as a snake, and that Panda and his great *indunas* think more of him than of any white man they know. He is unmarried also, though they say, too, that twice he had a wife, who died, and now he does not turn to look at women, which is strange in any man, and shows that he will escape trouble and succeed. Still, it must be remembered that they are all ugly down here in Zululand, cows, or heifers who will be cows. *Piff!* no more."

She paused for a little while, then went on in her dreamy, reflective voice: "Now, if he met a woman who is not merely a cow or a heifer, a woman cleverer than himself, even if she were not white, I wonder—"

At this point I thought it well to wake up. Turning my head I yawned, opened my eyes and looked at her vaguely, seeing which her expression changed in a flash from that of brooding power to one of moved and anxious girlhood; in short, it became most sweetly feminine.

"You are Mameena?" I said; "is it not so?"

"Oh, yes, *Inkoosi*," she answered, "that is my poor name. But how did you hear it, and how do you know me?"

"I heard it from one Saduko"—here she frowned a little—"and others, and I knew you because you are so beautiful"—an incautious speech at which she broke into a dazzling smile and tossed her deer like head.

"Am I?" she asked. "I never knew it, who am only a common Zulu girl to whom it pleases the great white chief to say kind things, for which I thank him"; and she made a graceful little reverence, just bending one knee. "But," she went on quickly, "whatever else I be, I am of no knowledge, not fit to tend you who are hurt. Shall I go and send my oldest mother?"

"Do you mean her whom your father calls the Worn-out-old-Cow, and whose ear he shot off?"

"Yes, it must be she from the description," she answered with a little shake of laughter, "though I never heard him give her that name."

"Or if you did, you have forgotten it," I said dryly. "Well, I think not, thank you. Why trouble her, when you will do quite as well? If there is milk in that gourd, perhaps you will give me a drink of it."

She flew to the bowl like a swallow, and next moment was kneeling at my side and holding it to my lips with one hand, while with the other she supported my head.

"I am honoured," she said. "I only came to the hut the moment before you woke, and seeing you still lost in swoon, I wept—look, my eyes are still wet (they were, though how she made them so I do not know)—for I feared lest that sleep should be but the beginning of the last."

"Quite so," I said; "it is very good of you. And now, since your fears are groundless—thanks be to the heavens—sit down, if you will, and tell me the story of how I came here."

She sat down, not, I noted, as a *Kafir* woman ordinarily does, in a kind of kneeling position, but on a stool.

"You were carried into the *kraal*, *Inkoosi*," she said, "on a litter of boughs. My heart stood still when I saw that litter coming; it was no more heart; it was cold iron, because I thought the dead or injured man was—" And she paused.

"Saduko?" I suggested.

"Not at all, *Inkoosi*—my father."

"Well, it wasn't either of them," I said, "so you must have felt happy."

"Happy! *Inkoosi*, when the guest of our house had been wounded, perhaps to death—the guest of whom I have heard so much, although by misfortune I was absent when he arrived."

"A difference of opinion with your eldest mother?" I suggested.

"Yes, *Inkoosi*; my own is dead, and I am not too well treated here. She called me a witch."

"Did she?" I answered. "Well, I do not altogether wonder at it; but please continue your story."

"There is none, *Inkoosi*. They brought you here, they told me how the evil brute of a buffalo had nearly killed you in the pool; that is all."

"Yes, yes, Mameena; but how did I get out of the pool?"

"Oh, it seems that your servant, Sikauli, the bastard, leapt into the water and engaged the attention of the buffalo which was kneading you into the mud, while Saduko got on to its back and drove his *assegai* down between its shoulders to the heart, so that it died. Then they pulled you out of the mud, crushed and almost drowned with water, and brought you to life again. But afterwards you became senseless, and so lay wandering in your speech until this hour."

"Ah, he is a brave man, is Saduko."

"Like others, neither more nor less," she replied with a shrug of her rounded shoulders. "Would you have had him let you die? I think the brave man was he who got in front of the bull and twisted its nose, not he who sat on its back and poked at it with a spear."

At this period in our conversation I became suddenly faint and lost count of things, even of the interesting Mameena. When I awoke again she was gone, and in her place was old Umbezi, who, I noticed, took down a mat from the side of the hut and folded it up to serve as a cushion before he sat himself upon the stool.

"Greeting, Macumazahn," he said when he saw that I was awake; "how are you?"

"As well as can be hoped," I answered; "and how are you, Umbezi?"

"Oh, bad, Macumazahn; even now I can scarcely sit down, for that bull had a very hard nose; also I am swollen up in front where Sikauli struck me when he tumbled out of the tree. Also my heart is cut in two because of our losses."

"What losses, Umbezi?"

"Wow! Macumazahn, the fire that those low fellows of mine lit got to our camp and burned up nearly everything—the meat, the skins, and even the ivory, which it cracked so that it is useless. That was an unlucky hunt, for although it began so well, we have come out of it quite naked; yes, with nothing at all except the head of the bull with the cleft horn, that I thought you might like to keep."

"Well, Umbezi, let us be thankful that we have come out with our lives—that is, if I am going to live," I added.

"Oh, Macumazahn, you will live without doubt, and be none the worse. Two of our doctors—very clever men—have looked at you and said so. One of them tied you up in all those skins, and I promised him a heifer for the business, if he cured you, and gave him a goat on account. But you must lie here for a month or more, so he says. Meanwhile Panda has sent for the hides which he demanded of me to be made into shields, and I have been obliged to kill twenty-five of my beasts to provide them—that is, of my own and of those of my headmen."

"Then I wish you and your headmen had killed them before we met those buffalo, Umbezi," I groaned, for my ribs were paining me very much. "Send Saduko and Sikauli here; I would thank them for saving my life."

So they came, next morning, I think, and I thanked them warmly enough.

"There, there, Baas," said Scowl, who was literally weeping tears of joy at my return from delirium and coma to the light of life and reason; not tears of Mameena's sort, but real ones, for I saw them running down his snub nose, that still bore marks of the eagle's claws. "There, there, say no more, I beseech you. If you were going to die, I wished to die, too, who, if you had left it, should only have wandered through the world without a heart. That is why I jumped into the pool, not because I am brave."

When I heard this my own eyes grew moist. Oh, it is the fashion to abuse natives, but from whom do we meet with more fidelity and love than from these poor wild *Kafirs* that so many of us talk of as black dirt which chances to be fashioned to the shape of man?

"As for myself, *Inkoosi*," added Saduko, "I only did my duty. How could I have held up my head again if the bull had killed you while

I walked away alive? Why, the very girls would have mocked at me. But, oh, his skin was tough. I thought that *assegai* would never get through it."

Observe the difference between these two men's characters. The one, although no hero in daily life, imperils himself from sheer, dog-like fidelity to a master who had given him many hard words and sometimes a flogging in punishment for drunkenness, and the other to gratify his pride, also perhaps because my death would have interfered with his plans and ambitions in which I had a part to play. No, that is a hard saying; still, there is no doubt that Saduko always first took his own interests into consideration, and how what he did would reflect upon his prospects and repute, or influence the attainment of his desires. I think this was so even when Mameena was concerned—at any rate, in the beginning—although certainly he always loved her with a single-hearted passion that is very rare among Zulus.

Presently Scowl left the hut to prepare me some broth, whereon Saduko at once turned the talk to this subject of Mameena. He understood that I had seen her. Did I not think her very beautiful?

"Yes, very beautiful," I answered; "indeed, the most beautiful Zulu woman I have ever seen."

And very clever—almost as clever as a white?

"Yes, and very clever—much cleverer than most whites."

And—anything else?

"Yes; very dangerous, and one who could turn like the wind and blow hot and blow cold."

"Ah!" he said, thought a while, then added: "Well, what do I care how she blows to others, so long as she blows hot to me."

"Well, Saduko, and does she blow hot for you?"

"Not altogether, Macumazahn." Another pause. "I think she blows rather like the wind before a great storm."

"That is a biting wind, Saduko, and when we feel it we know that the storm will follow."

"I dare say that the storm will follow, *Inkoosi*, for she was born in a storm and storm goes with her; but what of that, if she and I stand it out together? I love her, and I had rather die with her than live with any other woman."

"The question is, Saduko, whether she would rather die with you than live with any other man. Does she say so?"

"*Inkoosi*, Mameena's thought works in the dark; it is like a white ant in its tunnel of mud. You see the tunnel which shows that she is thinking, but you do not see the thought within. Still, sometimes, when she believes that no one beholds or hears her"—here I bethought me of the young lady's soliloquy over my apparently senseless self—"or when she is surprised, the true thought peeps out of its tunnel. It did so the other day, when I pleaded with her after she had heard that I killed the buffalo with the cleft horn.

"'Do I love you?' she said. 'I know not for sure. How can I tell? It is not our custom that a maiden should love before she is married, for if she did so most marriages would be things of the heart and not of cattle, and then half the fathers of Zululand would grow poor and refuse to rear girl-children who would bring them nothing. You are brave, you are handsome, you are well-born; I would sooner live with you than with any other man I know—that is, if you were rich and, better still, powerful. Become rich and powerful, Saduko, and I think that I shall love you.'

"'I will, Mameena,' I answered; 'but you must wait. The Zulu nation was not fashioned from nothing in a day. First Chaka had to come.'

"'Ah!' she said, and, my father, her eyes flashed. 'Ah! Chaka! There was a man! Be another Chaka, Saduko, and I will love you more—more than you can dream of—thus and thus,' and she flung her arms about me and kissed me as I was never kissed before, which, as you know, among us is a strange thing for a girl to do. Then she thrust me from her with a laugh, and added: 'As for the waiting, you must ask my father of that. Am I not his heifer, to be sold, and can I disobey my father?' And she was gone, leaving me empty, for it seemed as though she took my vitals with her. Nor will she talk thus any more, the white ant who has gone back into its tunnel."

"And did you speak to her father?"

"Yes, I spoke to him, but in an evil moment, for he had but just killed the cattle to furnish Panda's shields. He answered me very roughly. He said: 'You see these dead beasts which I and my people must slay for the king, or fall under his displeasure? Well, bring me five times their number, and we will talk of your marriage with my daughter, who is a maid in some request.'

"I answered that I understood and would try my best, whereon he became more gentle, for Umbezi has a kindly heart.

"'My son,' he said, 'I like you well, and since I saw you save Macumazahn, my friend, from that mad wild beast of a buffalo I like you better than before. Yet you know my case. I have an old name and am called the chief of a tribe, and many live on me. But I am poor, and this daughter of mine is worth much. Such a woman few men have bred. Well, I must make the best of her. My son-in-law must be one who will prop up my old age, one to whom, in my need or trouble, I could always go as to a dry log,[1] to break off some of its bark to make a fire to comfort me, not one who treads me into the mire as the buffalo did to Macumazahn. Now I have spoken, and I do not love such talk. Come back with the cattle, and I will listen to you, but meanwhile understand that I am not bound to you or to anyone; I shall take what my spirit sends me, which, if I may judge the future by the past, will not be much. One word more: Do not linger about this *kraal* too long, lest it should be said that you are the accepted suitor of Mameena. Go hence and do a man's work, and return with a man's reward, or not at all.'"

"Well, Saduko, that spear has an edge on it, has it not?" I answered. "And now, what is your plan?"

"My plan is, Macumazahn," he said, rising from his seat, "to go hence and gather those who are friendly to me because I am my father's son and still the chief of the Amangwane, or those who are left of them, although I have no *kraal* and no hoof of kine. Then, within a moon, I hope, I shall return here to find you strong again and once more a man, and we will start out against Bangu, as I have whispered to you, with the leave of a High One, who has said that, if I can take any cattle, I may keep them for my pains."

"I don't know about that, Saduko. I never promised you that I would make war upon Bangu—with or without the king's leave."

"No, you never promised, but Zikali the Dwarf, the Wise Little One, said that you would—and does Zikali lie? Ask yourself, who will remember a certain saying of his about a buffalo with a cleft horn, a pool and a dry river-bed. Farewell, O my father Macumazahn; I walk with the dawn, and I leave Mameena in your keeping."

"You mean that you leave me in Mameena's keeping," I began, but already he was crawling through the hole in the hut.

Well, Mameena kept me very comfortably. She was always in evidence, yet not too much so.

Heedless of her malice and abuse, she headed off the Worn-out-old-Cow, whom she knew I detested, from my presence. She saw personally to my bandages, as well as to the cooking of my food, over which matter she had several quarrels with the bastard, Scowl, who did not like her, for on him she never wasted any of her sweet looks. Also, as I grew stronger, she sat with me a good deal, talking, since, by common consent, Mameena the fair was exempted from all the field, and even

1. In Zululand a son-in-law is known as *isigodo so mkwenyana*, the "son-in-law log," for the reason stated in the text.—*Editor*

the ordinary household labours that fall to the lot of *Kafir* women. Her place was to be the ornament and, I may add, the advertisement of her father's *kraal*. Others might do the work, and she saw that they did it.

We discussed all sorts of things, from the Christian and other religions and European policy down, for her thirst for knowledge seemed to be insatiable. But what really interested her was the state of affairs in Zululand, with which she knew I was well acquainted, as a person who had played a part in its history and who was received and trusted at the Great House, and as a white man who understood the designs and plans of the Boers and of the Governor of Natal.

Now, if the old king, Panda, should chance to die, she would ask me, which of his sons did I think would succeed him—Umbelazi or Cetewayo, or another? Or, if he did not chance to die, which of them would he name his heir?

I replied that I was not a prophet, and that she had better ask Zikali the Wise.

"That is a very good idea," she said, "only I have no one to take me to him, since my father would not allow me to go with Saduko, his ward." Then she clapped her hands and added: "Oh, Macumazahn, will you take me? My father would trust me with you."

"Yes, I dare say," I answered; "but the question is, could I trust myself with you?"

"What do you mean?" she asked. "Oh, I understand. Then, after all, I am more to you than a black stone to play with?"

I think it was that unlucky joke of mine which first set Mameena thinking, "like a white ant in its tunnel," as Saduko said. At least, after it her manner towards me changed; she became very deferential; she listened to my words as though they were all wisdom; I caught her looking at me with her soft eyes as though I were quite an admirable object. She began to talk to me of her difficulties, her troubles and her ambitions. She asked me for my advice as to Saduko. On this point I replied to her that, if she loved him, and her father would allow it, presumably she had better marry him.

"I like him well enough, Macumazahn, although he wearies me at times; but love—Oh, tell me, *what* is love?" Then she clasped her slim hands and gazed at me like a fawn.

"Upon my word, young woman," I replied, "that is a matter upon which I should have thought you more competent to instruct me."

"Oh, Macumazahn," she said almost in a whisper, and letting her head droop like a fading lily, "you have never given me the chance, have you?" And she laughed a little, looking extremely attractive.

"Good gracious!"—or, rather, its Zulu equivalent—I answered, for I began to feel nervous. "What do you mean, Mameena? How could I—" There I stopped.

"I do not know what I mean, Macumazahn," she exclaimed wildly, "but I know well enough what you mean—that you are white as snow and I am black as soot, and that snow and soot don't mix well together."

"No," I answered gravely, "snow is good to look at, and so is soot, but mingled they make an ugly colour. Not that you are like soot," I added hastily, fearing to hurt her feelings. "That is your hue"—and I touched a copper bangle she was wearing—"a very lovely hue, Mameena, like everything else about you."

"Lovely," she said, beginning to weep a little, which upset me very much, for if there is one thing I hate, it is to see a woman cry. "How can a poor Zulu girl be lovely? Oh, Macumazahn, the spirits have dealt hardly with me, who have given me the colour of my people and the heart of yours. If I were white, now, what you are pleased to call this loveliness of mine would be of some use to me, for then—then—Oh, cannot you guess, Macumazahn?"

I shook my head and said that I could not, and next moment was sorry, for she proceeded to explain.

Sinking to her knees—for we were quite alone in the big hut and there was no one else about, all the other women being engaged on rural or domestic tasks, for which Mameena declared she had no time, as her business was to look after me—she rested her shapely head upon my knees and began to talk in a low, sweet voice that sometimes broke into a sob.

"Then I will tell you—I will tell you; yes, even if you hate me afterwards. I could teach you what love is very well, Macumazahn; you are quite right—because I love you." (Sob.) "No, you shall not stir till you have heard me out." Here she flung her arms about my legs and held them tight, so that without using great violence it was absolutely impossible for me to move. "When I saw you first, all shattered and senseless, snow seemed to fall upon my heart, and it stopped for a little while and has never been the same since. I think that something is growing in it, Macumazahn, that makes it big." (Sob.) "I used to like Saduko before that, but afterwards I did not like him at all—no, nor Masapo either—you know, he is the big chief who lives over the mountain, a very rich and powerful man, who, I believe, would like to marry me. Well, as I went on nursing you my heart grew bigger and bigger, and now you see it has burst." (Sob.) "Nay, stay still and do not try to speak. You *shall* hear me out. It is the least you can do, seeing that you have caused me all this pain. If you did not want me to love you, why did you not curse at me and strike me, as I am told white men do to *Kafir* girls?" She rose and went on:

"Now, hearken. Although I am the colour of copper, I am comely. I am well-bred also; there is no higher blood than ours in Zululand, both on my father's and my mother's side, and, Macumazahn, I have a fire in me that shows me things. I can be great, and I long for greatness. Take me to wife, Macumazahn, and I swear to you that in ten years I will make you king of the Zulus. Forget your pale white women and wed yourself to that fire which burns in me, and it shall eat up all that stands between you and the Crown, as flame eats up dry grass. More, I will make you happy. If you choose to take other wives, I will not be jealous, because I know that I should hold your spirit, and that, compared to me, they would be nothing in your thought—"

"But, Mameena," I broke in, "I don't want to be king of the Zulus."

"Oh, yes, yes, you do, for every man wants power, and it is better to rule over a brave, black people—thousands and thousands of them—than to be no one among the whites. Think, think! There is wealth in the land. By your skill and knowledge the *amabuto* (regiments) could be improved; with the wealth you would arm them with guns—yes, and 'by-and-byes' also with the throat of thunder" (that is, or was, the *Kafir* name for cannon).[2] "They would be invincible. Chaka's kingdom would be nothing to ours, for a hundred thousand warriors would sleep on their spears, waiting for your word. If you wished it even you could sweep out Natal and make the whites there your subjects, too. Or perhaps it would be safer to let them be, lest others should come across the green water to help them, and to strike northwards, where I am told there are great lands as rich and fair, in which none would dispute our sovereignty—"

"But, Mameena," I gasped, for this girl's titanic ambition literally overwhelmed me, "surely you are mad! How would you do all these things?"

"I am not mad," she answered; "I am only what is called great, and you know well enough that I can do them, not by myself, who am but a woman and tied with the ropes that bind women, but with you to cut those ropes and help me. I have a plan which will not fail. But, Macumazahn," she added in a changed voice, "until I know that you will be my partner in it I will not tell it even to you, for perhaps you might talk—in your sleep, and then the fire in my breast would soon go out—for ever."

2. Cannon were called "by-and-byes" by the natives, because when field-pieces first arrived in Natal inquisitive *Kafirs* pestered the soldiers to show them how they were fired. The answer given was always "By-and-bye!" Hence the name.—*Editor*

"I might talk now, for the matter of that, Mameena."

"No; for men like you do not tell tales of foolish girls who chance to love them. But if that plan began to work, and you heard say that kings or princes died, it might be otherwise. You might say, 'I think I know where the witch lives who causes these evils'—in your sleep, Macumazahn."

"Mameena," I said, "tell me no more. Setting your dreams on one side, can I be false to my friend, Saduko, who talks to me day and night of you?"

"Saduko! *Piff!*" she exclaimed, with that expressive gesture of her hand.

"And can I be false," I continued, seeing that Saduko was no good card to play, "to my friend, Umbezi, your father?"

"My father!" she laughed. "Why, would it not please him to grow great in your shadow? Only yesterday he told me to marry you, if I could, for then he would find a stick indeed to lean on, and be rid of Saduko's troubling."

Evidently Umbezi was a worse card even than Saduko, so I played another.

"And can I help you, Mameena, to tread a road that at the best must be red with blood?"

"Why not," she asked, "since with or without you I am destined to tread that road, the only difference being that with you it will lead to glory and without you perhaps to the jackals and the vultures? Blood! *Piff!* What is blood in Zululand?"

This card also having failed, I tabled my last.

"Glory or no glory, I do not wish to share it, Mameena. I will not make war among a people who have entertained me hospitably, or plot the downfall of their Great Ones. As you told me just now, I am nobody—just one grain of sand upon a white shore—but I had rather be that than a haunted rock which draws the heavens' lightnings and is drenched with sacrifice. I seek no throne over white or black, Mameena, who walk my own path to a quiet grave that shall perhaps not be without honour of its own, though other than you seek. I will keep your counsel, Mameena, but, because you are so beautiful and so wise, and because you say you are fond of me—for which I thank you—I pray you put away these fearful dreams of yours that in the end, whether they succeed or fail, will send you shivering from the world to give account of them to the Watcher-on-high."

"Not so, O Macumazana," she said, with a proud little laugh.

"When your Watcher sowed my seed—if thus he did—he sowed the dreams that are a part of me also, and I shall only bring him back his own, with the flower and the fruit by way of interest. But that is finished. You refuse the greatness. Now, tell me, if I sink those dreams in a great water, tying about them the stone of forgetfulness and saying: 'Sleep there, O dreams; it is not your hour'—if I do this, and stand before you just a woman who loves and who swears by the spirits of her fathers never to think or do that which has not your blessing—will you love me a little, Macumazahn?"

Now I was silent, for she had driven me to the last ditch, and I knew not what to say. Moreover, I will confess my weakness—I was strangely moved. This beautiful girl with the "fire in her heart," this woman who was different from all other women that I had ever known, seemed to have twisted her slender fingers into my heartstrings and to be drawing me towards her. It was a great temptation, and I bethought me of old Zikali's saying in the Black Kloof, and seemed to hear his giant laugh.

She glided up to me, she threw her arms about me and kissed me on the lips, and I think I kissed her back, but really I am not sure what I did or said, for my head swam. When it cleared again she was standing in front of me, looking at me reflectively.

"Now, Macumazahn," she said, with a little smile that both mocked and dazzled, "the poor black girl has you, the wise, experienced white man, in her net, and I will show you that she can be generous. Do you think that I do not read your heart, that I do not know that you believe I am dragging you down to shame and ruin? Well, I spare you, Macumazahn, since you have kissed me and spoken words which already you may have forgotten, but which I do not forget. Go your road, Macumazahn, and I go mine, since the proud white man shall not be stained with my black touch. Go your road; but one thing I forbid you—to believe that you have been listening to lies, and that I have merely played off a woman's arts upon you for my own ends. I love you, Macumazahn, as you will never be loved till you die, and I shall never love any other man, however many I may marry. Moreover, you shall promise me one thing—that once in my life, and once only, if I wish it, you shall kiss me again before all men. And now, lest you should be moved to folly and forget your white man's pride, I bid you farewell, O Macumazana. When we meet again it will be as friends only."

Then she went, leaving me feeling smaller than ever I felt in my life, before or since—even smaller than when I walked into the presence of old Zikali the Wise. Why, I wondered, had she first made a fool of me, and then thrown away the fruits of my folly? To this hour I cannot quite answer the question, though I believe the explanation to be that she did really care for me, and was anxious not to involve me in trouble and her plottings; also she may have been wise enough to see that our natures were as oil and water and would never blend.

Chapter 5

Two Bucks and the Doe

It may be thought that, as a sequel to this somewhat remarkable scene in which I was absolutely bowled over—perhaps bowled out would be a better term—by a *Kafir* girl who, after bending me to her will, had the genius to drop me before I repented, as she knew I would do so soon as her back was turned, thereby making me look the worst of fools, that my relations with that young lady would have been strained. But not a bit of it. When next we met, which was on the following morning, she was just her easy, natural self, attending to my hurts, which by now were almost well, joking about this and that, inquiring as to the contents of certain letters which I had received from Natal, and of some newspapers that came with them—for on all such matters she was very curious—and so forth.

Impossible, the clever critic will say—impossible that a savage could act with such finish. Well, friend critic, that is just where you are wrong. When you come to add it up there's very little difference in all main and essential matters between the savage and yourself.

To begin with, by what exact right do we call people like the Zulus savages? Setting aside the habit of polygamy, which, after all, is common among very highly civilised peoples in the East, they have a social system not unlike our own. They have, or had, their king, their nobles, and their commons. They have an ancient and elaborate law, and a system of morality in some ways as high as our own, and certainly more generally obeyed. They have their priests and their doctors; they are strictly upright, and observe the rites of hospitality.

Where they differ from us mainly is that they do not get drunk until the white man teaches them so to do, they wear less clothing, the climate being more genial, their towns at night are not disgraced by the sights that distinguish ours, they cherish and are never cruel to their children, although they may occasionally put a deformed infant or a twin out of the way, and when they go to war, which is often, they carry out the business with a terrible thoroughness, almost as terrible as that which prevailed in every nation in Europe a few generations ago.

Of course, there remain their witchcraft and the cruelties which result from their almost universal belief in the power and efficiency of magic. Well, since I lived in England I have been reading up this subject, and I find that quite recently similar cruelties were practised throughout Europe—that is in a part of the world which for over a thousand years has enjoyed the advantages of the knowledge and profession of the Christian faith.

Now, let him who is highly cultured take up a stone to throw at the poor, untaught Zulu, which I notice the most dissolute and drunken wretch of a white man is often ready to do, generally because he covets his land, his labour, or whatever else may be his.

But I wander from my point, which is that a clever man or woman among the people whom we call savages is in all essentials very much the same as a clever man or woman anywhere else.

Here in England every child is educated at the expense of the Country, but I have not observed that the system results in the production of more really able individuals. Ability is the gift of Nature, and that universal mother sheds her favours impartially over all who breathe. No, not quite impartially, perhaps, for the old Greeks and others were examples to the contrary. Still, the general rule obtains.

To return. Mameena was a very able person, as she chanced to be a very lovely one, a person who, had she been favoured by opportunity, would doubtless have played the part of a Cleopatra with equal or greater success, since she shared the beauty and the unscrupulousness of that famous lady and was, I believe, capable of her passion.

I scarcely like to mention the matter since it affects myself, and the natural vanity of man makes him prone to conclude that he is the particular object of sole and undying devotion. Could he know all the facts of the case, or cases, probably he would be much undeceived, and feel about as small as I did when Mameena walked, or rather crawled, out of the hut (she could even crawl gracefully). Still, to be honest—and why should I not, since all this business "went beyond" so long ago?—I do believe that there was a certain amount of truth in what she said—that, for Heaven knows what reason, she did take a fancy to me, which fancy continued during her short and stormy life. But the reader of her story may judge for himself.

Within a fortnight of the day of my discomfiture in the hut I was quite well and strong again, my ribs, or whatever part of me it was that the buffalo had injured with his iron knees, having mended up. Also, I was anxious to be going, having business to attend to in Natal, and, as no more had been seen or heard of Saduko, I determined to trek homewards, leaving a message that he knew where to find me if he wanted me. The truth is that I was by no means keen on being involved in his private war with Bangu. Indeed, I wished to wash my hands of the whole matter, including the fair Mameena and her mocking eyes.

So one morning, having already got up my oxen, I told Scowl to inspan them—an order which he received with joy, for he and the other boys wished to be off to civilisation and its delights. Just as the operation was beginning, however, a message came to me from old Umbezi, who begged me to delay my departure till after noon, as a friend of his, a big chief, had come to visit him who wished much to have the honour of making my acquaintance. Now, I wished the big chief farther off, but, as it seemed rude to refuse the request of one who had been so kind to me, I ordered the oxen to be unyoked but kept at hand, and in an irritable frame of mind walked up to the *kraal*. This was about half a mile from my place of outspan, for as soon as I was sufficiently recovered I had begun to sleep in my wagon, leaving the big hut to the Worn-out-Old-Cow.

There was no particular reason why I should be irritated, since time in those days was of no great account in Zululand, and it did not much matter to me whether I trekked in the morning or the afternoon. But the fact was that I could not get over the prophecy of Zikali, "the Little and Wise," that I was destined to share Saduko's expedition against Bangu, and, although he had been right about the buffalo and Mameena, I was determined to prove him wrong in this particular.

If I had left the country, obviously I could not go against Bangu, at any rate at present. But while I remained in it Saduko might return at any moment, and then, doubtless, I should find it hard to escape from the kind of half-promise that I had given to him.

Well, as soon as I reached the *kraal* I saw that some kind of festivity was in progress, for an ox had been killed and was being cooked, some of it in pots and some by roasting; also there were several strange Zulus present. Within the fence of the *kraal*, seated in its shadow, I found Umbezi and some of his headmen, and with them a great, brawny *ringed* native, who wore a tiger-skin *moocha* as a mark of rank, and some of *his* headmen. Also Mameena was standing near the gate, dressed in her best beads and holding a gourd of *Kafir* beer which, evidently, she had just been handing to the guests.

"Would you have run away without saying good-bye to me, Macumazahn?" she whispered to me as I came abreast of her. "That is unkind of you, and I should have wept much. However, it was not so fated."

"I was going to ride up and bid farewell when the oxen were inspanned," I answered. "But who is that man?"

"You will find out presently, Macumazahn. Look, my father is beckoning to us."

So I went on to the circle, and as I advanced Umbezi rose and, taking me by the hand, led me to the big man, saying:

"This is Masapo, chief of the Amansomi, of the Quabe race, who desires to know you, Macumazahn."

"Very kind of him, I am sure," I replied coolly, as I threw my eye over Masapo. He was, as I have said, a big man, and of about fifty years of age, for his hair was tinged with grey. To be frank, I took a great dislike to him at once, for there was something in his strong, coarse face, and his air of insolent pride, which repelled me. Then I was silent, since among the Zulus, when two strangers of more or less equal rank meet, he who speaks first acknowledges inferiority to the other. Therefore I stood and contemplated this new suitor of Mameena, waiting on events.

Masapo also contemplated me, then made some remark to one of his attendants, that I did not catch, which caused the fellow to laugh.

"He has heard that you are an *ipisi*" (a great hunter), broke in Umbezi, who evidently felt that the situation was growing strained, and that it was necessary to say something.

"Has he?" I answered. "Then he is more fortunate than I am, for I have never heard of him or what he is." This, I am sorry to say, was a fib, for it will be remembered that Mameena had mentioned him in the hut as one of her suitors, but among natives one must keep up one's dignity somehow. "Friend Umbezi," I went on, "I have come to bid you farewell, as I am about to trek for Durban."

At this juncture Masapo stretched out his great hand to me, but without rising, and said:

"*Siyakubona* (that is, good-day), white man."

"*Siyakubona*, black man," I answered, just touching his fingers, while Mameena, who had come up again with her beer, and was facing me, made a little grimace and tittered.

Now I turned on my heel to go, whereon Masapo said in a coarse, growling voice:

"O Macumazana, before you leave us I wish to speak with you on a certain matter. Will it please you to sit aside with me for a while?"

"Certainly, O Masapo." And I walked away a few yards out of hearing, whither he followed me.

"Macumazahn," he said (I give the gist of his remarks, for he did not come to the point at once), "I need guns, and I am told that you can provide them, being a trader."

"Yes, Masapo, I dare say that I can, at a price, though it is a risky business smuggling guns into Zululand. But might I ask what you need them for? is it to shoot elephants?"

"Yes, to shoot elephants," he replied, rolling his big eyes round him. "Macumazahn, I am told that you are discreet, that you do not shout from the top of a hut what you hear within it. Now, hearken to me. Our country is disturbed; we do not all of us love the seed of Senzangakona, of whom the present king, Panda, is one. For instance, you may know that we Quabies—for my tribe, the Amansomi, are of that race—suffered at the spear of Chaka. Well, we think that a time may come when we who live on shrubs like goats may again browse on tree-tops like giraffes, for Panda is no strong king, and he has sons who hate each other, one of whom may need our spears. Do you understand?"

"I understand that you want guns, O Masapo," I answered dryly. "Now, as to the price and place of delivery."

Then we bargained for a while, but the details of that business transaction of long ago will interest no one. Indeed, I only mention the matter to show that Masapo was plotting to bring trouble on the ruling house, whereof Panda was the representative at that time.

When we had concluded our rather nefarious negotiations, which were to the effect that I was to receive so many cattle in return for so many guns, if I could deliver them at a certain spot, namely, Umbezi's *kraal*, I returned to the circle where Umbezi, his followers and guests were sitting, purposing to bid him farewell. By now, however, meat had been served, and as I was hungry, having had little breakfast that morning, I stayed to eat. When I had finished my meal, and washed it down with a draught of *tshwala* (that is, *Kafir* beer), I rose to go, but just at that moment who should walk through the gate but Saduko?

"Piff!" said Mameena, who was standing near me, speaking in a voice that none but I could hear. "When two bucks meet, what happens, Macumazahn?"

"Sometimes they fight and sometimes one runs away. It depends very much on the doe," I answered in the same low voice, looking at her.

She shrugged her shoulders, folded her arms beneath her breast, nodded to Saduko as he passed, then leaned gracefully against the fence and awaited events.

"Greeting, Umbezi," said Saduko in his proud manner. "I see that you feast. Am I welcome here?"

"Of course you are always welcome, Saduko," replied Umbezi uneasily, "although, as it happens, I am entertaining a great man." And he looked towards Masapo.

"I see," said Saduko, eyeing the strangers. "But which of these may be the great man? I ask that I may salute him."

"You know well enough, *umfokazana*" (that is, low fellow), exclaimed Masapo angrily.

"I know that if you were outside this fence, Masapo, I would cram that word down your throat at the point of my *assegai*," replied Saduko in a fierce voice. "Oh, I can guess your business here, Masapo, and you can guess mine," and he glanced towards Mameena. "Tell me, Umbezi, is this little chief of the Amansomi your daughter's accepted suitor?"

"Nay, nay, Saduko," said Umbezi; "no one is her accepted suitor. Will you not sit down and take food with us? Tell us where you have been, and why you return here thus suddenly, and—uninvited?"

"I return here, O Umbezi, to speak with the white chief, Macumazahn. As to where I have been, that is my affair, and not yours or Masapo's."

"Now, if I were chief of this *kraal*," said Masapo, "I would hunt out of it this hyena with a mangy coat and without a hole who comes to devour your meat and, perhaps," he added with meaning, "to steal away your child."

"Did I not tell you, Macumazahn, that when two bucks met they would fight?" whispered Mameena suavely into my ear.

"Yes, Mameena, you did—or rather I told you. But you did not tell me what the doe would do."

"The doe, Macumazahn, will crouch in her form and see what happens—as is the fashion of does," and again she laughed softly.

"Why not do your own hunting, Masapo?" asked Saduko. "Come, now, I will promise you good sport. Outside this *kraal* there are other hyenas waiting who call me chief—a hundred or two of them—assembled for a certain purpose by the royal leave of King Panda, whose House, as we all know, you hate. Come, leave that beef and beer and begin your hunting of hyenas, O Masapo."

Now Masapo sat silent, for he saw that he who thought to snare a baboon had caught a tiger.

"You do not speak, O Chief of the little Amansomi," went on Saduko, who was beside himself with rage and jealousy. "You will not leave your beef and beer to hunt the hyenas who are captained by an *umfokazana*! Well, then, the *umfokazana* will speak," and, stepping up to Masapo, with the spear he carried poised in his right hand, Saduko grasped his rival's short beard with his left.

"Listen, Chief," he said. "You and I are enemies. You seek the woman I seek, and, mayhap, being rich, you will buy her. But if so, I tell you that I will kill you and all your House, you sneaking, half-bred dog!"

With these fierce words he spat in his face and tumbled him backwards. Then, before anyone could stop him, for Umbezi, and even Masapo's headmen, seemed paralysed with surprise, he stalked through the *kraal* gate, saying as he passed me:

"*Inkoosi*, I have words for you when you are at liberty."

"You shall pay for this," roared Umbezi after him, turning almost green with rage, for Masapo still lay upon his broad back, speechless, "you who dare to insult my guest in my own house."

"Somebody must pay," cried back Saduko from the gate, "but who it is only the unborn moons will see."

"Mameena," I said as I followed him, "you have set fire to the grass, and men will be burned in it."

"I meant to, Macumazahn," she answered calmly. "Did I not tell you that there was a flame in me, and it will break out sometimes? But, Macumazahn, it is you who have set fire to the grass, not I. Remember that when half Zululand is in ashes. Farewell, O Macumazana, till we meet again, and," she added softly, "whoever else must burn, may the spirits have *you* in their keeping."

At the gate, remembering my manners, I turned to bid that company a polite farewell. By now Masapo had gained his feet, and was roaring out like a bull:

"Kill him! Kill the hyena! Umbezi, will you sit still and see me, your guest—me, Masapo—struck and insulted under the shadow of your own hut? Go forth and kill him, I say!"

"Why not kill him yourself, Masapo," asked the agitated Umbezi, "or bid your headmen kill him? Who am I that I should take precedence of so great a chief in a matter of the spear?" Then he turned towards me, saying: "Oh, Macumazahn the crafty, if I have dealt well by you, come here and give me your counsel."

"I come, Eater-up-of-Elephants," I answered, and I did.

"What shall I do—what shall I do?" went on Umbezi, brushing the perspiration off his brow with one hand, while he wrung the other in his agitation. "There stands a friend of mine"—he pointed to the infuriated Masapo—"who wishes me to kill another friend of mine," and he jerked his thumb towards the *kraal* gate. "If I refuse I offend one friend, and if I consent I bring blood upon my hands which will call for blood, since, although Saduko is poor, without doubt he has those who love him."

"Yes," I answered, "and perhaps you will bring blood upon other parts of yourself besides your hands, since Saduko is not one to sit still like a sheep while his throat is cut. Also did he not say that he is not quite alone? Umbezi, if you will take my advice, you will leave Masapo to do his own killing."

"It is good; it is wise!" exclaimed Umbezi. "Masapo," he called to that warrior, "if you wish to fight, pray do not think of me. I see nothing, I hear nothing, and I promise proper burial to any who fall. Only you had best be swift, for Saduko is walking away all this time. Come, you and your people have spears, and the gate stands open."

"Am I to go without my meat in order to knock that hyena on the head?" asked Masapo in a brave voice. "No, he can wait my leisure. Sit still, my people. I tell you, sit still. Tell him, you Macumazahn, that I am coming for him presently, and be warned to keep yourself away from him, lest you should tumble into his hole."

"I will tell him," I answered, "though I know not who made me your messenger. But listen to me, you Speaker of big words and Doer of small deeds, if you dare to lift a finger against me I will teach you something about holes, for there shall be one or more through that great carcass of yours."

Then, walking up to him, I looked him in the face, and at the same time tapped the handle of the big double-barrelled pistol I carried.

He shrank back muttering something.

"Oh, don't apologise," I said, "only be more careful in future. And now I wish you a good dinner, Chief Masapo, and peace upon your *kraal*, friend Umbezi."

After this speech I marched off, followed by the clamour of Masapo's furious attendants and the sound of Mameena's light and mocking laughter.

"I wonder which of them she will marry?" I thought to myself, as I set out for the wagons.

As I approached my camp I saw that the oxen were being inspanned, as I supposed by the order of Scowl, who must have heard that there was a row up at the *kraal*, and thought it well to be ready to bolt. In this I was mistaken, however, for just then Saduko strolled out of a patch of bush and said:

"I ordered your boys to yoke up the oxen, *Inkoosi*."

"Have you? That's cool!" I answered. "Perhaps you will tell me why."

"Because we must make a good trek to the northward before night, *Inkoosi*."

"Indeed! I thought that I was heading south-east."

"Bangu does not live in the south or the east," he replied slowly.

"Oh, I had almost forgotten about Bangu," I said, with a rather feeble attempt at evasion.

"Is it so?" he answered in his haughty voice. "I never knew before that Macumazahn was a man who broke a promise to his friend."

"Would you be so kind as to explain your meaning, Saduko?"

"Is it needful?" he answered, shrugging his shoulders. "Unless my ears played me tricks, you agreed to go up with me against Bangu. Well, I have gathered the necessary men—with the king's leave—they await us yonder," and he pointed with his spear towards a dense patch of bush that lay some miles beneath us. "But," he added, "if you desire to change your mind I will go alone. Only then, I think, we had better bid each other good-bye, since I love not friends who change their minds when the *assegais* begin to shake."

Now, whether Saduko spoke thus by design I do not know. Certainly, however, he could have found no better way to ensure my companionship for what it was worth, since, although I had made no actual promise in this case, I have always prided myself on keeping even a half-bargain with a native.

"I will go with you," I said quietly, "and I hope that, when it comes to the pinch, your spear will be as sharp as your tongue, Saduko. Only do not speak to me again like that, lest we should quarrel." As I said this I saw a look of relief appear on his face, of very great relief.

"I pray your pardon, my lord Macumazahn," he said, seizing my hand, "but, oh! there is a hole in my heart. I think that Mameena means to play me false, and now that has happened with yonder dog, Masapo, which will make her father hate me."

"If you will take my advice, Saduko," I replied earnestly, "you will let this Mameena fall out of the hole in your heart; you will forget her name; you will have done with her. Ask me not why."

"Perhaps there is no need, O Macumazana. Perhaps she has been making love to you, and you have turned her away, as, being what you are, and my friend, of course you would do." (It is rather inconvenient to be set upon such a pedestal at times, but I did not attempt to assent or to deny anything, much less to enter into explanations.)

"Perhaps all this has happened," he continued, "or perhaps it is she who has sent for Masapo the Hog. I do not ask, because if you know you will not tell me. Moreover, it matters nothing. While I have a heart, Mameena will never drop out of it; while I can remember names, hers will never be forgotten by me. Moreover, I mean that she shall be my wife. Now, I am minded to take a few men and spear this hog, Masapo, before we go up against Bangu, for then he, at any rate, will be out of my road."

"If you do anything of the sort, Saduko, you will go up against Bangu alone, for I trek east at once, who will not be mixed up with murder."

"Then let it be, *Inkoosi*; unless he attacks me, as my Snake send that he may, the Hog can wait. After all, he will only be growing a little fatter. Now, if it pleases you order the wagons to trek. I will show the road, for we must camp in that bush to-night where my people wait me, and there I will tell you my plans; also you will find one with a message for you."

Chapter 6

The Ambush

We had reached the bush after six hours' downhill trek over a pretty bad track made by cattle—of course, there were no roads in Zululand at this date. I remember the place well. It was a kind of spreading woodland on a flat bottom, where trees of no great size grew sparsely. Some were mimosa thorns, others had deep green leaves and bore a kind of plum with an acid taste and a huge stone, and others silver-coloured leaves in their season. A river, too, low at this time of the year, wound through it, and in the scrub upon its banks were many guinea-fowl and other birds. It was a pleasing, lonely place, with lots of game in it, that came here in the winter to eat the grass, which was lacking on the higher *veld*. Also it gave the idea of vastness, since wherever one looked there was nothing to be seen except a sea of trees.

Well, we outspanned by the river, of which I forget the name, at a spot that Saduko showed us, and set to work to cook our food, that consisted of venison from a blue wildebeest, one of a herd of these wild-looking animals which I had been fortunate enough to shoot as they whisked past us, gambolling in and out between the trees.

While we were eating I observed that armed Zulus arrived continually in parties of from six to a score of men, and as they arrived lifted their spears, though whether in salutation to Saduko or to myself I did not know, and sat themselves down on an open space between us and the river-bank. Although it was difficult to say whence they came, for they appeared like ghosts out of the bush, I thought it well to take no notice of them, since I guessed that their coming was prearranged.

"Who are they?" I whispered to Scowl, as he brought me my tot of *squareface*.

"Saduko's wild men," he answered in the same low voice, "outlaws of his tribe who live among the rocks."

Now I scanned them sideways, while pretending to light my pipe and so forth, and certainly they seemed a remarkably savage set of people. Great, gaunt fellows with tangled hair, who wore tattered skins upon their shoulders and seemed to have no possessions save some snuff, a few sleeping-mats, and an ample supply of large fighting shields, hardwood *kerries* or knob-sticks, and broad *ixwas*, or stabbing *assegais*. Such was the look of them as they sat round us in silent semicircles, like aas-vogels—as the Dutch call vultures—sit round a dying ox.

Still I smoked on and took no notice.

At length, as I expected, Saduko grew weary of my silence and spoke. "These are men of the Amangwane tribe, Macumazahn; three hundred of them, all that Bangu left alive, for when their fathers were killed, the women escaped with some of the children, especially those of the outlying *kraals*. I have gathered them to be revenged upon Bangu, I who am their chief by right of blood."

"Quite so," I answered. "I see that you have gathered them; but do they wish to be revenged on Bangu at the risk of their own lives?"

"We do, white *Inkoosi*," came the deep-throated answer from the three hundred.

"And do they acknowledge you, Saduko, to be their chief?"

"We do," again came the answer. Then a spokesman stepped forward, one of the few grey-haired men among them, for most of these Amangwane were of the age of Saduko, or even younger.

"O Watcher-by-Night," he said, "I am Tshoza, the brother of Matiwane, Saduko's father, the only one of his brothers that escaped the slaughter on the night of the Great Killing. Is it not so?"

"It is so," exclaimed the serried ranks behind him.

"I acknowledge Saduko as my chief, and so do we all," went on Tshoza.

"So do we all," echoed the ranks.

"Since Matiwane died we have lived as we could, O Macumazana; like baboons among the rocks, without cattle, often without a hut to shelter us; here one, there one. Still, we have lived, awaiting the hour of vengeance upon Bangu, that hour which Zikali the Wise, who is of our blood, has promised to us. Now we believe that it has come, and one and all, from here, from there, from everywhere, we have gathered at the summons of Saduko to be led against Bangu and to conquer him or to die. Is it not so, Amangwane?"

"It is, it is so!" came the deep, unanimous answer, that caused the stirless leaves to shake in the still air.

"I understand, O Tshoza, brother of Matiwane and uncle of Saduko the chief," I replied. "But Bangu is a strong man, living, I am told, in a strong place. Still, let that go; for have you not said that you come out to conquer or to die, you who have nothing to lose; and if you conquer, you conquer; and if you die, you die and the tale is told. But supposing that you conquer. What will Panda, King of the Zulus, say to you, and to me also, who stir up war in his country?"

Now the Amangwane looked behind them, and Saduko cried out: "Appear, messenger from Panda the King!"

Before his words had ceased to echo I saw a little, withered man threading his way between the tall, gaunt forms of the Amangwane. He came and stood before me, saying:

"Hail, Macumazahn. Do you remember me?"

"Aye," I answered, "I remember you as Maputa, one of Panda's *indunas*."

"Quite so, Macumazahn; I am Maputa, one of his *indunas*, a member of his Council, a captain of his *impis* (that is, armies), as I was to his brothers who are gone, whose names it is not lawful that I should name. Well, Panda the King has sent me to you, at the request of Saduko there, with a message."

"How do I know that you are a true messenger?" I asked. "Have you brought me any token?"

"Aye," he answered, and, fumbling under his cloak, he produced something wrapped in dried leaves, which he undid and handed to me, saying:

"This is the token that Panda sends to you, Macumazahn, bidding me to tell you that you will certainly know it again; also that you are welcome to it, since the two little bullets which he swallowed as you directed made him very ill, and he needs no more of them."

I took the token, and, examining it in the moonlight, recognised it at once.

It was a cardboard box of strong calomel pills, on the top of which was written: "Allan Quatermain, Esq.: One *only* to be taken as directed." Without entering into explanations, I may state that I had taken "one as directed," and subsequently presented the rest of the box to King Panda, who was very anxious to "taste the white man's medicine."

"Do you recognise the token, Macumazahn?" asked the *induna*.

"Yes," I replied gravely; "and let the King return thanks to the spirits of his ancestors that he did not swallow three of the balls, for if he had done so, by now there would have been another Head in Zululand. Well, speak on, Messenger."

But to myself I reflected, not for the first time, how strangely these natives could mix up the sublime with the ridiculous. Here was a matter that must involve the death of many men, and the token sent to me by the autocrat who stood at the back of it all, to prove the good faith of his messenger, was a box of calomel pills! However, it served the purpose as well as anything else.

Maputa and I drew aside, for I saw that he wished to speak with me alone.

"O Macumazana," he said, when we were out of hearing of the others, "these are the words of Panda to you: 'I understand that you, Macumazahn, have promised to accompany Saduko, son of Matiwane, on an expedition of his against Bangu, chief of the Amakoba. Now, were anyone else concerned, I should forbid this expedition, and especially should I forbid you, a white man in my country, to share therein. But this dog of a Bangu is an evil-doer. Many years ago he worked on the Black One who went before me to send him to destroy Matiwane, my friend, filling the Black One's ears with false accusations; and thereafter he did treacherously destroy him and all his tribe save Saduko, his son, and some of the people and children who escaped. Moreover, of late he has been working against me, the King, striving to stir up rebellion against me, because he knows that I hate him for his crimes. Now I, Panda, unlike those who went before me, am a man of peace who do not wish to light the fire of civil war in the land, for who knows where such fires will stop, or whose *kraals* they will consume? Yet I do wish to see Bangu punished for his wickedness, and his pride abated. Therefore I give Saduko leave, and those people of the Amangwane who remain to him, to avenge their private wrongs upon Bangu if they can; and I give you leave, Macumazahn, to be of his party. Moreover, if any cattle are taken, I shall ask no account of them; you and Saduko may divide them as you wish. But understand, O Macumazana, that if you or your people are killed or wounded, or robbed of your goods, I know nothing of the matter, and am not responsible to you or to the white House of Natal; it is your own matter. These are my words. I have spoken.'"

"I see," I answered. "I am to pull Panda's hot iron out of the fire and to extinguish the fire. If I succeed I may keep a piece of the iron when it gets cool, and if I burn my fingers it is my own fault, and I or my House must not come crying to Panda."

"O Watcher-by-Night, you have speared the bull in the heart," replied Maputa, the messenger, nodding his shrewd old head. "Well, will you go up with Saduko?"

"Say to the King, O Messenger, that I will go up with Saduko because I promised him that I would, being moved by the tale of his wrongs, and not for the sake of the cattle, although it is true that if I hear any of them lowing in my camp I may keep them. Say to Panda also that if aught of ill befalls me he shall hear nothing of it, nor will I bring his high name into this business; but that he, on his part, must not blame me for anything that may happen afterwards. Have you the message?"

"I have it word for word; and may your Spirit be with you, Macumazahn, when you attack the strong mountain of Bangu, which, were I you," Maputa added reflectively, "I think I should do just at the dawn, since the Amakoba drink much beer and are heavy sleepers."

Then we took a pinch of snuff together, and he departed at once for Nodwengu, Panda's Great Place.

Fourteen days had gone by, and Saduko and I, with our ragged band of Amangwane, sat one morning, after a long night march, in the hilly country looking across a broad vale, which was sprinkled with trees like an English park, at that mountain on the side of which Bangu, chief of the Amakoba, had his *kraal*.

It was a very formidable mountain, and, as we had already observed, the paths leading up to the *kraal* were amply protected with stone walls in which the openings were quite narrow, only just big enough to allow one ox to pass through them at a time. Moreover, all these walls had been strengthened recently, perhaps because Bangu was aware that Panda looked upon him, a northern chief dwelling on the confines of his dominions, with suspicion and even active enmity, as he was also no doubt aware Panda had good cause to do.

Here in a dense patch of bush that grew in a kloof of the hills we held a council of war.

So far as we knew our advance had been unobserved, for I had left my wagons in the low *veld* thirty miles away, giving it out among the local natives that I was hunting game there, and bringing on with me only Scowl and four of my best hunters, all well-armed natives who could shoot. The three hundred Amangwane also had advanced in small parties, separated from each other, pretending to be *Kafirs* marching towards Delagoa Bay. Now, however, we had all met in this bush. Among our number were three Amangwane who, on the slaughter of their tribe, had fled with their mothers to this district and been brought up among the people of Bangu, but who at his summons had come back to Saduko. It was on these men that we relied at this juncture, for they alone knew the country. Long and anxiously did we consult with them. First they explained, and, so far as the moonlight would allow, for as yet the dawn had not broken, pointed out to us the various paths that led to Bangu's *kraal*.

"How many men are there in the town?" I asked.

"About seven hundred who carry spears," they answered, "together with others in outlying *kraals*. Moreover, watchmen are always set at the gateways in the walls."

"And where are the cattle?" I asked again.

"Here, in the valley beneath, Macumazahn," answered the spokesman. "If you listen you will hear them lowing. Fifty men, not less, watch them at night—two thousand head of them, or more."

"Then it would not be difficult to get round these cattle and drive them off, leaving Bangu to breed up a new herd?"

"It might not be difficult," interrupted Saduko, "but I came here to kill Bangu, as well as to seize his cattle, since with him I have a blood feud."

"Very good," I answered; "but that mountain cannot be stormed with three hundred men, fortified as it is with walls and *schanzes*. Our band would be destroyed before ever we came to the *kraal*, since, owing to the sentries who are set everywhere, it would be impossible to surprise the place. Also you have forgotten the dogs, Saduko. Moreover, even if it were possible, I will have nothing to do with the massacre of women and children, which must happen in an assault. Now, listen to me, O Saduko. I say let us leave the *kraal* of Bangu alone, and this coming night send fifty of our men, under the leadership of the guides, down to yonder bush, where they will lie hid. Then, after moonrise, when all are asleep, these fifty must rush the cattle *kraal*, killing any who may oppose them, should they be seen, and driving the herd out through yonder great pass by which we have entered the land. Bangu and his people, thinking that those who have taken the cattle are but common thieves of some wild tribe, will gather and follow the beasts to recapture them. But we, with the rest of the Amangwane, can set an ambush in the narrowest part of the pass among the rocks, where the grass is high and the euphorbia trees grow thick, and there, when they have passed the Nek, which I and my hunters will hold with our guns, we will give them battle. What say you?"

Now, Saduko answered that he would rather attack the *kraal*, which he wished to burn. But the old Amangwane, Tshoza, brother of the dead Matiwane, said:

"No, Macumazahn, Watcher-by-Night, is wise. Why should we waste our strength on stone walls, of which none know the number or can find the gates in the darkness, and thereby leave our skulls to be set up as ornaments on the fences of the accursed Amakoba? Let us draw the Amakoba out into the pass of the mountains, where they have no walls to protect them, and there fall on them when they are bewildered and settle the matter with them man to man. As for the women and children, with Macumazahn I say let them go; afterwards, perhaps, they will become *our* women and children."

"Aye," answered the Amangwane, "the plan of the white *Inkoosi* is good; he is clever as a weasel; we will have his plan and no other."

So Saduko was overruled and my counsel adopted.

All that day we rested, lighting no fires and remaining still as the dead in the dense bush. It was a very anxious day, for although the place was so wild and lonely, there was always the fear lest we should be discovered. It was true that we had travelled mostly by night in small parties, to avoid leaving a spoor, and avoided all *kraals*; still, some rumour of our approach might have reached the Amakoba, or a party of hunters might stumble on us, or those who sought for lost cattle.

Indeed, something of this sort did happen, for about midday we heard a footfall, and perceived the figure of a man, whom by his head-dress we knew for an Amakoba, threading his way through the bush. Before he saw us he was in our midst. For a moment he hesitated ere he turned to fly, and that moment was his last, for three of the Amangwane leapt on him silently as leopards leap upon a buck, and where he stood there he died. Poor fellow! Evidently he had been on a visit to some witch-doctor, for in his blanket we found medicine and love charms. This doctor cannot have been one of the stamp of Zikali the Dwarf, I thought to myself; at least, he had not warned him that he would never live to dose his beloved with that foolish medicine.

Meanwhile a few of us who had the quickest eyes climbed trees, and thence watched the town of Bangu and the valley that lay between us and it. Soon we saw that so far, at any rate, Fortune was playing into our hands, since herd after herd of kine were driven into the valley during the afternoon and enclosed in the stock-*kraals*. Doubtless Bangu intended on the morrow to make his half-yearly inspection of all the cattle of the tribe, many of which were herded at a distance from his town.

At length the long day drew to its close and the shadows of the evening thickened. Then we made ready for our dreadful game, of which the stake was the lives of all of us, since, should we fail, we could expect no mercy. The fifty picked men were gathered and ate food in silence. These men were placed under the command of Tshoza, for he was the most experienced of the Amangwane, and led by the three guides who had dwelt among the Amakoba, and who "knew every ant-heap in the land," or so they swore. Their duty, it will be remembered, was to cross the valley, separate themselves into small parties, unbar the various cattle *kraals*, kill or hunt off the herdsmen, and drive the beasts back across the valley into the pass. A second fifty men, under the command of Saduko, were to be left just at the end of this pass where it opened out into the valley, in order to help and reinforce the cattle-lifters, or, if need be, to check the following Amakoba while the great herds of beasts were got away, and then fall back on the rest of us in our ambush nearly two miles distant. The management of this ambush was to be my charge—a heavy one indeed.

Now, the moon would not be up till midnight. But two hours before that time we began our moves, since the cattle must be driven out of the *kraals* as soon as she appeared and gave the needful light. Otherwise the fight in the pass would in all probability be delayed till after sunrise, when the Amakoba would see how small was the number of their foes. Terror, doubt, darkness—these must be our allies if our desperate venture was to succeed.

All was arranged at last and the time had come. We, the three captains of our divided force, bade each other farewell, and passed the word down the ranks that, should we be separated by the accidents of war, my wagons were the meeting-place of any who survived.

Tshoza and his fifty glided away into the shadow silently as ghosts and were gone. Presently the fierce-faced Saduko departed also with his fifty. He carried the double-barrelled gun I had given him, and was accompanied by one of my best hunters, a Natal native, who was also armed with a heavy smooth-bore loaded with slugs. Our hope was that the sound of these guns might terrify the foe, should there be occasion to use them before our forces joined up again, and make them think they had to do with a body of raiding Dutch white men, of whose *roers*—as the heavy elephant guns of that day were called—all natives were much afraid.

So Saduko went with his fifty, leaving me wondering whether I should ever see his face again. Then I, my bearer Scowl, the two remaining hunters, and the ten score Amangwane who were left turned and soon were following the road by which we had come down the rugged pass. I call it a road, but, in fact, it was nothing but a water-washed gully strewn with boulders, through which we must pick our way as best we could in the darkness, having first removed the percussion cap from the nipple of every gun, for fear lest the accidental discharge of one of them should warn the Amakoba, confuse our other parties, and bring all our deep-laid plans to nothing.

Well, we accomplished that march somehow, walking in three long lines, so that each man might keep touch with him in front, and just as the moon began to rise reached the spot that I had chosen for the ambush.

Certainly it was well suited to that purpose. Here the track or gully bed narrowed to a width of not more than a hundred feet, while the steep slopes of the kloof on either side were clothed with scattered bushes and finger-like *euphorbias* which grew among stones. Behind these stones and bushes we hid ourselves, a hundred men on one side and a hundred on the other, whilst I and my three hunters, who were armed with guns, took up a position under shelter of a great boulder nearly five feet thick that lay but a little to the right of the gully itself, up which we expected the cattle would come. This place I chose for two reasons: first, that I might keep touch with both wings of my force, and, secondly, that we might be able to fire straight down the path on the pursuing Amakoba.

These were the orders that I gave to the Amangwane, warning them that he who disobeyed would be punished with death. They were not to stir until I, or, if I should be killed, one of my hunters, fired a shot; for my fear was lest, growing excited, they might leap out before the time and kill some of our own people, who very likely would be mixed up with the first of the pursuing Amakoba. Secondly, when the cattle had passed and the signal had been given, they were to rush on the Amakoba, throwing themselves across the gully, so that the enemy would have to fight upwards on a steep slope.

That was all I told them, since it is not wise to confuse natives by giving too many orders. One thing I added, however—that they must conquer or they must die. There was no mercy for them; it was a case of death or victory. Their spokesman—for these people always find a spokesman—answered that they thanked me for my advice; that they understood, and that they would do their best. Then they lifted their spears to me in salute. A wild lot of men they looked in the moonlight as they departed to take shelter behind the rocks and trees and wait.

That waiting was long, and I confess that before the end it got upon my nerves. I began to think of all sorts of things, such as whether I should live to see the sun rise again; also I reflected upon the legitimacy of this remarkable enterprise. What right had I to involve myself in a quarrel between these savages?

Why had I come here? To gain cattle as a trader? No, for I was not at all sure that I would take them if gained. Because Saduko had twitted me with faithlessness to my words? Yes, to a certain extent; but that was by no means the whole reason. I had been moved by the recital of the cruel wrongs inflicted upon Saduko and his tribe by this Bangu, and therefore had not been loath to associate myself with his attempted vengeance upon a wicked murderer. Well, that was sound enough so far as it went; but now a new consideration suggested itself to me. Those wrongs had been worked many years ago; probably most of the men who had aided and abetted them by now were dead or very aged, and it was their sons upon whom the vengeance would be wreaked.

What right had I to assist in visiting the sins of the fathers upon the sons? Frankly I could not say. The thing seemed to me to be a part of the problem of life, neither less nor more. So I shrugged my shoulders sadly and consoled myself by reflecting that very likely the issue would go against me, and that my own existence would pay the price of the venture and expound its moral. This consideration soothed my conscience somewhat, for when a man backs his actions with the risk of his life, right or wrong, at any rate he plays no coward's part.

The time went by very slowly and nothing happened. The waning moon shone brightly in a clear sky, and as there was no wind the silence seemed peculiarly intense. Save for the laugh of an occasional hyena and now and again for a sound which I took for the coughing of a distant lion, there was no stir between sleeping earth and moonlit heaven in which little clouds floated beneath the pale stars.

At length I thought that I heard a noise, a kind of murmur far away. It grew, it developed.

It sounded like a thousand sticks tapping upon something hard, very faintly. It continued to grow, and I knew the sound for that of the beating hoofs of animals galloping. Then there were isolated noises, very faint and thin; they might be shouts; then something that I could not mistake—shots fired at a distance. So the business was afoot; the cattle were moving, Saduko and my hunter were firing. There was nothing for it but to wait.

The excitement was very fierce; it seemed to consume me, to eat into my brain. The sound of the tapping upon the rocks grew louder until it merged into a kind of rumble, mixed with an echo as of that of very distant thunder, which presently I knew to be not thunder, but the bellowing of a thousand frightened beasts.

Nearer and nearer came the galloping hoofs and the rumble of bellowings; nearer and nearer the shouts of men, affronting the stillness of the solemn night. At length a single animal appeared, a *koodoo* buck that somehow had got mixed up with the cattle. It went past us like a flash, and was followed a minute or so later by a bull that, being young and light, had outrun its companions. That, too, went by, foam on its lips and its tongue hanging from its jaws.

Then the herd appeared—a countless herd it seemed to me—plunging up the incline—cows, heifers, calves, bulls, and oxen, all mixed together in one inextricable mass, and every one of them snorting, bellowing, or making some other kind of sound. The din was fearful, the sight bewildering, for the beasts were of all colours, and their long horns flashed like ivory in the moonlight. Indeed, the only thing in the least like it which I have ever seen was the rush of the buffaloes from the reed camp on that day when I got my injury.

They were streaming past us now, a mighty and moving mass so closely packed that a man might have walked upon their backs. In fact, some of the calves which had been thrust up by the pressure were being carried along in this fashion. Glad was I that none of us were in their path, for their advance seemed irresistible. No fence or wall could have saved us, and even stout trees that grew in the gully were snapped or thrust over.

At length the long line began to thin, for now it was composed of stragglers and weak or injured beasts, of which there were many. Other sounds, too, began to dominate the bellowings of the animals, those of the excited cries of men. The first of our companions, the cattle-lifters, appeared, weary and gasping, but waving their spears in triumph. Among them was old Tshoza. I stepped upon my rock, calling to him by name. He heard me, and presently was lying at my side panting.

"We have got them all!" he gasped. "Not a hoof is left save those that are trodden down. Saduko is not far behind with the rest of our brothers, except some that have been killed. All the Amakoba tribe are after us. He holds them back to give the cattle time to get away."

"Well done!" I answered. "It is very good. Now make your men hide among the others that they may find their breath before the fight."

So he stopped them as they came. Scarcely had the last of them vanished into the bushes when the gathering volume of shouts, amongst which I heard a gun go off, told us that Saduko and his band and the pursuing Amakoba were not far away. Presently they, too, appeared—that is the handful of Amangwane did—not fighting now, but running as hard as they could, for they knew they were approaching the ambush and wished to pass it so as not to be mixed up with the Amakoba. We let them go through us. Among the last of them came Saduko, who was wounded, for the blood ran down his side, supporting my hunter, who was also wounded, more severely as I feared.

I called to him.

"Saduko," I said, "halt at the crest of the path and rest there so that you may be able to help us presently."

He waved the gun in answer, for he was too breathless to speak, and went on with those who were left of his following—perhaps thirty men in all—in the track of the cattle. Before he was out of sight the Amakoba arrived, a mob of five or six hundred men mixed up together and advancing without order or discipline, for they seemed to have lost their heads as well as their cattle. Some of them had shields and some had none, some broad and some throwing *assegais*, while many were quite naked, not having stayed to put on their *moocha*s and much less their war finery. Evidently they were mad with rage, for the sounds that issued from them seemed to concentrate into one mighty curse.

The moment had come, though to tell the truth I heartily wished that it had not. I wasn't exactly afraid, although I never set up for great courage, but I did not quite like the business. After all we were stealing these people's cattle, and now were going to kill as many of them as we could. I had to recall Saduko's dreadful story of the massacre of his tribe before I could make up my mind to give the signal. That hardened me, and so did the reflection that after all they outnumbered us enormously and very likely would prove victors in the end. Anyhow it was too late to repent. What a tricky and uncomfortable thing is conscience, that nearly always begins to trouble us at the moment of, or after, the event, not before, when it might be of some use.

I raised myself upon the rock and fired both barrels of my gun into the advancing horde, though whether I killed anyone or no I cannot say. I have always hoped that I did not; but as the mark was large and I am a fair shot, I fear that is scarcely possible. Next moment, with a howl that sounded like that of wild beasts, from either side of the gorge the fierce Amangwane free-spears—for that is what they were—leapt out of their hiding-places and hurled themselves upon their hereditary foes. They were fighting for more than cattle; they were fighting for hate and for revenge since these Amakoba had slaughtered their fathers and their mothers, their sisters and their brothers, and they alone remained to pay them back blood for blood.

Great heaven! how they did fight, more like devils than human beings. After that first howl which shaped itself to the word "Saduko," they were silent as bulldogs. Though they were so few, at first their terrible rush drove back the Amakoba. Then, as these recovered from their surprise, the weight of numbers began to tell, for they, too, were brave men who did not give way to panic. Scores of them went down at once, but the remainder pushed the Amangwane before them up the hill. I took little share in the fight, but was thrust backward with the others, only firing when I was obliged to save my own life. Foot by foot we were pushed back till at length we drew near to the crest of the pass.

Then, while the issue hung in the balance, there was another shout of "Saduko!" and that chief himself, followed by his thirty, rushed upon the Amakoba.

This charge decided the battle, for not knowing how many more were coming, those who were left of the Amakoba turned and fled, nor did we pursue them far.

We mustered on the hill-top, not more than two hundred of us now, the rest were fallen or desperately wounded, my poor hunter, whom I had lent to Saduko, being among the dead. Although wounded, he died fighting to the last, then fell down, shouting to me:

"Chief, have I done well?" and expired.

I was breathless and spent, but as in a dream I saw some Amangwane drag up a gaunt old savage, crying:

"Here is Bangu, Bangu the Butcher, whom we have caught alive."

Saduko stepped up to him.

"Ah! Bangu," he said, "now say, why should I not kill you as you would have killed the little lad Saduko long ago, had not Zikali saved him? See, here is the mark of your spear."

"Kill," said Bangu. "Your Spirit is stronger than mine. Did not Zikali foretell it? Kill, Saduko."

"Nay," answered Saduko. "If you are weary I am weary, too, and wounded as well. Take a spear, Bangu, and we will fight."

So they fought there in the moonlight, man to man; fought fiercely while all watched, till presently I saw Bangu throw his arms wide and fall backwards.

Saduko was avenged. I have always been glad that he slew his enemy thus, and not as it might have been expected that he would do.

Chapter 7

Saduko Brings the Marriage Gift

We reached my wagons in the early morning of the following day, bringing with us the cattle and our wounded. Thus encumbered it was a most toilsome march, and an anxious one also, for it was always possible that the remnant of the Amakoba might attempt pursuit. This, however, they did not do, for very many of them were dead or wounded, and those who remained had no heart left in them. They went back to their mountain home and lived there in shame and wretchedness, for I do not believe there were fifty head of cattle left among the tribe, and *Kafirs* without cattle are nothing. Still, they did not starve, since there were plenty of women to work the fields, and we had not touched their corn. The end of them was that Panda gave them to their conqueror, Saduko, and he incorporated them with the Amangwane. But that did not happen until some time afterwards.

When we had rested a while at the wagons the captured beasts were mustered, and on being counted were found to number a little over twelve hundred head, not reckoning animals that had been badly hurt in the flight, which we killed for beef. It was a noble prize, truly, and, notwithstanding the wound in his thigh, which hurt him a good deal now that it had stiffened, Saduko stood up and surveyed them with glistening eyes. No wonder, for he who had been so poor was now rich, and would remain so even after he had paid over whatever number of cows Umbezi chose to demand as the price of Mameena's hand. Moreover, he was sure, and I shared his confidence, that in these changed circumstances both that young woman and her father would look upon his suit with very favourable eyes. He had, so to speak, succeeded to the title and the family estates by means of a lawsuit brought in the "Court of the *Assegai*," and therefore there was hardly a father in Zululand who would shut his *kraal* gate upon him. We forgot, both of us, the proverb that points out how numerous are the slips between the cup and the lip, which, by the way, is one that has its Zulu equivalents. One of them, if I remember right at the moment, is: "However loud the hen cackles, the housewife does not always get the egg."

As it chanced, although Saduko's hen was cackling very loudly just at this time, he was not destined to find the coveted egg. But of that matter I will speak in its place.

I, too, looked at those cattle, wondering whether Saduko would remember our bargain, under which some six hundred head of them belonged to me. Six hundred head! Why, putting them at £5 apiece all round—and as oxen were very scarce just at that time, they were worth quite as much, if not more—that meant £3,000, a larger sum of money than I had ever owned at one time in all my life. Truly the paths of violence were profitable! But would he remember? On the whole I thought probably not, since *Kafirs* are not fond of parting with cattle.

Well, I did him an injustice, for presently he turned and said, with something of an effort:

"Macumazahn, half of all these belong to you, and truly you have earned them, for it was your cunning and good counsel that gained us the victory. Now we will choose them beast by beast."

So I chose a fine ox, then Saduko chose one; and so it went on till I had eight of my number driven out. As the eighth was taken I turned to Saduko and said:

"There, that will do. These oxen I must have to replace those in my teams which died on the trek, but I want no more."

"Wow!" said Saduko, and all those who stood with him, while one of them added—I think it was old Tshoza:

"He refuses six hundred cattle which are fairly his! He must be mad!"

"No friends," I answered, "I am not mad, but neither am I bad. I accompanied Saduko on this raid because he is dear to me and stood by me once in the hour of danger. But I do not love killing men with whom I have no quarrel, and I will not take the price of blood."

"Wow!" said old Tshoza again, for Saduko seemed too astonished to speak, "he is a spirit, not a man. He is *holy!*"

"Not a bit of it," I answered. "If you think that, ask Mameena"—a dark saying which they did not understand. "Now, listen. I will not take those cattle because I do not think as you *Kafirs* think. But as they are mine, according to your law, I am going to dispose of them. I give ten head to each of my hunters, and fifteen head to the relations of him who was killed. The rest I give to Tshoza and to the other men of the Amangwane who fought with us, to be divided among them in such proportions as they may agree, I being the judge in the event of any quarrel arising."

Now these men raised a great cry of *"Inkoosi!"* and, running up, old Tshoza seized my hand and kissed it.

"Your heart is big," he cried; "you drop fatness! Although you are so small, the spirit of a king lives in you, and the wisdom of the heavens."

Thus he praised me, while all the others joined in, till the din was awful. Saduko thanked me also in his magnificent manner. Yet I do not think that he was altogether pleased, although my great gift relieved him from the necessity of sharing up the spoil with his companions. The truth was, or so I believe, that he understood that henceforth the Amangwane would love me better than they loved him. This, indeed, proved to be the case, for I am sure that there was no man among all those wild fellows who would not have served me to the death, and to this day my name is a power among them and their descendants. Also it has grown into something of a proverb among all those *Kafirs* who know the story. They talk of any great act of liberality in an idiom as "a gift of Macumazana," and in the same way of one who makes any remarkable renunciation, as "a wearer of Macumazana's blanket," or as "he who has stolen Macumazana's shadow."

Thus did I earn a great reputation very cheaply, for really I could not have taken those cattle; also I am sure that had I done so they would have brought me bad luck. Indeed, one of the regrets of my life is that I had anything whatsoever to do with the business.

Our journey back to Umbezi's *kraal*—for thither we were heading—was very slow, hampered as we were with wounded and by a vast herd of cattle. Of the latter, indeed, we got rid after a while, for, except those which I had given to my men, and a hundred or so of the best beasts that Saduko took with him for a certain purpose, they were sent away to a place which he had chosen, in charge of about half of his people, under the command of his uncle, Tshoza, there to await his coming.

Over a month had gone by since the night of the ambush when at last we outspanned quite close to Umbezi's, in that bush where first I had met the Amangwane free-spears. A very different set of men they looked on this triumphant day to those fierce fellows who had slipped out of the trees at the call of their chief. As we went through the country Saduko had bought fine *moochas* and blankets for them; also head-dresses had been made with the long black feathers of the *sakabuli* finch, and shields and leglets of the hides and tails of oxen. Moreover, having fed plentifully and travelled easily, they were fat and well-favoured, as, given good food, natives soon become after a period of abstinence.

The plan of Saduko was to lie quiet in the bush that night, and on the following morning to advance in all his grandeur, accompanied by his spears, present the hundred head of cattle that had been demanded, and formally ask his daughter's hand from Umbezi. As the reader may have gathered already, there was a certain histrionic vein in Saduko; also when he was in feather he liked to show off his plumage.

Well, this plan was carried out to the letter. On the following morning, after the sun was well up, Saduko, as a great chief does, sent forward two bedizened heralds to announce his approach to Umbezi, after whom followed two other men to sing his deeds and praises. (By the way, I observed that they had clearly been instructed to avoid any mention of a person called Macumazahn.) Then we advanced in force. First went Saduko, splendidly apparelled as a chief, carrying a small *assegai* and adorned with plumes, leglets and a leopard-skin kilt. He was attended by about half a dozen of the best-looking of his followers, who posed as *indunas* or councillors. Behind these I walked, a dusty, insignificant little fellow, attended by the ugly, snub-nosed Scowl in a very greasy pair of trousers, worn-out European boots through which his toes peeped, and nothing else, and by my three surviving hunters, whose appearance was even more disreputable. After us marched about four score of the transformed Amangwane, and after them came the hundred picked cattle driven by a few herdsmen.

In due course we arrived at the gate of the *kraal*, where we found the heralds and the praisers prancing and shouting.

"Have you seen Umbezi?" asked Saduko of them.

"No," they answered; "he was asleep when we got here, but his people say that he is coming out presently."

"Then tell his people that he had better be quick about it, or I shall turn him out," replied the proud Saduko.

Just at this moment the *kraal* gate opened and through it appeared Umbezi, looking extremely fat and foolish; also, it struck me, frightened, although this he tried to conceal.

"Who visits me here," he said, "with so much—um—ceremony?" and with the carved dancing-stick he carried he pointed doubtfully at the lines of armed men. "Oh, it is you, is it, Saduko?" and he looked him up and down, adding: "How grand you are to be sure. Have you been robbing anybody? And you, too, Macumazahn. Well, *you* do not look grand. You look like an old cow that has been suckling two calves on the winter *veld*. But tell me, what are all these warriors for? I ask because I have not food for so many, especially as we have just had a feast here."

"Fear nothing, Umbezi," answered Saduko in his grandest manner. "I have brought food for my own men. As for my business, it is simple. You asked a hundred head of cattle as the *lobola* (that is, the marriage gift) of your daughter, Mameena. They are there. Go send your servants to the *kraal* and count them."

"Oh, with pleasure," Umbezi replied nervously, and he gave some orders to certain men behind him. "I am glad to see that you have become rich in this sudden fashion, Saduko, though how you have done so I cannot understand."

"Never mind how I have become rich," answered Saduko. "I *am* rich; that is enough for the present. Be pleased to send for Mameena, for I would talk with her."

"Yes, yes, Saduko, I understand that you would talk with Mameena; but"—and he looked round him desperately—"I fear that she is still asleep. As you know, Mameena was always a late riser, and, what is more, she hates to be disturbed. Don't you think that you could come back, say, to-morrow morning? She will be sure to be up by then; or, better still, the day after?"

"In which hut is Mameena?" asked Saduko sternly, while I, smelling a rat, began to chuckle to myself.

"I really do not know, Saduko," replied Umbezi. "Sometimes she sleeps in one, sometimes in another, and sometimes she goes several hours' journey away to her aunt's *kraal* for a change. I should not be in the least surprised if she had done so last night. I have no control over Mameena."

Before Saduko could answer, a shrill, rasping voice broke upon our ears, which after some search I saw proceeded from an ugly and ancient female seated in the shadow, in whom I recognised the lady who was known by the pleasing name of "Worn-out-Old-Cow."

"He lies!" screeched the voice. "He lies. Thanks be to the spirit of my ancestors that wild cat Mameena has left this *kraal* for good. She slept last night, not with her aunt, but with her husband, Masapo, to whom Umbezi gave her in marriage two days ago, receiving in payment a hundred and twenty head of cattle, which was twenty more than *you* bid, Saduko."

Now when Saduko heard these words I thought that he would really go mad with rage. He turned quite grey under his dark skin and for a while trembled like a leaf, looking as though he were about to fall to the ground. Then he leapt as a lion leaps, and seizing Umbezi by the throat, hurled him backwards, standing over him with raised spear.

"You dog!" he cried in a terrible voice. "Tell me the truth or I will rip you up. What have you done with Mameena?"

"Oh! Saduko," answered Umbezi in choking tones, "Mameena has chosen to get married. It was no fault of mine; she would have her way."

He got no farther, and had I not intervened by throwing my arms about Saduko and dragging him back, that moment would have been Umbezi's last, for Saduko was about to pin him to the earth with his spear. As it proved, I was just in time, and Saduko, being weak with emotion, for I felt his heart going like a sledge-hammer, could not break from my grasp before his reason returned to him.

At length he recovered himself a little and threw down his spear as though to put himself out of temptation. Then he spoke, always in the same terrible voice, asking:

"Have you more to say about this business, Umbezi? I would hear all before I answer you."

"Only this, Saduko," replied Umbezi, who had risen to his feet and was shaking like a reed. "I did no more than any other father would have done. Masapo is a very powerful chief, one who will be a good stick for me to lean on in my old age. Mameena declared that she wished to marry him—"

"He lies!" screeched the Old Cow. "What Mameena said was that she had no will towards marriage with any Zulu in the land, so I suppose she is looking after a white man," and she leered in my direction. "She said, however, that if her father wished to marry her to Masapo, she must be a dutiful daughter and obey him, but that if blood and trouble came of that marriage, let it be on his head and not on hers."

"Would you also stick your claws into me, cat?" shouted Umbezi, catching the old woman a savage cut across the back with the light dancing-stick which he still held in his hand, whereon she fled away screeching and cursing him.

"Oh, Saduko," he went on, "let not your ears be poisoned by these falsehoods. Mameena never said anything of the sort, or if she did it was not to me. Well, the moment that my daughter had consented to take Masapo as her husband his people drove a hundred and twenty of the most beautiful cattle over the hill, and would you have had me refuse them, Saduko? I am sure that when you have seen them you will say that I was quite right to accept such a splendid *lobola* in return for one sharp-tongued girl. Remember, Saduko, that although you had promised a hundred head, that is less by twenty, at the time you did not own one, and where you were to get them from I could not guess. Moreover," he added with a last, desperate, imaginative effort, for I think he saw that his arguments were making no impression, "some strangers who called here told me that both you and Macumazahn had been killed by certain evil-doers in the mountains. There, I have spoken, and, Saduko, if you now have cattle, why, on my part, I have another daughter, not quite so good-looking perhaps, but a much better worker in the field. Come and drink a sup of beer, and I will send for her."

"Stop talking about your other daughter and your beer and listen to me," replied Saduko, looking at the *assegai* which he had thrown to the ground so ominously that I set my foot on it. "I am now a greater chief than the boar Masapo. Has Masapo such a bodyguard as these Eaters-up-of-Enemies?" and he jerked his thumb backwards towards the serried lines of fierce-faced Amangwane who stood listening behind us. "Has Masapo as many cattle as I have, whereof those which you see are but a tithe brought as a *lobola* gift to the father of her who had been promised to me as wife? Is Masapo Panda's friend? I think that I have heard otherwise. Has Masapo just conquered a countless tribe by his courage and his wit? Is Masapo young and of high blood, or is he but an old, low-born boar of the mountains?

"You do not answer, Umbezi, and perhaps you do well to be silent. Now listen again. Were it not for Macumazahn here, whom I do not desire to mix up with my quarrels, I would bid my men take you and beat you to death with the handles of their spears, and then go on and serve the Boar in the same fashion in his mountain sty. As it is, these things must wait a little while, especially as I have other matters to attend to first. Yet the day is not far off when I will attend to them also. Therefore my counsel to you, Cheat, is to make haste to die or to find courage to fall upon a spear, unless you would learn how it feels to be brayed with sticks like a green hide until none can know that you were once a man. Send now and tell my words to Masapo the Boar. And to Mameena say that soon I will come to take her with spears and not with cattle. Do you understand? Oh! I see that you do, since already you weep with fear like a woman. Then farewell to you till that day when I return with the sticks, O Umbezi the cheat and the liar, Umbezi, 'Eater-up-of-Elephants,'" and turning, Saduko stalked away.

I was about to follow in a great hurry, having had enough of this very unpleasant scene, when poor old Umbezi sprang at me and clasped me by the arm.

"O Macumazana," he exclaimed, weeping in his terror, "O Macumazana, if ever I have been a friend to you, help me out of this deep pit into which I have fallen through the tricks of that monkey of a daughter of mine, who I think is a witch born to bring trouble upon men. Macumazahn, if she had been your daughter and a powerful chief had appeared with a hundred and twenty head of such beautiful cattle, you would have given her to him, would you not, although he is of mixed blood and not very young, especially as she did not mind who only cares for place and wealth?"

"I think not," I answered; "but then it is not our custom to sell women in that fashion."

"No, no, I forgot; in this as in other matters you white men are mad and, Macumazahn, to tell you the truth, I believe it is you she really cares for; she said as much to me once or twice. Well, why did you not take her away when I was not looking? We could have settled matters afterwards, and I should have been free of her witcheries and not up to my neck in this hole as I am now."

"Because some people don't do that kind of thing, Umbezi."

"No, no, I forgot. Oh! why can I not remember that you are *quite* mad and therefore that it must not be expected of you to act as though you were sane. Well, at least you are that tiger Saduko's friend, which again shows that you must be very mad, for most people would sooner try to milk a cow buffalo than walk hand in hand with him. Don't you see, Macumazahn, that he means to kill me, Macumazahn, to bray me like a green hide? Ugh! to beat me to death with sticks. Ugh! And what is more, that unless you prevent him, he will certainly do it, perhaps to-morrow or the next day. Ugh! Ugh! Ugh!"

"Yes, I see, Umbezi, and I think that he *will* do it. But what I do not see is how I am to prevent him. Remember that you let Mameena grow into his heart and behaved badly to him, Umbezi."

"I never promised her to him, Macumazahn. I only said that if he brought a hundred cattle, then I might promise."

"Well, he has wiped out the Amakoba, the enemies of his House, and there are the hundred cattle whereof he has many more, and now it is too late for you to keep your share of the bargain. So I think you must make yourself as comfortable as you can in the hole that your hands dug, Umbezi, which I would not share for all the cattle in Zululand."

"Truly you are not one from whom to seek comfort in the hour of distress," groaned poor Umbezi, then added, brightening up: "But perhaps Panda will kill him because he has wiped out Bangu in a time of peace. Oh Macumazahn, can you not persuade Panda to kill him? If so, I now have more cattle than I really want—"

"Impossible," I answered. "Panda is his friend, and between ourselves I may tell you that he ate up the Amakoba by his especial wish. When the King hears of it he will call to Saduko to sit in his shadow and make him great, one of his councillors, probably with power of life and death over little people like you and Masapo."

"Then it is finished," said Umbezi faintly, "and I will try to die like a man. But to be brayed like a hide! And with thin sticks! Oh!" he added, grinding his teeth, "if only I can get hold of Mameena I will not leave much of that pretty hair of hers upon her head. I will tie her hands and shut her up with the Old Cow, who loves her as a meer-cat loves a mouse. No; I will kill her. There—do you hear, Macumazahn, unless you do something to help me, I will kill Mameena, and you won't like that, for I am sure she is dear to you, although you were not man enough to run away with her as she wished."

"If you touch Mameena," I said, "be certain, my friend, that Saduko's sticks and your skin will not be far apart, for I will report you to Panda myself as an unnatural evil-doer. Now hearken to me, you old fool. Saduko is so fond of your daughter, on this point being mad, as you say I am, that if only he could get her I think he might overlook the fact of her having been married before. What you have to do is to try to buy her back from Masapo. Mind you, I say buy her back—not get her by bloodshed—which you might do by persuading Masapo to put her away. Then, if he knew that you were trying to do this, I think that Saduko might leave his sticks uncut for a while."

"I will try. I will indeed, Macumazahn. I will try very hard. It is true Masapo is an obstinate pig; still, if he knows that his own life is at stake, he might give way. Moreover, when she learns that Saduko has grown rich and great, Mameena might help me. Oh, I thank you, Macumazahn; you are indeed the prop of my hut, and it and all in it are yours. Farewell, farewell, Macumazahn, if you must go. But why—why did you not run away with Mameena, and save me all this fear and trouble?"

So I and that old humbug, Umbezi, Eater-up-of-Elephants, parted for a while, and never did I know him in a more chastened frame of mind, except once, as I shall tell.

Chapter 7

The King's Daughter

When I got back to my wagons after this semi-tragical interview with that bombastic and self-seeking old windbag, Umbezi, it was to find that Saduko and his warriors had already marched for the King's *kraal*, Nodwengu. A message awaited me, however, to the effect that it was hoped that I would follow, in order to make report of the affair of the destruction of the Amakoba. This, after reflection, I determined to do, really, I think, because of the intense human interest of the whole business. I wanted to see how it would work out.

Also, in a way, I read Saduko's mind and understood that at the moment he did not wish to discuss the matter of his hideous disappointment. Whatever else may have been false in this man's nature, one thing rang true, namely, his love or his infatuation for the girl Mameena. Throughout his life she was his guiding star—about as evil a star as could have arisen upon any man's horizon; the fatal star that was to light him down to doom. Let me thank Providence, as I do, that I was so fortunate as to escape its baneful influences, although I admit that they attracted me not a little.

So, seduced thither by my curiosity, which has so often led me into trouble, I trekked to Nodwengu, full of many doubts not unmingled with amusement, for I could not rid my mind of recollections of the utter terror of the "Eater-up-of-Elephants" when he was brought face to face with the dreadful and concentrated rage of the robbed Saduko and the promise of his vengeance. Ultimately I arrived at the Great Place without experiencing any adventure that is worthy of record, and camped in a spot that was appointed to me by some *induna* whose name I forget, but who evidently knew of my approach, for I found him awaiting me at some distance from the town. Here I sat for quite a long while, two or three days, if I remember right, amusing myself with killing or missing turtle-doves with a shotgun, and similar pastimes, until something should happen, or I grew tired and started for Natal.

In the end, just as I was about to trek seawards, an old friend, Maputa, turned up at my wagons—that same man who had brought me the message from Panda before we started to attack Bangu.

"Greeting, Macumazahn," he said. "What of the Amakoba? I see they did not kill you."

"No," I answered, handing him some snuff, "they did not quite kill me, for here I am. What is your pleasure with me?"

"O Macumazana, only that the King wishes to know whether you have any of those little balls left in the box which I brought back to you, since, if so, he thinks he would like to swallow one of them in this hot weather."

I proffered him the whole box, but he would not take it, saying that the King would like me to give it to him myself. Now I understood that this was a summons to an audience, and asked when it would please Panda to receive me and "the-little-black-stones-that-work-wonders." He answered—at once.

So we started, and within an hour I stood, or rather sat, before Panda.

Like all his family, the King was an enormous man, but, unlike Chaka and those of his brothers whom I had known, one of a kindly countenance. I saluted him by lifting my cap, and took my place upon a wooden stool that had been provided for me outside the great hut, in the shadow of which he sat within his *isi-gohlo*, or private enclosure.

"Greeting, O Macumazana," he said. "I am glad to see you safe and well, for I understand that you have been engaged upon a perilous adventure since last we met."

"Yes, King," I answered; "but to which adventure do you refer—that of the buffalo, when Saduko helped me, or that of the Amakoba, when I helped Saduko?"

"The latter, Macumazahn, of which I desire to hear all the story."

So I told it to him, he and I being alone, for he commanded his councillors and servants to retire out of hearing.

"Wow!" he said, when I had finished, "you are clever as a baboon, Macumazahn. That was a fine trick to set a trap for Bangu and his Amakoba dogs and bait it with his own cattle. But they tell me that you refused your share of those cattle. Now, why was that, Macumazahn?"

By way of answer I repeated to Panda my reasons, which I have set out already.

"Ah!" he exclaimed, when I had finished. "Every one seeks greatness in his own way, and perhaps yours is better than ours. Well, the

White man walks one road—or some of them do—and the Black man another. They both end at the same place, and none will know which is the right road till the journey is done. Meanwhile, what you lose Saduko and his people gain. He is a wise man, Saduko, who knows how to choose his friends, and his wisdom has brought him victory and gifts. But to you, Macumazahn, it has brought nothing but honour, on which, if a man feeds only, he will grow thin."

"I like to be thin, O Panda," I answered slowly.

"Yes, yes, I understand," replied the King, who, in common with most natives, was quick enough to seize a point, "and I, too, like people who keep thin on such food as yours, people, also, whose hands are always clean. We Zulus trust you, Macumazahn, as we trust few white men, for we have known for years that your lips say what your heart thinks, and that your heart always thinks the thing which is good. You may be named Watcher-by-Night, but you love light, not darkness."

Now, at these somewhat unusual compliments I bowed, and felt myself colouring a little as I did so, even through my sunburn, but I made no answer to them, since to do so would have involved a discussion of the past and its tragical events, into which I had no wish to enter. Panda, too, remained silent for a while. Then he called to a messenger to summon the princes, Cetewayo and Umbelazi, and to bid Saduko, the son of Matiwane, to wait without, in case he should wish to speak with him.

A few minutes later the two princes arrived. I watched their coming with interest, for they were the most important men in Zululand, and already the nation debated fiercely which of them would succeed to the throne. I will try to describe them a little.

They were both of much the same age—it is always difficult to arrive at a Zulu's exact years—and both fine young men. Cetewayo, however, had the stronger countenance. It was said that he resembled that fierce and able monster, Chaka the Wild Beast, his uncle, and certainly I perceived in him a likeness to his other uncle, Dingaan, Umpanda's predecessor, whom I had known but too well when I was a lad. He had the same surly eyes and haughty bearing; also, when he was angry his mouth shut itself in the same iron fashion.

Of Umbelazi it is difficult for me to speak without enthusiasm. As Mameena was the most beautiful woman I ever saw in Zululand—although it is true that old war-dog, Umslopogaas, a friend of mine who does not come into this story, used to tell me that Nada the Lily, whom I have mentioned, was even lovelier—so Umbelazi was by far the most splendid man. Indeed, the Zulus named him Umbelazi the

Handsome, and no wonder. To begin with, he stood at least three inches above the tallest of them; from a quarter of a mile away I have recognised him by his great height, even through the dust of a desperate battle, and his breadth was proportionate to his stature. Then he was perfectly made, his great, shapely limbs ending, like Saduko's, in small hands and feet. His face, too, was well-cut and open, his colour lighter than Cetewayo's, and his eyes, which always seemed to smile, were large and dark.

Even before they passed the small gate of the inner fence it was easy for me to see that this royal pair were not upon the best of terms, for each of them tried to get through it first, to show his right of precedence. The result was somewhat ludicrous, for they jammed in the gateway. Here, however, Umbelazi's greater weight told, for, putting out his strength, he squeezed his brother into the reeds of the fence, and won through a foot or so in front of him.

"You grow too fat, my brother," I heard Cetewayo say, and saw him scowl as he spoke. "If I had held an *assegai* in my hand you would have been cut."

"I know it, my brother," answered Umbelazi, with a good-humoured laugh, "but I knew also that none may appear before the King armed. Had it been otherwise, I would rather have followed after you."

Now, at this hint of Umbelazi's, that he would not trust his brother behind his back with a spear, although it seemed to be conveyed in jest, I saw Panda shift uneasily on his seat, while Cetewayo scowled even more ominously than before. However, no further words passed between them, and, walking up to the King side by side, they saluted him with raised hands, calling out "Baba!"—that is, Father.

"Greeting, my children," said Panda, adding hastily, for he foresaw a quarrel as to which of them should take the seat of honour on his right: "Sit there in front of me, both of you, and, Macumazahn, do you come hither," and he pointed to the coveted place. "I am a little deaf in my left ear this morning."

So these brothers sat themselves down in front of the King; nor were they, I think, grieved to find this way out of their rivalry; but first they shook hands with me, for I knew them both, though not well, and even in this small matter the old trouble arose, since there was some difficulty as to which of them should first offer me his hand. Ultimately, I remember, Cetewayo won this trick.

When these preliminaries were finished, Panda addressed the princes, saying:

"My sons, I have sent for you to ask your counsel upon a certain matter—not a large matter, but one that may grow." And he paused to take snuff, whereon both of them ejaculated:

"We hear you, Father."

"Well, my sons, the matter is that of Saduko, the son of Matiwane, chief of the Amangwane, whom Bangu, chief of the Amakoba, ate up years ago by leave of Him who went before me. Now, this Bangu, as you know, has for some time been a thorn in my foot—a thorn that caused it to fester—and yet I did not wish to make war on him. So I spoke a word in the ear of Saduko, saying, 'He is yours, if you can kill him; and his cattle are yours.' Well, Saduko is not dull. With the help of this white man, Macumazahn, our friend from of old, he has killed Bangu and taken his cattle, and already my foot is beginning to heal."

"We have heard it," said Cetewayo.

"It was a great deed," added Umbelazi, a more generous critic.

"Yes," continued Panda, "I, too, think it was a great deed, seeing that Saduko had but a small regiment of wanderers to back him—"

"Nay," interrupted Cetewayo, "it was not those eaters of rats who won him the day, it was the wisdom of this Macumazahn."

"Macumazahn's wisdom would have been of little use without the courage of Saduko and his rats," commented Umbelazi, and from this moment I saw that the two brothers were taking sides for and against Saduko, as they did upon every other matter, not because they cared for the right of whatever was in question, but because they wished to oppose each other.

"Quite so," went on the King; "I agree with both of you, my sons. But the point is this: I think Saduko a man of promise, and one who should be advanced that he may learn to love us all, especially as his House has suffered wrong from our House, since He-who-is-gone listened to the evil counsel of Bangu, and allowed him to kill out Matiwane's tribe without just cause. Therefore, in order to wipe away this stain and bind Saduko to us, I think it well to re-establish Saduko in the chieftainship of the Amangwane, with the lands that his father held, and to give him also the chieftainship of the Amakoba, of whom it seems that the women and children, with some of the men, remain, although he already holds their cattle which he has captured in war."

"As the King pleases," said Umbelazi, with a yawn, for he was growing weary of listening to the case of Saduko.

But Cetewayo said nothing, for he appeared to be thinking of something else.

"I think also," went on Panda in a rather uncertain voice, "in order to bind him so close that the bonds may never be broken, it would be wise to give him a woman of our family in marriage."

"Why should this little Amangwane be allowed to marry into the royal House?" asked Cetewayo, looking up. "If he is dangerous, why not kill him, and have done?"

"For this reason, my son. There is trouble ahead in Zululand, and I do not wish to kill those who may help us in that hour, nor do I wish them to become our enemies. I wish that they may be our friends; and therefore it seems to me wise, when we find a seed of greatness, to water it, and not to dig it up or plant it in a neighbour's garden. From his deeds I believe that this Saduko is such a seed."

"Our father has spoken," said Umbelazi; "and I like Saduko, who is a man of mettle and good blood. Which of our sisters does our father propose to give to him?"

"She who is named after the mother of our race, O Umbelazi; she whom your own mother bore—your sister Nandie" (in English, the Sweet).

"A great gift, O my Father, since Nandie is both fair and wise. Also, what does she think of this matter?"

"She thinks well of it, Umbelazi, for she has seen Saduko and taken a liking to him. She told me herself that she wishes no other husband."

"Is it so?" replied Umbelazi indifferently. "Then if the King commands, and the King's daughter desires, what more is there to be said?"

"Much, I think," broke in Cetewayo. "I hold that it is out of place that this little man, who has but conquered a little tribe by borrowing the wit of Macumazahn here, should be rewarded not only with a chieftainship, but with the hand of the wisest and most beautiful of the King's daughters, even though Umbelazi," he added, with a sneer, "should be willing to throw him his own sister like a bone to a passing dog."

"Who threw the bone, Cetewayo?" asked Umbelazi, awaking out of his indifference. "Was it the King, or was it I, who never heard of the matter till this moment? And who are we that we should question the King's decrees? Is it our business to judge or to obey?"

"Has Saduko perchance made you a present of some of those cattle which he stole from the Amakoba, Umbelazi?" asked Cetewayo. "As our father asks no *lobola*, perhaps you have taken the gift instead."

"The only gift that I have taken from Saduko," said Umbelazi, who, I could see, was hard pressed to keep his temper, "is that of his service. He is my friend, which is why you hate him, as you hate all my friends."

"Must I then love every stray cur that licks your hand, Umbelazi? Oh, no need to tell me he is your friend, for I know it was you who put it into our father's heart to allow him to kill Bangu and steal his cattle, which I hold to be an ill deed, for now the Great House is thatched with his reeds and Bangu's blood is on its doorposts. Moreover, he who wrought the wrong is to come and dwell therein, and for aught I know to be called a prince, like you and me. Why should he not, since the Princess Nandie is to be given to him in marriage? Certainly, Umbelazi, you would do well to take the cattle which this white trader has refused, for all men know that you have earned them."

Now Umbelazi sprang up, straightening himself to the full of his great height, and spoke in a voice that was thick with passion.

"I pray your leave to withdraw, O King," he said, "since if I stay here longer I shall grow sorry that I have no spear in my hand. Yet before I go I will tell the truth. Cetewayo hates Saduko, because, knowing him to be a chief of wit and courage, who will grow great, he sought him for his man, saying, 'Sit you in my shadow,' after he had promised to sit in mine. Therefore it is that he heaps these taunts upon me. Let him deny it if he can."

"That I shall not trouble to do, Umbelazi," answered Cetewayo, with a scowl. "Who are you that spy upon my doings, and with a mouth full of lies call me to account before the King? I will hear no more of it. Do you bide here and pay Saduko his price with the person of our sister. For, as the King has promised her, his word cannot be changed. Only let your dog know that I keep a stick for him, if he should snarl at me. Farewell, my Father. I go upon a journey to my own lordship, the land of Gikazi, and there you will find me when you want me, which I pray may not be till after this marriage is finished, for on that I will not trust my eyes to look."

Then, with a salute, he turned and departed, bidding no good-bye to his brother.

My hand, however, he shook in farewell, for Cetewayo was always friendly to me, perhaps because he thought I might be useful to him. Also, as I learned afterwards, he was very pleased with me for the reason that I had refused my share of the Amakoba cattle, and that he knew I had no part in this proposed marriage between Saduko and Nandie, of which, indeed, I now heard for the first time.

"My Father," said Umbelazi, when Cetewayo had gone, "is this to be borne? Am I to blame in the matter? You have heard and seen—answer me, my Father."

"No, you are not to blame this time, Umbelazi," replied the King, with a heavy sigh. "But oh! my sons, my sons, where will your quarrelling end? I think that only a river of blood can quench so fierce a fire, and then which of you will live to reach its bank?"

For a while he looked at Umbelazi, and I saw love and fear in his eye, for towards him Panda always had more affection than for any of his other children.

"Cetewayo has behaved ill," he said at length; "and before a white man, who will report the matter, which makes it worse. He has no right to dictate to me to whom I shall or shall not give my daughters in marriage. Moreover, I have spoken; nor do I change my word because he threatens me. It is known throughout the land that I never change my word; and the white men know it also, do they not, O Macumazana?"

I answered yes, they did. Also, this was true, for, like most weak men, Panda was very obstinate, and honest, too, in his own fashion.

He waved his hand, to show that the subject was ended, then bade Umbelazi go to the gate and send a messenger to bring in "the son of Matiwane."

Presently Saduko arrived, looking very stately and composed as he lifted his right hand and gave Panda the *Bayete*—the royal salute.

"Be seated," said the King. "I have words for your ear."

Thereon, with the most perfect grace, without hurrying and without undue delay, Saduko crouched himself down upon his knees, with one of his elbows resting on the ground, as only a native knows how to do without looking absurd, and waited.

"Son of Matiwane," said the King, "I have heard all the story of how, with a small company, you destroyed Bangu and most of the men of the Amakoba, and ate up their cattle every one."

"Your pardon, Black One," interrupted Saduko. "I am but a boy, I did nothing. It was Macumazahn, Watcher-by-Night, who sits yonder. His wisdom taught me how to snare the Amakoba, after they were decoyed from their mountain, and it was Tshoza, my uncle, who loosed the cattle from the *kraals*. I say that I did nothing, except to strike a blow or two with a spear when I must, just as a baboon throws stones at those who would steal its young."

"I am glad to see that you are no boaster, Saduko," said Panda. "Would that more of the Zulus were like you in that matter, for then I must not listen to so many loud songs about little things. At least, Bangu was killed and his proud tribe humbled, and, for reasons of state, I am glad that this happened without my moving a regiment or being mixed up with the business, for I tell you that there are some of my family who loved Bangu. But I—I loved your father, Matiwane, whom Bangu butchered, for we were brought up together as boys—yes, and served together in the same regiment, the Amawombe, when the Wild One, my brother, ruled" (he meant Chaka, for among the Zulus the names of dead kings are *hlonipa*—that is, they must not be spoken if it can be avoided). "Therefore," went on Panda, "for this reason, and for others, I am glad that Bangu has been punished, and that, although vengeance has crawled after him like a footsore bull, at length he has been tossed with its horns and crushed with its knees."

"Yebo, Ngonyama!" (Yes, O Lion!) said Saduko.

"Now, Saduko," went on Panda, "because you are your father's son, and because you have shown yourself a man, although you are still little in the land, I am minded to advance you. Therefore I give to you the chieftainship over those who remain of the Amakoba and over all of the Amangwane blood whom you can gather."

"*Bayete*! As the King pleases," said Saduko.

"And I give you leave to become a *kehla*—a wearer of the head-ring—although, as you have said, you are still but a boy, and with it a place upon my Council."

"*Bayete*! As the King pleases," said Saduko, still apparently unmoved by the honours that were being heaped upon him.

"And, Son of Matiwane," went on Panda, "you are still unmarried, are you not?"

Now, for the first time, Saduko's face changed. "Yes, Black One," he said hurriedly, "but—"

Here he caught my eye, and, reading some warning in it, was silent.

"But," repeated Panda after him, "doubtless you would like to be? Well, it is natural in a young man who wishes to found a House, and therefore I give you leave to marry."

"Yebo, Silo!" (Yes, O Wild Beast!) "I thank the King, but—"

Here I sneezed loudly, and he ceased.

"But," repeated Panda, "of course, you do not know where to find a wife between the time the hawk stoops and the rat squeaks in its claws. How should you who have never thought of the matter? Also," he continued, with a smile, "it is well that you have not thought of it, since she whom I shall give to you could not live in the second hut in your *kraal* and call another *Inkosikazi* (that is, head lady or chieftainess). Umbelazi, my son, go fetch her of whom we have thought as a bride for this boy."

Now Umbelazi rose, and went with a broad smile upon his face, while Panda, somewhat fatigued with all his speech-making—for he was very fat and the day was very hot—leaned his head back against the hut and closed his eyes.

"O Black One! O thou who consumeth with rage! (*Dhlangamandhla*)" broke out Saduko, who, I could see, was much disturbed. "I have something to say to you."

"No doubt, no doubt," answered Panda drowsily, "but save up your thanks till you have seen, or you will have none left afterwards," and he snored slightly.

Now I, perceiving that Saduko was about to ruin himself, thought it well to interfere, though what business of mine it was to do so I cannot say. At any rate, if only I had held my tongue at this moment, and allowed Saduko to make a fool of himself, as he wished to do—for where Mameena was concerned he never could be wise—I verily believe that all the history of Zululand would have run a different course, and that many thousands of men, white and black, who are now dead would be alive to-day. But Fate ordered it otherwise. Yes, it was not I who spoke, but Fate. The Angel of Doom used my throat as his trumpet.

Seeing that Panda dozed, I slipped behind Saduko and gripped him by the arm.

"Are you mad?" I whispered into his ear. "Will you throw away your fortune, and your life also?"

"But Mameena," he whispered back. "I would marry none save Mameena."

"Fool!" I answered. "Mameena has betrayed and spat upon you. Take what the Heavens send you and give thanks. Would you wear Masapo's soiled blanket?"

"Macumazahn," he said in a hollow voice, "I will follow your head, and not my own heart. Yet you sow a strange seed, Macumazahn, or so you may think when you see its fruit." And he gave me a wild look—a look that frightened me.

There was something in this look which caused me to reflect that I might do well to go away and leave Saduko, Mameena, Nandie, and the rest of them to "dree their weirds," as the Scotch say, for, after all, what was my finger doing in that very hot stew? Getting burnt, I thought, and not collecting any stew.

Yet, looking back on these events, how could I foresee what would be the end of the madness of Saduko, of the fearful machinations of Mameena, and of the weakness of Umbelazi when she snared him in the net of her beauty, thus bringing about his ruin, through the hate of Saduko and the ambition of Cetewayo? How could I know that, at the back of all these events, stood the old dwarf, Zikali the Wise, working night and day to slake the enmity and fulfil the vengeance which long ago he had conceived and planned against the royal House of Senzangakona and the Zulu people over whom it ruled?

Yes, he stood there like a man behind a great stone upon the brow of a mountain, slowly, remorselessly, with infinite skill, labour, and patience, pushing that stone to the edge of the cliff, whence at length, in the appointed hour, it would thunder down upon those who dwelt beneath, to leave them crushed and no more a people. How could I guess that we, the actors in this play, were all the while helping him to push that stone, and that he cared nothing how many of us were carried with it into the abyss, if only we brought about the triumph of his secret, unutterable rage and hate?

Now I see and understand all these things, as it is easy to do, but then I was blind; nor did the Voices reach my dull ears to warn me, as, how or why I cannot tell, they did, I believe, reach those of Zikali.

Oh, what was the sum of it? Just this, I think, and nothing more—that, as Saduko and the others were Mameena's tools, and as all of them and their passions were Zikali's tools, so he himself was the tool of some unseen Power that used him and us to accomplish its design. Which, I suppose, is fatalism, or, in other words, all these things happened because they must happen. A poor conclusion to reach after so much thought and striving, and not complimentary to man and his boasted powers of free will; still, one to which many of us are often driven, especially if we have lived among savages, where such dramas work themselves out openly and swiftly, unhidden from our eyes by the veils and subterfuges of civilisation. At least, there is this comfort about it—that, if we are but feathers blown by the wind, how can the individual feather be blamed because it did not travel against, turn or keep back the wind?

Well, let me return from these speculations to the history of the facts that caused them.

Just as—a little too late—I had made up my mind that I would go after my own business, and leave Saduko to manage his, through the fence gateway appeared the great, tall Umbelazi leading by the hand a woman. As I saw in a moment, it did not need certain bangles of copper, ornaments of ivory and of very rare pink beads, called *infibinga*, which only those of the royal House were permitted to wear, to proclaim her a person of rank, for dignity and high blood were apparent in her face, her carriage, her gestures, and all that had to do with her.

Nandie the Sweet was not a great beauty, as was Mameena, although her figure was fine, and her stature like that of all the race of Senzangakona—considerably above the average. To begin with, she was darker in hue, and her lips were rather thick, as was her nose; nor were her eyes large and liquid like those of an antelope. Further, she lacked the informing mystery of Mameena's face, that at times was broken and lit up by flashes of alluring light and quick, sympathetic perception, as a heavy evening sky, that seems to join the dim earth to the dimmer heavens, is illuminated by pulsings of fire, soft and many-hued, suggesting, but not revealing, the strength and splendour that it veils. Nandie had none of these attractions, which, after all, anywhere upon the earth belong only to a few women in each generation. She was a simple, honest-natured, kindly, affectionate young woman of high birth, no more; that is, as these qualities are understood and expressed among her people.

Umbelazi led her forward into the presence of the King, to whom she bowed gracefully enough. Then, after casting a swift, sidelong glance at Saduko, which I found it difficult to interpret, and another of inquiry at me, she folded her hands upon her breast and stood silent, with bent head, waiting to be addressed.

The address was brief enough, for Panda was still sleepy.

"My daughter," he said, with a yawn, "there stands your husband," and he jerked his thumb towards Saduko. "He is a young man and a brave, and unmarried; also one who should grow great in the shadow of our House, especially as he is a friend of your brother, Umbelazi. I understand also that you have seen him and like him. Unless you have anything to say against it, for as, not being a common father, the King receives no cattle—at least in this case—I am not prejudiced, but will listen to your words," and he chuckled in a drowsy fashion. "I propose that the marriage should take place to-morrow. Now, my daughter, have you anything to say? For if so, please say it at once, as I am tired. The eternal wranglings between your brethren, Cetewayo and Umbelazi, have worn me out."

Now Nandie looked about her in her open, honest fashion, her gaze resting first on Saduko, then on Umbelazi, and lastly upon me.

"My Father," she said at length, in her soft, steady voice, "tell me, I beseech you, who proposes this marriage? Is it the Chief Saduko, is it the Prince Umbelazi, or is it the white lord whose true name I do not know, but who is called Macumazahn, Watcher-by-Night?"

"I can't remember which of them proposed it," yawned Panda. "Who can keep on talking about things from night till morning? At any rate, I propose it, and I will make your husband a big man among our people. Have you anything to say against it?"

"I have nothing to say, my Father. I have met Saduko, and like him well—for the rest, you are the judge. But," she added slowly, "does Saduko like me? When he speaks my name, does he feel it here?" and she pointed to her throat.

"I am sure I do not know what he feels in his throat," Panda replied testily, "but I feel that mine is dry. Well, as no one says anything, the matter is settled. To-morrow Saduko shall give the *umqoliso* (the Ox of the Girl), that makes marriage—if he has not got one here I will lend it to him, and you can take the new, big hut that I have built in the outer *kraal* to dwell in for the present. There will be a dance, if you wish it; if not, I do not care, for I have no wish for ceremony just now, who am too troubled with great matters. Now I am going to sleep."

Then sinking from his stool on to his knees, Panda crawled through the doorway of his great hut, which was close to him, and vanished.

Umbelazi and I departed also through the gateway of the fence, leaving Saduko and the Princess Nandie alone together, for there were no attendants present. What happened between them I am sure I do not know, but I gather that, in one way or another, Saduko made himself sufficiently agreeable to the princess to persuade her to take him to husband. Perhaps, being already enamoured of him, she was not difficult to persuade. At any rate, on the morrow, without any great feasting or fuss, except the customary dance, the *umqoliso*, the Ox of the Girl, was slaughtered, and Saduko became the husband of a royal maiden of the House of Senzangakona.

Certainly, as I remember reflecting, it was a remarkable rise in life for one who, but a few months before, had been without possessions or a home.

I may add that, after our brief talk in the King's *kraal*, while Panda was dozing, I had no further words with Saduko on this matter of his marriage, for between its proposal and the event he avoided me, nor did I seek him out. On the day of the marriage also, I trekked for Natal, and for a whole year heard no more of Saduko, Nandie, and Mameena; although, to be frank, I must admit I thought of the last of these persons more often, perhaps, than I should have done.

The truth is that Mameena was one of those women who sticks in a man's mind even more closely than a "Wait-a-bit" thorn does in his coat.

Chapter 9

Allan Returns to Zululand

A whole year had gone by, in which I did, or tried to do, various things that have no connection with this story, when once more I found myself in Zululand—at Umbezi's *kraal* indeed. Hither I had trekked in fulfilment of a certain bargain, already alluded to, that was concerned with ivory and guns, which I had made with the old fellow, or, rather, with Masapo, his son-in-law, whom he represented in this matter. Into the exact circumstances of that bargain I do not enter, since at the moment I cannot recall whether I ever obtained the necessary permit to import those guns into Zululand, although now that I am older I earnestly hope that I did so, since it is wrong to sell weapons to natives that may be put to all sorts of unforeseen uses.

At any rate, there I was, sitting alone with the Headman in his hut discussing a dram of *squareface* that I had given to him, for the *trade* was finished to our mutual satisfaction, and Scowl, my body servant, with the hunters, had just carried off the ivory—a fine lot of tusks—to my wagons.

"Well, Umbezi," I said, "and how has it fared with you since we parted a year ago? Have you seen anything of Saduko, who, you may remember, left you in some wrath?"

"Thanks be to my Spirit, I have seen nothing of that wild man, Macumazahn," answered Umbezi, shaking his fat old head in a fashion which showed great anxiety. "Yet I have heard of him, for he sent me a message the other day to tell me that he had not forgotten what he owed me."

"Did he mean the sticks with which he promised to bray you like a green hide?" I inquired innocently.

"I think so, Macumazahn—I think so, for certainly he owes me nothing else. And the worst of it is that, there at Panda's *kraal*, he has grown like a pumpkin on a dung heap—great, great!"

"And therefore is now one who can pay any debt that he owes, Umbezi," I said, taking a pull at the *squareface* and looking at him over the top of the pannikin.

"Doubtless he can, Macumazahn, and, between you and me, that is the real reason why I—or rather Masapo—was so anxious to get those guns. They were not for hunting, as he told you by the messenger, or for war, but to protect us against Saduko, in case he should attack. Well, now I hope we shall be able to hold our own."

"You and Masapo must teach your people to use them first, Umbezi. But I expect Saduko has forgotten all about both of you now that he is the husband of a princess of the royal blood. Tell me, how goes it with Mameena?"

"Oh, well, well, Macumazahn. For is she not the head lady of the Amasomi? There is nothing wrong with her—nothing at all, except that as yet she has no child; also that—," and he paused.

"That what?" I asked.

"That she hates the very sight of her husband, Masapo, and says that she would rather be married to a baboon—yes, to a baboon—than to him, which gives him offence, after he has paid so many cattle for her. But what of this, Macumazahn? There is always a grain missing upon the finest head of corn. Nothing is *quite* perfect in the world, Macumazahn, and if Mameena does not chance to love her husband—" and he shrugged his shoulders and drank some *squareface.*

"Of course it does not matter in the least, Umbezi, except to Mameena and her husband, who no doubt will settle down in time, now that Saduko is married to a princess of the Zulu House."

"I hope so, Macumazahn, but, to tell the truth, I wish you had brought more guns, for I live amongst a terrible lot of people. Masapo, who is furious with Mameena because she will have none of him, and therefore with me, as though I could control Mameena; Mameena, who is mad with Masapo, and therefore with me, because I gave her in marriage to him; Saduko, who foams at the mouth at the name of Masapo, because he has married Mameena, whom, it is said, he still loves, and therefore at me, because I am her father and did my best to settle her in the world. Oh, give me some more of that fire-water, Macumazahn, for it makes me forget all these things, and especially that my guardian spirit made me the father of Mameena, with whom you would not run away when you might have done so. Oh, Macumazahn, why did you not run away with Mameena, and turn her into a quiet white woman who ties herself up in sacks, sings songs to the 'Great-Great' in the sky—(that is, hymns to the Power above us)—and never thinks of any man who is not her husband?"

"Because if I had done so, Umbezi, I should have ceased to be a quiet white man. Yes, yes, my friend, I should have been in some such place as yours to-day, and that is the last thing that I wish. And now, Umbezi, you have had quite enough *squareface*, so I will take the bottle away with me. Good-night."

On the following morning I trekked very early from Umbezi's *kraal*—before he was up indeed, for the *squareface* made him sleep sound. My destination was Nodwengu, Panda's Great Place, where I hoped to do some trading, but, as I was in no particular hurry, my plan was to go round by Masapo's, and see for myself how it fared between him and Mameena. Indeed, I reached the borders of the Amasomi territory, whereof Masapo was chief, by evening, and camped there. But with the night came reflection, and reflection told me that I should do well to keep clear of Mameena and her domestic complications, if she had any. So I changed my mind, and next morning trekked on to Nodwengu by the only route that my guides reported to be practicable, one which took me a long way round.

That day, owing to the roughness of the road—if road it could be called—and an accident to one of the wagons, we only covered about fifteen miles, and as night fell were obliged to outspan at the first spot where we could find water. When the oxen had been unyoked I looked about me, and saw that we were in a place that, although I had approached it from a somewhat different direction, I recognised at once as the mouth of the Black Kloof, in which, over a year before, I had interviewed Zikali the Little and Wise. There was no mistaking the spot; that blasted valley, with the piled-up columns of boulders and the overhanging cliff at the end of it, have, so far as I am aware, no exact counterparts in Africa.

I sat upon the box of the first wagon, eating my food, which consisted of some *biltong* and biscuit, for I had not bothered to shoot any game that day, which was very hot, and wondering whether Zikali were still alive, also whether I should take the trouble to walk up the kloof and find out. On the whole I thought that I would not, as the place repelled me, and I did not particularly wish to hear any more of his prophecies and fierce, ill-omened talk. So I just sat there studying the wonderful effect of the red evening light pouring up between those walls of fantastic rocks.

Presently I perceived, far away, a single human figure—whether it were man or woman I could not tell—walking towards me along the path which ran at the bottom of the cleft. In those gigantic surroundings it looked extraordinarily small and lonely, although perhaps because of the intense red light in which it was bathed, or perhaps just because it was human, a living thing in the midst of all that still, inanimate grandeur, it caught and focused my attention. I grew greatly interested in it; I wondered if it were that of man or woman, and what it was doing here in this haunted valley.

The figure drew nearer, and now I saw it was slender and tall, like that of a lad or of a well-grown woman, but to which sex it belonged I could not see, because it was draped in a cloak of beautiful grey fur. Just then Scowl came to the other side of the wagon to speak to me about something, which took off my attention for the next two minutes. When I looked round again it was to see the figure standing within three yards of me, its face hidden by a kind of hood which was attached to the fur cloak.

"Who are you, and what is your business?" I asked, whereon a gentle voice answered:

"Do you not know me, O Macumazana?"

"How can I know one who is tied up like a gourd in a mat? Yet is it not—is it not—"

"Yes, it is Mameena, and I am very pleased that you should remember my voice, Macumazahn, after we have been separated for such a long, long time," and, with a sudden movement, she threw back the *kaross*, hood and all, revealing herself in all her strange beauty.

I jumped down off the wagon-box and took her hand.

"O Macumazana," she said, while I still held it—or, to be accurate, while she still held mine—"indeed my heart is glad to see a friend again," and she looked at me with her appealing eyes, which, in the red light, I could see appeared to float in tears.

"A friend, Mameena!" I exclaimed. "Why, now you are so rich, and the wife of a big chief, you must have plenty of friends."

"Alas! Macumazahn, I am rich in nothing except trouble, for my husband saves, like the ants for winter. Why, he even grudged me this poor *kaross*; and as for friends, he is so jealous that he will not allow me any."

"He cannot be jealous of women, Mameena!"

"Oh, women! *Piff!* I do not care for women; they are very unkind to me, because—because—well, perhaps you can guess why, Macumazahn," she answered, glancing at her own reflection in a little travelling looking-glass that hung from the woodwork of the wagon, for I had been using it to brush my hair, and smiled very sweetly.

"At least you have your husband, Mameena, and I thought that perhaps by this time—"

She held up her hand.

"My husband! Oh, I would that I had him not, for I hate him, Macumazahn; and as for the rest—never! The truth is that I never cared for any man except one whose name *you* may chance to remember, Macumazahn."

"I suppose you mean Saduko—" I began.

"Tell me, Macumazahn," she inquired innocently, "are white people very stupid? I ask because you do not seem as clever as you used to be. Or have you perhaps a bad memory?"

Now I felt myself turning red as the sky behind me, and broke in hurriedly:

"If you did not like your husband, Mameena, you should not have married him. You know you need not unless you wished."

"When one has only two thorn bushes to sit on, Macumazahn, one chooses that which seems to have the fewest prickles, to discover sometimes that they are still there in hundreds, although one did not see them. You know that at length everyone gets tired of standing."

"Is that why you have taken to walking, Mameena? I mean, what are you doing here alone?"

"I? Oh, I heard that you were passing this way, and came to have a talk with you. No, from you I cannot hide even the least bit of the truth. I came to talk with you, but also I came to see Zikali and ask him what a wife should do who hates her husband."

"Indeed! And what did he answer you?"

"He answered that he thought she had better run away with another man, if there were one whom she did not hate—out of Zululand, of course," she replied, looking first at me and then at my wagon and the two horses that were tied to it.

"Is that all he said, Mameena?"

"No. Have I not told you that I cannot hide one grain of the truth from you? He added that the only other thing to be done was to sit still and drink my sour milk, pretending that it is sweet, until my Spirit gives me a new cow. He seemed to think that my Spirit would be bountiful in the matter of new cows—one day."

"Anything more?" I inquired.

"One little thing. Have I not told you that you shall have all—all the truth? Zikali seemed to think also that at last every one of my herd of cows, old and new, would come to a bad end. He did not tell me to what end."

She turned her head aside, and when she looked up again I saw that she was weeping, really weeping this time, not just making her eyes swim, as she did before.

"Of course they will come to a bad end, Macumazahn," she went on in a soft, thick voice, "for I and all with whom I have to do were *torn out of the reeds* (*i.e.* created) that way. And that's why I won't tempt you to run away with me any more, as I meant to do when I saw you, because it is true, Macumazahn you are the only man I ever liked or ever shall like; and you know I could make you run away with me if I chose, although I am black and you are white—oh, yes, before to-morrow morning. But I won't do it; for why should I catch you in my unlucky web and bring you into all sorts of trouble among my people and your own? Go you your road, Macumazahn, and I will go mine as the wind blows me. And now give me a cup of water and let me be away—a cup of water, no more. Oh, do not be afraid for me, or melt too much, lest I should melt also. I have an escort waiting over yonder hill. There, thank you for your water, Macumazahn, and good night. Doubtless we shall meet again ere long, and—I forgot; the Little Wise One said he would like to have a talk with you. Good night, Macumazahn, good night. I trust that you did a profitable trade with Umbezi my father and Masapo my husband. I wonder why such men as these should have been chosen to be my father and my husband. Think it over, Macumazahn, and tell me when next we meet. Give me that pretty mirror, Macumazahn; when I look in it I shall see you as well as myself, and that will please me—you don't know how much. I thank you. Good night."

In another minute I was watching her solitary little figure, now wrapped again in the hooded *kaross*, as it vanished over the brow of the rise behind us, and really, as she went, I felt a lump rising in my throat. Notwithstanding all her wickedness—and I suppose she was wicked—there was something horribly attractive about Mameena.

When she had gone, taking my only looking-glass with her, and the lump in my throat had gone also, I began to wonder how much fact there was in her story. She had protested so earnestly that she told me all the truth that I felt sure there must be something left behind. Also I remembered she had said Zikali wanted to see me. Well, the end of it was I took a moonlight walk up that dreadful gorge, into which not even Scowl would accompany me, because he declared that the place was well known to be haunted by *imikovu*, or spectres who have been raised from the dead by wizards.

It was a long and disagreeable walk, and somehow I felt very depressed and insignificant as I trudged on between those gigantic cliffs, passing now through patches of bright moonlight and now through deep pools of shadow, threading my way among clumps of bush or round the bases of tall pillars of piled-up stones, till at length I came to the overhanging cliffs at the end, which frowned down on me like the brows of some titanic demon.

Well, I got to the end at last, and at the gate of the *kraal* fence was met by one of those fierce and huge men who served the dwarf as guards. Suddenly he emerged from behind a stone, and having scanned me for a moment in silence, beckoned to me to follow him, as though I were expected. A minute later I found myself face to face with Zikali, who was seated in the clear moonlight just outside the shadow of his hut, and engaged, apparently, in his favourite occupation of carving wood with a rough native knife of curious shape.

For a while he took no notice of me; then suddenly looked up, shaking back his braided grey locks, and broke into one of his great laughs.

"So it is you, Macumazahn," he said. "Well, I knew you were passing my way and that Mameena would send you here. But why do you come to see the 'Thing-that-should-not-have-been-born'? To tell me how you fared with the buffalo with the split horn, eh?"

"No, Zikali, for why should I tell you what you know already? Mameena said you wished to talk with me, that was all."

"Then Mameena lied," he answered, "as is her nature, in whose throat live four false words for every one of truth. Still, sit down, Macumazahn. There is beer made ready for you by that stool; and give me the knife and a pinch of the white man's snuff that you have brought for me as a present."

I produced these articles, though how he knew that I had them with me I cannot tell, nor did I think it worth while to inquire. The snuff, I remember, pleased him very much, but of the knife he said that it was a pretty toy, but he would not know how to use it. Then we fell to talking.

"What was Mameena doing here?" I asked boldly.

"What was she doing at your wagons?" he asked. "Oh, do not stop to tell me; I know, I know. That is a very good Snake of yours, Macumazahn, which always just lets you slip through her fingers, when, if she chose to close her hand—Well, well, I do not betray the secrets of my clients; but I say this to you—go on to the *kraal* of the son of Senzangakona, and you will see things happen that will make you laugh, for Mameena will be there, and the mongrel Masapo, her husband. Truly she hates him well, and, after all, I would rather be loved than hated by Mameena, though both are dangerous. Poor Mongrel! Soon the jackals will be chewing his bones."

"Why do you say that?" I asked.

"Only because Mameena tells me that he is a great wizard, and the jackals eat many wizards in Zululand. Also he is an enemy of Panda's House, is he not?"

"You have been giving her some bad counsel, Zikali," I said, blurting out the thought in my mind.

"Perhaps, perhaps, Macumazahn; only I may call it good counsel. I have my own road to walk, and if I can find some to clear away the thorns that would prick my feet, what of it? Also she will get her pay, who finds life dull up there among the Amasomi, with one she hates for a hut-fellow. Go you and watch, and afterwards, when you have an hour to spare, come and tell me what happens—that is, if I do not chance to be there to see for myself."

"Is Saduko well?" I asked to change the subject, for I did not wish to become privy to the plots that filled the air.

"I am told that his tree grows great, that it overshadows all the royal *kraal*. I think that Mameena wishes to sleep in the shade of it. And now you are weary, and so am I. Go back to your wagons, Macumazahn, for I have nothing more to say to you to-night. But be sure to return and tell me what chances at Panda's *kraal*. Or, as I have said, perhaps I shall meet you there. Who knows, who knows?"

Now, it will be observed that there was nothing very remarkable in this conversation between Zikali and myself. He did not tell me any deep secrets or make any great prophecy. It may be wondered, indeed, when there is so much to record, why I set it down at all.

My answer is, because of the extraordinary impression that it produced upon me. Although so little was said, I felt all the while that those few words were a veil hiding terrible events to be. I was sure that some dreadful scheme had been hatched between the old dwarf and Mameena whereof the issue would soon become apparent, and that he had sent me away in a hurry after he learned that she had told me nothing, because he feared lest I should stumble on its cue and perhaps cause it to fail.

At any rate, as I walked back to my wagons by moonlight down that dreadful gorge, the hot, thick air seemed to me to have a physical taste and smell of blood, and the dank foliage of the tropical trees that grew there, when now and again a puff of wind stirred them, moaned like the fabled *imikovu*, or as men might do in their last faint agony. The effect upon my nerves was quite strange, for when at last I reached my wagons I was shaking like a reed, and a cold perspiration, unnatural enough upon that hot night, poured from my face and body.

Well, I took a couple of stiff tots of *squareface* to pull myself together, and at length went to sleep, to awake before dawn with a headache. Looking out of the wagon, to my surprise I saw Scowl and the hunters, who should have been snoring, standing in a group and talking to each other in frightened whispers. I called Scowl to me and asked what was the matter.

"Nothing, Baas," he said with a shamefaced air; "only there are so many spooks about this place. They have been passing in and out of it all night."

"Spooks, you idiot!" I answered. "Probably they were people going to visit the *Nyanga*, Zikali."

"Perhaps, Baas; only then we do not know why they should all look like dead people—princes, some of them, by their dress—and walk upon the air a man's height from the ground."

"Pooh!" I replied. "Do you not know the difference between owls in the mist and dead kings? Make ready, for we trek at once; the air here is full of fever."

"Certainly, Baas," he said, springing off to obey; and I do not think I ever remember two wagons being got under way quicker than they were that morning.

I merely mention this nonsense to show that the Black Kloof could affect other people's nerves as well as my own.

In due course I reached Nodwengu without accident, having sent forward one of my hunters to report my approach to Panda. When my wagons arrived outside the Great Place they were met by none other than my old friend, Maputa, he who had brought me back the pills before our attack upon Bangu.

"Greeting, Macumazahn," he said. "I am sent by the King to say that you are welcome and to point you out a good place to outspan; also to give you permission to trade as much as you will in this town, since he knows that your dealings are always fair."

I returned my thanks in the usual fashion, adding that I had brought a little present for the King which I would deliver when it pleased him to receive me. Then I invited Maputa, to whom I also offered some trifle which delighted him very much, to ride with me on the wagon-box till we came to the selected outspan.

This, by the way, proved, to be a very good place indeed, a little valley full of grass for the cattle—for by the King's order it had not been grazed—with a stream of beautiful water running down it.

Moreover it overlooked a great open space immediately in front of the main gate of the town, so that I could see everything that went on and all who arrived or departed.

"You will be comfortable here, Macumazahn," said Maputa, "during your stay, which we hope will be long, since, although there will soon be a mighty crowd at Nodwengu, the King has given orders that none except your own servants are to enter this valley."

"I thank the King; but why will there be a crowd, Maputa?"

"Oh!" he answered with a shrug of the shoulders, "because of a new thing. All the tribes of the Zulus are to come up to be reviewed. Some say that Cetewayo has brought this about, and some say that it is Umbelazi. But I am sure that it is the work of neither of these, but of Saduko, your old friend, though what his object is I cannot tell you. I only trust," he added uneasily, "that it will not end in bloodshed between the Great Brothers."

"So Saduko has grown tall, Maputa?"

"Tall as a tree, Macumazahn. His whisper in the King's ear is louder than the shouts of others. Moreover, he has become a 'self-eater' (that is a Zulu term which means one who is very haughty). You will have to wait on him, Macumazahn; he will not wait on you."

"Is it so?" I answered. "Well, tall trees are blown down sometimes."

He nodded his wise old head. "Yes, Macumazahn; I have seen plenty grow and fall in my time, for at last the swimmer goes with the stream. Anyhow, you will be able to do a good trade among so many, and, whatever happens, none will harm you whom all love. And now farewell; I bear your messages to the King, who sends an ox for you to kill lest you should grow hungry in his house."

That same evening I saw Saduko and the others, as I shall tell. I had been up to visit the King and give him my present, a case of English table-knives with bone handles, which pleased him greatly, although he did not in the least know how to use them. Indeed, without their accompanying forks these are somewhat futile articles. I found the old fellow very tired and anxious, but as he was surrounded by *indunas*, I had no private talk with him. Seeing that he was busy, I took my leave as soon as I could, and when I walked away whom should I meet but Saduko.

I saw him while he was a good way off, advancing towards the inner gate with a train of attendants like a royal personage, and knew very well that he saw me. Making up my mind what to do at once, I walked straight on to him, forcing him to give me the path, which he did not wish to do before so many people, and brushed past him as though he were a stranger. As I expected, this treatment had the desired effect, for after we had passed each other he turned and said:

"Do you not know me, Macumazahn?"

"Who calls?" I asked. "Why, friend, your face is familiar to me. How are you named?"

"Have you forgotten Saduko?" he said in a pained voice.

"No, no, of course not," I answered. "I know you now, although you seem somewhat changed since we went out hunting and fighting together—I suppose because you are fatter. I trust that you are well, Saduko? Good-bye. I must be going back to my wagons. If you wish to see me you will find me there."

These remarks, I may add, seemed to take Saduko very much aback. At any rate, he found no reply to them, even when old Maputa, with whom I was walking, and some others sniggered aloud. There is nothing that Zulus enjoy so much as seeing one whom they consider an upstart set in his place.

Well, a couple of hours afterwards, just as the sun was sinking, who should walk up to my wagons but Saduko himself, accompanied by a woman whom I recognised at once as his wife, the Princess Nandie, who carried a fine baby boy in her arms. Rising, I saluted Nandie and offered her my camp-stool, which she looked at suspiciously and declined, preferring to seat herself on the ground after the native fashion. So I took it back again, and after I had sat down on it, not before, stretched out my hand to Saduko, who by this time was quite humble and polite.

Well, we talked away, and by degrees, without seeming too much interested in them, I was furnished with a list of all the advancements which it had pleased Panda to heap upon Saduko during the past year. In their way they were remarkable enough, for it was much as though some penniless country gentleman in England had been promoted in that short space of time to be one of the premier peers of the kingdom and endowed with great offices and estates. When he had finished the count of them he paused, evidently waiting for me to congratulate him. But all I said was:

"By the Heavens above I am sorry for you, Saduko! How many enemies you must have made! What a long way there will be for you to fall one night!"—a remark at which the quiet Nandie broke into a low laugh that I think pleased her husband even less than my sarcasm. "Well," I went on, "I see that you have got a baby, which is much better than all these titles. May I look at it, *Inkosazana*?"

Of course she was delighted, and we proceeded to inspect the baby, which evidently she loved more than anything on earth. Whilst we were examining the child and chatting about it, Saduko sitting by meanwhile in the sulks, who on earth should appear but Mameena and her fat and sullen-looking husband, the chief Masapo.

"Oh, Macumazahn," she said, appearing to notice no one else, "how pleased I am to see you after a whole long year!"

I stared at her and my jaw dropped. Then I recovered myself, thinking she must have made a mistake and meant to say "week."

"Twelve moons," she went on, "and, Macumazahn, not one of them has gone by but I have thought of you several times and wondered if we should ever meet again. Where have you been all this while?"

"In many places," I answered; "amongst others at the Black Kloof, where I called upon the dwarf, Zikali, and lost my looking-glass."

"The *Nyanga*, Zikali! Oh, how often have I wished to see him. But, of course, I cannot, for I am told he will not receive any women."

"I don't know, I am sure," I replied, "but you might try; perhaps he would make an exception in your favour."

"I think I will, Macumazahn," she murmured, whereon I collapsed into silence, feeling that things were getting beyond me.

When I recovered myself a little it was to hear Mameena greeting Saduko with much effusion, and complimenting him on his rise in life, which she said she had always foreseen. This remark seemed to bowl out Saduko also, for he made no answer to it, although I noticed that he could not take his eyes off Mameena's beautiful face. Presently, however, he seemed to become aware of Masapo, and instantly his whole demeanour changed, for it grew proud and even terrible. Masapo tendered him some greeting; whereon Saduko turned upon him and said:

"What, chief of the Amasomi, do you give the good-day to an *umfokazana* and a mangy hyena? Why do you do this? Is it because the low *umfokazana* has become a noble and the mangy hyena has put on a tiger's coat?" And he glared at him like a veritable tiger.

Masapo made no answer that I could catch. Muttering some inaudible words, he turned to depart, and in doing so—quite innocently, I think—struck Nandie, knocking her over on to her back and causing the child to fall out of her arms in such fashion that its tender head struck against a pebble with sufficient force to cause it to bleed.

Saduko leapt at him, smiting him across the shoulders with the little stick that he carried. For a moment Masapo paused, and I thought that he was going to show fight. If he had any such intention, however, he changed his mind, for without a word, or showing any resentment at the insult which he had received, he broke into a heavy run and vanished among the evening shadows. Mameena, who had observed all, broke into something else, namely, a laugh.

"Piff! My husband is big yet not brave," she said, "but I do not think he meant to hurt you, woman."

"Do you speak to me, wife of Masapo?" asked Nandie with gentle dignity, as she gained her feet and picked up the stunned child. "If so, my name and titles are the *Inkosazana* Nandie, daughter of the Black One and wife of the lord Saduko."

"Your pardon," replied Mameena humbly, for she was cowed at once. "I did not know who you were, *Inkosazana*."

"It is granted, wife of Masapo. Macumazahn, give me water, I pray you, that I may bathe the head of my child."

The water was brought, and presently, when the little one seemed all right again, for it had only received a scratch, Nandie thanked me and departed to her own huts, saying with a smile to her husband as she passed that there was no need for him to accompany her, as she had servants waiting at the *kraal* gate. So Saduko stayed behind, and Mameena stayed also. He talked with me for quite a long while, for he had much to tell me, although all the time I felt that his heart was not in his talk. His heart was with Mameena, who sat there and smiled continually in her mysterious way, only putting in a word now and again, as though to excuse her presence.

At length she rose and said with a sigh that she must be going back to where the Amasomi were in camp, as Masapo would need her to see to his food. By now it was quite dark, although I remember that from time to time the sky was lit up by sheet lightning, for a storm was brewing. As I expected, Saduko rose also, saying that he would see me on the morrow, and went away with Mameena, walking like one who dreams.

A few minutes later I had occasion to leave the wagons in order to inspect one of the oxen which was tied up by itself at a distance, because it had shown signs of some sickness that might or might not be catching. Moving quietly, as I always do from a hunter's habit, I walked alone to the place where the beast was tethered behind some mimosa thorns. Just as I reached these thorns the broad lightning shone out vividly, and showed me Saduko holding the unresisting shape of Mameena in his arms and kissing her passionately.

Then I turned and went back to the wagons even more quietly than I had come.

I should add that on the morrow I found out that, after all, there was nothing serious the matter with my ox.

Chapter 10
The Smelling-Out

After these events matters went on quietly for some time. I visited Saduko's huts—very fine huts—about the doors of which sat quite a number of his tribesmen, who seemed glad to see me again. Here I learned from the Lady Nandie that her babe, whom she loved dearly, was none the worse for its little accident. Also I learned from Saduko himself, who came in before I left, attended like a prince by several notable men, that he had made up his quarrel with Masapo, and, indeed, apologised to him, as he found that he had not really meant to insult the princess, his wife, having only thrust her over by accident. Saduko added indeed that now they were good friends, which was well for Masapo, a man whom the King had no cause to like. I said that I was glad to hear it, and went on to call upon Masapo, who received me with enthusiasm, as also did Mameena.

Here I noted with pleasure that this pair seemed to be on much better terms than I understood had been the case in the past, for Mameena even addressed her husband on two separate occasions in very affectionate language, and fetched something that he wanted without waiting to be asked. Masapo, too, was in excellent spirits, because, as he told me, the old quarrel between him and Saduko was thoroughly made up, their reconciliation having been sealed by an interchange of gifts. He added that he was very glad that this was the case, since Saduko was now one of the most powerful men in the country, who could harm him much if he chose, especially as some secret enemy had put it about of late that he, Masapo, was an enemy of the King's House, and an evil-doer who practised witchcraft. In proof of his new friendship, however, Saduko had promised that these slanders should be looked into and their originator punished, if he or she could be found.

Well, I congratulated him and took my departure, "thinking furiously," as the Frenchman says. That there was a tragedy pending I was sure; this weather was too calm to last; the water ran so still because it was preparing to leap down some hidden precipice.

Yet what could I do? Tell Masapo I had seen his wife being embraced by another man? Surely that was not my business; it was Masapo's business to attend to her conduct. Also they would both deny it, and I had no witness. Tell him that Saduko's reconciliation with him was not sincere, and that he had better look to himself? How did I know it was not sincere? It might suit Saduko's book to make friends with Masapo, and if I interfered I should only make enemies and be called a liar who was working for some secret end.

Go to Panda and confide my suspicions to him? He was far too anxious and busy about great matters to listen to me, and if he did, would only laugh at this tale of a petty flirtation. No, there was nothing to be done except sit still and wait. Very possibly I was mistaken, after all, and things would smooth themselves out, as they generally do.

Meanwhile the *reviewing*, or whatever it may have been, was in progress, and I was busy with my own affairs, making hay while the sun shone. So great were the crowds of people who came up to Nodwengu that in a week I had sold everything I had to sell in the two wagons, that were mostly laden with cloth, beads, knives and so forth. Moreover, the prices I got were splendid, since the buyers bid against each other, and before I was cleared out I had collected quite a herd of cattle, also a quantity of ivory. These I sent on to Natal with one of the wagons, remaining behind myself with the other, partly because Panda asked me to do so—for now and again he would seek my advice on sundry questions—and partly from curiosity.

There was plenty to be curious about up at Nodwengu just then, since no one was sure that civil war would not break out between the princes Cetewayo and Umbelazi, whose factions were present in force.

It was averted for the time, however, by Umbelazi keeping away from the great gathering under pretext of being sick, and leaving Saduko and some others to watch his interests. Also the rival regiments were not allowed to approach the town at the same time. So that public cloud passed over, to the enormous relief of everyone, especially of Panda the King. As to the private cloud whereof this history tells, it was otherwise.

As the tribes came up to the Great Place they were reviewed and sent away, since it was impossible to feed so vast a multitude as would have collected had they all remained. Thus the Amasomi, a small people who were amongst the first to arrive, soon left. Only, for some reason which I never quite understood, Masapo, Mameena and a few of Masapo's children and headmen were detained there; though perhaps, if she had chosen, Mameena could have given an explanation.

Well, things began to happen. Sundry personages were taken ill, and some of them died suddenly; and soon it was noted that all these people either lived near to where Masapo's family was lodged or had at some time or other been on bad terms with him. Thus Saduko himself was taken ill, or said he was; at any rate, he vanished from public gaze for three days, and reappeared looking very sorry for himself, though I could not observe that he had lost strength or weight. These catastrophes I pass over, however, in order to come to the greatest of them, which is one of the turning points of this chronicle.

After recovering from his alleged sickness Saduko gave a kind of thanksgiving feast, at which several oxen were killed. I was present at this feast, or rather at the last part of it, for I only put in what may be called a complimentary appearance, having no taste for such native gorgings. As it drew near its close Saduko sent for Nandie, who at first refused to come as there were no women present—I think because he wished to show his friends that he had a princess of the royal blood for his wife, who had borne him a son that one day would be great in the land. For Saduko, as I have said, had become a *self-eater*, and this day his pride was inflamed by the adulation of the company and by the beer that he had drunk.

At length Nandie did come, carrying her babe, from which she never would be parted. In her dignified, ladylike fashion (although it seems an odd term to apply to a savage, I know none that describes her better) she greeted first me and then sundry of the other guests, saying a few words to each of them. At length she came opposite to Masapo, who had dined not wisely but too well, and to him, out of her natural courtesy, spoke rather longer than to the others, inquiring after his wife, Mameena, and others. At the moment it occurred to me that she did this in order to assure him that she bore no malice because of the accident of a while before, and was a party to her husband's reconciliation with him.

Masapo, in a hazy way, tried to reciprocate these kind intentions. Rising to his feet, his fat, coarse body swaying to and fro because of the beer that he had drunk, he expressed satisfaction at the feast that had been prepared in her house. Then, his eyes falling on the child, he began to declaim about its size and beauty, until he was stopped by the murmured protests of others, since among natives it is held to be not fortunate to praise a young child. Indeed, the person who does so is apt to be called an *umtakati*, or bewitcher, who will bring evil upon its head, a word that I heard murmured by several near to me. Not satisfied with this serious breach of etiquette, the intoxicated Masapo snatched the infant from its mother's arms under pretext of looking for the hurt that had been caused to its brow when it fell to the ground at my camp, and finding none, proceeded to kiss it with his thick lips.

Nandie dragged it from him, saying: "Would you bring death upon my son, O Chief of the Amasomi?"

Then, turning, she walked away from the feasters, upon whom there fell a certain hush.

Fearing lest something unpleasant should ensue, for I saw Saduko biting his lips with rage not unmixed with fear, and remembering Masapo's reputation as a wizard, I took advantage of this pause to bid a general good night to the company and retire to my camp.

What happened immediately after I left I do not know, but just before dawn on the following morning I was awakened from sleep in my wagon by my servant Scowl, who said that a messenger had come from the huts of Saduko, begging that I would proceed there at once and bring the white man's medicines, as his child was very ill. Of course I got up and went, taking with me some *ipecacuanha* and a few other remedies that I thought might be suitable for infantile ailments.

Outside the huts, which I reached just as the sun began to rise, I was met by Saduko himself, who was coming to seek me, as I saw at once, in a state of terrible grief.

"What is the matter?" I asked.

"O Macumazana," he answered, "that dog Masapo has bewitched my boy, and unless you can save him he dies."

"Nonsense," I said, "why do you utter wind? If the babe is sick, it is from some natural cause."

"Wait till you see it," he replied.

Well, I went into the big hut, and there found Nandie and some other women, also a native doctor or two. Nandie was seated on the floor looking like a stone image of grief, for she made no sound, only pointed with her finger to the infant that lay upon a mat in front of her.

A single glance showed me that it was dying of some disease of which I had no knowledge, for its dusky little body was covered with red blotches and its tiny face twisted all awry. I told the women to heat water, thinking that possibly this might be a case of convulsions, which a hot bath would mitigate; but before it was ready the poor babe uttered a thin wail and died.

Then, when she saw that her child was gone, Nandie spoke for the first time.

"The wizard has done his work well," she said, and flung herself face downwards on the floor of the hut.

As I did not know what to answer, I went out, followed by Saduko.

"What has killed my son, Macumazahn?" he asked in a hollow voice, the tears running down his handsome face, for he had loved his firstborn.

"I cannot tell," I replied; "but had he been older I should have thought he had eaten something poisonous, which seems impossible."

"Yes, Macumazahn, and the poison that he has eaten came from the breath of a wizard whom you may chance to have seen kiss him last night. Well, his life shall be avenged."

"Saduko," I exclaimed, "do not be unjust. There are many sicknesses that may have killed your son of which I have no knowledge, who am not a trained doctor."

"I will not be unjust, Macumazahn. The babe has died by witchcraft, like others in this town of late, but the evil-doer may not be he whom I suspect. That is for the smellers-out to decide," and without more words he turned and left me.

Next day Masapo was put upon his trial before a Court of Councillors, over which the King himself presided, a very unusual thing for him to do, and one which showed the great interest he took in the case.

At this court I was summoned to give evidence, and, of course, confined myself to answering such questions as were put to me. Practically these were but two. What had passed at my wagons when Masapo had knocked over Nandie and her child, and Saduko had struck him, and what had I seen at Saduko's feast when Masapo had kissed the infant? I told them in as few words as I could, and after some slight cross-examination by Masapo, made with a view to prove that the upsetting of Nandie was an accident and that he was drunk at Saduko's feast, to both of which suggestions I assented, I rose to go. Panda, however, stopped me and bade me describe the aspect of the child when I was called in to give it medicine.

I did so as accurately as possible, and could see that my account made a deep impression on the mind of the court. Then Panda asked me if I had ever seen any similar case, to which I was obliged to reply: "No, I have not."

After this the Councillors consulted privately, and when we were called back the King gave his judgment, which was very brief. It was evident, he said, that there had been events which might have caused enmity to arise in the mind of Masapo against Saduko, by whom Masapo had been struck with a stick. Therefore, although a reconciliation had taken place, there seemed to be a possible motive for revenge. But if Masapo killed the child, there was no evidence to show how he had done so. Moreover, that infant, his own grandson, had not died of any known disease. He had, however, died of a similar disease to that which had carried off certain others with whom Masapo had been mixed up, whereas more, including Saduko himself, had been sick and recovered, all of which seemed to make a strong case against Masapo.

Still, he and his Councillors wished not to condemn without full proof. That being so, they had determined to call in the services of some great witch-doctor, one who lived at a distance and knew nothing of the circumstances. Who that doctor should be was not yet settled. When it was and he had arrived, the case would be re-opened, and meanwhile Masapo would be kept a close prisoner. Finally, he prayed that the white man, Macumazahn, would remain at his town until the matter was settled.

So Masapo was led off, looking very dejected, and, having saluted the King, we all went away.

I should add that, except for the remission of the case to the court of the witch-doctor, which, of course, was an instance of pure *Kafir* superstition, this judgment of the King's seemed to me well reasoned and just, very different indeed from what would have been given by Dingaan or Chaka, who were wont, on less evidence, to make a clean sweep not only of the accused, but of all his family and dependents.

About eight days later, during which time I had heard nothing of the matter and seen no one connected with it, for the whole thing seemed to have become *Zila*—that is, not to be talked about—I received a summons to attend the *smelling-out*, and went, wondering what witch-doctor had been chosen for that bloody and barbarous ceremony. Indeed, I had not far to go, since the place selected for the occasion was outside the fence of the town of Nodwengu, on that great open stretch of ground which lay at the mouth of the valley where I was camped. Here, as I approached, I saw a vast multitude of people crowded together, fifty deep or more, round a little oval space not much larger than the pit of a theatre. On the inmost edge of this ring were seated many notable people, male and female, and as I was conducted to the side of it which was nearest to the gate of the town, I observed among them Saduko, Masapo, Mameena and others, and mixed up with them a number of soldiers, who were evidently on duty.

Scarcely had I seated myself on a camp-stool, carried by my servant Scowl, when through the gate of the *kraal* issued Panda and certain of his Council, whose appearance the multitude greeted with the royal salute of *Bayete*, that came from them in a deep and simultaneous roar of sound. When its echoes died away, in the midst of a deep silence Panda spoke, saying:

"Bring forth the *Nyanga* (doctor). Let the *umhlahlo* (that is, the witch-trial) begin!"

There was a long pause, and then in the open gateway appeared a solitary figure that at first sight seemed to be scarcely human, the figure of a dwarf with a gigantic head, from which hung long, white hair, plaited into locks. It was Zikali, no other!

Quite unattended, and naked save for his *moocha*, for he had on him none of the ordinary paraphernalia of the witch-doctor, he waddled forward with a curious toad-like gait till he had passed through the Councillors and stood in the open space of the ring. Halting there, he looked about him slowly with his deep-set eyes, turning as he looked, till at length his glance fell upon the King.

"What would you have of me, Son of Senzangakona?" he asked. "Many years have passed since last we met. Why do you drag me from my hut, I who have visited the *kraal* of the King of the Zulus but twice since the Black One (Chaka) sat upon the throne—once when the Boers were killed by him who went before you, and once when I was brought forth to see all who were left of my race, shoots of the royal Dwandwe stock, slain before my eyes. Do you bear me hither that I may follow them into the darkness, O Child of Senzangakona? If so I am ready; only then I have words to say that it may not please you to hear."

His deep, rumbling voice echoed into silence, while the great audience waited for the King's answer. I could see that they were all afraid of this man, yes, even Panda was afraid, for he shifted uneasily upon his stool. At length he spoke, saying:

"Not so, O Zikali. Who would wish to do hurt to the wisest and most ancient man in all the land, to him who touches the far past with one hand and the present with the other, to him who was old before our grandfathers began to be? Nay, you are safe, you on whom not even the 'Black One' dared to lay a finger, although you were his enemy and he hated you. As for the reason why you have been brought here, tell it to us, O Zikali. Who are we that we should instruct you in the ways of wisdom?"

When the dwarf heard this he broke into one of his great laughs.

"So at last the House of Senzangakona acknowledges that I have wisdom. Then before all is done they will think me wise indeed."

He laughed again in his ill-omened fashion and went on hurriedly, as though he feared that he should be called upon to explain his words:

"Where is the fee? Where is the fee? Is the King so poor that he expects an old Dwandwe doctor to divine for nothing, just as though he were working for a private friend?"

Panda made a motion with his hand, and ten fine heifers were driven into the circle from some place where they had been kept in waiting.

"Sorry beasts!" said Zikali contemptuously, "compared to those we used to breed before the time of Senzangakona"—a remark which caused a loud *"Wow!"* of astonishment to be uttered by the multitude that heard it. "Still, such as they are, let them be taken to my *kraal*, with a bull, for I have none."

The cattle were driven away, and the ancient dwarf squatted himself down and stared at the ground, looking like a great black toad. For a long while—quite ten minutes, I should think—he stared thus, till I, for one, watching him intently, began to feel as though I were mesmerised.

At length he looked up, tossing back his grey locks, and said:

"I see many things in the dust. Oh, yes, it is alive, it is alive, and tells me many things. Show that you are alive, O Dust. Look!"

As he spoke, throwing his hands upwards, there arose at his very feet one of those tiny and incomprehensible whirlwinds with which all who know South Africa will be familiar. It drove the dust together; it lifted it in a tall, spiral column that rose and rose to a height of fifty feet or more. Then it died away as suddenly as it had come, so that the dust fell down again over Zikali, over the King, and over three of his sons who sat behind him. Those three sons, I remember, were named Tshonkweni, Dabulesinye, and Mantantashiya. As it chanced, by a strange coincidence all of these were killed at the great battle of the Tugela of which I have to tell.

Now again an exclamation of fear and wonder rose from the audience, who set down this lifting of the dust at Zikali's very feet not to natural causes, but to the power of his magic. Moreover, those on whom it had fallen, including the King, rose hurriedly and shook and brushed it from their persons with a zeal that was not, I think, inspired by a mere desire for cleanliness. But Zikali only laughed again in his terrible fashion and let it lie on his fresh-oiled body, which it turned to the dull, dead hue of a grey adder.

He rose and, stepping here and there, examined the new-fallen dust. Then he put his hand into a pouch he wore and produced from it a dried human finger, whereof the nail was so pink that I think it must have been coloured—a sight at which the circle shuddered.

"Be clever," he said, "O Finger of her I loved best; be clever and write in the dust as yonder Macumazana can write, and as some of the Dwandwe used to write before we became slaves and bowed ourselves down before the Great Heavens." (By this he meant the Zulus, whose name means the Heavens.) "Be clever, dear Finger which caressed me once, me, the *Thing-that-should-not-have-been-born*, as more will think before I die, and write those matters that it pleases the House of Senzangakona to know this day."

Then he bent down, and with the dead finger at three separate spots made certain markings in the fallen dust, which to me seemed to consist of circles and dots; and a strange and horrid sight it was to see him do it.

"I thank you, dear Finger. Now sleep, sleep, your work is done," and slowly he wrapped the relic up in some soft material and restored it to his pouch.

Then he studied the first of the markings and asked: "What am I here for? What am I here for? Does he who sits upon the Throne desire to know how long he has to reign?"

Now, those of the inner circle of the spectators, who at these smellings-out act as a kind of chorus, looked at the King, and, seeing that he shook his head vigorously, stretched out their right hands, holding the thumb downwards, and said simultaneously in a cold, low voice:

"Izwa!" (That is, "We hear you.")

Zikali stamped upon this set of markings.

"It is well," he said. "He who sits upon the Throne does not desire to know how long he has to reign, and therefore the dust has forgotten and shows it not to me."

Then he walked to the next markings and studied them.

"Does the Child of Senzangakona desire to know which of his sons shall live and which shall die; aye, and which of them shall sleep in his hut when he is gone?"

Now a great roar of *"Izwa!"* accompanied by the clapping of hands, rose from all the outer multitude who heard, for there was no information that the Zulu people desired so earnestly as this at the time of which I write.

But again Panda, who, I saw, was thoroughly alarmed at the turn things were taking, shook his head vigorously, whereon the obedient chorus negatived the question in the same fashion as before.

Zikali stamped upon the second set of markings, saying:

"The people desire to know, but the Great Ones are afraid to learn, and therefore the dust has forgotten who in the days to come shall sleep in the hut of the King and who shall sleep in the bellies of the jackals and the crops of the vultures after they have 'gone beyond' by the bridge of spears."

Now, at this awful speech (which, both because of all that it implied of bloodshed and civil war and of the wild, wailing voice in which it was spoken, that seemed quite different from Zikali's, caused everyone who heard it, including myself, I am afraid, to gasp and shiver) the King sprang from his stool as though to put a stop to such doctoring. Then, after his fashion, he changed his mind and sat down again. But Zikali, taking no heed, went to the third set of marks and studied them.

"It would seem," he said, "that I am awakened from sleep in my Black House yonder to tell of a very little matter, that might well have been dealt with by any common *Nyanga* born but yesterday. Well, I have taken my fee, and I will earn it, although I thought that I was brought here to speak of great matters, such as the death of princes and the fortunes of peoples. Is it desired that my Spirit should speak of wizardries in this town of Nodwengu?"

"Izwa!" said the chorus in a loud voice.

Zikali nodded his great head and seemed to talk with the dust, waiting now and again for an answer.

"Good," he said; "they are many, and the dust has told them all to me. Oh, they are very many"—and he glared around him—"so many that if I spoke them all the hyenas of the hills would be full to-night—"

Here the audience began to show signs of great apprehension.

"But," looking down at the dust and turning his head sideways, "what do you say, what do you say? Speak more plainly, Little Voices, for you know I grow deaf. Oh! now I understand. The matter is even smaller than I thought. Just of one wizard—"

"Izwa!" (loudly).

"—just of a few deaths and some sicknesses."

"Izwa!"

"Just of one death, one principal death."

"Izwa!" (very loudly).

"Ah! So we have it—one death. Now, was it a man?"

"Izwa!" (very coldly).

"A woman?"

"Izwa!" (still more coldly).

"Then a child? It must be a child, unless indeed it is the death of a spirit. But what do you people know of spirits? A child! A child! Ah! you hear me—a child. A male child, I think. Do you not say so, O Dust?"

"Izwa!" (emphatically).

"A common child? A bastard? The son of nobody?"

"Izwa!" (very low).

"A well-born child? One who would have been great? O Dust, I hear, I hear; a royal child, a child in whom ran the blood of the Father of the Zulus, he who was my friend? The blood of Senzangakona, the blood of the 'Black One,' the blood of Panda."

He stopped, while both from the chorus and from the thousands of the circle gathered around went up one roar of *"Izwa!"* emphasised by a mighty movement of outstretched arms and down-pointing thumbs.

Then silence, during which Zikali stamped upon all the remaining markings, saying:

"I thank you, O Dust, though I am sorry to have troubled you for so small a matter. So, so," he went on presently, "a royal boy-child is dead, and you think by witchcraft. Let us find out if he died by witchcraft or as others die, by command of the Heavens that need them. What! Here is one mark which I have left. Look! It grows red, it is full of spots! The child died with a twisted face."

"Izwa! Izwa! Izwa!" (*crescendo*).

"This death was not natural. Now, was it witchcraft or was it poison? Both, I think, both. And whose was the child? Not that of a son of the King, I think. Oh, yes, you hear me, People, you hear me; but be silent; I do not need your help. No, not of a son; of a daughter, then." He turned and, looked about him till his eye fell upon a group of women, amongst whom sat Nandie, dressed like a common person. "Of a daughter, a daughter—" He walked to the group of women. "Why, none of these are royal; they are the children of low people. And yet—and yet I seem to smell the blood of Senzangakona."

He sniffed at the air as a dog does, and as he sniffed drew ever nearer to Nandie, till at last he laughed and pointed to her.

"*Your* child, Princess, whose name I do not know. Your firstborn child, whom you loved more than your own heart."

She rose.

"Yes, yes, *Nyanga*," she cried. "I am the Princess Nandie, and he was my child, whom I loved more than my own heart."

"Haha!" said Zikali. "Dust, you did not lie to me. My Spirit, you did not lie to me. But now, tell me, Dust—and tell me, my Spirit—who killed this child?"

He began to waddle round the circle, an extraordinary sight, covered as he was with grey grime, varied with streaks of black skin where the perspiration had washed the dust away.

Presently he came opposite to me, and, to my dismay, paused, sniffing at me as he had at Nandie.

"Ah! ah! O Macumazana," he said, "you have something to do with this matter," a saying at which all that audience pricked their ears.

Then I rose up in wrath and fear, knowing my position to be one of some danger.

"Wizard, or smeller-out of wizards, whichever you name yourself," I called in a loud voice, "if you mean that *I* killed Nandie's child, you lie!"

"No, no, Macumazahn," he answered, "but you tried to save it, and therefore you had something to do with the matter, had you not? Moreover, I think that you, who are wise like me, know who did kill it. Won't you tell me, Macumazahn? No? Then I must find out for myself. Be at peace. Does not all the land know that your hands are white as your heart?"

Then, to my great relief, he passed on, amidst a murmur of approbation, for, as I have said, the Zulus liked me. Round and round he wandered, to my surprise passing both Mameena and Masapo without taking any particular note of them, although he scanned them both, and I thought that I saw a swift glance of recognition pass between him and Mameena. It was curious to watch his progress, for as he went those in front of him swayed in their terror like corn before a puff of wind, and when he had passed they straightened themselves as the corn does when the wind has gone by.

At length he had finished his journey and returned to his starting-point, to all appearance completely puzzled.

"You keep so many wizards at your *kraal*, King," he said, addressing Panda, "that it is hard to say which of them wrought this deed. It would have been easier to tell you of greater matters. Yet I have taken your fee, and I must earn it—I must earn it. Dust, you are dumb. Now, my *Idhlozi*, my Spirit, do you speak?" and, holding his head sideways, he turned his left ear up towards the sky, then said presently, in a curious, matter-of-fact voice:

"Ah! I thank you, Spirit. Well, King, your grandchild was killed by the House of Masapo, your enemy, chief of the Amasomi."

Now a roar of approbation went up from the audience, among whom Masapo's guilt was a foregone conclusion.

When this had died down Panda spoke, saying:

"The House of Masapo is a large house; I believe that he has several wives and many children. It is not enough to smell out the House, since I am not as those who went before me were, nor will I slay the innocent with the guilty. Tell us, O Opener-of-Roads, who among the House of Masapo has wrought this deed?"

"That's just the question," grumbled Zikali in a deep voice. "All that I know is that it was done by poisoning, and I smell the poison. It is here."

Then he walked to where Mameena sat and cried out:

"Seize that woman and search her hair."

Executioners who were in waiting sprang forward, but Mameena waved them away.

"Friends," she said, with a little laugh, "there is no need to touch me," and, rising, she stepped forward to the centre of the ring. Here, with a few swift motions of her hands, she flung off first the cloak she wore, then the *moocha* about her middle, and lastly the fillet that bound her long hair, and stood before that audience in all her naked beauty—a wondrous and a lovely sight.

"Now," she said, "let women come and search me and my garments, and see if there is any poison hid there."

Two old crones stepped forward—though I do not know who sent them—and carried out a very thorough examination, finally reporting that they had found nothing. Thereon Mameena, with a shrug of her shoulders, resumed such clothes as she wore, and returned to her place.

Zikali appeared to grow angry. He stamped upon the ground with his big feet; he shook his braided grey locks and cried out:

"Is my wisdom to be defeated in such a little matter? One of you tie a bandage over my eyes."

Now a man—it was Maputa, the messenger—came out and did so, and I noted that he tied it well and tight. Zikali whirled round upon his heels, first one way and then another, and, crying aloud: "Guide me, my Spirit!" marched forward in a zigzag fashion, as a blindfolded man does, with his arms stretched out in front of him. First he went to the right, then to the left, and then straight forward, till at length, to my astonishment, he came exactly opposite the spot where Masapo sat and, stretching out his great, groping hands, seized the *kaross* with which he was covered and, with a jerk, tore it from him.

"Search this!" he cried, throwing it on the ground, and a woman searched.

Presently she uttered an exclamation, and from among the fur of one of the tails of the *kaross* produced a tiny bag that appeared to be made out of the bladder of a fish. This she handed to Zikali, whose eyes had now been unbandaged.

He looked at it, then gave it to Maputa, saying:

"There is the poison—there is the poison, but who gave it I do not say. I am weary. Let me go."

Then, none hindering him, he walked away through the gate of the *kraal*.

Soldiers seized upon Masapo, while the multitude roared: "Kill the wizard!"

Masapo sprang up, and, running to where the King sat, flung himself upon his knees, protesting his innocence and praying for mercy. I also, who had doubts as to all this business, ventured to rise and speak.

"O King," I said, "as one who has known this man in the past, I plead with you. How that powder came into his *kaross* I know not, but perchance it is not poison, only harmless dust."

"Yes, it is but wood dust which I use for the cleaning of my nails," cried Masapo, for he was so terrified I think he knew not what he said.

"So you own to knowledge of the medicine?" exclaimed Panda. "Therefore none hid it in your *kaross* through malice."

Masapo began to explain, but what he said was lost in a mighty roar of "Kill the wizard!"

Panda held up his hand and there was silence.

"Bring milk in a dish," commanded the King, and it, was brought, and, at a further word from him, dusted with the powder.

"Now, O Macumazana," said Panda to me, "if you still think that yonder man is innocent, will you drink this milk?"

"I do not like milk, O King," I answered, shaking my head, whereon all who heard me laughed.

"Will Mameena, his wife, drink it, then?" asked Panda.

She also shook her head, saying:

"O King, I drink no milk that is mixed with dust."

Just then a lean, white dog, one of those homeless, mangy beasts that stray about *kraals* and live upon carrion, wandered into the ring. Panda made a sign, and a servant, going to where the poor beast stood staring about it hungrily, set down the wooden dish of milk in front of it. Instantly the dog lapped it up, for it was starving, and as it finished the last drop the man slipped a leathern thong about its neck and held it fast.

Now all eyes were fixed upon the dog, mine among them. Presently the beast uttered a long and melancholy howl which thrilled me through, for I knew it to be Masapo's death warrant, then began to scratch the ground and foam at the mouth. Guessing what would follow, I rose, bowed to the King, and walked away to my camp, which, it will be remembered, was set up in a little kloof commanding this place, at a distance only of a few hundred yards. So intent was all the multitude upon watching the dog that I doubt whether anyone saw me go. As for that poor beast, Scowl, who stayed behind, told me that it did not die for about ten minutes, since before its end a red rash appeared upon it similar to that which I had seen upon Saduko's child, and it was seized with convulsions.

Well, I reached my tent unmolested, and, having lit my pipe, engaged myself in making business entries in my note-book, in order to divert my mind as much as I could, when suddenly I heard a most devilish clamour. Looking up, I saw Masapo running towards me with a speed that I should have thought impossible in so fat a man, while after him raced the fierce-faced executioners, and behind came the mob.

"Kill the evil-doer!" they shouted.

Masapo reached me. He flung himself on his knees before me, gasping:

"Save me, Macumazahn! I am innocent. Mameena, the witch! Mameena—"

He got no farther, for the slayers had leapt on him like hounds upon a buck and dragged him from me.

Then I turned and covered up my eyes.

Next morning I left Nodwengu without saying good-bye to anyone, for what had happened there made me desire a change. My servant, Scowl, and one of my hunters remained, however, to collect some cattle that were still due to me.

A month or more later, when they joined me in Natal, bringing the cattle, they told me that Mameena, the widow of Masapo, had entered the house of Saduko as his second wife. In answer to a question which I put to them, they added that it was said that the Princess Nandie did not approve of this choice of Saduko, which she thought would not be fortunate for him or bring him happiness. As her husband seemed to be much enamoured of Mameena, however, she had waived her objections, and when Panda asked if she gave her consent had told him that, although she would prefer that Saduko should choose some other woman who had not been mixed up with the wizard who killed her child, she was prepared to take Mameena as her sister, and would know how to keep her in her place.

Chapter 11

The Sin of Umbelazi

About eighteen months had gone by, and once again, in the autumn of the year 1856, I found myself at old Umbezi's *kraal*, where there seemed to be an extraordinary market for any kind of gas-pipe that could be called a gun. Well, as a trader who could not afford to neglect profitable markets, which are hard things to find, there I was.

Now, in eighteen months many things become a little obscured in one's memory, especially if they have to do with savages, in whom, after all, one takes only a philosophical and a business interest. Therefore I may perhaps be excused if I had more or less forgotten a good many of the details of what I may call the Mameena affair. These, however, came back to me very vividly when the first person that I met—at some distance from the *kraal*, where I suppose she had been taking a country walk—was the beautiful Mameena herself. There she was, looking quite unchanged and as lovely as ever, sitting under the shade of a wild fig-tree and fanning herself with a handful of its leaves.

Of course I jumped off my wagon-box and greeted her.

"*Siyakubona* (that is, good morrow), Macumazahn," she said. "My heart is glad to see you."

"*Siyakubona*, Mameena," I answered, leaving out all reference to *my* heart. Then I added, looking at her: "Is it true that you have a new husband?"

"Yes, Macumazahn, an old lover of mine has become a new husband. You know whom I mean—Saduko. After the death of that evildoer, Masapo, he grew very urgent, and the King, also the *Inkosazana* Nandie, pressed it on me, and so I yielded. Also, to be honest, Saduko was a good match, or seemed to be so."

By now we were walking side by side, for the train of wagons had gone ahead to the old outspan. So I stopped and looked her in the face.

"'Seemed to be,'" I repeated. "What do you mean by 'seemed to be'? Are you not happy this time?"

"Not altogether, Macumazahn," she answered, with a shrug of her shoulders. "Saduko is very fond of me—fonder than I like indeed, since it causes him to neglect Nandie, who, by the way, has another son, and, although she says little, that makes Nandie cross. In short," she added, with a burst of truth, "I am the plaything, Nandie is the great lady, and that place suits me ill."

"If you love Saduko, you should not mind, Mameena."

"Love," she said bitterly. *"Piff!* What is love? But I have asked you that question once before."

"Why are you here, Mameena?" I inquired, leaving it unanswered.

"Because Saduko is here, and, of course, Nandie, for she never leaves him, and he will not leave me; because the Prince Umbelazi is coming; because there are plots afoot and the great war draws near—that war in which so many must die."

"Between Cetewayo and Umbelazi, Mameena?"

"Aye, between Cetewayo and Umbelazi. Why do you suppose those wagons of yours are loaded with guns for which so many cattle must be paid? Not to shoot game with, I think. Well, this little *kraal* of my father's is just now the headquarters of the Umbelazi faction, the Isigqosa, as the princedom of Gikazi is that of Cetewayo. My poor father!" she added, with her characteristic shrug, "he thinks himself very great to-day, as he did after he had shot the elephant—before I nursed you, Macumazahn—but often I wonder what will be the end of it—for him and for all of us, Macumazahn, including yourself."

"I!" I answered. "What have I to do with your Zulu quarrels?"

"That you will know when you have done with them, Macumazahn. But here is the *kraal*, and before we enter it I wish to thank you for trying to protect that unlucky husband of mine, Masapo."

"I only did so, Mameena, because I thought him innocent."

"I know, Macumazahn; and so did I, although, as I always told you, I hated him, the man with whom my father forced me to marry. But I am afraid, from what I have learned since, that he was not altogether innocent. You see, Saduko had struck him, which he could not forget. Also, he was jealous of Saduko, who had been my suitor, and wished to injure him. But what I do not understand," she added, with a burst of confidence, "is why he did not kill Saduko instead of his child."

"Well, Mameena, you may remember it was said he tried to do so."

"Yes, Macumazahn; I had forgotten that. I suppose that he did try, and failed. Oh, now I see things with both eyes. Look, yonder is my father. I will go away. But come and talk to me sometimes, Macumazahn, for otherwise Nandie will be careful that I should hear nothing—I who am the plaything, the beautiful woman of the House, who must sit and smile, but must not think."

So she departed, and I went on to meet old Umbezi, who came gambolling towards me like an obese goat, reflecting that, whatever might be the truth or otherwise of her story, her advancement in the world did not seem to have brought Mameena greater happiness and contentment.

Umbezi, who greeted me warmly, was in high spirits and full of importance. He informed me that the marriage of Mameena to Saduko, after the death of the wizard, her husband, whose tribe and cattle had been given to Saduko in compensation for the loss of his son, was a most fortunate thing for him.

I asked why.

"Because as Saduko grows great so I, his father-in-law, grow great with him, Macumazahn, especially as he has been liberal to me in the matter of cattle, passing on to me a share of the herds of Masapo, so that I, who have been poor so long, am getting rich at last. Moreover, my *kraal* is to be honoured with a visit from Umbelazi and some of his brothers to-morrow, and Saduko has promised to lift me up high when the Prince is declared heir to the throne."

"Which prince?" I asked.

"Umbelazi, Macumazahn. Who else? Umbelazi, who without doubt will conquer Cetewayo."

"Why without doubt, Umbezi? Cetewayo has a great following, and if *he* should conquer I think that you will only be lifted up in the crops of the vultures."

At this rough suggestion Umbezi's fat face fell.

"O Macumazana," he said, "if I thought that, I would go over to Cetewayo, although Saduko is my son-in-law. But it is not possible, since the King loves Umbelazi's mother most of all his wives, and, as I chance to know, has sworn to her that he favours Umbelazi's cause, since he is the dearest to him of all his sons, and will do everything that he can to help him, even to the sending of his own regiment to his assistance, if there should be need. Also, it is said that Zikali, Opener-of-Roads, who has all wisdom, has prophesied that Umbelazi will win more than he ever hoped for."

"The King!" I said, "a straw blown hither and thither between two great winds, waiting to be wafted to rest by that which is strongest! The prophecy of Zikali! It seems to me that it can be read two ways, if, indeed, he ever made one. Well, Umbezi, I hope that you are right, for, although it is no affair of mine, who am but a white trader in your country, I like Umbelazi better than Cetewayo, and think that he has a kinder heart. Also, as you have chosen his side, I advise you to stick to it, since traitors to a cause seldom come to any good, whether it wins or loses. And now, will you take count of the guns and powder which I have brought with me?"

Ah! better would it have been for Umbezi if he had listened to my advice and remained faithful to the leader he had chosen, for then, even if he had lost his life, at least he would have kept his good name. But of him presently, as they say in pedigrees.

Next day I went to pay my respects to Nandie, whom I found engaged in nursing her new baby and as quiet and stately in her demeanour as ever. Still, I think that she was very glad to see me, because I had tried to save the life of her first child, whom she could not forget, if for no other reason. Whilst I was talking to her of that sad matter, also of the political state of the country, as to which I think she wished to say something to me, Mameena entered the hut, without waiting to be asked, and sat down, whereon Nandie became suddenly silent.

This, however, did not trouble Mameena, who talked away about anything and everything, completely ignoring the head-wife. For a while Nandie bore it with patience, but at length she took advantage of a pause in the conversation to say in her firm, low voice:

"This is my hut, daughter of Umbezi, a thing which you remember well enough when it is a question whether Saduko, our husband, shall visit you or me. Can you not remember it now when I would speak with the white chief, Watcher-by-Night, who has been so good as to take the trouble to come to see me?"

On hearing these words Mameena leapt up in a rage, and I must say I never saw her look more lovely.

"You insult me, daughter of Panda, as you always try to do, because you are jealous of me."

"Your pardon, sister," replied Nandie. "Why should I, who am Saduko's *Inkosikazi*, and, as you say, daughter of Panda, the King, be jealous of the widow of the wizard, Masapo, and the daughter of the headman, Umbezi, whom it has pleased our husband to take into his house to be the companion of his leisure?"

"Why? Because you know that Saduko loves my little finger more than he does your whole body, although you are of the King's blood and have borne him brats," she answered, looking at the infant with no kindly eye.

"It may be so, daughter of Umbezi, for men have their fancies, and without doubt you are fair. Yet I would ask you one thing—if Saduko loves you so much, how comes it he trusts you so little that you must learn any matter of weight by listening at my door, as I found you doing the other day?"

"Because you teach him not to do so, O Nandie. Because you are ever telling him not to consult with me, since she who has betrayed one husband may betray another. Because you make him believe my place is that of his toy, not that of his companion, and this although I am cleverer than you and all your House tied into one bundle, as you may find out some day."

"Yes," answered Nandie, quite undisturbed, "I do teach him these things, and I am glad that in this matter Saduko has a thinking head and listens to me. Also I agree that it is likely I shall learn many more ill things through and of you one day, daughter of Umbezi. And now, as it is not good that we should wrangle before this white lord, again I say to you that this is my hut, in which I wish to speak alone with my guest."

"I go, I go!" gasped Mameena; "but I tell you that Saduko shall hear of this."

"Certainly he will hear of it, for I shall tell him when he comes to-night."

Another instant and Mameena was gone, having shot out of the hut like a rabbit from its burrow.

"I ask your pardon, Macumazahn, for what has happened," said Nandie, "but it had become necessary that I should teach my sister, Mameena, upon which stool she ought to sit. I do not trust her, Macumazahn. I think that she knows more of the death of my child than she chooses to say, she who wished to be rid of Masapo for a reason you can guess. I think also she will bring shame and trouble upon Saduko, whom she has bewitched with her beauty, as she bewitches all men—perhaps even yourself a little, Macumazahn. And now let us talk of other matters."

To this proposition I agreed cordially, since, to tell the truth, if I could have managed to do so with any decent grace, I should have been out of that hut long before Mameena. So we fell to conversing on the condition of Zululand and the dangers that lay ahead for all who were connected with the royal House—a state of affairs which troubled Nandie much, for she was a clear-headed woman, and one who feared the future.

"Ah! Macumazahn," she said to me as we parted, "I would that I were the wife of some man who did not desire to grow great, and that no royal blood ran in my veins."

On the next day the Prince Umbelazi arrived, and with him Saduko and a few other notable men. They came quite quietly and without any ostensible escort, although Scowl, my servant, told me he heard that the bush at a little distance was swarming with soldiers of the Isigqosa party. If I remember rightly, the excuse for the visit was that Umbezi had some of a certain rare breed of white cattle whereof the prince wished to secure young bulls and heifers to improve his herd.

Once inside the *kraal*, however, Umbelazi, who was a very open-natured man, threw off all pretence, and, after greeting me heartily enough, told me with plainness that he was there because this was a convenient spot on which to arrange the consolidation of his party.

Almost every hour during the next two weeks messengers—many of whom were chiefs disguised—came and went. I should have liked to follow their example—that is, so far as their departure was concerned—for I felt that I was being drawn into a very dangerous vortex. But, as a matter of fact, I could not escape, since I was obliged to wait to receive payment for my stuff, which, as usual, was made in cattle.

Umbelazi talked with me a good deal at that time, impressing upon me how friendly he was towards the English white men of Natal, as distinguished from the Boers, and what good treatment he was prepared to promise to them, should he ever attain to authority in Zululand. It was during one of the earliest of these conversations, which, of course, I saw had an ultimate object, that he met Mameena, I think, for the first time.

We were walking together in a little natural glade of the bush that bordered one side of the *kraal*, when, at the end of it, looking like some wood nymph of classic fable in the light of the setting sun, appeared the lovely Mameena, clothed only in her girdle of fur, her necklace of blue beads and some copper ornaments, and carrying upon her head a gourd.

Umbelazi noted her at once, and, ceasing his political talk, of which he was obviously tired, asked me who that beautiful *intombi* (that is, girl) might be.

"She is not an *intombi*, Prince," I answered. "She is a widow who is again a wife, the second wife of your friend and councillor, Saduko, and the daughter of your host, Umbezi."

"Is it so, Macumazahn? Oh, then I have heard of her, though, as it chances, I have never met her before. No wonder that my sister Nandie is jealous, for she is beautiful indeed."

"Yes," I answered, "she looks pretty against the red sky, does she not?"

By now we were drawing near to Mameena, and I greeted her, asking if she wanted anything.

"Nothing, Macumazahn," she answered in her delicate, modest way, for never did I know anyone who could seem quite so modest as Mameena, and with a swift glance of her shy eyes at the tall and splendid Umbelazi, "nothing. Only," she added, "I was passing with the milk of one of the few cows my father gave me, and saw you, and I thought that perhaps, as the day has been so hot, you might like a drink of it."

Then, lifting the gourd from her head, she held it out to me.

I thanked her, drank some—who could do less?—and returned it to her, whereon she made as though she would hasten to depart.

"May I not drink also, daughter of Umbezi?" asked Umbelazi, who could scarcely take his eyes off her.

"Certainly, sir, if you are a friend of Macumazahn," she replied, handing him the gourd.

"I am that, Lady, and more than that, since I am a friend of your husband, Saduko, also, as you will know when I tell you that my name is Umbelazi."

"I thought it must be so," she replied, "because of your—of your stature. Let the Prince accept the offering of his servant, who one day hopes to be his subject," and, dropping upon her knee, she held out the gourd to him. Over it I saw their eyes meet. He drank, and as he handed back the vessel she said:

"O Prince, may I be granted a word with you? I have that to tell which you would perhaps do well to hear, since news sometimes reaches the ears of humble women that escapes those of the men, our masters."

He bowed his head in assent, whereon, taking a hint which Mameena gave me with her eyes, I muttered something about business and made myself scarce. I may add that Mameena must have had a great deal to tell Umbelazi. Fully an hour and a half had gone by before, by the light of the moon, from a point of vantage on my wagon-box, whence, according to my custom, I was keeping a lookout on things in general, I saw her slip back to the *kraal* silently as a snake, followed at a little distance by the towering form of Umbelazi.

Apparently Mameena continued to be the recipient of information which she found it necessary to communicate in private to the prince. At any rate, on sundry subsequent evenings the dullness of my vigil on the wagon-box was relieved by the sight of her graceful figure gliding home from the kloof that Umbelazi seemed to find a very suitable spot for reflection after sunset. On one of the last of these occasions I remember that Nandie chanced to be with me, having come to my wagon for some medicine for her baby.

"What does it mean, Macumazahn?" she asked, when the pair had gone by, as they thought unobserved, since we were standing where they could not see us.

"I don't know, and I don't want to know," I answered sharply.

"Neither do I, Macumazahn; but without doubt we shall learn in time. If the crocodile is patient and silent the buck always drops into its jaws at last."

On the day after Nandie made this wise remark Saduko started on a mission, as I understood, to win over several doubtful chiefs to the cause of Indhlovu-ene-sihlonti (the elephant-with-the-tuft-of-hair), as the Prince Umbelazi was called among the Zulus, though not to his face. This mission lasted ten days, and before it was concluded an important event happened at Umbezi's *kraal*.

One evening Mameena came to me in a great rage, and said that she could bear her present life no longer. Presuming on her rank and position as head-wife, Nandie treated her like a servant—nay, like a little dog, to be beaten with a stick. She wished that Nandie would die.

"It will be very unlucky for you if she does," I answered, "for then, perhaps, Zikali will be summoned to look into the matter, as he was before."

What was she to do, she went on, ignoring my remark.

"Eat the porridge that you have made in your own pot, or break the pot" (*i.e.* go away), I suggested. "There was no need for you to marry Saduko, any more than there was for you to marry Masapo."

"How can you talk to me like that, Macumazahn," she answered, stamping her foot, "when you know well it is your fault if I married anyone? *Piff!* I hate them all, and, since my father would only beat me if I took my troubles to him, I will run off, and live in the wilderness alone and become a witch-doctoress."

"I am afraid you will find it very dull, Mameena," I began in a bantering tone, for, to tell the truth, I did not think it wise to show her too much sympathy while she was so excited.

Mameena never waited for the end of the sentence, but, sobbing out that I was false and cruel, she turned and departed swiftly. Oh! little did I foresee how and where we should meet again.

Next morning I was awakened shortly after sunrise by Scowl, whom I had sent out with another man the night before to look for a lost ox.

"Well, have you found the ox?" I asked.

"Yes, Baas; but I did not waken you to tell you that. I have a message for you, Baas, from Mameena, wife of Saduko, whom I met about four hours ago upon the plain yonder."

I bade him set it out.

"These were the words of Mameena, Baas: 'Say to Macumazahn, your master, that Indhlovu-ene-sihlonti, taking pity on my wrongs and loving me with his heart, has offered to take me into his House and that I have accepted his offer, since I think it better to become the *Inkosazana* of the Zulus, as I shall one day, than to remain a servant in the house of Nandie. Say to Macumazahn that when Saduko returns he is to tell him that this is all his fault, since if he had kept Nandie in her place I would have died rather than leave him. Let him say to Saduko also that, although from henceforth we can be no more than friends, my heart is still tender towards him, and that by day and by night I will strive to water his greatness, so that it may grow into a tree that shall shade the land. Let Macumazahn bid him not to be angry with me, since what I do I do for his good, as he would have found no happiness while Nandie and I dwelt in one house. Above all, also let him not be angry with the Prince, who loves him more than any man, and does but travel whither the wind that I breathe blows him. Bid Macumazahn think of me kindly, as I shall of him while my eyes are open.'"

I listened to this amazing message in silence, then asked if Mameena was alone.

"No, Baas; Umbelazi and some soldiers were with her, but they did not hear her words, for she stepped aside to speak with me. Then she returned to them, and they walked away swiftly, and were swallowed up in the night."

"Very good, Sikauli," I said. "Make me some coffee, and make it strong."

I dressed and drank several cups of the coffee, all the while "thinking with my head," as the Zulus say. Then I walked up to the *kraal* to see Umbezi, whom I found just coming out of his hut, yawning.

"Why do you look so black upon this beautiful morning, Macumazahn?" asked the genial old scamp. "Have you lost your best cow, or what?"

"No, my friend," I answered; "but you and another have lost your best cow." And word for word I repeated to him Mameena's message. When I had finished really I thought that Umbezi was about to faint.

"Curses be on the head of this Mameena!" he exclaimed. "Surely some evil spirit must have been her father, not I, and well was she called Child of Storm.[1] What shall I do now, Macumazahn? Thanks be to my Spirit," he added, with an air of relief, "she is too far gone for me to try to catch her; also, if I did, Umbelazi and his soldiers would kill me."

"And what will Saduko do if you don't?" I asked.

"Oh, of course he will be angry, for no doubt he is fond of her. But, after all, I am used to that. You remember how he went mad when she married Masapo. At least, he cannot say that I made her run away with Umbelazi. After all, it is a matter which they must settle between them."

"I think it may mean great trouble," I said, "at a time when trouble is not needed."

"Oh, why so, Macumazahn? My daughter did not get on with the Princess Nandie—we could all see that—for they would scarcely speak to each other. And if Saduko is fond of her—well, after all, there are other beautiful women in Zululand. I know one or two of them myself whom I will mention to Saduko—or rather to Nandie. Really, as things were, I am not sure but that he is well rid of her."

"But what do you think of the matter as her father?" I asked, for I wanted to see to what length his accommodating morality would stretch.

"As her father—well, of course, Macumazahn, as her father I am sorry, because it will mean talk, will it not, as the Masapo business did? Still, there is this to be said for Mameena," he added, with a brightening face, "she always runs away up the tree, not down. When she got rid of Masapo—I mean when Masapo was killed for his witchcraft—she married Saduko, who was a bigger man—Saduko, whom she would not marry when Masapo was the bigger man. And now, when she has got rid of Saduko, she enters the hut of Umbelazi, who will one day be King of the Zulus, the biggest man in all the world, which means that she will be the biggest woman, for remember, Macumazahn, she will walk round and round that great Umbelazi till whatever way he looks he will see her and no one else. Oh, she will grow great, and carry up her poor old father in the blanket on her back. Oh, the sun still shines behind the cloud, Macumazahn, so let us make the best of the cloud, since we know that it will break out presently."

---

1. That, if I have not said so already, was the meaning which the Zulus gave to the word "Mameena", although as I know the language I cannot get any such interpretation out of the name, I believe that it was given to her, however, because she was born just before a terrible tempest, when the wind wailing round the hut made a sound like the word "Ma-mee-na".—*A. Q.*

"Yes, Umbezi; but other things besides the sun break out from clouds sometimes—lightning, for instance; lightning which kills."

"You speak ill-omened words, Macumazahn; words that take away my appetite, which is generally excellent at this hour. Well, if Mameena is bad it is not my fault, for I brought her up to be good. After all," he added with an outburst of petulance, "why do you scold me when it is your fault? If you had run away with the girl when you might have done so, there would have been none of this trouble."

"Perhaps not," I answered; "only then I am sure I should have been dead to-day, as I think that all who have to do with her will be ere long. And now, Umbezi, I wish you a good breakfast."

On the following morning, Saduko returned and was told the news by Nandie, whom I had carefully avoided. On this occasion, however, I was forced to be present, as the person to whom the sinful Mameena had sent her farewell message. It was a very painful experience, of which I do not remember all the details. For a while after he learned the truth Saduko sat still as a stone, staring in front of him, with a face that seemed to have become suddenly old. Then he turned upon Umbezi, and in a few terrible words accused him of having arranged the matter in order to advance his own fortunes at the price of his daughter's dishonour. Next, without listening to his ex-father-in-law's voluble explanations, he rose and said that he was going away to kill Umbelazi, the evil-doer who had robbed him of the wife he loved, with the connivance of all three of us, and by a sweep of his hand he indicated Umbezi, the Princess Nandie and myself.

This was more than I could stand, so I, too, rose and asked him what he meant, adding in the irritation of the moment that if I had wished to rob him of his beautiful Mameena, I thought I could have done so long ago—a remark that staggered him a little.

Then Nandie rose also, and spoke in her quiet voice.

"Saduko, my husband," she said, "I, a Princess of the Zulu House, married you who are not of royal blood because I loved you, and although Panda the King and Umbelazi the Prince wished it, for no other reason whatsoever. Well, I have been faithful to you through some trials, even when you set the widow of a wizard—if, indeed, as I have reason to suspect, she was not herself the wizard—before me, and although that wizard had killed our son, lived in her hut rather than in mine. Now this woman of whom you thought so much has deserted you for your friend and my brother, the Prince Umbelazi—Umbelazi who is called the Handsome, and who, if the fortune of war goes with him, as it may or may not, will succeed to Panda, my father. This she has done because she alleges that I, your *Inkosikazi* and the King's daughter, treated her as a servant, which is a lie. I kept her in her place, no more, who, if she could have had her will, would have ousted me from mine, perhaps by death, for the wives of wizards learn their arts. On this pretext she has left you; but that is not her real reason. She has left you because the Prince, my brother, whom she has befooled with her tricks and beauty, as she has befooled others, or tried to"—and she glanced at me—"is a bigger man than you are. You, Saduko, may become great, as my heart prays that you will, but my brother may become a king. She does not love him any more than she loved you, but she does love the place that may be his, and therefore hers—she who would be the first doe of the herd. My husband, I think that you are well rid of Mameena, for I think also that if she had stayed with us there would have been more deaths in our House; perhaps mine, which would not matter, and perhaps yours, which would matter much. All this I say to you, not from jealousy of one who is fairer than I, but because it is the truth. Therefore my counsel to you is to let this business pass over and keep silent. Above all, seek not to avenge yourself upon Umbelazi, since I am sure that he has taken vengeance to dwell with him in his own hut. I have spoken."

That this moderate and reasoned speech of Nandie's produced a great effect upon Saduko I could see, but at the time the only answer he made to it was:

"Let the name of Mameena be spoken no more within hearing of my ears. Mameena is dead."

So her name was heard no more in the Houses of Saduko and of Umbezi, and when it was necessary for any reason to refer to her, she was given a new name, a composite Zulu word, "O-we-Zulu", I think it was, which is "Storm-child" shortly translated, for "Zulu" means a storm as well as the sky.

I do not think that Saduko spoke of her to me again until towards the climax of this history, and certainly I did not mention her to him. But from that day forward I noted that he was a changed man. His pride and open pleasure in his great success, which had caused the Zulus to name him the Self-eater, were no longer marked. He became cold and silent, like a man who is thinking deeply, but who shutters his thoughts lest some should read them through the windows of his eyes. Moreover, he paid a visit to Zikali the Little and Wise, as I found out by accident; but what advice that cunning old dwarf gave to him I did not find out—then.

The only other event which happened in connection with this

elopement was that a message came from Umbelazi to Saduko, brought by one of the princes, a brother of Umbelazi, who was of his party. As I know, for I heard it delivered, it was a very humble message when the relative positions of the two men are considered—that of one who knew that he had done wrong, and, if not repentant, was heartily ashamed of himself.

"Saduko," it said, "I have stolen a cow of yours, and I hope you will forgive me, since that cow did not love the pasture in your *kraal*, but in mine she grows fat and is content. Moreover, in return I will give you many other cows. Everything that I have to give, I will give to you who are my friend and trusted councillor. Send me word, O Saduko, that this wall which I have built between us is broken down, since ere long you and I must stand together in war."

To this message Saduko's answer was:

"O Prince, you are troubled about a very little thing. That cow which you have taken was of no worth to me, for who wishes to keep a beast that is ever tearing and lowing at the gates of the *kraal*, disturbing those who would sleep inside with her noise? Had you asked her of me, I would have given her to you freely. I thank you for your offer, but I need no more cows, especially if, like this one, they have no calves. As for a wall between us, there is none, for how can two men who, if the battle is to be won, must stand shoulder to shoulder, fight if divided by a wall? O Son of the King, I am dreaming by day and night of the battle and the victory, and I have forgotten all about the barren cow that ran away after you, the great bull of the herd. Only do not be surprised if one day you find that this cow has a sharp horn."

Chapter 12

Panda's Prayer

About six weeks later, in the month of November, 1856, I chanced to be at Nodwengu when the quarrel between the princes came to a head. Although none of the regiments was actually allowed to enter the town—that is, as a regiment—the place was full of people, all of them in a state of great excitement, who came in during the daytime and went to sleep in the neighbouring military *kraals* at night. One evening, as some of these soldiers—about a thousand of them, if I remember right—were returning to the Ukubaza *kraal*, a fight occurred between them, which led to the final outbreak.

As it happened, at that time there were two separate regiments stationed at this *kraal*. I think that they were the Imkulutshana and the Hlaba, one of which favoured Cetewayo and the other Umbelazi. As certain companies of each of these regiments marched along together in parallel lines, two of their captains got into dispute on the eternal subject of the succession to the throne. From words they came to blows, and the end of it was that he who favoured Umbelazi killed him who favoured Cetewayo with his *kerry*. Thereon the comrades of the slain man, raising a shout of "Usutu," which became the war-cry of Cetewayo's party, fell upon the others, and a dreadful combat ensued. Fortunately the soldiers were only armed with sticks, or the slaughter would have been very great; but as it was, after an indecisive engagement, about fifty men were killed and many more injured.

Now, with my usual bad luck, I, who had gone out to shoot a few birds for the pot—*pauw*, or bustard, I think they were—was returning across this very plain to my old encampment in the kloof where Masapo had been executed, and so ran into the fight just as it was beginning. I saw the captain killed and the subsequent engagement. Indeed, as it happened, I did more. Not knowing where to go or what to do, for I was quite alone, I pulled up my horse behind a tree and waited till I could escape the horrors about me; for I can assure anyone who may ever read these words that it is a very horrible sight to see a thousand men engaged in fierce and deadly combat. In truth, the fact that they had no spears, and could only batter each other to death with their heavy *kerries*, made it worse, since the duels were more desperate and prolonged.

Everywhere men were rolling on the ground, hitting at each other's heads, until at last some blow went home and one of them threw out his arms and lay still, either dead or senseless. Well, there I sat watching all this shocking business from the saddle of my trained shooting pony, which stood like a stone, till presently I became aware of two great fellows rushing at me with their eyes starting out of their heads and shouting as they came:

"Kill Umbelazi's white man! Kill! Kill!"

Then, seeing that the matter was urgent and that it was a question of my life or theirs, I came into action.

In my hand I held a double-barrelled shotgun loaded with what we used to call *loopers*, or B. B. shot, of which but a few went to each charge, for I had hoped to meet with a small buck on my way to camp. So, as these soldiers came, I lifted the gun and fired, the right barrel at one of them and the left barrel at the other, aiming in each case at the centre of the small dancing shields, which from force of habit they held stretched out to protect their throats and breasts. At that distance, of course, the *loopers* sank through the soft hide of the shields and deep into the bodies of those who carried them, so that both of them dropped dead, the left-hand man being so close that he fell against my pony, his uplifted *kerry* striking me upon the thigh and bruising me.

When I saw what I had done, and that my danger was over for the moment, without waiting to reload I dug the spurs into my horse's sides and galloped off to Nodwengu, passing between the groups of struggling men. On arriving unharmed at the town, I went instantly to the royal huts and demanded to see the King, who sent word that I was to be admitted. On coming before him I told him exactly what had happened—that I had killed two of Cetewayo's men in order to save my own life, and on that account submitted myself to his justice.

"O Macumazana," said Panda in great distress, "I know well that you are not to blame, and already I have sent out a regiment to stop this fighting, with command that those who caused it should be brought before me to-morrow for judgment. I am glad indeed, Macumazahn, that you have escaped without harm, but I must tell you that I fear henceforth your life will be in danger, since all the Usutu party will hold it forfeit if they can catch you. While you are in my town I can protect you, for I will set a strong guard about your camp; but here you will have to stay until these troubles are done with, since if you leave you may be murdered on the road."

"I thank you for your kindness, King," I answered; "but all this is very awkward for me, who hoped to trek for Natal to-morrow."

"Well, there it is, Macumazahn, you will have to stay here unless you wish to be killed. He who walks into a storm must put up with the hailstones."

So it came about that once again Fate dragged me into the Zulu maelstrom.

On the morrow I was summoned to the trial, half as a witness and half as one of the offenders. Going to the head of the Nodwengu *kraal*, where Panda was sitting in state with his Council, I found the whole great space in front of him crowded with a dense concourse of fierce-faced partisans, those who favoured Cetewayo—the Usutu—sitting on the right, and those who favoured Umbelazi—the Isigqosa—sitting on the left. At the head of the right-hand section sat Cetewayo, his brethren and chief men. At the head of the left-hand section sat Umbelazi, his brethren and his chief men, amongst whom I saw Saduko take a place immediately behind the Prince, so that he could whisper into his ear.

To myself and my little band of eight hunters, who by Panda's express permission, came armed with their guns, as I did also, for I was determined that if the necessity arose we would sell our lives as dearly as we could, was appointed a place almost in front of the King and between the two factions. When everyone was seated the trial began, Panda demanding to know who had caused the tumult of the previous night.

I cannot set out what followed in all its details, for it would be too long; also I have forgotten many of them. I remember, however, that Cetewayo's people said that Umbelazi's men were the aggressors, and that Umbelazi's people said that Cetewayo's men were the aggressors, and that each of their parties backed up these statements, which were given at great length, with loud shouts.

"How am I to know the truth?" exclaimed Panda at last. "Macumazahn, you were there; step forward and tell it to me."

So I stood out and told the King what I had seen, namely that the captain who favoured Cetewayo had begun the quarrel by striking the captain who favoured Umbelazi, but that in the end Umbelazi's man had killed Cetewayo's man, after which the fighting commenced.

"Then it would seem that the Usutu are to blame," said Panda.

"Upon what grounds do you say so, my father?" asked Cetewayo, springing up. "Upon the testimony of this white man, who is well known to be the friend of Umbelazi and of his henchman Saduko, and who himself killed two of those who called me chief in the course of the fight?"

"Yes, Cetewayo," I broke in, "because I thought it better that I should kill them than that they should kill me, whom they attacked quite unprovoked."

"At any rate, you killed them, little White Man," shouted Cetewayo, "for which cause your blood is forfeit. Say, did Umbelazi give you leave to appear before the King accompanied by men armed with guns, when we who are his sons must come with sticks only? If so, let him protect you!"

"That I will do if there is need!" exclaimed Umbelazi.

"Thank you, Prince," I said; "but if there is need I will protect myself as I did yesterday," and, cocking my double-barrelled rifle, I looked full at Cetewayo.

"When you leave here, then at least I will come even with you, Macumazahn!" threatened Cetewayo, spitting through his teeth, as was his way when mad with passion.

For he was beside himself, and wished to vent his temper on someone, although in truth he and I were always good friends.

"If so I shall stop where I am," I answered coolly, "in the shadow of the King, your father. Moreover, are you so lost in folly, Cetewayo, that you should wish to bring the English about your ears? Know that if I am killed you will be asked to give account of my blood."

"Aye," interrupted Panda, "and know that if anyone lays a finger on Macumazana, who is my guest, he shall die, whether he be a common man or a prince and my son. Also, Cetewayo, I fine you twenty head of cattle, to be paid to Macumazana because of the unprovoked attack which your men made upon him when he rightly slew them."

"The fine shall be paid, my father," said Cetewayo more quietly, for he saw that in threatening me he had pushed matters too far.

Then, after some more talk, Panda gave judgment in the cause, which judgment really amounted to nothing. As it was impossible to decide which party was most to blame, he fined both an equal number of cattle, accompanying the fine with a lecture on their ill-behaviour, which was listened to indifferently.

After this matter was disposed of the real business of the meeting began.

Rising to his feet, Cetewayo addressed Panda.

"My father," he said, "the land wanders and wanders in darkness, and you alone can give light for its feet. I and my brother, Umbelazi, are at variance, and the quarrel is a great one, namely, as to which of us is to sit in your place when you are 'gone down,' when we call and you do not answer. Some of the nation favour one of us and some favour the other, but you, O King, and you alone, have the voice of judgment. Still, before you speak, I and those who stand with me would bring this to your mind. My mother, Umqumbazi, is your *Inkosikazi*, your head-wife, and therefore, according to our law, I, her eldest son, should be your heir. Moreover, when you fled to the Boers before the fall of him who sat in your place before you (Dingaan), did not they, the white Amabunu, ask you which amongst your sons was your heir, and did you not point me out to the white men? And thereon did not the Amabunu clothe me in a dress of honour because I was the King to be? But now of late the mother of Umbelazi has been whispering in your ear, as have others"—and he looked at Saduko and some of Umbelazi's brethren—"and your face has grown cold towards me, so cold that many say that you will point out Umbelazi to be King after you and stamp on my name. If this is so, my father, tell me at once, that I may know what to do."

Having finished this speech, which certainly did not lack force and dignity, Cetewayo sat down again, awaiting the answer in sullen silence. But, making none, Panda looked at Umbelazi, who, on rising, was greeted with a great cheer, for although Cetewayo had the larger following in the land, especially among the distant chiefs, the Zulus individually loved Umbelazi more, perhaps because of his stature, beauty and kindly disposition—physical and moral qualities that naturally appeal to a savage nation.

"My father," he said, "like my brother, Cetewayo, I await your word. Whatever you may have said to the Amabunu in haste or fear, I do not admit that Cetewayo was ever proclaimed your heir in the hearing of the Zulu people. I say that my right to the succession is as good as his, and that it lies with you, and you alone, to declare which of us shall put on the royal *kaross* in days that my heart prays may be distant. Still, to save bloodshed, I am willing to divide the land with Cetewayo" (here both Panda and Cetewayo shook their heads and the audience roared "Nay"), "or, if that does not please him, I am willing to meet Cetewayo man to man and spear to spear and fight till one of us be slain."

"A safe offer!" sneered Cetewayo, "for is not my brother named

Elephant, and the strongest warrior among the Zulus? No, I will not set the fortunes of those who cling to me on the chance of a single stab, or on the might of a man's muscles. Decide, O father; say which of the two of us is to sit at the head of your *kraal* after you have gone over to the Spirits and are but an ancestor to be worshipped."

Now, Panda looked much disturbed, as was not wonderful, since, rushing out from the fence behind which they had been listening, Umqumbazi, Cetewayo's mother, whispered into one of his ears, while Umbelazi's mother whispered into the other. What advice each of them gave I do not know, although obviously it was not the same advice, since the poor man rolled his eyes first at one and then at the other, and finally put his hands over his ears that he might hear no more.

"Choose, choose, O King!" shouted the audience. "Who is to succeed you, Cetewayo or Umbelazi?"

Watching Panda, I saw that he fell into a kind of agony; his fat sides heaved, and, although the day was cold, sweat ran from his brow.

"What would the white men do in such a case?" he said to me in a hoarse, low voice, whereon I answered, looking at the ground and speaking so that few could hear me:

"I think, O King, that a white man would do nothing. He would say that others might settle the matter after he was dead."

"Would that I could say so, too," muttered Panda; "but it is not possible."

Then followed a long pause, during which all were silent, for every man there felt that the hour was big with doom. At length Panda rose with difficulty, because of his unwieldy weight, and uttered these fateful words, that were none the less ominous because of the homely idiom in which they were couched:

"When two young bulls quarrel they must fight it out."

Instantly in one tremendous roar volleyed forth the royal salute of *Bayete*, a signal of the acceptance of the King's word—the word that meant civil war and the death of many thousands.

Then Panda turned and, so feebly that I thought he would fall, walked through the gateway behind him, followed by the rival queens. Each of these ladies struggled to be first after him in the gate, thinking that it would be an omen of success for her son. Finally, however, to the disappointment of the multitude, they only succeeded in passing it side by side.

When they had gone the great audience began to break up, the men of each party marching away together as though by common consent, without offering any insult or molestation to their adversaries. I think that this peaceable attitude arose, however, from the knowledge that matters had now passed from the stage of private quarrel into that of public war. It was felt that their dispute awaited decision, not with sticks outside the Nodwengu *kraal*, but with spears upon some great battlefield, for which they went to prepare.

Within two days, except for those regiments which Panda kept to guard his person, scarcely a soldier was to be seen in the neighbourhood of Nodwengu. The princes also departed to muster their adherents, Cetewayo establishing himself among the Mandhlakazi that he commanded, and Umbelazi returning to the *kraal* of Umbezi, which happened to stand almost in the centre of that part of the nation which adhered to him.

Whether he took Mameena with him there I am not certain. I believe, however, that, fearing lest her welcome at her birthplace should be warmer than she wished, she settled herself at some retired and outlying *kraal* in the neighbourhood, and there awaited the crisis of her fortune. At any rate, I saw nothing of her, for she was careful to keep out of my way.

With Umbelazi and Saduko, however, I did have an interview. Before they left Nodwengu they called on me together, apparently on the best of terms, and said in effect that they hoped for my support in the coming war.

I answered that, however well I might like them personally, a Zulu civil war was no affair of mine, and that, indeed, for every reason, including the supreme one of my own safety, I had better get out of the way at once.

They argued with me for a long while, making great offers and promises of reward, till at length, when he saw that my determination could not be shaken, Umbelazi said:

"Come, Saduko, let us humble ourselves no more before this white man. After all, he is right; the business is none of his, and why should we ask him to risk his life in our quarrel, knowing as we do that white men are not like us; they think a great deal of their lives. Farewell, Macumazahn. If I conquer and grow great you will always be welcome in Zululand, whereas if I fail perhaps you will be best over the Tugela river."

Now, I felt the hidden taunt in this speech very keenly. Still, being determined that for once I would be wise and not allow my natural curiosity and love of adventure to drag me into more risks and trouble, I replied:

"The Prince says that I am not brave and love my life, and what he says is true. I fear fighting, who by nature am a trader with the heart of a trader, not a warrior with the heart of a warrior, like the great Indhlovu-ene-Sihlonti"—words at which I saw the grave Saduko smile faintly. "So farewell to you, Prince, and may good fortune attend you."

Of course, to call the Prince to his face by this nickname, which referred to a defect in his person, was something of an insult; but I had been insulted, and meant to give him "a Roland for his Oliver." However, he took it in good part.

"What is good fortune, Macumazahn?" Umbelazi replied as he grasped my hand. "Sometimes I think that to live and prosper is good fortune, and sometimes I think that to die and sleep is good fortune, for in sleep there is neither hunger nor thirst of body or of spirit. In sleep there come no cares; in sleep ambitions are at rest; nor do those who look no more upon the sun smart beneath the treacheries of false women or false friends. Should the battle turn against me, Macumazahn, at least that good fortune will be mine, for never will I live to be crushed beneath Cetewayo's heel."

Then he went. Saduko accompanied him for a little way, but, making some excuse to the Prince, came back and said to me:

"Macumazahn, my friend, I dare say that we part for the last time, and therefore I make a request to you. It is as to one who is dead to me. Macumazahn, I believe that Umbelazi the thief"—these words broke from his lips with a hiss—"has given her many cattle and hidden her away either in the kloof of Zikali the Wise, or near to it, under his care. Now, if the war should go against Umbelazi and I should be killed in it, I think evil will fall upon that woman's head, I who have grown sure that it was she who was the wizard and not Masapo the Boar. Also, as one connected with Umbelazi, who has helped him in his plots, she will be killed if she is caught. Macumazahn, hearken to me. I will tell you the truth. My heart is still on fire for that woman. She has bewitched me; her eyes haunt my sleep and I hear her voice in the wind. She is more to me than all the earth and all the sky, and although she has wronged me I do not wish that harm should come to her. Macumazahn, I pray you if I die, do your best to befriend her, even though it be only as a servant in your house, for I think that she cares more for you than for anyone, who only ran away with him"—and he pointed in the direction that Umbelazi had taken—"because he is a prince, who, in her folly, she believes will be a king. At least take her to Natal, Macumazahn, where, if you wish to be free of her, she can marry whom she will and will live safe until night comes. Panda loves you much, and, whoever conquers in the war, will give you her life if you ask it of him."

Then this strange man drew the back of his hand across his eyes, from which I saw the tears were running, and, muttering, "If you would have good fortune remember my prayer," turned and left me before I could answer a single word.

As for me, I sat down upon an ant-heap and whistled a whole hymn tune that my mother had taught me before I could think at all. To be left the guardian of Mameena! Talk of a *damnosa hereditas*, a terrible and mischievous inheritance—why, this was the worst that ever I heard of. A servant in my house indeed, knowing what *I* did about her! Why, I had sooner share the "good fortune" which Umbelazi anticipated beneath the sod. However, that was not in the question, and without it the alternative of acting as her guardian was bad enough, though I comforted myself with the reflection that the circumstances in which this would become necessary might never arise. For, alas! I was sure that if they did arise I should have to live up to them. True, I had made no promise to Saduko with my lips, but I felt, as I knew he felt, that this promise had passed from my heart to his.

"That thief Umbelazi!" Strange words to be uttered by a great vassal of his lord, and both of them about to enter upon a desperate enterprise. "A prince whom in her folly she believes will be a king." Stranger words still. Then Saduko did not believe that he *would* be a king! And yet he was about to share the fortunes of his fight for the throne, he who said that his heart was still on fire for the woman whom "Umbelazi the thief" had stolen. Well, if I were Umbelazi, thought I to myself, I would rather that Saduko were not my chief councillor and general. But, thank Heaven! I was not Umbelazi, or Saduko, or any of them! And, thank Heaven still more, I was going to begin my trek from Zululand on the morrow!

Man proposes but God disposes. I did not trek from Zululand for many a long day. When I got back to my wagons it was to find that my oxen had mysteriously disappeared from the *veld* on which they were accustomed to graze. They were lost; or perhaps they had felt the urgent need of trekking from Zululand back to a more peaceful country. I sent all the hunters I had with me to look for them, only Scowl and I remaining at the wagons, which in those disturbed times I did not like to leave unguarded.

Four days went by, a week went by, and no sign of either hunters or oxen. Then at last a message, which reached me in some roundabout fashion, to the effect that the hunters had found the oxen a long way off, but on trying to return to Nodwengu had been driven by some of the Usutu—that is, by Cetewayo's party—across the Tugela into Natal, whence they dared not attempt to return.

For once in my life I went into a rage and cursed that nondescript kind of messenger, sent by I know not whom, in language that I think he will not forget. Then, realising the futility of swearing at a mere tool, I went up to the Great House and demanded an audience with Panda himself. Presently the *inceku*, or household servant, to whom I gave my message, returned, saying that I was to be admitted at once, and on entering the enclosure I found the King sitting at the head of the *kraal* quite alone, except for a man who was holding a large shield over him in order to keep off the sun.

He greeted me warmly, and I told him my trouble about the oxen, whereon he sent away the shield-holder, leaving us two together.

"Watcher-by-Night," he said, "why do you blame me for these events, when you know that I am nobody in my own House? I say that I am a dead man, whose sons fight for his inheritance. I cannot tell you for certain who it was that drove away your oxen. Still, I am glad that they are gone, since I believe that if you had attempted to trek to Natal just now you would have been killed on the road by the Usutu, who believe you to be a councillor of Umbelazi."

"I understand, O King," I answered, "and I dare say that the accident of the loss of my oxen is fortunate for me. But tell me now, what am I to do? I wish to follow the example of John Dunn (another white man in the country who was much mixed up with Zulu politics) and leave the land. Will you give me more oxen to draw my wagons?"

"I have none that are broken in, Macumazahn, for, as you know, we Zulus possess few wagons; and if I had I would not lend them to you, who do not desire that your blood should be upon my head."

"You are hiding something from me, O King," I said bluntly. "What is it that you want me to do? Stay here at Nodwengu?"

"No, Macumazahn. When the trouble begins I want you to go with a regiment of my own that I shall send to the assistance of my son, Umbelazi, so that he may have the benefit of your wisdom. O Macumazana, I will tell you the truth. My heart loves Umbelazi, and I fear me that he is overmatched by Cetewayo. If I could I would save his life, but I know not how to do so, since I must not seem to take sides too openly. But I can send down a regiment as your escort, if you choose to go to view the battle as my agent and make report to me. Say, will you not go?"

"Why should I go?" I answered, "seeing that whoever wins I may be killed, and that if Cetewayo wins I shall certainly be killed, and all for no reward."

"Nay, Macumazahn; I will give orders that whoever conquers, the man that dares to lift a spear against you shall die. In this matter, at least, I shall not be disobeyed. Oh! I pray you, do not desert me in my trouble. Go down with the regiment that I shall send and breathe your wisdom into the ear of my son, Umbelazi. As for your reward, I swear to you by the head of the Black One (Chaka) that it shall be great. I will see to it that you do not leave Zululand empty-handed, Macumazahn."

Still I hesitated, for I mistrusted me of this business.

"O Watcher-by-Night," exclaimed Panda, "you will not desert me, will you? I am afraid for the son of my heart, Umbelazi, whom I love above all my children; I am much afraid for Umbelazi," and he burst into tears before me.

It was foolish, no doubt, but the sight of the old King weeping for his best-beloved child, whom he believed to be doomed, moved me so much that I forgot my caution.

"If you wish it, O Panda," I said, "I will go down to the battle with your regiment and stand there by the side of the Prince Umbelazi."

Chapter 13
Umbelazi the Fallen

So I stayed on at Nodwengu, who, indeed, had no choice in the matter, and was very wretched and ill at ease. The place was almost deserted, except for a couple of regiments which were quartered there, the Sangqu and the Amawombe. This latter was the royal regiment, a kind of Household Guards, to which the Kings Chaka, Dingaan and Panda all belonged in turn. Most of the headmen had taken one side or the other, and were away raising forces to fight for Cetewayo or Umbelazi, and even the greater part of the women and children had gone to hide themselves in the bush or among the mountains, since none knew what would happen, or if the conquering army would not fall upon and destroy them.

A few councillors, however, remained with Panda, among whom was old Maputa, the general, who had once brought me the "message of the pills." Several times he visited me at night and told me the rumours that were flying about. From these I gathered that some skirmishes had taken place and the battle could not be long delayed; also that Umbelazi had chosen his fighting ground, a plain near the banks of the Tugela.

"Why has he done this," I asked, "seeing that then he will have a broad river behind him, and if he is defeated water can kill as well as spears?"

"I know not for certain," answered Maputa; "but it is said because of a dream that Saduko, his general, has dreamed thrice, which dream declares that there and there alone Umbelazi will find honour. At any rate, he has chosen this place; and I am told that all the women and children of his army, by thousands, are hidden in the bush along the banks of the river, so that they may fly into Natal if there is need."

"Have they wings," I asked, "wherewith to fly over the Tugela 'in wrath,' as it well may be after the rains? Oh, surely his Spirit has turned from Umbelazi!"

"Aye, Macumazahn," he answered, "I, too, think that *ufulatewe idhlozi* (that is, his own spirit) has turned its back on him. Also I think that Saduko is no good councillor. Indeed, were I the prince," added the old fellow shrewdly, "I would not keep him whose wife I had stolen as the whisperer in my ear."

"Nor I, Maputa," I answered as I bade him good-bye.

Two days later, early in the morning, Maputa came to me again and said that Panda wished to see me. I went to the head of the *kraal*, where I found the King seated and before him the captains of the royal Amawombe regiment.

"Watcher-by-Night," he said, "I have news that the great battle between my sons will take place within a few days. Therefore I am sending down this, my own royal regiment, under the command of Maputa the skilled in war to spy out the battle, and I pray that you will go with it, that you may give to the General Maputa and to the captains the help of your wisdom. Now these are my orders to you, Maputa, and to you, O captains—that you take no part in the fight unless you should see that the Elephant, my son Umbelazi, is fallen into a pit, and that then you shall drag him out if you can and save him alive. Now repeat my words to me."

So they repeated the words, speaking with one voice.

"Your answer, O Macumazana," he said when they had spoken.

"O King, I have told you that I will go—though I do not like war—and I will keep my promise," I replied.

"Then make ready, Macumazahn, and be back here within an hour, for the regiment marches ere noon."

So I went up to my wagons and handed them over to the care of some men whom Panda had sent to take charge of them. Also Scowl and I saddled our horses, for this faithful fellow insisted upon accompanying me, although I advised him to stay behind, and got out our rifles and as much ammunition as we could possibly need, and with them a few other necessaries. These things done, we rode back to the gathering-place, taking farewell of the wagons with a sad heart, since I, for one, never expected to see them again.

As we went I saw that the regiment of the Amawombe, picked men every one of them, all fifty years of age or over, nearly four thousand strong, was marshalled on the dancing-ground, where they stood company by company. A magnificent sight they were, with their white fighting-shields, their gleaming spears, their otter-skin caps, their kilts and armlets of white bulls' tails, and the snowy egret plumes which they wore upon their brows. We rode to the head of them, where I saw

Maputa, and as I came they greeted me with a cheer of welcome, for in those days a white man was a power in the land. Moreover, as I have said, the Zulus knew and liked me well. Also the fact that I was to watch, or perchance to fight with them, put a good heart into the Amawombe.

There we stood until the lads, several hundreds of them, who bore the mats and cooking vessels and drove the cattle that were to be our commissariat, had wended away in a long line. Then suddenly Panda appeared out of his hut, accompanied by a few servants, and seemed to utter some kind of prayer, as he did so throwing dust or powdered medicine towards us, though what this ceremony meant I did not understand.

When he had finished Maputa raised a spear, whereon the whole regiment, in perfect time, shouted out the royal salute, *Bayete*, with a sound like that of thunder. Thrice they repeated this tremendous and impressive salute, and then were silent. Again Maputa raised his spear, and all the four thousand voices broke out into the *Ingoma*, or national chant, to which deep, awe-inspiring music we began our march. As I do not think it has ever been written down, I will quote the words. They ran thus:

Ba ya m'zonda,
Ba ya m'loyisa,
Izizwe zonke,
Ba zond',
Inkoosi.[1]

The spirit of this fierce *Ingoma*, conveyed by sound, gesture and inflection of voice, not the exact words, remember, which are very rude and simple, leaving much to the imagination, may perhaps be rendered somewhat as follows. An exact translation into English verse is almost impossible—at any rate, to me:

Loud on their lips is lying,
Red are their eyes with hate;
Rebels their King defying.
Lo! where our impis wait
There shall be dead and dying,
Vengeance insatiate!

---

1. Literally translated, this famous chant, now, I think, published for the first time, which, I suppose, will never again pass the lips of a Zulu *impi*, means:
They (*i.e.* the enemy) bear him (*i.e.* the King) hatred,
They call down curses on his head,
All of them throughout this land
Abhor our King.
The *Ingoma* when sung by twenty or thirty thousand men rushing down to battle must, indeed, have been a song to hear.—*Editor*

It was early on the morning of the 2nd of December, a cold, miserable morning that came with wind and driving mist, that I found myself with the Amawombe at the place known as Endondakusuka, a plain with some *kopjes* in it that lies within six miles of the Natal border, from which it is separated by the Tugela river.

As the orders of the Amawombe were to keep out of the fray if that were possible, we had taken up a position about a mile to the right of what proved to be the actual battlefield, choosing as our camping ground a rising knoll that looked like a huge tumulus, and was fronted at a distance of about five hundred yards by another smaller knoll. Behind us stretched bush-land, or rather broken land, where mimosa thorns grew in scattered groups, sloping down to the banks of the Tugela about four miles away.

Shortly after dawn I was roused from the place where I slept, wrapped up in some blankets, under a mimosa tree—for, of course, we had no tents—by a messenger, who said that the Prince Umbelazi and the white man, John Dunn, wished to see me. I rose and tidied myself as best I could, since, if I can avoid it, I never like to appear before natives in a dishevelled condition. I remember that I had just finished brushing my hair when Umbelazi arrived.

I can see him now, looking a veritable giant in that morning mist. Indeed, there was something quite unearthly about his appearance as he arose out of those rolling vapours, such light as there was being concentrated upon the blade of his big spear, which was well known as the broadest carried by any warrior in Zululand, and a copper torque he wore about his throat.

There he stood, rolling his eyes and hugging his *kaross* around him because of the cold, and something in his anxious, indeterminate expression told me at once that he knew himself to be a man in terrible danger. Just behind him, dark and brooding, his arms folded on his breast, his eyes fixed upon the ground, looking, to my moved imagination, like an evil genius, stood the stately and graceful Saduko. On his left was a young and sturdy white man carrying a rifle and smoking a pipe, whom I guessed to be John Dunn, a gentleman whom, as it chanced, I had never met, while behind were a force of Natal Government Zulus, clad in some kind of uniform and armed with guns, and with them a number of natives, also from Natal—*kraal Kafirs*, who carried stabbing *assegais*. One of these led John Dunn's horse.

Of those Government men there may have been thirty or forty, and of the *kraal Kafirs* anything between two and three hundred.

I shook Umbelazi's hand and gave him good-day.

"That is an ill day upon which no sun shines, O Macumazana," he answered—words that struck me as ominous. Then he introduced me to John Dunn, who seemed glad to meet another white man. Next, not knowing what to say, I asked the exact object of their visit, whereon Dunn began to talk. He said that he had been sent over on the previous afternoon by Captain Walmsley, who was an officer of the Natal Government stationed across the border, to try to make peace between the Zulu factions, but that when he spoke of peace one of Umbelazi's brothers—I think it was Mantantashiya—had mocked at him, saying that they were quite strong enough to cope with the Usutu—that was Cetewayo's party. Also, he added, that when he suggested that the thousands of women and children and the cattle should be got across the Tugela drift during the previous night into safety in Natal, Mantantashiya would not listen, and Umbelazi being absent, seeking the aid of the Natal Government, he could do nothing.

"Quem Deus vult perdere prius dementat" (whom God wishes to destroy, He first makes mad), quoted I to myself beneath my breath. This was one of the Latin tags that my old father, who was a scholar, had taught me, and at that moment it came back to my mind. But as I suspected that John Dunn knew no Latin, I only said aloud:

"What an infernal fool!" (We were talking in English.) "Can't you get Umbelazi to do it now?" (I meant, to send the women and children across the river.)

"I fear it is too late, Mr. Quatermain," he answered. "The Usutu are in sight. Look for yourself." And he handed me a telescope which he had with him.

I climbed on to some rocks and scanned the plain in front of us, from which just then a puff of wind rolled away the mist. It was black with advancing men! As yet they were a considerable distance away—quite two miles, I should think—and coming on very slowly in a great half-moon with thin horns and a deep breast; but a ray from the sun glittered upon their countless spears. It seemed to me that there must be quite twenty or thirty thousand of them in this breast, which was in three divisions, commanded, as I learned afterwards, by Cetewayo, Uzimela, and by a young Boer named Groening.

"There they are, right enough," I said, climbing down from my rocks. "What are you going to do, Mr. Dunn?"

"Obey orders and try to make peace, if I can find anyone to make peace with; and if I can't—well, fight, I suppose. And you, Mr. Quatermain?"

"Oh, obey orders and stop here, I suppose. Unless," I added doubtfully, "these Amawombe take the bit between their teeth and run away with me."

"They'll do that before nightfall, Mr. Quatermain, if I know anything of the Zulus. Look here, why don't you get on your horse and come off with me? This is a queer place for you."

"Because I promised not to," I answered with a groan, for really, as I looked at those savages round me, who were already fingering their spears in a disagreeable fashion, and those other thousands of savages advancing towards us, I felt such little courage as I possessed sinking into my boots.

"Very well, Mr. Quatermain, you know your own business best; but I hope you will come out of it safely, that is all."

"Same to you," I replied.

Then John Dunn turned, and in my hearing asked Umbelazi what he knew of the movements of the Usutu and of their plan of battle.

The Prince replied, with a shrug of his shoulders:

"Nothing at present, Son of Mr. Dunn, but doubtless before the sun is high I shall know much."

As he spoke a sudden gust of wind struck us, and tore the nodding ostrich plume from its fastening on Umbelazi's head-ring. Whilst a murmur of dismay rose from all who saw what they considered this very ill-omened accident, away it floated into the air, to fall gently to the ground at the feet of Saduko. He stooped, picked it up, and reset it in its place, saying as he did so, with that ready wit for which some *Kafirs* are remarkable:

"So may I live, O Prince, to set the crown upon the head of Panda's favoured son!"

This apt speech served to dispel the general gloom caused by the incident, for those who heard it cheered, while Umbelazi thanked his captain with a nod and a smile. Only I noted that Saduko did not mention the name of "Panda's favoured son" upon whose head he hoped to live to set the crown. Now, Panda had many sons, and that day would show which of them was favoured.

A minute or two later John Dunn and his following departed, as he said, to try to make peace with the advancing Usutu. Umbelazi, Saduko and their escort departed also towards the main body of the host of the Isigqosa, which was massed to our left, "sitting on their spears," as the natives say, and awaiting the attack. As for me, I remained alone with the Amawombe, drinking some coffee that Scowl had brewed for me, and forcing myself to swallow food.

I can say honestly that I do not ever remember partaking of a more unhappy meal. Not only did I believe that I was looking on the last sun I should ever see—though by the way, there was uncommonly little of that orb visible—but what made the matter worse was that, if so, I should be called upon to die alone among savages, with not a single white face near to comfort me. Oh, how I wished I had never allowed myself to be dragged into this dreadful business. Yes, and I was even mean enough to wish that I had broken my word to Panda and gone off with John Dunn when he invited me, although now I thank goodness that I did not yield to that temptation and thereby sacrifice my self-respect.

Soon, however, things grew so exciting that I forgot these and other melancholy reflections in watching the development of events from the summit of our tumulus-like knoll, whence I had a magnificent view of the whole battle. Here, after seeing that his regiment made a full meal, as a good general should, old Maputa joined me, whom I asked whether he thought there would be any fighting for him that day.

"I think so, I think so," he answered cheerfully. "It seems to me that the Usutu greatly outnumber Umbelazi and the Isigqosa, and, of course, as you know, Panda's orders are that if he is in danger we must help him. Oh, keep a good heart, Macumazahn, for I believe I can promise you that you will see our spears grow red to-day. You will not go hungry from this battle to tell the white people that the Amawombe are cowards whom you could not flog into the fight. No, no, Macumazahn, my Spirit looks towards me this morning, and I who am old and who thought that I should die at length like a cow, shall see one more great fight—my twentieth, Macumazahn; for I fought with this same Amawombe in all the Black One's big battles, and for Panda against Dingaan also."

"Perhaps it will be your last," I suggested.

"I dare say, Macumazahn; but what does that matter if only I and the royal regiment can make an end that shall be spoken of? Oh, cheer up, cheer up, Macumazahn; your Spirit, too, looks towards you, as I promise that we all will do when the shields meet; for know, Macumazahn, that we poor black soldiers expect that you will show us how to fight this day, and, if need be, how to fall hidden in a heap of the foe."

"Oh!" I replied, "so this is what you Zulus mean by the 'giving of counsel,' is it?—you infernal, bloodthirsty old scoundrel," I added in English.

But I think Maputa never heard me. At any rate, he only seized my arm and pointed in front, a little to the left, where the horn of the great Usutu army was coming up fast, a long, thin line alive with twinkling spears; their moving arms and legs causing them to look like spiders, of which the bodies were formed by the great war shields.

"See their plan?" he said. "They would close on Umbelazi and gore him with their horns and then charge with their head. The horn will pass between us and the right flank of the Isigqosa. Oh! awake, awake, Elephant! Are you asleep with Mameena in a hut? Unloose your spears, Child of the King, and at them as they mount the slope. Behold!" he went on, "it is the son of Dunn that begins the battle! Did I not tell you that we must look to the white men to show us the way? Peep through your tube, Macumazahn, and tell me what passes."

So I "peeped," and, the telescope which John Dunn had kindly left with me being good though small, saw everything clearly enough. He rode up almost to the point of the left horn of the Usutu, waving a white handkerchief and followed by his small force of police and Natal *Kafirs*. Then from somewhere among the Usutu rose a puff of smoke. Dunn had been fired at.

He dropped the handkerchief and leapt to the ground. Now he and his police were firing rapidly in reply, and men fell fast among the Usutu. They raised their war shout and came on, though slowly, for they feared the bullets. Step by step John Dunn and his people were thrust back, fighting gallantly against overwhelming odds. They were level with us, not a quarter of a mile to our left. They were pushed past us. They vanished among the bush behind us, and a long while passed before ever I heard what became of them, for we met no more that day.

Now, the horns having done their work and wrapped themselves round Umbelazi's army as the nippers of a wasp close about a fly (why did not Umbelazi cut off those horns, I wondered), the Usutu bull began his charge. Twenty or thirty thousand strong, regiment after regiment, Cetewayo's men rushed up the slope, and there, near the crest of it, were met by Umbelazi's regiments springing forward to repel the onslaught and shouting their battle-cry of *"Laba! Laba! Laba! Laba!"*

The noise of their meeting shields came to our ears like that of the roll of thunder, and the sheen of their stabbing-spears shone as shines the broad summer lightning. They hung and wavered on the slope; then from the Amawombe ranks rose a roar of

"Umbelazi wins!"

Watching intently, we saw the Usutu giving back. Down the slope they went, leaving the ground in front of them covered with black spots which we knew to be dead or wounded men.

"Why does not the Elephant charge home?" said Maputa in a perplexed voice. "The Usutu bull is on his back! Why does he not trample him?"

"Because he is afraid, I suppose," I answered, and went on watching.

There was plenty to see, as it happened. Finding that they were not pursued, Cetewayo's *impi* reformed swiftly at the bottom of the slope, in preparation for another charge. Among that of Umbelazi, above them, rapid movements took place of which I could not guess the meaning, which movements were accompanied by much noise of angry shouting. Then suddenly, from the midst of the Isigqosa army, emerged a great body of men, thousands strong, which ran swiftly, but in open order, down the slope towards the Usutu, holding their spears reversed. At first I thought that they were charging independently, till I saw the Usutu ranks open to receive them with a shout of welcome.

"Treachery!" I said. "Who is it?"

"Saduko, with the Amakoba and Amangwane soldiers and others. I know them by their head-dresses," answered Maputa in a cold voice.

"Do you mean that Saduko has gone over to Cetewayo with all his following?" I asked excitedly.

"What else, Macumazahn? Saduko is a traitor: Umbelazi is finished," and he passed his hand swiftly across his mouth—a gesture that has only one meaning among the Zulus.

As for me, I sat down upon a stone and groaned, for now I understood everything.

Presently the Usutu raised fierce, triumphant shouts, and once again their *impi*, swelled with Saduko's power, began to advance up the slope. Umbelazi, and those of the Isigqosa party who clung to him—now, I should judge, not more than eight thousand men—never stayed to wait the onslaught. They broke! They fled in a hideous rout, crashing through the thin, left horn of the Usutu by mere weight of numbers, and passing behind us obliquely on their road to the banks of the Tugela. A messenger rushed up to us, panting.

"These are the words of Umbelazi," he gasped. "O Watcher-by-Night and O Maputa, Indhlovu-ene-sihlonti prays that you will hold back the Usutu, as the King bade you do in case of need, and so give to him and those who cling to him time to escape with the women and children into Natal. His general, Saduko, has betrayed him, and gone over with three regiments to Cetewayo, and therefore we can no longer stand against the thousands of the Usutu."

"Go tell the prince that Macumazahn, Maputa, and the Amawombe regiment will do their best," answered Maputa calmly. "Still, this is our advice to him, that he should cross the Tugela swiftly with the women and the children, seeing that we are few and Cetewayo is many."

The messenger leapt away, but, as I heard afterwards, he never found Umbelazi, since the poor man was killed within five hundred yards of where we stood.

Then Maputa gave an order, and the Amawombe formed themselves into a triple line, thirteen hundred men in the first line, thirteen hundred men in the second line, and about a thousand in the third, behind whom were the carrier boys, three or four hundred of them. The place assigned to me was in the exact centre of the second line, where, being mounted on a horse, it was thought, as I gathered, that I should serve as a convenient rallying-point.

In this formation we advanced a few hundred yards to our left, evidently with the object of interposing ourselves between the routed *impi* and the pursuing Usutu, or, if the latter should elect to go round us, with that of threatening their flank. Cetewayo's generals did not leave us long in doubt as to what they would do. The main body of their army bore away to the right in pursuit of the flying foe, but three regiments, each of about two thousand five hundred spears, halted. Five minutes passed perhaps while they marshalled, with a distance of some six hundred yards between them. Each regiment was in a triple line like our own.

To me that seemed a very long five minutes, but, reflecting that it was probably my last on earth, I tried to make the best of it in a fashion that can be guessed. Strange to say, however, I found it impossible to keep my mind fixed upon those matters with which it ought to have been filled. My eyes and thoughts would roam. I looked at the ranks of the veteran Amawombe, and noted that they were still and solemn as men about to die should be, although they showed no sign of fear. Indeed, I saw some of those near me passing their snuffboxes to each other. Two grey-haired men also, who evidently were old friends, shook hands as people do who are parting before a journey, while two others discussed in a low voice the possibility of our wiping out most of the Usutu before we were wiped out ourselves.

"It depends," said one of them, "whether they attack us regiment by regiment or all together, as they will do if they are wise."

Then an officer bade them be silent, and conversation ceased. Maputa passed through the ranks giving orders to the captains. From a distance his withered old body, with a fighting shield held in front of it, looked like that of a huge black ant carrying something in its mouth. He came to where Scowl and I sat upon our horses.

"Ah! I see that you are ready, Macumazahn," he said in a cheerful voice. "I told you that you should not go away hungry, did I not?"

"Maputa," I said in remonstrance, "what is the use of this? Umbelazi is defeated, you are not of his *impi*, why send all these"—and I waved my hand—"down into the darkness? Why not go to the river and try to save the women and children?"

"Because we shall take many of those down into the darkness with us, Macumazahn," and he pointed to the dense masses of the Usutu. "Yet," he added, with a touch of compunction, "this is not your quarrel. You and your servant have horses. Slip out, if you will, and gallop hard to the lower drift. You may get away with your lives."

Then my white man's pride came to my aid.

"Nay," I answered, "I will not run while others stay to fight."

"I never thought you would, Macumazahn, who, I am sure, do not wish to earn a new and ugly name. Well, neither will the Amawombe run to become a mock among their people. The King's orders were that we should try to help Umbelazi, if the battle went against him. We obey the King's orders by dying where we stand. Macumazahn, do you think that you could hit that big fellow who is shouting insults at us there? If so, I should be obliged to you, as I dislike him very much," and he showed me a captain who was swaggering about in front of the lines of the first of the Usutu regiments, about six hundred yards away.

"I will try," I answered, "but it's a long shot." Dismounting, I climbed a pile of stones and, resting my rifle on the topmost of them, took a very full sight, aimed, held my breath, and pressed the trigger. A second afterwards the shouter of insults threw his arms wide, letting fall his spear, and pitched forward on to his face.

A roar of delight rose from the watching Amawombe, while old Maputa clapped his thin brown hands and grinned from ear to ear.

"Thank you, Macumazahn. A very good omen! Now I am sure that, whatever those Isigqosa dogs of Umbelazi's may do, we King's men shall make an excellent end, which is all that we can hope. Oh, what a beautiful shot! It will be something to think of when I am an *idhlozi*, a spirit-snake, crawling about my own *kraal*. Farewell, Macumazahn," and he took my hand and pressed it. "The time has come. I go to lead the charge. The Amawombe have orders to defend you to the last, for I wish you to see the finish of this fight. Farewell."

Then off he hurried, followed by his orderlies and staff-officers.

I never saw him again alive, though I think that once in after years I did meet his *idhlozi* in his *kraal* under strange circumstances. But that has nothing to do with this history.

As for me, having reloaded, I mounted my horse again, being afraid lest, if I went on shooting, I should miss and spoil my reputation. Besides, what was the use of killing more men unless I was obliged? There were plenty ready to do that.

Another minute, and the regiment in front of us began to move, while the other two behind it ostentatiously sat themselves down in their ranks, to show that they did not mean to spoil sport. The fight was to begin with a duel between about six thousand men.

"Good!" muttered the warrior who was nearest me. "They are in our bag."

"Aye," answered another, "those little boys" (used as a term of contempt) "are going to learn their last lesson."

For a few seconds there was silence, while the long ranks leant forward between the hedges of lean and cruel spears. A whisper went down the line; it sounded like the noise of wind among trees, and was the signal to prepare. Next a far-off voice shouted some word, which was repeated again and again by other voices before and behind me. I became aware that we were moving, quite slowly at first, then more quickly. Being lifted above the ranks upon my horse I could see the whole advance, and the general aspect of it was that of a triple black wave, each wave crowned with foam—the white plumes and shields of the Amawombe were the foam—and alive with sparkles of light—their broad spears were the light.

We were charging now—and oh! the awful and glorious excitement of that charge! Oh, the rush of the bending plumes and the dull thudding of eight thousand feet! The Usutu came up the slope to meet us. In silence we went, and in silence they came. We drew near to each other. Now we could see their faces peering over the tops of their mottled shields, and now we could see their fierce and rolling eyes.

Then a roar—a rolling roar such as at that time I had never heard: the thunder of the roar of the meeting shields—and a flash—a swift, simultaneous flash, the flash of the lightning of the stabbing spears. Up went the cry of:

"Kill, Amawombe, kill!" answered by another cry of:

"Toss, Usutu, toss!"

After that, what happened? Heaven knows alone—or at least I do not. But in later years Mr. Osborn, afterwards the resident magistrate at Newcastle, in Natal, who, being young and foolish in those days, had swum his horse over the Tugela and hidden in a little kopje quite near to us in order to see the battle, told me that it looked as though some huge breaker—that breaker being the splendid Amawombe—rolling in towards the shore with the weight of the ocean behind it, had suddenly struck a ridge of rock and, rearing itself up, submerged and hidden it.

At least, within three minutes that Usutu regiment was no more. We had killed them every one, and from all along our lines rose a fierce hissing sound of *"S'gee, S'gee"* (*Zhi* in the Zulu) uttered as the spears went home in the bodies of the conquered.

That regiment had gone, taking nearly a third of our number with it, for in such a battle as this the wounded were as good as dead. Practically our first line had vanished in a fray that did not last more than a few minutes. Before it was well over the second Usutu regiment sprang up and charged. With a yell of victory we rushed down the slope towards them. Again there was the roar of the meeting shields, but this time the fight was more prolonged, and, being in the front rank now, I had my share of it. I remember shooting two Usutu who stabbed at me, after which my gun was wrenched from my hand. I remember the melee swinging backwards and forwards, the groans of the wounded, the shouts of victory and despair, and then Scowl's voice saying:

"We have beat them, Baas, but here come the others."

The third regiment was on our shattered lines. We closed up, we fought like devils, even the bearer boys rushed into the fray. From all sides they poured down upon us, for we had made a ring; every minute men died by hundreds, and, though their numbers grew few, not one of the Amawombe yielded. I was fighting with a spear now, though how it came into my hand I cannot remember for certain. I think, however, I wrenched it from a man who rushed at me and was stabbed before he could strike. I killed a captain with this spear, for as he fell I recognised his face. It was that of one of Cetewayo's companions to whom I had sold some cloth at Nodwengu. The fallen were piled up quite thick around me—we were using them as a breastwork, friend and foe together. I saw Scowl's horse rear into the air and fall. He slipped over its tail, and next instant was fighting at my side, also with a spear, muttering Dutch and English oaths as he struck.

"Beetje varm! (a little hot) *Beetje varm, Baas!"* I heard him say. Then my horse screamed aloud and something hit me hard upon the head—I suppose it was a thrown *kerry*—after which I remember nothing for a while, except a sensation of passing through the air.

I came to myself again, and found that I was still on the horse, which was ambling forward across the *veld* at a rate of about eight miles an hour, and that Scowl was clinging to my stirrup leather and running at my side. He was covered with blood, so was the horse, and so was I. It may have been our own blood, for all three were more or less wounded, or it may have been that of others; I am sure I do not know, but we were a terrible sight. I pulled upon the reins, and the horse stopped among some thorns. Scowl felt in the saddlebags and found a large flask of Hollands gin and water—half gin and half water—which he had placed there before the battle. He uncorked and gave it to me. I took a long pull at the stuff, that tasted like veritable nectar, then handed it to him, who did likewise. New life seemed to flow into my veins. Whatever teetotallers may say, alcohol is good at such a moment.

"Where are the Amawombe?" I asked.

"All dead by now, I think, Baas, as we should be had not your horse bolted. Wow! but they made a great fight—one that will be told of! They have carried those three regiments away upon their spears."

"That's good," I said. "But where are we going?"

"To Natal, I hope, Baas. I have had enough of the Zulus for the present. The Tugela is not far away, and we will swim it. Come on, before our hurts grow stiff."

So we went on, till presently we reached the crest of a rise of ground overlooking the river, and there saw and heard dreadful things, for beneath us those devilish Usutu were massacring the fugitives and the camp-followers. These were being driven by the hundred to the edge of the water, there to perish on the banks or in the stream, which was black with drowned or drowning forms.

And oh! the sounds! Well, these I will not attempt to describe.

"Keep up stream," I said shortly, and we struggled across a kind of donga, where only a few wounded men were hidden, into a somewhat denser patch of bush that had scarcely been entered by the flying Isigqosa, perhaps because here the banks of the river were very steep and difficult; also, between them its waters ran swiftly, for this was above the drift.

For a while we went on in safety, then suddenly I heard a noise. A great man plunged past me, breaking through the bush like a buffalo, and came to a halt upon a rock which overhung the Tugela, for the floods had eaten away the soil beneath.

"Umbelazi!" said Scowl, and as he spoke we saw another man following as a wild dog follows a buck.

"Saduko!" said Scowl.

I rode on. I could not help riding on, although I knew it would be safer to keep away. I reached the edge of that big rock. Saduko and Umbelazi were fighting there.

In ordinary circumstances, strong and active as he was, Saduko would have had no chance against the most powerful Zulu living. But the prince was utterly exhausted; his sides were going like a blacksmith's bellows, or those of a fat eland bull that has been galloped to a standstill. Moreover, he seemed to me to be distraught with grief, and, lastly, he had no shield left, nothing but an *assegai.*

A stab from Saduko's spear, which he partially parried, wounded him slightly on the head, and cut loose the fillet of his ostrich plume, that same plume which I had seen blown off in the morning, so that it fell to the ground. Another stab pierced his right arm, making it helpless. He snatched the *assegai* with his left hand, striving to continue the fight, and just at that moment we came up.

"What are you doing, Saduko?" I cried. "Does a dog bite his own master?"

He turned and stared at me; both of them stared at me.

"Aye, Macumazahn," he answered in an icy voice, "sometimes when it is starving and that full-fed master has snatched away its bone. Nay, stand aside, Macumazahn" (for, although I was quite unarmed, I had stepped between them), "lest you should share the fate of this woman-thief."

"Not I, Saduko," I cried, for this sight made me mad, "unless you murder me."

Then Umbelazi spoke in a hollow voice, sobbing out his words:

"I thank you, White Man, yet do as this snake bids you—this snake that has lived in my *kraal* and fed out of my cup. Let him have his fill of vengeance because of the woman who bewitched me—yes, because of the sorceress who has brought me and thousands to the dust. Have you heard, Macumazahn, of the great deed of this son of Matiwane? Have you heard that all the while he was a traitor in the pay of Cetewayo, and that he went over, with the regiments of his command, to the Usutu just when the battle hung upon the turn? Come, Traitor, here is my heart—the heart that loved and trusted you. Strike—strike hard!"

"Out of the way, Macumazahn!" hissed Saduko. But I would not stir.

He sprang at me, and, though I put up the best fight that I could in my injured state, got his hands about my throat and began to choke me. Scowl ran to help me, but his wound—for he was hurt—or his utter exhaustion took effect on him. Or perhaps it was excitement. At any rate, he fell down in a fit. I thought that all was over, when again I heard Umbelazi's voice, and felt Saduko's grip loosen at my throat, and sat up.

"Dog," said the Prince, "where is your *assegai*?" And as he spoke he threw it from him into the river beneath, for he had picked it up while we struggled, but, as I noted, retained his own. "Now, dog, why do I not kill you, as would have been easy but now? I will tell you. Because I will not mix the blood of a traitor with my own. See!" He set the haft of his broad spear upon the rock and bent forward over the blade. "You and your witch-wife have brought me to nothing, O Saduko. My blood, and the blood of all who clung to me, is on your head. Your name shall stink for ever in the nostrils of all true men, and I whom you have betrayed—I, the Prince Umbelazi—will haunt you while you live; yes, my spirit shall enter into you, and when you die—ah! then we'll meet again. Tell this tale to the white men, Macumazahn, my friend, on whom be honour and blessings."

He paused, and I saw the tears gush from his eyes—tears mingled with blood from the wound in his head. Then suddenly he uttered the battle-cry of *"Laba! Laba!"* and let his weight fall upon the point of the spear.

It pierced him through and through. He fell on to his hands and knees. He looked up at us—oh, the piteousness of that look!—and then rolled sideways from the edge of the rock.

A heavy splash, and that was the end of Umbelazi the Fallen—Umbelazi, about whom Mameena had cast her net.

A sad story in truth. Although it happened so many years ago I weep as I write it—I weep as Umbelazi wept.

Chapter 14
Umbezi and the Blood Royal

After this I think that some of the Usutu came up, for it seemed to me that I heard Saduko say:

"Touch not Macumazahn or his servant. They are my prisoners. He who harms them dies, with all his House."

So they put me, fainting, on my horse, and Scowl they carried away upon a shield.

When I came to I found myself in a little cave, or rather beneath some overhanging rocks, at the side of a kopje, and with me Scowl, who had recovered from his fit, but seemed in a very bewildered condition. Indeed, neither then nor afterwards did he remember anything of the death of Umbelazi, nor did I ever tell him that tale. Like many others, he thought that the Prince had been drowned in trying to swim the Tugela.

"Are they going to kill us?" I asked of him, since, from the triumphant shouting without, I knew that we must be in the midst of the victorious Usutu.

"I don't know, Baas," he answered. "I hope not; after we have gone through so much it would be a pity. Better to have died at the beginning of the battle."

I nodded my head in assent, and just at that moment a Zulu, who had very evidently been fighting, entered the place carrying a dish of toasted lumps of beef and a gourd of water.

"Cetewayo sends you these, Macumazahn," he said, "and is sorry that there is no milk or beer. When you have eaten a guard waits without to escort you to him." And he went.

"Well," I said to Scowl, "if they were going to kill us, they would scarcely take the trouble to feed us first. So let us keep up our hearts and eat."

"Who knows?" answered poor Scowl, as he crammed a lump of

beef into his big mouth. "Still, it is better to die on a full than on an empty stomach."

So we ate and drank, and, as we were suffering more from exhaustion than from our hurts, which were not really serious, our strength came back to us. As we finished the last lump of meat, which, although it had been only half cooked upon the point of an *assegai*, tasted very good, the Zulu put his head into the mouth of the shelter and asked if we were ready. I nodded, and, supporting each other, Scowl and I limped from the place. Outside were about fifty soldiers, who greeted us with a shout that, although it was mixed with laughter at our pitiable appearance, struck me as not altogether unfriendly. Amongst these men was my horse, which stood with its head hanging down, looking very depressed. I was helped on to its back, and, Scowl clinging to the stirrup leather, we were led a distance of about a quarter of a mile to Cetewayo.

We found him seated, in the full blaze of the evening sun, on the eastern slope of one of the land-waves of the *veld*, with the open plain in front of him. It was a strange and savage scene. There sat the victorious prince, surrounded by his captains and *indunas*, while before him rushed the triumphant regiments, shouting his titles in the most extravagant language. *Izimbongi* also—that is, professional praisers—were running up and down before him dressed in all sorts of finery, telling his deeds, calling him Eater-up-of-the-Earth, and yelling out the names of those great ones who had been killed in the battle.

Meanwhile parties of bearers were coming up continually, carrying dead men of distinction upon shields and laying them out in rows, as game is laid out at the end of a day's shooting in England. It seems that Cetewayo had taken a fancy to see them, and, being too tired to walk over the field of battle, ordered that this should be done. Among these, by the way, I saw the body of my old friend, Maputa, the general of the Amawombe, and noted that it was literally riddled with spear thrusts, every one of them in front; also that his quaint face still wore a smile.

At the head of these lines of corpses were laid six dead, all men of large size, in whom I recognised the brothers of Umbelazi, who had fought on his side, and the half-brothers of Cetewayo. Among them were those three princes upon whom the dust had fallen when Zikali, the prophet, smelt out Masapo, the husband of Mameena.

Dismounting from my horse, with the help of Scowl, I limped through and over the corpses of these fallen royalties, cut in the Zulu fashion to free their spirits, which otherwise, as they believed, would haunt the slayers, and stood in front of Cetewayo.

"*Siyakubona*, Macumazahn," he said, stretching out his hand to me, which I took, though I could not find it in my heart to wish *him* "good day."

"I hear that you were leading the Amawombe, whom my father, the King, sent down to help Umbelazi, and I am very glad that you have escaped alive. Also my heart is proud of the fight that they made, for you know, Macumazahn, once, next to the King, I was general of that regiment, though afterwards we quarrelled. Still, I am pleased that they did so well, and I have given orders that every one of them who remains alive is to be spared, that they may be officers of a new Amawombe which I shall raise. Do you know, Macumazahn, that you have nearly wiped out three whole regiments of the Usutu, killing many more people than did all my brother's army, the Isigqosa? Oh, you are a great man. Had it not been for the loyalty"—this word was spoken with just a tinge of sarcasm—"of Saduko yonder, you would have won the day for Umbelazi. Well, now that this quarrel is finished, if you will stay with me I will make you general of a whole division of the King's army, since henceforth I shall have a voice in affairs."

"You are mistaken, O Son of Panda," I answered; "the splendour of the Amawombe's great stand against a multitude is on the name of Maputa, the King's councillor and the *induna* of the Black One (Chaka), who is gone. He lies yonder in his glory," and I pointed to Maputa's pierced body. "I did but fight as a soldier in his ranks."

"Oh, yes, we know that, we know all that, Macumazahn; and Maputa was a clever monkey in his way, but we know also that you taught him how to jump. Well, he is dead, and nearly all the Amawombe are dead, and of my three regiments but a handful is left; the vultures have the rest of them. That is all finished and forgotten, Macumazahn, though by good fortune the spears went wide of you, who doubtless are a magician, since otherwise you and your servant and your horse would not have escaped with a few scratches when everyone else was killed. But you did escape, as you have done before in Zululand; and now you see here lie certain men who were born of my father. Yet one is missing—he against whom I fought, aye, and he whom, although we fought, I loved the best of all of them. Now, it has been whispered in my ear that you alone know what became of him, and, Macumazahn, I would learn whether he lives or is dead; also, if he is dead, by whose hand he died, who would reward that hand."

Now, I looked round me, wondering whether I should tell the truth or hold my tongue, and as I looked my eyes met those of Saduko, who, cold and unconcerned, was seated among the captains, but at a little distance from any of them—a man apart; and I remembered that he and I alone knew the truth of the end of Umbelazi.

Why, I do not know, but it came into my mind that I would keep the secret. Why should I tell the triumphant Cetewayo that Umbelazi had been driven to die by his own hand; why should I lay bare Saduko's victory and shame? All these matters had passed into the court of a different tribunal. Who was I that I should reveal them or judge the actors of this terrible drama?

"O Cetewayo," I said, "as it chanced I saw the end of Umbelazi. No enemy killed him. He died of a broken heart upon a rock above the river; and for the rest of the story go ask the Tugela into which he fell."

For a moment Cetewayo hid his eyes with his hand.

"Is it so?" he said presently. "Wow! I say again that had it not been for Saduko, the son of Matiwane, yonder, who had some quarrel with Indhlovu-ene-Sihlonti about a woman and took his chance of vengeance, it might have been I who died of a broken heart upon a rock above the river. Oh, Saduko, I owe you a great debt and will pay you well; but you shall be no friend of mine, lest we also should chance to quarrel about a woman, and *I* should find myself dying of a broken heart on a rock above a river. O my brother Umbelazi, I mourn for you, my brother, for, after all, we played together when we were little and loved each other once, who in the end fought for a toy that is called a throne, since, as our father said, two bulls cannot live in the same yard, my brother. Well, you are gone and I remain, yet who knows but that at the last your lot may be happier than mine. You died of a broken heart, Umbelazi, but of what shall *I* die, I wonder?"[1]

I have given this interview in detail, since it was because of it that the saying went abroad that Umbelazi died of a broken heart. So in truth he did, for before his spear pierced it his heart was broken.

Now, seeing that Cetewayo was in one of his soft moods, and that he seemed to look upon me kindly, though I had fought against him, I reflected that this would be a good opportunity to ask his leave to depart. To tell the truth, my nerves were quite shattered with all I had gone through, and I longed to be away from the sights and sounds of that terrible battlefield, on and about which so many thousand people had perished this fateful day, as I had seldom longed for anything before. But while I was making up my mind as to the best way to approach him, something happened which caused me to lose my chance.

---

1. That history of Cetewayo's fall and tragic death and of Zikali's vengeance I hope to write one day, for in these events also I was destined to play a part.—*A. Q.*

Hearing a noise behind me, I looked round, to see a stout man arrayed in a very fine war dress, and waving in one hand a gory spear and in the other a head-plume of ostrich feathers, who was shouting out:

"Give me audience of the son of the King! I have a song to sing to the Prince. I have a tale to tell to the conqueror, Cetewayo."

I stared. I rubbed my eyes. It could not be—yes, it was—Umbezi, "Eater-up-of-Elephants," the father of Mameena. In a few seconds, without waiting for leave to approach, he had bounded through the line of dead princes, stopping to kick one of them on the head and address his poor clay in some words of shameful insult, and was prancing about before Cetewayo, shouting his praises.

"Who is this *umfokazana*?" (that is, low fellow) growled the Prince. "Bid him cease his noise and speak, lest he should be silent for ever."

"O Calf of the Black Cow, I am Umbezi, Eater-up-of-Elephants, chief captain of Saduko the Cunning, he who won you the battle, father of Mameena the Beautiful, whom Saduko wed and whom the dead dog, Umbelazi, stole away from him."

"Ah!" said Cetewayo, screwing up his eyes in a fashion he had when he meant mischief, which among the Zulus caused him to be named the "Bull-who-shuts-his-eyes-to-toss," "and what have you to tell me, 'Eater-up-of-Elephants' and father of Mameena, whom the dead dog, Umbelazi, took away from your master, Saduko the Cunning?"

"This, O Mighty One; this, O Shaker of the Earth, that well am I named Eater-up-of-Elephants, who have eaten up Indhlovu-ene-Sihlonti—the Elephant himself."

Now Saduko seemed to awake from his brooding and started from his place; but Cetewayo sharply bade him be silent, whereon Umbezi, the fool, noting nothing, continued his tale.

"O Prince, I met Umbelazi in the battle, and when he saw me he fled from me; yes, his heart grew soft as water at the sight of me, the warrior whom he had wronged, whose daughter he had stolen."

"I hear you," said Cetewayo. "Umbelazi's heart turned to water at the sight of you because he had wronged you—you who until this morning, when you deserted him with Saduko, were one of his jackals. Well, and what happened then?"

"He fled, O Lion with the Black Mane; he fled like the wind, and I, I flew after him like—a stronger wind. Far into the bush he fled, till at length he came to a rock above the river and was obliged to stand. Then there we fought. He thrust at me, but I leapt over his spear *thus*," and he gambolled into the air. "He thrust at me again, but I bent myself *thus*," and he ducked his great head. "Then he grew tired and my time came. He turned and ran round the rock, and I, I ran after him, stabbing him through the back, *thus*, and *thus*, and *thus*, till he fell, crying for mercy, and rolled off the rock into the river; and as he rolled I snatched away his plume. See, is it not the plume of the dead dog Umbelazi?"

Cetewayo took the ornament and examined it, showing it to one or two of the captains near him, who nodded their heads gravely.

"Yes," he said, "this is the war plume of Umbelazi, beloved of the King, strong and shining pillar of the Great House; we know it well, that war plume at the sight of which many a knee has loosened. And so you killed him, 'Eater-up-of-Elephants,' father of Mameena, you who this morning were one of the meanest of his jackals. Now, what reward shall I give you for this mighty deed, O Umbezi?"

"A great reward, O Terrible One," began Umbezi, but in an awful voice Cetewayo bade him be silent.

"Yes," he said, "a great reward. Hearken, Jackal and Traitor. Your own words bear witness against you. You, *you* have dared to lift your hand against the blood-royal, and with your foul tongue to heap lies and insults upon the name of the mighty dead."

Now, understanding at last, Umbezi began to babble excuses, yes, and to declare that all his tale was false. His fat cheeks fell in, he sank to his knees.

But Cetewayo only spat towards the man, after his fashion when enraged, and looked round him till his eye fell upon Saduko.

"Saduko," he said, "take away this slayer of the Prince, who boasts that he is red with my own blood, and when he is dead cast him into the river from that rock on which he says he stabbed Panda's son."

Saduko looked round him wildly and hesitated.

"Take him away," thundered Cetewayo, "and return ere dark to make report to me."

Then, at a sign from the Prince, soldiers flung themselves upon the miserable Umbezi and dragged him thence, Saduko going with them; nor was the poor liar ever seen again. As he passed by me he called to me, for Mameena's sake, to save him; but I could only shake my head and bethink me of the warning I had once given to him as to the fate of traitors.

It may be said that this story comes straight from the history of Saul and David, but I can only answer that it happened. Circumstances that were not unlike ended in a similar tragedy, that is all. What David's exact motives were, naturally I cannot tell; but it is easy to guess those of Cetewayo, who, although he could make war upon his brother to secure the throne, did not think it wise to let it go abroad that the royal blood might be lightly spilt. Also, knowing that I was a witness of the Prince's death, he was well aware that Umbezi was but a boastful liar who hoped thus to ingratiate himself with an all-powerful conqueror.

Well, this tragic incident had its sequel. It seems—to his honour, be it said—that Saduko refused to be the executioner of his father-in-law, Umbezi; so those with him performed this office and brought him back a prisoner to Cetewayo.

When the Prince learned that his direct order, spoken in the accustomed and fearful formula of *"Take him away,"* had been disobeyed, his rage was, or seemed to be, great. My own conviction is that he was only seeking a cause of quarrel against Saduko, who, he thought, was a very powerful man, who would probably treat him, should opportunity arise, as he had treated Umbelazi, and perhaps now that the most of Panda's sons were dead, except himself and the lads M'tonga, Sikota and M'kungo, who had fled into Natal, might even in future days aspire to the throne as the husband of the King's daughter. Still, he was afraid or did not think it politic at once to put out of his path this master of many legions, who had played so important a part in the battle. Therefore he ordered him to be kept under guard and taken back to Nodwengu, that the whole matter might be investigated by Panda the King, who still ruled the land, though henceforth only in name. Also he refused to allow me to depart into Natal, saying that I, too, must come to Nodwengu, as there my testimony might be needed.

So, having no choice, I went, it being fated that I should see the end of the drama.

Chapter 15

Mameena Claims the Kiss

When I reached Nodwengu I was taken ill and laid up in my wagon for about a fortnight. What my exact sickness was I do not know, for I had no doctor at hand to tell me, as even the missionaries had fled the country. Fever resulting from fatigue, exposure and excitement, and complicated with fearful headache—caused, I presume, by the blow which I received in the battle—were its principal symptoms.

When I began to get better, Scowl and some Zulu friends who came to see me informed me that the whole land was in a fearful state of disorder, and that Umbelazi's adherents, the Isigqosa, were still being hunted out and killed. It seems that it was even suggested by some of the Usutu that I should share their fate, but on this point Panda was firm. Indeed, he appears to have said publicly that whoever lifted a spear against me, his friend and guest, lifted it against him, and would be the cause of a new war. So the Usutu left me alone, perhaps because they were satisfied with fighting for a while, and thought it wisest to be content with what they had won.

Indeed, they had won everything, for Cetewayo was now supreme—by right of the *assegai*—and his father but a cipher. Although he remained the *head* of the nation, Cetewayo was publicly declared to be its *feet*, and strength was in these active *feet*, not in the bowed and sleeping *head*. In fact, so little power was left to Panda that he could not protect his own household. Thus one day I heard a great tumult and shouting proceeding apparently from the *Isigodhlo*, or royal enclosure, and on inquiring what it was afterwards, was told that Cetewayo had come from the Amangwe *kraal* and denounced Nomantshali, the King's wife, as *umtakati*, or a witch. More, in spite of his father's prayers and tears, he had caused her to be put to death before his eyes—a dreadful and a savage deed. At this distance of time I cannot remember whether Nomantshali was the mother of Umbelazi or of one of the other fallen princes.[1]

A few days later, when I was up and about again, although I had not ventured into the *kraal*, Panda sent a messenger to me with a present of an ox. On his behalf this man congratulated me on my recovery, and told me that, whatever might have happened to others, I was to have no fear for my own safety. He added that Cetewayo had sworn to the King that not a hair of my head should be harmed, in these words:

"Had I wished to kill Watcher-by-Night because he fought against me, I could have done so down at Endondakusuka; but then I ought to kill you also, my father, since you sent him thither against his will with your own regiment. But I like him well, who is brave and who brought me good tidings that the Prince, my enemy, was dead of a broken heart. Moreover, I wish to have no quarrel with the White House (the English) on account of Macumazahn, so tell him that he may sleep in peace."

The messenger said further that Saduko, the husband of the King's daughter, Nandie, and Umbelazi's chief *induna*, was to be put upon his trial on the morrow before the King and his council, together with Mameena, daughter of Umbezi, and that my presence was desired at this trial.

I asked what was the charge against them. He replied that, so far as Saduko was concerned, there were two: first, that he had stirred up civil war in the land, and, secondly, that having pushed on Umbelazi into a fight in which many thousands perished, he had played the traitor, deserting him in the midst of the battle, with all his following—a very heinous offence in the eyes of Zulus, to whatever party they may belong.

Against Mameena there were three counts of indictment. First, that it was she who had poisoned Saduko's child and others, not Masapo, her first husband, who had suffered for that crime. Secondly, that she had deserted Saduko, her second husband, and gone to live with another man, namely, the late Prince Umbelazi. Thirdly, that she was a witch, who had enmeshed Umbelazi in the web of her sorceries and thereby caused him to aspire to the succession to the throne, to which he had no right, and made the *isililo*, or cry of mourning for the dead, to be heard in every *kraal* in Zululand.

"With three such pitfalls in her narrow path, Mameena will have to walk carefully if she would escape them all," I said.

---

1. On re-reading this history it comes back to me that she was the mother of M'tonga, who was much younger than Umbelazi.—*A. Q.*

"Yes, *Inkoosi*, especially as the pitfalls are dug from side to side of the path and have a pointed stake set at the bottom of each of them. Oh, Mameena is already as good as dead, as she deserves to be, who without doubt is the greatest *umtakati* north of the Tugela."

I sighed, for somehow I was sorry for Mameena, though why she should escape when so many better people had perished because of her I did not know; and the messenger went on:

"The Black One (that is, Panda) sent me to tell Saduko that he would be allowed to see you, Macumazahn, before the trial, if he wished, for he knew that you had been a friend of his, and thought that you might be able to give evidence in his favour."

"And what did Saduko say to that?" I asked.

"He said that he thanked the King, but that it was not needful for him to talk with Macumazahn, whose heart was white like his skin, and whose lips, if they spoke at all, would tell neither more nor less than the truth. The Princess Nandie, who is with him—for she will not leave him in his trouble, as all others have done—on hearing these words of Saduko's, said that they were true, and that for this reason, although you were her friend, she did not hold it necessary to see you either."

Upon this intimation I made no comment, but "my head thought," as the natives say, that Saduko's real reason for not wishing to see me was that he felt ashamed to do so, and Nandie's that she feared to learn more about her husband's perfidies than she knew already.

"With Mameena it is otherwise," went on the messenger, "for as soon as she was brought here with Zikali the Little and Wise, with whom, it seems, she has been sheltering, and learned that you, Macumazahn, were at the *kraal*, she asked leave to see you—"

"And is it granted?" I broke in hurriedly, for I did not at all wish for a private interview with Mameena.

"Nay, have no fear, *Inkoosi*," replied the messenger with a smile; "it is refused, because the King said that if once she saw you she would bewitch you and bring trouble on you, as she does on all men. It is for this reason that she is guarded by women only, no man being allowed to go near to her, for on women her witcheries will not bite. Still, they say that she is merry, and laughs and sings a great deal, declaring that her life has been dull up at old Zikali's, and that now she is going to a place as gay as the *veld* in spring, after the first warm rain, where there will be plenty of men to quarrel for her and make her great and happy. That is what she says, the witch who knows perhaps what the Place of Spirits is like."

Then, as I made no remarks or suggestions, the messenger departed, saying that he would return on the morrow to lead me to the place of trial.

Next morning, after the cows had been milked and the cattle loosed from their *kraals*, he came accordingly, with a guard of about thirty men, all of them soldiers who had survived the great fight of the Amawombe. These warriors, some of whom had wounds that were scarcely healed, saluted me with loud cries of "*Inkoosi*!" and *"Baba"* as I stepped out of the wagon, where I had spent a wretched night of unpleasant anticipation, showing me that there were at least some Zulus with whom I remained popular. Indeed, their delight at seeing me, whom they looked upon as a comrade and one of the few survivors of the great adventure, was quite touching. As we went, which we did slowly, their captain told me of their fears that I had been killed with the others, and how rejoiced they were when they learned that I was safe. He told me also that, after the third regiment had attacked them and broken up their ring, a small body of them, from eighty to a hundred only, managed to cut a way through and escape, running, not towards the Tugela, where so many thousands had perished, but up to Nodwengu, where they reported themselves to Panda as the only survivors of the Amawombe.

"And are you safe now?" I asked of the captain.

"Oh, yes," he answered. "You see, we were the King's men, not Umbelazi's, so Cetewayo bears us no grudge. Indeed, he is obliged to us, because we gave the Usutu their stomachs full of good fighting, which is more than did those cows of Umbelazi's. It is towards Saduko that he bears a grudge, for you know, my father, one should never pull a drowning man out of the stream—which is what Saduko did, for had it not been for his treachery, Cetewayo would have sunk beneath the water of Death—especially if it is only to spite a woman who hates him. Still, perhaps Saduko will escape with his life, because he is Nandie's husband, and Cetewayo fears Nandie, his sister, if he does not love her. But here we are, and those who have to watch the sky all day will be able to tell of the evening weather" (in other words, those who live will learn).

As he spoke we passed into the private enclosure of the *isigohlo*, outside of which a great many people were gathered, shouting, talking and quarrelling, for in those days all the usual discipline of the Great Place was relaxed. Within the fence, however, that was strongly guarded on its exterior side, were only about a score of councillors, the King, the Prince Cetewayo, who sat upon his right, the Princess Nandie, Saduko's wife, a few attendants, two great, silent fellows armed with clubs, whom I guessed to be executioners, and, seated in the shade in a corner, that ancient dwarf, Zikali, though how he came to be there I did not know.

Obviously the trial was to be quite a private affair, which accounted for the unusual presence of the two *slayers*. Even my Amawombe guard was left outside the gate, although I was significantly informed that if I chose to call upon them they would hear me, which was another way of saying that in such a small gathering I was absolutely safe.

Walking forward boldly towards Panda, who, though he was as fat as ever, looked very worn and much older than when I had last seen him, I made my bow, whereon he took my hand and asked after my health. Then I shook Cetewayo's hand also, as I saw that it was stretched out to me. He seized the opportunity to remark that he was told that I had suffered a knock on the head in some scrimmage down by the Tugela, and he hoped that I felt no ill effects. I answered: No, though I feared that there were a few others who had not been so fortunate, especially those who had stumbled against the Amawombe regiment, with whom I chanced to be travelling upon a peaceful mission of inquiry.

It was a bold speech to make, but I was determined to give him a quid pro quo, and, as a matter of fact, he took it in very good part, laughing heartily at the joke.

After this I saluted such of the councillors present as I knew, which was not many, for most of my old friends were dead, and sat down upon the stool that was placed for me not very far from the dwarf Zikali, who stared at me in a stony fashion, as though he had never seen me before.

There followed a pause. Then, at some sign from Panda, a side gate in the fence was opened, and through it appeared Saduko, who walked proudly to the space in front of the King, to whom he gave the salute of *Bayete*, and, at a sign, sat himself down upon the ground. Next, through the same gate, to which she was conducted by some women, came Mameena, quite unchanged and, I think, more beautiful than she had ever been. So lovely did she look, indeed, in her cloak of grey fur, her necklet of blue beads, and the gleaming rings of copper which she wore upon her wrists and ankles, that every eye was fixed upon her as she glided gracefully forward to make her obeisance to Panda.

This done, she turned and saw Nandie, to whom she also bowed, as she did so inquiring after the health of her child. Without waiting for an answer, which she knew would not be vouchsafed, she advanced to me and grasped my hand, which she pressed warmly, saying how glad she was to see me safe after going through so many dangers, though she thought I looked even thinner than I used to be.

Only of Saduko, who was watching her with his intent and melancholy eyes, she took no heed whatsoever. Indeed, for a while I thought that she could not have seen him. Nor did she appear to recognise Cetewayo, although he stared at her hard enough. But, as her glance fell upon the two executioners, I thought I saw her shudder like a shaken reed. Then she sat down in the place appointed to her, and the trial began.

The case of Saduko was taken first. An officer learned in Zulu law—which I can assure the reader is a very intricate and well-established law—I suppose that he might be called a kind of attorney-general, rose and stated the case against the prisoner. He told how Saduko, from a nobody, had been lifted to a great place by the King and given his daughter, the Princess Nandie, in marriage. Then he alleged that, as would be proved in evidence, the said Saduko had urged on Umbelazi the Prince, to whose party he had attached himself, to make war upon Cetewayo. This war having begun, at the great battle of Endondakusuka, he had treacherously deserted Umbelazi, together with three regiments under his command, and gone over to Cetewayo, thereby bringing Umbelazi to defeat and death.

This brief statement of the case for the prosecution being finished, Panda asked Saduko whether he pleaded guilty or not guilty.

"Guilty, O King," he answered, and was silent.

Then Panda asked him if he had anything to say in excuse of his conduct.

"Nothing, O King, except that I was Umbelazi's man, and when you, O King, had given the word that he and the Prince yonder might fight, I, like many others, some of whom are dead and some alive, worked for him with all my ten fingers that he might have the victory."

"Then why did you desert my son the Prince in the battle?" asked Panda.

"Because I saw that the Prince Cetewayo was the stronger bull and wished to be on the winning side, as all men do—for no other reason," answered Saduko calmly.

Now, everyone present stared, not excepting Cetewayo. Panda, who, like the rest of us, had heard a very different tale, looked extremely puzzled, while Zikali, in his corner, set up one of his great laughs.

After a long pause, at length the King, as supreme judge, began to pass sentence. At least, I suppose that was his intention, but before three words had left his lips Nandie rose and said:

"My Father, ere you speak that which cannot be unspoken, hear me. It is well known that Saduko, my husband, was my brother Umbelazi's general and councillor, and if he is to be killed for clinging to the Prince, then I should be killed also, and countless others in Zululand who still remain alive because they were not in or escaped the battle. It is well known also, my Father, that during that battle Saduko went over to my brother Cetewayo, though whether this brought about the defeat of Umbelazi I cannot say. Why did he go over? He tells you because he wished to be on the winning side. It is not true. He went over in order to be revenged upon Umbelazi, who had taken from him yonder witch"—and she pointed with her finger at Mameena—"yonder witch, whom he loved and still loves, and whom even now he would shield, even though to do so he must make his own name shameful. Saduko sinned; I do not deny it, my Father, but there sits the real traitress, red with the blood of Umbelazi and with that of thousands of others who have *tshonile'd* (gone down to keep him company among the ghosts). Therefore, O King, I beseech you, spare the life of Saduko, my husband, or, if he must die, learn that I, your daughter, will die with him. I have spoken, O King."

And very proudly and quietly she sat herself down again, waiting for the fateful words.

But those words were not spoken, since Panda only said: "Let us try the case of this woman, Mameena."

Thereon the law officer rose again and set out the charges against Mameena, namely, that it was she who had poisoned Saduko's child, and not Masapo; that, after marrying Saduko, she had deserted him and gone to live with the Prince Umbelazi; and that finally she had bewitched the said Umbelazi and caused him to make civil war in the land.

"The second charge, if proved, namely, that this woman deserted her husband for another man, is a crime of death," broke in Panda abruptly as the officer finished speaking; "therefore, what need is there to hear the first and the third until that is examined. What do you plead to that charge, woman?"

Now, understanding that the King did not wish to stir up these other matters of murder and witchcraft for some reason of his own, we all turned to hear Mameena's answer.

"O King," she said in her low, silvery voice, "I cannot deny that I left Saduko for Umbelazi the Handsome, any more than Saduko can deny that he left Umbelazi the beaten for Cetewayo the conqueror."

"Why did you leave Saduko?" asked Panda.

"O King, perhaps because I loved Umbelazi; for was he not called the Handsome? Also *you* know that the Prince, your son, was one to be loved." Here she paused, looking at poor Panda, who winced. "Or, perhaps, because I wished to be great; for was he not of the Blood Royal, and, had it not been for Saduko, would he not one day have been a king? Or, perhaps, because I could no longer bear the treatment that the Princess Nandie dealt out to me; she who was cruel to me and threatened to beat me, because Saduko loved my hut better than her own. Ask Saduko; he knows more of these matters than I do," and she gazed at him steadily. Then she went on: "How can a woman tell her reasons, O King, when she never knows them herself?"—a question at which some of her hearers smiled.

Now Saduko rose and said slowly:

"Hear me, O King, and I will give the reason that Mameena hides. She left me for Umbelazi because I bade her to do so, for I knew that Umbelazi desired her, and I wished to tie the cord tighter which bound me to one who at that time I thought would inherit the Throne. Also, I was weary of Mameena, who quarrelled night and day with the Princess Nandie, my *Inkosikazi*."

Now Nandie gasped in astonishment (and so did I), but Mameena laughed and said:

"Yes, O King, those were the two real reasons that I had forgotten. I left Saduko because he bade me, as he wished to make a present to the Prince. Also, he was tired of me; for many days at a time he would scarcely speak to me, because, however kind she might be, I could not help quarrelling with the Princess Nandie. Moreover, there was another reason which I have forgotten: I had no child, and not having any child I did not think it mattered whether I went or stayed. If Saduko searches, he will remember that I told him so, and that he agreed with me."

Again she looked at Saduko, who said hurriedly:

"Yes, yes, I told her so; I told her that I wished for no barren cows in my *kraal*."

Now some of the audience laughed outright, but Panda frowned.

"It seems," he said, "that my ears are being stuffed with lies, though which of these two tells them I cannot say. Well, if the woman left the man by his own wish, and that his ends might be furthered, as he says, he had put her away, and therefore the fault, if any, is his, not hers. So that charge is ended. Now, woman, what have you to tell us of the witchcraft which it is said you practised upon the Prince who is gone, thereby causing him to make war in the land?"

"Little that you would wish to hear, O King, or that it would be seemly for me to speak," she answered, drooping her head modestly. "The only witchcraft that ever I practised upon Umbelazi lies here"—and she touched her beautiful eyes—"and here"—and she touched her curving lips—"and in this poor shape of mine which some have thought so fair. As for the war, what had I to do with war, who never spoke to Umbelazi, who was so dear to me"—and she looked up with tears running down her face—"save of love? O King, is there a man among you all who would fear the witcheries of such a one as I; and because the Heavens made me beautiful with the beauty that men must follow, am I also to be killed as a sorceress?"

Now, to this argument neither Panda nor anyone else seemed to find an answer, especially as it was well known that Umbelazi had cherished his ambition to the succession long before he met Mameena. So that charge was dropped, and the first and greatest of the three proceeded with; namely, that it was she, Mameena, and not her husband, Masapo, who had murdered Nandie's child.

When this accusation was made against her, for the first time I saw a little shade of trouble flit across Mameena's soft eyes.

"Surely, O King," she said, "that matter was settled long ago, when the Ndwande, Zikali, the great *Nyanga*, smelt out Masapo the wizard, he who was my husband, and brought him to his death for this crime. Must I then be tried for it again?"

"Not so, woman," answered Panda. "All that Zikali smelt out was the poison that wrought the crime, and as some of that poison was found upon Masapo, he was killed as a wizard. Yet it may be that it was not he who used the poison."

"Then surely the King should have thought of that before he died," murmured Mameena. "But I forget: It is known that Masapo was always hostile to the House of Senzangakona."

To this remark Panda made no answer, perhaps because it was unanswerable, even in a land where it was customary to kill the supposed wizard first and inquire as to his actual guilt afterwards, or not at all. Or perhaps he thought it politic to ignore the suggestion that he had been inspired by personal enmity. Only, he looked at his daughter, Nandie, who rose and said:

"Have I leave to call a witness on this matter of the poison, my Father?"

Panda nodded, whereon Nandie said to one of the councillors:

"Be pleased to summon my woman, Nahana, who waits without."

The man went, and presently returned with an elderly female who, it appeared, had been Nandie's nurse, and, never having married, owing to some physical defect, had always remained in her service, a person well known and much respected in her humble walk of life.

"Nahana," said Nandie, "you are brought here that you may repeat to the King and his council a tale which you told to me as to the coming of a certain woman into my hut before the death of my first-born son, and what she did there. Say first, is this woman present here?"

"Aye, *Inkosazana*," answered Nahana, "yonder she sits. Who could mistake her?" and she pointed to Mameena, who was listening to every word intently, as a dog listens at the mouth of an ant-bear hole when the beast is stirring beneath.

"Then what of the woman and her deeds?" asked Panda.

"Only this, O King. Two nights before the child that is dead was taken ill, I saw Mameena creep into the hut of the lady Nandie, I who was asleep alone in a corner of the big hut out of reach of the light of the fire. At the time the lady Nandie was away from the hut with her son. Knowing the woman for Mameena, the wife of Masapo, who was on friendly terms with the *Inkosazana*, whom I supposed she had come to visit, I did not declare myself; nor did I take any particular note when I saw her sprinkle a little mat upon which the babe, Saduko's son, was wont to be laid, with some medicine, because I had heard her promise to the *Inkosazana* a powder which she said would drive away insects. Only, when I saw her throw some of this powder into the vessel of warm water that stood by the fire, to be used for the washing of the child, and place something, muttering certain words that I could not catch, in the straw of the doorway, I thought it strange, and was about to question her when she left the hut. As it happened, O King, but a little while afterwards, before one could count ten tens indeed, a messenger came to the hut to tell me that my old mother lay dying at her *kraal* four days' journey from Nodwengu, and prayed to see me before she died. Then I forgot all about Mameena and the powder, and, running out to seek the Princess Nandie, I craved her leave to go with the messenger to my mother's *kraal*, which she granted to me, saying that I need not return until my mother was buried.

"So I went. But, oh! my mother took long to die. Whole moons passed before I shut her eyes, and all this while she would not let me go; nor, indeed, did I wish to leave her whom I loved. At length it was over, and then came the days of mourning, and after those some more days of rest, and after them again the days of the division of the cattle, so that in the end six moons or more had gone by before I returned to the service of the Princess Nandie, and found that

Mameena was now the second wife of the lord Saduko. Also I found that the child of the lady Nandie was dead, and that Masapo, the first husband of Mameena, had been smelt out and killed as the murderer of the child. But as all these things were over and done with, and as Mameena was very kind to me, giving me gifts and sparing me tasks, and as I saw that Saduko my lord loved her much, it never came into my head to say anything of the matter of the powder that I saw her sprinkle on the mat.

"After she had run away with the Prince who is dead, however, I did tell the lady Nandie. Moreover, the lady Nandie, in my presence, searched in the straw of the doorway of the hut and found there, wrapped in soft hide, certain medicines such as the *Nyangas* sell, wherewith those who consult them can bewitch their enemies, or cause those whom they desire to love them or to hate their wives or husbands. That is all I know of the story, O King."

"Do my ears hear a true tale, Nandie?" asked Panda. "Or is this woman a liar like others?"

"I think not, my Father; see, here is the *muti* (medicine) which Nahana and I found hid in the doorway of the hut that I have kept unopened till this day."

And she laid on the ground a little leather bag, very neatly sewn with sinews, and fastened round its neck with a fibre string.

Panda directed one of the councillors to open the bag, which the man did unwillingly enough, since evidently he feared its evil influence, pouring out its contents on to the back of a hide shield, which was then carried round so that we might all look at them. These, so far as I could see, consisted of some withered roots, a small piece of human thigh bone, such as might have come from the skeleton of an infant, that had a little stopper of wood in its orifice, and what I took to be the fang of a snake.

Panda looked at them and shrank away, saying:

"Come hither, Zikali the Old, you who are skilled in magic, and tell us what is this medicine."

Then Zikali rose from the corner where he had been sitting so silently, and waddled heavily across the open space to where the shield lay in front of the King. As he passed Mameena, she bent down over the dwarf and began to whisper to him swiftly; but he placed his hands upon his big head, covering up his ears, as I suppose, that he might not hear her words.

"What have I to do with this matter, O King?" he asked.

"Much, it seems, O Opener-of-Roads," said Panda sternly, "seeing that you were the doctor who smelt out Masapo, and that it was in your *kraal* that yonder woman hid herself while her lover, the Prince, my son, who is dead, went down to the battle, and that she was brought thence with you. Tell us, now, the nature of this *muti*, and, being wise, as you are, be careful to tell us truly, lest it should be said, O Zikali, that you are not a *Nyanga* only, but an *umtakati* as well. For then," he added with meaning, and choosing his words carefully, "perchance, O Zikali, I might be tempted to make trial of whether or no it is true that you cannot be killed like other men, especially as I have heard of late that your heart is evil towards me and my House."

For a moment Zikali hesitated—I think to give his quick brain time to work, for he saw his great danger. Then he laughed in his dreadful fashion and said:

"Oho! the King thinks that the otter is in the trap," and he glanced at the fence of the *isigohlo* and at the fierce executioners, who stood watching him sternly. "Well, many times before has this otter seemed to be in a trap, yes, ere your father saw light, O Son of Senzangakona, and after it also. Yet here he stands living. Make no trial, O King, of whether or no I be mortal, lest if Death should come to such a one as I, he should take many others with him also. Have you not heard the saying that when the Opener-of-Roads comes to the end of his road there will be no more a King of the Zulus, as when he began his road there was no King of the Zulus, since the days of his manhood are the days of *all* the Zulu kings?"

Thus he spoke, glaring at Panda and at Cetewayo, who shrank before his gaze.

"Remember," he went on, "that the Black One who is 'gone down' long ago, the Wild Beast who fathered the Zulu herd, threatened him whom he named the 'Thing-that-should-not-have-been-born,' aye, and slew those whom he loved, and afterwards was slain by others, who also are 'gone down,' and that you alone, O Panda, did not threaten him, and that you alone, O Panda, have not been slain. Now, if you would make trial of whether I die as other men die, bid your dogs fall on, for Zikali is ready," and he folded his arms and waited.

Indeed, all of us waited breathlessly, for we understood that the terrible dwarf was matching himself against Panda and Cetewayo and defying them both. Presently it became obvious that he had won the game, since Panda only said:

"Why should I slay one whom I have befriended in the past, and why do you speak such heavy words of death in my ears, O, Zikali the

Wise, which of late have heard so much of death?" He sighed, adding: "Be pleased now, to tell us of this medicine, or, if you will not, go, and I will send for other *Nyangas*."

"Why should I not tell you, when you ask me softly and without threats, O King? See"—and Zikali took up some of the twisted roots—"these are the roots of a certain poisonous herb that blooms at night on the tops of mountains, and woe be to the ox that eats thereof. They have been boiled in gall and blood, and ill will befall the hut in which they are hidden by one who can speak the words of power. This is the bone of a babe that has never lived to cut its teeth—I think of a babe that was left to die alone in the bush because it was hated, or because none would father it. Such a bone has strength to work ill against other babes; moreover, it is filled with a charmed medicine. Look!" and, pulling out the plug of wood, he scattered some grey powder from the bone, then stopped it up again. "This," he added, picking up the fang, "is the tooth of a deadly serpent, that, after it has been doctored, is used by women to change the heart of a man from another to herself. I have spoken."

And he turned to go.

"Stay!" said the King. "Who set these foul charms in the doorway of Saduko's hut?"

"How can I tell, O King, unless I make preparation and cast the bones and smell out the evil-doer? You have heard the story of the woman Nahana. Accept it or reject it as your heart tells you."

"If that story be true, O Zikali, how comes it that you yourself smelt out, not Mameena, the wife of Masapo, but Masapo, her husband, himself, and caused him to be slain because of the poisoning of the child of Nandie?"

"You err, O King. I, Zikali, smelt out the House of Masapo. Then I smelt out the poison, searching for it first in the hair of Mameena, and finding it in the *kaross* of Masapo. I never smelt out that it was Masapo who gave the poison. That was the judgment of you and of your Council, O King. Nay, I knew well that there was more in the matter, and had you paid me another fee and bade me to continue to use my wisdom, without doubt I should have found this magic stuff hidden in the hut, and mayhap have learned the name of the hider. But I was weary, who am very old; and what was it to me if you chose to kill Masapo or chose to let him go? Masapo, who, being your secret enemy, was a man who deserved to die—if not for this matter, then for others."

Now, all this while I had been watching Mameena, who sat, in the

Zulu fashion, listening to this deadly evidence, a slight smile upon her face, and without attempting any interruption or comment. Only I saw that while Zikali was examining the medicine, her eyes were seeking the eyes of Saduko, who remained in his place, also silent, and, to all appearance, the least interested of anyone present. He tried to avoid her glance, turning his head uneasily; but at length her eyes caught his and held them. Then his heart began to beat quickly, his breast heaved, and on his face there grew a look of dreamy content, even of happiness. From that moment forward, till the end of the scene, Saduko never took his eyes off this strange woman, though I think that, with the exception of the dwarf, Zikali, who saw everything, and of myself, who am trained to observation, none noted this curious by-play of the drama.

The King began to speak. "Mameena," he said, "you have heard. Have you aught to say? For if not it would seem that you are a witch and a murderess, and one who must die."

"Yea, a little word, O King," she answered quietly. "Nahana speaks truth. It is true that I entered the hut of Nandie and set the medicine there. I say it because by nature I am not one who hides the truth or would attempt to throw discredit even upon a humble serving-woman," and she glanced at Nahana.

"Then from between your own teeth it is finished," said Panda.

"Not altogether, O King. I have said that I set the medicine in the hut. I have not said, and I will not say, how and why I set it there. That tale I call upon Saduko yonder to tell to you, he who was my husband, that I left for Umbelazi, and who, being a man, must therefore hate me. By the words he says I will abide. If he declares that I am guilty, then I am guilty, and prepared to pay the price of guilt. But if he declares that I am innocent, then, O King and O Prince Cetewayo, without fear I trust myself to your justness. Now speak, O Saduko; speak the whole truth, whatever it may be, if that is the King's will."

"It is my will," said Panda.

"And mine also," added Cetewayo, who, I could see, like everyone else, was much interested in this matter.

Saduko rose to his feet, the same Saduko that I had always known, and yet so changed. All the life and fire had gone from him; his pride in himself was no more; none could have known him for that ambitious, confident man who, in his day of power, the Zulus named the Self-Eater. He was a mere mask of the old Saduko, informed by some new, some alien, spirit. With dull, lack-lustre eyes fixed always upon the lovely eyes of Mameena, in slow and hesitating tones he began his tale.

"It is true, O Lion," he said, "that Mameena spread the poison upon my child's mat. It is true that she set the deadly charms in the doorway of Nandie's hut. These things she did, not knowing what she did, and it was I who instructed her to do them. This is the case. From the beginning I have always loved Mameena as I have loved no other woman and as no other woman was ever loved. But while I was away with Macumazahn, who sits yonder, to destroy Bangu, chief of the Amakoba, he who had killed my father, Umbezi, the father of Mameena, he whom the Prince Cetewayo gave to the vultures the other day because he had lied as to the death of Umbelazi, he, I say, forced Mameena, against her will, to marry Masapo the Boar, who afterwards was executed for wizardry. Now, here at your feast, when you reviewed the people of the Zulus, O King, after you had given me the lady Nandie as wife, Mameena and I met again and loved each other more than we had ever done before. But, being an upright woman, Mameena thrust me away from her, saying:

"'I have a husband, who, if he is not dear to me, still is my husband, and while he lives to him I will be true.' Then, O King, I took counsel with the evil in my heart, and made a plot in myself to be rid of the Boar, Masapo, so that when he was dead I might marry Mameena. This was the plot that I made—that my son and Princess Nandie's should be poisoned, and that Masapo should seem to poison him, so that he might be killed as a wizard and I marry Mameena."

Now, at this astounding statement, which was something beyond the experience of the most cunning and cruel savage present there, a gasp of astonishment went up from the audience; even old Zikali lifted his head and stared. Nandie, too, shaken out of her usual calm, rose as though to speak; then, looking first at Saduko and next at Mameena, sat herself down again and waited. But Saduko went on again in the same cold, measured voice:

"I gave Mameena a powder which I had bought for two heifers from a great doctor who lived beyond the Tugela, but who is now dead, which powder I told her was desired by Nandie, my *Inkosikazi*, to destroy the little beetles than ran about the hut, and directed her where she was to spread it. Also, I gave her the bag of medicine, telling her to thrust it into the doorway of the hut, that it might bring a blessing upon my House. These things she did ignorantly to please me, not knowing that the powder was poison, not knowing that the medicine was bewitched. So my child died, as I wished it to die, and, indeed, I myself fell sick because by accident I touched the powder.

"Afterwards Masapo was smelt out as a wizard by old Zikali, I having caused a bag of the poison to be sewn in his *kaross* in order to deceive Zikali, and killed by your order, O King, and Mameena was given to me as a wife, also by your order, O King, which was what I desired. Later on, as I have told you, I wearied of her, and wishing to please the Prince who has wandered away, I commanded her to yield herself to him, which Mameena did out of her love for me and to advance my fortunes, she who is blameless in all things."

Saduko finished speaking and sat down again, as an automaton might do when a wire is pulled, his lack-lustre eyes still fixed upon Mameena's face.

"You have heard, O King," said Mameena. "Now pass judgment, knowing that, if it be your will, I am ready to die for Saduko's sake."

But Panda sprang up in a rage.

"Take him away!" he said, pointing to Saduko. "Take away that dog who is not fit to live, a dog who eats his own child that thereby he may cause another to be slain unjustly and steal his wife."

The executioners leapt forward, and, having something to say, for I could bear this business no longer, I began to rise to my feet. Before I gained them, however, Zikali was speaking.

"O King," he said, "it seems that you have killed one man unjustly on this matter, namely, Masapo. Would you do the same by another?" and he pointed to Saduko.

"What do you mean?" asked Panda angrily. "Have you not heard this low fellow, whom I made great, giving him the rule over tribes and my daughter in marriage, confess with his own lips that he murdered his child, the child of my blood, in order that he might eat a fruit which grew by the roadside for all men to nibble at?" and he glared at Mameena.

"Aye, Child of Senzangakona," answered Zikali, "I heard Saduko say this with his own lips, but the voice that spoke from the lips was not the voice of Saduko, as, were you a skilled *Nyanga* like me, you would have known as well as I do, and as well as does the white man, Watcher-by-Night, who is a reader of hearts.

"Hearken now, O King, and you great ones around the King, and I will tell you a story. Matiwane, the father of Saduko, was my friend, as he was yours, O King, and when Bangu slew him and his people, by leave of the Wild Beast (Chaka), I saved the child, his son, aye, and brought him up in my own House, having learned to love him. Then, when he became a man, I, the Opener-of-Roads, showed him two roads, down either of which he might choose to walk—the Road of Wisdom and the Road of War and Women: the white road that runs through peace to knowledge, and the red road that runs through blood to death.

"But already there stood one upon this red road who beckoned him, she who sits yonder, and he followed after her, as I knew he would. From the beginning she was false to him, taking a richer man for her husband. Then, when Saduko grew great, she grew sorry, and came to ask my counsel as to how she might be rid of Masapo, whom she swore she hated. I told her that she could leave him for another man, or wait till her Spirit moved him from her path; but I never put evil into her heart, seeing that it was there already.

"Then she and no other, having first made Saduko love her more than ever, murdered the child of Nandie, his *Inkosikazi*; and so brought about the death of Masapo and crept into Saduko's arms. Here she slept a while, till a new shadow fell upon her, that of the 'Elephant-with-the-tuft-of-hair,' who will walk the woods no more. Him she beguiled that she might grow great the quicker, and left the house of Saduko, taking his heart with her, she who was destined to be the doom of men.

"Now, into Saduko's breast, where his heart had been, entered an evil spirit of jealousy and of revenge, and in the battle of Endondakusuka that spirit rode him as a white man rides a horse. As he had arranged to do with the Prince Cetewayo yonder—nay, deny it not, O Prince, for I know all; did you not make a bargain together, on the third night before the battle, among the bushes, and start apart when the buck leapt out between you?" (Here Cetewayo, who had been about to speak, threw the corner of his *kaross* over his face.) "As he had arranged to do, I say, he went over with his regiments from the Isigqosa to the Usutu, and so brought about the fall of Umbelazi and the death of many thousands. Yes, and this he did for one reason only—because yonder woman had left him for the Prince, and he cared more for her than for all the world could give him, for her who had filled him with madness as a bowl is filled with milk. And now, O King, you have heard this man tell you a story, you have heard him shout out that he is viler than any man in all the land; that he murdered his own child, the child he loved so well, to win this witch; that afterwards he gave her to his friend and lord to buy more of his favour, and that lastly he deserted that lord because he thought that there was another lord from whom he could buy more favour. Is it not so, O King?"

"It is so," answered Panda, "and therefore must Saduko be thrown out to the jackals."

"Wait a while, O King. I say that Saduko has spoken not with his own voice, but with the voice of Mameena. I say that she is the greatest witch in all the land, and that she has drugged him with the medicine of her eyes, so that he knows not what he says, even as she drugged the Prince who is dead."

"Then prove it, or he dies!" exclaimed the King.

Now the dwarf went to Panda and whispered in his ear, whereon Panda whispered in turn into the ears of two of his councillors. These men, who were unarmed, rose and made as though to leave the *isigohlo*. But as they passed Mameena one of them suddenly threw his arms about her, pinioning her arms, the other tearing off the *kaross* he wore—for the weather was cold—flung it over her head and knotted it behind her so that she was hidden except for her ankles and feet. Then, although she did not move or struggle, they caught hold of her and stood still.

Now Zikali hobbled to Saduko and bade him rise, which he did. Then he looked at him for a long while and made certain movements with his hands before his face, after which Saduko uttered a great sigh and stared about him.

"Saduko," said Zikali, "I pray you tell me, your foster-father, whether it is true, as men say, that you sold your wife, Mameena, to the Prince Umbelazi in order that his favour might fall on you like heavy rain?"

"Wow! Zikali," said Saduko, with a start of rage, "If were you as others are I would kill you, you toad, who dare to spit slander on my name. She ran away with the Prince, having beguiled him with the magic of her beauty."

"Strike me not, Saduko," went on Zikali, "or at least wait to strike until you have answered one more question. Is it true, as men say, that in the battle of Endondakusuka you went over to the Usutu with your regiments because you thought that Indhlovu-ene-Sihlonti would be beaten, and wished to be on the side of him who won?"

"What, Toad! More slander?" cried Saduko. "I went over for one reason only—to be revenged upon the Prince because he had taken from me her who was more to me than life or honour. Aye, and when I went over Umbelazi was winning; it was because I went that he lost and died, as I meant that he should die, though now," he added sadly, "I would that I had not brought him to ruin and the dust, who think that, like myself, he was but wet clay in a woman's fingers.

"O King," he added, turning to Panda, "kill me, I pray you, who am not worthy to live, since to him whose hand is red with the blood of his friend, death alone is left, who, while he breathes, must share his sleep with ghosts that watch him with their angry eyes."

Then Nandie sprang up and said:

"Nay, Father, listen not to him who is mad, and therefore holy.[2] What he has done, he has done, who, as he has said, was but a tool in another's hand. As for our babe, I know well that he would have died sooner than harm it, for he loved it much, and when it was taken away, for three whole days and nights he wept and would touch no food. Give this poor man to me, my Father—to me, his wife, who loves him—and let us go hence to some other land, where perchance we may forget."

"Be silent, daughter," said the King; "and you, O Zikali, the *Nyanga*, be silent also."

They obeyed, and, after thinking awhile, Panda made a motion with his hand, whereon the two councillors lifted the *kaross* from off Mameena, who looked about her calmly and asked if she were taking part in some child's game.

"Aye, woman," answered Panda, "you are taking part in a great game, but not, I think, such as is played by children—a game of life and death. Now, have you heard the tale of Zikali the Little and Wise, and the words of Saduko, who was once your husband, or must they be repeated to you?"

"There is no need, O King; my ears are too quick to be muffled by a fur bag, and I would not waste your time."

"Then what have you to say, woman?"

"Not much," she answered with a shrug of her shoulders, "except that I have lost in this game. You will not believe me, but if you had left me alone I should have told you so, who did not wish to see that poor fool, Saduko, killed for deeds he had never done. Still, the tale he told you was not told because I had bewitched him; it was told for love of me, whom he desired to save. It was Zikali yonder; Zikali, the enemy of your house, who in the end will destroy your House, O Son of Senzangakona, that bewitched him, as he has bewitched you all, and forced the truth out of his unwilling heart.

"Now, what more is there to say? Very little, as I think. I did the things that are laid to my charge, and worse things which have not been stated. Oh, I played for great stakes, I, who meant to be the *Inkosazana* of the Zulus, and, as it chances, by the weight of a hair I have lost. I thought that I had counted everything, but the hair's

2. The Zulus suppose that insane people are inspired.—*A. Q.*

weight which turned the balance against me was the mad jealousy of this fool, Saduko, upon which I had not reckoned. I see now that when I left Saduko I should have left him dead. Thrice I had thought of it. Once I mixed the poison in his drink, and then he came in, weary with his plottings, and kissed me ere he drank; and my woman's heart grew soft and I overset the bowl that was at his lips. Do you not remember, Saduko?

"So, so! For that folly alone I deserve to die, for she who would reign"—and her beautiful eyes flashed royally—"must have a tiger's heart, not that of a woman. Well, because I was too kind I must die; and, after all is said, it is well to die, who go hence awaited by thousands upon thousands that I have sent before me, and who shall be greeted presently by your son, Indhlovu-ene-Sihlonti, and his warriors, greeted as the *Inkosazana* of Death, with red, lifted spears and with the royal salute!

"Now, I have spoken. Walk your little road, O King and Prince and Councillors, till you reach the gulf into which I sink, that yawns for all of you. O King, when you meet me again at the bottom of that gulf, what a tale you will have to tell me, you who are but the shadow of a king, you whose heart henceforth must be eaten out by a worm that is called Love-of-the-Lost. O Prince and Conqueror Cetewayo, what a tale you will have to tell me when I greet you at the bottom of that gulf, you who will bring your nation to a wreck and at last die as I must die—only the servant of others and by the will of others. Nay, ask me not how. Ask old Zikali, my master, who saw the beginning of your House and will see its end. Oh, yes, as you say, I am a witch, and I know, I know! Come, I am spent. You men weary me, as men have always done, being but fools whom it is so easy to make drunk, and who when drunk are so unpleasing. Piff! I am tired of you sober and cunning, and I am tired of you drunken and brutal, you who, after all, are but beasts of the field to whom Mvelingangi, the Creator, has given heads which can think, but which always think wrong.

"Now, King, before you unchain your dogs upon me, I ask one moment. I said that I hated all men, yet, as you know, no woman can tell the truth—quite. There is a man whom I do not hate, whom I never hated, whom I think I love because he would not love me. He sits there," and to my utter dismay, and the intense interest of that company, she pointed at me, Allan Quatermain!

"Well, once by my 'magic,' of which you have heard so much, I got the better of this man against his will and judgment, and, because of that soft heart of mine, I let him go; yes, I let the rare fish go when he was on my hook. It is well that I should have let him go, since, had I kept him, a fine story would have been spoiled and I should have become nothing but a white hunter's servant, to be thrust away behind the door when the white *Inkosikazi* came to eat his meat—I, Mameena, who never loved to stand out of sight behind a door. Well, when he was at my feet and I spared him, he made me a promise, a very small promise, which yet I think he will keep now when we part for a little while. Macumazahn, did you not promise to kiss me once more upon the lips whenever and wherever I should ask you?"

"I did," I answered in a hollow voice, for in truth her eyes held me as they had held Saduko.

"Then come now, Macumazahn, and give me that farewell kiss. The King will permit it, and since I have now no husband, who take Death to husband, there is none to say you nay."

I rose. It seemed to me that I could not help myself. I went to her, this woman surrounded by implacable enemies, this woman who had played for great stakes and lost them, and who knew so well how to lose. I stood before her, ashamed and yet not ashamed, for something of her greatness, evil though it might be, drove out my shame, and I knew that my foolishness was lost in a vast tragedy.

Slowly she lifted her languid arm and threw it about my neck; slowly she bent her red lips to mine and kissed me, once upon the mouth and once upon the forehead. But between those two kisses she did a thing so swiftly that my eyes could scarcely follow what she did. It seemed to me that she brushed her left hand across her lips, and that I saw her throat rise as though she swallowed something. Then she thrust me from her, saying:

"Farewell, O Macumazana, you will never forget this kiss of mine; and when we meet again we shall have much to talk of, for between now and then your story will be long. Farewell, Zikali. I pray that all your plannings may succeed, since those you hate are those I hate, and I bear you no grudge because you told the truth at last. Farewell, Prince Cetewayo. You will never be the man your brother would have been, and your lot is very evil, you who are doomed to pull down a House built by One who was great. Farewell, Saduko the fool, who threw away your fortune for a woman's eyes, as though the world were not full of women. Nandie the Sweet and the Forgiving will nurse you well until your haunted end. Oh! why does Umbelazi lean over your shoulder, Saduko, and look at me so strangely? Farewell, Panda the Shadow. Now let loose your slayers. Oh! let them loose swiftly, lest they should be balked of my blood!"

Panda lifted his hand and the executioners leapt forward, but ere ever they reached her, Mameena shivered, threw wide her arms and fell back—dead. The poisonous drug she had taken worked well and swiftly.

Such was the end of Mameena, Child of Storm.

A deep silence followed, a silence of awe and wonderment, till suddenly it was broken by a sound of dreadful laughter. It came from the lips of Zikali the Ancient, Zikali, the "Thing-that-should-never-have-been-born."

CHAPTER 16

Mameena—Mameena—Mameena!

That evening at sunset, just as I was about to trek, for the King had given me leave to go, and at that time my greatest desire in life seemed to be to bid good-bye to Zululand and the Zulus—I saw a strange, beetle-like shape hobbling up the hill towards me, supported by two big men. It was Zikali.

He passed me without a word, merely making a motion that I was to follow him, which I did out of curiosity, I suppose, for Heaven knows I had seen enough of the old wizard to last me for a lifetime. He reached a flat stone about a hundred yards above my camp, where there was no bush in which anyone could hide, and sat himself down, pointing to another stone in front of him, on which I sat myself down. Then the two men retired out of earshot, and, indeed, of sight, leaving us quite alone.

"So you are going away, O Macumazana?" he said.

"Yes, I am," I answered with energy, "who, if I could have had my will, would have gone away long ago."

"Yes, yes, I know that; but it would have been a great pity, would it not? If you had gone, Macumazahn, you would have missed seeing the end of a strange little story, and you, who love to study the hearts of men and women, would not have been so wise as you are to-day."

"No, nor as sad, Zikali. Oh! the death of that woman!" And I put my hand before my eyes.

"Ah! I understand, Macumazahn; you were always fond of her, were you not, although your white pride would not suffer you to admit that black fingers were pulling at your heartstrings? She was a wonderful witch, was Mameena; and there is this comfort for you—that she pulled at other heartstrings as well. Masapo's, for instance; Saduko's, for instance; Umbelazi's, for instance, none of whom got any luck from her pulling—yes, and even at mine."

Now, as I did not think it worth while to contradict his nonsense so far as I was concerned personally, I went off on this latter point.

"If you show affection as you did towards Mameena to-day, Zikali, I pray my Spirit that you may cherish none for me," I said.

He shook his great head pityingly as he answered:

"Did you never love a lamb and kill it afterwards when you were hungry, or when it grew into a ram and butted you, or when it drove away your other sheep, so that they fell into the hands of thieves? Now, I am very hungry for the fall of the House of Senzangakona, and the lamb, Mameena, having grown big, nearly laid me on my back to-day within the reach of the slayer's spear. Also, she was hunting my sheep, Saduko, into an evil net whence he could never have escaped. So, somewhat against my will, I was driven to tell the truth of that lamb and her tricks."

"I daresay," I exclaimed; "but, at any rate, she is done with, so what is the use of talking about her?"

"Ah! Macumazahn, she is done with, or so you think, though that is a strange saying for a white man who believes in much that we do not know; but at least her work remains, and it has been a great work. Consider now. Umbelazi and most of the princes, and thousands upon thousands of the Zulus, whom I, the *Dwande*, hate, dead, dead! *Mameena's work*, Macumazahn! Panda's hand grown strengthless with sorrow and his eyes blind with tears. *Mameena's work*, Macumazahn! Cetewayo, king in all but name; Cetewayo, who shall bring the House of Senzangakona to the dust. *Mameena's work*, Macumazahn! Oh! a mighty work. Surely she has lived a great and worthy life, and she died a great and worthy death! And how well she did it! Had you eyes to see her take the poison which I gave her—a good poison, was it not?—between her kisses, Macumazahn?"

"I believe it was your work, and not hers," I blurted out, ignoring his mocking questions. "You pulled the strings; you were the wind that caused the grass to bend till the fire caught it and set the town in flames—the town of your foes."

"How clever you are, Macumazahn! If your wits grow so sharp, one day they will cut your throat, as, indeed, they have nearly done several times already. Yes, yes, I know how to pull strings till the trap falls, and to blow grass until the flame catches it, and how to puff at that flame until it burns the House of Kings. And yet this trap would have fallen without me, only then it might have snared other rats; and this grass would have caught fire if I had not blown, only then it might have burnt another House. I did not make these forces,

Macumazahn; I did but guide them towards a great end, for which the White House (that is, the English) should thank me one day." He brooded a while, then went on: "But what need is there to talk to you of these matters, Macumazahn, seeing that in a time to come you will have your share in them and see them for yourself? After they are finished, then we will talk."

"I do not wish to talk of them," I answered. "I have said so already. But for what other purpose did you take the trouble to come here?"

"Oh, to bid you farewell for a little while, Macumazahn. Also to tell you that Panda, or rather Cetewayo, for now Panda is but his voice, since the Head must go where the Feet carry it, has spared Saduko at the prayer of Nandie and banished him from the land, giving him his cattle and any people who care to go with him to wherever he may choose to live from henceforth. At least, Cetewayo says it was at Nandie's prayer, and at mine and yours, but what he means is that, after all that has happened, he thought it wise that Saduko should die of himself."

"Do you mean that he should kill himself, Zikali?"

"No, no; I mean that his own *idhlozi*, his Spirit, should be left to kill him, which it will do in time. You see, Macumazahn, Saduko is now living with a ghost, which he calls the ghost of Umbelazi, whom he betrayed."

"Is that your way of saying he is mad, Zikali?"

"Oh, yes, he lives with a ghost, or the ghost lives in him, or he is mad—call it which you will. The mad have a way of living with ghosts, and ghosts have a way of sharing their food with the mad. Now you understand everything, do you not?"

"Of course," I answered; "it is as plain as the sun."

"Oh! did I not say you were clever, Macumazahn, you who know where madness ends and ghosts begin, and why they are just the same thing? Well, the sun is no longer plain. Look, it has sunk; and you would be on your road who wish to be far from Nodwengu before morning. You will pass the plain of Endondakusuka, will you not, and cross the Tugela by the drift? Have a look round, Macumazahn, and see if you can recognise any old friends. Umbezi, the knave and traitor, for instance; or some of the princes. If so, I should like to send them a message. What! You cannot wait? Well, then, here is a little present for you, some of my own work. Open it when it is light again, Macumazahn; it may serve to remind you of the strange little tale of Mameena with the Heart of Fire. I wonder where she is now? Sometimes, sometimes—" And he rolled his great eyes about him and sniffed at the air like a hound. "Farewell till we meet again. Farewell, Macumazahn. Oh! if you had only run away with Mameena, how different things might have been to-day!"

I jumped up and fled from that terrible old dwarf, whom I verily believe—No; where is the good of my saying what I believe? I fled from him, leaving him seated on the stone in the shadows, and as I fled, out of the darkness behind me there arose the sound of his loud and eerie laughter.

Next morning I opened the packet which he had given me, after wondering once or twice whether I should not thrust it down an ant-bear hole as it was. But this, somehow, I could not find the heart to do, though now I wish I had. Inside, cut from the black core of the umzimbiti wood, with just a little of the white sap left on it to mark the eyes, teeth and nails, was a likeness of Mameena. Of course, it was rudely executed, but it was—or rather is, for I have it still—a wonderfully good portrait of her, for whether Zikali was or was not a wizard, he was certainly a good artist. There she stands, her body a little bent, her arms outstretched, her head held forward with the lips parted, just as though she were about to embrace somebody, and in one of her hands, cut also from the white sap of the umzimbiti, she grasps a human heart—Saduko's, I presume, or perhaps Umbelazi's.

Nor was this all, for the figure was wrapped in a woman's hair, which I knew at once for that of Mameena, this hair being held in place by the necklet of big blue beads she used to wear about her throat.

* * * * * * * *

Some five years had gone by, during which many things had happened to me that need not be recorded here, when one day I found myself in a rather remote part of the Umvoti district of Natal, some miles to the east of a mountain called the Eland's Kopje, whither I had gone to carry out a big deal in *mealies*, over which, by the way, I lost a good bit of money. That has always been my fate when I plunged into commercial ventures.

One night my wagons, which were overloaded with these confounded weevilly *mealies*, got stuck in the drift of a small tributary of the Tugela that most inopportunely had come down in flood. Just as darkness fell I managed to get them up the bank in the midst of a pelting rain that soaked me to the bone. There seemed to be no prospect of lighting a fire or of obtaining any decent food, so I was about to go to bed supperless when a flash of lightning showed me a large *kraal* situated upon a hillside about half a mile away, and an idea entered my mind.

"Who is the headman of that *kraal*?" I asked of one of the *Kafirs* who had collected round us in our trouble, as such idle fellows always do.

"Tshoza, *Inkoosi*," answered the man.

"Tshoza! Tshoza!" I said, for the name seemed familiar to me. "Who is Tshoza?"

"*Ikona* (I don't know), *Inkoosi*. He came from Zululand some years ago with Saduko the Mad."

Then, of course, I remembered at once, and my mind flew back to the night when old Tshoza, the brother of Matiwane, Saduko's father, had cut out the cattle of the Bangu and we had fought the battle in the pass.

"Oh!" I said, "is it so? Then lead me to Tshoza, and I will give you a 'Scotchman.'" (That is, a two-shilling piece, so called because some enterprising emigrant from Scotland passed off a vast number of them among the simple natives of Natal as substitutes for half-crowns.)

Tempted by this liberal offer—and it was very liberal, because I was anxious to get to Tshoza's *kraal* before its inhabitants went to bed—the meditative *Kafir* consented to guide me by a dark and devious path that ran through bush and dripping fields of corn. At length we arrived—for if the *kraal* was only half a mile away, the path to it covered fully two miles—and glad enough was I when we had waded the last stream and found ourselves at its gate.

In response to the usual inquiries, conducted amid a chorus of yapping dogs, I was informed that Tshoza did not live there, but somewhere else; that he was too old to see anyone; that he had gone to sleep and could not be disturbed; that he was dead and had been buried last week, and so forth.

"Look here, my friend," I said at last to the fellow who was telling me all these lies, "you go to Tshoza in his grave and say to him that if he does not come out alive instantly, Macumazahn will deal with his cattle as once he dealt with those of Bangu."

Impressed with the strangeness of this message, the man departed, and presently, in the dim light of the rain-washed moon, I perceived a little old man running towards me; for Tshoza, who was pretty ancient at the beginning of this history, had not been made younger by a severe wound at the battle of the Tugela and many other troubles.

"Macumazahn," he said, "is that really you? Why, I heard that you were dead long ago; yes, and sacrificed an ox for the welfare of your Spirit."

"And ate it afterwards, I'll be bound," I answered.

"Oh! it must be you," he went on, "who cannot be deceived, for it is true we ate that ox, combining the sacrifice to your Spirit with a feast; for why should anything be wasted when one is poor? Yes,

yes, it must be you, for who else would come creeping about a man's *kraal* at night, except the Watcher-by-Night? Enter, Macumazahn, and be welcome."

So I entered and ate a good meal while we talked over old times.

"And now, where is Saduko?" I asked suddenly as I lit my pipe.

"Saduko?" he answered, his face changing as he spoke. "Oh! of course he is here. You know I came away with him from Zululand. Why? Well, to tell the truth, because after the part we had played—against my will, Macumazahn—at the battle of Endondakusuka, I thought it safer to be away from a country where those who have worn their *karosses* inside out find many enemies and few friends."

"Quite so," I said. "But about Saduko?"

"Oh, I told you, did I not? He is in the next hut, and dying!"

"Dying! What of, Tshoza?"

"I don't know," he answered mysteriously; "but I think he must be bewitched. For a long while, a year or more, he has eaten little and cannot bear to be alone in the dark; indeed, ever since he left Zululand he has been very strange and moody."

Now I remembered what old Zikali had said to me years before to the effect that Saduko was living with a ghost which would kill him.

"Does he think much about Umbelazi, Tshoza?" I asked.

"O Macumazana, he thinks of nothing else; the Spirit of Umbelazi is in him day and night."

"Indeed," I said. "Can I see him?"

"I don't know, Macumazahn. I will go and ask the lady Nandie at once, for, if you can, I believe there is no time to lose." And he left the hut.

Ten minutes later he returned with a woman, Nandie the Sweet herself, the same quiet, dignified Nandie whom I used to know, only now somewhat worn with trouble and looking older than her years.

"Greeting, Macumazahn," she said. "I am pleased to see you, although it is strange, very strange, that you should come here just at this time. Saduko is leaving us—on a long journey, Macumazahn."

I answered that I had heard so with grief, and wondered whether he would like to see me.

"Yes, very much, Macumazahn; only be prepared to find him different from the Saduko whom you knew. Be pleased to follow me."

So we went out of Tshoza's hut, across a courtyard to another large hut, which we entered. It was lit with a good lamp of European make; also a bright fire burned upon the hearth, so that the place was as light as day. At the side of the hut a man lay upon some blankets, watched by a woman. His eyes were covered with his hand, and he was moaning:

"Drive him away! Drive him away! Cannot he suffer me to die in peace?"

"Would you drive away your old friend, Macumazahn, Saduko?" asked Nandie very gently, "Macumazahn, who has come from far to see you?"

He sat up, and, the blankets falling off him, showed me that he was nothing but a living skeleton. Oh! how changed from that lithe and handsome chief whom I used to know. Moreover, his lips quivered and his eyes were full of terrors.

"Is it really you, Macumazahn?" he said in a weak voice. "Come, then, and stand quite close to me, so that he may not get between us," and he stretched out his bony hand.

I took the hand; it was icy cold.

"Yes, yes, it is I, Saduko," I said in a cheerful voice; "and there is no man to get between us; only the lady Nandie, your wife, and myself are in the hut; she who watched you has gone."

"Oh, no, Macumazahn, there is another in the hut whom you cannot see. There he stands," and he pointed towards the hearth. "Look! The spear is through him and his plume lies on the ground!"

"Through whom, Saduko?"

"Whom? Why, the Prince Umbelazi, whom I betrayed for Mameena's sake."

"Why do you talk wind, Saduko?" I asked. "Years ago I saw Indhlovu-ene-Sihlonti die."

"Die, Macumazahn! We do not die; it is only our flesh that dies. Yes, yes, I have learned that since we parted. Do you not remember his last words: 'I will haunt you while you live, and when you cease to live, ah! then we shall meet again'? Oh! from that hour to this he *has* haunted me, Macumazahn—he and the others; and now, now we are about to meet as he promised."

Then once more he hid his eyes and groaned.

"He is mad," I whispered to Nandie.

"Perhaps. Who knows?" she answered, shaking her head.

Saduko uncovered his eyes.

"Make 'the-thing-that-burns' brighter," he gasped, "for I do not perceive him so clearly when it is bright. Oh! Macumazahn, he is looking at you and whispering. To whom is he whispering? I see! to Mameena, who also looks at you and smiles. They are talking. Be silent. I must listen."

Now, I began to wish that I were out of that hut, for really a little of this uncanny business went a long way. Indeed, I suggested going, but Nandie would not allow it.

"Stay with me till the end," she muttered. So I had to stay, wondering what Saduko heard Umbelazi whispering to Mameena, and on which side of me he saw her standing.

He began to wander in his mind.

"That was a clever pit you dug for Bangu, Macumazahn; but you would not take your share of the cattle, so the blood of the Amakoba is not on your head. Ah! what a fight was that which the Amawombe made at Endondakusuka. You were with them, you remember, Macumazahn; and why was I not at your side? Oh! then we would have swept away the Usutu as the wind sweeps ashes. Why was I not at your side to share the glory? I remember now—because of the Daughter of Storm. She betrayed me for Umbelazi, and I betrayed Umbelazi for her; and now he haunts me, whose greatness I brought to the dust; and the Usutu wolf, Cetewayo, curls himself up in his form and grows fat on his food. And—and, Macumazahn, it has all been done in vain, for Mameena hates me. Yes, I can read it in her eyes. She mocks and hates me worse in death than she did in life, and she says that—that it was not all her fault—because she loves—because she loves—"

A look of bewilderment came upon his face—his poor, tormented face; then suddenly Saduko threw his arms wide, and sobbed in an ever-weakening voice:

"All—all done in vain! Oh! *Mameena, Ma—mee—na, Ma—meena!*" and fell back dead.

"Saduko has gone away," said Nandie, as she drew a blanket over his face. "But I wonder," she added with a little hysterical smile, "oh! how I wonder who it was the Spirit of Mameena told him that she loved—Mameena, who was born without a heart?"

I made no answer, for at that moment I heard a very curious sound, which seemed to me to proceed from somewhere above the hut. Of what did it remind me? Ah! I knew. It was like the sound of the dreadful laughter of Zikali, Opener-of-Roads—Zikali, the "Thing-that-should-never-have-been-born."

Doubtless, however, it was only the cry of some storm-driven night bird. Or perhaps it was an hyena that laughed—an hyena that scented death.

Allan and the Holy Flower

Chapter 1

Brother John

I do not suppose that anyone who knows the name of Allan Quatermain would be likely to associate it with flowers, and especially with orchids. Yet as it happens it was once my lot to take part in an orchid hunt of so remarkable a character that I think its details should not be lost. At least I will set them down, and if in the after days anyone cares to publish them, well—he is at liberty to do so.

It was in the year—oh! never mind the year, it was a long while ago when I was much younger, that I went on a hunting expedition to the north of the Limpopo River which borders the Transvaal. My companion was a gentleman of the name of Scroope, Charles Scroope. He had come out to Durban from England in search of sport. At least, that was one of his reasons. The other was a lady whom I will call Miss Margaret Manners, though that was not her name.

It seems that these two were engaged to be married, and really attached to each other. Unfortunately, however, they quarrelled violently about another gentlemen with whom Miss Manners danced four consecutive dances, including two that were promised to her fiancé at a Hunt ball in Essex, where they all lived. Explanations, or rather argument, followed. Mr. Scroope said that he would not tolerate such conduct. Miss Manners replied that she would not be dictated to; she was her own mistress and meant to remain so. Mr. Scroope exclaimed that she might so far as he was concerned. She answered that she never wished to see his face again. He declared with emphasis that she never should and that he was going to Africa to shoot elephants.

What is more, he went, starting from his Essex home the next day without leaving any address. As it transpired afterwards, long afterwards, had he waited till the post came in he would have received a letter that might have changed his plans. But they were high-spirited young people, both of them, and played the fool after the fashion of those in love.

Well, Charles Scroope turned up in Durban, which was but a poor place then, and there we met in the bar of the Royal Hotel.

"If you want to kill big game," I heard some one say, who it was I really forget, "there's the man to show you how to do it—Hunter Quatermain; the best shot in Africa and one of the finest fellows, too."

I sat still, smoking my pipe and pretending to hear nothing. It is awkward to listen to oneself being praised, and I was always a shy man.

Then after a whispered colloquy Mr. Scroope was brought forward and introduced to me. I bowed as nicely as I could and ran my eye over him. He was a tall young man with dark eyes and a rather romantic aspect (that was due to his love affair), but I came to the conclusion that I liked the cut of his jib. When he spoke, that conclusion was affirmed. I always think there is a great deal in a voice; personally, I judge by it almost as much as by the face. This voice was particularly pleasant and sympathetic, though there was nothing very original or striking in the words by which it was, so to speak, introduced to me. These were:

"How do you do, sir. Will you have a split?"

I answered that I never drank spirits in the daytime, or at least not often, but that I should be pleased to take a small bottle of beer.

When the beer was consumed we walked up together to my little house on which is now called the Berea, the same in which, amongst others, I received my friends, Curtis and Good, in after days, and there we dined. Indeed, Charlie Scroope never left that house until we started on our shooting expedition.

Now I must cut all this story short, since it is only incidentally that it has to do with the tale I am going to tell. Mr. Scroope was a rich man and as he offered to pay all the expenses of the expedition while I was to take all the profit in the shape of ivory or anything else that might accrue, of course I did not decline his proposal.

Everything went well with us on that trip until its unfortunate end. We only killed two elephants, but of other game we found plenty. It was when we were near Delagoa Bay on our return that the accident happened.

We were out one evening trying to shoot something for our dinner, when between the trees I caught sight of a small buck. It vanished round a little promontory of rock which projected from the side of the kloof, walking quietly, not running in alarm. We followed after it. I was the first, and had just wriggled round these rocks and perceived the buck standing about ten paces away (it was a bush-*bok*), when I heard a rustle among the bushes on the top of the rock not a dozen feet above my head, and Charlie Scroope's voice calling:

"Look out, Quatermain! He's coming."

"Who's coming?" I answered in an irritated tone, for the noise had made the buck run away.

Then it occurred to me, all in an instant of course, that a man would not begin to shout like that for nothing; at any rate when his supper was concerned. So I glanced up above and behind me. To this moment I can remember exactly what I saw. There was the granite water-worn boulder, or rather several boulders, with ferns growing in their cracks of the maiden-hair tribe, most of them, but some had a silver sheen on the under side of their leaves. On one of these leaves, bending it down, sat a large beetle with red wings and a black body engaged in rubbing its antenna with its front paws. And above, just appearing over the top of the rock, was the head of an extremely fine leopard. As I write to seem to perceive its square jowl outlined against the arc of the quiet evening sky with the saliva dropping from its lips.

This was the last thing which I did perceive for a little while, since at that moment the leopard—we call them tigers in South Africa—dropped upon my back and knocked me flat as a pancake. I presume that it also had been stalking the buck and was angry at my appearance on the scene. Down I went, luckily for me, into a patch of mossy soil.

"All up!" I said to myself, for I felt the brute's weight upon my back pressing me down among the moss, and what was worse, its hot breath upon my neck as it dropped its jaws to bite me in the head. Then I heard the report of Scroope's rifle, followed by furious snarling from the leopard, which evidently had been hit. Also it seemed to think that I had caused its injuries, for it seized me by the shoulder. I felt its teeth slip along my skin, but happily they only fastened in the shooting coat of tough corduroy that I was wearing. It began to shake me, then let go to get a better grip. Now, remembering that Scroope only carried a light, single-barrelled rifle, and therefore could not fire again, I knew, or thought I knew, that my time had come. I was not exactly afraid, but the sense of some great, impending chance became very vivid. I remembered—not my whole life, but one or two odd little things connected with my infancy. For instance, I seemed to see myself seated on my mother's knee, playing with a little jointed gold-fish which she wore upon her watch-chain.

After this I muttered a word or two of supplication, and, I think, lost consciousness. If so, it can only have been for a few seconds. Then my mind returned to me and I saw a strange sight. The leopard and Scroope were fighting each other. The leopard, standing on one hind leg, for the other was broken, seemed to be boxing Scroope, whilst

Scroope was driving his big hunting knife into the brute's carcase. They went down, Scroope undermost, the leopard tearing at him. I gave a wriggle and came out of that mossy bed—I recall the sucking sound my body made as it left the ooze.

Close by was my rifle, uninjured and at full cock as it had fallen from my hand. I seized it, and in another second had shot the leopard through the head just as it was about to seize Scroope's throat.

It fell stone dead on the top of him. One quiver, one contraction of the claws (in poor Scroope's leg) and all was over. There it lay as though it were asleep, and underneath was Scroope.

The difficulty was to get it off him, for the beast was very heavy, but I managed this at last with the help of a thorn bough I found which some elephant had torn from a tree. This I used as a lever. There beneath lay Scroope, literally covered with blood, though whether his own or the leopard's I could not tell. At first I thought that he was dead, but after I had poured some water over him from the little stream that trickled down the rock, he sat up and asked inconsequently:

"What am I now?"

"A hero," I answered. (I have always been proud of that repartee.)

Then, discouraging further conversation, I set to work to get him back to the camp, which fortunately was close at hand.

When we had proceeded a couple of hundred yards, he still making inconsequent remarks, his right arm round my neck and my left arm round his middle, suddenly he collapsed in a dead faint, and as his weight was more than I could carry, I had to leave him and fetch help.

In the end I got him to the tents by aid of the *Kaffirs* and a blanket, and there made an examination. He was scratched all over, but the only serious wounds were a bite through the muscles of the left upper arm and three deep cuts in the right thigh just where it joins the body, caused by a stroke of the leopard's claws. I gave him a dose of laudanum to send him to sleep and dressed these hurts as best I could. For three days he went on quite well. Indeed, the wounds had begun to heal healthily when suddenly some kind of fever took him, caused, I suppose, by the poison of the leopard's fangs or claws.

Oh! what a terrible week was that which followed! He became delirious, raving continually of all sorts of things, and especially of Miss Margaret Manners. I kept up his strength as well as was possible with soup made from the flesh of game, mixed with a little brandy which I had. But he grew weaker and weaker. Also the wounds in the thigh began to suppurate.

The *Kaffirs* whom we had with us were of little use in such a case, so that all the nursing fell on me. Luckily, beyond a shaking, the leopard had done me no hurt, and I was very strong in those days. Still the lack of rest told on me, since I dared not sleep for more than half an hour or so at a time. At length came a morning when I was quite worn out. There lay poor Scroope turning and muttering in the little tent, and there I sat by his side, wondering whether he would live to see another dawn, or if he did, for how long I should be able to tend him. I called to a *Kaffir* to bring me my coffee, and just was I was lifting the pannikin to my lips with a shaking hand, help came.

It arrived in a very strange shape. In front of our camp were two thorn trees, and from between these trees, the rays from the rising sun falling full on him, I saw a curious figure walking towards me in a slow, purposeful fashion. It was that of a man of uncertain age, for though the beard and long hair were white, the face was comparatively youthful, save for the wrinkles round the mouth, and the dark eyes were full of life and vigour. Tattered garments, surmounted by a torn *kaross* or skin rug, hung awkwardly upon his tall, thin frame. On his feet were *veld-schoen* of untanned hide, on his back a battered tin case was strapped, and in his bony, nervous hand he clasped a long staff made of the black and white wood the natives call *unzimbiti*, on the top of which was fixed a butterfly net. Behind him were some *Kaffirs* who carried cases on their heads.

I knew him at once, since we had met before, especially on a certain occasion in Zululand, when he calmly appeared out of the ranks of a hostile native *impi*. He was one of the strangest characters in all South Africa. Evidently a gentleman in the true sense of the word, none knew his history (although I know it now, and a strange story it is), except that he was an American by birth, for in this matter at times his speech betrayed him. Also he was a doctor by profession, and to judge from his extraordinary skill, one who must have seen much practice both in medicine and in surgery. For the rest he had means, though where they came from was a mystery, and for many years past had wandered about South and Eastern Africa, collecting butterflies and flowers.

By the natives, and I might add by white people also, he was universally supposed to be mad. This reputation, coupled with his medical skill, enabled him to travel wherever he would without the slightest fear of molestation, since the *Kaffirs* look upon the mad as inspired by God. Their name for him was Dogeetah, a ludicrous corruption of the English word *doctor*, whereas white folk called him indifferently Brother John, Uncle Jonathan, or Saint John. The second appellation he got from his extraordinary likeness (when cleaned up and nicely dressed) to the figure by which the great American nation is typified in comic papers, as England is typified by John Bull. The first and third arose in the well-known goodness of his character and a taste he was supposed to possess for living on locusts and wild honey, or their local equivalents. Personally, however, he preferred to be addressed as Brother John.

Oh! who can tell the relief with which I saw him; an angel from heaven could scarcely have been more welcome. As he came I poured out a second jorum of coffee, and remembering that he liked it sweet, put in plenty of sugar.

"How do you do, Brother John?" I said, proffering him the coffee.

"Greeting, Brother Allan," he answered—in those days he affected a kind of old Roman way of speaking, as I imagine it. Then he took the coffee, put his long finger into it to test the temperature and stir up the sugar, drank it off as though it were a dose of medicine, and handed back the tin to be refilled.

"Bug-hunting?" I queried.

He nodded. "That and flowers and observing human nature and the wonderful works of God. Wandering around generally."

"Where from last?" I asked.

"Those hills nearly twenty miles away. Left them at eight in the evening; walked all night."

"Why?" I said, looking at him.

"Because it seemed as though someone were calling me. To be plain, you, Allan."

"Oh! you heard about my being here and the trouble?"

"No, heard nothing. Meant to strike out for the coast this morning. Just as I was turning in, at 8.5 exactly, got your message and started. That's all."

"My message——" I began, then stopped, and asking to see his watch, compared it with mine. Oddly enough, they showed the same time to within two minutes.

"It is a strange thing," I said slowly, "but at 8.05 last night I did try to send a message for some help because I thought my mate was dying," and I jerked my thumb towards the tent. "Only it wasn't to you or any other man, Brother John. Understand?"

"Quite. Message was expressed on, that's all. Expressed and I guess registered as well."

I looked at Brother John and Brother John looked at me, but at the time we made no further remark. The thing was too curious, that is, unless he lied. But nobody had ever known him to lie. He was a truthful person, painfully truthful at times. And yet there are people who do not believe in prayer.

"What is it?" he asked.

"Mauled by leopard. Wounds won't heal, and fever. I don't think he can last long."

"What do you know about it? Let me see him."

Well, he saw him and did wonderful things. That tin box of his was full of medicines and surgical instruments, which latter he boiled before he used them. Also he washed his hands till I thought the skin would come off them, using up more soap than I could spare. First he gave poor Charlie a dose of something that seemed to kill him; he said he had that drug from the *Kaffirs*. Then he opened up those wounds upon his thigh and cleaned them out and bandaged them with boiled herbs. Afterwards, when Scroope came to again, he gave him a drink that threw him into a sweat and took away the fever. The end of it was that in two days' time his patient sat up and asked for a square meal, and in a week we were able to begin to carry him to the coast.

"Guess that message of yours saved Brother Scroope's life," said old John, as he watched him start.

I made no answer. Here I may state, however, that through my own men I inquired a little as to Brother John's movements at the time of what he called the message. It seemed that he *had* arranged to march towards the coast on the next morning, but that about two hours after sunset suddenly he ordered them to pack up everything and follow him. This they did and to their intense disgust those *Kaffirs* were forced to trudge all night at the heels of Dogeetah, as they called him. Indeed, so weary did they become, that had they not been afraid of being left alone in an unknown country in the darkness, they said they would have thrown down their loads and refused to go any further.

That is as far as I was able to take the matter, which may be explained by telepathy, inspiration, instinct, or coincidence. It is one as to which the reader must form his own opinion.

During our week together in camp and our subsequent journey to Delagoa Bay and thence by ship to Durban, Brother John and I grew very intimate, with limitations. Of his past, as I have said, he never talked, or of the real object of his wanderings which I learned afterwards, but of his natural history and ethnological (I believe that is the word) studies he spoke a good deal. As, in my humble way, I also am an observer of such matters and know something about African natives and their habits from practical experience, these subjects interested me.

Amongst other things, he showed me many of the specimens that he had collected during his recent journey; insects and beautiful butterflies neatly pinned into boxes, also a quantity of dried flowers pressed between sheets of blotting paper, amongst them some which he told me were orchids. Observing that these attracted me, he asked me if I would like to see the most wonderful orchid in the whole world. Of course I said yes, whereon he produced out of one of his cases a flat package about two feet six square. He undid the grass mats in which it was wrapped, striped, delicately woven mats such as they make in the neighbourhood of Zanzibar. Within these was the lid of a packing-case. Then came more mats and some copies of *The Cape Journal* spread out flat. Then sheets of blotting paper, and last of all between two pieces of cardboard, a flower and one leaf of the plant on which it grew.

Even in its dried state it was a wondrous thing, measuring twenty-four inches from the tip of one wing or petal to the tip of the other, by twenty inches from the top of the back sheath to the bottom of the pouch. The measurement of the back sheath itself I forget, but it must have been quite a foot across. In colour it was, or had been, bright golden, but the back sheath was white, barred with lines of black, and in the exact centre of the pouch was a single black spot shaped like the head of a great ape. There were the overhanging brows, the deep recessed eyes, the surly mouth, the massive jaws—everything.

Although at that time I had never seen a gorilla in the flesh, I had seen a coloured picture of the brute, and if that picture had been photographed on the flower the likeness could not have been more perfect.

"What is it?" I asked, amazed.

"Sir," said Brother John, sometimes he used this formal term when excited, "it is the most marvellous *Cypripedium* in the whole earth, and, sir, I have discovered it. A healthy root of that plant will be worth £20,000."

"That's better than gold mining," I said. "Well, have you got the root?"

Brother John shook his head sadly as he answered:

"No such luck."

"How's that as you have the flower?"

"I'll tell you, Allan. For a year past and more I have been collecting in the district back of Kilwa and found some wonderful things, yes, wonderful. At last, about three hundred miles inland, I came to a tribe, or rather, a people, that no white man had ever visited. They are called the Mazitu, a numerous and warlike people of bastard Zulu blood."

"I have heard of them," I interrupted. "They broke north before the days of Senzangakona, two hundred years or more ago."

"Well, I could make myself understood among them because they still talk a corrupt Zulu, as do all the tribes in those parts. At first they wanted to kill me, but let me go because they thought that I was mad. Everyone thinks that I am mad, Allan; it is a kind of public delusion, whereas I think that I am sane and that most other people are mad."

"A private delusion," I suggested hurriedly, as I did not wish to discuss Brother John's sanity. "Well, go on about the Mazitu."

"Later they discovered that I had skill in medicine, and their king, Bausi, came to me to be treated for a great external tumour. I risked an operation and cured him. It was anxious work, for if he had died I should have died too, though that would not have troubled me very much," and he sighed. "Of course, from that moment I was supposed to be a great magician. Also Bausi made a blood brotherhood with me, transfusing some of his blood into my veins and some of mine into his. I only hope he has not inoculated me with his tumours, which are congenital. So I became Bausi and Bausi became me. In other words, I was as much chief of the Mazitu as he was, and shall remain so all my life."

"That might be useful," I said, reflectively, "but go on."

"I learned that on the western boundary of the Mazitu territory were great swamps; that beyond these swamps was a lake called Kirua, and beyond that a large and fertile land supposed to be an island, with a mountain in its centre. This land is known as Pongo, and so are the people who live there."

"That is a native name for the gorilla, isn't it?" I asked. "At least so a fellow who had been on the West Coast told me."

"Indeed, then that's strange, as you will see. Now these Pongo are supposed to be great magicians, and the god they worship is said to be a gorilla, which, if you are right, accounts for their name. Or rather," he went on, "they have two gods. The other is that flower you see there. Whether the flower with the monkey's head on it was the first god and suggested the worship of the beast itself, or *vice versa*, I don't know. Indeed I know very little, just what I was told by the Mazitu and a man who called himself a Pongo chief, no more."

"What did they say?"

"The Mazitu said that the Pongo people are devils who came by the secret channels through the reeds in canoes and stole their children and women, whom they sacrificed to their gods. Sometimes, too, they made raids upon them at night, howling like hyenas. The men they killed and the women and children they took away. The Mazitu want to attack them but cannot do so, because they are not water people and have no canoes, and therefore are unable to reach the island, if it is an island. Also they told me about the wonderful flower which grows in the place where the ape-god lives, and is worshipped like the god. They had the story of it from some of their people who had been enslaved and escaped."

"Did you try to get to the island?" I asked.

"Yes, Allan. That is, I went to the edge of the reeds which lie at the end of a long slope of plain, where the lake begins. Here I stopped for some time catching butterflies and collecting plants. One night when I was camped there by myself, for none of my men would remain so near the Pongo country after sunset, I woke up with a sense that I was no longer alone. I crept out of my tent and by the light of the moon, which was setting, for dawn drew near, I saw a man who leant upon the handle of a very wide-bladed spear which was taller than himself, a big man over six feet two high, I should say, and broad in proportion. He wore a long, white cloak reaching from his shoulders almost to the ground. On his head was a tight-fitting cap with lappets, also white. In his ears were rings of copper or gold, and on his wrists bracelets of the same metal. His skin was intensely black, but the features were not at all negroid. They were prominent and finely-cut, the nose being sharp and the lips quite thin; indeed of an Arab type. His left hand was bandaged, and on his face was an expression of great anxiety. Lastly, he appeared to be about fifty years of age. So still did he stand that I began to wonder whether he were one of those ghosts which the Mazitu swore the Pongo wizards send out to haunt their country.

"For a long while we stared at each other, for I was determined that I would not speak first or show any concern. At last he spoke in a low, deep voice and in Mazitu, or a language so similar that I found it easy to understand.

"'Is not your name Dogeetah, O White Lord, and are you not a master of medicine?'

"'Yes,' I answered, 'but who are you who dare to wake me from my sleep?'

"'Lord, I am the *Kalubi*, the Chief of the Pongo, a great man in my own land yonder.'

"'Then why do you come here alone at night, *Kalubi*, Chief of the Pongo?'

"'Why do *you* come here alone, White Lord?' he answered evasively.

"'What do you want, anyway?' I asked.

"'O! Dogeetah, I have been hurt, I want you to cure me,' and he looked at his bandaged hand.

"'Lay down that spear and open your robe that I may see you have no knife.'

"He obeyed, throwing the spear to some distance.

"'Now unwrap the hand.'

"He did so. I lit a match, the sight of which seemed to frighten him greatly, although he asked no questions about it, and by its light examined the hand. The first joint of the second finger was gone. From the appearance of the stump which had been cauterized and was tied tightly with a piece of flexible grass, I judged that it had been bitten off.

"'What did this?' I asked.

"'Monkey,' he answered, 'poisonous monkey. Cut off the finger, O Dogeetah, or tomorrow I die.'

"'Why do you not tell your own doctors to cut off the finger, you who are *Kalubi*, Chief of the Pongo?'

"'No, no,' he replied, shaking his head. 'They cannot do it. It is not lawful. And I, I cannot do it, for if the flesh is black the hand must come off too, and if the flesh is black at the wrist, then the arm must be cut off.'

"I sat down on my camp stool and reflected. Really I was waiting for the sun to rise, since it was useless to attempt an operation in that light. The man, *Kalubi*, thought that I had refused his petition and became terribly agitated.

"'Be merciful, White Lord,' he prayed, 'do not let me die. I am afraid to die. Life is bad, but death is worse. O! If you refuse me, I will kill myself here before you and then my ghost will haunt you till you die also of fear and come to join me. What fee do you ask? Gold or ivory or slaves? Say and I will give it.'

"'Be silent,' I said, for I saw that if he went on thus he would throw himself into a fever, which might cause the operation to prove fatal. For the same reason I did not question him about many things I should have liked to learn. I lit my fire and boiled the instruments—he thought I was making magic. By the time that everything was ready the sun was up.

"'Now,' I said, 'let me see how brave you are.'

"Well, Allan, I performed that operation, removing the finger at the base where it joins the hand, as I thought there might be something in his story of the poison. Indeed, as I found afterwards on dissection, and can show you, for I have the thing in spirits, there was, for the blackness of which he spoke, a kind of mortification, I presume, had crept almost to the joint, though the flesh beyond was healthy enough. Certainly that *Kalubi* was a plucky fellow. He sat like a rock and never even winced. Indeed, when he saw that the flesh was sound he uttered a great sigh of relief. After it was all over he turned a little faint, so I gave him some spirits of wine mixed with water which revived him.

"'O Lord Dogeetah,' he said, as I was bandaging his hand, 'while I live I am your slave. Yet, do me one more service. In my land there is a terrible wild beast, that which bit off my finger. It is a devil; it kills us and we fear it. I have heard that you white men have magic weapons which slay with a noise. Come to my land and kill me that wild beast with your magic weapon. I say, Come, Come, for I am terribly afraid,' and indeed he looked it.

"'No,' I answered, 'I shed no blood; I kill nothing except butterflies, and of these only a few. But if you fear this brute why do you not poison it? You black people have many drugs.'

"'No use, no use,' he replied in a kind of wail. 'The beast knows poisons, some it swallows and they do not harm it. Others it will not touch. Moreover, no black man can do it hurt. It is white, and it has been known from of old that if it dies at all, it must be by the hand of one who is white.'

"'A very strange animal,' I began, suspiciously, for I felt sure that he was lying to me. But just at that moment I heard the sound of my men's voices. They were advancing towards me through the giant grass, singing as they came, but as yet a long way off. The *Kalubi* heard it also and sprang up.

"'I must be gone,' he said. 'None must see me here. What fee, O Lord of medicine, what fee?'

"'I take no payment for my medicine,' I said. 'Yet—stay. A wonderful flower grows in your country, does it not? A flower with wings and a cup beneath. I would have that flower.'

"'Who told you of the Flower?' he asked. 'The Flower is holy. Still, O White Lord, still for you it shall be risked. Oh, return and bring with you one who can kill the beast and I will make you rich. Return and call to the reeds for the *Kalubi*, and the *Kalubi* will hear and come to you.'

"Then he ran to his spear, snatched it from the ground and vanished among the reeds. That was the last I saw, or am ever likely to see, of him."

"But, Brother John, you got the flower somehow."

"Yes, Allan. About a week later when I came out of my tent one morning, there it was standing in a narrow-mouthed, earthenware pot filled with water. Of course I meant that he was to send me the plant, roots and all, but I suppose he understood that I wanted a bloom. Or perhaps he dared not send the plant. Anyhow, it is better than nothing."

"Why did you not go into the country and get it for yourself?"

"For several reasons, Allan, of which the best is that it was impossible. The Mazitu swear that if anyone sees that flower he is put to death. Indeed, when they found that I had a bloom of it, they forced me to move to the other side of the country seventy miles away. So I thought that I would wait till I met with some companions who would accompany me. Indeed, to be frank, Allan, it occurred to me that you were the sort of man who would like to interview this wonderful beast that bites off people's fingers and frightens them to death," and Brother John stroked his long, white beard and smiled, adding, "Odd that we should have met so soon afterwards, isn't it?"

"Did you?" I replied, "now did you indeed? Brother John, people say all sorts of things about you, but I have come to the conclusion that there's nothing the matter with your wits."

Again he smiled and stroked his long, white beard.

CHAPTER 2

The Auction Room

I do not think that this conversion about the Pongo savages who were said to worship a Gorilla and a Golden Flower was renewed until we reached my house at Durban. Thither of course I took Mr. Charles Scroope, and thither also came Brother John who, as bedroom accommodation was lacking, pitched his tent in the garden.

One night we sat on the step smoking; Brother John's only concession to human weakness was that he smoked. He drank no wine or spirits; he never ate meat unless he was obliged, but I rejoice to say that he smoked cigars, like most Americans, when he could get them.

"John," said I, "I have been thinking over that yarn of yours and have come to one or two conclusions."

"What may they be, Allan?"

"The first is that you were a great donkey not to get more out of the *Kalubi* when you had the chance."

"Agreed, Allan, but, amongst other things, I am a doctor and the operation was uppermost in my mind."

"The second is that I believe this *Kalubi* had charge of the gorilla-god, as no doubt you've guessed; also that it was the gorilla which bit off his finger."

"Why so?"

"Because I have heard of great monkeys called *sokos* that live in Central East Africa which are said to bite off men's toes and fingers. I have heard too that they are very like gorillas."

"Now you mention it, so have I, Allan. Indeed, once I saw a *soko*, though some way off, a huge, brown ape which stood on its hind legs and drummed upon its chest with its fists. I didn't see it for long because I ran away."

"The third is that this yellow orchid would be worth a great deal of money if one could dig it up and take it to England."

"I think I told you, Allan, that I valued it at £20,000, so that conclusion of yours is not original."

"The fourth is that I should like to dig up that orchid and get a share of the £20,000."

Brother John became intensely interested.

"Ah!" he said, "now we are getting to the point. I have been wondering how long it would take you to see it, Allan, but if you are slow, you are sure."

"The fifth is," I went on, "that such an expedition to succeed would need a great deal of money, more than you or I could find. Partners would be wanted, active or sleeping, but partners with cash."

Brother John looked towards the window of the room in which Charlie Scroope was in bed, for being still weak he went to rest early.

"No," I said, "he's had enough of Africa, and you told me yourself that it will be two years before he is really strong again. Also there's a lady in this case. Now listen. I have taken it on myself to write to that lady, whose address I found out while he didn't know what he was saying. I have said that he was dying, but that I hoped he might live. Meanwhile, I added, I thought she would like to know that he did nothing but rave of her; also that he was a hero, with a big H twice underlined. My word! I did lay it on about the hero business with a spoon, a real hotel gravy spoon. If Charlie Scroope knows himself again when he sees my description of him, well, I'm a Dutchman, that's all. The letter caught the last mail and will, I hope, reach the lady in due course. Now listen again. Scroope wants me to go to England with him to look after him on the voyage—that's what he says. What he means is that he hopes I might put in a word for him with the lady, if I should chance to be introduced to her. He offers to pay all my expenses and to give me something for my loss of time. So, as I haven't seen England since I was three years old, I think I'll take the chance."

Brother John's face fell. "Then how about the expedition, Allan?" he asked.

"This is the first of November," I answered, "and the wet season in those parts begins about now and lasts till April. So it would be no use trying to visit your Pongo friends till then, which gives me plenty of time to go to England and come out again. If you'll trust that flower to me I'll take it with me. Perhaps I might be able to find someone who would be willing to put down money on the chance of getting the plant on which it grew. Meanwhile, you are welcome to this house if you care to stay here."

"Thank you, Allan, but I can't sit still for so many months. I'll go somewhere and come back." He paused and a dreamy look came into his dark eyes, then went on, "You see, Brother, it is laid on me to wander and wander through all this great land until—I know."

"Until you know what?" I asked, sharply.

He pulled himself together with a jerk, as it were, and answered with a kind of forced carelessness.

"Until I know every inch of it, of course. There are lots of tribes I have not yet visited."

"Including the Pongo," I said. "By the way, if I can get the money together for a trip up there, I suppose you mean to come too, don't you? If not, the thing's off so far as I am concerned. You see, I am reckoning on you to get us through the Mazitu and into Pongo-land by the help of your friends."

"Certainly I mean to come. In fact, if you don't go, I shall start alone. I intend to explore Pongo-land even if I never come out of it again."

Once more I looked at him as I answered:

"You are ready to risk a great deal for a flower, John. Or are you looking for more than a flower? If so, I hope you will tell me the truth."

This I said as I was aware that Brother John had a foolish objection to uttering, or even acting lies.

"Well, Allan, as you put it like that, the truth is that I heard something more about the Pongo than I told you up country. It was after I had operated on that *Kalubi*, or I would have tried to get in alone. But this I could not do then as I have said."

"And what did you hear?"

"I heard that they had a white goddess as well as a white god."

"Well, what of it? A female gorilla, I suppose."

"Nothing, except that goddesses have always interested me. Good night."

"You are an odd old fish," I remarked after him, "and what is more you have got something up your sleeve. Well, I'll have it down one day. Meanwhile, I wonder whether the whole thing is a lie, no; not a lie, an hallucination. It can't be—because of that orchid. No one can explain away the orchid. A queer people, these Pongo, with their white god and goddess and their Holy Flower. But after all Africa is a land of queer people, and of queer gods too."

* * * * * * * *

And now the story shifts away to England. (Don't be afraid, my adventurous reader, if ever I have one, it is coming back to Africa again in a very few pages.)

Mr. Charles Scroope and I left Durban a day or two after my last conversation with Brother John. At Cape Town we caught the mail, a wretched little boat you would think it now, which after a long and wearisome journey at length landed us safe at Plymouth. Our companions on that voyage were very dull. I have forgotten most of them, but one lady I do remember. I imagine that she must have commenced life as a barmaid, for she had the orthodox tow hair and blowsy appearance. At any rate, she was the wife of a wine-merchant who had made a fortune at the Cape. Unhappily, however, she had contracted too great a liking for her husband's wares, and after dinner was apt to become talkative. For some reason or other she took a particular aversion to me. Oh! I can see her now, seated in that saloon with the oil lamp swinging over her head (she always chose the position under the oil lamp because it showed off her diamonds). And I can hear her too. "Don't bring any of your elephant-hunting manners here, Mr. Allan" (with an emphasis on the Allan) "Quatermain, they are not fit for polite society. You should go and brush your hair, Mr. Quatermain." (I may explain that my hair sticks up naturally.)

Then would come her little husband's horrified "Hush! hush! you are quite insulting, my dear."

Oh! why do I remember it all after so many years when I have even forgotten the people's names? One of those little things that stick in the mind, I suppose. The Island of Ascension, where we called, sticks also with its long swinging rollers breaking in white foam, its bare mountain peak capped with green, and the turtles in the ponds. Those poor turtles. We brought two of them home, and I used to look at them lying on their backs in the forecastle flapping their fins feebly. One of them died, and I got the butcher to save me the shell. Afterwards I gave it as a wedding present to Mr. and Mrs. Scroope, nicely polished and lined. I meant it for a work-basket, and was overwhelmed with confusion when some silly lady said at the marriage, and in the hearing of the bride and bridegroom, that it was the most beautiful cradle she had ever seen. Of course, like a fool, I tried to explain, whereon everybody tittered.

But why do I write of such trifles that have nothing to do with my story?

I mentioned that I had ventured to send a letter to Miss Margaret Manners about Mr. Charles Scroope, in which I said incidentally that if the hero should happen to live I should probably bring him home by the next mail. Well, we got into Plymouth about eight o'clock in the morning, on a mild, November day, and shortly afterwards a tug arrived to take off the passengers and mails; also some cargo. I, being an early riser, watched it come and saw upon the deck a stout lady wrapped in furs, and by her side a very pretty, fair-haired young woman clad in a neat serge dress and a pork-pie hat. Presently a steward told me that someone wished to speak to me in the saloon. I went and found these two standing side by side.

"I believe you are Mr. Allan Quatermain," said the stout lady. "Where is Mr. Scroope whom I understand you have brought home? Tell me at once."

Something about her appearance and fierce manner of address alarmed me so much that I could only answer feebly:

"Below, madam, below."

"There, my dear," said the stout lady to her companion, "I warned you to be prepared for the worst. Bear up; do not make a scene before all these people. The ways of Providence are just and inscrutable. It is your own temper that was to blame. You should never have sent the poor man off to these heathen countries."

Then, turning to me, she added sharply: "I suppose he is embalmed; we should like to bury him in Essex."

"Embalmed!" I gasped. "Embalmed! Why, the man is in his bath, or was a few minutes ago."

In another second that pretty young lady who had been addressed was weeping with her head upon my shoulder.

"Margaret!" exclaimed her companion (she was a kind of heavy aunt), "I told you not to make a scene in public. Mr. Quatermain, as Mr. Scroope is alive, would you ask him to be so good as to come here."

Well, I fetched him, half-shaved, and the rest of the business may be imagined. It is a very fine thing to be a hero with a big H. Henceforth (thanks to me) that was Charlie Scroope's lot in life. He has grandchildren now, and they all think him a hero. What is more, he does not contradict them. I went down to the lady's place in Essex, a fine property with a beautiful old house. On the night I arrived there was a dinner-party of twenty-four people. I had to make a speech about Charlie Scroope and the leopard. I think it was a good speech. At any rate everybody cheered, including the servants, who had gathered at the back of the big hall.

I remember that to complete the story I introduced several other leopards, a mother and two three-part-grown cubs, also a wounded buffalo, and told how Mr. Scroope finished them off one after the other with a hunting knife. The thing was to watch his face as the history proceeded. Luckily he was sitting next to me and I could kick him under the table. It was all very amusing, and very happy also, for these two really loved each other. Thank God that I, or rather Brother John, was able to bring them together again.

It was during that stay of mine in Essex, by the way, that I first met Lord Ragnall and the beautiful Miss Holmes with whom I was destined to experience some very strange adventures in the after years.

* * * * * * * *

After this interlude I got to work. Someone told me that there was a firm in the City that made a business of selling orchids by auction, flowers which at this time were beginning to be very fashionable among rich horticulturists. This, thought I, would be the place for me to show my treasure. Doubtless Messrs. May and Primrose—that was their world-famed style—would be able to put me in touch with opulent orchidists who would not mind venturing a couple of thousands on the chance of receiving a share in a flower that, according to Brother John, should be worth untold gold. At any rate, I would try.

So on a certain Friday, about half-past twelve, I sought out the place of business of Messrs. May and Primrose, bearing with me the golden *Cypripedium*, which was now enclosed in a flat tin case.

As it happened I chose an unlucky day and hour, for on arriving at the office and asking for Mr. May, I was informed that he was away in the country valuing.

"Then I would like to see Mr. Primrose," I said.

"Mr. Primrose is round at the Rooms selling," replied the clerk, who appeared to be very busy.

"Where are the Rooms?" I asked.

"Out of the door, turn to the left, turn to the left again and under the clock," said the clerk, and closed the shutter.

So disgusted was I with his rudeness that I nearly gave up the enterprise. Thinking better of it, however, I followed the directions given, and in a minute or two found myself in a narrow passage that led to a large room. To one who had never seen anything of the sort before, this room offered a curious sight. The first thing I observed was a notice on the wall to the effect that customers were not allowed to smoke pipes. I thought to myself that orchids must be curious flowers if they could distinguish between the smoke of a cigar and a pipe, and stepped into the room. To my left was a long table covered with pots of the most beautiful flowers that I had ever seen; all of them orchids. Along the wall and opposite were other tables closely packed with withered roots which I concluded were also those of orchids. To my inexperienced eye the whole lot did not look worth five shillings, for they seemed to be dead.

At the head of the room stood the rostrum, where sat a gentleman with an extremely charming face. He was engaged in selling by auction so rapidly that the clerk at his side must have had difficulty in keeping a record of the lots and their purchasers. In front of him was a horseshoe table, round which sat buyers. The end of this table was left unoccupied so that the porters might exhibit each lot before it was put up for sale. Standing under the rostrum was yet another table, a small one, upon which were about twenty pots of flowers, even more wonderful than those on the large table. A notice stated that these would be sold at one-thirty precisely. All about the room stood knots of men (such ladies as were present sat at the table), many of whom had lovely orchids in their buttonholes. These, I found out afterwards, were dealers and amateurs. They were a kindly-faced set of people, and I took a liking to them.

The whole place was quaint and pleasant, especially by contrast with the horrible London fog outside. Squeezing my small person into a corner where I was in nobody's way, I watched the proceedings for a while. Suddenly an agreeable voice at my side asked me if I would like a look at the catalogue. I glanced at the speaker, and in a sense fell in love with him at once—as I have explained before, I am one of those to whom a first impression means a great deal. He was not very tall, though strong-looking and well-made enough. He was not very handsome, though none so ill-favoured. He was just an ordinary fair young Englishman, four or five-and-twenty years of age, with merry blue eyes and one of the pleasantest expressions that I ever saw. At once I felt that he was a sympathetic soul and full of the milk of human kindness. He was dressed in a rough tweed suit rather worn, with the orchid that seemed to be the badge of all this tribe in his buttonhole. Somehow the costume suited his rather pink and white complexion and rumpled fair hair, which I could see as he was sitting on his cloth hat.

"Thank you, no," I answered, "I did not come here to buy. I know nothing about orchids," I added by way of explanation, "except a few I have seen growing in Africa, and this one," and I tapped the tin case which I held under my arm.

"Indeed," he said. "I should like to hear about the African orchids. What is it you have in the case, a plant or flowers?"

"One flower only. It is not mine. A friend in Africa asked me to—well, that is a long story which might not interest you."

"I'm not sure. I suppose it must be a *Cymbidium scape* from the size."

I shook my head. "That's not the name my friend mentioned. He called it a *Cypripedium*."

The young man began to grow curious. "One *Cypripedium* in all that large case? It must be a big flower."

"Yes, my friend said it is the biggest ever found. It measures twenty-four inches across the wings, petals I think he called them, and about a foot across the back part."

"Twenty-four inches across the petals and a foot across the dorsal sepal!" said the young man in a kind of gasp, "and a *Cypripedium*! Sir, surely you are joking?"

"Sir," I answered indignantly, "I am doing nothing of the sort. Your remark is tantamount to telling me that I am speaking a falsehood. But, of course, for all I know, the thing may be some other kind of flower."

"Let me see it. In the name of the goddess Flora let me see it!"

I began to undo the case. Indeed it was already half-open when two other gentlemen, who had either overheard some of our conversation or noted my companion's excited look, edged up to us. I observed that they also wore orchids in their buttonholes.

"Hullo! Somers," said one of them in a tone of false geniality, "what have you got there?"

"What has your friend got there?" asked the other.

"Nothing," replied the young man who had been addressed as Somers, "nothing at all; that is—only a case of tropical butterflies."

"Oh! butterflies," said No. 1 and sauntered away. But No. 2, a keen-looking person with the eye of a hawk, was not so easily satisfied.

"Let us see these butterflies," he said to me.

"You can't," ejaculated the young man. "My friend is afraid lest the damp should injure their colours. Ain't you, Brown?"

"Yes, I am, Somers," I replied, taking his cue and shutting the tin case with a snap.

Then the hawk-eyed person departed, also grumbling, for that story about the damp stuck in his throat.

"Orchidist!" whispered the young man. "Dreadful people, orchidists, so jealous. Very rich, too, both of them. Mr. Brown—I hope that is your name, though I admit the chances are against it."

"They are," I replied, "my name is Allan Quatermain."

"Ah! much better than Brown. Well, Mr. Allan Quatermain, there's a private room in this place to which I have admittance. Would you mind coming with that——" here the hawk-eyed gentleman strolled past again, "that case of butterflies?"

"With pleasure," I answered, and followed him out of the auction chamber down some steps through the door to the left, and ultimately into a little cupboard-like room lined with shelves full of books and ledgers.

He closed the door and locked it.

"Now," he said in a tone of the villain in a novel who at last has come face to face with the virtuous heroine, "now we are alone. Mr. Quatermain, let me see—those butterflies."

I placed the case on a deal table which stood under a skylight in the room. I opened it; I removed the cover of wadding, and there, pressed between two sheets of glass and quite uninjured after all its journeyings, appeared the golden flower, glorious even in death, and by its side the broad green leaf.

The young gentleman called Somers looked at it till I thought his eyes would really start out of his head. He turned away muttering something and looked again.

"Oh! Heavens," he said at last, "oh! Heavens, is it possible that such a thing can exist in this imperfect world? You haven't faked it, Mr. Half—I mean Quatermain, have you?"

"Sir," I said, "for the second time you are making insinuations. Good morning," and I began to shut up the case.

"Don't be offhanded," he exclaimed. "Pity the weaknesses of a poor sinner. You don't understand. If only you understood, you would understand."

"No," I said, "I am bothered if I do."

"Well, you will when you begin to collect orchids. I'm not mad, really, except perhaps on this point, Mr. Quatermain,"—this in a low and thrilling voice—"that marvellous *Cypripedium*—your friend is right, it is a *Cypripedium*—is worth a gold mine."

"From my experience of gold mines I can well believe that," I said tartly, and, I may add, prophetically.

"Oh! I mean a gold mine in the figurative and colloquial sense, not as the investor knows it," he answered. "That is, the plant on which it grew is priceless. Where is the plant, Mr. Quatermain?"

"In a rather indefinite locality in Africa east by south," I replied. "I can't place it to within three hundred miles."

"That's vague, Mr. Quatermain. I have no right to ask it, seeing that you know nothing of me, but I assure you I am respectable, and in short, would you mind telling me the story of this flower?"

"I don't think I should," I replied, a little doubtfully. Then, after another good look at him, suppressing all names and exact localities,

I gave him the outline of the tale, explaining that I wanted to find someone who would finance an expedition to the remote and romantic spot where this particular *Cypripedium* was believed to grow.

Just as I finished my narrative, and before he had time to comment on it, there came a violent knocking at the door.

"Mr. Stephen," said a voice, "are you there, Mr. Stephen?"

"By Jove! that's Briggs," exclaimed the young man. "Briggs is my father's manager. Shut up the case, Mr. Quatermain. Come in, Briggs," he went on, unlocking the door slowly. "What is it?"

"It is a good deal," replied a thin and agitated person who thrust himself through the opening door. "Your father, I mean Sir Alexander, has come to the office unexpectedly and is in a nice taking because he didn't find you there, sir. When he discovered that you had gone to the orchid sale he grew furious, sir, furious, and sent me to fetch you."

"Did he?" replied Mr. Somers in an easy and unruffled tone. "Well, tell Sir Alexander I am coming at once. Now please go, Briggs, and tell him I am coming at once."

Briggs departed not too willingly.

"I must leave you, Mr. Quatermain," said Mr. Somers as he shut the door behind him. "But will you promise me not to show that flower to anyone until I return? I'll be back within half an hour."

"Yes, Mr. Somers. I'll wait half an hour for you in the sale room, and I promise that no one shall see that flower till you return."

"Thank you. You are a good fellow, and I promise you shall lose nothing by your kindness if I can help it."

We went together into the sale room, where some thought suddenly struck Mr. Somers.

"By Jove!" he said, "I nearly forgot about that *Odontoglossum*. Where's Woodden? Oh! come here, Woodden, I want to speak to you."

The person called Woodden obeyed. He was a man of about fifty, indefinite in colouring, for his eyes were very light-blue or grey and his hair was sandy, tough-looking and strongly made, with big hands that showed signs of work, for the palms were horny and the nails worn down. He was clad in a suit of shiny black, such as folk of the labouring class wear at a funeral. I made up my mind at once that he was a gardener.

"Woodden," said Mr. Somers, "this gentleman here has got the most wonderful orchid in the whole world. Keep your eye on him and see that he isn't robbed. There are people in this room, Mr. Quatermain, who would murder you and throw your body into the Thames for that flower," he added, darkly.

On receipt of this information Woodden rocked a little on his feet as though he felt the premonitory movements of an earthquake. It was a habit of his whenever anything astonished him. Then, fixing his pale eye upon me in a way which showed that my appearance surprised him, he pulled a lock of his sandy hair with his thumb and finger and said:

"'Servant, sir, and where might this horchid be?"

I pointed to the tin case.

"Yes, it's there," went on Mr. Somers, "and that's what you've got to watch. Mr. Quatermain, if anyone attempts to rob you, call for Woodden and he will knock them down. He's my gardener, you know, and entirely to be trusted, especially if it is a matter of knocking anyone down."

"Aye, I'll knock him down surely," said Woodden, doubling his great fist and looking round him with a suspicious eye.

"Now listen, Woodden. Have you looked at that *Odontoglossum Pavo*, and if so, what do you think of it?" and he nodded towards a plant which stood in the centre of the little group that was placed on the small table beneath the auctioneer's desk. It bore a spray of the most lovely white flowers. On the top petal (if it is a petal), and also on the lip of each of these rounded flowers was a blotch or spot of which the general effect was similar to the iridescent eye on the tail feathers of a peacock, whence, I suppose, the flower was named "*Pavo*," or Peacock.

"Yes, master, and I think it the beautifullest thing that ever I saw. There isn't a *'glossum* in England like that there *'glossum Paving*," he added with conviction, and rocked again as he said the word. "But there's plenty after it. I say they're a-smelling round that blossom like, like—dawgs round a rat hole. And" (this triumphantly) "they don't do that for nothing."

"Quite so, Woodden, you have got a logical mind. But, look here, we must have that *Pavo* whatever it costs. Now the Governor has sent for me. I'll be back presently, but I might be detained. If so, you've got to bid on my behalf, for I daren't trust any of these agents. Here's your authority," and he scribbled on a card, *Woodden, my gardener, has directions to bid for me.—S.S.* "Now, Woodden," he went on, when he had given the card to an attendant who passed it up to the auctioneer, "don't you make a fool of yourself and let that *Pavo* slip through your fingers."

In another instant he was gone.

"What did the master say, sir?" asked Woodden of me. "That I was to get that there *Paving* whatever it cost?"

"Yes," I said, "that's what he said. I suppose it will fetch a good deal—several pounds."

"Maybe, sir, can't tell. All I know is that I've got to buy it as you can bear me witness. Master, he ain't one to be crossed for money. What he wants, he'll have, that is if it be in the orchid line."

"I suppose you are fond of orchids, too, Mr. Woodden?"

"Fond of them, sir? Why, I loves 'em!" (Here he rocked.) "Don't feel for nothing else in the same way; not even for my old woman" (then with a burst of enthusiasm) "no, not even for the master himself, and I'm fond enough of him, God knows! But, begging your pardon, sir" (with a pull at his forelock), "would you mind holding that tin of yours a little tighter? I've got to keep an eye on that as well as on *O. Paving*, and I just see'd that chap with the tall hat alooking at it suspicious."

After this we separated. I retired into my corner, while Woodden took his stand by the table, with one eye fixed on what he called the *O. Paving* and the other on me and my tin case.

An odd fish truly, I thought to myself. Positive, the old woman; Comparative, his master; Superlative, the orchid tribe. Those were his degrees of affection. Honest and brave and a good fellow though, I bet.

The sale languished. There were so many lots of one particular sort of dried orchid that buyers could not be found for them at a reasonable price, and many had to be bought in. At length the genial Mr. Primrose in the rostrum addressed the audience.

"Gentlemen," he said, "I quite understand that you didn't come here today to buy a rather poor lot of *Cattleya Mossiæ*. You came to buy, or to bid for, or to see sold the most wonderful *Odontoglossum* that has ever been flowered in this country, the property of a famous firm of importers whom I congratulate upon their good fortune in having obtained such a gem. Gentlemen, this miraculous flower ought to adorn a royal greenhouse. But there it is, to be taken away by whoever will pay the most for it, for I am directed to see that it will be sold without reserve. Now, I think," he added, running his eye over the company, "that most of our great collectors are represented in this room today. It is true that I do not see that spirited and liberal young orchidist, Mr. Somers, but he has left his worthy head-gardener, Mr. Woodden, than whom there is no finer judge of an orchid in England" (here Woodden rocked violently) "to bid for him, as I hope, for the glorious flower of which I have been speaking. Now, as it is exactly half-past one, we will proceed to business. Smith, hand the *Odontoglossum Pavo* round, that everyone may inspect its beauties, and be careful you don't let it fall. Gentlemen, I must ask you not to touch it or to defile its purity with tobacco smoke. Eight perfect flowers in bloom, gentlemen, and four—no, five more to open. A strong plant in perfect health, six pseudo-bulbs with leaves, and three without. Two black leads which I am advised can be separated off at the proper time. Now, what bids for the *Odontoglossum Pavo*. Ah! I wonder who will have the honour of becoming the owner of this perfect, this unmatched production of nature. Thank you, sir—three hundred. Four. Five. Six. Seven in three places. Eight. Nine. Ten. Oh! gentlemen, let us get on a little faster. Thank you, sir—fifteen. Sixteen. It is against you, Mr Woodden. Ah! thank you, seventeen."

There came a pause in the fierce race for *O. Pavo*, which I occupied in reducing seventeen hundred shillings to pounds sterling.

My word! I thought to myself, £85 is a goodish price to pay for one plant, however rare. Woodden is acting up to his instructions with a vengeance.

The pleading voice of Mr. Primrose broke in upon my meditations.

"Gentlemen, gentlemen!" he said, "surely you are not going to allow the most wondrous production of the floral world, on which I repeat there is no reserve, to be knocked down at this miserable figure. Come, come. Well, if I must, I must, though after such a disgrace I shall get no sleep tonight. One," and his hammer fell for the first time. "Think, gentlemen, upon my position, think what the eminent owners, who with their usual delicacy have stayed away, will say to me when I am obliged to tell them the disgraceful truth. Two," and his hammer fell a second time. "Smith, hold up that flower. Let the company see it. Let them know what they are losing."

Smith held up the flower at which everybody glared. The little ivory hammer circled round Mr. Primrose's head. It was about to fall, when a quiet man with a long beard who hitherto had not joined in the bidding, lifted his head and said softly:

"Eighteen hundred."

"Ah!" exclaimed Mr. Primrose, "I thought so. I thought that the owner of the greatest collection in England would not see this treasure slip from his grasp without a struggle. Against you, Mr. Woodden."

"Nineteen, sir," said Woodden in a stony voice.

"Two thousand," echoed the gentleman with the long beard.

"Twenty-one hundred," said Woodden.

"That's right, Mr. Woodden," cried Mr. Primrose, "you are indeed representing your principal worthily. I feel sure that you do not mean to stop for a few miserable pounds."

"Not if I knows it," ejaculated Woodden. "I has my orders and I acts up to them."

"Twenty-two hundred," said Long-beard.

"Twenty-three," echoed Woodden.

"Oh, damn!" shouted Long-beard and rushed from the room.

"*Odontoglossum Pavo* is going for twenty-three hundred, only twenty-tree hundred," cried the auctioneer. "Any advance on twenty-three hundred? What? None? Then I must do my duty. One. Two. For the last time—no advance? Three. Gone to Mr. Woodden, bidding for his principal, Mr. Somers."

The hammer fell with a sharp tap, and at this moment my young friend sauntered into the room.

"Well, Woodden," he said, "have they put the *Pavo* up yet?"

"It's up and it's down, sir. I've bought him right enough."

"The deuce you have! What did it fetch?"

Woodden scratched his head.

"I don't rightly know, sir, never was good at figures, not having much book learning, but it's twenty-three something."

"£23? No, it would have brought more than that. By Jingo! it must be £230. That's pretty stiff, but still, it may be worth it."

At this moment Mr. Primrose, who, leaning over his desk, was engaged in animated conversation with an excited knot of orchid fanciers, looked up:

"Oh! there you are, Mr. Somers," he said. "In the name of all this company let me congratulate you on having become the owner of the matchless *Odontoglossum Pavo* for what, under all the circumstances, I consider the quite moderate price of £2,300."

Really that young man took it very well. He shivered slightly and turned a little pale, that is all. Woodden rocked to and fro like a tree about to fall. I and my tin box collapsed together in the corner. Yes, I was so surprised that my legs seemed to give way under me. People began to talk, but above the hum of the conversation I heard young Somers say in a low voice:

"Woodden, you're a born fool." Also the answer: "That's what my mother always told me, master, and she ought to know if anyone did. But what's wrong now? I obeyed orders and bought *O. Paving*."

"Yes. Don't bother, my good fellow, it's my fault, not yours. I'm the born fool. But heavens above! how am I to face this?" Then, recovering himself, he strolled up to the rostrum and said a few words to the auctioneer. Mr. Primrose nodded, and I heard him answer:

"Oh, that will be all right, sir, don't bother. We can't expect an account like this to be settled in a minute. A month hence will do."

Then he went on with the sale.

Chapter 3

Sir Alexander and Stephen

It was just at this moment that I saw standing by me a fine-looking, stout man with a square, grey beard and a handsome, but not very good-tempered face. He was looking about him as one does who finds himself in a place to which he is not accustomed.

"Perhaps you could tell me, sir," he said to me, "whether a gentleman called Mr. Somers is in this room. I am rather short-sighted and there are a great many people."

"Yes," I answered, "he has just bought the wonderful orchid called *Odontoglossum Pavo*. That is what they are all talking about."

"Oh, has he? Has he indeed? And pray what did he pay for the article?"

"A huge sum," I answered. "I thought it was two thousand three hundred shillings, but it appears it was £2,300."

The handsome, elderly gentleman grew very red in the face, so red that I thought he was going to have a fit. For a few moments he breathed heavily.

"A rival collector," I thought to myself, and went on with the story which, it occurred to me, might interest him.

"You see, the young gentleman was called away to an interview with his father. I heard him instruct his gardener, a man named Wooden, to buy the plant at any price."

"At any price! Indeed. Very interesting; continue, sir."

"Well, the gardener bought it, that's all, after tremendous competition. Look, there he is packing it up. Whether his master meant him to go as far as he did I rather doubt. But here he comes. If you know him——"

The youthful Mr. Somers, looking a little pale and *distrait*, strolled up apparently to speak to me; his hands were in his pockets and an unlighted cigar was in his mouth. His eyes fell upon the elderly gentleman, a sight that caused him to shape his lips as though to whistle and drop the cigar.

"Hullo, father," he said in his pleasant voice. "I got your message and have been looking for you, but never thought that I should find you here. Orchids aren't much in your line, are they?"

"Didn't you, indeed!" replied his parent in a choked voice. "No, I haven't much use for—this stinking rubbish," and he waved his umbrella at the beautiful flowers. "But it seems that you have, Stephen. This little gentlemen here tells me you have just bought a very fine specimen."

"I must apologize," I broke in, addressing Mr. Somers. "I had not the slightest idea that this—big gentleman," here the son smiled faintly, "was your intimate relation."

"Oh! pray don't, Mr. Quatermain. Why should you not speak of what will be in all the papers. Yes, father, I have bought a very fine specimen, the finest known, or at least Woodden has on my behalf, while I was hunting for you, which comes to the same thing."

"Indeed, Stephen, and what did you pay for this flower? I have heard a figure, but think that there must be some mistake."

"I don't know what you heard, father, but it seems to have been knocked down to me at £2,300. It's a lot more than I can find, indeed, and I was going to ask you to lend me the money for the sake of the family credit, if not for my own. But we can talk about that afterwards."

"Yes, Stephen, we can talk of that afterwards. In fact, as there is no time like the present, we will talk of it now. Come to my office. And, sir" (this was to me) "as you seem to know something of the circumstances, I will ask you to come also; and you too, Blockhead" (this was to Woodden, who just then approached with the plant).

Now, of course, I might have refused an invitation conveyed in such a manner. But, as a matter of fact, I didn't. I wanted to see the thing out; also to put in a word for young Somers, if I got the chance. So we all departed from that room, followed by a titter of amusement from those of the company who had overheard the conversation. In the street stood a splendid carriage and pair; a powdered footman opened its door. With a ferocious bow Sir Alexander motioned to me to enter, which I did, taking one of the back seats as it gave more room for my tin case. Then came Mr. Stephen, then Woodden bundled in holding the precious plant in front of him like a wand of office, and last of all, Sir Alexander, having seen us safe, entered also.

"Where to, sir?" asked the footman.

"Office," he snapped, and we started.

Four disappointed relatives in a funeral coach could not have been more silent. Our feelings seemed to be too deep for words. Sir Alexander, however, did make one remark and to me. It was:

"If you will remove the corner of that infernal tin box of yours from my ribs I shall be obliged to you, sir."

"Your pardon," I exclaimed, and in my efforts to be accommodating, dropped it on his toe. I will not repeat the remark he made, but I may explain that he was gouty. His son suddenly became afflicted with a sense of the absurdity of the situation. He kicked me on the shin, he even dared to wink, and then began to swell visibly with suppressed laughter. I was in agony, for if he had exploded I do not know what would have happened. Fortunately, at this moment the carriage stopped at the door of a fine office. Without waiting for the footman Mr. Stephen bundled out and vanished into the building—I suppose to laugh in safety. Then I descended with the tin case; then, by command, followed Woodden with the flower, and lastly came Sir Alexander.

"Stop here," he said to the coachman; "I shan't be long. Be so good as to follow me, Mr. What's-your-name, and you, too, Gardener."

We followed, and found ourselves in a big room luxuriously furnished in a heavy kind of way. Sir Alexander Somers, I should explain, was an enormously opulent bullion-broker, whatever a bullion-broker may be. In this room Mr. Stephen was already established; indeed, he was seated on the window-sill swinging his leg.

"Now we are alone and comfortable," growled Sir Alexander with sarcastic ferocity.

"As the boa-constrictor said to the rabbit in the cage," I remarked.

I did not mean to say it, but I had grown nervous, and the thought leapt from my lips in words. Again Mr. Stephen began to swell. He turned his face to the window as though to contemplate the wall beyond, but I could see his shoulders shaking. A dim light of intelligence shone in Woodden's pale eyes. About three minutes later the joke got home. He gurgled something about boa-constrictors and rabbits and gave a short, loud laugh. As for Sir Alexander, he merely said:

"I did not catch your remark, sir, would you be so good as to repeat it?"

As I appeared unwilling to accept the invitation, he went on:

"Perhaps, then, you would repeat what you told me in that saleroom?"

"Why should I?" I asked. "I spoke quite clearly and you seemed to understand."

"You are right," replied Sir Alexander; "to waste time is useless." He wheeled round on Woodden, who was standing near the door still holding the paper-wrapped plant in front of him. "Now, blockhead," he shouted, "tell me why you brought that thing."

Woodden made no answer, only rocked a little. Sir Alexander reiterated his command. This time Woodden set the plant upon a table and replied:

"If you're aspeaking to me, sir, that baint my name, and what's more, if you calls me so again, I'll punch your head, whoever you be," and very deliberately he rolled up the sleeves on his brawny arms, a sight at which I too began to swell with inward merriment.

"Look here, father," said Mr. Stephen, stepping forward. "What's the use of all this? The thing's perfectly plain. I did tell Woodden to buy the plant at any price. What is more I gave him a written authority which was passed up to the auctioneer. There's no getting out of it. It is true it never occurred to me that it would go for anything like £2,300—the odd £300 was more my idea, but Woodden only obeyed his orders, and ought not to be abused for doing so."

"There's what I call a master worth serving," remarked Woodden.

"Very well, young man," said Sir Alexander, "you have purchased this article. Will you be so good as to tell me how you propose it should be paid for."

"I propose, father, that you should pay for it," replied Mr. Stephen sweetly. "Two thousand three hundred pounds, or ten times that amount, would not make you appreciably poorer. But if, as is probable, you take a different view, then I propose to pay for it myself. As you know a certain sum of money came to me under my mother's will in which you have only a life interest. I shall raise the amount upon that security—or otherwise."

If Sir Alexander had been angry before, now he became like a mad bull in a china shop. He pranced round the room; he used language that should not pass the lips of any respectable merchant of bullion; in short, he did everything that a person in his position ought not to do. When he was tired he rushed to a desk, tore a cheque from a book and filled it in for a sum of £2,300 to bearer, which cheque he blotted, crumpled up and literally threw at the head of his son.

"You worthless, idle young scoundrel," he bellowed. "I put you in this office here that you may learn respectable and orderly habits and in due course succeed to a very comfortable business. What happens? You don't take a ha'porth of interest in bullion-broking, a subject of which I believe you to remain profoundly ignorant. You don't even spend your money, or rather my money, upon any gentleman-like vice, such as horse-racing, or cards, or even—well, never mind. No, you take to flowers, miserable, beastly flowers, things that a cow eats and clerks grow in back gardens."

"An ancient and Arcadian taste. Adam is supposed to have lived in a garden," I ventured to interpolate.

"Perhaps you would ask your friend with the stubbly hair to remain quiet," snorted Sir Alexander. "I was about to add, although for the sake of my name I meet your debts, that I have had enough of this kind of thing. I disinherit you, or will do if I live till 4 p.m. when the lawyer's office shuts, for thank God! there are no entailed estates, and I dismiss you from the firm. You can go and earn your living in any way you please, by orchid-hunting if you like." He paused, gasping for breath.

"Is that all, father?" asked Mr. Stephen, producing a cigar from his pocket.

"No, it isn't, you cold-blooded young beggar. That house you occupy at Twickenham is mine. You will be good enough to clear out of it; I wish to take possession."

"I suppose, father, I am entitled to a week's notice like any other tenant," said Mr. Stephen, lighting the cigar. "In fact," he added, "if you answer no, I think I shall ask you to apply for an ejection order. You will understand that I have arrangements to make before taking a fresh start in life."

"Oh! curse your cheek, you—you—cucumber!" raged the infuriated merchant prince. Then an inspiration came to him. "You think more of an ugly flower than of your father, do you? Well, at least I'll put an end to that," and he made a dash at the plant on the table with the evident intention of destroying the same.

But the watching Woodden saw. With a kind of lurch he interposed his big frame between Sir Alexander and the object of his wrath.

"Touch *O. Paving* and I knocks yer down," he drawled out.

Sir Alexander looked at *O. Paving*, then he looked at Woodden's leg-of-mutton fist, and—changed his mind.

"Curse *O. Paving*," he said, "and everyone who has to do with it," and swung out of the room, banging the door behind him.

"Well, that's over," said Mr. Stephen gently, as he fanned himself with a pocket-handkerchief. "Quite exciting while it lasted, wasn't it, Mr. Quatermain—but I have been there before, so to speak. And now what do you say to some luncheon? Pym's is close by, and they have very good oysters. Only I think we'll drive round by the bank and hand in this cheque. When he's angry my parent is capable of anything. He might even stop it. Woodden, get off down to Twickenham with *O. Pavo*. Keep it warm, for it feels rather like frost. Put it in the stove for tonight and give it a little, just a little tepid water, but be careful not to touch the flower. Take a four-wheeled cab, it's slow but safe, and mind you keep the windows up and don't smoke. I shall be home for dinner."

Woodden pulled his forelock, seized the pot in his left hand, and departed with his right fist raised—I suppose in case Sir Alexander should be waiting for him round the corner.

Then we departed also and, after stopping for a minute at the bank to pay in the cheque, which I noted, notwithstanding its amount, was accepted without comment, ate oysters in a place too crowded to allow of conversation.

"Mr. Quatermain," said my host, "it is obvious that we cannot talk here, and much less look at that orchid of yours, which I want to study at leisure. Now, for a week or so at any rate I have a roof over my head, and in short, will you be my guest for a night or two? I know nothing about you, and of me you only know that I am the disinherited son of a father, to whom I have failed to give satisfaction. Still it is possible that we might pass a few pleasant hours together talking of flowers and other things; that is, if you have no previous engagement."

"I have none," I answered. "I am only a stranger from South Africa lodging at an hotel. If you will give me time to call for my bag, I will pass the night at your house with pleasure."

By the aid of Mr. Somers' smart dog-cart, which was waiting at a city mews, we reached Twickenham while there was still half an hour of daylight. The house, which was called Verbena Lodge, was small, a square, red-brick building of the early Georgian period, but the gardens covered quite an acre of ground and were very beautiful, or must have been so in summer. Into the greenhouse we did not enter, because it was too late to see the flowers. Also, just when we came to them, Woodden arrived in his four-wheeled cab and departed with his master to see to the housing of *O. Pavo*."

Then came dinner, a very pleasant meal. My host had that day been turned out upon the world, but he did not allow this circumstance to interfere with his spirits in the least. Also he was evidently determined to enjoy its good things while they lasted, for his champagne and port were excellent.

"You see, Mr. Quatermain," he said, "it's just as well we had the row which has been boiling up for a long while. My respected father has made so much money that he thinks I should go and do likewise. Now I don't see it. I like flowers, especially orchids, and I hate bullion-broking. To me the only decent places in London are that sale-room where we met and the Horticultural Gardens."

"Yes," I answered rather doubtfully, "but the matter seems a little serious. Your parent was very emphatic as to his intentions, and after this kind of thing," and I pointed to the beautiful silver and the port, "how will you like roughing it in a hard world?"

"Don't think I shall mind a bit; it would be rather a pleasant change. Also, even if my father doesn't alter his mind, as he may, for he likes me at bottom because I resemble my dear mother, things ain't so very bad. I have got some money that she left me, £6,000 or £7,000, and I'll sell that *Odontoglossum Pavo* for what it will fetch to Sir Joshua Tredgold—he was the man with the long beard who you tell me ran up Woodden to over £2,000—or failing him to someone else. I'll write about it tonight. I don't think I have any debts to speak of, for the Governor has been allowing me £3,000 a year, at least that is my share of the profits paid to me in return for my bullion-broking labours, and except flowers, I have no expensive tastes. So the devil take the past, here's to the future and whatever it may bring," and he polished off the glass of port he held and laughed in his jolly fashion.

Really he was a most attractive young man, a little reckless, it is true, but then recklessness and youth mix well, like brandy and soda.

I echoed the toast and drank off my port, for I like a good glass of wine when I can get it, as would anyone who has had to live for months on rotten water, although I admit that agrees with me better than the port.

"Now, Mr. Quatermain," he went on, "if you have done, light your pipe and let's go into the other room and study that *Cypripedium* of yours. I shan't sleep tonight unless I see it again first. Stop a bit, though, we'll get hold of that old ass, Woodden, before he turns in."

"Woodden," said his master, when the gardener had arrived, "this gentleman, Mr. Quatermain, is going to show you an orchid that is ten times finer than *O. Pavo!*"

"Beg pardon, sir," answered Woodden, "but if Mr. Quatermain says that, he lies. It ain't in nature; it don't bloom nowhere."

I opened the case and revealed the golden *Cypripedium*. Woodden stared at it and rocked. Then he stared again and felt his head as though to make sure it was on his shoulders. Then he gasped.

"Well, if that there flower baint made up, it's a *master one*! If I could see that there flower ablowing on the plant I'd die happy."

"Woodden, stop talking, and sit down," exclaimed his master. "Yes, there, where you can look at the flower. Now, Mr. Quatermain, will you tell us the story of that orchid from beginning to end. Of course omitting its habitat if you like, for it isn't fair to ask that secret. Woodden can be trusted to hold his tongue, and so can I."

I remarked that I was sure they could, and for the next half-hour talked almost without interruption, keeping nothing back and explaining that I was anxious to find someone who would finance an expedition to search for this particular plant; as I believed, the only one of its sort that existed in the world.

"How much will it cost?" asked Mr. Somers.

"I lay it at £2,000," I answered. "You see, we must have plenty of men and guns and stores, also trade goods and presents."

"I call that cheap. But supposing, Mr. Quatermain, that the expedition proves successful and the plant is secured, what then?"

"Then I propose that Brother John, who found it and of whom I have told you, should take one-third of whatever it might sell for, that I as captain of the expedition should take one-third, and that whoever finds the necessary money should take the remaining third."

"Good! That's settled."

"What's settled?" I asked.

"Why, that we should divide in the proportions you named, only I bargain to be allowed to take my whack in kind—I mean in plant, and to have the first option of purchasing the rest of the plant at whatever value may be agreed upon."

"But, Mr. Somers, do you mean that you wish to find £2,000 and make this expedition in person?"

"Of course I do. I thought you understood that. That is, if you will have me. Your old friend, the lunatic, you and I will together seek for and find this golden flower. I say that's settled."

On the morrow accordingly, it was settled with the help of a document, signed in duplicate by both of us.

Before these arrangements were finally concluded, however, I insisted that Mr. Somers should meet my late companion, Charlie Scroope, when I was not present, in order that the latter might give him a full and particular report concerning myself. Apparently the interview was satisfactory, at least so I judged from the very cordial and even respectful manner in which young Somers met me after it was over. Also I thought it my duty to explain to him with much clearness in the presence of Scroope as a witness, the great dangers of such an enterprise as that on which he proposed to embark. I told him straight out that he must be prepared to find his death in it from starvation, fever, wild beasts or at the hands of savages, while success was quite problematical and very likely would not be attained.

"*You* are taking these risks," he said.

"Yes," I answered, "but they are incident to the rough trade I follow, which is that of a hunter and explorer. Moreover, my youth is past, and I have gone through experiences and bereavements of which you know nothing, that cause me to set a very slight value on life. I care little whether I die or continue in the world for some few added years. Lastly, the excitement of adventure has become a kind of necessity for me. I do not think that I could live in England for very long. Also I'm a fatalist. I believe that when my time comes I must go, that this hour is foreordained and that nothing I can do will either hasten or postpone it by one moment. Your circumstances are different. You are quite young. If you stay here and approach your father in a proper spirit, I have no doubt but that he will forget all the rough words he said to you the other day, for which indeed you know you gave him some provocation. Is it worth while throwing up such prospects and undertaking such dangers for the chance of finding a rare flower? I say this to my own disadvantage, since I might find it hard to discover anyone else who would risk £2,000 upon such a venture, but I do urge you to weigh my words."

Young Somers looked at me for a little while, then he broke into one of his hearty laughs and exclaimed, "Whatever else you may be, Mr. Allan Quatermain, you are a gentleman. No bullion-broker in the City could have put the matter more fairly in the teeth of his own interests."

"Thank you," I said.

"For the rest," he went on, "I too am tired of England and want to see the world. It isn't the golden *Cypripedium* that I seek, although I should like to win it well enough. That's only a symbol. What I seek are adventure and romance. Also, like you I am a fatalist. God chose His own time to send us here, and I presume that He will choose His own time to take us away again. So I leave the matter of risks to Him."

"Yes, Mr. Somers," I replied rather solemnly. "You may find adventure and romance, there are plenty of both in Africa. Or you may find a nameless grave in some fever-haunted swamp. Well, you have chosen, and I like your spirit."

Still I was so little satisfied about this business, that a week or so before we sailed, after much consideration, I took it upon myself to write a letter to Sir Alexander Somers, in which I set forth the whole matter as clearly as I could, not blinking the dangerous nature of our undertaking. In conclusion, I asked him whether he thought it wise to allow his only son to accompany such an expedition, mainly because of a not very serious quarrel with himself.

As no answer came to this letter I went on with our preparations. There was money in plenty, since the re-sale of *O. Pavo* to Sir Joshua

Tredgold, at some loss, had been satisfactorily carried out, which enabled me to invest in all things needful with a cheerful heart. Never before had I been provided with such an outfit as that which preceded us to the ship.

At length the day of departure came. We stood on the platform at Paddington waiting for the Dartmouth train to start, for in those days the African mail sailed from that port. A minute or two before the train left, as we were preparing to enter our carriage I caught sight of a face that I seemed to recognise, the owner of which was evidently searching for someone in the crowd. It was that of Briggs, Sir Alexander's clerk, whom I had met in the sale-room.

"Mr. Briggs," I said as he passed me, "are you looking for Mr. Somers? If so, he is in here."

The clerk jumped into the compartment and handed a letter to Mr. Somers. Then he emerged again and waited. Somers read the letter and tore off a blank sheet from the end of it, on which he hastily wrote some words. He passed it to me to give to Briggs, and I could not help seeing what was written. It was: "Too late now. God bless you, my dear father. I hope we may meet again. If not, try to think kindly of your troublesome and foolish son, Stephen."

In another minute the train had started.

"By the way," he said, as we steamed out of the station, "I have heard from my father, who enclosed this for you."

I opened the envelope, which was addressed in a bold, round hand that seemed to me typical of the writer, and read as follows:

> *My Dear Sir,*—I appreciate the motives which caused you to write to me and I thank you very heartily for your letter, which shows me that you are a man of discretion and strict honour. As you surmise, the expedition on which my son has entered is not one that commends itself to me as prudent. Of the differences between him and myself you are aware, for they came to a climax in your presence. Indeed, I feel that I owe you an apology for having dragged you into an unpleasant family quarrel. Your letter only reached me today having been forwarded to my place in the country from my office. I should have at once come to town, but unfortunately I am laid up with an attack of gout which makes it impossible for me to stir. Therefore, the only thing I can do is to write to my son hoping that the letter which I send by a special messenger will reach him in time and avail to alter his determination to undertake this journey. Here

I may add that although I have differed and do differ from him on various points, I still have a deep affection for my son and earnestly desire his welfare. The prospect of any harm coming to him is one upon which I cannot bear to dwell.

Now I am aware that any change of his plans at this eleventh hour would involve you in serious loss and inconvenience. I beg to inform you formally, therefore, that in this event I will make good everything and will in addition write off the £2,000 which I understand he has invested in your joint venture. It may be, however, that my son, who has in him a vein of my own obstinacy, will refuse to change his mind. In that event, under a *higher power* I can only commend him to your care and beg that you will look after him as though he were your own child. I can ask and you can do no more. Tell him to write me as opportunity offers, as perhaps you will too; also that, although I hate the sight of them, I will look after the flowers which he has left at the house at Twickenham.

Your obliged servant,
Alexander Somers

This letter touched me much, and indeed made me feel very uncomfortable. Without a word I handed it to my companion, who read it through carefully.

"Nice of him about the orchids," he said. "My dad has a good heart, although he lets his temper get the better of him, having had his own way all his life."

"Well, what will you do?" I asked.

"Go on, of course. I've put my hand to the plough and I am not going to turn back. I should be a cur if I did, and what's more, whatever he might say he'd think none the better of me. So please don't try to persuade me, it would be no good."

For quite a while afterwards young Somers seemed to be comparatively depressed, a state of mind that in his case was rare indeed. At last, he studied the wintry landscape through the carriage window and said nothing. By degrees, however, he recovered, and when we reached Dartmouth was as cheerful as ever, a mood that I could not altogether share.

Before we sailed I wrote to Sir Alexander telling him exactly how things stood, and so I think did his son, though he never showed me the letter.

At Durban, just as we were about to start up country, I received an answer from him, sent by some boat that followed us very closely. In it he said that he quite understood the position, and whatever happened would attribute no blame to me, whom he should always regard with friendly feelings. He told me that, in the event of any difficulty or want of money, I was to draw on him for whatever might be required, and that he had advised the African Bank to that effect. Further, he added, that at least his son had shown grit in this matter, for which he respected him.

And now for a long while I must bid good-bye to Sir Alexander Somers and all that has to do with England.

Chapter 4
Mavovo and Hans

We arrived safely at Durban at the beginning of March and took up our quarters at my house on the Berea, where I expected that Brother John would be awaiting us. But no Brother John was to be found. The old, lame Griqua, Jack, who looked after the place for me and once had been one of my hunters, said that shortly after I went away in the ship, Dogeetah, as he called him, had taken his tin box and his net and walked off inland, he knew not where, leaving, as he declared, no message or letter behind him. The cases full of butterflies and dried plants were also gone, but these, I found he had shipped to some port in America, by a sailing vessel bound for the United States which chanced to put in at Durban for food and water. As to what had become of the man himself I could get no clue. He had been seen at Maritzburg and, according to some *Kaffirs* whom I knew, afterwards on the borders of Zululand, where, so far as I could learn, he vanished into space.

This, to say the least of it, was disconcerting, and a question arose as to what was to be done. Brother John was to have been our guide. He alone knew the Mazitu people; he alone had visited the borders of the mysterious Pongo-land, I scarcely felt inclined to attempt to reach that country without his aid.

When a fortnight had gone by and still there were no signs of him, Stephen and I held a solemn conference. I pointed out the difficulties and dangers of the situation to him and suggested that, under the circumstances, it might be wise to give up this wild orchid-chase and go elephant hunting instead in a certain part of Zululand, where in those days these animals were still abundant.

He was inclined to agree with me, since the prospect of killing elephants had attractions for him.

"And yet," I said, after reflection, "it's curious, but I never remember making a successful trip after altering plans at the last moment, that is, unless one was driven to it."

"I vote we toss up," said Somers; "it gives providence a chance. Now then, heads for the Golden Cyp, and tails for the elephants."

He spun a half-crown into the air. It fell and rolled under a great, yellow-wood chest full of curiosities that I had collected, which it took all our united strength to move. We dragged it aside and not without some excitement, for really a good deal hung upon the chance, I lit a match and peered into the shadow. There in the dust lay the coin.

"What is it?" I asked of Somers, who was stretched on his stomach on the chest.

"Orchid—I mean head," he answered. "Well, that's settled, so we needn't bother any more."

The next fortnight was a busy time for me. As it happened there was a schooner in the bay of about one hundred tons burden which belonged to a Portuguese trader named Delgado, who dealt in goods that he carried to the various East African ports and Madagascar. He was a villainous-looking person whom I suspected of having dealings with the slave traders, who were very numerous and a great power in those days, if indeed he were not one himself. But as he was going to Kilwa whence we proposed to start inland, I arranged to make use of him to carry our party and the baggage. The bargain was not altogether easy to strike for two reasons. First, he did not appear to be anxious that we should hunt in the districts at the back of Kilwa, where he assured me there was no game, and secondly, he said that he wanted to sail at once. However, I overcame his objections with an argument he could not resist—namely, money, and in the end he agreed to postpone his departure for fourteen days.

Then I set about collecting our men, of whom I had made up my mind there must not be less than twenty. Already I had sent messengers summoning to Durban from Zululand and the upper districts of Natal various hunters who had accompanied me on other expeditions. To the number of a dozen or so they arrived in due course. I have always had the good fortune to be on the best of terms with my *Kaffirs*, and where I went they were ready to go without asking any questions. The man whom I had selected to be their captain under me was a Zulu of the name of Mavovo. He was a short fellow, past middle age, with an enormous chest. His strength was proverbial; indeed, it was said that he could throw an ox by the horns, and myself I have seen him hold down the head of a wounded buffalo that had fallen, until I could come up and shoot it.

When I first knew Mavovo he was a petty chief and witch doctor in Zululand. Like myself, he had fought for the Prince Umbelazi in the great battle of the Tugela, a crime which Cetewayo never forgave him. About a year afterwards he got warning that he had been smelt out as a wizard and was going to be killed. He fled with two of his wives and a child. The slayers overtook them before he could reach the Natal border, and stabbed the elder wife and the child of the second wife. They were four men, but, made mad by the sight, Mavovo turned on them and killed them all. Then, with the remaining wife, cut to pieces as he was, he crept to the river and through it to Natal. Not long after this wife died also; it was said from grief at the loss of her child. Mavovo did not marry again, perhaps because he was now a man without means, for Cetewayo had taken all his cattle; also he was made ugly by an assegai wound which had cut off his right nostril. Shortly after the death of his second wife he sought me out and told me he was a chief without a *kraal* and wished to become my hunter. So I took him on, a step which I never had any cause to regret, since although morose and at times given to the practice of uncanny arts, he was a most faithful servant and brave as a lion, or rather as a buffalo, for a lion is not always brave.

Another man whom I did not send for, but who came, was an old Hottentot named Hans, with whom I had been more or less mixed up all my life. When I was a boy he was my father's servant in the Cape Colony and my companion in some of those early wars. Also he shared some very terrible adventures with me which I have detailed in the history I have written of my first wife, Marie Marais. For instance, he and I were the only persons who escaped from the massacre of Retief and his companions by the Zulu king, Dingaan. In the subsequence campaigns, including the Battle of the Blood River, he fought at my side and ultimately received a good share of captured cattle. After this he retired and set up a native store at a place called Pinetown, about fifteen miles out of Durban. Here I am afraid he got into bad ways and took to drink more or less; also to gambling. At any rate, he lost most of his property, so much of it indeed that he scarcely knew which way to turn. Thus it happened that one evening when I went out of the house where I had been making up my accounts, I saw a yellow-faced white-haired old fellow squatted on the veranda smoking a pipe made out of a corn-cob.

"Good day, Baas," he said, "here am I, Hans."

"So I see," I answered, rather coldly. "And what are you doing here, Hans? How can you spare time from your drinking and gambling at Pinetown to visit me here, Hans, after I have not seen you for three years?"

"Baas, the gambling is finished, because I have nothing more to stake, and the drinking is done too, because but one bottle of Cape Smoke makes me feel quite ill next morning. So now I only take water and as little of that as I can, water and some tobacco to cover up its taste."

"I am glad to hear it, Hans. If my father, the Predikant who baptised you, were alive now, he would have much to say about your conduct as indeed I have no doubt he will presently when you have gone into a hole (*i.e.*, a grave). For there in the hole he will be waiting for you, Hans."

"I know, I know, Baas. I have been thinking of that and it troubles me. Your reverend father, the Predikant, will be very cross indeed with me when I join him in the Place of Fires where he sits awaiting me. So I wish to make my peace with him by dying well, and in your service, Baas. I hear that the Baas is going on an expedition. I have come to accompany the Baas."

"To accompany me! Why, you are old, you are not worth five shillings a month and your *scoff* (food). You are a shrunken old brandy cask that will not even hold water."

Hans grinned right across his ugly face.

"Oh! Baas, I am old, but I am clever. All these years I have been gathering wisdom. I am as full of it as a bee's nest is with honey when the summer is done. And, Baas, I can stop those leaks in the cask."

"Hans, it is no good, I don't want you. I am going into great danger. I must have those about me whom I can trust."

"Well, Baas, and who can be better trusted than Hans? Who warned you of the attack of the Quabies on Maraisfontein, and so saved the life of——"

"Hush!" I said.

"I understand. I will not speak the name. It is holy not to be mentioned. It is the name of one who stands with the white angels before God; not to be mentioned by poor drunken Hans. Still, who stood at your side in that great fight? Ah! it makes me young again to think of it, when the roof burned; when the door was broken down; when we met the Quabies on the spears; when you held the pistol to the head of the Holy One whose name must not be mentioned, the Great One who knew how to die. Oh! Baas, our lives are twisted up together like the creeper and the tree, and where you go, there I must go also. Do not turn me away. I ask no wages, only a bit of food and a handful of tobacco, and the light of your face and a word now and again of the memories that belong to both of us. I am still very strong. I can shoot well—well, Baas, who was it that put it into your mind to aim at the tails of the vultures on the Hill of Slaughter yonder in Zululand, and so saved the lives of all the Boer people, and of her whose holy name must not be mentioned? Baas, you will not turn me away?"

"No," I answered, "you can come. But you will swear by the spirit of my father, the Predikant, to touch no liquor on this journey."

"I swear by his spirit and by that of the Holy One," and he flung himself forward on to his knees, took my hand and kissed it. Then he rose and said in a matter-of-fact tone, "If the Baas can give me two blankets, I shall thank him, also five shillings to buy some tobacco and a new knife. Where are the Baas's guns? I must go to oil them. I beg that the Baas will take with him that little rifle which is named *Intombi* (Maiden), the one with which he shot the vultures on the Hill of Slaughter, the one that killed the geese in the Goose Kloof when I loaded for him and he won the great match against the Boer whom Dingaan called Two-faces."

"Good," I said. "Here are the five shillings. You shall have the blankets and a new gun and all things needful. You will find the guns in the little back room and with them those of the Baas, my companion, who also is your master. Go see to them."

At length all was ready, the cases of guns, ammunition, medicines, presents and food were on board the *Maria*. So were four donkeys that I had bought in the hope that they would prove useful, either to ride or as pack beasts. The donkey, be it remembered, and man are the only animals which are said to be immune from the poisonous effects of the bite of tsetse fly, except, of course, the wild game. It was our last night at Durban, a very beautiful night of full moon at the end of March, for the Portuguese Delgado had announced his intention of sailing on the following afternoon. Stephen Somers and I were seated on the *stoep* smoking and talking things over.

"It is a strange thing," I said, "that Brother John should never have turned up. I know that he was set upon making this expedition, not only for the sake of the orchid, but also for some other reason of which he would not speak. I think that the old fellow must be dead."

"Very likely," answered Stephen (we had become intimate and I called him Stephen now), "a man alone among savages might easily come to grief and never be heard of again. Hark! What's that?" and he pointed to some gardenia bushes in the shadow of the house near by, whence came a sound of something that moved.

"A dog, I expect, or perhaps it is Hans. He curls up in all sorts of places near to where I may be. Hans, are you there?"

A figure arose from the gardenia bushes.

"*Ja*, I am here, Baas."

"What are you doing, Hans?"

"I am doing what the dog does, Baas—watching my master."

"Good," I answered. Then an idea struck me. "Hans, you have heard of the white Baas with the long beard whom the *Kaffirs* call Dogeetah?"

"I have heard of him and once I saw him, a few moons ago passing through Pinetown. A *Kaffir* with him told me that he was going over the Drakensberg to hunt for things that crawl and fly, being quite mad, Baas."

"Well, where is he now, Hans? He should have been here to travel with us."

"Am I a spirit that I can tell the Baas whither a white man has wandered. Yet, stay. Mavovo may be able to tell. He is a great doctor, he can see through distance, and even now, this very night his Snake of divination has entered into him and he is looking into the future, yonder, behind the house. I saw him form the circle."

I translated what Hans said to Stephen, for he had been talking in Dutch, then asked him if he would like to see some *Kaffir* magic.

"Of course," he answered, "but it's all bosh, isn't it?"

"Oh, yes, all bosh, or so most people say," I answered evasively. "Still, sometimes these *Inyangas* tell one strange things."

Then, led by Hans, we crept round the house to where there was a five-foot stone wall at the back of the stable. Beyond this wall, within the circle of some huts where my *Kaffirs* lived, was an open space with an ant-heap floor where they did their cooking. Here, facing us, sat Mavovo, while in a ring around him were all the hunters who were to accompany us; also Jack, the lame Griqua, and the two house-boys. In front of Mavovo burned a number of little wood fires. I counted them and found that there were fourteen, which, I reflected, was the exact number of our hunters, plus ourselves. One of the hunters was engaged in feeding these fires with little bits of stick and handfuls of dried grass so as to keep them burning brightly. The others sat round perfectly silent and watched with rapt attention. Mavovo himself looked like a man who is asleep. He was crouched on his haunches with his big head resting almost upon his knees. About his middle was a snake-skin, and round his neck an ornament that appeared to be made of human teeth. On his right side lay a pile of feathers from the wings of vultures, and on his left a little heap of silver money—I suppose the fees paid by the hunters for whom he was divining.

After we had watched him for some while from our shelter behind the wall he appeared to wake out of his sleep. First he muttered; then he looked up to the moon and seemed to say a prayer of which I could not catch the words. Next he shuddered three times convulsively and exclaimed in a clear voice:

"My Snake has come. It is within me. Now I can hear, now I can see."

Three of the little fires, those immediately in front of him, were larger than the others. He took up his bundle of vultures' feathers, selected one with care, held it towards the sky, then passed it through the flame of the centre one of the three fires, uttering as he did so, my native name, Macumazana. Withdrawing it from the flame he examined the charred edges of the feather very carefully, a proceeding that caused a cold shiver to go down my back, for I knew well that he was inquiring of his *Spirit* what would be my fate upon this expedition. How it answered, I cannot tell, for he laid the feather down and took another, with which he went through the same process. This time, however, the name he called out was Mwamwazela, which in its shortened form of Wazela, was the *Kaffir* appellation that the natives had given to Stephen Somers. It means a Smile, and no doubt was selected for him because of his pleasant, smiling countenance.

Having passed it through the right-hand fire of the three, he examined it and laid it down.

So it went on. One after another he called out the names of the hunters, beginning with his own as captain; passed the feather which represented each of them through the particular fire of his destiny, examined and laid it down. After this he seemed to go to sleep again for a few minutes, then woke up as a man does from a natural slumber, yawned and stretched himself.

"Speak," said his audience, with great anxiety. "Have you seen? Have you heard? What does your Snake tell you of me? Of me? Of me? Of me?"

"I have seen, I have heard," he answered. "My Snake tells me that this will be a very dangerous journey. Of those who go on it six will die by the bullet, by the spear or by sickness, and others will be hurt."

"Ow?" said one of them, "but which will die and which will come out safe? Does not your Snake tell you that, O Doctor?"

"Yes, of course my Snake tells me that. But my Snake tells me also to hold my tongue on the matter, lest some of us should be turned to cowards. It tells me further that the first who should ask me more, will be one of those who must die. Now do you ask? Or you? Or you? Or you? Ask if you will."

Strange to say no one accepted the invitation. Never have I seen a body of men so indifferent to the future, at least to every appearance. One and all they seemed to come to the conclusion that so far as they were concerned it might be left to look after itself.

"My Snake told me something else," went on Mavovo. "It is that if among this company there is any jackal of a man who, thinking that he might be one of the six to die, dreams to avoid his fate by deserting, it will be of no use. For then my Snake will point him out and show me how to deal with him."

Now with one voice each man present there declared that desertion from the lord Macumazana was the last thing that could possibly occur to him. Indeed, I believe that those brave fellows spoke truth. No doubt they put faith in Mavovo's magic after the fashion of their race. Still the death he promised was some way off, and each hoped he would be one of the six to escape. Moreover, the Zulu of those days was too accustomed to death to fear its terrors over much.

One of them did, however, venture to advance the argument, which Mavovo treated with proper contempt, that the shillings paid for this divination should be returned by him to the next heirs of such of them as happened to decease. Why, he asked, should these pay a shilling in order to be told that they must die? It seemed unreasonable.

Certainly the Zulu *Kaffirs* have a queer way of looking at things.

"Hans," I whispered, "is your fire among those that burn yonder?"

"Not so, Baas," he wheezed back into my ear. "Does the Baas think me a fool? If I must die, I must die; if I am to live, I shall live. Why then should I pay a shilling to learn what time will declare? Moreover, yonder Mavovo takes the shillings and frightens everybody, but tells nobody anything. *I* call it cheating. But, Baas, do you and the Baas Wazela have no fear. You did not pay shillings, and therefore Mavovo, though without doubt he is a great *Inyanga*, cannot really prophesy concerning you, since his Snake will not work without a fee."

The argument seems remarkably absurd. Yet it must be common, for now that I come to think of it, no gipsy will tell a "true fortune" unless her hand is crossed with silver.

"I say, Quatermain," said Stephen idly, "since our friend Mavovo seems to know so much, ask him what has become of Brother John, as Hans suggested. Tell me what he says afterwards, for I want to see something."

So I went through the little gate in the wall in a natural kind of way, as though I had seen nothing, and appeared to be struck by the sight of the little fires.

"Well, Mavovo," I said, "are you doing doctor's work? I thought that it had brought you into enough trouble in Zululand."

"That is so, *Baba*," replied Mavovo, who had a habit of calling me *father*, though he was older than I. "It cost me my chieftainship and my cattle and my two wives and my son. It made of me a wanderer who is glad to accompany a certain Macumazana to strange lands where many things may befall me, yes," he added with meaning, "even the last of all things. And yet a gift is a gift and must be used. You, *Baba*, have a gift of shooting and do you cease to shoot? You have a gift of wandering and can you cease to wander?"

He picked up one of the burnt feathers from the little pile by his side and looked at it attentively. "Perhaps, *Baba*, you have been told—my ears are very sharp, and I thought I heard some such words floating through the air just now—that we poor *Kaffir Inyangas* can prophesy nothing true unless we are paid, and perhaps that is a fact so far as something of the moment is concerned. And yet the Snake in the *Inyanga*, jumping over the little rock which hides the present from it, may see the path that winds far and far away through the valleys, across the streams, up the mountains, till it is lost in the 'heaven above.' Thus on this feather, burnt in my magic fire, I seem to see something of your future, O my father Macumazana. Far and far your road runs," and he drew his finger along the feather. "Here is a journey," and he flicked away a carbonised flake, "here is another, and another, and another," and he flicked off flake after flake. "Here is one that is very successful, it leaves you rich; and here is yet one more, a wonderful journey this in which you see strange things and meet strange people. Then"—and he blew on the feather in such a fashion that all the charred filaments (Brother John says that *laminae* is the right word for them) fell away from it—"then, there is nothing left save such a pole as some of my people stick upright on a grave, the Shaft of Memory they call it. O, my father, you will die in a distant land, but you will leave a great memory behind you that will live for hundreds of years, for see how strong is this quill over which the fire has had no power. With some of these others it is quite different," he added.

"I daresay," I broke in, "but, Mavovo, be so good as to leave me out of your magic, for I don't at all want to know what is going to happen to me. Today is enough for me without studying next month and next year. There is a saying in our holy book which runs: *Sufficient to the day is its evil.*"

"Quite so, O Macumazana. Also that is a very good saying as some of those hunters of yours are thinking now. Yet an hour ago they were forcing their shillings on me that I might tell them of the future. And *you*, too, want to know something. You did not come through that gate to quote to me the wisdom of your holy book. What is it, *Baba*? Be quick, for my Snake is getting very tired. He wishes to go back to his hole in the world beneath."

"Well, then," I answered in rather a shamefaced fashion, for Mavovo had an uncanny way of seeing into one's secret motives, "I should like to know, if you can tell me, which you can't, what has become of the white man with the long beard whom you black people call Dogeetah? He should have been here to go on this journey with us; indeed, he was to be our guide and we cannot find him. Where is he and why is he not here?"

"Have you anything about you that belonged to Dogeetah, Macumazana?"

"No," I answered; "that is, yes," and from my pocket I produced the stump of pencil that Brother John had given me, which, being economical, I had saved up ever since. Mavovo took it, and after considering it carefully as he had done in the case of the feathers, swept up a pile of ashes with his horny hand from the edge of the largest of the little fires, that indeed which had represented myself. These ashes he patted flat. Then he drew on them with the point of the pencil, tracing what seemed to me to be the rough image of a man, such as children scratch upon whitewashed walls. When he had finished he sat up and contemplated his handiwork with all the satisfaction of an artist. A breeze had risen from the sea and was blowing in little gusts, so that the fine ashes were disturbed, some of the lines of the picture being filled in and others altered or enlarged.

For a while Mavovo sat with his eyes shut. Then he opened them, studied the ashes and what remained of the picture, and taking a blanket that lay near by, threw it over his own head and over the ashes. Withdrawing it again presently he cast it aside and pointed to the picture which was now quite changed. Indeed, in the moonlight, it looked more like a landscape than anything else.

"All is clear, my father," he said in a matter-of-fact voice. "The white wanderer, Dogeetah, is not dead. He lives, but he is sick. Something is the matter with one of his legs so that he cannot walk. Perhaps a bone is broken or some beast has bitten him. He lies in a hut such as *Kaffirs* make, only this hut has a veranda round it like your *stoep*, and there are drawings on the wall. The hut is a long way off, I don't know where."

"Is that all?" I asked, for he paused.

"No, not all. Dogeetah is recovering. He will join us in that country whither we journey, at a time of trouble. That is all, and the fee is half-a-crown."

"You mean one shilling," I suggested.

"No, my father Macumazana. One shilling for simple magic such as foretelling the fate of common black people. Half-a-crown for very difficult magic that has to do with white people, magic of which only great doctors, like me, Mavovo, are the masters."

I gave him the half-crown and said:

"Look here, friend Mavovo, I believe in you as a fighter and a hunter, but as a magician I think you are a humbug. Indeed, I am so sure of it that if ever Dogeetah turns up at a time of trouble in that land whither we are journeying, I will make you a present of that double-barrelled rifle of mine which you admired so much."

One of his rare smiles appeared upon Mavovo's ugly face.

"Then give it to me now, *Baba*," he said, "for it is already earned. My Snake cannot lie—especially when the fee is half-a-crown."

I shook my head and declined, politely but with firmness.

"Ah!" said Mavovo, "you white men are very clever and think that you know everything. But it is not so, for in learning so much that is new, you have forgotten more that is old. When the Snake that is in you, Macumazana, dwelt in a black savage like me a thousand thousand years ago, you could have done and did what I do. But now you can only mock and say, 'Mavovo the brave in battle, the great hunter, the loyal man, becomes a liar when he blows the burnt feather, or reads what the wind writes upon the charmed ashes.'"

"I do not say that you are a liar, Mavovo, I say that you are deceived by your own imaginings. It is not possible that man can know what is hidden from man."

"Is it indeed so, O Macumazana, Watcher by Night? Am I, Mavovo, the pupil of Zikali, the Opener of Roads, the greatest of wizards, indeed deceived by my own imaginings? And has man no other eyes but those in his head, that he cannot see what is hidden from man? Well, you say so and all we black people know that you are very clever, and why should I, a poor Zulu, be able to see what you cannot see? Yet when tomorrow one sends you a message from the ship in which we are to sail, begging you to come fast because there is trouble on the ship, then bethink you of your words and my words, and whether or no man can see what is hidden from man in the blackness of the future. Oh! that rifle of yours is mine already, though you will not give it to me now, you who think that I am a cheat. Well, my father Macumazana, because you think I am a cheat, never again will I blow the feather or read what the wind writes upon the ashes for you or any who eat your food."

Then he rose, saluted me with uplifted right hand, collected his little pile of money and bag of medicines and marched off to the sleeping hut.

On our way round the house we met my old lame caretaker, Jack.

"*Inkoosi*," he said, "the white chief Wazela bade me say that he and the cook, Sam, have gone to sleep on board the ship to look after the goods. Sam came up just now and fetched him away; he says he will show you why tomorrow."

I nodded and passed on, wondering to myself why Stephen had suddenly determined to stay the night on the *Maria*.

Chapter 5

Hassan

I suppose it must have been two hours after dawn on the following morning that I was awakened by knocks upon the door and the voice of Jack saying that Sam, the cook, wanted to speak to me.

Wondering what he could be doing there, as I understood he was sleeping on the ship, I called out that he was to come in. Now this Sam, I should say, hailed from the Cape, and was a person of mixed blood. The original stock, I imagine, was Malay which had been crossed with Indian coolie. Also, somewhere or other, there was a dash of white and possibly, but of this I am not sure, a little Hottentot. The result was a person of few vices and many virtues. Sammy, I may say at once, was perhaps the biggest coward I ever met. He could not help it, it was congenital, though, curiously enough, this cowardice of his never prevented him from rushing into fresh danger. Thus he knew that the expedition upon which I was engaged would be most hazardous; remembering his weakness I explained this to him very clearly. Yet that knowledge did not deter him from imploring that he might be allowed to accompany me. Perhaps this was because there was some mutual attachment between us, as in the case of Hans. Once, a good many years before, I had rescued Sammy from a somewhat serious scrape by declining to give evidence against him. I need not enter into the details, but a certain sum of money over which he had control had disappeared. I will merely say, therefore, that at the time he was engaged to a coloured lady of very expensive tastes, whom in the end he never married.

After this, as it chanced, he nursed me through an illness. Hence the attachment of which I have spoken.

Sammy was the son of a native Christian preacher, and brought up upon what he called "The Word." He had received an excellent education for a person of his class, and in addition to many native dialects with which a varied career had made him acquainted, spoke English perfectly, though in the most bombastic style. Never would he use a short word if a long one came to his hand, or rather to his tongue. For several years of his life he was, I believe, a teacher in a school at Capetown where coloured persons received their education; his "department," as he called it, being "English Language and Literature."

Wearying of or being dismissed from his employment for some reason that he never specified, he had drifted up the coast to Zanzibar, where he turned his linguistic abilities to the study of Arabic and became the manager or head cook of an hotel. After a few years he lost this billet, I know not how or why, and appeared at Durban in what he called a *reversed position*. Here it was that we met again, just before my expedition to Pongo-land.

In manners he was most polite, in disposition most religious; I believe he was a Baptist by faith, and in appearance a small, brown dandy of a man of uncertain age, who wore his hair parted in the middle and, whatever the circumstances, was always tidy in his garments.

I took him on because he was in great distress, an excellent cook, the best of nurses, and above all for the reason that, as I have said, we were in a way attached to each other. Also, he always amused me intensely, which goes for something on a long journey of the sort that I contemplated.

Such in brief was Sammy.

As he entered the room I saw that his clothes were very wet and asked him at once if it were raining, or whether he had got drunk and been sleeping in the damp grass.

"No, Mr. Quatermain," he answered, "the morning is extremely fine, and like the poor Hottentot, Hans, I have abjured the use of intoxicants. Though we differ on much else, in this matter we agree."

"Then what the deuce is up?" I interrupted, to cut short his flow of fine language.

"Sir, there is trouble on the ship" (remembering Mavovo I started at these words) "where I passed the night in the company of Mr. Somers at his special request." (It was the other way about really.) "This morning before the dawn, when he thought that everybody was asleep, the Portuguese captain and some of his Arabs began to weigh the anchor quite quietly; also to hoist the sails. But Mr. Somers and I, being very much awake, came out of the cabin and he sat upon the capstan with a revolver in his hand, saying—well, sir, I will not repeat what he said."

"No, don't. What happened then?"

"Then, sir, there followed much noise and confusion. The Portuguese and the Arabs threatened Mr. Somers, but he, sir, continued to sit upon the capstan with the stern courage of a rock in a rushing stream, and remarked that he would see them all somewhere before they touched it. After this, sir, I do not know what occurred, since while I watched from the bulwarks someone knocked me head over heels into the sea and being fortunately, a good swimmer, I gained the shore and hurried here to advise you."

"And did you advise anyone else, you idiot?" I asked.

"Yes, sir. As I sped along I communicated to an officer of the port that there was the devil of a mess upon the *Maria* which he would do well to investigate."

By this time I was in my shirt and trousers and shouting to Mavovo and the others. Soon they arrived, for as the costume of Mavovo and his company consisted only of a *moocha* and a blanket, it did not take them long to dress.

"Mavovo," I began, "there is trouble on the ship——"

"O *Baba*," he interrupted with something resembling a grin, "it is very strange, but last night I dreamed that I told you——"

"Curse your dreams," I said. "Gather the men and go down—no, that won't work, there would be murder done. Either it is all over now or it is all right. Get the hunters ready; I come with them. The luggage can be fetched afterwards."

Within less than an hour we were at that wharf off which the *Maria* lay in what one day will be the splendid port of Durban, though in those times its shipping arrangements were exceedingly primitive. A strange-looking band we must have been. I, who was completely dressed, and I trust tidy, marched ahead. Next came Hans in the filthy wide-awake hat which he usually wore and greasy corduroys and after him the oleaginous Sammy arrayed in European reach-me-downs, a billy-cock and a bright blue tie striped with red, garments that would have looked very smart had it not been for his recent immersion. After him followed the fierce-looking Mavovo and his squad of hunters, all of whom wore the *ring* or *isicoco*, as the Zulus call it; that is, a circle of polished black wax sewn into their short hair. They were a grim set of fellows, but as, according to a recent law it was not allowable for them to appear armed in the town, their guns had already been shipped, while their broad stabbing spears were rolled up in their sleeping mats, the blades wrapped round with dried grass.

Each of them, however, bore in his hand a large *knobkerry* of redwood, and they marched four by four in martial fashion. It is true that when we embarked on the big boat to go to the ship much of their warlike ardour evaporated, since these men, who feared nothing on the land, were terribly afraid of that unfamiliar element, the water.

We reached the *Maria*, an unimposing kind of tub, and climbed aboard. On looking aft the first thing that I saw was Stephen seated on the capstan with a pistol in his hand, as Sammy had said. Near by, leaning on the bulwark was the villainous-looking Portuguese, Delgado, apparently in the worst of tempers and surrounded by a number of equally villainous-looking Arab sailors clad in dirty white. In front was the Captain of the port, a well-known and esteemed gentleman of the name of Cato, like myself a small man who had gone through many adventures. Accompanied by some attendants, he was seated on the after-skylight, smoking, with his eyes fixed upon Stephen and the Portuguese.

"Glad to see you, Quatermain," he said. "There's some row on here, but I have only just arrived and don't understand Portuguese, and the gentleman on the capstan won't leave it to explain."

"What's up, Stephen?" I asked, after shaking Mr. Cato by the hand.

"What's up?" replied Somers. "This man," and he pointed to Delgado, "wanted to sneak out to sea with all our goods, that's all, to say nothing of me and Sammy, whom, no doubt, he'd have chucked overboard, as soon as he was out of sight of land. However, Sammy, who knows Portuguese, overheard his little plans and, as you see, I objected."

Well, Delgado was asked for his version of the affair, and, as I expected, explained that he only intended to get a little nearer to the bar and there wait till we arrived. Of course he lied and knew that we were aware of the fact and that his intention had been to slip out to sea with all our valuable property, which he would sell after having murdered or marooned Stephen and the poor cook. But as nothing could be proved, and we were now in strong enough force to look after ourselves and our belongings, I did not see the use of pursuing the argument. So I accepted the explanation with a smile, and asked everybody to join in a morning nip.

Afterwards Stephen told me that while I was engaged with Mavovo on the previous night, a message had reached him from Sammy who was on board the ship in charge of our belongings, saying that he would be glad of some company. Knowing the cook's nervous nature, fortunately enough he made up his mind at once to go and sleep upon the *Maria*. In the morning trouble arose as Sammy had told me. What he did not tell me was that he was not knocked overboard, as he said, but took to the water of his own accord, when complications with Delgado appeared imminent.

"I understand the position," I said, "and all's well that ends well. But it's lucky you thought of coming on board to sleep."

After this everything went right. I sent some of the men back in the charge of Stephen for our remaining effects, which they brought safely aboard, and in the evening we sailed. Our voyage up to Kilwa was beautiful, a gentle breeze driving us forward over a sea so calm that not even Hans, who I think was one of the worst sailors in the world, or the Zulu hunters were really sick, though as Sammy put it, they "declined their food."

I think it was on the fifth night of our voyage, or it may have been the seventh, that we anchored one afternoon off the island of Kilwa, not very far from the old Portuguese fort. Delgado, with whom we had little to do during the passage, hoisted some queer sort of signal. In response a boat came off containing what he called the Port officials, a band of cut-throat, desperate-looking, black fellows in charge of a pock-marked, elderly half-breed who was introduced to us as the Bey Hassan-ben-Mohammed. That Mr. Hassan-ben-Mohammed entirely disapproved of our presence on the ship, and especially of our proposed landing at Kilwa, was evident to me from the moment that I set eyes upon his ill-favoured countenance. After a hurried conference with Delgado, he came forward and addressed me in Arabic, of which I could not understand a word. Luckily, however, Sam the cook, who, as I think I said, was a great linguist, had a fair acquaintance with this tongue, acquired, it appears, while at the Zanzibar hotel; so, not trusting Delgado, I called on him to interpret.

"What is he saying, Sammy?" I asked.

He began to talk to Hassan and replied presently:

"Sir, he makes you many compliments. He says that he has heard what a great man who are from his friend, Delgado, also that you and Mr. Somers are English, a nation which he adores."

"Does he?" I exclaimed. "I should never have thought it from his looks. Thank him for his kind remarks and tell him that we are going to land here and march up country to shoot."

Sammy obeyed, and the conversation went on somewhat as follows:

"With all humility I (*i.e.* Hassan) request you not to land. This country is not a fit place for such noble gentlemen. There is nothing to eat and no head of game has been seen for years. The people in the interior are savages of the worst sort, whom hunger has driven to take to cannibalism. I would not have your blood upon my head. I beg of you, therefore, to go on in this ship to Delagoa Bay, where you will find a good hotel, or to any other place you may select."

A.Q.: "Might I ask you, noble sir, what is your position at Kilwa, that you consider yourself responsible for our safety?"

H.: "Honoured English lord, I am a trader here of Portuguese nationality, but born of an Arab mother of high birth and brought up among that people. I have gardens on the mainland, tended by my native servants who are as children to me, where I grow palms and cassava and ground nuts and plantains and many other kinds of produce. All the tribes in this district look upon me as their chief and venerated father."

A.Q.: "Then, noble Hassan, you will be able to pass us through them, seeing that we are peaceful hunters who wish to harm no one."

(A long consultation between Hassan and Delgado, during which I ordered Mavovo to bring his Zulus on deck with their guns.)

H.: "Honoured English lord, I cannot allow you to land."

A.Q.: "Noble son of the Prophet, I intend to land with my friend, my followers, my donkeys and my goods early tomorrow morning. If I can do so with your leave I shall be glad. If not——" and I glanced at the fierce group of hunters behind me.

H.: "Honoured English lord, I shall be grieved to use force, but let me tell you that in my peaceful village ashore I have at least a hundred men armed with rifles, whereas here I see under twenty."

A.Q., after reflection and a few words with Stephen Somers: "Can you tell me, noble sir, if from your peaceful village you have yet sighted the English man-of-war, *Crocodile*; I mean the steamer that is engaged in watching for the dhows of wicked slavers? A letter from her captain informed me that he would be in these waters by yesterday. Perhaps, however, he has been delayed for a day or two."

If I had exploded a bomb at the feet of the excellent Hassan its effect could scarcely have been more remarkable than that of this question. He turned—not pale, but a horrible yellow, and exclaimed:

"English man-of-war! *Crocodile*! I thought she had gone to Aden to refit and would not be back at Zanzibar for four months."

A.Q.: "You have been misinformed, noble Hassan. She will not refit till October. Shall I read you the letter?" and I produced a piece of paper from my pocket. "It may be interesting since my friend, the captain, whom you remember is named Flowers, mentions you in it. He says——"

Hassan waved his hand. "It is enough. I see, honoured lord, that you are a man of mettle not easily to be turned from your purpose. In the name of God the Compassionate, land and go wheresoever you like."

A.Q.: "I think that I had almost rather wait until the *Crocodile* comes in."

H.: "Land! Land! Captain Delgado, get up the cargo and man your boat. Mine too is at the service of these lords. You, Captain, will like to get away by this night's tide. There is still light, Lord Quatermain, and such hospitality as I can offer is at your service."

A.Q.: "Ah! I knew Bey Hassan, that you were only joking with me when you said that you wished us to go elsewhere. An excellent jest, truly, from one whose hospitality is so famous. Well, to fall in with your wishes, we will come ashore this evening, and if the Captain Delgado chances to sight the Queen's ship *Crocodile* before he sails, perhaps he will be so good as to signal to us with a rocket."

"Certainly, certainly," interrupted Delgado, who up to this time had pretended that he understood no English, the tongue in which I was speaking to the interpreter, Sammy.

Then he turned and gave orders to his Arab crew to bring up our belongings from the hold and to lower the *Maria*'s boat.

Never did I see goods transferred in quicker time. Within half an hour every one of our packages was off that ship, for Stephen Somers kept a count of them. Our personal baggage went into the *Maria*'s boat, and the goods together with the four donkeys which were lowered on to the top of them, were rumbled pell-mell into the barge-like punt belonging to Hassan. Here also I was accommodated, with about half of our people, the rest taking their seats in the smaller boat under the charge of Stephen.

At length all was ready and we cast off.

"Farewell, Captain," I cried to Delgado. "If you should sight the *Crocodile*——"

At this point Delgado broke into such a torrent of bad language in Portuguese, Arabic and English that I fear the rest of my remarks never reached him.

As we rowed shorewards I observed that Hans, who was seated near to me under the stomach of a jackass, was engaged in sniffing at the sides and bottom of the barge, as a dog might do, and asked him what he was about.

"Very odd smell in this boat," he whispered back in Dutch. "It stinks of *Kaffir* man, just like the hold of the *Maria*. I think this boat is used to carry slaves."

"Be quiet," I whispered back, "and stop nosing at those planks." But to myself I thought, Hans is right, we are in a nest of slave-traders, and this Hassan is their leader.

We rowed past the island, on which I observed the ruins of an old Portuguese fort and some long grass-roofed huts, where, I reflected, the slaves were probably kept until they could be shipped away. Observing my glance fixed upon these, Hassan hastened to explain, through Sammy, that they were storehouses in which he dried fish and hides, and kept goods.

"How interesting!" I answered. "Further south we dry hides in the sun."

Crossing a narrow channel we arrived at a rough jetty where we disembarked, whence we were led by Hassan not to the village which I now saw upon our left, but to a pleasant looking, though dilapidated house that stood a hundred yards from the shore. Something about the appearance of this house impressed me with the idea that it was never built by slavers; the whole look of the place with its veranda and garden suggested taste and civilisation. Evidently educated people had designed it and resided here. I glanced about me and saw, amidst a grove of neglected orange trees that were surrounded with palms of some age, the ruins of a church. About this there was no doubt, for there, surmounted by a stone cross, was a little pent-house in which still hung the bell that once summoned the worshippers to prayer.

"Tell the English lord," said Hassan to Sammy, "that these buildings were a mission station of the Christians, who abandoned them more than twenty years ago. When I came here I found them empty."

"Indeed," I answered, "and what were the names of those who dwelt in them?"

"I never heard," said Hassan; "they had been gone a long while when I came."

Then we went up to the house, and for the next hour and more were engaged with our baggage which was piled in a heap in what had been the garden and in unpacking and pitching two tents for the hunters which I caused to be placed immediately in front of the rooms that were assigned to us. Those rooms were remarkable in their way. Mine had evidently been a sitting chamber, as I judged from some such broken articles of furniture, that appeared to be of American make. That which Stephen occupied had once served as a sleeping-place, for the bedstead of iron still remained there. Also there were a hanging book-case, now fallen, and some tattered remnants of books. One of these, that oddly enough was well-preserved, perhaps because the white ants or other creatures did not like the taste of its morocco binding, was a Keble's *Christian Year*, on the title-page of which was written, *To my dearest Elizabeth on her birthday, from her husband.* I took the liberty to put it in my pocket. On the wall, moreover, still hung the small watercolour picture of a very pretty young woman with fair hair and blue eyes, in the corner of which picture was written in the same handwriting as that in the book, "Elizabeth, aged twenty." This also I annexed, thinking that it might come in useful as a piece of evidence.

"Looks as if the owners of this place had left it in a hurry, Quatermain," said Stephen.

"That's it, my boy. Or perhaps they didn't leave; perhaps they stopped here."

"Murdered?"

I nodded and said, "I dare say friend Hassan could tell us something about the matter. Meanwhile as supper isn't ready yet, let us have a look at that church while it is light."

We walked through the palm and orange grove to where the building stood finely placed upon a mound. It was well-constructed of a kind of coral rock, and a glance showed us that it had been gutted by fire; the discoloured walls told their own tale. The interior was now full of shrubs and creepers, and an ugly, yellowish snake glided from what had been the stone altar. Without, the graveyard was enclosed by a broken wall, only we could see no trace of graves. Near the gateway, however, was a rough mound.

"If we could dig into that," I said, "I expect we should find the bones of the people who inhabited this place. Does that suggest anything to you, Stephen?"

"Nothing, except that they were probably killed."

"You should learn to draw inferences. It is a useful art, especially in Africa. It suggests to me that, if you are right, the deed was not done by natives, who would never take the trouble to bury the dead. Arabs, on the contrary, might do so, especially if there were any bastard Portuguese among them who called themselves Christians. But whatever happened must have been a long while ago," and I pointed to a self-sown hardwood tree growing from the mound which could scarcely have been less than twenty years old.

We returned to the house to find that our meal was ready. Hassan had asked us to dine with him, but for obvious reasons I preferred that Sammy should cook our food and that he should dine with us. He appeared full of compliments, though I could see hate and suspicion in his eye, and we fell to on the kid that we had bought from him, for I did not wish to accept any gifts from this fellow. Our drink was square-face gin, mixed with water that I sent Hans to fetch with his own hands from the stream that ran by the house, lest otherwise it should be drugged.

At first Hassan, like a good Mohammedan, refused to touch any spirits, but as the meal went on he politely relented upon this point, and I poured him out a liberal tot. The appetite comes in eating, as the Frenchman said, and the same thing applies to drinking. So at least it was in Hassan's case, who probably thought that the quantity swallowed made no difference to his sin. After the third dose of square-face he grew quite amiable and talkative. Thinking the opportunity a good one, I sent for Sammy, and through him told our host that we were anxious to hire twenty porters to carry our packages. He declared that there was not such a thing as a porter within a hundred miles, whereon I gave him some more gin. The end of it was that we struck a bargain, I forget for how much, he promising to find us twenty good men who were to stay with us for as long as we wanted them.

Then I asked him about the destruction of the mission station, but although he was half-drunk, on this point he remained very close. All he would say was that he had heard that twenty years ago the people called the Mazitu, who were very fierce, had raided right down to the coast and killed those who dwelt there, except a white man and his wife who had fled inland and never been seen again.

"How many of them were buried in that mound by the church?" I asked quickly.

"Who told you they were buried there?" he replied, with a start, but seeing his mistake, went on, "I do not know what you mean. I never heard of anyone being buried. Sleep well, honoured lords, I must go and see to the loading of my goods upon the *Maria*." Then rising, he salaamed and walked, or rather rolled, away.

"So the *Maria* hasn't sailed after all," I said, and whistled in a certain fashion. Instantly Hans crept into the room out of the darkness, for this was my signal to him.

"Hans," I said, "I hear sounds upon that island. Slip down to the shore and spy out what is happening. No one will see you if you are careful."

"No, Baas," he answered with a grin, "I do not think that anyone will see Hans if he is careful, especially at night," and he slid away as quietly as he had come.

Now I went out and spoke to Mavovo, telling him to keep a good watch and to be sure that every man had his gun ready, as I thought that these people were slave-traders and might attack us in the night.

In that event, I said, they were to fall back upon the *stoep*, but not to fire until I gave the word.

"Good, my father," he answered. "This is a lucky journey; I never thought there would be hope of war so soon. My Snake forgot to mention it the other night. Sleep safe, Macumazana. Nothing that walks shall reach you while we live."

"Don't be so sure," I answered, and we lay down in the bedroom with our clothes on and our rifles by our sides.

The next thing I remember was someone shaking me by the shoulder. I thought it was Stephen, who had agreed to keep awake for the first part of the night and to call me at one in the morning. Indeed, he was awake, for I could see the glow from the pipe he smoked.

"Baas," whispered the voice of Hans, "I have found out everything. They are loading the *Maria* with slaves, taking them in big boats from the island."

"So," I answered. "But how did you get here? Are the hunters asleep without?"

He chuckled. "No, they are not asleep; they look with all their eyes and listen with all their ears, yet old Hans passed through them; even the Baas Somers did not hear him."

"That I didn't," said Stephen; "thought a rat was moving, no more."

I stepped through the place where the door had been on to the *stoep*. By the light of the fire which the hunters had lit without I could see Mavovo sitting wide awake, his gun upon his knees, and beyond him two sentries. I called him and pointed to Hans.

"See," I said, "what good watchmen you are when one can step over your heads and enter my room without your knowing it!"

Mavovo looked at the Hottentot and felt his clothes and boots to see whether they were wet with the night dew.

"Ow!" he exclaimed in a surly voice, "I said that nothing which walks could reach you, Macumazana, but this yellow snake has crawled between us on his belly. Look at the new mud that stains his waistcoat."

"Yet snakes can bite and kill," answered Hans with a snigger. "Oh! you Zulus think that you are very brave, and shout and flourish spears and battleaxes. One poor Hottentot dog is worth a whole *impi* of you after all. No, don't try to strike me, Mavovo the warrior, since we both serve the same master in our separate ways. When it comes to fighting I will leave the matter to you, but when it is a case of watching or spying, do you leave it to Hans. Look here, Mavovo," and he opened his hand in which was a horn snuff-box such as Zulus sometimes carry in their ears. "To whom does this belong?"

"It is mine," said Mavovo, "and you have stolen it."

"Yes," jeered Hans, "it is yours. Also I stole it from your ear as I passed you in the dark. Don't you remember that you thought a gnat had tickled you and hit up at your face?"

"It is true," growled Mavovo, "and you, snake of a Hottentot, are great in your own low way. Yet next time anything tickles me, I shall strike, not with my hand, but with a spear."

Then I turned them both out, remarking to Stephen that this was a good example of the eternal fight between courage and cunning. After this, as I was sure that Hassan and his friends were too busy to interfere with us that night, we went to bed and slept the sleep of the just.

When I got up the next morning I found that Stephen Somers had already risen and gone out, nor did he appear until I was half through my breakfast.

"Where on earth have you been?" I asked, noting that his clothes were torn and covered with wet moss.

"Up the tallest of those palm trees, Quatermain. Saw an Arab climbing one of them with a rope and got another Arab to teach me the trick. It isn't really difficult, though it looks alarming."

"What in the name of goodness——" I began.

"Oh!" he interrupted, "my ruling passion. Looking through the glasses I thought I caught sight of an orchid growing near the crown, so went up. It wasn't an orchid after all, only a mass of yellow pollen. But I learned something for my pains. Sitting in the top of that palm I saw the *Maria* working out from under the lee of the island. Also, far away, I noted a streak of smoke, and watching it through the glasses, made out what looked to me uncommonly like a man-of-war steaming slowly along the coast. In fact, I am sure it was, and English too. Then the mist came up and I lost sight of them."

"My word!" I said, "that will be the *Crocodile*. What I told our host, Hassan, was not altogether bunkum. Mr. Cato, the port officer at Durban, mentioned to me that the *Crocodile* was expected to call there within the next fortnight to take in stores after a slave hunting cruise down the coast. Now it would be odd if she chanced to meet the *Maria* and asked to have a look at her cargo, wouldn't it?"

"Not at all, Quatermain, for unless one or the other of them changes her course that is just what she must do within the next hour or so, and I jolly well hope she will. I haven't forgiven that beast, Delgado, the trick he tried to play on us by slipping away with our goods, to say nothing of those poor devils of slaves. Pass the coffee, will you?"

For the next ten minutes we ate in silence, for Stephen had an excellent appetite and was hungry after his morning climb.

Just as we finished our meal Hassan appeared, looking even more villainous than he had done the previous day. I saw also that he was in a truculent mood, induced perhaps by the headache from which he was evidently suffering as a result of his potations. Or perhaps the fact that the *Maria* had got safe away with the slaves, as he imagined unobserved by us, was the cause of the change of his demeanour. A third alternative may have been that he intended to murder us during the previous night and found no safe opportunity of carrying out his amiable scheme.

We saluted him courteously, but without *salaaming* in reply he asked me bluntly through Sammy when we intended to be gone, as such "Christian dogs defiled his house," which he wanted for himself.

I answered, as soon as the twenty bearers whom he had promised us appeared, but not before.

"You lie," he said. "I never promised you bearers; I have none here."

"Do you mean that you shipped them all away in the *Maria* with the slaves last night?" I asked, sweetly.

My reader, have you ever taken note of the appearance and proceedings of a tom-cat of established age and morose disposition when a little dog suddenly disturbs it on the prowl? Have you observed how it contorts itself into arched but unnatural shapes, how it swells visibly to almost twice its normal size, how its hair stands up and its eyes flash, and the stream of unmentionable language that proceeds from its open mouth? If so, you will have a very good idea of the effect produced upon Hassan by this remark of mine. The fellow looked as though he were going to burst with rage. He rolled about, his bloodshot eyes seemed to protrude, he cursed us horribly, he put his hand upon the hilt of the great knife he wore, and finally he did what the tom-cat does, he spat.

Now, Stephen was standing with me, looking as cool as a cucumber and very much amused, and being, as it chanced, a little nearer to Hassan than I was, received the full benefit of this rude proceeding. My word! didn't it wake him up. He said something strong, and the next second flew at the half-breed like a tiger, landing him a beauty straight upon the nose. Back staggered Hassan, drawing his knife as he did so, but Stephen's left in the eye caused him to drop it, as he dropped himself. I pounced upon the knife, and since it was too late to interfere, for the mischief had been done, let things take their course and held back the Zulus who had rushed up at the noise.

Hassan rose and, to do him credit, came on like a man, head down. His great skull caught Stephen, who was the lighter of the two, in the chest and knocked him over, but before the Arab could follow up the advantage, he was on his feet again. Then ensued a really glorious mill. Hassan fought with head and fists and feet, Stephen with fists alone. Dodging his opponent's rushes, he gave it to him as he passed, and soon his coolness and silence began to tell. Once he was knocked over by a hooked one under the jaw, but in the next round he sent the Arab literally flying head over heels. Oh! how those Zulus cheered, and I, too, danced with delight. Up Hassan came again, spitting out several teeth and, adopting new tactics, grabbed Stephen round the middle. To and fro they swung, the Arab trying to kick the Englishman with his knees and to bite him also, till the pain reminded him of the absence of his front teeth. Once he nearly got him down—nearly, but not quite, for the collar by which he had gripped him (his object was to strangle) burst and, at that juncture, Hassan's turban fell over his face, blinding him for a moment.

Then Stephen gripped him round the middle with his left arm and with his right pummelled him unmercifully till he sank in a sitting position to the ground and held up his hand in token of surrender.

"The noble English lord has beaten me," he gasped.

"Apologise!" yelled Stephen, picking up a handful of mud, "or I shove this down your dirty throat."

He seemed to understand. At any rate, he bowed till his forehead touched the ground, and apologised very thoroughly.

"Now that is over," I said cheerfully to him, "so how about those bearers?"

"I have no bearers," he answered.

"You dirty liar," I exclaimed; "one of my people has been down to your village there and says it is full of men."

"Then go and take them for yourself," he replied, viciously, for he knew that the place was stockaded.

Now I was in a fix. It was all very well to give a slave-dealer the thrashing he deserved, but if he chose to attack us with his Arabs we should be in a poor way. Watching me with the eye that was not bunged up, Hassan guessed my perplexity.

"I have been beaten like a dog," he said, his rage returning to him with his breath, "but God is compassionate and just, He will avenge in due time."

The words had not left his lips for one second when from somewhere out at sea there floated the sullen boom of a great gun. At this moment, too, an Arab rushed up from the shore, crying:

"Where is the Bey Hassan?"

"Here," I said, pointing at him.

The Arab stared until I thought his eyes would drop out, for the Bey Hassan was indeed a sight to see. Then he gabbled in a frightened voice:

"Captain, an English man-of-war is chasing the *Maria*."

Boom went the great gun for the second time. Hassan said nothing, but his jaw dropped, and I saw that he had lost exactly three teeth.

"That is the *Crocodile*," I remarked slowly, causing Sammy to translate, and as I spoke, produced from my inner pocket a Union Jack which I had placed there after I heard that the ship was sighted. "Stephen," I went on as I shook it out, "if you have got your wind, would you mind climbing up that palm tree again and signalling with this to the *Crocodile* out at sea?"

"By George! that's a good idea," said Stephen, whose jovial face, although swollen, was now again wreathed in smiles. "Hans, bring me a long stick and a bit of string."

But Hassan did not think it at all a good idea.

"English lord," he gasped, "you shall have the bearers. I will go to fetch them."

"No, you won't," I said, "you will stop here as a hostage. Send that man."

Hassan uttered some rapid orders and the messenger sped away, this time towards the stockaded village on the right.

As he went another messenger arrived, who also stared amazedly at the condition of his chief.

"Bey—if you are the Bey," he said, in a doubtful voice, for by now the amiable face of Hassan had begun to swell and colour, "with the telescope we have seen that the English man-of-war has sent a boat and boarded the *Maria*."

"God is great!" muttered the discomfited Hassan, "and Delgado, who is a thief and a traitor from his mother's breast, will tell the truth. The English sons of Satan will land here. All is finished; nothing is left but flight. Bid the people fly into the bush and take the slaves—I mean their servants. I will join them."

"No, you won't," I interrupted, through Sammy; "at any rate, not at present. You will come with us."

The miserable Hassan reflected, then he asked:

"Lord Quatermain" (I remember the title, because it is the nearest I ever got, or am likely to get, to the peerage), "if I furnish you with the twenty bearers and accompany you for some days on your journey inland, will you promise not to signal to your countrymen on the ship and bring them ashore?"

"What do you think?" I asked of Stephen.

"Oh!" he answered, "I think I'd agree. This scoundrel has had a pretty good dusting, and if once the *Crocodile* people land, there'll be an end of our expedition. As sure as eggs are eggs they will carry us off to Zanzibar or somewhere to give evidence before a slave court. Also nothing will be gained, for by the time the sailors get here, all these rascals will have bolted, except our friend, Hassan. You see it isn't as though we were sure he would be hung. He'd probably escape after all. International law, subject of a foreign Power, no direct proof—that kind of thing, you know."

"Give me a minute or two," I said, and began to reflect very deeply.

Whilst I was thus engaged several things happened. I saw twenty natives being escorted towards us, doubtless the bearers who had been promised; also I saw many others, accompanied by other natives, flying from the village into the bush. Lastly, a third messenger arrived, who announced that the *Maria* was sailing away, apparently in charge of a prize-crew, and that the man-of-war was putting about as though to accompany her. Evidently she had no intention of effecting a landing upon what was, nominally at any rate, Portuguese territory. Therefore, if anything was to be done, we must act at once.

Well, the end of it was that, like a fool, I accepted Stephen's advice and did nothing, always the easiest course and generally that which leads to most trouble. Ten minutes afterwards I changed my mind, but then it was too late; the *Crocodile* was out of signalling distance. This was subsequent to a conversation with Hans.

"Baas," said that worthy, in his leery fashion, "I think you have made a mistake. You forget that these yellow devils in white robes who have run away will come back again, and that when you return from up country, they may be waiting for you. Now if the English man-of-war had destroyed their town, and their slave-sheds, they might have gone somewhere else. However," he added, as an afterthought, glancing at the disfigured Hassan, "we have their captain, and of course you mean to hang him, Baas. Or if you don't like to, leave it to me. I can hang men very well. Once, when I was young, I helped the executioner at Cape Town."

"Get out," I said, but, nevertheless, I knew that Hans was right.

CHAPTER 6

The Slave Road

The twenty bearers having arrived, in charge of five or six Arabs armed with guns, we went to inspect them, taking Hassan with us, also the hunters. They were a likely lot of men, though rather thin and scared-looking, and evidently, as I could see from their physical appearance and varying methods of dressing the hair, members of different tribes. Having delivered them, the Arabs, or rather one of them, entered into excited conversation with Hassan. As Sammy was not at hand I do not know what was said, although I gathered that they were contemplating his rescue. If so, they gave up the idea and began to run away as their companions had done. One of them, however, a bolder fellow than the rest, turned and fired at me. He missed by some yards, as I could tell from the sing of the bullet, for these Arabs are execrable shots. Still his attempt at murder irritated me so much that I determined he should not go scot-free. I was carrying the little rifle called *Intombi*, that with which, as Hans had reminded me, I shot the vultures at Dingaan's *kraal* many years before. Of course, I could have killed the man, but this I did not wish to do. Or I could have shot him through the leg, but then we should have had to nurse him or leave him to die! So I selected his right arm, which was outstretched as he fled, and at about fifty paces put a bullet through it just above the elbow.

"There," I said to the Zulus as I saw it double up, "that low fellow will never shoot at anyone again."

"Pretty, Macumazana, very pretty!" said Mavovo, "but as you can aim so well, why not have chosen his head? That bullet is half-wasted."

Next I set to work to get into communication with the bearers, who thought, poor devils, that they had been but sold to a new master. Here I may explain that they were slaves not meant for exportation, but men kept to cultivate Hassan's gardens. Fortunately I found that two of them belonged to the Mazitu people, who it may be remembered are of the same blood as the Zulus, although they separated from the parent stock generations ago. These men talked a dialect that I could understand, though at first not very easily. The foundation of it was Zulu, but it had become much mixed with the languages of other tribes whose women the Mazitu had taken to wife.

Also there was a man who could speak some bastard Arabic, sufficiently well for Sammy to converse with him.

I asked the Mazitus if they knew the way back to their country. They answered yes, but it was far off, a full month's journey. I told them that if they would guide us thither, they should receive their freedom and good pay, adding that if the other men served us well, they also should be set free when we had done with them. On receiving this information the poor wretches smiled in a sickly fashion and looked at Hassan-ben-Mohammed, who glowered at them and us from the box on which he was seated in charge of Mavovo.

How can we be free while that man lives, their look seemed to say. As though to confirm their doubts Hassan, who understood or guessed what was passing, asked by what right we were promising freedom to his slaves.

"By right of that," I answered, pointing to the Union Jack which Stephen still had in his hand. "Also we will pay you for them when we return, according as they have served us."

"Yes," he muttered, "you will pay me for them when you return, or perhaps before that, Englishman."

It was three o'clock in the afternoon before we were able to make a start. There was so much to be arranged that it might have been wiser to wait till the morrow, had we not determined that if we could help it nothing would induce us to spend another night in that place. Blankets were served out to each of the bearers who, poor naked creatures, seemed quite touched at the gift of them; the loads were apportioned, having already been packed at Durban in cases such as one man could carry. The pack saddles were put upon the four donkeys which proved to be none the worse for their journey, and burdens to a weight of about 100 lbs. each fixed on them in waterproof hide bags, besides cooking calabashes and sleeping mats which Hans produced from somewhere. Probably he stole them out of the deserted village, but as they were necessary to us I confess I asked no questions. Lastly, six or eight goats which were wandering about were captured to take with us for food till we could find game. For these I offered to pay Hassan, but when I handed him the money he threw it down in a rage, so I picked it up and put it in my pocket again with a clear conscience.

At length everything was more or less ready, and the question arose as to what was to be done with Hassan. The Zulus, like Hans, wished to kill him, as Sammy explained to him in his best Arabic. Then this murderous fellow showed what a coward he was at heart. He flung himself upon his knees, he wept, he invoked us in the name of the Compassionate Allah who, he explained, was after all the same God that we worshipped, till Mavovo, growing impatient of the noise, threatened him with his *kerry*, whereon he became silent. The easy-natured Stephen was for letting him go, a plan that seemed to have advantages, for then at least we should be rid of his abominable company. After reflection, however, I decided that we had better take him along with us, at any rate for a day or so, to hold as a hostage in case the Arabs should follow and attack us. At first he refused to stir, but the assegai of one of the Zulu hunters pressed gently against what remained of his robe, furnished an argument that he could not resist.

At length we were off. I with the two guides went ahead. Then came the bearers, then half of the hunters, then the four donkeys in charge of Hans and Sammy, then Hassan and the rest of the hunters, except Mavovo, who brought up the rear with Stephen. Needless to say, all our rifles were loaded, and generally we were prepared for any emergency. The only path, that which the guides said we must follow, ran by the seashore for a few hundred yards and then turned inland through Hassan's village where he lived, for it seemed that the old mission house was not used by him. As we marched along a little rocky cliff—it was not more than ten feet high—where a deep-water channel perhaps fifty yards in breadth separated the mainland from the island whence the slaves had been loaded on to the *Maria*, some difficulty arose about the donkeys. One of these slipped its load and another began to buck and evinced an inclination to leap into the sea with its precious burden. The rearguard of hunters ran to get hold of it, when suddenly there was a splash.

The brute's in! I thought to myself, till a shout told me that not the ass, but Hassan had departed over the cliff's edge. Watching his opportunity and being, it was clear, a first-rate swimmer, he had flung himself backwards in the midst of the confusion and falling into deep water, promptly dived. About twenty yards from the shore he came up for a moment, then dived again heading for the island. I dare say I could have potted him through the head with a snap shot, but somehow I did not like to kill a man swimming for his life as though he were a hippopotamus or a crocodile. Moreover, the boldness of the manoeuvre appealed to me. So I refrained from firing and called to the others to do likewise.

As our late host approached the shore of the island I saw Arabs running down the rocks to help him out of the water. Either they had not left the place, or had re-occupied it as soon as H.M.S. *Crocodile* had vanished with her prize. As it was clear that to recapture Hassan would involve an attack upon the garrison of the island which we were in no position to carry out, I gave orders for the march to be resumed. These, the difficulty with the donkey having been overcome, were obeyed at once.

It was fortunate that we did not delay, for scarcely had the caravan got into motion when the Arabs on the island began to fire at us. Luckily no one was hit, and we were soon round a point and under cover; also their shooting was as bad as usual. One missile, however, it was a pot-leg, struck a donkey-load and smashed a bottle of good brandy and a tin of preserved butter. This made me angry, so motioning to the others to proceed I took shelter behind a tree and waited till a torn and dirty turban, which I recognised as that of Hassan, poked up above a rock. Well, I put a bullet through that turban, for I saw the thing fly, but unfortunately, not through the head beneath it. Having left this P.P.C. card on our host, I bolted from the rock and caught up the others.

Presently we passed round the village; through it I would not go for fear of an ambuscade. It was quite a big place, enclosed with a strong fence, but hidden from the sea by a rise in the intervening land. In the centre was a large eastern-looking house, where doubtless Hassan dwelt with his harem. After we had gone a little way further, to my astonishment I saw flames breaking out from the palm-leaf roof of this house. At the time I could not imagine how this happened, but when, a day or two later, I observed Hans wearing a pair of large and very handsome gold pendants in his ears and a gold bracelet on his wrist, and found that he and one of the hunters were extremely well set up in the matter of British sovereigns—well, I had my doubts. In due course the truth came out. He and the hunter, an adventurous spirit, slipped through a gate in the fence without being observed, ran across the deserted village to the house, stole the ornaments and money from the women's apartments and as they departed, fired the place "in exchange for the bottle of good brandy," as Hans explained.

I was inclined to be angry, but after all, as we had been fired on, Hans's exploit became an act of war rather than a theft. So I made him and his companion divide the gold equally with the rest of the hunters, who no doubt had kept their eyes conveniently shut, not forgetting Sammy, and said no more. They netted £8 apiece, which pleased them very much. In addition to this I gave £1 each, or rather goods to that value, to the bearers as their share of the loot.

Hassan, I remarked, was evidently a great agriculturist, for the gardens which he worked by slave labour were beautiful, and must have brought him in a large revenue.

Passing through these gardens we came to sloping land covered with bush. Here the track was not too good, for the creepers hampered our progress. Indeed, I was very glad when towards sunset we reached the crest of a hill and emerged upon a tableland which was almost clear of trees and rose gradually till it met the horizon. In that bush we might easily have been attacked, but in this open country I was not so much afraid, since the loss to the Arabs would have been great before we were overpowered. As a matter of fact, although spies dogged us for days no assault was ever attempted.

Finding a convenient place by a stream we camped for the night, but as it was so fine, did not pitch the tents. Afterwards I was sorry that we had not gone further from the water, since the mosquitoes bred by millions in the marshes bordering the stream gave us a dreadful time. On poor Stephen, fresh from England, they fell with peculiar ferocity, with the result that in the morning what between the bruises left by Hassan and their bites, he was a spectacle for men and angels. Another thing that broke our rest was the necessity of keeping a strict watch in case the slave-traders should elect to attack us in the hours of darkness; also to guard against the possibility of our bearers running away and perhaps stealing the goods. It is true that before they went to sleep I explained to them very clearly that any of them who attempted to give us the slip would certainly be seen and shot, whereas if they remained with us they would be treated with every kindness. They answered through the two Mazitu that they had nowhere to go, and did not wish to fall again into the power of Hassan, of whom they spoke literally with shudders, pointing the while to their scarred backs and the marks of the slave yokes upon their necks. Their protestations seemed and indeed proved to be sincere, but of this of course we could not then be sure.

As I was engaged at sunrise in making certain that the donkeys had not strayed and generally that all was well, I noted through the thin mist a little white object, which at first I thought was a small bird sitting on an upright stick about fifty yards from the camp. I went towards it and discovered that it was not a bird but a folded piece of paper stuck in a cleft wand, such as natives often use for the carrying of letters. I opened the paper and with great difficulty, for the writing within was bad Portuguese, read as follows:

> English Devils.—Do not think that you have escaped me. I know where you are going, and if you live through the journey it will be but to die at my hands after all. I tell you that I have at my command three hundred brave men armed with guns who worship Allah and thirst for the blood of Christian dogs. With these I will follow, and if you fall into my hands alive, you shall learn what it is to die by fire or pinned over ant-heaps in the sun. Let us see if your English man-of-war will help you then, or your false God either. Misfortune go with you, white-skinned robbers of honest men!

This pleasing epistle was unsigned, but its anonymous author was not hard to identify. I showed it to Stephen who was so infuriated at its contents that he managed to dab some ammonia with which he was treating his mosquito bites into his eye. When at length the pain was soothed by bathing, we concocted this answer:

> Murderer, known among men as Hassan-ben-Mohammed—Truly we sinned in not hanging you when you were in our power. Oh! wolf who grows fat upon the blood of the innocent, this is a fault that we shall not commit again. Your death is near to you and we believe at our hands. Come with all your villains whenever you will. The more there are of them the better we shall be pleased, who would rather rid the world of many fiends than of a few.
> Till we meet again,
> Allan Quatermain
> Stephen Somers

"Neat, if not Christian," I said when I had read the letter over.

"Yes," replied Stephen, "but perhaps just a little bombastic in tone. If that gentleman did arrive with three hundred armed men—eh?"

"Then, my boy," I answered, "in this way or in that we shall thrash him. I don't often have an inspiration, but I've got one now, and it is to the effect that Mr. Hassan has not very long to live and that we shall be intimately connected with his end. Wait till you have seen a slave caravan and you will understand my feelings. Also I know these gentry. That little prophecy of ours will get upon his nerves and give him a foretaste of things. Hans, go and set this letter in that cleft stick. The postman will call for it before long."

****

As it happened, within a few days we did see a slave caravan, some of the merchandise of the estimable Hassan.

We had been making good progress through a beautiful and healthy country, steering almost due west, or rather a little to the north of west. The land was undulating and rich, well-watered and only bush-clad in the neighbourhood of the streams, the higher ground being open, of a park-like character, and dotted here and there with trees. It was evident that once, and not very long ago, the population had been dense, for we came to the remains of many villages, or rather towns with large market-places. Now, however, these were burned with fire, or deserted, or occupied only by a few old bodies who got a living from the overgrown gardens. These poor people, who sat desolate and crooning in the sun, or perhaps worked feebly at the once fertile fields, would fly screaming at our approach, for to them men armed with guns must of necessity be slave-traders.

Still from time to time we contrived to catch some of them, and through one member of our party or the other to get at their stories. Really it was all one story. The slaving Arabs, on this pretext or on that, had set tribe against tribe. Then they sided with the stronger and conquered the weaker by aid of their terrible guns, killing out the old folk and taking the young men, women and children (except the infants whom they butchered) to be sold as slaves. It seemed that the business had begun about twenty years before, when Hassan-ben-Mohammed and his companions arrived at Kilwa and drove away the missionary who had built a station there.

At first this trade was extremely easy and profitable, since the raw material lay near at hand in plenty. By degrees, however, the neighbouring communities had been worked out. Countless numbers of them were killed, while the pick of the population passed under the slave yoke, and those of them who survived, vanished in ships to unknown lands. Thus it came about that the slavers were obliged to go further afield and even to conduct their raids upon the borders of the territory of the great Mazitu people, the inland race of Zulu origin of whom I have spoken. According to our informants, it was even rumoured that they proposed shortly to attack these Mazitus in force, relying on their guns to give them the victory and open to them a new and almost inexhaustible store of splendid human merchandise. Meanwhile they were cleaning out certain small tribes which hitherto had escaped them, owing to the fact that they had their residence in bush or among difficult hills.

The track we followed was the recognised slave road. Of this we soon became aware by the numbers of skeletons which we found lying in the tall grass at its side, some of them with heavy slave-sticks still upon their wrists. These, I suppose, had died from exhaustion, but others, as their split skulls showed had been disposed of by their captors.

On the eighth day of our march we struck the track of a slave caravan. It had been travelling towards the coast, but for some reason or other had turned back. This may have been because its leaders had been warned of the approach of our party. Or perhaps they had heard that another caravan, which was at work in a different district, was drawing near, bringing its slaves with it, and wished to wait for its arrival in order that they might join forces.

The spoor of these people was easy to follow. First we found the body of a boy of about ten. Then vultures revealed to us the remains of two young men, one of whom had been shot and the other killed by a blow from an axe. Their corpses were roughly hidden beneath some grass, I know not why. A mile or two further on we heard a child wailing and found it by following its cries. It was a little girl of about four who had been pretty, though now she was but a living skeleton. When she saw us she scrambled away on all fours like a monkey. Stephen followed her, while I, sick at heart, went to get a tin of preserved milk from our stores. Presently I heard him call to me in a horrified voice. Rather reluctantly, for I knew that he must have found something dreadful, I pushed my way through the bush to where he was. There, bound to the trunk of a tree, sat a young woman, evidently the mother of the child, for it clung to her leg.

Thank God she was still living, though she must have died before another day dawned. We cut her loose, and the Zulu hunters, who are kind folk enough when they are not at war, carried her to camp. In the end with much trouble we saved the lives of that mother and child. I sent for the two Mazitus, with whom I could by now talk fairly well, and asked them why the slavers did these things.

They shrugged their shoulders and one of them answered with a rather dreadful laugh:

"Because, Chief, these Arabs, being black-hearted, kill those who can walk no more, or tie them up to die. If they let them go they might recover and escape, and it makes the Arabs sad that those who have been their slaves should live to be free and happy."

"Does it? Does it indeed?" exclaimed Stephen with a snort of rage that reminded me of his father. "Well, if ever I get a chance I'll make them sad with a vengeance."

Stephen was a tender-hearted young man, and for all his soft and indolent ways, an awkward customer when roused.

Within forty-eight hours he got his chance, thus: That day we camped early for two reasons. The first was that the woman and child we had rescued was so weak they could not walk without rest, and we had no men to spare to carry them; the second that we came to an ideal spot to pass the night. It was, as usual, a deserted village through which ran a beautiful stream of water. Here we took possession of some outlying huts with a fence round them, and as Mavovo had managed to shoot a fat eland cow and her half-grown calf, we prepared to have a regular feast. Whilst Sammy was making some broth for the rescued woman, and Stephen and I smoked our pipes and watched him, Hans slipped through the broken gate of the thorn fence, or *boma*, and announced that Arabs were coming, two lots of them with many slaves.

We ran out to look and saw that, as he had said, two caravans were approaching, or rather had reached the village, but at some distance from us, and were now camping on what had once been the market-place. One of these was that whose track we had followed, although during the last few hours of our march we had struck away from it, chiefly because we could not bear such sights as I have described. It seemed to comprise about two hundred and fifty slaves and over forty guards, all black men carrying guns, and most of them by their dress Arabs, or bastard Arabs. In the second caravan, which approached from another direction, were not more than one hundred slaves and about twenty or thirty captors.

"Now," I said, "let us eat our dinner and then, if you like, we will go to call upon those gentlemen, just to show that we are not afraid of them. Hans, get the flag and tie it to the top of that tree; it will show them to what country we belong."

Up went the Union Jack duly, and presently through our glasses we saw the slavers running about in a state of excitement; also we saw the poor slaves turn and stare at the bit of flapping bunting and then begin to talk to each other. It struck me as possible that some-one among their number had seen a Union Jack in the hands of an English traveller, or had heard of it as flying upon ships or at points on the coast, and what it meant to slaves. Or they may have understood some of the remarks of the Arabs, which no doubt were pointed and explanatory. At any rate, they turned and stared till the Arabs ran among them with *sjambocks*, that is, whips of hippopotamus hide, and suppressed their animated conversation with many blows.

At first I thought that they would break camp and march away; indeed, they began to make preparations to do this, then abandoned the idea, probably because the slaves were exhausted and there was no other water they could reach before nightfall. In the end they settled down and lit cooking fires. Also, as I observed, they took precautions against attack by stationing sentries and forcing the slaves to construct a *boma* of thorns about their camp.

"Well," said Stephen, when we had finished our dinner, "are you ready for that call?"

"No!" I answered, "I do not think that I am. I have been considering things, and concluded that we had better leave well alone. By this time those Arabs will know all the story of our dealings with their worthy master, Hassan, for no doubt he has sent messengers to them. Therefore, if we go to their camp, they may shoot us at sight. Or, if they receive us well, they may offer hospitality and poison us, or cut our throats suddenly. Our position might be better, still it is one that I believe they would find difficult to take. So, in my opinion, we had better stop still and await developments."

Stephen grumbled something about my being over-cautious, but I took no heed of him. One thing I did do, however. Sending for Hans, I told him to take one of the Mazitu—I dared not risk them both for they were our guides—and another of the natives whom we had borrowed from Hassan, a bold fellow who knew all the local languages, and creep down to the slavers' camp as soon as it was quite dark. There I ordered him to find out what he could, and if possible to mix with the slaves and explain that we were their friends. Hans nodded, for this was exactly the kind of task that appealed to him, and went off to make his preparations.

Stephen and I also made some preparations in the way of strengthening our defences, building large watch-fires and setting sentries.

The night fell, and Hans with his companions departed stealthily as snakes. The silence was intense, save for the occasional wailings of the slaves, which now and again broke out in bursts of melancholy sound, *"La-lu-La-lua!"* and then died away, to be followed by horrid screams as the Arabs laid their lashes upon some poor wretch. Once too, a shot was fired.

"They have seen Hans," said Stephen.

"I think not," I answered, "for if so there would have been more than one shot. Either it was an accident or they were murdering a slave."

After this nothing more happened for a long while, till at length Hans seemed to rise out of the ground in front of me, and behind him I saw the figures of the Mazitu and the other man.

"Tell your story," I said.

"Baas, it is this. Between us we have learned everything. The Arabs know all about you and what men you have. Hassan has sent them orders to kill you. It is well that you did not go to visit them, for certainly you would have been murdered. We crept near and overheard their talk. They purpose to attack us at dawn tomorrow morning unless we leave this place before, which they will know of as we are being watched."

"And if so, what then?" I asked.

"Then, Baas, they will attack as we are making up the caravan, or immediately afterwards as we begin to march."

"Indeed. Anything more, Hans?"

"Yes, Baas. These two men crept among the slaves and spoke with them. They are very sad, those slaves, and many of them have died of heart-pain because they have been taken from their homes and do not know where they are going. I saw one die just now; a young woman. She was talking to another woman and seemed quite well, only tired, till suddenly she said in a loud voice, 'I am going to die, that I may come back as a spirit and bewitch these devils till they are spirits too.' Then she called upon the fetish of her tribe, put her hands to her breast and fell down dead. At least," added Hans, spitting reflectively, "she did not fall quite down because the slave-stick held her head off the ground. The Arabs were very angry, both because she had cursed them and was dead. One of them came and kicked her body and afterwards shot her little boy who was sick, because the mother had cursed them. But fortunately he did not see us, because we were in the dark far from the fire."

"Anything more, Hans?"

"One thing, Baas. These two men lent the knives you gave them to two of the boldest among the slaves that they might cut the cords of the slave-sticks and the other cords with which they were tied, and then pass them down the lines, that their brothers might do the same. But perhaps the Arabs will find it out, and then the Mazitu and the other must lose their knives. That is all. Has the Baas a little tobacco?"

"Now, Stephen," I said when Hans had gone and I had explained everything, "there are two courses open to us. Either we can try to give these gentlemen the slip at once, in which case we must leave the woman and child to their fate, or we can stop where we are and wait to be attacked."

"I won't run," said Stephen sullenly; "it would be cowardly to desert that poor creature. Also we should have a worse chance marching. Remember Hans said that they are watching us."

"Then you would wait to be attacked?"

"Isn't there a third alternative, Quatermain? To attack them?"

"That's the idea," I said. "Let us send for Mavovo."

Presently he came and sat down in front of us, while I set out the case to him.

"It is the fashion of my people to attack rather than to be attacked, and yet, my father, in this case my heart is against it. Hans" (he called him *Inblatu*, a Zulu word which means Spotted Snake, that was the Hottentot's *Kaffir* name) "says that there are quite sixty of the yellow dogs, all armed with guns, whereas we have not more than fifteen, for we cannot trust the slave men. Also he says that they are within a strong fence and awake, with spies out, so that it will be difficult to surprise them. But here, father, we are in a strong fence and cannot be surprised. Also men who torture and kill women and children, except in war must, I think, be cowards, and will come on faintly against good shooting, if indeed they come at all. Therefore, I say, 'Wait till the buffalo shall either charge or run.' But the word is with you, Macumazana, wise Watcher-by-Night, not with me, your hunter. Speak, you who are old in war, and I will obey."

"You argue well," I answered; "also another reason comes to my mind. Those Arab brutes may get behind the slaves, of whom we should butcher a lot without hurting them. Stephen, I think we had better see the thing through here."

"All right, Quatermain. Only I hope that Mavovo is wrong in thinking that those blackguards may change their minds and run away."

"Really, young man, you are becoming very blood-thirsty—for an orchid grower," I remarked, looking at him. "Now, for my part, I devoutly hope that Mavovo is right, for let me tell you, if he isn't it may be a nasty job."

"I've always been peaceful enough up to the present," replied Stephen. "But the sight of those unhappy wretches of slaves with their heads cut open, and of the woman tied to a tree to starve——"

"Make you wish to usurp the functions of God Almighty," I said. "Well, it is a natural impulse and perhaps, in the circumstances, one that will not displease Him. And now, as we have made up our minds what we are going to do, let's get to business so that these Arab gentlemen may find their breakfast ready when they come to call."

Chapter 7

The Rush of the Slaves

Well, we did all that we could in the way of making ready. After we had strengthened the thorn fence of our *boma* as much as possible and lit several large fires outside of it to give us light, I allotted his place to each of the hunters and saw that their rifles were in order and that they had plenty of ammunition. Then I made Stephen lie down to sleep, telling him that I would wake him to watch later on. This, however, I had no intention of doing as I wanted him to rise fresh and with a steady nerve on the occasion of his first fight.

As soon as I saw that his eyes were shut I sat down on a box to think. To tell the truth, I was not altogether happy in my mind. To begin with I did not know how the twenty bearers would behave under fire. They might be seized with panic and rush about, in which case I determined to let them out of the *boma* to take their chance, for panic is a catching thing.

A worse matter was our rather awkward position. There were a good many trees round the camp among which an attacking force could take cover. But what I feared much more than this, or even than the reedy banks of the stream along which they could creep out of reach of our bullets, was a sloping stretch of land behind us, covered with thick grass and scrub and rising to a crest about two hundred yards away. Now if the Arabs got round to this crest they would fire straight into our *boma* and make it untenable. Also if the wind were in their favour, they might burn us out or attack under the clouds of smoke. As a matter of fact, by the special mercy of Providence, none of these things happened, for a reason which I will explain presently.

In the case of a night, or rather a dawn attack, I have always found that hour before the sky begins to lighten very trying indeed. As a rule everything that can be done is done, so that one must sit idle. Also it is then that both the physical and the moral qualities are at their lowest ebb, as is the mercury in the thermometer. The night is dying, the day is not yet born. All nature feels the influence of that hour. Then bad dreams come, then infants wake and call, then memories of those who are lost to us arise, then the hesitating soul often takes its plunge into the depths of the Unknown. It is not wonderful, therefore, that on this occasion the wheels of Time drave heavily for me. I knew that the morning was at hand by many signs. The sleeping bearers turned and muttered in their sleep, a distant lion ceased its roaring and departed to its own place, an alert-minded cock crew somewhere, and our donkeys rose and began to pull at their tether-ropes. As yet, however, it was quite dark. Hans crept up to me; I saw his wrinkled, yellow face in the light of the watch-fire.

"I smell the dawn," he said and vanished again.

Mavovo appeared, his massive frame silhouetted against the blackness.

"Watcher-by-Night, the night is done," he said. "If they come at all, the enemy should soon be here."

Saluting, he too passed away into the dark, and presently I heard the sounds of spear-blades striking together and of rifles being cocked.

I went to Stephen and woke him. He sat up yawning, muttered something about greenhouses; then remembering, said:

"Are those Arabs coming? We are in for a fight at last. Jolly, old fellow, isn't it?"

"You are a jolly old fool!" I answered inconsequently; and marched off in a rage.

My mind was uneasy about this inexperienced young man. If anything should happen to him, what should I say to his father? Well, in that event, it was probable that something would happen to me too. Very possibly we should both be dead in an hour. Certainly I had no intention of allowing myself to be taken alive by those slaving devils. Hassan's remarks about fires and ant-heaps and the sun were too vividly impressed upon my memory.

In another five minutes everybody was up, though it required kicks to rouse most of the bearers from their slumbers. They, poor men, were accustomed to the presence of Death and did not suffer him to disturb their sleep. Still I noted that they muttered together and seemed alarmed.

"If they show signs of treachery, you must kill them," I said to Mavovo, who nodded in his grave, silent fashion.

Only we left the rescued slave-woman and her child plunged in the stupor of exhaustion in a corner of the camp. What was the use of disturbing her?

Sammy, who seemed far from comfortable, brought two pannikins of coffee to Stephen and myself.

"This is a momentous occasion, Messrs. Quatermain and Somers," he said as he gave us the coffee, and I noted that his hand shook and his teeth chattered. "The cold is extreme," he went on in his copybook English by way of explaining these physical symptoms which he saw I had observed. "Mr. Quatermain, it is all very well for you to paw the ground and smell the battle from afar, as is written in the Book of Job. But I was not brought up to the trade and take it otherwise. Indeed I wish I was back at the Cape, yes, even within the whitewashed walls of the Place of Detention."

"So do I," I muttered, keeping my right foot on the ground with difficulty.

But Stephen laughed outright and asked:

"What will you do, Sammy, when the fighting begins?"

"Mr. Somers," he answered, "I have employed some wakeful hours in making a hole behind that tree-trunk, through which I hope bullets will not pass. There, being a man of peace, I shall pray for our success."

"And if the Arabs get in, Sammy?"

"Then, sir, under Heaven, I shall trust to the fleetness of my legs."

I could stand it no longer, my right foot flew up and caught Sammy in the place at which I had aimed. He vanished, casting a reproachful look behind him.

Just then a terrible clamour arose in the slavers' camp which hitherto had been very silent, and just then also the first light of dawn glinted on the barrels of our guns.

"Look out!" I cried, as I gulped down the last of my coffee, "there's something going on there."

The clamour grew louder and louder till it seemed to fill the skies with a concentrated noise of curses and shrieking. Distinct from it, as it were, I heard shouts of alarm and rage, and then came the sounds of gunshots, yells of agony and the thud of many running feet. By now the light was growing fast, as it does when once it comes in these latitudes. Three more minutes, and through the grey mist of the dawn we saw dozens of black figures struggling up the slope towards us. Some seemed to have logs of wood tied behind them, others crawled along on all fours, others dragged children by the hand, and all yelled at the top of their voices.

"The slaves are attacking us," said Stephen, lifting his rifle.

"Don't shoot," I cried. "I think they have broken loose and are taking refuge with us."

I was right. These unfortunates had used the two knives which our men smuggled to them to good purpose. Having cut their bonds during the night they were running to seek the protection of the Englishmen and their flag. On they surged, a hideous mob, the slave-sticks still fast to the necks of many of them, for they had not found time or opportunity to loose them all, while behind came the Arabs firing. The position was clearly very serious, for if they burst into our camp, we should be overwhelmed by their rush and fall victims to the bullets of their captors.

"Hans," I cried, "take the men who were with you last night and try to lead those slaves round behind us. Quick! Quick now before we are stamped flat."

Hans darted away, and presently I saw him and the two other men running towards the approaching crowd, Hans waving a shirt or some other white object to attract their attention. At the time the foremost of them had halted and were screaming, "Mercy, English! Save us, English!" having caught sight of the muzzles of our guns.

This was a fortunate occurrence indeed, for otherwise Hans and his companions could never have stopped them. The next thing I saw was the white shirt bearing away to the left on a line which led past the fence of our *boma* into the scrub and high grass behind the camp. After it struggled and scrambled the crowd of slaves like a flock of sheep after the bell-wether. To them Hans's shirt was a kind of "white helmet of Navarre."

So that danger passed by. Some of the slaves had been struck by the Arab bullets or trodden down in the rush or collapsed from weakness, and at those of them who still lived the pursuers were firing. One woman, who had fallen under the weight of the great slave-stick which was fastened about her throat, was crawling forward on her hands and knees. An Arab fired at her and the bullet struck the ground under her stomach but without hurting her, for she wriggled forward more quickly. I was sure that he would shoot again, and watched. Presently, for by now the light was good, I saw him, a tall fellow in a white robe, step from behind the shelter of a banana-tree about a hundred and fifty yards away, and take a careful aim at the woman. But I too took aim and—well, I am not bad at this kind of snap-shooting when I try. That Arab's gun never went off. Only he went up two feet or more into the air and fell backwards, shot through the head which was the part of his person that I had covered.

The hunters uttered a low *"Ow!"* of approval, while Stephen, in a sort of ecstasy, exclaimed:

"Oh! what a heavenly shot!"

"Not bad, but I shouldn't have fired it," I answered, "for they haven't attacked us yet. It is a kind of declaration of war, and," I added, as Stephen's sun-helmet leapt from his head, "there's the answer. Down, all of you, and fire through the loopholes."

Then the fight began. Except for its grand finale it wasn't really much of a fight when compared with one or two we had afterwards on this expedition. But, on the other hand, its character was extremely awkward for us. The Arabs made one rush at the beginning, shouting on Allah as they came. But though they were plucky villains they did not repeat that experiment. Either by good luck or good management Stephen knocked over two of them with his double-barrelled rifle, and I also emptied my large-bore breech-loader—the first I ever owned—among them, not without results, while the hunters made a hit or two.

After this the Arabs took cover, getting behind trees and, as I had feared, hiding in the reeds on the banks of the stream. Thence they harassed us a great deal, for amongst them were some very decent shots. Indeed, had we not taken the precaution of lining the thorn fence with a thick bank of earth and sods, we should have fared badly. As it was, one of the hunters was killed, the bullet passing through the loophole and striking him in the throat as he was about to fire, while the unfortunate bearers who were on rather higher ground, suffered a good deal, two of them being dispatched outright and four wounded. After this I made the rest of them lie flat on the ground close against the fence, in such a fashion that we could fire over their bodies.

Soon it became evident that there were more of these Arabs than we had thought, for quite fifty of them were firing from different places. Moreover, by slow degrees they were advancing with the evident object of outflanking us and gaining the high ground behind. Some of them, of course, we stopped as they rushed from cover to cover, but this kind of shooting was as difficult as that at bolting rabbits across a woodland ride, and to be honest, I must say that I alone was much good at the game, for here my quick eye and long practice told.

Within an hour the position had grown very serious indeed, so much so that we found it necessary to consider what should be done. I pointed out that with our small number a charge against the scattered riflemen, who were gradually surrounding us, would be worse than useless, while it was almost hopeless to expect to hold the *boma* till nightfall. Once the Arabs got behind us, they could rake us from the higher ground. Indeed, for the last half-hour we had directed all our efforts to preventing them from passing this *boma*, which, fortunately, the stream on the one side and a stretch of quite open land on the other made it very difficult for them to do without more loss than they cared to face.

"I fear there is only one thing for it," I said at length, during a pause in the attack while the Arabs were either taking counsel or waiting for more ammunition, "to abandon the camp and everything and bolt up the hill. As those fellows must be tired and we are all good runners, we may save our lives in that way."

"How about the wounded," asked Stephen, "and the slave-woman and child?"

"I don't know," I answered, looking down.

Of course I did know very well, but here, in an acute form, arose the ancient question: Were we to perish for the sake of certain individuals in whom we had no great interest and whom we could not save by remaining with them? If we stayed where we were our end seemed fairly certain, whereas if we ran for it, we had a good chance of escape. But this involved the desertion of several injured bearers and a woman and child whom we had picked up starving, all of whom would certainly be massacred, save perhaps the woman and child.

As these reflections flitted through my brain I remembered that a drunken Frenchman named Leblanc, whom I had known in my youth and who had been a friend of Napoleon, or so he said, told me that the great emperor when he was besieging Acre in the Holy Land, was forced to retreat. Being unable to carry off his wounded men, he left them in a monastery on Mount Carmel, each with a dose of poison by his side. Apparently they did not take the poison, for according to Leblanc, who said he was present there (not as a wounded man), the Turks came and butchered them. So Napoleon chose to save his own life and that of his army at the expense of his wounded. But, after all, I reflected, he was no shining example to Christian men and I hadn't time to find any poison. In a few words I explained the situation to Mavovo, leaving out the story of Napoleon, and asked his advice.

"We must run," he answered. "Although I do not like running, life is more than stores, and he who lives may one day pay his debts."

"But the wounded, Mavovo; we cannot carry them."

"I will see to them, Macumazana; it is the fortune of war. Or if they prefer it, we can leave them—to be nursed by the Arabs," which of course was just Napoleon and his poison over again.

I confess that I was about to assent, not wishing that I and Stephen, especially Stephen, should be potted in an obscure engagement with some miserable slave-traders, when something happened.

It will be remembered that shortly after dawn Hans, using a shirt for a flag, had led the fugitive slaves past the camp up to the hill behind. There he and they had vanished, and from that moment to this we had seen nothing of him or them. Now of a sudden he reappeared still waving the shirt. After him rushed a great mob of naked men, two hundred of them perhaps, brandishing slave-sticks, stones and the boughs of trees. When they had almost reached the *boma* whence we watched them amazed, they split into two bodies, half of them passing to our left, apparently under the command of the Mazitu who had accompanied Hans to the slave-camp, and the other half to the right following the old Hottentot himself. I stared at Mavovo, for I was too thunderstruck to speak.

"Ah!" said Mavovo, "that Spotted Snake of yours" (he referred to Hans), "is great in his own way, for he has even been able to put courage into the hearts of slaves. Do you not understand, my father, that they are about to attack those Arabs, yes, and to pull them down, as wild dogs do a buffalo calf?"

It was true: this was the Hottentot's superb design. Moreover, it succeeded. Up on the hillside he had watched the progress of the fight and seen how it must end. Then, through the interpreter who was with him, he harangued those slaves, pointing out to them that we, their white friends, were about to be overwhelmed, and that they must either strike for themselves, or return to the yoke. Among them were some who had been warriors in their own tribes, and through these he stirred the others. They seized the slave-sticks from which they had been freed, pieces of rock, anything that came to their hands, and at a given signal charged, leaving only the women and children behind them.

Seeing them come the scattered Arabs began to fire at them, killing some, but thereby revealing their own hiding-places. At these the slaves rushed. They hurled themselves upon the Arabs; they tore them, they dashed out their brains in such fashion that within another five minutes quite two-thirds of them were dead; and the rest, of whom we took some toll with our rifles as they bolted from cover, were in full flight.

It was a terrible vengeance. Never did I witness a more savage scene than that of these outraged men wreaking their wrongs upon their tormentors. I remember that when most of the Arabs had been killed and a few were escaped, the slaves found one, I think it was the captain of the gang, who had hidden himself in a little patch of dead reeds washed up by the stream. Somehow they managed to fire these; I expect that Hans, who had remained discreetly in the background after the fighting began, emerged when it was over and gave them a match. In due course out came the wretched Arab. Then they flung themselves on him as marching ants do upon a caterpillar, and despite his cries for mercy, tore him to fragments, literally to fragments. Being what they were, it was hard to blame them. If we had seen our parents shot, our infants pitilessly butchered, our homes destroyed and our women and children marched off in the slave-sticks to be sold into bondage, should we not have done the same? I think so, although we are not ignorant savages.

Thus our lives were saved by those whom we had tried to save, and for once justice was done even in those dark parts of Africa, for in that time they were dark indeed. Had it not been for Hans and the courage which he managed to inspire into the hearts of these crushed blacks, I have little doubt but that before nightfall we should have been dead, for I do not think that any attempt at retreat would have proved successful. And if it had, what would have happened to us in that wild country surrounded by enemies and with only the few rounds of ammunition that we could have carried in our flight?

"Ah! Baas," said the Hottentot a little while later, squinting at me with his bead-like eyes, "after all you did well to listen to my prayer and bring me with you. Old Hans is a drunkard, yes, or at least he used to be, and old Hans gambles, yes, and perhaps old Hans will go to hell. But meanwhile old Hans can think, as he thought one day before the attack on Maraisfontein, as he thought one day on the Hill of Slaughter by Dingaan's *kraal*, and as he thought this morning up there among the bushes. Oh! he knew how it must end. He saw that those dogs of Arabs were cutting down a tree to make a bridge across that deep stream and get round to the high ground at the back of you, whence they would have shot you all in five minutes. And now, Baas, my stomach feels very queer. There was no breakfast on the hillside and the sun was very hot. I think that just one tot of brandy—oh! I know, I promised not to drink, but if *you* give it me the sin is yours, not mine."

Well, I gave him the tot, a stiff one, which he drank quite neat, although it was against my principles, and locked up the bottle afterwards. Also I shook the old fellow's hand and thanked him, which seemed to please him very much, for he muttered something to the effect that it was nothing, since if I had died he would have died too, and therefore he was thinking of himself, not of me. Also two big tears trickled down his snub nose, but these may have been produced by the brandy.

Well, we were the victors and elated as may be imagined, for we knew that the few slavers who had escaped would not attack us again. Our first thought was for food, for it was now past midday and we were starving. But dinner presupposed a cook, which reminded us of Sammy. Stephen, who was in such a state of jubilation that he danced rather than walked, the helmet with a bullet-hole through it stuck ludicrously upon the back of his head, started to look for him, and presently called to me in an alarmed voice. I went to the back of the camp and, staring into a hole like a small grave, that had been hollowed behind a solitary thorn tree, at the bottom of which lay a huddled heap, I found him. It was Sammy to all appearance. We got hold of him, and up he came, limp, senseless, but still holding in his hand a large, thick *Bible*, bound in boards. Moreover, in the exact centre of this *Bible* was a bullet-hole, or rather a bullet which had passed through the stout cover and buried itself in the paper behind. I remember that the point of it reached to the First Book of Samuel.

As for Sammy himself, he seemed to be quite uninjured, and indeed after we had poured some water on him—he was never fond of water—he revived quickly enough. Then we found out what had happened.

"Gentlemen," he said, "I was seated in my place of refuge, being as I have told you a man of peace, enjoying the consolation of religion"—he was very pious in times of trouble. "At length the firing slackened, and I ventured to peep out, thinking that perhaps the foe had fled, holding the Book in front of my face in case of accidents. After that I remember no more."

"No," said Stephen, "for the bullet hit the *Bible* and the *Bible* hit your head and knocked you silly."

"Ah!" said Sammy, "how true is what I was taught that the Book shall be a shield of defence to the righteous. Now I understand why I was moved to bring the thick old *Bible* that belonged to my mother in heaven, and not the little thin one given to me by the Sunday school teacher, through which the ball of the enemy would have passed."

Then he went off to cook the dinner.

Certainly it was a wonderful escape, though whether this was a direct reward of his piety, as he thought, is another matter.

As soon as we had eaten, we set to work to consider our position, of which the crux was what to do with the slaves. There they sat in groups outside the fence, many of them showing traces of the recent conflict, and stared at us stupidly. Then of a sudden, as though with one voice, they began to clamour for food.

"How are we to feed several hundred people?" asked Stephen.

"The slavers must have done it somehow," I answered. "Let's go and search their camp."

So we went, followed by our hungry clients, and, in addition to many more things, to our delight found a great store of rice, *mealies* and other grain, some of which was ground into meal. Of this we served out an ample supply together with salt, and soon the cooking pots were full of porridge. My word! how those poor creatures did eat, nor, although it was necessary to be careful, could we find it in our hearts to stint them of the first full meal that had passed their lips after weeks of starvation. When at length they were satisfied we addressed them, thanking them for their bravery, telling them that they were free and asking what they meant to do.

Upon this point they seemed to have but one idea. They said that they would come with us who were their protectors. Then followed a great *indaba*, or consultation, which really I have not time to set out. The end of it was that we agreed that so many of them as wished should accompany us till they reached country that they knew, when they would be at liberty to depart to their own homes. Meanwhile we divided up the blankets and other stores of the Arabs, such as trade goods and beads, among them, and then left them to their own devices, after placing a guard over the foodstuffs. For my part I hoped devoutly that in the morning we should find them gone.

After this we returned to our *boma* just in time to assist at a sad ceremony, that of the burial of my hunter who had been shot through the head. His companions had dug a deep hole outside the fence and within a few yards of where he fell. In this they placed him in a sitting position with his face turned towards Zululand, setting by his side two gourds that belonged to him, one filled with water and the other with grain. Also they gave him a blanket and his two assegais, tearing the blanket and breaking the handles of the spears, to "kill" them as they said. Then quietly enough they threw in the earth about him and filled the top of the hole with large stones to prevent the hyenas from digging him up. This done, one by one, they walked past the grave, each man stopping to bid him farewell by name. Mavovo, who came last, made a little speech, telling the deceased to *namba kachle*, that is, go comfortably to the land of ghosts, as, he added, no doubt he would do who had died as a man should. He requested him, moreover, if he returned as a spirit, to bring good and not ill-fortune on us, since otherwise when he, Mavovo, became a spirit in his turn, he would have words to say to him on the matter. In conclusion, he remarked that as his, Mavovo's Snake, had foretold this event at Durban, a fact with which the deceased would now be acquainted he, the said deceased, could never complain of not having received value for the shilling he had paid as a divining fee.

"Yes," exclaimed one of the hunters with a note of anxiety in his voice, "but your Snake mentioned six of us to you, O doctor!"

"It did," replied Mavovo, drawing a pinch of snuff up his uninjured nostril, "and our brother there was the first of the six. Be not afraid, the other five will certainly join him in due course, for my Snake must speak the truth. Still, if anyone is in a hurry," and he glared round the little circle, "let him stop and talk with me alone. Perhaps I could arrange that his turn——" here he stopped, for they were all gone.

"Glad *I* didn't pay a shilling to have my fortune told by Mavovo," said Stephen, when we were back in the *boma*, "but why did they bury his pots and spears with him?"

"To be used by the spirit on its journey," I answered. "Although they do not quite know it, these Zulus believe, like all the rest of the world, that man lives on elsewhere."

Chapter 8

The Magic Mirror

I did not sleep very well that night, for now that the danger was over I found that the long strain of it had told upon my nerves. Also there were many noises. Thus, the bearers who were shot had been handed over to their companions, who disposed of them in a simple fashion, namely by throwing them into the bush where they attracted the notice of hyenas. Then the four wounded men who lay near to me groaned a good deal, or when they were not groaning uttered loud prayers to their local gods. We had done the best we could for these unlucky fellows. Indeed, that kind-hearted little coward, Sammy, who at some time in his career served as a dresser in a hospital, had tended their wounds, none of which were mortal, very well indeed, and from time to time rose to minister to them.

But what disturbed me most was the fearful hubbub which came from the camp below. Many of the tropical African tribes are really semi-nocturnal in their habits, I suppose because there the night is cooler than the day, and on any great occasion this tendency asserts itself.

Thus every one of these freed slaves seemed to be howling his loudest to an accompaniment of clashing iron pots or stones, which, lacking their native drums, they beat with sticks.

Moreover, they had lit large fires, about which they flitted in an ominous and unpleasant fashion, that reminded me of some mediaeval pictures of hell, which I had seen in an old book.

At last I could stand it no longer, and kicking Hans who, curled up like a dog, slept at my feet, asked him what was going on. His answer caused me to regret the question.

"Plenty of those slaves cannibal men, Baas. Think they eat the Arabs and like them very much," he said with a yawn, then went to sleep again.

I did not continue the conversation.

When at length we made a start on the following morning the sun was high over us. Indeed, there was a great deal to do. The guns and ammunition of the dead Arabs had to be collected; the ivory, of which they carried a good store, must be buried, for to take it with us was impossible, and the loads apportioned.[1] Also it was necessary to make litters for the wounded, and to stir up the slaves from their debauch, into the nature of which I made no further inquiries, was no easy task. On mustering them I found that a good number had vanished during the night, where to I do not know. Still a mob of well over two hundred people, a considerable portion of whom were women and children, remained, whose one idea seemed to be to accompany us wherever we might wander. So with this miscellaneous following at length we started.

To describe our adventures during the next month would be too long if not impossible, for to tell the truth, after the lapse of so many years, these have become somewhat entangled in my mind. Our great difficulty was to feed such a multitude, for the store of rice and grain, upon which we were quite unable to keep a strict supervision, they soon devoured. Fortunately the country through which we passed, at this time of the year (the end of the wet season) was full of game, of which, travelling as we did very slowly, we were able to shoot a great deal. But this game killing, delightful as it may be to the sportsman, soon palled on us as a business. To say nothing of the expenditure of ammunition, it meant incessant work.

Against this the Zulu hunters soon began to murmur, for, as Stephen and I could rarely leave the camp, the burden of it fell on them. Ultimately I hit upon this scheme. Picking out thirty or forty of the likeliest men among the slaves, I served out to each of them ammunition and one of the Arab guns, in the use of which we drilled them as best we could. Then I told them that they must provide themselves and their companions with meat. Of course accidents happened. One man was accidentally shot and three others were killed by a cow elephant and a wounded buffalo. But in the end they learned to handle their rifles sufficiently well to supply the camp. Moreover, day by day little parties of the slaves disappeared, I presume to seek their own homes, so that when at last we entered the borders of the Mazitu country there were not more than fifty of them left, including seventeen of those whom we had taught to shoot.

Then it was that our real adventures began.

---

1. To my sorrow we never saw this ivory again.—*A.Q.*

One evening, after three days' march through some difficult bush in which lions carried off a slave woman, killed one of the donkeys and mauled another so badly that it had to be shot, we found ourselves upon the edge of a great grassy plateau that, according to my aneroid, was 1,640 feet above sea level.

"What place is this?" I asked of the two Mazitu guides, those same men whom we had borrowed from Hassan.

"The land of our people, Chief," they answered, "which is bordered on one side by the bush and on the other by the great lake where live the Pongo wizards."

I looked about me at the bare uplands that already were beginning to turn brown, on which nothing was visible save vast herds of buck such as were common further south. A dreary prospect it was, for a slight rain was falling, accompanied by mist and a cold wind.

"I do not see your people or their *kraals*," I said; "I only see grass and wild game."

"Our people will come," they replied, rather nervously. "No doubt even now their spies watch us from among the tall grass or out of some hole."

"The deuce they do," I said, or something like it, and thought no more of the matter. When one is in conditions in which anything *may* happen, such as, so far as I am concerned, have prevailed through most of my life, one grows a little careless as to what *will* happen. For my part I have long been a fatalist, to a certain extent. I mean I believe that the individual, or rather the identity which animates him, came out from the Source of all life a long while, perhaps hundreds of thousands or millions of years ago, and when his career is finished, perhaps hundreds of thousands or millions of years hence, or perhaps tomorrow, will return perfected, but still as an individual, to dwell in or with that Source of Life. I believe also that his various existences, here or elsewhere, are fore-known and fore-ordained, although in a sense he may shape them by the action of his free will, and that nothing which he can do will lengthen or shorten one of them by a single hour. Therefore, so far as I am concerned, I have always acted up to the great injunction of our Master and taken no thought for the morrow.

However, in this instance, as in many others of my experience, the morrow took plenty of thought for itself. Indeed, before the dawn, Hans, who never seemed really to sleep any more than a dog does, woke me up with the ominous information that he heard a sound which he thought was caused by the tramp of hundreds of marching men.

"Where?" I asked, after listening without avail—to look was useless, for the night was dark as pitch.

He put his ear to the ground and said:

"There."

I put *my* ear to the ground, but although my senses are fairly acute, could hear nothing.

Then I sent for the sentries, but these, too, could hear nothing. After this I gave the business up and went to sleep again.

However, as it proved, Hans was quite right; in such matters he generally was right, for his senses were as keen as those of any wild beast. At dawn I was once more awakened, this time by Mavovo, who reported that we were being surrounded by a regiment, or regiments. I rose and looked out through the mist. There, sure enough, in dim and solemn outline, though still far off, I perceived rank upon rank of men, armed men, for the light glimmered faintly upon their spears.

"What is to be done, Macumazana?" asked Mavovo.

"Have breakfast, I think," I answered. "If we are going to be killed it may as well be after breakfast as before," and calling the trembling Sammy, I instructed him to make the coffee. Also I awoke Stephen and explained the situation to him.

"Capital!" he answered. "No doubt these are the Mazitu, and we have found them much more easily than we expected. People generally take such a lot of hunting for in this confounded great country."

"That's not such a bad way of looking at things," I answered, "but would you be good enough to go round the camp and make it clear that not on any account is anyone to fire without orders. Stay, collect all the guns from those slaves, for heaven knows what they will do with them if they are frightened!"

Stephen nodded and sauntered off with three or four of the hunters. While he was gone, in consultation with Mavovo, I made certain little arrangements of my own, which need not be detailed. They were designed to enable us to sell our lives as dearly as possible, should things come to the worst. One should always try to make an impression upon the enemy in Africa, for the sake of future travellers if for no other reason.

In due course Stephen and the hunters returned with the guns, or most of them, and reported that the slave people were in great state of terror, and showed a disposition to bolt.

"Let them bolt," I answered. "They would be of no use to us in a row and might even complicate matters. Call in the Zulus who are watching at once."

He nodded, and a few minutes later I heard—for the mist which hung about the bush to the east of the camp was still too dense to allow of my seeing anything—a clamour of voices, followed by the sound of scuttling feet. The slave people, including our bearers, had gone, every one of them. They even carried away the wounded. Just as the soldiers who surrounded us were completing their circle they bolted between the two ends of it and vanished into the bush out of which we had marched on the previous evening. Often since then I have wondered what became of them. Doubtless some perished, and the rest worked their way back to their homes or found new ones among other tribes. The experiences of those who escaped must be interesting to them if they still live. I can well imagine the legends in which these will be embodied two or three generations hence.

Deducting the slave people and the bearers whom we had wrung out of Hassan, we were now a party of seventeen, namely eleven Zulu hunters including Mavovo, two white men, Hans and Sammy, and the two Mazitus who had elected to remain with us, while round us was a great circle of savages which closed in slowly.

As the light grew—it was long in coming on that dull morning—and the mist lifted, I examined these people, without seeming to take any particular notice of them. They were tall, much taller than the average Zulu, and slighter in their build, also lighter in colour. Like the Zulus they carried large hide shields and one very broad-bladed spear. Throwing assegais seemed to be wanting, but in place of them I saw that they were armed with short bows, which, together with a quiver of arrows, were slung upon their backs. The officers wore a short skin cloak or *kaross*, and the men also had cloaks, which I found out afterwards were made from the inner bark of trees.

They advanced in the most perfect silence and very slowly. Nobody said anything, and if orders were given this must have been done by signs. I could not see that any of them had firearms.

"Now," I said to Stephen, "perhaps if we shot and killed some of those fellows, they might be frightened and run away. Or they might not; or if they did they might return."

"Whatever happened," he remarked sagely, "we should scarcely be welcome in their country afterwards, so I think we had better do nothing unless we are obliged."

I nodded, for it was obvious that we could not fight hundreds of men, and told Sammy, who was perfectly livid with fear, to bring the breakfast. No wonder he was afraid, poor fellow, for we were in great danger. These Mazitu had a bad name, and if they chose to attack us we should all be dead in a few minutes.

The coffee and some cold buck's flesh were put upon our little camp-table in front of the tent which we had pitched because of the rain, and we began to eat. The Zulu hunters also ate from a bowl of *mealie* porridge which they had cooked on the previous night, each of them with his loaded rifle upon his knees. Our proceedings appeared to puzzle the Mazitu very much indeed. They drew quite near to us, to within about forty yards, and halted there in a dead circle, staring at us with their great round eyes. It was like a scene in a dream; I shall never forget it.

Everything about us appeared to astonish them, our indifference, the colour of Stephen and myself (as a matter of fact at that date Brother John was the only white man they had ever seen), our tent and our two remaining donkeys. Indeed, when one of these beasts broke into a bray, they showed signs of fright, looking at each other and even retreating a few paces.

At length the position got upon my nerves, especially as I saw that some of them were beginning to fiddle with their bows, and that their General, a tall, one-eyed old fellow, was making up his mind to do something. I called to one of the two Mazitus, whom I forgot to say we had named Tom and Jerry, and gave him a pannikin of coffee.

"Take that to the captain there with my good wishes, Jerry, and ask him if he will drink with us," I said.

Jerry, who was a plucky fellow, obeyed. Advancing with the steaming coffee, he held it under the Captain's nose. Evidently he knew the man's name, for I heard him say:

"O Babemba, the white lords, Macumazana and Wazela, ask if you will share their holy drink with them?"

I could perfectly understand the words, for these people spoke a dialect so akin to Zulu that by now it had no difficulty for me.

"Their holy drink!" exclaimed the old fellow, starting back. "Man, it is hot red-water. Would these white wizards poison me with *mwavi*?"

Here I should explain that *mwavi* or *mkasa*, as it is sometimes called, is the liquor distilled from the inner bark of a sort of mimosa tree or sometimes from a root of the strychnos tribe, which is administered by the witch-doctors to persons accused of crime. If it makes them sick they are declared innocent. If they are thrown into convulsions or stupor they are clearly guilty and die, either from the effects of the poison or afterwards by other means.

"This is no *mwavi*, O Babemba," said Jerry. "It is the divine liquor that makes the white lords shoot straight with their wonderful guns which kill at a thousand paces. See, I will swallow some of it," and he did, though it must have burnt his tongue.

Thus encouraged, old Babemba sniffed at the coffee and found it fragrant. Then he called a man, who from his peculiar dress I took to be a doctor, made him drink some, and watched the results, which were that the doctor tried to finish the pannikin. Snatching it away indignantly Babemba drank himself, and as I had half-filled the cup with sugar, found the mixture good.

"It is indeed a holy drink," he said, smacking his lips. "Have you any more of it?"

"The white lords have more," said Jerry. "They invite you to eat with them."

Babemba stuck his finger into the tin, and covering it with the sediment of sugar, sucked and reflected.

"It's all right," I whispered to Stephen. "I don't think he'll kill us after drinking our coffee, and what's more, I believe he is coming to breakfast."

"This may be a snare," said Babemba, who now began to lick the sugar out of the pannikin.

"No," answered Jerry with creditable resource; "though they could easily kill you all, the white lords do not hurt those who have partaken of their holy drink, that is unless anyone tries to harm them."

"Cannot you bring some more of the holy drink here?" he asked, giving a final polish to the pannikin with his tongue.

"No," said Jerry, "if you want it you must go there. Fear nothing. Would I, one of your own people, betray you?"

"True!" exclaimed Babemba. "By your talk and your face you are a Mazitu. How came you—well, we will speak of that afterwards. I am very thirsty. I will come. Soldiers, sit down and watch, and if any harm happens to me, avenge it and report to the king."

Now, while all this was going on, I had made Hans and Sammy open one of the boxes and extract therefrom a good-sized mirror in a wooden frame with a support at the back so that it could be stood anywhere. Fortunately it was unbroken; indeed, our packing had been so careful that none of the looking-glasses or other fragile things were injured. To this mirror I gave a hasty polish, then set it upright upon the table.

Old Babemba came along rather suspiciously, his one eye rolling over us and everything that belonged to us. When he was quite close it fell upon the mirror. He stopped, he stared, he retreated, then drawn by his overmastering curiosity, came on again and again stood still.

"What is the matter?" called his second in command from the ranks.

"The matter is," he answered, "that here is great magic. Here I see myself walking towards myself. There can be no mistake, for one eye is gone in my other self."

"Advance, O Babemba," cried the doctor who had tried to drink all the coffee, "and see what happens. Keep your spear ready, and if your witch-self attempts to harm you, kill it."

Thus encouraged, Babemba lifted his spear and dropped it again in a great hurry.

"That won't do, fool of a doctor," he shouted back. "My other self lifts a spear also, and what is more all of you who should be behind are in front of me. The holy drink has made me drunk; I am bewitched. Save me!"

Now I saw that the joke had gone too far, for the soldiers were beginning to string their bows in confusion. Luckily at this moment, the sun at length came out almost opposite to us.

"O Babemba," I said in a solemn voice, "it is true that this magic shield, which we have brought as a gift to you, gives you another self. Henceforth your labours will be halved, and your pleasures doubled, for when you look into this shield you will be not one but two. Also it has other properties—see," and lifting the mirror I used it as a heliograph, flashing the reflected sunlight into the eyes of the long half-circle of men in front of us. My word! didn't they run.

"Wonderful!" exclaimed old Babemba, "and can I learn to do that also, white lord?"

"Certainly," I answered, "come and try. Now, hold it so while I say the spell," and I muttered some hocus-pocus, then directed it towards certain of the Mazitu who were gathering again. "There! Look! Look! You have hit them in the eye. You are a master of magic. They run, they run!" and run they did indeed. "Is there anyone yonder whom you dislike?"

"Yes, plenty," answered Babemba with emphasis, "especially that witch-doctor who drank nearly all the holy drink."

"Very well; by-and-by I will show you how you can burn a hole in him with this magic. No, not now, not now. For a while this mocker of the sun is dead. Look," and dipping the glass beneath the table I produced it back first. "You cannot see anything, can you?"

"Nothing except wood," replied Babemba, staring at the deal slip with which it was lined.

Then I threw a dish-cloth over it and, to change the subject, offered him another pannikin of the "holy drink" and a stool to sit on.

The old fellow perched himself very gingerly upon the stool, which was of the folding variety, stuck the iron-tipped end of his great spear in the ground between his knees and took hold of the pannikin. Or rather he took hold of a pannikin and not the right one. So ridiculous was his appearance that the light-minded Stephen, who, forgetting the perils of the situation, had for the last minute or two been struggling with inward laughter, clapped down his coffee on the table and retired into the tent, where I heard him gurgling in unseemly merriment. It was this coffee that in the confusion of the moment Sammy gave to old Babemba. Presently Stephen reappeared, and to cover his confusion seized the pannikin meant for Babemba and drank it, or most of it. Then Sammy, seeing his mistake, said:

"Mr. Somers, I regret that there is an error. You are drinking from the cup which that stinking savage has just licked clean."

The effect was dreadful and instantaneous, for then and there Stephen was violently sick.

"Why does the white lord do that?" asked Babemba. "Now I see that you are truly deceiving me, and that what you are giving me to swallow is nothing but hot *mwavi*, which in the innocent causes vomiting, but that in those who mean evil, death."

"Stop that foolery, you idiot," I muttered to Stephen, kicking him on the shins, "or you'll get our throats cut." Then, collecting myself with an effort, I said:

"Oh! not at all, General. This white lord is the priest of the holy drink and—what you see is a religious rite."

"Is it so," said Babemba. "Then I hope that the rite is not catching."

"Never," I replied, proffering him a biscuit. "And now, General Babemba, tell me, why do you come against us with about five hundred armed men?"

"To kill you, white lords—oh! how hot is this holy drink, yet pleasant. You said that it was not catching, did you not? For I feel——"

"Eat the cake," I answered. "And why do you wish to kill us? Be so good as to tell me the truth now, or I shall read it in the magic shield which portrays the inside as well as the out," and lifting the cloth I stared at the glass.

"If you can read my thoughts, white lord, why trouble me to tell them?" asked Babemba sensibly enough, his mouth full of biscuit. "Still, as that bright thing may lie, I will set them out. Bausi, king of our people, has sent me to kill you, because news has reached him that you are great slave dealers who come hither with guns to capture the Mazitus and take them away to the Black Water to be sold and sent across it in big canoes that move of themselves. Of this he has been warned by messengers from the Arab men. Moreover, we know that it is true, for last night you had with you many slaves who, seeing our spears, ran away not an hour ago."

Now I stared hard at the looking-glass and answered coolly:

"This magic shield tells a somewhat different story. It says that your king, Bausi, for whom by the way we have many things as presents, told you to lead us to him with honour, that we might talk over matters with him."

The shot was a good one. Babemba grew confused.

"It is true," he stammered, "that—I mean, the king left it to my judgment. I will consult the witch-doctor."

"If he left it to your judgment, the matter is settled," I said, "since certainly, being so great a noble, you would never try to murder those of whose holy drink you have just partaken. Indeed if you did so," I added in a cold voice, "you would not live long yourself. One secret word and that drink will turn to *muwavi* of the worst sort inside of you."

"Oh! yes, white lord, it is settled," exclaimed Babemba, "it is settled. Do not trouble the secret word. I will lead you to the king and you shall talk with him. By my head and my father's spirit you are safe from me. Still, with your leave, I will call the great doctor, Imbozwi, and ratify the agreement in his presence, and also show him the magic shield."

So Imbozwi was sent for, Jerry taking the message. Presently he arrived. He was a villainous-looking person of uncertain age, humpbacked like the picture of Punch, wizened and squint-eyed. His costume was of the ordinary witch-doctor type being set off with snake skins, fish bladders, baboon's teeth and little bags of medicine. To add to his charms a broad strip of pigment, red ochre probably, ran down his forehead and the nose beneath, across the lips and chin, ending in a red mark the size of a penny where the throat joins the chest. His woolly hair also, in which was twisted a small ring of black gum, was soaked with grease and powdered blue. It was arranged in a kind of horn, coming to a sharp point about five inches above the top of the skull. Altogether he looked extremely like the devil. What was more, he was a devil in a bad temper, for the first words he said embodied a reproach to us for not having asked him to partake of our "holy drink" with Babemba.

We offered to make him some more, but he refused, saying that we should poison him.

Then Babemba set the matter out, rather nervously I thought, for evidently he was afraid of this old wizard, who listened in complete silence. When Babemba explained that without the king's direct order it would be foolish and unjustifiable to put to death such magicians as we were, Imbozwi spoke for the first time, asking why he called us magicians.

Babemba instanced the wonders of the shining shield that showed pictures.

"Pooh!" said Imbozwi, "does not calm water or polished iron show pictures?"

"But this shield will make fire," said Babemba. "The white lords say it can burn a man up."

"Then let it burn me up," replied Imbozwi with ineffable contempt, "and I will believe that these white men are magicians worthy to be kept alive, and not common slave-traders such as we have often heard of."

"Burn him, white lords, and show him that I am right," exclaimed the exasperated Babemba, after which they fell to wrangling. Evidently they were rivals, and by this time both of them had lost their tempers.

The sun was now very hot, quite sufficiently so to enable us to give Mr. Imbozwi a taste of our magic, which I determined he should have. Not being certain whether an ordinary mirror would really reflect enough heat to scorch, I drew from my pocket a very powerful burning-glass which I sometimes used for the lighting of fires in order to save matches, and holding the mirror in one hand and the burning-glass in the other, I worked myself into a suitable position for the experiment. Babemba and the witch-doctor were arguing so fiercely that neither of them seemed to notice what I was doing. Getting the focus right, I directed the concentrated spark straight on to Imbozwi's greased top-knot, where I knew he would feel nothing, my plan being to char a hole in it. But as it happened this top-knot was built up round something of a highly inflammable nature, reed or camphor-wood, I expect. At any rate, about thirty seconds later the top-knot was burning like a beautiful torch.

"Ow!" said the *Kaffirs* who were watching. "My Aunt!" exclaimed Stephen. "Look, look!" shouted Babemba in tones of delight. "Now will you believe, O blown-out bladder of a man, that there are greater magicians than yourself in the world?"

"What is the matter, son of a dog, that you make a mock of me?" screeched the infuriated Imbozwi, who alone was unaware of anything unusual.

As he spoke some suspicion rose in his mind which caused him to put his hand to his top-knot, and withdraw it with a howl. Then he sprang up and began to dance about, which of course only fanned the fire that had now got hold of the grease and gum. The Zulus applauded; Babemba clapped his hands; Stephen burst into one of his idiotic fits of laughter. For my part I grew frightened. Near at hand stood a large wooden pot such as the *Kaffirs* make, from which the coffee kettle had been filled, that fortunately was still half-full of water. I seized it and ran to him.

"Save me, white lord!" he howled. "You are the greatest of magicians and I am your slave."

Here I cut him short by clapping the pot bottom upwards on his burning head, into which it vanished as a candle does into an extinguisher. Smoke and a bad smell issued from beneath the pot, the water from which ran all over Imbozwi, who stood quite still. When I was sure the fire was out, I lifted the pot and revealed the discomfited wizard, but without his elaborate head-dress. Beyond a little scorching he was not in the least hurt, for I had acted in time; only he was bald, for when touched the charred hair fell off at the roots.

"It is gone," he said in an amazed voice after feeling at his scalp.

"Yes," I answered, "quite. The magic shield worked very well, did it not?"

"Can you put it back again, white lord?" he asked.

"That will depend upon how you behave," I replied.

Then without another word he turned and walked back to the soldiers, who received him with shouts of laughter. Evidently Imbozwi was not a popular character, and his discomfiture delighted them.

Babemba also was delighted. Indeed, he could not praise our magic enough, and at once began to make arrangements to escort us to the king at his head town, which was called Beza, vowing that we need fear no harm at his hands or those of his soldiers. In fact, the only person who did not appreciate our black arts was Imbozwi himself. I caught a look in his eye as he marched off which told me that he hated us bitterly, and reflected to myself that perhaps I had been foolish to use that burning-glass, although in truth I had not intended to set his head on fire.

"My father," said Mavovo to me afterwards, "it would have been better to let that snake burn to death, for then you would have killed his poison. I am something of a doctor myself, and I tell you there is nothing our brotherhood hates so much as being laughed at. You have made a fool of him before all his people and he will not forget it, Macumazana."

CHAPTER 9

Bausi the King

About midday we made a start for Beza Town where King Bausi lived, which we understood we ought to reach on the following evening. For some hours the regiment marched in front, or rather round us, but as we complained to Babemba of the noise and dust, with a confidence that was quite touching, he sent it on ahead. First, however, he asked us to pass our word "by our mothers," which was the most sacred of oaths among many African peoples, that we would not attempt to escape. I confess that I hesitated before giving an answer, not being entirely enamoured of the Mazitu and of our prospects among them, especially as I had discovered through Jerry that the discomfited Imbozwi had departed from the soldiers on some business of his own. Had the matter been left to me, indeed, I should have tried to slip back into the bush over the border, and there put in a few months shooting during the dry season, while working my way southwards. This, too, was the wish of the Zulu hunters, of Hans, and I need not add of Sammy. But when I mentioned the matter to Stephen, he implored me to abandon the idea.

"Look here, Quatermain," he said, "I have come to this God-forsaken country to get that great *Cypripedium*, and get it I will or die in the attempt. Still," he added after surveying our rather blank faces, "I have no right to play with your lives, so if you think the thing too dangerous I will go on alone with this old boy, Babemba. Putting everything else aside, I think that one of us ought to visit Bausi's *kraal* in case the gentleman who you call Brother John should turn up there. In short, I have made up my mind, so it is no use talking."

I lit my pipe, and for quite a time contemplated this obstinate young man while considering the matter from every point of view. Finally, I came to the conclusion that he was right and I was wrong. It was true that by bribing Babemba, or otherwise, there was still an excellent prospect of effecting a masterly retreat and of avoiding many perils. On the other hand, we had not come to this wild place in order to retreat. Further, at whose expense had we come here? At that of Stephen Somers who wished to proceed. Lastly, to say nothing of the chance of meeting Brother John, to whom I felt no obligation since he had given us the slip at Durban, I did not like the idea of being beaten. We had started out to visit some mysterious savages who worshipped a monkey and a flower, and we might as well go on till circumstances were too much for us. After all, dangers are everywhere; those who turn back because of dangers will never succeed in any life that we can imagine.

"Mavovo," I said presently, pointing to Stephen with my pipe, "the *inkoosi* Wazela does not wish to try to escape. He wishes to go on to the country of the Pongo people if we can get there. And, Mavovo, remember that he has paid for everything; we are his hired servants. Also that he says that if we run back he will walk forward alone with these Mazitus. Still, if any of you hunters desire to slip off, he will not look your way, nor shall I. What say you?"

"I say, Macumazana, that, though young, Wazela is a chief with a great heart, and that where you and he go, I shall go also, as I think will the rest of us. I do not like these Mazitu, for if their fathers were Zulus their mothers were low people. They are bastards, and of the Pongo I hear nothing but what is evil. Still, no good ox ever turns in the yoke because of a mud-hole. Let us go on, for if we sink in the swamp what does it matter? Moreover, my Snake tells me that we shall not sink, at least not all of us."

So it was arranged that no effort should be made to return. Sammy, it is true, wished to do so, but when it came to the point and he was offered one of the remaining donkeys and as much food and ammunition as he could carry, he changed his mind.

"I think it better, Mr. Quatermain," he said, "to meet my end in the company of high-born, lofty souls than to pursue a lonely career towards the inevitable in unknown circumstances."

"Very well put, Sammy," I answered; "so while waiting for the inevitable, please go and cook the dinner."

Having laid aside our doubts, we proceeded on the journey comfortably enough, being well provided with bearers to take the place of those who had run away. Babemba, accompanied by a single orderly, travelled with us, and from him we collected much information. It seemed that the Mazitu were a large people who could muster from five to seven thousand spears. Their tradition was that they came from the south and were of the same stock as the Zulus, of whom they had heard vaguely. Indeed, many of their customs, to say nothing of their language, resembled those of that country. Their military organisation, however, was not so thorough, and in other ways they struck me as a lower race. In one particular, it is true, that of their houses, they were more advanced, for these, as we saw in the many *kraals* that we passed, were better built, with doorways through which one could walk upright, instead of the *Kaffir* bee-holes.

We slept in one of these houses on our march, and should have found it very comfortable had it not been for the innumerable fleas which at length drove us out into the courtyard. For the rest, these Mazitu much resembled the Zulus. They had *kraals* and were breeders of cattle; they were ruled by headmen under the command of a supreme chief or king; they believed in witchcraft and offered sacrifice to the spirits of their ancestors, also in some kind of a vague and mighty god who dominated the affairs of the world and declared his will through the doctors. Lastly, they were, and I dare say still are, a race of fighting men who loved war and raided the neighbouring peoples upon any and every pretext, killing their men and stealing their women and cattle. They had their virtues, too, being kindly and hospitable by nature, though cruel enough to their enemies. Moreover, they detested dealing in slaves and those who practised it, saying that it was better to kill a man than to deprive him of his freedom. Also they had a horror of the cannibalism which is so common in the dark regions of Africa, and for this reason, more than any other, loathed the Pongo folk who were supposed to be eaters of men.

On the evening of the second day of our march, during which we had passed through a beautiful and fertile upland country, very well watered, and except in the valleys, free from bush, we arrived at Beza. This town was situated on a wide plain surrounded by low hills and encircled by a belt of cultivated land made beautiful by the crops of maize and other cereals which were then ripe to harvest. It was fortified in a way. That is, a tall, unclimbable palisade of timber surrounded the entire town, which fence was strengthened by prickly pears and cacti planted on its either side.

Within this palisade the town was divided into quarters more or less devoted to various trades. Thus one part of it was called the Ironsmiths' Quarter; another the Soldiers' Quarter; another the Quarter of the Land-tillers; another that of the Skin-dressers, and so on. The king's dwelling and those of his women and dependents were near the North gate, and in front of these, surrounded by semi-circles of huts, was a wide space into which cattle could be driven if necessary. This, however, at the time of our visit, was used as a market and a drilling ground.

We entered the town, that must in all have contained a great number of inhabitants, by the South gate, a strong log structure facing a wooded slope through which ran a road. Just as the sun was setting we marched to the guest-huts up a central street lined with the population of the place who had gathered to stare at us. These huts were situated in the Soldiers' Quarter, not far from the king's house and surrounded by an inner fence to keep them private.

None of the people spoke as we passed them, for the Mazitu are polite by nature; also it seemed to me that they regarded us with awe tempered by curiosity. They only stared, and occasionally those of them who were soldiers saluted us by lifting their spears. The huts into which we were introduced by Babemba, with whom we had grown very friendly, were good and clean.

Here all our belongings, including the guns which we had collected just before the slaves ran away, were placed in one of the huts over which a Mazitu mounted guard, the donkeys being tied to the fence at a little distance. Outside this fence stood another armed Mazitu, also on guard.

"Are we prisoners here?" I asked of Babemba.

"The king watches over his guests," he answered enigmatically. "Have the white lords any message for the king whom I am summoned to see this night?"

"Yes," I answered. "Tell the king that we are the brethren of him who more than a year ago cut a swelling from his body, whom we have arranged to meet here. I mean the white lord with a long beard who among you black people is called Dogeetah."

Babemba started. "You are the brethren of Dogeetah! How comes it then that you never mentioned his name before, and when is he going to meet you here? Know that Dogeetah is a great man among us, for with him alone of all men the king has made blood-brotherhood. As the king is, so is Dogeetah among the Mazitu."

"We never mentioned him because we do not talk about everything at once, Babemba. As to when Dogeetah will meet us I am not sure; I am only sure that he is coming."

"Yes, lord Macumazana, but when, when? That is what the king will want to know and that is what you must tell him. Lord," he added, dropping his voice, "you are in danger here where you have many enemies, since it is not lawful for white men to enter this land. If you would save your lives, be advised by me and be ready to tell the king tomorrow when Dogeetah, whom he loves, will appear here to vouch for you, and see that he does appear very soon and by the day you name. Since otherwise when he comes, if come he does, he may not find you able to talk to him. Now I, your friend, have spoken and the rest is with you."

Then without another word he rose, slipped through the door of the hut and out by the gateway of the fence from which the sentry moved aside to let him pass. I, too, rose from the stool on which I sat and danced about the hut in a perfect fury.

"Do you understand what that infernal (I am afraid I used a stronger word) old fool told me?" I exclaimed to Stephen. "He says that we must be prepared to state exactly when that other infernal old fool, Brother John, will turn up at Beza Town, and that if we don't we shall have our throats cut as indeed has already been arranged."

"Rather awkward," replied Stephen. "There are no express trains to Beza, and if there were we couldn't be sure that Brother John would take one of them. I suppose there *is* a Brother John?" he added reflectively. "To me he seems to be—intimately connected with Mrs. Harris."

"Oh! there is, or there was," I explained. "Why couldn't the confounded ass wait quietly for us at Durban instead of fooling off butterfly hunting to the north of Zululand and breaking his leg or his neck there if he has done anything of the sort?"

"Don't know, I am sure. It's hard enough to understand one's own motives, let alone Brother John's."

Then we sat down on our stools again and stared at each other. At this moment Hans crept into the hut and squatted down in front of us. He might have walked in as there was a doorway, but he preferred to creep on his hands and knees, I don't know why.

"What is it, you ugly little toad?" I asked viciously, for that was just what he looked like; even the skin under his jaw moved like a toad's.

"The Baas is in trouble?" remarked Hans.

"I should think he was," I answered, "and so will you be presently when you are wriggling on the point of a Mazitu spear."

"They are broad spears that would make a big hole," remarked Hans again, whereupon I rose to kick him out, for his ideas were, as usual, unpleasant.

"Baas," he went on, "I have been listening—there is a very good hole in this hut for listening if one lies against the wall and pretends to be asleep. I have heard all and understood most of your talk with that one-eyed savage and the Baas Stephen."

"Well, you little sneak, what of it?"

"Only, Baas, that if we do not want to be killed in this place from which there is no escape, it is necessary that you should find out exactly on what day and at what hour Dogeetah is going to arrive."

"Look here, you yellow idiot," I exclaimed, "if you are beginning that game too, I'll——" then I stopped, reflecting that my temper was getting the better of me and that I had better hear what Hans had to say before I vented it on him.

"Baas, Mavovo is a great doctor; it is said that his Snake is the straightest and the strongest in all Zululand save that of his master, Zikali, the old slave. He told you that Dogeetah was laid up somewhere with a hurt leg and that he was coming to meet you here; no doubt therefore he can tell you also *when* he is coming. I would ask him, but he won't set his Snake to work for me. So you must ask him, Baas, and perhaps he will forget that you laughed at his magic and that he swore you would never see it again."

"Oh! blind one," I answered, "how do I know that Mavovo's story about Dogeetah was not all nonsense?"

Hans stared at me amazed.

"Mavovo's story nonsense! Mavovo's Snake a liar! Oh! Baas, that is what comes of being too much a Christian. Now, thanks to your father the Predikant, I am a Christian too, but not so much that I have forgotten how to know good magic from bad. Mavovo's Snake a liar, and after he whom we buried yonder was the first of the hunters whom the feathers named to him at Durban!" and he began to chuckle in intense amusement, then added, "Well, Baas, there it is. You must either ask Mavovo, and very nicely, or we shall all be killed. *I* don't mind much, for I should rather like to begin again a little younger somewhere else, but just think what a noise Sammy will make!" and turning he crept out as he had crept in.

"Here's a nice position," I groaned to Stephen when he had gone. "I, a white man, who, in spite of some coincidences with which I am acquainted, know that all this *Kaffir* magic is bosh am to beg a savage to tell me something of which he *must* be ignorant. That is, unless we educated people have got hold of the wrong end of the stick altogether. It is humiliating; it isn't Christian, and I'm hanged if I'll do it!"

"I dare say you will be—hanged I mean—whether you do it or whether you don't," replied Stephen with his sweet smile. "But I say, old fellow, how do you know it is all bosh? We are told about lots of miracles which weren't bosh, and if miracles ever existed, why can't they exist now? But there, I know what you mean and it is no use arguing. Still, if you're proud, I ain't. I'll try to soften the stony heart of Mavovo—we are rather pals, you know—and get him to unroll the book of his occult wisdom," and he went.

A few minutes later I was called out to receive a sheep which, with milk, native beer, some corn, and other things, including green forage for the donkeys, Bausi had sent for us to eat. Here I may remark that while we were among the Mazitu we lived like fighting cocks. There was none of that starvation which is, or was, so common in East Africa where the traveller often cannot get food for love or money—generally because there is none.

When this business was settled by my sending a message of thanks to the king with an intimation that we hoped to wait upon him on the morrow with a few presents, I went to seek Sammy in order to tell him to kill and cook the sheep. After some search I found, or rather heard him beyond a reed fence which divided two of the huts. He was acting as interpreter between Stephen Somers and Mavovo.

"This Zulu man declares, Mr. Somers," he said, "that he quite understands everything you have been explaining, and that it is probable that we shall all be butchered by this savage Bausi, if we cannot tell him when the white man, Dogeetah, whom he loves, will arrive here. He says also that he thinks that by his magic he could learn when this will happen—if it is to happen at all—(which of course, Mr. Somers, for your private information only, is a mighty lie of the ignorant heathen). He adds, however, that he does not care one brass farthing—his actual expression, Mr. Somers, is 'one grain of corn on a *mealie*-cob'—about his or anybody else's life, which from all I have heard of his proceedings I can well believe to be true. He says in his vulgar language that there is no difference between the belly of a Mazitu-land hyena and that of any other hyena, and that the earth of Mazitu-land is as welcome to his bones as any other earth, since the earth is the wickedest of all hyenas, in that he has observed that soon or late it devours everlastingly everything which once it bore. You must forgive me for reproducing his empty and childish talk, Mr. Somers, but you bade me to render the words of this savage with exactitude. In fact, Mr. Somers, this reckless person intimates, in short that some power with which he is not acquainted—he calls it the 'Strength that makes the Sun to shine and broiders the blanket of the night with stars' (forgive me for repeating his silly words), caused him 'to be born into this world, and, at an hour already appointed, will draw him from this world back into its dark, eternal bosom, there to be rocked in sleep, or nursed to life again, according to its unknown will'—I translate exactly, Mr. Somers, although I do not know what it all means—and that he does not care a curse when this happens. Still, he says that whereas he is growing old and has known many sorrows—he alludes here, I gather, to some nigger wives of his whom another savage knocked on the head; also to a child to whom he appears to have been attached—you are young with all your days and, he hopes, joys, before you. Therefore he would gladly do anything in his power to save your life, because although you are white and he is black he has conceived an affection for you and looks on you as his child. Yes, Mr. Somers, although I blush to repeat it, this black fellow says he looks upon you as his child. He adds, indeed, that if the opportunity arises, he will gladly give his life to save your life, and that it cuts his heart in two to refuse you anything. Still he must refuse this request of yours, that he will ask the creature he calls his Snake—what he means by that, I don't know, Mr. Somers—to declare when the white man, named Dogeetah, will arrive in this place. For this reason, that he told Mr. Quatermain when he laughed at him about his divinations that he would make no more magic for him or any of you, and that he will die rather than break his word. That's all, Mr. Somers, and I dare say you will think—quite enough, too."

"I understand," replied Stephen. "Tell the chief, Mavovo" (I observed he laid an emphasis on the word, *chief*) "that I *quite* understand, and that I thank him very much for explaining things to me so fully. Then ask him whether, as the matter is so important, there is no way out of this trouble?"

Sammy translated into Zulu, which he spoke perfectly, as I noted without interpolations or additions.

"Only one way," answered Mavovo in the intervals of taking snuff. "It is that Macumazana himself shall ask me to do this thing, Macumazana is my old chief and friend, and for his sake I will forget what in the case of others I should always remember. If he will come and ask me, without mockery, to exercise my skill on behalf of all of us, I will try to exercise it, although I know very well that he believes it to be but as an idle little whirlwind that stirs the dust, that raises the dust and lets it fall again without purpose or meaning, forgetting, as the wise white men forget, that even the wind which blows the dust is the same that breathes in our nostrils, and that to it, we also are as is the dust."

Now I, the listener, thought for a moment or two. The words of this fighting savage, Mavovo, even those of them of which I had heard only the translation, garbled and beslavered by the mean comments of the unutterable Sammy, stirred my imagination. Who was I that I should dare to judge of him and his wild, unknown gifts? Who was I that I should mock at him and by my mockery intimate that I believed him to be a fraud?

Stepping through the gateway of the fence, I confronted him.

"Mavovo," I said, "I have overheard your talk. I am sorry if I laughed at you in Durban. I do not understand what you call your magic. It is beyond me and may be true or may be false. Still, I shall be grateful to you if you will use your power to discover, if you can, whether Dogeetah is coming here, and if so, when. Now, do as it may please you; I have spoken."

"And I have heard, Macumazana, my father. Tonight I will call upon my Snake. Whether it will answer or what it will answer, I cannot say."

Well, he did call upon his Snake with due and portentous ceremony and, according to Stephen, who was present, which I declined to be, that mystic reptile declared that Dogeetah, alias Brother John, would arrive in Beza Town precisely at sunset on the third day from that night. Now as he had divined on Friday, according to our almanac, this meant that we might hope to see him—hope exactly described my state of mind on the matter—on the Monday evening in time for supper.

"All right," I said briefly. "Please do not talk to me any more about this *impi*ous rubbish, for I want to go to sleep."

Next morning early we unpacked our boxes and made a handsome selection of gifts for the king, Bausi, hoping thus to soften his royal heart. It included a bale of calico, several knives, a musical box, a cheap American revolver, and a bundle of tooth-picks; also several pounds of the best and most fashionable beads for his wives. This truly noble present we sent to the king by our two Mazitu servants, Tom and Jerry, who were marched off in the charge of several sentries, for I hoped that these men would talk to their compatriots and tell them what good fellows we were. Indeed I instructed them to do so.

Imagine our horror, therefore, when about an hour later, just as we were tidying ourselves up after breakfast, there appeared through the gate, not Tom and Jerry, for they had vanished, but a long line of Mazitu soldiers each of whom carried one of the articles that we had sent. Indeed the last of them held the bundle of toothpicks on his fuzzy head as though it were a huge faggot of wood. One by one they set them down upon the lime flooring of the veranda of the largest hut. Then their captain said solemnly:

"Bausi, the Great Black One, has no need of the white men's gifts."

"Indeed," I replied, for my dander was up. "Then he won't get another chance at them."

The men turned away without more words, and presently Babemba turned up with a company of about fifty soldiers.

"The king is waiting to see you, white lords," he said in a voice of very forced jollity, "and I have come to conduct you to him."

"Why would he not accept our presents?" I asked, pointing to the row of them.

"Oh! that is because of Imbozwi's story of the magic shield. He said he wanted no gifts to burn his hair off. But, come, come. He will explain for himself. If the Elephant is kept waiting he grows angry and trumpets."

"Does he?" I said. "And how many of us are to come?"

"All, all, white lord. He wishes to see every one of you."

"Not me, I suppose?" said Sammy, who was standing close by. "I must stop to make ready the food."

"Yes, you too," replied Babemba. "The king would look on the mixer of the holy drink."

Well, there was no way out of it, so off we marched, all well armed as I need not say, and were instantly surrounded by the soldiers. To give an unusual note to the proceedings I made Hans walk first, carrying on his head the rejected musical box from which flowed the touching melody of "Home, Sweet Home." Then came Stephen bearing the Union Jack on a pole, then I in the midst of the hunters and accompanied by Babemba, then the reluctant Sammy, and last of all the two donkeys led by Mazitus, for it seemed that the king had especially ordered that these should be brought also.

It was a truly striking cavalcade, the sight of which under any other circumstances would have made me laugh. Nor did it fail in its effect, for even the silent Mazitu people through whom we wended our way, were moved to something like enthusiasm. "Home, Sweet Home" they evidently thought heavenly, though perhaps the two donkeys attracted them most, especially when these brayed.

"Where are Tom and Jerry?" I asked of Babemba.

"I don't know," he answered; "I think they have been given leave to go to see their friends."

Imbozwi is suppressing evidence in our favour, I thought to myself, and said no more.

Presently we reached the gate of the royal enclosure. Here to my dismay the soldiers insisted on disarming us, taking away our rifles, our revolvers, and even our sheath knives. In vain did I remonstrate, saying that we were not accustomed to part with these weapons. The answer was that it was not lawful for any man to appear before the king armed even with so much as a dancing-stick. Mavovo and the Zulus showed signs of resisting and for a minute I thought there was going to be a row, which of course would have ended in our massacre, for although the Mazitus feared guns very much, what could we have done against hundreds of them? I ordered him to give way, but for once he was on the point of disobeying me. Then by a happy thought I reminded him that, according to his Snake, Dogeetah was coming, and that therefore all would be well. So he submitted with an ill grace, and we saw our precious guns borne off we knew not where.

Then the Mazitu soldiers piled their spears and bows at the gate of the *kraal* and we proceeded with only the Union Jack and the musical box, which was now discoursing "Britannia rules the waves."

Across the open space we marched to where several broad-leaved trees grew in front of a large native house. Not far from the door of this house a fat, middle-aged and angry-looking man was seated on a stool, naked except for a *moocha* of cat-skins about his loins and a string of large blue beads round his neck.

"Bausi, the King," whispered Babemba.

At his side squatted a little hunchbacked figure, in whom I had no difficulty in recognising Imbozwi, although he had painted his scorched scalp white with vermillion spots and adorned his snub nose with a purple tip, his dress of ceremony I presume. Round and behind there were a number of silent councillors. At some signal or on reaching a given spot, all the soldiers, including old Babemba, fell upon their hands and knees and began to crawl. They wanted us to do the same, but here I drew the line, feeling that if once we crawled we must always crawl.

So at my word we advanced upright, but with slow steps, in the midst of all this wriggling humanity and at length found ourselves in the august presence of Bausi, "the Beautiful Black One," King of the Mazitu.

Chapter 10

The Sentence

We stared at Bausi and Bausi stared at us.

"I am the Black Elephant Bausi," he exclaimed at last, worn out by our solid silence, "and I trumpet! I trumpet! I trumpet!" (It appeared that this was the ancient and hallowed formula with which a Mazitu king was wont to open a conversation with strangers.)

After a suitable pause I replied in a cold voice:

"We are the white lions, Macumazana and Wazela, and we roar! we roar! we roar!"

"I can trample," said Bausi.

"And we can bite," I said haughtily, though how we were to bite or do anything else effectual with nothing but a Union Jack, I did not in the least know.

"What is that thing?" asked Bausi, pointing to the flag.

"That which shadows the whole earth," I answered proudly, a remark that seemed to impress him, although he did not at all understand it, for he ordered a soldier to hold a palm leaf umbrella over him to prevent it from shadowing *him*.

"And that," he asked again, pointing to the music box, "which is not alive and yet makes a noise?"

"That sings the war-song of our people," I said. "We sent it to you as a present and you returned it. Why do you return our presents, O Bausi?"

Then of a sudden this potentate grew furious.

"Why do you come here, white men," he asked, "uninvited and against the law of my land, where only one white man is welcome, my brother Dogeetah, who cured me of sickness with a knife? I know who you are. You are dealers in men. You come here to steal my people and sell them into slavery. You had many slaves with you on the borders of my country, but you sent them away. You shall die, you shall die, you who call yourselves lions, and the painted rag which you say shadows the world, shall rot with your bones. As for that box which sings a war-song, I will smash it; it shall not bewitch me as your magic shield bewitched my great doctor, Imbozwi, burning off his hair."

Then springing up with wonderful agility for one so fat, he knocked the musical box from Hans' head, so that it fell to the ground and after a little whirring grew silent.

"That is right," squeaked Imbozwi. "Trample on their magic, O Elephant. Kill them, O Black One; burn them as they burned my hair."

Now things were, I felt, very serious, for already Bausi was looking about him as though to order his soldiers to make an end of us. So I said in desperation:

"O King, you mentioned a certain white man, Dogeetah, a doctor of doctors, who cured you of sickness with a knife, and called him your brother. Well, he is our brother also, and it was by his invitation that we have come to visit you here, where he will meet us presently."

"If Dogeetah is your friend, then you are my friends," answered Bausi, "for in this land he rules as I rule, he whose blood flows in my veins, as my blood flows in his veins. But you lie. Dogeetah is no brother of slave-dealers, his heart is good and yours are evil. You say that he will meet you here. When will he meet you? Tell me, and if it is soon, I will hold my hand and wait to hear his report of you before I put you to death, for if he speaks well of you, you shall not die."

Now I hesitated, as well I might, for I felt that looking at our case from his point of view, Bausi, believing us to be slave-traders, was not angry without cause. While I was racking my brains for a reply that might be acceptable to him and would not commit us too deeply, to my astonishment Mavovo stepped forward and confronted the king.

"Who are you, fellow?" shouted Bausi.

"I am a warrior, O King, as my scars show," and he pointed to the assegai wounds upon his breast and to his cut nostril. "I am a chief of a people from whom your people sprang and my name is Mavovo, Mavovo who is ready to fight you or any man whom you may name, and to kill him or you if you will. Is there one here who wishes to be killed?"

No one answered, for the mighty-chested Zulu looked very formidable.

"I am a doctor also," went on Mavovo, "one of the greatest of doctors who can open the 'Gates of Distance' and read that which is hid in the womb of the Future. Therefore I will answer your questions which you put to the lord Macumazana, the great and wise white man whom I serve, because we have fought together in many battles. Yes, I will be his mouth, I will answer. The white man Dogeetah, who is your blood-brother and whose word is your word among the Mazitu, will arrive here at sunset on the second day from now. I have spoken."

Bausi looked at me in question.

"Yes," I exclaimed, feeling that I must say something and that it did not much matter what I said, "Dogeetah will arrive here on the second day from now within half an hour after sunset."

Something, I know not what, prompted me to allow that extra half-hour, which in the event, saved all our lives. Now Bausi consulted a while with the execrable Imbozwi and also with the old one-eyed General Babemba while we watched, knowing that our fate hung upon the issue.

At length he spoke.

"White men," he said, "Imbozwi, the head of the witch-finders here, whose hair you burnt off by your evil magic, says that it would be better to kill you at once as your hearts are bad and you are planning mischief against my people. So I think also. But Babemba my General, with whom I am angry because he did not obey my orders and put you to death on the borders of my country when he met you there with your caravan of slaves, thinks otherwise. He prays me to hold my hand, first because you have bewitched him into liking you and secondly because if you should happen to be speaking the truth—which we do not believe—and to have come here at the invitation of my brother Dogeetah, he, Dogeetah, would be pained if he arrived and found you dead, nor could even he bring you to life again. This being so, since it matters little whether you die now or later, my command is that you be kept prisoners till sunset of the second day from this, and that then you will be led out and tied to stakes in the market-place, there to wait till the approach of darkness, by when you say Dogeetah will be here. If he arrives and owns you as his brethren, well and good; if he does not arrive, or disowns you—better still, for then you shall be shot to death with arrows as a warning to all other stealers of men not to cross the borders of the Mazitu."

I listened to this atrocious sentence with horror, then gasped out:

"We are not stealers of men, O King, we are freers of men, as Tom and Jerry of your own people could tell you."

"Who are Tom and Jerry?" he asked, indifferently. "Well, it does not matter, for doubtless they are liars like the rest of you. I have spoken. Take them away, feed them well and keep them safe till within an hour of sunset on the second day from this."

Then, without giving us any further opportunity of speaking, Bausi rose, and followed by Imbozwi and his councillors, marched off into his big hut. We too, were marched off, this time under a double guard commanded by someone whom I had not seen before. At the gate of the *kraal* we halted and asked for the arms that had been taken from us. No answer was given; only the soldiers put their hands upon our shoulders and thrust us along.

"This is a nice business," I whispered to Stephen.

"Oh! it doesn't matter," he answered. "There are lots more guns in the huts. I am told that these Mazitus are dreadfully afraid of bullets. So all we have to do is just to break out and shoot our way through them, for of course they will run when we begin to fire."

I looked at him but did not answer, for to tell the truth I felt in no mood for argument.

Presently we arrived at our quarters, where the soldiers left us, to camp outside. Full of his warlike plan, Stephen went at once to the hut in which the slavers' guns had been stored with our own spare rifles and all the ammunition. I saw him emerge looking very blank indeed and asked him what was the matter.

"Matter!" he answered in a voice that for once really was full of dismay. "The matter is that those Mazitu have stolen all the guns and all the ammunition. There's not enough powder left to make a blue devil."

"Well," I replied, with the kind of joke one perpetrates under such circumstances, "we shall have plenty of blue devils without making any more."

Truly ours was a dreadful situation. Let the reader imagine it. Within a little more than forty-eight hours we were to be shot to death with arrows if an erratic old gentleman who, for aught I knew might be dead, did not turn up at what was then one of the remotest and most inaccessible spots in Central Africa. Moreover, our only hope that such a thing would happen, if hope it could be called, was the prophecy of a *Kaffir* witch-doctor.

To rely on this in any way was so absurd that I gave up thinking of it and set my mind to considering if there were any possible means of escape. After hours of reflection I could find none. Even Hans, with all his experience and nearly superhuman cunning, could suggest none. We were unarmed and surrounded by thousands of savages, all of whom save perhaps Babemba, believed us to be slave-traders, a race that very properly they held in abhorrence, who had visited the country with the object of stealing their women and children. The king, Bausi, a very prejudiced fellow, was dead against us. Also by a piece of foolishness which I now bitterly regretted, as indeed I regretted the whole expedition, or at any rate entering on it in the absence of

Brother John, we had made an implacable enemy of the head medicine-man, who to these folk was a sort of Archbishop of Canterbury. Short of a miracle, there was no hope for us. All that we could do was to say our prayers and prepare for the end.

Mavovo, it is true, remained cheerful. His faith in his "Snake" was really touching. He offered to go through that divination process again in our presence and demonstrate that there was no mistake. I declined because I had no faith in divinations, and Stephen also declined, for another reason, namely that the result might prove to be different, which, he held, would be depressing. The other Zulus oscillated between belief and scepticism, as do the unstable who set to work to study the evidences of Christianity. But Sammy did not oscillate, he literally howled, and prepared the food which poured in upon us so badly that I had to turn on Hans to do the cooking, for however little appetite we might have, it was necessary that we should keep up our strength by eating.

"What, Mr. Quatermain," asked Sammy between his tears, "is the use of dressing viands that our systems will never have time to thoroughly assimilate?"

The first night passed somehow, and so did the next day and the next night which heralded our last morning. I got up quite early and watched the sunrise. Never, I think, had I realised before what a beautiful thing the sunrise is, at least not to the extent I did now when I was saying good-bye to it for ever. Unless indeed there should prove to be still lovelier sunrises beyond the dark of death! Then I went into our hut, and as Stephen, who had the nerves of a rhinoceros, was still sleeping like a tortoise in winter, I said my prayers earnestly enough, mourned over my sins which proved to be so many that at last I gave up the job in despair, and then tried to occupy myself by reading the Old Testament, a book to which I have always been extremely attached.

As a passage that I lit on described how the prophet Samuel for whom I could not help reading "Imbozwi," hewed Agag in pieces after Bausi—I mean Saul—had relented and spared his life, I cannot say that it consoled me very much. Doubtless, I reflected, these people believe that I, like Agag, had "made women childless" by my sword, so there remained nothing save to follow the example of that unhappy king and walk "delicately" to doom.

Then, as Stephen was still sleeping—how *could* he do it, I wondered—I set to work to make up the accounts of the expedition to date. It had already cost £1,423. Just fancy expending £1,423 in order to be tied to a post and shot to death with arrows. And all to get a rare orchid! Oh! I reflected to myself, if by some marvel I should escape, or if I should live again in any land where these particular flowers flourish, I would never even look at them. And as a matter of fact I never have.

At length Stephen did wake up and, as criminals are reported to do in the papers before execution, made an excellent breakfast.

"What's the good of worrying?" he said presently. "I shouldn't if it weren't for my poor old father. It must have come to this one day, and the sooner it is over the sooner to sleep, as the song says. When one comes to think of it there are enormous advantages in sleep, for that's the only time one is quite happy. Still, I should have liked to see that *Cypripedium* first."

"Oh! drat the *Cypripedium*!" I exclaimed, and blundered from the hut to tell Sammy that if he didn't stop his groaning I would punch his head.

"Jumps! Regular jumps! Who'd have thought it of Quatermain?" I heard Stephen mutter in the intervals of lighting his pipe.

The morning went "like lightning that is greased," as Sammy remarked. Three o'clock came and Mavovo and his following sacrificed a kid to the spirits of their ancestors, which, as Sammy remarked again, was "a horrible, heathen ceremony much calculated to prejudice our cause with Powers Above."

When it was over, to my delight, Babemba appeared. He looked so pleasant that I jumped to the conclusion that he brought the best of news with him. Perhaps that the king had pardoned us, or perhaps—blessed thought—that Brother John had really arrived before his time.

But not a bit of it! All he had to say was that he had caused inquiries to be made along the route that ran to the coast and that certainly for a hundred miles there was at present no sign of Dogeetah. So as the Black Elephant was growing more and more enraged under the stirrings up of Imbozwi, it was obvious that that evening's ceremony must be performed. Indeed, as it was part of his duty to superintend the erection of the posts to which we were to be tied and the digging of our graves at their bases, he had just come to count us again to be sure that he had not made any mistake as to the number. Also, if there were any articles that we would like buried with us, would we be so kind as to point them out and he would be sure to see to the matter. It would be soon over, and not painful, he added, as he had selected the very best archers in Beza Town who rarely missed and could, most of them, send an arrow up to the feather into a buffalo.

Then he chatted a little about other matters, as to where he should find the magic shield I had given him, which he would always value as a souvenir, etc., took a pinch of snuff with Mavovo and departed, saying that he would be sure to return again at the proper time.

It was now four o'clock, and as Sammy was quite beyond it, Stephen made himself some tea. It was very good tea, especially as we had milk to put in it, although I did not remember what it tasted like till afterwards.

Now, having abandoned hope, I went into a hut alone to compose myself to meet my end like a gentleman, and seated there in silence and semi-darkness my spirit grew much calmer. After all, I reflected, why should I cling to life? In the country whither I travelled, as the reader who has followed my adventures will know, were some whom I clearly longed to see again, notably my father and my mother, and two noble women who were even more to me. My boy, it is true, remained (he was alive then), but I knew that he would find friends, and as I was not so badly off at that time, I had been able to make a proper provision for him. Perhaps it was better that I should go, seeing that if I lived on it would only mean more troubles and more partings.

What was about to befall me of course I could not tell, but I knew then as I know now, that it was not extinction or even that sleep of which Stephen had spoken. Perhaps I was passing to some place where at length the clouds would roll away and I should understand; whence, too, I should see all the landscape of the past and future, as an eagle does watching from the skies, and be no longer like one struggling through dense bush, wild-beast and serpent haunted, beat upon by the storms of heaven and terrified with its lightnings, nor knowing whither I hewed my path. Perhaps in that place there would be no longer what St. Paul describes as another law in my members warring against the law of my mind, and bringing me into captivity to the law of sin. Perhaps there the past would be forgiven by the Power which knows whereof we are made, and I should become what I have always longed to be—good in every sense and even find open to me new and better roads of service. I take these thoughts from a note that I made in my pocket-book at the time.

Thus I reflected and then wrote a few lines of farewell in the fond and foolish hope that somehow they might find those to whom they were addressed (I have those letters still and very oddly they read today). This done, I tried to throw out my mind towards Brother John if he still lived, as indeed I had done for days past, so that I might inform him of our plight and, I am afraid, reproach him for having brought us to such an end by his insane carelessness or want of faith.

Whilst I was still engaged thus Babemba arrived with his soldiers to lead us off to execution. It was Hans who came to tell me that he was there. The poor old Hottentot shook me by the hand and wiped his eyes with his ragged coat-sleeve.

"Oh! Baas, this is our last journey," he said, "and you are going to be killed, Baas, and it is all my fault, Baas, because I ought to have found a way out of the trouble which is what I was hired to do. But I can't, my head grows so stupid. Oh! if only I could come even with Imbozwi I shouldn't mind, and I will, I *will*, if I have to return as a ghost to do it. Well, Baas, you know the Predikant, your father, told us that we don't go out like a fire, but burn again for always elsewhere——"

("I hope not," I thought to myself.)

"And that quite easily without anything to pay for the wood. So I hope that we shall always burn together, Baas. And meanwhile, I have brought you a little something," and he produced what looked like a peculiarly obnoxious horse ball. "You swallow this now and you will never feel anything; it is a very good medicine that my grandfather's grandfather got from the Spirit of his tribe. You will just go to sleep as nicely as though you were very drunk, and wake up in the beautiful fire which burns without any wood and never goes out for ever and ever, Amen."

"No, Hans," I said, "I prefer to die with my eyes open."

"And so would I, Baas, if I thought there was any good in keeping them open, but I don't, for I can't believe any more in the Snake of that black fool, Mavovo. If it had been a good Snake, it would have told him to keep clear of Beza Town, so I will swallow one of these pills and give the other to the Baas Stephen," and he crammed the filthy mess into his mouth and with an effort got it down, as a young turkey does a ball of meal that is too big for its throat.

Then, as I heard Stephen calling me, I left him invoking a most comprehensive and polyglot curse upon the head of Imbozwi, to whom he rightly attributed all our woes.

"Our friend here says it is time to start," said Stephen, rather shakily, for the situation seemed to have got a hold of him at last, and nodding towards old Babemba, who stood there with a cheerful smile looking as though he were going to conduct us to a wedding.

"Yes, white lord," said Babemba, "it is time, and I have hurried so as not to keep you waiting. It will be a very fine show, for the Black Elephant himself is going to do you the honour to be present, as will all the people of Beza Town and those for many miles round."

"Hold your tongue, you old idiot," I said, "and stop your grinning.

If you had been a man and not a false friend you would have got us out of this trouble, knowing as you do very well that we are no sellers of men, but rather the enemy of those who do such things."

"Oh! white lord," said Babemba, in a changed voice, "believe me I only smile to make you happy up to the end. My lips smile, but I am crying inside. I know that you are good and have told Bausi so, but he will not believe me, who thinks that I have been bribed by you. What can I do against that evil-hearted Imbozwi, the head of the witch-doctors, who hates you because he thinks you have better magic than he has and who whispers day and night into the king's ear, telling him that if he does not kill you, all our people will be slain or sold for slaves, as you are only the scouts or a big army that is coming. Only last night Imbozwi held a great divination *indaba*, and read this and a great deal more in the enchanted water, making the king think he saw it in pictures, whereas I, looking over his shoulder, could see nothing at all, except the ugly face of Imbozwi reflected in the water. Also he swore that his spirit told me that Dogeetah, the king's blood brother, being dead, would never come to Beza Town again. I have done my best. Keep your heart white towards me, O Macumazana, and do not haunt me, for I tell you I have done my best, and if ever I should get a chance against Imbozwi, which I am afraid I shan't, as he will poison me first, I will pay him back. Oh! he shall not die quickly as you will."

"I wish I could get a chance at him," I muttered, for even in this solemn moment I could cultivate no Christian spirit towards Imbozwi.

Feeling that he was honest after all, I shook old Babemba's hand and gave him the letters I had written, asking him to try and get them to the coast. Then we started on our last walk.

The Zulu hunters were already outside the fence, seated on the ground, chatting and taking snuff. I wondered if this was because they really believed in Mavovo's confounded Snake, or from bravado, inspired by the innate courage of their race. When they saw me they sprang to their feet and, lifting their right hands, gave me a loud and hearty salute of "*Inkoosi*! Baba! *Inkoosi*! Macumazana!" Then, at a signal from Mavovo, they broke into some Zulu war-chant, which they kept up till we reached the stakes. Sammy, too, broke into a chant, but one of quite a different nature.

"Be quiet!" I said to him. "Can't you die like a man?"

"No, indeed I cannot, Mr. Quatermain," he answered, and went on howling for pity in about twenty different languages.

Stephen and I walked together, he still carrying the Union Jack, of which no one tried to deprive him. I think the Mazitu believed it was his fetish. We didn't talk much, though once he said:

"Well, the love of orchids has brought many a man to a bad end. I wonder whether the Governor will keep my collection or sell it."

After this he relapsed into silence, and not knowing and indeed not caring what would happen to his collection, I made no answer.

We had not far to go; personally I could have preferred a longer walk. Passing with our guards down a kind of by-street, we emerged suddenly at the head of the market-place, to find that it was packed with thousands of people gathered there to see our execution. I noticed that they were arranged in orderly companies and that a broad open roadway was left between them, running to the southern gate of the market, I suppose to facilitate the movements of so large a crowd.

All this multitude received us in respectful silence, though Sammy's howls caused some of them to smile, while the Zulu war-chant appeared to excite their wonder, or admiration. At the head of the marketplace, not far from the king's enclosure, fifteen stout posts had been planted on as many mounds. These mounds were provided so that everyone might see the show and, in part at any rate, were made of soil hollowed from fifteen deep graves dug almost at the foot of the mounds. Or rather there were seventeen posts, an extra large one being set at each end of the line in order to accommodate the two donkeys, which it appeared were also to be shot to death. A great number of soldiers kept a space clear in front of the posts. On this space were gathered Bausi, his councillors, some of his head wives, Imbozwi more hideously painted than usual, and perhaps fifty or sixty picked archers with strung bows and an ample supply of arrows, whose part in the ceremony it was not difficult for us to guess.

"King Bausi," I said as I was led past that potentate, "you are a murderer and Heaven Above will be avenged upon you for this crime. If our blood is shed, soon you shall die and come to meet us where *we* have power, and your people shall be destroyed."

My words seemed to frighten the man, for he answered:

"I am no murderer. I kill you because you are robbers of men. Moreover, it is not I who have passed sentence on you. It is Imbozwi here, the chief of the doctors, who has told me all about you, and whose spirit says you must die unless my brother Dogeetah appears to save you. If Dogeetah comes, which he cannot do because he is dead, and vouches for you, then I shall know that Imbozwi is a wicked liar, and as you were to die, so he shall die."

"Yes, yes," screeched Imbozwi. "If Dogeetah comes, as that false wizard prophesies," and he pointed to Mavovo, "then I shall be ready to die in your place, white slave-dealers. Yes, yes, then you may shoot *me* with arrows."

"King, take note of those words, and people, take note of those words, that they may be fulfilled if Dogeetah comes," said Mavovo in a great, deep voice.

"I take note of them," answered Bausi, "and I swear by my mother on behalf of all the people, that they shall be fulfilled—if Dogeetah comes."

"Good," exclaimed Mavovo, and stalked on to the stake which had been pointed out to him.

As he went he whispered something into Imbozwi's ear that seemed to frighten that limb of Satan, for I saw him start and shiver. However, he soon recovered, for in another minute he was engaged in superintending those whose business it was to lash us to the posts.

This was done simply and effectively by tying our wrists with a grass rope behind these posts, each of which was fitted with two projecting pieces of wood that passed under our arms and practically prevented us from moving. Stephen and I were given the places of honour in the middle, the Union Jack being fixed, by his own request, to the top of Stephen's stake. Mavovo was on my right, and the other Zulus were ranged on either side of us. Hans and Sammy occupied the end posts respectively (except those to which the poor jackasses were bound). I noted that Hans was already very sleepy and that shortly after he was fixed up, his head dropped forward on his breast. Evidently his medicine was working, and almost I regretted that I had not taken some while I had the chance.

When we were all fastened, Imbozwi came round to inspect. Moreover, with a piece of white chalk he made a round mark on the breast of each of us; a kind of bull's eye for the archers to aim at.

"Ah! white man," he said to me as he chalked away at my shooting coat, "you will never burn anyone's hair again with your magic shield. Never, never, for presently I shall be treading down the earth upon you in that hole, and your goods will belong to me."

I did not answer, for what was the use of talking to this vile brute when my time was so short. So he passed on to Stephen and began to chalk him. Stephen, however, in whom the natural man still prevailed, shouted: "Take your filthy hands off me," and lifting his leg, which was unfettered, gave the painted witch-doctor such an awful kick in the stomach, that he vanished backwards into the grave beneath him.

"Ow! Well done, Wazela!" said the Zulus, "we hope that you have killed him."

"I hope so too," said Stephen, and the multitude of spectators gasped to see the sacred person of the head witch-doctor, of whom they evidently went in much fear, treated in such a way. Only Babemba grinned, and even the king Bausi did not seem displeased.

But Imbozwi was not to be disposed of so easily, for presently, with the help of sundry myrmidons, minor witch-doctors, he scrambled out of the grave, cursing and covered with mud, for it was wet down there. After that I took no more heed of him or of much else. Seeing that I had only half an hour to live, as may be imagined, I was otherwise engaged.

CHAPTER 11

The Coming of Dogeetah

The sunset that day was like the sunrise, particularly fine, although as in the case of the tea, I remembered little of it till afterwards. In fact, thunder was about, which always produces grand cloud effects in Africa.

The sun went down like a great red eye, over which there dropped suddenly a black eyelid of cloud with a fringe of purple lashes.

There's the last I shall see of you, my old friend, thought I to myself, unless I catch you up presently.

The gloom began to gather. The king looked about him, also at the sky overhead, as though he feared rain, then whispered something to Babemba, who nodded and strolled up to my post.

"White lord," he said, "the Elephant wishes to know if you are ready, as presently the light will be very bad for shooting?"

"No," I answered with decision, "not till half an hour after sundown as was agreed."

Babemba went to the king and returned to me.

"White lord, the king says that a bargain is a bargain, and he will keep to his word. Only you must not then blame him if the shooting is bad, since of course he did not know that the night would be so cloudy, which is not usual at this time of year."

It grew darker and darker, till at length we might have been lost in a London fog. The dense masses of the people looked like banks, and the archers, flitting to and fro as they made ready, might have been shadows in Hades. Once or twice lightning flashed and was followed after a pause by the distant growling of thunder. The air, too, grew very oppressive. Dense silence reigned. In all those multitudes no one spoke or stirred; even Sammy ceased his howling, I suppose because he had become exhausted and fainted away, as people often do just before they are hanged. It was a most solemn time. Nature seemed to be adapting herself to the mood of sacrifice and making ready for us a mighty pall.

At length I heard the sound of arrows being drawn from their quivers, and then the squeaky voice of Imbozwi, saying:

"Wait a little, the cloud will lift. There is light behind it, and it will be nicer if they can see the arrows coming."

The cloud did begin to lift, very slowly, and from beneath it flowed a green light like that in a cat's eye.

"Shall we shoot, Imbozwi?" asked the voice of the captain of the archers.

"Not yet, not yet. Not till the people can watch them die."

The edge of cloud lifted a little more; the green light turned to a fiery red thrown by the sunk sun and reflected back upon the earth from the dense black cloud above. It was as though all the landscape had burst into flames, while the heaven over us remained of the hue of ink. Again the lightning flashed, showing the faces and staring eyes of the thousands who watched, and even the white teeth of a great bat that flittered past. That flash seemed to burn off an edge of the lowering cloud and the light grew stronger and stronger, and redder and redder.

Imbozwi uttered a hiss like a snake. I heard a bow-string twang, and almost at the same moment the thud of an arrow striking my post just above my head. Indeed, by lifting myself I could touch it. I shut my eyes and began to see all sorts of queer things that I had forgotten for years and years. My brain swam and seemed to melt into a kind of confusion. Through the intense silence I thought I heard the sound of some animal running heavily, much as a fat bull eland does when it is suddenly disturbed. Someone uttered a startled exclamation, which caused me to open my eyes again. The first thing I saw was the squad of savage archers lifting their bows—evidently that first arrow had been a kind of trial shot. The next, looking absolutely unearthly in that terrible and ominous light, was a tall figure seated on a white ox shambling rapidly towards us along the open roadway that ran from the southern gate of the market-place.

Of course, I knew that I dreamed, for this figure exactly resembled Brother John. There was his long, snowy beard. There in his hand was his butterfly net, with the handle of which he seemed to be prodding the ox. Only he was wound about with wreaths of flowers as were the great horns of the ox, and on either side of him and before and behind him ran girls, also wreathed with flowers. It was a vision, nothing else, and I shut my eyes again awaiting the fatal arrow.

"Shoot!" screamed Imbozwi.

"Nay, shoot not!" shouted Babemba. *"Dogeetah is come!"*

A moment's pause, during which I heard arrows falling to the ground; then from all those thousands of throats a roar that shaped itself to the words:

"Dogeetah! Dogeetah is come to save the white lords."

I must confess that after this my nerve, which is generally pretty good, gave out to such an extent that I think I fainted for a few minutes. During that faint I seemed to be carrying on a conversation with Mavovo, though whether it ever took place or I only imagined it I am not sure, since I always forgot to ask him.

He said, or I thought he said, to me:

"And now, Macumazana, my father, what have you to say? Does my Snake stand upon its tail or does it not? Answer, I am listening."

To which I replied, or seemed to reply:

"Mavovo, my child, certainly it appears as though your Snake *does* stand upon its tail. Still, I hold that all this is a fantasy; that we live in a land of dream in which nothing is real except those things which we cannot see or touch or hear. That there is no me and no you and no Snake at all, nothing but a Power in which we move, that shows us pictures and laughs when we think them real."

Whereon Mavovo said, or seemed to say:

"Ah! at last you touch the truth, O Macumazana, my father. All things are a shadow and we are shadows in a shadow. But what throws the shadow, O Macumazana, my father? Why does Dogeetah appear to come hither riding on a white ox and why do all these thousands think that my Snake stands so very stiff upon its tail?"

"I'm hanged if I know," I replied and woke up.

There, without doubt, *was* old Brother John with a wreath of flowers—I noted in disgust that they were orchids—hanging in a bacchanalian fashion from his dinted sun-helmet over his left eye. He was in a furious rage and reviling Bausi, who literally crouched before him, and I was in a furious rage and reviling him. What I said I do not remember, but he said, his white beard bristling with indignation while he threatened Bausi with the handle of the butterfly net:

"You dog! You savage, whom I saved from death and called Brother. What were you doing to these white men who are in truth my brothers, and to their followers? Were you about to kill them? Oh! if so, I will forget my vow, I will forget the bond that binds us and——"

"Don't, pray don't," said Bausi. "It is all a horrible mistake; I am not to be blamed at all. It is that witch-doctor, Imbozwi, whom by the ancient law of the land I must obey in such matters. He consulted his Spirit and declared that you were dead; also that these white lords were the most wicked of men, slave-traders with spotted hearts, who came hither to spy out the Mazitu people and to destroy them with magic and bullets."

"Then he lied," thundered Brother John, "and he knew that he lied."

"Yes, yes, it is evident that he lied," answered Bausi. "Bring him here, and with him those who serve him."

Now by the light of the moon which was shining brightly in the heavens, for the thunder-clouds had departed with the last glow of sunset, soldiers began an active search for Imbozwi and his confederates. Of these they caught eight or ten, all wicked-looking fellows hideously painted and adorned like their master, but Imbozwi himself they could not find.

I began to think that in the confusion he had given us the slip, when presently from the far end of the line, for we were still all tied to our stakes, I heard the voice of Sammy, hoarse, it is true, but quite cheerful now, saying:

"Mr. Quatermain, in the interests of justice, will you inform his Majesty that the treacherous wizard for whom he is seeking, is now peeping and muttering at the bottom of the grave which was dug to receive my mortal remains."

I did inform his Majesty, and in double-quick time our friend Imbozwi was once more fished out of a grave by the strong arms of Babemba and his soldiers, and dragged into the presence of the irate Bausi.

"Loose the white lords and their followers," said Bausi, "and let them come here."

So our bonds were undone and we walked to where the king and Brother John stood, the miserable Imbozwi and his attendant doctors huddled in a heap before them.

"Who is this?" said Bausi to him, pointing at Brother John. "Is it not he whom you vowed was dead?"

Imbozwi did not seem to think that the question required an answer, so Bausi continued:

"What was the song that you sang in our ears just now—that if Dogeetah came you would be ready to be shot to death with arrows in the place of these white lords whose lives you swore away, was it not?"

Again Imbozwi made no answer, although Babemba called his attention to the king's query with a vigorous kick. Then Bausi shouted:

"By your own mouth are you condemned, O liar, and that shall be done to you which you have yourself decreed," adding almost in the words of Elijah after he had triumphed over the priests of Baal, "Take away these false prophets. Let them not escape. Say you not so, O people?"

"Aye," roared the multitude fiercely, "take them away."

"Not a popular character, Imbozwi," Stephen remarked to me in a reflective voice. "Well, he is going to be served hot on his own toast now, and serve the brute right."

"Who is the false doctor now?" mocked Mavovo in the silence that followed. "Who is about to sup on arrow-heads, O Painter-of-white-spots?" and he pointed to the mark that Imbozwi had so gleefully chalked over his heart as a guide to the arrows of the archers.

Now, seeing that all was lost, the little humpbacked villain with a sudden twist caught me by the legs and began to plead for mercy. So piteously did he plead, that being already softened by the fact of our wonderful escape from those black graves, my heart was melted in me. I turned to ask the king to spare his life, though with little hope that the prayer would be granted, for I saw that Bausi feared and hated the man and was only too glad of the opportunity to be rid of him. Imbozwi, however, interpreted my movement differently, since among savages the turning of the back always means that a petition is refused. Then, in his rage and despair, the venom of his wicked heart boiled over. He leapt to his feet, and drawing a big, carved knife from among his witch-doctor's trappings, sprang at me like a wild cat, shouting:

"At least you shall come too, white dog!"

Most mercifully Mavovo was watching him, for that is a good Zulu saying which declares that "Wizard is Wizard's fate." With one bound he was on him. Just as the knife touched me—it actually pricked my skin though without drawing blood, which was fortunate as probably it was poisoned—he gripped Imbozwi's arm in his grasp of iron and hurled him to the ground as though he were but a child.

After this of course all was over.

"Come away," I said to Stephen and Brother John; "this is no place for us." So we went and gained our huts without molestation and indeed quite unobserved, for the attention of everyone in Beza Town was fully occupied elsewhere. From the market-place behind us rose so hideous a clamour that we rushed into my hut and shut the door to escape or lessen the sound. It was dark in the hut, for which I was really thankful, for the darkness seemed to soothe my nerves. Especially was this so when Brother John said:

"Friend, Allan Quatermain, and you, young gentleman, whose name I don't know, I will tell you what I think I never mentioned to you before, that, in addition to being a doctor, I am a clergyman of the American Episcopalian Church. Well, as a clergyman, I will ask your leave to return thanks for your very remarkable deliverance from a cruel death."

"By all means," I muttered for both of us, and he did so in a most earnest and beautiful prayer. Brother John may or may not have been a little touched in the head at this time of his life, but he was certainly an able and a good man.

Afterwards, as the shrieks and shouting had now died down to a confused murmur of many voices, we went and sat outside under the projecting eaves of the hut, where I introduced Stephen Somers to Brother John.

"And now," I said, "in the name of goodness, where do you come from tied up in flowers like a Roman priest at sacrifice, and riding on a bull like the lady called Europa? And what on earth do you mean by playing us such a scurvy trick down there in Durban, leaving us without a word after you had agreed to guide us to this hellish hole?"

Brother John stroked his long beard and looked at me reproachfully.

"I guess, Allan," he said in his American fashion, "there is a mistake somewhere. To answer the last part of your question first, I did not leave you without a word; I gave a letter to that lame old Griqua gardener of yours, Jack, to be handed to you when you arrived."

"Then the idiot either lost it and lied to me, as Griquas will, or he forgot all about it."

"That is likely. I ought to have thought of that, Allan, but I didn't. Well, in that letter I said that I would meet you here, where I should have been six weeks ago awaiting you. Also I sent a message to Bausi to warn him of your coming in case I should be delayed, but I suppose that something happened to it on the road."

"Why did you not wait and come with us like a sensible man?"

"Allan, as you ask me straight out, I will tell you, although the subject is one of which I do not care to speak. I knew that you were going to journey by Kilwa; indeed it was your only route with a lot of people and so much baggage, and I did not wish to visit Kilwa." He paused, then went on: "A long while ago, nearly twenty-three years to be accurate, I went to live at Kilwa as a missionary with my young wife. I built a mission station and a church there, and we were happy and fairly successful in our work. Then on one evil day the Swahili and other Arabs came in dhows to establish a slave-dealing station. I resisted them, and the end of it was that they attacked us, killed most of my people and enslaved the rest. In that attack I received a cut from a sword on the head—look, here is the mark of it," and drawing his white hair apart he showed us a long scar that was plainly visible in the moonlight.

"The blow knocked me senseless just about sunset one evening. When I came to myself again it was broad daylight and everybody was gone, except one old woman who was tending me. She was half-crazed with grief because her husband and two sons had been killed, and another son, a boy, and a daughter had been taken away. I asked her where my young wife was. She answered that she, too, had been taken away eight or ten hours before, because the Arabs had seen the lights of a ship out at sea, and thought they might be those of a British man-of-war that was known to be cruising on the coast. On seeing these they had fled inland in a hurry, leaving me for dead, but killing the wounded before they went. The old woman herself had escaped by hiding among some rocks on the seashore, and after the Arabs had gone had crept back to the house and found me still alive.

"I asked her where my wife had been taken. She said she did not know, but some others of our people told her that they had heard the Arabs say they were going to some place a hundred miles inland, to join their leader, a half-bred villain named Hassan-ben-Mohammed, to whom they were carrying my wife as a present.

"Now we knew this wretch, for after the Arabs landed at Kilwa, but before actual hostilities broke out between us, he had fallen sick of smallpox and my wife had helped to nurse him. Had it not been for her, indeed, he would have died. However, although the leader of the band, he was not present at the attack, being engaged in some slave-raiding business in the interior.

"When I learned this terrible news, the shock of it, or the loss of blood, brought on a return of insensibility, from which I only awoke two days later to find myself on board a Dutch trading vessel that was sailing for Zanzibar. It was the lights of this ship that the Arabs had seen and mistaken for those of an English man-of-war. She had put into Kilwa for water, and the sailors, finding me on the veranda of the house and still living, in the goodness of their hearts carried me on board. Of the old woman they had seen nothing; I suppose that at their approach she ran away.

"At Zanzibar, in an almost dying condition, I was handed over to a clergyman of our mission, in whose house I lay desperately ill for a long while. Indeed six months went by before I fully recovered my right mind. Some people say that I have never recovered it; perhaps you are one of them, Allan.

"At last the wound in my skull healed, after a clever English naval surgeon had removed some bits of splintered bone, and my strength came back to me. I was and still am an American subject, and in those days we had no consul at Zanzibar, if there is one there now, of which I am not sure, and of course no warship. The English made what inquiries they could for me, but could find out little or nothing, since all the country about Kilwa was in possession of Arab slave-traders who were supported by a ruffian who called himself the Sultan of Zanzibar."

Again he paused, as though saddened by his recollections.

"Did you never hear any more of your wife?" asked Stephen.

"Yes, Mr. Somers; I heard at Zanzibar from a slave whom our mission bought and freed, that he had seen a white woman who answered to her description alive and apparently well, at some place I was unable to identify. He could only tell me that it was fifteen days' journey from the coast. She was then in charge of some black people, he did not know of what tribe, who, he believed, had found her wandering in the bush. He noted that the black people seemed to treat her with the greatest reverence, although they could not understand what she said. On the following day, whilst searching for six lost goats, he was captured by Arabs who, he heard afterwards, were out looking for this white woman. The day after the man had told me this, he was seized with inflammation of the lungs, of which, being in a weak state from his sufferings in the slave gang, he quickly died. Now you will understand why I was not particularly anxious to revisit Kilwa."

"Yes," I said, "we understand that, and a good deal more of which we will talk later. But, to change the subject, where do you come from now, and how did you happen to turn up just in the nick of time?"

"I was journeying here across country by a route I will show you on my map," he answered, "when I met with an accident to my leg" (here Stephen and I looked at each other) "which kept me laid up in a *Kaffir* hut for six weeks. When I got better, as I could not walk very well I rode upon oxen that I had trained. That white beast you saw is the last of them; the others died of the bite of the tsetse fly. A fear which I could not define caused me to press forward as fast as possible; for the last twenty-four hours I have scarcely stopped to eat or sleep. When I got into the Mazitu country this morning I found the *kraals* empty, except for some women and girls, who knew me again, and threw these flowers over me. They told me that all the men had gone to Beza Town for a great feast, but what the feast was they either did not know or would not reveal. So I hurried on and arrived in time—thank God in time! It is a long story; I will tell you the details afterwards. Now we are all too tired. What's that noise?"

I listened and recognised the triumphant song of the Zulu hunters, who were returning from the savage scene in the market-place. Presently they arrived, headed by Sammy, a very different Sammy from the wailing creature who had gone out to execution an hour or two before. Now he was the gayest of the gay, and about his neck were strung certain weird ornaments which I identified as the personal property of Imbozwi.

"Virtue is victorious and justice has been done, Mr. Quatermain. These are the spoils of war," he said, pointing to the trappings of the late witch-doctor.

"Oh! get out, you little cur! We want to know nothing more," I said. "Go, cook us some supper," and he went, not in the least abashed.

The hunters were carrying between them what appeared to be the body of Hans. At first I was frightened, thinking that he must be dead, but examination showed that he was only in a state of insensibility such as might be induced by laudanum. Brother John ordered him to be wrapped up in a blanket and laid by the fire, and this was done.

Presently Mavovo approached and squatted down in front of us.

"Macumazana, my father," he said quietly, "what words have you for me?"

"Words of thanks, Mavovo. If you had not been so quick, Imbozwi would have finished me. As it is, the knife only touched my skin without breaking it, for Dogeetah has looked to see."

Mavovo waved his hand as though to sweep this little matter aside, and asked, looking me straight in the eyes:

"And what other words, Macumazana? As to my Snake I mean."

"Only that you were right and I was wrong," I answered shamefacedly. "Things have happened as you foretold, how or why I do not understand."

"No, my father, because you white men are so vain" ("blown out was his word), "that you think you have all wisdom. Now you have learned that this is not so. I am content. The false doctors are all dead, my father, and I think that Imbozwi——"

I held up my hand, not wishing to hear details. Mavovo rose, and with a little smile, went about his business.

"What does he mean about his Snake?" inquired Brother John curiously.

I told him as briefly as I could, and asked him if he could explain the matter. He shook his head.

"The strangest example of native vision that I have ever heard of," he answered, "and the most useful. Explain! There is no explanation, except the old one that there are more things in heaven and earth, etc., and that God gives different gifts to different men."

Then we ate our supper; I think one of the most joyful meals of which I have ever partaken. It is wonderful how good food tastes when one never expected to swallow another mouthful. After it was finished the others went to bed but, with the still unconscious Hans for my only companion, I sat for a while smoking by the fire, for on this high tableland the air was chilly. I felt that as yet I could not sleep; if for no other reason because of the noise that the Mazitu were making in the town, I suppose in celebration of the execution of the terrible witch-doctors and the return of Dogeetah. Suddenly Hans awoke, and sitting up, stared at me through the bright flame which I had recently fed with dry wood.

"Baas," he said in a hollow voice, "there you are, here I am, and there is the fire which never goes out, a very good fire. But, Baas, why are we not inside of it as your father the Predikant promised, instead of outside here in the cold?"

"Because you are still in the world, you old fool, and not where you deserve to be," I answered. "Because Mavovo's Snake was a snake with a true tongue after all, and Dogeetah came as it foretold. Because we are all alive and well, and it is Imbozwi with his spawn who are dead upon the posts. That is why, Hans, as you would have seen for yourself if you had kept awake, instead of swallowing filthy medicine like a frightened woman, just because you were afraid of death, which at your age you ought to have welcomed."

"Oh! Baas," broke in Hans, "don't tell me that things are so and that we are really alive in what your honoured father used to call this gourd full of tears. Don't tell me, Baas, that I made a coward of myself and swallowed that beastliness—if you knew what it was made of you would understand, Baas—for nothing but a bad headache. Don't tell me that Dogeetah came when my eyes were not open to see him, and worst of all, that Imbozwi and his children were tied to those poles when I was not able to help them out of the bottle of tears into the fire that burns for ever and ever. Oh! it is too much, and I swear, Baas, that however often I have to die, henceforward it shall always be with my eyes open," and holding his aching head between his hands he rocked himself to and fro in bitter grief.

Well might Hans be sad, seeing that he never heard the last of the incident. The hunters invented a new and gigantic name for him, which meant "The little-yellow-mouse-who-feeds-on-sleep-while-the-black-rats-eat-up-their-enemies." Even Sammy made a mock of him, showing him the spoils which he declared he had wrenched unaided from the mighty master of magic, Imbozwi. As indeed he had—after the said Imbozwi was stone dead at the stake.

It was very amusing until things grew so bad that I feared Hans would kill Sammy, and had to put a stop to the joke.

Chapter 12
Brother John's Story

Although I went to bed late I was up before sunrise. Chiefly because I wished to have some private conversation with Brother John, whom I knew to be a very early riser. Indeed, he slept less than any man I ever met.

As I expected, I found him astir in his hut; he was engaged in pressing flowers by candlelight.

"John," I said, "I have brought you some property which I think you have lost," and I handed him the morocco-bound *Christian Year* and the water-colour drawing which we had found in the sacked mission house at Kilwa. He looked first at the picture and then at the book; at least, I suppose he did, for I went outside the hut for a while—to observe the sunrise. In a few minutes he called me, and when the door was shut, said in an unsteady voice:

"How did you come by these relics, Allan?"

I told him the story from beginning to end. He listened without a word, and when I had finished said:

"I may as well tell what perhaps you have guessed, that the picture is that of my wife, and the book is her book."

"Is!" I exclaimed.

"Yes, Allan. I say *is* because I do not believe that she is dead. I cannot explain why, any more than I could explain last night how that great Zulu savage was able to prophesy my coming. But sometimes we can wring secrets from the Unknown, and I believe that I have won this truth in answer to my prayers, that my wife still lives."

"After twenty years, John?"

"Yes, after twenty years. Why do you suppose," he asked almost fiercely, "that for two-thirds of a generation I have wandered about among African savages, pretending to be crazy because these wild people revere the mad and always let them pass unharmed?"

"I thought it was to collect butterflies and botanical specimens."

"Butterflies and botanical specimens! These were the pretext. I have been and am searching for my wife. You may think it a folly, especially considering what was her condition when we separated—she was expecting a child, Allan—but I do not. I believe that she is hidden away among some of these wild peoples."

"Then perhaps it would be as well not to find her," I answered, bethinking me of the fate which had overtaken sundry white women in the old days, who had escaped from shipwrecks on the coast and become the wives of *Kaffirs*.

"Not so, Allan. On that point I fear nothing. If God has preserved my wife, He has also protected her from every harm. And now," he went on, "you will understand why I wish to visit these Pongo—the Pongo who worship a white goddess!"

"I understand," I said and left him, for having learned all there was to know, I thought it best not to prolong a painful conversation. To me it seemed incredible that this lady should still live, and I feared the effect upon him of the discovery that she was no more. How full of romance is this poor little world of ours! Think of Brother John (Eversley was his real name as I discovered afterwards), and what his life had been. A high-minded educated man trying to serve his Faith in the dark places of the earth, and taking his young wife with him, which for my part I have never considered a right thing to do. Neither tradition nor Holy Writ record that the Apostles dragged their wives and families into the heathen lands where they went to preach, although I believe that some of them were married. But this is by the way.

Then falls the blow; the mission house is sacked, the husband escapes by a miracle and the poor young lady is torn away to be the prey of a vile slave-trader. Lastly, according to the quite unreliable evidence of some savage already in the shadow of death, she is seen in the charge of other unknown savages. On the strength of this the husband, playing the part of a mad botanist, hunts for her for a score of years, enduring incredible hardships and yet buoyed up by a high and holy trust. To my mind it was a beautiful and pathetic story. Still, for reasons which I have suggested, I confess that I hoped that long ago she had returned into the hands of the Power which made her, for what would be the state of a young white lady who for two decades had been at the mercy of these black brutes?

And yet, and yet, after my experience of Mavovo and his Snake, I did not feel inclined to dogmatise about anything. Who and what was I, that I should venture not only to form opinions, but to thrust them down the throats of others? After all, how narrow are the limits of the knowledge upon which we base our judgments. Perhaps the great sea of intuition that surrounds us is safer to float on than are these little islets of individual experience, whereon we are so wont to take our stand.

Meanwhile my duty was not to speculate on the dreams and mental attitudes of others, but like a practical hunter and trader, to carry to a successful issue an expedition that I was well paid to manage, and to dig up a certain rare flower root, if I could find it, in the marketable value of which I had an interest. I have always prided myself upon my entire lack of imagination and all such mental fantasies, and upon an aptitude for hard business and an appreciation of the facts of life, that after all are the things with which we have to do. This is the truth; at least, I hope it is. For if I were to be *quite* honest, which no one ever has been, except a gentleman named Mr. Pepys, who, I think, lived in the reign of Charles II, and who, to judge from his memoirs, which I have read lately, did not write for publication, I should have to admit that there is another side to my nature. I sternly suppress it, however, at any rate for the present.

While we were at breakfast Hans who, still suffering from headache and remorse, was lurking outside the gateway far from the madding crowd of critics, crept in like a beaten dog and announced that Babemba was approaching followed by a number of laden soldiers. I was about to advance to receive him. Then I remembered that, owing to a queer native custom, such as that which caused Sir Theophilus Shepstone, whom I used to know very well, to be recognised as the holder of the spirit of the great Chaka and therefore as the equal of the Zulu monarchs, Brother John was the really important man in our company. So I gave way and asked him to be good enough to take my place and to live up to that station in savage life to which it had pleased God to call him.

I am bound to say he rose to the occasion very well, being by nature and appearance a dignified old man. Swallowing his coffee in a hurry, he took his place at a little distance from us, and stood there in a statuesque pose. To him entered Babemba crawling on his hands and knees, and other native gentlemen likewise crawling, also the burdened soldiers in as obsequious an attitude as their loads would allow.

"O King Dogeetah," said Babemba, "your brother king, Bausi, returns the guns and fire-goods of the white men, your children, and sends certain gifts."

"Glad to hear it, General Babemba," said Brother John, "although it would be better if he had never taken them away. Put them down and get on to your feet. I do not like to see men wriggling on their stomachs like monkeys."

The order was obeyed, and we checked the guns and ammunition; also our revolvers and the other articles that had been taken away from us. Nothing was missing or damaged; and in addition there were four fine elephant's tusks, an offering to Stephen and myself, which, as a business man, I promptly accepted; some *karosses* and Mazitu weapons, presents to Mavovo and the hunters, a beautiful native bedstead with ivory legs and mats of finely-woven grass, a gift to Hans in testimony to his powers of sleep under trying circumstances (the Zulus roared when they heard this, and Hans vanished cursing behind the huts), and for Sammy a weird musical instrument with a request that in future he would use it in public instead of his voice.

Sammy, I may add, did not see the joke any more than Hans had done, but the rest of us appreciated the Mazitu sense of humour very much.

"It is very well, Mr. Quatermain," he said, "for these black babes and sucklings to sit in the seat of the scornful. On such an occasion silent prayers would have been of little use, but I am certain that my loud crying to Heaven delivered you all from the bites of the heathen arrows."

"O Dogeetah and white lords," said Babemba, "the king invites your presence that he may ask your forgiveness for what has happened, and this time there will be no need for you to bring arms, since henceforward no hurt can come to you from the Mazitu people."

So presently we set out once more, taking with us the gifts that had been refused. Our march to the royal quarters was a veritable triumphal progress. The people prostrated themselves and clapped their hands slowly in salutation as we passed, while the girls and children pelted us with flowers as though we were brides going to be married. Our road ran by the place of execution where the stakes, at which I confess I looked with a shiver, were still standing, though the graves had been filled in.

On our arrival Bausi and his councillors rose and bowed to us. Indeed, the king did more, for coming forward he seized Brother John by the hand, and insisted upon rubbing his ugly black nose against that of this revered guest. This, it appeared, was the Mazitu method of embracing, an honour which Brother John did not seem at all to appreciate. Then followed long speeches, washed down with draughts of thick native beer. Bausi explained that his evil proceedings were entirely due to the wickedness of the deceased Imbozwi and his disciples, under whose tyranny the land had groaned for long, since the people believed them to speak "with the voice of Heaven Above."

Brother John, on our behalf, accepted the apology, and then read a lecture, or rather preached a sermon, that took exactly twenty-five minutes to deliver (he is rather long in the wind), in which he demonstrated the evils of superstition and pointed to a higher and a better path. Bausi replied that he would like to hear more of that path another time which, as he presumed that we were going to spend the rest of our lives in his company, could easily be found—say during the next spring when the crops had been sown and the people had leisure on their hands.

After this we presented our gifts, which now were eagerly accepted. Then I took up my parable and explained to Bausi that so far from stopping in Beza Town for the rest of our lives, we were anxious to press forward at once to Pongo-land. The king's face fell, as did those of his councillors.

"Listen, O lord Macumazana, and all of you," he said. "These Pongo are horrible wizards, a great and powerful people who live by themselves amidst the swamps and mix with none. If the Pongo catch Mazitu or folk of any other tribe, either they kill them or take them as prisoners to their own land where they enslave them, or sometimes sacrifice them to the devils they worship."

"That is so," broke in Babemba, "for when I was a lad I was a slave to the Pongo and doomed to be sacrificed to the White Devil. It was in escaping from them that I lost this eye."

Needless to say, I made a note of this remark, though I did not think the moment opportune to follow the matter up. If Babemba has once been to Pongo-land, I reflected to myself, Babemba can go again or show us the way there.

"And if we catch any of the Pongo," went on Bausi, "as sometimes we do when they come to hunt for slaves, we kill them. Ever since the Mazitu have been in this place there has been hate and war between them and the Pongo, and if I could wipe out those evil ones, then I should die happily."

"That you will never do, O King, while the White Devil lives," said Babemba. "Have you not heard the Pongo prophecy, that while the White Devil lives and the Holy Flower blooms, they will live. But when the White Devil dies and the Holy Flower ceases to bloom, then their women will become barren and their end will be upon them."

"Well, I suppose that this White Devil will die some day," I said.

"Not so, Macumazana. It will never die of itself. Like its wicked Priest, it has been there from the beginning and will always be there unless it is killed. But who is there that can kill the White Devil?"

I thought to myself that I would not mind trying, but again I did not pursue the point.

"My brother Dogeetah and lords," exclaimed Bausi, "it is not possible that you should visit these wizards except at the head of an army. But how can I send an army with you, seeing that the Mazitu are a land people and have no canoes in which to cross the great lake, and no trees whereof to make them?"

We answered that we did not know but would think the matter over, as we had come from our own place for this purpose and meant to carry it out.

Then the audience came to an end, and we returned to our huts, leaving Dogeetah to converse with his "brother Bausi" on matters connected with the latter's health. As I passed Babemba I told him that I should like to see him alone, and he said that he would visit me that evening after supper. The rest of the day passed quietly, for we had asked that people might be kept away from our encampment.

We found Hans, who had not accompanied us, being a little shy of appearing in public just then, engaged in cleaning the rifles, and this reminded me of something. Taking the double-barrelled gun of which I have spoken, I called Mavovo and handed it to him, saying:

"It is yours, O true prophet."

"Yes, my father," he answered, "it is mine for a little while, then perhaps it will be yours again."

The words struck me, but I did not care to ask their meaning. Somehow I wanted to hear no more of Mavovo's prophecies.

Then we dined, and for the rest of that afternoon slept, for all of us, including Brother John, needed rest badly. In the evening Babemba came, and we three white men saw him alone.

"Tell us about the Pongo and this white devil they worship," I said.

"Macumazana," he answered, "fifty years have gone by since I was in that land and I see things that happened to me there as through a mist. I went to fish amongst the reeds when I was a boy of twelve, and tall men robed in white came in a canoe and seized me. They led me to a town where there were many other such men, and treated me very well, giving me sweet things to eat till I grew fat and my skin shone. Then in the evening I was taken away, and we marched all night to the mouth of a great cave. In this cave sat a horrible old man about whom danced robed people, performing the rites of the White Devil.

"The old man told me that on the following morning I was to be cooked and eaten, for which reason I had been made so fat. There was a canoe at the mouth of the cave, beyond which lay water. While all were asleep I crept to the canoe. As I loosed the rope one of the priests woke up and ran at me. But I hit him on the head with the paddle, for though only a boy I was bold and strong, and he fell into the water. He came up again and gripped the edge of the canoe, but I struck his fingers with the paddle till he let go. A great wind was blowing that night, tearing off boughs from the trees which grew upon the other shore of the water. It whirled the canoe round and round and one of the boughs struck me in the eye. I scarcely felt it at the time, but afterwards the eye withered. Or perhaps it was a spear or a knife that struck me in the eye, I do not know. I paddled till I lost my senses and always that wind blew. The last thing that I remember was the sound of the canoe being driven by the gale through reeds. When I woke up again I found myself near a shore, to which I waded through the mud, scaring great crocodiles. But this must have been some days later, for now I was quite thin. I fell down upon the shore, and there some of our people found me and nursed me till I recovered. That is all."

"And quite enough too," I said. "Now answer me. How far was the town from the place where you were captured in Mazitu-land?"

"A whole day's journey in the canoe, Macumazana. I was captured in the morning early and we reached the harbour in the evening at a place where many canoes were tied up, perhaps fifty of them, some of which would hold forty men."

"And how far was the town from this harbour?"

"Quite close, Macumazana."

Now Brother John asked a question.

"Did you hear anything about the land beyond the water by the cave?"

"Yes, Dogeetah. I heard then, or afterwards—for from time to time rumours reach us concerning these Pongo—that it is an island where grows the Holy Flower, of which you know, for when last you were here you had one of its blooms. I heard, too, that this Holy Flower was tended by a priestess named Mother of the Flower, and her servants, all of whom were virgins."

"Who was the priestess?"

"I do not know, but I heave heard that she was one of those people who, although their parents are black, are born white, and that if any females among the Pongo are born white, or with pink eyes, or deaf and dumb, they are set apart to be the servants of the priestess. But this priestess must now be dead, seeing that when I was a boy she was already old, very, very old, and the Pongo were much concerned because there was no one of white skin who could be appointed to succeed her. Indeed she *is* dead, since many years ago there was a great feast in Pongo-land and numbers of slaves were eaten, because the priests had found a beautiful new princess who was white with yellow hair and had finger-nails of the right shape."

Now I bethought me that this finding of the priestess named "Mother of the Flower," who must be distinguished by certain personal peculiarities, resembled not a little that of the finding of the Apis bull-god, which also must have certain prescribed and holy markings, by the old Egyptians, as narrated by Herodotus. However, I said nothing about it at the time, because Brother John asked sharply:

"And is this priestess also dead?"

"I do not know, Dogeetah, but I think not. If she were dead I think that we should have heard some rumour of the Feast of the eating of the dead Mother."

"Eating the dead mother!" I exclaimed.

"Yes, Macumazana. It is the law among the Pongo that, for a certain sacred reason, the body of the Mother of the Flower, when she dies, must be partaken of by those who are privileged to the holy food."

"But the White Devil neither dies nor is eaten?" I said.

"No, as I have told you, he never dies. It is he who causes others to die, as if you go to Pongo-land doubtless you will find out," Babemba added grimly.

Upon my word, thought I to myself, as the meeting broke up because Babemba had nothing more to say, if I had my way I would leave Pongo-land and its white devil alone. Then I remembered how Brother John stood in reference to this matter, and with a sigh resigned myself to fate. As it proved it, I mean Fate, was quite equal to the occasion. The very next morning, early, Babemba turned up again.

"Lords, lords," he said, "a wonderful thing has happened! Last night we spoke of the Pongo and now behold! an embassy from the Pongo is here; it arrived at sunrise."

"What for?" I asked.

"To propose peace between their people and the Mazitu. Yes, they ask that Bausi should send envoys to their town to arrange a lasting peace. As if anyone would go!" he added.

"Perhaps some might dare to," I answered, for an idea occurred to me, "but let us go to see Bausi."

Half an hour later we were seated in the king's enclosure, that is, Stephen and I were, for Brother John was already in the royal hut, talking to Bausi. As we went a few words had passed between us.

"Has it occurred to you, John," I asked, "that if you really wish to visit Pongo-land here is perhaps what you would call a providential opportunity. Certainly none of these Mazitu will go, since they fear lest they should find a permanent peace—inside of the Pongo. Well, you are a blood-brother to Bausi and can offer to play the part of Envoy Extraordinary, with us as the members of your staff."

"I have already thought of it, Allan," he replied, stroking his long beard.

We sat down among a few of the leading councillors, and presently Bausi came out of his hut accompanied by Brother John, and having greeted us, ordered the Pongo envoys to be admitted. They were led in at once, tall, light-coloured men with regular and Semitic features, who were clothed in white linen like Arabs, and wore circles of gold or copper upon their necks and wrists.

In short, they were imposing persons, quite different from ordinary Central African natives, though there was something about their appearance which chilled and repelled me. I should add that their spears had been left outside, and that they saluted the king by folding their arms upon their breasts and bowing in a dignified fashion.

"Who are you?" asked Bausi, "and what do you want?"

"I am Komba," answered their spokesman, quite a young man with flashing eyes, "the Accepted-of-the-Gods, who, in a day to come that perhaps is near, will be the *Kalubi* of the Pongo people, and these are my servants. I have come here bearing gifts of friendship which are without, by the desire of the holy *Motombo*, the High Priest of the gods——"

"I thought that the *Kalubi* was the priest of your gods," interrupted Bausi.

"Not so. The *Kalubi* is the King of the Pongo as you are the King of the Mazitu. The *Motombo*, who is seldom seen, is King of the spirits and the Mouth of the gods."

Bausi nodded in the African fashion, that is by raising the chin, not depressing it, and Komba went on:

"I have placed myself in your power, trusting to your honour. You can kill me if you wish, though that will avail nothing, since there are others waiting to become *Kalubi* in my place."

"Am I a Pongo that I should wish to kill messengers and eat them?" asked Bausi, with sarcasm, a speech at which I noticed the Pongo envoys winced a little.

"King, you are mistaken. The Pongo only eat those whom the White God has chosen. It is a religious rite. Why should they who have cattle in plenty desire to devour men?"

"I don't know," grunted Bausi, "but there is one here who can tell a different story," and he looked at Babemba, who wriggled uncomfortably.

Komba also looked at him with his fierce eyes.

"It is not conceivable," he said, "that anybody should wish to eat one so old and bony, but let that pass. I thank you, King, for your promise of safety. I have come here to ask that you should send envoys to confer with the *Kalubi* and the *Motombo*, that a lasting peace may be arranged between our peoples."

"Why do not the *Kalubi* and the *Motombo* come here to confer?" asked Bausi.

"Because it is not lawful that they should leave their land, O King. Therefore they have sent me who am the *Kalubi*-to-come. Hearken. There has been war between us for generations. It began so long ago that only the *Motombo* knows of its beginning which he has from the gods. Once the Pongo people owned all this land and only had their sacred places beyond the water. Then your forefathers came and fell on them, killing many, enslaving many and taking their women to wife. Now, say the *Motombo* and the *Kalubi*, in the place of war let there be peace; where there is but barren sand, there let corn and flowers grow; let the darkness, wherein men lose their way and die, be changed to pleasant light in which they can sit in the sun holding each other's hands."

"Hear, hear!" I muttered, quite moved by this eloquence. But Bausi was not at all moved; indeed, he seemed to view these poetic proposals with the darkest suspicion.

"Give up killing our people or capturing them to be sacrificed to your White Devil, and then in a year or two we may listen to your words that are smeared with honey," he said. "As it is, we think that they are but a trap to catch flies. Still, if there are any of our councillors willing to visit your *Motombo* and your *Kalubi* and hear what they have to propose, taking the risk of whatever may happen to them there, I do not forbid it. Now, O my Councillors, speak, not altogether, but one by one, and be swift, since to the first that speaks shall be given this honour."

I think I never heard a denser silence than that which followed this invitation. Each of the *indunas* looked at his neighbour, but not one of them uttered a single word.

"What!" exclaimed Bausi, in affected surprise. "Do none speak? Well, well, you are lawyers and men of peace. What says the great general, Babemba?"

"I say, O King, that I went once to Pongo-land when I was young, taken by the hair of my head, to leave an eye there and that I do not wish to visit it again walking on the soles of my feet."

"It seems, O Komba, that since none of my people are willing to act as envoys, if there is to be talk of peace between us, the *Motombo* and the *Kalubi* must come here under safe conduct."

"I have said that cannot be, O King."

"If so, all is finished, O Komba. Rest, eat of our food and return to your own land."

Then Brother John rose and said:

"We are blood-brethren, Bausi, and therefore I can speak for you. If you and your councillors are willing, and these Pongos are willing, I and my friends do not fear to visit the *Motombo* and the *Kalubi*, to talk with them of peace on behalf of your people, since we love to see new lands and new races of mankind. Say, Komba, if the king allows, will you accept us as ambassadors?"

"It is for the king to name his own ambassadors," answered Komba. "Yet the *Kalubi* has heard of the presence of you white lords in Mazitu-land and bade me say that if it should be your pleasure to accompany the embassy and visit him, he would give you welcome. Only when the matter was laid before the *Motombo*, the oracle spoke thus:

"'Let the white men come if come they will, or let them stay away. But if they come, let them bring with them none of those iron tubes, great or small, whereof the land has heard, that vomit smoke with a noise and cause death from afar. They will not need them to kill meat, for meat shall be given to them in plenty; moreover, among the Pongo they will be safe, unless they offer insult to the god.'"

These words Komba spoke very slowly and with much emphasis, his piercing eyes fixed upon my face as though to read the thoughts it hid. As I heard them my courage sank into my boots. Well, I knew that the *Kalubi* was asking us to Pongo-land that we might kill this Great White Devil that threatened his life, which, I took it, was a monstrous ape. And how could we face that or some other frightful brute without firearms? My mind was made up in a minute.

"O Komba," I said, "my gun is my father, my mother, my wife and all my other relatives. I do not stir from here without it."

"Then, white lord," answered Komba, "you will do well to stop in this place in the midst of your family, since, if you try to bring it with you to Pongo-land, you will be killed as you set foot upon the shore."

Before I could find an answer Brother John spoke, saying:

"It is natural that the great hunter, Macumazana, should not wish to be parted from what which to him is as a stick to a lame man. But with me it is different. For years I have used no gun, who kill nothing that God made, except a few bright-winged insects. I am ready to visit your country with naught save this in my hand," and he pointed to the butterfly net that leaned against the fence behind him.

"Good, you are welcome," said Komba, and I thought that I saw his eyes gleam with unholy joy. There followed a pause, during which I explained everything to Stephen, showing that the thing was madness. But here, to my horror, that young man's mulish obstinacy came in.

"I say, you know, Quatermain," he said, "we can't let the old boy go alone, or at least I can't. It's another matter for you who have a son dependent on you. But putting aside the fact that I mean to get——" he was about to add, "the orchid," when I nudged him. Of course, it was ridiculous, but an uneasy fear took me lest this Komba should in some mysterious way understand what he was saying. "What's up? Oh! I see, but the beggar can't understand English. Well, putting aside everything else, it isn't the game, and there you are, you know. If Mr. Brother John goes, I'll go too, and indeed if he doesn't go, I'll go alone."

"You unutterable young ass," I muttered in a stage aside.

"What is it the young white lord says he wishes in our country?" asked the cold Komba, who with diabolical acuteness had read some of Stephen's meaning in his face.

"He says that he is a harmless traveller who would like to study the scenery and to find out if you have any gold there," I answered.

"Indeed. Well, he shall study the scenery and we have gold," and he touched the bracelets on his arm, "of which he shall be given as much as he can carry away. But perchance, white lords, you would wish to talk this matter over alone. Have we your leave to withdraw a while, O King?"

Five minutes later we were seated in the king's "great house" with Bausi himself and Babemba. Here there was a mighty argument. Bausi implored Brother John not to go, and so did I. Babemba said that to go would be madness, as he smelt witchcraft and murder in the air, he who knew the Pongo.

Brother John replied sweetly that he certainly intended to avail himself of this heaven-sent opportunity to visit one of the few remaining districts in this part of Africa through which he had not yet wandered. Stephen yawned and fanned himself with a pocket-handkerchief, for the hut was hot, and remarked that having come so far after a certain rare flower he did not mean to return empty-handed.

"I perceive, Dogeetah," said Bausi at last, "that you have some reason for this journey which you are hiding from me. Still, I am minded to hold you here by force."

"If you do, it will break our brotherhood," answered Brother John. "Seek not to know what I would hide, Bausi, but wait till the future shall declare it."

Bausi groaned and gave in. Babemba said that Dogeetah and Wazela were bewitched, and that I, Macumazana, alone retained my senses.

"Then that's settled," exclaimed Stephen. "John and I are to go as envoys to the Pongo, and you, Quatermain, will stop here to look after the hunters and the stores."

"Young man," I replied, "do you wish to insult me? After your father put you in my charge, too! If you two are going, I shall come also, if I have to do so mother-naked. But let me tell you once and for all in the most emphatic language I can command, that I consider you a brace of confounded lunatics, and that if the Pongo don't eat you, it will be more than you deserve. To think that at my age I should be dragged among a lot of cannibal savages without even a pistol, to fight some unknown brute with my bare hands! Well, we can only die once—that is, so far as we know at present."

"How true," remarked Stephen; "how strangely and profoundly true!"

Oh! I could have boxed his ears.

We went into the courtyard again, whither Komba was summoned with his attendants. This time they came bearing gifts, or having them borne for them. These consisted, I remember, of two fine tusks of ivory which suggested to me that their country could not be entirely surrounded by water, since elephants would scarcely live upon an island; gold dust in a gourd and copper bracelets, which showed that it was mineralized; white native linen, very well woven, and some really beautiful decorated pots, indicating that the people had artistic tastes. Where did they get them from, I wonder, and what was the origin of their race? I cannot answer the question, for I never found out with any certainty. Nor do I think they knew themselves.

The *indaba* was resumed. Bausi announced that we three white men with a servant apiece (I stipulated for this) would visit Pongo-land as his envoys, taking no firearms with us, there to discuss terms of peace between the two peoples, and especially the questions of trade and intermarriage. Komba was very insistent that this should be included; at the time I wondered why. He, Komba, on behalf of the *Motombo* and the *Kalubi*, the spiritual and temporal rulers of his land, guaranteed us safe conduct on the understanding that we attempted no insult or violence to the gods, a stipulation from which there was no escape, though I liked it little. He swore also that we should be delivered safe and sound in the Mazitu country within six days of our having left its shores.

Bausi said that it was good, adding that he would send five hundred armed men to escort us to the place where we were to embark, and to receive us on our return; also that if any hurt came to us he would wage war upon the Pongo people for ever until he found means to destroy them.

So we parted, it being agreed that we were to start upon our journey on the following morning.

Chapter 13

Rica Town

As a matter of fact we did not leave Beza Town till twenty-four hours later than had been arranged, since it took some time for old Babemba, who was to be in charge of it, to collect and provision our escort of five hundred men.

Here, I may mention, that when we got back to our huts we found the two Mazitu bearers, Tom and Jerry, eating a hearty meal, but looking rather tired. It appeared that in order to get rid of their favourable evidence, the ceased witch-doctor, Imbozwi, who for some reason or other had feared to kill them, caused them to be marched off to a distant part of the land where they were imprisoned. On the arrival of the news of the fall and death of Imbozwi and his subordinates, they were set at liberty, and at once returned to us at Beza Town. Of course it became necessary to explain to our servants what we were about to do. When they understood the nature of our proposed expedition they shook their heads, and when they learned that we had promised to leave our guns behind us, they were speechless with amazement.

"Kransick! Kransick!" which means *ill in the skull*, or *mad*, exclaimed Hans to the others as he tapped his forehead significantly. "They have caught it from Dogeetah, one who lives on insects which he entangles in a net, and carries no gun to kill game. Well, I knew they would."

The hunters nodded in assent, and Sammy lifted his arms to Heaven as though in prayer. Only Mavovo seemed indifferent. Then came the question of which of them was to accompany us.

"So far as I am concerned that is soon settled," said Mavovo. "I go with my father, Macumazana, seeing that even without a gun I am still strong and can fight as my male ancestors fought with a spear."

"And I, too, go with the Baas Quatermain," grunted Hans, "seeing that even without a gun I am cunning, as *my* female ancestors were before me."

"Except when you take medicine, Spotted Snake, and lose yourself in the mist of sleep," mocked one of the Zulus. "Does that fine bedstead which the king sent you go with you?"

"No, son of a fool!" answered Hans. "I'll lend it to you who do not understand that there is more wisdom within me when I am asleep than there is in you when you are awake."

It remained to be decided who the third man should be. As neither of Brother John's two servants, who had accompanied him on his cross-country journey, was suitable, one being ill and the other afraid, Stephen suggested Sammy as the man, chiefly because he could cook.

"No, Mr. Somers, no," said Sammy, with earnestness. "At this proposal I draw the thick rope. To ask one who can cook to visit a land where he will be cooked, is to seethe the offspring in its parent's milk."

So we gave him up, and after some discussion fixed upon Jerry, a smart and plucky fellow, who was quite willing to accompany us. The rest of that day we spent in making our preparations which, if simple, required a good deal of thought. To my annoyance, at the time I wanted to find Hans to help me, he was not forthcoming. When at length he appeared I asked him where he had been. He answered, to cut himself a stick in the forest, as he understood we should have to walk a long way. Also he showed me the stick, a long, thick staff of a hard and beautiful kind of bamboo which grows in Mazitu-land.

"What do you want that clumsy thing for," I said, "when there are plenty of sticks about?"

"New journey, new stick! Baas. Also this kind of wood is full of air and might help me to float if we are upset into the water."

"What an idea!" I exclaimed, and dismissed the matter from my mind.

At dawn, on the following day, we started, Stephen and I riding on the two donkeys, which were now fat and lusty, and Brother John upon his white ox, a most docile beast that was quite attached to him. All the hunters, fully armed, came with us to the borders of the Mazitu country, where they were to await our return in company with the Mazitu regiment. The king himself went with us to the west gate of the town, where he bade us all, and especially Brother John, an affectionate farewell. Moreover, he sent for Komba and his attendants, and again swore to him that if any harm happened to us, he would not rest till he had found a way to destroy the Pongo, root and branch.

"Have no fear," answered the cold Komba, "in our holy town of Rica we do not tie innocent guests to stakes to be shot to death with arrows."

The repartee, which was undoubtedly neat, irritated Bausi, who was not fond of allusions to this subject.

"If the white men are so safe, why do you not let them take their guns with them?" he asked, somewhat illogically.

"If we meant evil, King, would their guns help them, they being but few among so many. For instance, could we not steal them, as you did when you plotted the murder of these white lords. It is a law among the Pongo that no such magic weapon shall be allowed to enter their land."

"Why?" I asked, to change the conversation, for I saw that Bausi was growing very wrath and feared complications.

"Because, my lord Macumazana, there is a prophecy among us that when a gun is fired in Pongo-land, its gods will desert us, and the *Motombo*, who is their priest, will die. That saying is very old, but until a little while ago none knew what it meant, since it spoke of 'a hollow spear that smoked,' and such a weapon was not known to us."

"Indeed," I said, mourning within myself that we should not be in a position to bring about the fulfilment of that prophecy, which, as Hans said, shaking his head sadly, "was a great pity, a very great pity!"

Three days' march over country that gradually sloped downwards from the high tableland on which stood Beza Town, brought us to the lake called Kirua, a word which, I believe, means The Place of the Island. Of the lake itself we could see nothing, because of the dense brake of tall reeds which grew out into the shallow water for quite a mile from the shore and was only pierced here and there with paths made by the hippopotami when they came to the mainland at night to feed. From a high mound which looked exactly like a tumulus and, for aught I know, may have been one, however, the blue waters beyond were visible, and in the far distance what, looked at through glasses, appeared to be a tree-clad mountain top. I asked Komba what it might be, and he answered that it was the Home of the gods in Pongo-land.

"What gods?" I asked again, whereon he replied like a black Herodotus, that of these it was not lawful to speak.

I have rarely met anyone more difficult to pump than that frigid and un-African Komba.

On the top of this mound we planted the Union Jack, fixed to the tallest pole that we could find. Komba asked suspiciously why we did so, and as I was determined to show this unsympathetic person that there were others as unpumpable as himself, I replied that it was the god of our tribe, which we set up there to be worshipped, and that anyone who tried to insult or injure it, would certainly die, as the witch-doctor, Imbozwi, and his children had found out. For once Komba seemed a little impressed, and even bowed to the bunting as he passed by.

What I did not inform him was that we had set the flag there to be a sign and a beacon to us in case we should ever be forced to find our way back to this place unguided and in a hurry. As a matter of fact, this piece of forethought, which oddly enough originated with the most reckless of our party, Stephen, proved our salvation, as I shall tell later on. At the foot of the mound we set our camp for the night, the Mazitu soldiers under Babemba, who did not mind mosquitoes, making theirs nearer to the lake, just opposite to where a wide hippopotamus lane pierced the reeds, leaving a little canal of clear water.

I asked Komba when and how we were to cross the lake. He said that we must start at dawn on the following morning when, at this time of the year, the wind generally blew off shore, and that if the weather were favourable, we should reach the Pongo town of Rica by nightfall. As to how we were to do this, he would show me if I cared to follow him. I nodded, and he led me four or five hundred yards along the edge of the reeds in a southerly direction.

As we went, two things happened. The first of these was that a very large, black rhinoceros, which was sleeping in some bushes, suddenly got our wind and, after the fashion of these beasts, charged down on us from about fifty yards away. Now I was carrying a heavy, single-barrelled rifle, for as yet we and our weapons were not parted. On came the rhinoceros, and Komba, small blame to him for he only had a spear, started to run. I cocked the rifle and waited my chance.

When it was not more than fifteen paces away the rhinoceros threw up its head, at which, of course, it was useless to fire because of the horn, and I let drive at the throat. The bullet hit it fair, and I suppose penetrated to the heart. At any rate, it rolled over and over like a shot rabbit, and with a single stretch of its limbs, expired almost at my feet.

Komba was much impressed. He returned; he stared at the dead rhinoceros and at the hole in its throat; he stared at me; he stared at the still smoking rifle.

"The great beast of the plains killed with a noise!" he muttered. "Killed in an instant by this little monkey of a white man" (I thanked him for that and made a note of it) "and his magic. Oh! the *Motombo* was wise when he commanded——" and with an effort he stopped.

"Well, friend, what is the matter?" I asked. "You see there was no need for you to run. If you had stepped behind me you would have been as safe as you are now—after running."

"It is so, lord Macumazana, but the thing is strange to me. Forgive me if I do not understand."

"Oh! I forgive you, my lord *Kalubi*—that is—to be. It is clear that you have a good deal to learn in Pongo-land."

"Yes, my lord Macumazana, and so perhaps have you," he replied dryly, having by this time recovered his nerve and sarcastic powers.

Then after telling Mavovo, who appeared mysteriously at the sound of the shot—I think he was stalking us in case of accidents—to fetch men to cut up the rhinoceros, Komba and I proceeded on our walk.

A little further on, just by the edge of the reeds, I caught sight of a narrow, oblong trench dug in a patch of stony soil, and of a rusted mustard tin half-hidden by some scanty vegetation.

"What is that?" I asked, in seeming astonishment, though I knew well what it must be.

"Oh!" replied Komba, who evidently was not yet quite himself, "that is where the white lord Dogeetah, Bausi's blood-brother, set his little canvas house when he was here over twelve moons ago."

"Really!" I exclaimed, "he never told me he was here." (This was a lie, but somehow I was not afraid of lying to Komba.) "How do you know that he was here?"

"One of our people who was fishing in the reeds saw him."

"Oh! that explains it, Komba. But what an odd place for him to fish in; so far from home; and I wonder what he was fishing for. When you have time, Komba, you must explain to me what it is that you catch amidst the roots of thick reeds in such shallow water."

Komba replied that he would do so with pleasure—when he had time. Then, as though to avoid further conversation he ran forward, and thrusting the reeds apart, showed me a great canoe, big enough to hold thirty or forty men, which with infinite labour had been hollowed out of the trunk of a single, huge tree. This canoe differed from the majority of those that personally I have seen used on African lakes and rivers, in that it was fitted for a mast, now unshipped. I looked at it and said it was a fine boat, whereon Komba replied that there were a hundred such at Rica Town, though not all of them were so large.

Ah! thought I to myself as we walked back to the camp. Then, allowing an average of twenty to a canoe, the Pongo tribe number about two thousand males old enough to paddle, an estimate which turned out to be singularly correct.

Next morning at dawn we started, with some difficulty. To begin with, in the middle of the night old Babemba came to the canvas shelter under which I was sleeping, woke me up and in a long speech implored me not to go. He said he was convinced that the Pongo intended foul play of some sort and that all this talk of peace was a mere trick to entrap us white men into the country, probably in order to sacrifice us to its gods for a religious reason.

I answered that I quite agreed with him, but that as my companions insisted upon making this journey, I could not desert them. All that I could do was to beg him to keep a sharp look-out so that he might be able to help us in case we got into trouble.

"Here I will stay and watch for you, lord Macumazana," he answered, "but if you fall into a snare, am I able to swim through the water like a fish, or to fly through the air like a bird to free you?"

After he had gone one of the Zulu hunters arrived, a man named Ganza, a sort of lieutenant to Mavovo, and sang the same song. He said that it was not right that I should go without guns to die among devils and leave him and his companions wandering alone in a strange land.

I answered that I was much of the same opinion, but that Dogeetah insisted upon going and that I had no choice.

"Then let us kill Dogeetah, or at any rate tie him up, so that he can do no more mischief in his madness," Ganza suggested blandly, whereon I turned him out.

Lastly Sammy arrived and said:

"Mr. Quatermain, before you plunge into this deep well of foolishness, I beg that you will consider your responsibilities to God and man, and especially to us, your household, who are now but lost sheep far from home, and further, that you will remember that if anything disagreeable should overtake you, you are indebted to me to the extent of two months' wages which will probably prove unrecoverable."

I produced a little leather bag from a tin box and counted out to Sammy the wages due to him, also those for three months in advance.

To my astonishment he began to weep. "Sir," he said, "I do not seek filthy lucre. What I mean is that I am afraid you will be killed by these Pongo, and, alas! although I love you, sir, I am too great a coward to come and be killed with you, for God made me like that. I pray you not to go, Mr. Quatermain, because I repeat, I love you, sir."

"I believe you do, my good fellow," I answered, "and I also am afraid of being killed, who only seem to be brave because I must. However, I hope we shall come through all right. Meanwhile, I am going to give this box and all the gold in it, of which there is a great deal, into your charge, Sammy, trusting to you, if anything happens to us, to get it safe back to Durban if you can."

"Oh! Mr. Quatermain," he exclaimed, "I am indeed honoured, especially as you know that once I was in jail for—embezzlement—with extenuating circumstances, Mr. Quatermain. I tell you that although I am a coward, I will die before anyone gets his fingers into that box."

"I am sure that you will, Sammy my boy," I said. "But I hope, although things look queer, that none of us will be called upon to die just yet."

****

The morning came at last, and the six of us marched down to the canoe which had been brought round to the open waterway. Here we had to undergo a kind of customs-house examination at the hands of Komba and his companions, who seemed terrified lest we should be smuggling firearms.

"You know what rifles are like," I said indignantly. "Can you see any in our hands? Moreover, I give you my word that we have none."

Komba bowed politely, but suggested that perhaps some "little guns," by which he meant pistols, remained in our baggage—by accident. Komba was a most suspicious person.

"Undo all the loads," I said to Hans, who obeyed with an enthusiasm which I confess struck me as suspicious.

Knowing his secretive and tortuous nature, this sudden zeal for openness seemed almost unnatural. He began by unrolling his own blanket, inside of which appeared a miscellaneous collection of articles. I remember among them a spare pair of very dirty trousers, a battered tin cup, a wooden spoon such as *Kaffirs* use to eat their *scoff* with, a bottle full of some doubtful compound, sundry roots and other native medicines, an old pipe I had given him, and last but not least, a huge head of yellow tobacco in the leaf, of a kind that the Mazitu, like the Pongos, cultivate to some extent.

"What on earth do you want so much tobacco for, Hans?" I asked.

"For us three black people to smoke, Baas, or to take as snuff, or to chew. Perhaps where we are going we may find little to eat, and then tobacco is a food on which one can live for days. Also it brings sleep at nights."

"Oh! that will do," I said, fearing lest Hans, like a second Walter Raleigh, was about to deliver a long lecture upon the virtue of tobacco.

"There is no need for the yellow man to take this weed to our land," interrupted Komba, "for there we have plenty. Why does he cumber himself with the stuff?" and he stretched out his hand idly as though to take hold of and examine it closely.

At this moment, however, Mavovo called attention to his bundle which he had undone, whether on purpose or by accident, I do not know, and forgetting the tobacco, Komba turned to attend to him. With a marvellous celerity Hans rolled up his blanket again. In less than a minute the lashings were fast and it was hanging on his back. Again suspicion took me, but an argument which had sprung up between Brother John and Komba about the former's butterfly net, which Komba suspected of being a new kind of gun or at least a magical instrument of a dangerous sort, attracted my notice. After this dispute, another arose over a common garden trowel that Stephen had thought fit to bring with him. Komba asked what it was for. Stephen replied through Brother John that it was to dig up flowers.

"Flowers!" said Komba. "One of our gods is a flower. Does the white lord wish to dig up our god?"

Of course this was exactly what Stephen did desire to do, but not unnaturally he kept the fact to himself. The squabble grew so hot that finally I announced that if our little belongings were treated with so much suspicion, it might be better that we should give up the journey altogether.

"We have passed our word that we have no firearms," I said in the most dignified manner that I could command, "and that should be enough for you, O Komba."

Then Komba, after consultation with his companions, gave way. Evidently he was anxious that we should visit Pongo-land.

So at last we started. We three white men and our servants seated ourselves in the stern of the canoe on grass cushions that had been provided. Komba went to the bows and his people, taking the broad paddles, rowed and pushed the boat along the water-way made by the hippopotami through the tall and matted reeds, from which ducks and other fowl rose in multitudes with a sound like thunder. A quarter of an hour or so of paddling through these weed-encumbered shallows brought us to the deep and open lake. Here, on the edge of the reeds a tall pole that served as a mast was shipped, and a square sail, made of closely-woven mats, run up. It filled with the morning off-land breeze and presently we were bowling along at a rate of quite eight miles the hour. The shore grew dim behind us, but for a long while above the clinging mists I could see the flag that we had planted on the mound. By degrees it dwindled till it became a mere speck and vanished. As it grew smaller my spirits sank, and when it was quite gone, I felt very low indeed.

Another of your fool's errands, Allan my boy, I said to myself. I wonder how many more you are destined to survive.

The others, too, did not seem in the best of spirits. Brother John stared at the horizon, his lips moving as though he were engaged in prayer, and even Stephen was temporarily depressed. Jerry had fallen asleep, as a native generally does when it is warm and he has nothing to do. Mavovo looked very thoughtful. I wondered whether he had been consulting his Snake again, but did not ask him. Since the episode of our escape from execution by bow and arrow I had grown somewhat afraid of that unholy reptile. Next time it might foretell our immediate doom, and if it did I knew that I should believe.

As for Hans, he looked much disturbed, and was engaged in wildly hunting for something in the flap pockets of an antique corduroy waistcoat which, from its general appearance, must, I imagine, years ago have adorned the person of a British game-keeper.

"Three," I heard him mutter. "By my great grandfather's spirit! only three left."

"Three what?" I asked in Dutch.

"Three charms, Baas, and there ought to have been quite twenty-four. The rest have fallen out through a hole that the devil himself made in this rotten stuff. Now we shall not die of hunger, and we shall not be shot, and we shall not be drowned, at least none of those things will happen to me. But there are twenty-one other things that may finish us, as I have lost the charms to ward them off. Thus——"

"Oh! stop your rubbish," I said, and fell again into the depths of my uncomfortable reflections. After this I, too, went to sleep. When I woke it was past midday and the wind was falling. However, it held while we ate some food we had brought with us, after which it died away altogether, and the Pongo people took to their paddles. At my suggestion we offered to help them, for it occurred to me that we might just as well learn how to manage these paddles. So six were given to us, and Komba, who now I noted was beginning to speak in a somewhat imperious tone, instructed us in their use. At first we made but a poor hand at the business, but three or four hours' steady practice taught us a good deal. Indeed, before our journey's end, I felt that we should be quite capable of managing a canoe, if ever it became necessary for us to do so.

By three in the afternoon the shores of the island we were approaching—if it really was an island, a point that I never cleared up—were well in sight, the mountain top that stood some miles inland having been visible for hours. In fact, through my glasses, I had been able to make out its configuration almost from the beginning of the voyage. About five we entered the mouth of a deep bay fringed on either side with forests, in which were cultivated clearings with small villages of the ordinary African stamp. I observed from the smaller size of the trees adjacent to these clearings, that much more land had once been under cultivation here, probably within the last century, and asked Komba why this was so.

He answered in an enigmatic sentence which impressed me so much that I find I entered it verbatim in my notebook.

"When man dies, corn dies. Man is corn, and corn is man."

Under this entry I see that I wrote "Compare the saying, 'Bread is the staff of life.'"

I could not get any more out of him. Evidently he referred, however, to a condition of shrinking in the population, a circumstance which he did not care to discuss.

After the first few miles the bay narrowed sharply, and at its end came to a point where a stream of no great breadth fell into it. On either side of this stream that was roughly bridged in many places stood the town of Rica. It consisted of a great number of large huts roofed with palm leaves and constructed apparently of whitewashed clay, or rather, as we discovered afterwards, of lake mud mixed with chopped straw or grass.

Reaching a kind of wharf which was protected from erosion by piles formed of small trees driven into the mud, to which were tied a fleet of canoes, we landed just as the sun was beginning to sink. Our approach had doubtless been observed, for as we drew near the wharf a horn was blown by someone on the shore, whereon a considerable number of men appeared. I suppose out of the huts, and assisted to make the canoe fast. I noted that these all resembled Komba and his companions in build and features; they were so like each other that, except for the difference of their ages, it was difficult to tell them apart. They might all have been members of one family; indeed, this was practically the case, owing to constant intermarriage carried on for generations.

There was something in the appearance of these tall, cold, sharp-featured, white-robed men that chilled my blood, something unnatural and almost inhuman. Here was nothing of the usual African jollity. No one shouted, no one laughed or chattered. No one crowded on us, trying to handle our persons or clothes. No one appeared afraid or even astonished. Except for a word or two they were silent, merely contemplating us in a chilling and distant fashion, as though the arrival of three white men in a country where before no white man had ever set foot were an everyday occurrence.

Moreover, our personal appearance did not seem to impress them, for they smiled faintly at Brother John's long beard and at my stubbly hair, pointing these out to each other with their slender fingers or with the handles of their big spears. I remarked that they never used the blade of the spear for this purpose, perhaps because they thought that we might take this for a hostile or even a warlike demonstration. It is humiliating to have to add that the only one of our company who seemed to move them to wonder or interest was Hans. His extremely ugly and wrinkled countenance, it was clear, did appeal to them to some extent, perhaps because they had never seen anything in the least like it before, or perhaps for another reason which the reader may guess in due course.

At any rate, I heard one of them, pointing to Hans, ask Komba whether the ape-man was our god or only our captain. The compliment seemed to please Hans, who hitherto had never been looked on either as a god or a captain. But the rest of us were not flattered; indeed, Mavovo was indignant, and told Hans outright that if he heard any more such talk he would beat him before these people, to show them that he was neither a captain nor a god.

"Wait till I claim to be either, O butcher of a Zulu, before you threaten to treat me thus!" ejaculated Hans, indignantly. Then he added, with his peculiar Hottentot snigger, "Still, it is true that before all the meat is eaten (*i.e.* before all is done) you may think me both," a dark saying which at the time we did not understand.

When we had landed and collected our belongings, Komba told us to follow him, and led us up a wide street that was very tidily kept and bordered on either side by the large huts whereof I have spoken. Each of these huts stood in a fenced garden of its own, a thing I have rarely seen elsewhere in Africa. The result of this arrangement was that although as a matter of fact it had but a comparatively small population, the area covered by Rica was very great. The town, by the way, was not surrounded with any wall or other fortification, which showed that the inhabitants feared no attack. The waters of the lake were their defence.

For the rest, the chief characteristic of this place was the silence that brooded there. Apparently they kept no dogs, for none barked, and no poultry, for I never heard a cock crow in Pongo-land. Cattle and native sheep they had in abundance, but as they did not fear any enemy, these were pastured outside the town, their milk and meat being brought in as required. A considerable number of people were gathered to observe us, not in a crowd, but in little family groups which collected separately at the gates of the gardens.

For the most part these consisted of a man and one or more wives, finely formed and handsome women. Sometimes they had children with them, but these were very few; the most I saw with any one family was three, and many seemed to possess none at all. Both the women and the children, like the men, were decently clothed in long, white garments, another peculiarity which showed that these natives were no ordinary African savages.

Oh! I can see Rica Town now after all these many years: the wide street swept and garnished, the brown-roofed, white-walled huts in their fertile, irrigated gardens, the tall, silent folk, the smoke from the cooking fires rising straight as a line in the still air, the graceful palms and other tropical trees, and at the head of the street, far away to the north, the rounded, towering shape of the forest-clad mountain that was called House of the Gods. Often that vision comes back to me in my sleep, or at times in my waking hours when some heavy odour reminds me of the overpowering scent of the great trumpet-like blooms which hung in profusion upon broad leaved bushes that were planted in almost every garden.

On we marched till at last we reached a tall, live fence that was covered with brilliant scarlet flowers, arriving at its gate just as the last red glow of day faded from the sky and night began to fall. Komba pushed open the gate, revealing a scene that none of us are likely to forget. The fence enclosed about an acre of ground of which the back part was occupied by two large huts standing in the usual gardens.

In front of these, not more than fifteen paces from the gate, stood another building of a totally different character. It was about fifty feet in length by thirty broad and consisted only of a roof supported upon carved pillars of wood, the spaces between the pillars being filled with grass mats or blinds. Most of these blinds were pulled down, but four exactly opposite the gate were open. Inside the shed forty or fifty men, who wore white robes and peculiar caps and who were engaged in chanting a dreadful, melancholy song, were gathered on three sides of a huge fire that burned in a pit in the ground. On the fourth side, that facing the gate, a man stood alone with his arms outstretched and his back towards us.

Of a sudden he heard our footsteps and turned round, springing to the left, so that the light might fall on us. Now we saw by the glow of the great fire, that over it was an iron grid not unlike a small bedstead, and that on this grid lay some fearful object. Stephen, who was a little ahead, stared, then exclaimed in a horrified voice:

"My God! it is a woman!"

In another second the blinds fell down, hiding everything, and the singing ceased.

Chapter 14

The Kalubi's Oath

"Be silent!" I whispered, and all understood my tone if they did not catch the words. Then steadying myself with an effort, for this hideous vision, which might have been a picture from hell, made me feel faint, I glanced at Komba, who was a pace or two in front of us. Evidently he was much disturbed—the motions of his back told me this—by the sense of some terrible mistake that he had made. For a moment he stood still, then wheeled round and asked me if we had seen anything.

"Yes," I answered indifferently, "we saw a number of men gathered round a fire, nothing more."

He tried to search our faces, but luckily the great moon, now almost at her full, was hidden behind a thick cloud, so that he could not read them well. I heard him sigh in relief as he said:

"The *Kalubi* and the head men are cooking a sheep; it is their custom to feast together on those nights when the moon is about to change. Follow me, white lords."

Then he led us round the end of the long shed at which we did not even look, and through the garden on its farther side to the two fine huts I have mentioned. Here he clapped his hands and a woman appeared, I know not whence. To her he whispered something. She went away and presently returned with four or five other women who carried clay lamps filled with oil in which floated a wick of palm fibre. These lamps were set down in the huts that proved to be very clean and comfortable places, furnished after a fashion with wooden stools and a kind of low table of which the legs were carved to the shape of antelope's feet. Also there was a wooden platform at the end of the hut whereon lay beds covered with mats and stuffed with some soft fibre.

"Here you may rest safe," he said, "for, white lords, are you not the honoured guests of the Pongo people? Presently food" (I shuddered at the word) "will be brought to you, and after you have eaten well, if it is your pleasure, the *Kalubi* and his councillors will receive you in yonder feast-house and you can talk with them before you sleep. If you need aught, strike upon that jar with a stick," and he pointed to what looked like a copper cauldron that stood in the garden of the hut near the place where the women were already lighting a fire, "and some will wait on you. Look, here are your goods; none are missing, and here comes water in which you may wash. Now I must go to make report to the *Kalubi*," and with a courteous bow he departed.

So after a while did the silent, handsome women—to fetch our meal, I understood one of them to say, and at length we were alone.

"My aunt!" said Stephen, fanning himself with his pocket-handkerchief, "did you see that lady toasting? I have often heard of cannibals, those slaves, for instance, but the actual business! Oh! my aunt!"

"It is no use addressing your absent aunt—if you have got one. What did you expect if you would insist on coming to a hell like this?" I asked gloomily.

"Can't say, old fellow. Don't trouble myself much with expectations as a rule. That's why I and my poor old father never could get on. I always quoted the text 'Sufficient to the day is the evil thereof' to him, until at length he sent for the family *Bible* and ruled it out with red ink in a rage. But I say, do you think that we shall be called upon to understudy St. Lawrence on that grid?"

"Certainly, I do," I replied, "and, as old Babemba warned you, you can't complain."

"Oh! but I will and I can. And so will you, won't you, Brother John?"

Brother John woke up from a reverie and stroked his long beard.

"Since you ask me, Mr. Somers," he said, reflectively, "if it were a case of martyrdom for the Faith, like that of the saint to whom you have alluded, I should not object—at any rate in theory. But I confess that, speaking from a secular point of view, I have the strongest dislike to being cooked and eaten by these very disagreeable savages. Still, I see no reason to suppose that we shall fall victims to their domestic customs."

I, being in a depressed mood, was about to argue to the contrary, when Hans poked his head into the hut and said:

"Dinner coming, Baas, very fine dinner!"

So we went out into the garden where the tall, impassive ladies were arranging many wooden dishes on the ground. Now the moon was clear of clouds, and by its brilliant light we examined their contents. Some were cooked meat covered with a kind of sauce that made its nature indistinguishable. As a matter of fact, I believe it was mutton, but—who could say? Others were evidently of a vegetable nature. For instance, there was a whole platter full of roasted *mealie* cobs and a great boiled pumpkin, to say nothing of some bowls of curdled milk. Regarding this feast I became aware of a sudden and complete conversion to those principles of vegetarianism which Brother John was always preaching to me.

"I am sure you are quite right," I said to him, nervously, "in holding that vegetables are the best diet in a hot climate. At any rate I have made up my mind to try the experiment for a few days," and throwing manners to the winds, I grabbed four of the upper *mealie* cobs and the top of the pumpkin which I cut off with a knife. Somehow I did not seem to fancy that portion of it which touched the platter, for who knew what those dishes might have contained and how often they were washed.

Stephen also appeared to have found salvation on this point, for he, too, patronized the *mealie* cobs and the pumpkin; so did Mavovo, and so did even that inveterate meat-eater, Hans. Only the simple Jerry tackled the fleshpots of Egypt, or rather of Pongo-land, with appetite, and declared that they were good. I think that he, being the last of us through the gateway, had not realized what it was which lay upon the grid.

At length we finished our simple meal—when you are very hungry it takes a long time to fill oneself with squashy pumpkin, which is why I suppose ruminants and other grazing animals always seem to be eating—and washed it down with water in preference to the sticky-looking milk which we left to the natives.

"Allan," said Brother John to me in a low voice as we lit our pipes, "that man who stood with his back to us in front of the gridiron was the *Kalubi*. Against the firelight I saw the gap in his hand where I cut away the finger."

"Well, if we want to get any further, you must cultivate him," I answered. "But the question is, shall we get further than—that grid? I believe we have been trapped here to be eaten."

Before Brother John could reply, Komba arrived, and after inquiring whether our appetites had been good, intimated that the *Kalubi* and head men were ready to receive us. So off we went with the exception of Jerry, whom we left to watch our things, taking with us the presents we had prepared.

Komba led us to the feast-house, where the fire in the pit was out, or had been covered over, and the grid and its horrible burden had disappeared. Also now all the mats were rolled up, so that the clear moonlight flowed into and illuminated the place. Seated in a semicircle on wooden stools with their faces towards the gateway were the *Kalubi*, who occupied the centre, and eight councillors, all of them grey-haired men. This *Kalubi* was a tall, thin individual of middle age with, I think, the most nervous countenance that I ever saw. His features twitched continually and his hands were never still. The eyes, too, as far as I could see them in that light, were full of terrors.

He rose and bowed, but the councillors remained seated, greeting us with a long-continued and soft clapping of the hands, which, it seemed, was the Pongo method of salute.

We bowed in answer, then seated ourselves on three stools that had been placed for us, Brother John occupying the middle stool. Mavovo and Hans stood behind us, the latter supporting himself with his large bamboo stick. As soon as these preliminaries were over the *Kalubi* called upon Komba, whom he addressed in formal language as *You-who-have-passed-the-god*, and *You-the-Kalubi-to-be* (I thought I saw him wince as he said these words), to give an account of his mission and of how it came about that they had the honour of seeing the white lords there.

Komba obeyed. After addressing the *Kalubi* with every possible title of honour, such as *Absolute Monarch, Master whose feet I kiss, He whose eyes are fire and whose tongue is a sword, He at whose nod people die, Lord of the Sacrifice, first Taster of the Sacred meat, Beloved of the gods* (here the *Kalubi* shrank as though he had been pricked with a spear), *Second to none on earth save the Motombo the most holy, the most ancient, who comes from heaven and speaks with the voice of heaven*, etc., etc., he gave a clear but brief account of all that had happened in the course of his mission to Beza Town.

Especially did he narrate how, in obedience to a message which he had received from the *Motombo*, he had invited the white lords to Pongo-land, and even accepted them as envoys from the Mazitu when none would respond to King Bausi's invitation to fill that office. Only he had stipulated that they should bring with them none of their magic weapons which vomited out smoke and death, as the *Motombo* had commanded. At this information the expressive countenance of the *Kalubi* once more betrayed mental disturbance that I think Komba noted as much as we did. However, he said nothing, and after a pause, Komba went on to explain that no such weapons had been brought, since, not satisfied with our word that this was so, he and his companions had searched our baggage before we left Mazitu-land.

Therefore, he added, there was no cause to fear that we should bring about the fulfilment of the old prophecy that when a gun was fired among the Pongo the gods would desert the land and the people cease to be a people.

Having finished his speech, he sat down in a humble place behind us. Then the *Kalubi*, after formally accepting us as ambassadors from Bausi, King of the Mazitu, discoursed at length upon the advantages which would result to both peoples from a lasting peace between them. Finally he propounded the articles of such a peace. These, it was clear, had been carefully prepared, but to set them out would be useless, since they never came to anything, and I doubt whether it was intended that they should. Suffice it to say that they provided for intermarriage, free trade between the countries, blood-brotherhood, and other things that I have forgotten, all of which was to be ratified by Bausi taking a daughter of the *Kalubi* to wife, and the *Kalubi* taking a daughter of Bausi.

We listened in silence, and when he had finished, after a pretended consultation between us, I spoke as the Mouth of Brother John, who, I explained, was too grand a person to talk himself, saying that the proposals seemed fair and reasonable, and that we should be happy to submit them to Bausi and his council on our return.

The *Kalubi* expressed great satisfaction at this statement, but remarked incidentally that first of all the whole matter must be laid before the *Motombo* for his opinion, without which no State transaction had legal weight among the Pongo. He added that with our approval he proposed that we should visit his Holiness on the morrow, starting when the sun was three hours old, as he lived at a distance of a day's journey from Rica. After further consultation we replied that although we had little time to spare, as we understood that the *Motombo* was old and could not visit us, we, the white lords, would stretch a point and call on him. Meanwhile we were tired and wished to go to bed. Then we presented our gifts, which were gracefully accepted, with an intimation that return presents would be made to us before we left Pongo-land.

After this the *Kalubi* took a little stick and broke it, to intimate that the conference was at an end, and having bade him and his councillors good night we retired to our huts.

I should add, because it has a bearing on subsequent events, that on this occasion we were escorted, not by Komba, but by two of the councillors. Komba, as I noted for the first time when we rose to say good-bye, was no longer present at the council. When he left it I cannot say, since it will be remembered that his seat was behind us in the shadow, and none of us saw him go.

* * * * * * * *

"What do you make of all that?" I asked the others when the door was shut.

Brother John merely shook his head and said nothing, for in those days he seemed to be living in a kind of dreamland.

Stephen answered. "Bosh! Tommy rot! All my eye and my elbow! Those man-eating Johnnies have some game up their wide sleeves, and whatever it may be, it isn't peace with the Mazitu."

"I agree," I said. "If the real object were peace they would have haggled more, stood out for better terms, or hostages, or something. Also they would have got the consent of this *Motombo* beforehand. Clearly he is the master of the situation, not the *Kalubi*, who is only his tool; if business were meant he should have spoken first, always supposing that he exists and isn't a myth. However, if we live we shall learn, and if we don't, it doesn't matter, though personally I think we should be wise to leave *Motombo* alone and to clear out to Mazitu-land by the first canoe tomorrow morning."

"I intend to visit this *Motombo*," broke in Brother John with decision.

"Ditto, ditto," exclaimed Stephen, "but it's no use arguing that all over again."

"No," I replied with irritation. "It is, as you remark, of no use arguing with lunatics. So let's go to bed, and as it will probably be our last, have a good night's sleep."

"Hear, hear!" said Stephen, taking off his coat and placing it doubled up on the bed to serve as a pillow. "I say," he added, "stand clear a minute while I shake this blanket. It's covered with bits of something," and he suited the action to the word.

"Bits of something?" I said suspiciously. "Why didn't you wait a minute to let me see them. I didn't notice any bits before."

"Rats running about the roof, I expect," said Stephen carelessly.

Not being satisfied, I began to examine this roof and the clay walls, which I forgot to mention were painted over in a kind of pattern with whorls in it, by the feeble light of the primitive lamps. While I was thus engaged there was a knock on the door. Forgetting all about the dust, I opened it and Hans appeared.

"One of these man-eating devils wants to speak to you, Baas. Mavovo keeps him without."

"Let him in," I said, since in this place fearlessness seemed our best game, "but watch well while he is with us."

Hans whispered a word over his shoulder, and next moment a tall man wrapped from head to foot in white cloth, so that he looked like a ghost, came or rather shot into the hut and closed the door behind him.

"Who are you?" I asked.

By way of answer he lifted or unwrapped the cloth from about his face, and I saw that the *Kalubi* himself stood before us.

"I wish to speak alone with the white lord, Dogeetah," he said in a hoarse voice, "and it must be now, since afterwards it will be impossible."

Brother John rose and looked at him.

"How are you, *Kalubi*, my friend?" he asked. "I see that your wound has healed well."

"Yes, yes, but I would speak with you alone."

"Not so," replied Brother John. "If you have anything to say, you must say it to all of us, or leave it unsaid, since these lords and I are one, and that which I hear, they hear."

"Can I trust them?" muttered the *Kalubi*.

"As you can trust me. Therefore speak, or go. Yet, first, can we be overheard in this hut?"

"No, Dogeetah. The walls are thick. There is no one on the roof, for I have looked all round, and if any strove to climb there, we should hear. Also your men who watch the door would see him. None can hear us save perhaps the gods."

"Then we will risk the gods, *Kalubi*. Go on; my brothers know your story."

"My lords," he began, rolling his eyes about him like a hunted creature, "I am in a terrible pass. Once, since I saw you, Dogeetah, I should have visited the White God that dwells in the forest on the mountain yonder, to scatter the sacred seed. But I feigned to be sick, and Komba, the *Kalubi*-to-be, 'who has passed the god,' went in my place and returned unharmed. Now tomorrow, the night of the full moon, as *Kalubi*, I must visit the god again and once more scatter the seed and—Dogeetah, he will kill me whom he has once bitten. He will certainly kill me unless I can kill him. Then Komba will rule as *Kalubi* in my stead, and he will kill you in a way you can guess, by the 'Hot death,' as a sacrifice to the gods, that the women of the Pongo may once more become the mothers of many children. Yes, yes, unless we can kill the god who dwells in the forest, we all must die," and he paused, trembling, while the sweat dropped from him to the floor.

"That's pleasant," said Brother John, "but supposing that we kill the god how would that help us or you to escape from the *Motombo* and these murdering people of yours? Surely they would slay us for the sacrilege."

"Not so, Dogeetah. If the god dies, the *Motombo* dies. It is known from of old, and therefore the *Motombo* watches over the god as a mother over her child. Then, until a new god is found, the Mother of the Holy Flower rules, she who is merciful and will harm none, and I rule under her and will certainly put my enemies to death, especially that wizard Komba."

Here I thought I heard a faint sound in the air like the hiss of a snake, but as it was not repeated and I could see nothing, concluded that I was mistaken.

"Moreover," he went on, "I will load you with gold dust and any gifts you may desire, and set you safe across the water among your friends, the Mazitu."

"Look here," I broke in, "let us understand matters clearly, and, John, do you translate to Stephen. Now, friend *Kalubi*, first of all, who and what is this god you talk of?"

"Lord Macumazana, he is a huge ape white with age, or born white, I know not which. He is twice as big as any man, and stronger than twenty men, whom he can break in his hands, as I break a reed, or whose heads he can bite off in his mouth, as he bit off my finger for a warning. For that is how he treats the *Kalubis* when he wearies of them. First he bites off a finger and lets them go, and next he breaks them like a reed, as also he breaks those who are doomed to sacrifice before the fire."

"Ah!" I said, "a great ape! I thought as much. Well, and how long has this brute been a god among you?"

"I do not know how long. From the beginning. He was always there, as the *Motombo* was always there, for they are one."

"That's a lie any way," I said in English, then went on. "And who is this Mother of the Holy Flower? Is she also always there, and does she live in the same place as the ape god?"

"Not so, lord Macumazana. She dies like other mortals, and is succeeded by one who takes her place. Thus the present Mother is a white woman of your race, now of middle age. When she dies she will be succeeded by her daughter, who also is a white woman and very beautiful. After she dies another who is white will be found, perhaps one who is of black parents but born white."

"How old is this daughter?" interrupted Brother John in a curiously intent voice, "and who is her father?"

"The daughter was born over twenty years ago, Dogeetah, after the Mother of the Flower was captured and brought here. She says that the father was a white man to whom she was married, but who is dead."

Brother John's head dropped upon his chest, and his eyes shut as though he had gone to sleep.

"As for where the Mother lives," went on the *Kalubi*, "it is on the island in the lake at the top of the mountain that is surrounded by water. She has nothing to do with the White God, but those women who serve her go across the lake at times to tend the fields where grows the seed that the *Kalubi* sows, of which the corn is the White God's food."

"Good," I said, "now we understand—not much, but a little. Tell us next what is your plan? How are we to come into the place where this great ape lives? And if we come there, how are we to kill the beast, seeing that your successor, Komba, was careful to prevent us from bringing our firearms to your land?"

"Aye, lord Macumazana, may the teeth of the god meet in his brain for that trick; yes, may he die as I know how to make him die. That prophecy of which he told you is no prophecy from of old. It arose in the land within the last moon only, though whether it came from Komba or from the *Motombo* I know not. None save myself, or at least very few here, had heard of the iron tubes that throw out death, so how should there be a prophecy concerning them?"

"I am sure I don't know, *Kalubi*, but answer the rest of the question."

"As to your coming into the forest—for the White God lives in a forest on the slopes of the mountain, lords—that will be easy since the *Motombo* and the people will believe that I am trapping you there to be a sacrifice, such as they desire for sundry reasons," and he looked at the plump Stephen in a very suggestive way. "As to how you are to kill the god without your tubes of iron, that I do not know. But you are very brave and great magicians. Surely you can find a way."

Here Brother John seemed to wake up again.

"Yes," he said, "we shall find a way. Have no fear of that, O *Kalubi*. We are not afraid of the big ape whom you call a god. Yet it must be at a price. We will not kill this beast and try to save your life, save at a price."

"What price?" asked the *Kalubi* nervously. "There are wives and cattle—no, you do not want the wives, and the cattle cannot be taken across the lake. There are gold dust and ivory. I have already promised these, and there is nothing more that I can give."

"The price is, O *Kalubi*, that you hand over to us to be taken away the white woman who is called Mother of the Holy Flower, with her daughter——"

"And," interrupted Stephen, to whom I had been interpreting, "the Holy Flower itself, all of it dug up by the roots."

When he heard these modest requests the poor *Kalubi* became like one upon the verge of madness.

"Do you understand," he gasped, "do you understand that you are asking for the gods of my country?"

"Quite," replied Brother John with calmness; "for the gods of your country—nothing more nor less."

The *Kalubi* made as though he would fly from the hut, but I caught him by the arm and said:

"See, friend, things are thus. You ask us, at great danger to ourselves, to kill one of the gods of your country, the highest of them, in order to save your life. Well, in payment we ask you to make a present of the remaining gods of your country, and to see us and them safe across the lake. Do you accept or refuse?"

"I refuse," answered the *Kalubi* sullenly. "To accept would mean the last curse upon my spirit; that is too horrible to tell."

"And to refuse means the first curse upon your body; namely, that in a few hours it must be broken and chewed by a great monkey which you call a god. Yes, broken and chewed, and afterwards, I think, cooked and eaten as a sacrifice. Is it not so?"

The *Kalubi* nodded his head and groaned.

"Yet," I went on, "for our part we are glad that you have refused, since now we shall be rid of a troublesome and dangerous business and return in safety to Mazitu land."

"How will you return in safety, O lord Macumazana, you who are doomed to the 'Hot Death' if you escape the fangs of the god?"

"Very easily, O *Kalubi*, by telling Komba, the *Kalubi*-to-be, of your plots against this god of yours, and how we have refused to listen to your wickedness. In fact, I think this may be done at once while you are here with us, O *Kalubi*, where perhaps you do not expect to be found. I will go strike upon the pot without the door; doubtless though it is late, some will hear. Nay, man, stand you still; we have knives and our servants have spears," and I made as though to pass him.

"Lord," he said, "I will give you the Mother of the Holy Flower and her daughter; aye, and the Holy Flower itself dug up by the roots, and I swear that if I can, I will set you and them safe across the lake, only asking that I may come with you, since here I dare not stay. Yet the curse will come too, but if so, it is better to die of a curse in a day to be, than tomorrow at the fangs of the god. Oh! why was I born! Why was I born!" and he began to weep.

"That is a question many have asked and none have been able to answer, O friend *Kalubi*, though mayhap there is an answer somewhere," I replied in a kind voice.

For my heart was stirred with pity of this poor wretch lost in his hell of superstition; this potentate who could not escape from the trappings of a hateful power, save by the door of a death too horrible to contemplate; this priest whose doom it was to be slain by the very hands of his god, as those who went before him had been slain, and as those who came after him would be slain.

"Yet," I went on, "I think you have chosen wisely, and we hold you to your word. While you are faithful to us, we will say nothing. But of this be sure—that if you attempt to betray us, we who are not so helpless as we seem, will betray you, and it shall be you who die, not us. Is it a bargain?"

"It is a bargain, white lord, although blame me not if things go wrong, since the gods know all, and they are devils who delight in human woe and mock at bargains and torment those who would injure them. Yet, come what will, I swear to keep faith with you thus, by the oath that may not be broken," and drawing a knife from his girdle, he thrust out the tip of his tongue and pricked it. From the puncture a drop of blood fell to the floor.

"If I break my oath," he said, "may my flesh grow cold as that blood grows cold, and may it rot as that blood rots! Aye, and may my spirit waste and be lost in the world of ghosts as that blood wastes into the air and is lost in the dust of the world!"

It was a horrible scene and one that impressed me very much, especially as even then there fell upon me a conviction that this unfortunate man was doomed, that a fate which he could not escape was upon him.

We said nothing, and in another moment he had thrown his white wrappings over his face and slipped through the door.

"I am afraid we are playing it rather low down on that jumpy old boy," said Stephen remorsefully.

"The white woman, the white woman and her daughter," muttered Brother John.

"Yes," reflected Stephen aloud. "One is justified in doing anything to get two white women out of this hell, if they exist. So one may as well have the orchid also, for they'd be lonely without it, poor things, wouldn't they? Glad I thought of that, it's soothing to the conscience."

"I hope you'll find it so when we are all on that iron grid which I noticed is wide enough for three," I remarked sarcastically. "Now be quiet, I want to go to sleep."

I am sorry to have to add that for the most of that night Want remained my master. But if I couldn't sleep, I could, or rather was obliged to, think, and I thought very hard indeed.

First I reflected on the Pongo and their gods. What were these and why did they worship them? Soon I gave it up, remembering that the problem was one which applied equally to dozens of the dark religions of this vast African continent, to which none could give an answer, and least of all their votaries. That answer indeed must be sought in the horrible fears of the unenlightened human heart, which sees death and terror and evil around it everywhere and, in this grotesque form or in that, personifies them in gods, or rather in devils who must be propitiated. For always the fetish or the beast, or whatever it may be, is not the real object of worship. It is only the thing or creature which is inhabited by the spirit of the god or devil, the temple, as it were, that furnishes it with a home, which temple is therefore holy. And these spirits are diverse, representing sundry attributes or qualities.

Thus the great ape might be Satan, a prince of evil and blood. The Holy Flower might symbolise fertility and the growth of the food of man from the bosom of the earth. The Mother of the Flower might represent mercy and goodness, for which reason it was necessary that she should be white in colour, and dwell, not in the shadowed forest, but on a soaring mountain, a figure of light, in short, as opposed to darkness. Or she might be a kind of African Ceres, a goddess of the corn and harvest which were symbolised in the beauteous bloom she tended. Who could tell? Not I, either then or afterwards, for I never found out.

As for the Pongo themselves, their case was obvious. They were a dying tribe, the last descendants of some higher race, grown barren from intermarriage. Probably, too, they were at first only cannibals occasionally and from religious reasons. Then in some time of dearth they became very religious in that respect, and the habit overpowered them. Among cannibals, at any rate in Africa, as I knew, this dreadful food is much preferred to any other meat. I had not the slightest doubt that although the *Kalubi* himself had brought us here in the wild hope that we might save him from a terrible death at the hands of the Beelzebub he served, Komba and the councillors, inspired thereto by the prophet called *Motombo*, designed that we should be murdered and eaten as an offering to the gods. How we were to escape this fate, being unarmed, I could not imagine, unless some special protection were vouchsafed to us. Meanwhile, we must go on to the end, whatever it might be.

Brother John, or to give him his right name, the Reverend John Eversley, was convinced that the white woman imprisoned in the mountain was none other than the lost wife for whom he had searched for twenty weary years, and that the second white woman of whom we had heard that night was, strange as it might seem, her daughter and his own. Perhaps he was right and perhaps he was wrong. But even in the latter case, if two white persons were really languishing in this dreadful land, our path was clear. We must go on in faith until we saved them or until we died.

"Our life is granted, not in Pleasure's round, Or even Love's sweet dream, to lapse, content; Duty and Faith are words of solemn sound, And to their echoes must the soul be bent," as some one or other once wrote, very nobly I think. Well, there was but little of "Pleasure's round" about the present entertainment, and any hope of "Love's sweet dream" seemed to be limited to Brother John (here I was quite mistaken, as I so often am). Probably the "echoes" would be my share; indeed, already I seemed to hear their ominous thunder.

At last I did go to sleep and dreamed a very curious dream. It seemed to me that I was disembodied, although I retained all my powers of thought and observation; in fact, dead and yet alive. In this state I hovered over the people of the Pongo who were gathered together on a great plain under an inky sky. They were going about their business as usual, and very unpleasant business it often was. Some of them were worshipping a dim form that I knew was the devil; some were committing murders; some were feasting—at that on which they feasted I would not look; some were labouring or engaged in barter; some were thinking. But I, who had the power of looking into them, saw within the breast of each a tiny likeness of the man or woman or child as it might be, humbly bent upon its knees with hands together in an attitude of prayer, and with imploring, tear-stained face looking upwards to the black heaven.

Then in that heaven there appeared a single star of light, and from this star flowed lines of gentle fire that spread and widened till all the immense arc was one flame of glory. And now from the pulsing heart of the Glory, which somehow reminded me of moving lips, fell countless flakes of snow, each of which followed an appointed path till it lit upon the forehead of one of the tiny, imploring figures hidden within those savage breasts, and made it white and clean.

Then the Glory shrank and faded till there remained of it only the similitude of two transparent hands stretched out as though in blessing—and I woke up wondering how on earth I found the fancy to invent such a vision, and whether it meant anything or nothing.

Afterwards I repeated it to Brother John, who was a very spiritually minded as well as a good man—the two things are often quite different—and asked him to be kind enough to explain. At the time he shook his head, but some days later he said to me:

"I think I have read your riddle, Allan; the answer came to me quite of a sudden. In all those sin-stained hearts there is a seed of good and an aspiration towards the right. For every one of them also there is at last mercy and forgiveness, since how could they learn who never had a teacher? Your dream, Allan, was one of the ultimate redemption of even the most evil of mankind, by gift of the Grace that shall one day glow through the blackness of the night in which they wander."

That is what he said, and I only hope that he was right, since at present there is something very wrong with the world, especially in Africa.

Also we blame the blind savage for many things, but on the balance are we so much better, considering our lights and opportunities? Oh! the truth is that the devil—a very convenient word that—is a good fisherman. He has a large book full of flies of different sizes and colours, and well he knows how to suit them to each particular fish. But white or black, every fish takes one fly or the other, and then comes the question—is the fish that has swallowed the big gaudy lure so much worse or more foolish than that which has fallen to the delicate white moth with the same sharp barb in its tail?

In short, are we not all miserable sinners as the Prayer Book says, and in the eye of any judge who can average up the elemental differences of those waters wherein we were bred and are called upon to swim, is there so much to choose between us? Do we not all need those outstretched Hands of Mercy which I saw in my dream?

But there, there! What right has a poor old hunter to discuss things that are too high for him?

Chapter 15

The Motombo

After my dream I went to sleep again, till I was finally aroused by a strong ray of light hitting me straight in the eye.

Where the dickens does that come from? thought I to myself, for these huts had no windows.

Then I followed the ray to its source, which I perceived was a small hole in the mud wall some five feet above the floor. I rose and examined the said hole, and noted that it appeared to have been freshly made, for the clay at the sides of it was in no way discoloured. I reflected that if anyone wanted to eavesdrop, such an aperture would be convenient, and went outside the hut to pursue my investigations. Its wall, I found, was situated about four feet from the eastern part of the encircling reed fence, which showed no signs of disturbance, although there, in the outer face of the wall, was the hole, and beneath it on the lime flooring lay some broken fragments of plaster. I called Hans and asked him if he had kept watch round the hut when the wrapped-up man visited us during the night. He answered yes, and that he could swear that no one had come near it, since several times he had walked to the back and looked.

Somewhat comforted, though not satisfied, I went in to wake up the others, to whom I said nothing of this matter since it seemed foolish to alarm them for no good purpose. A few minutes later the tall, silent women arrived with our hot water. It seemed curious to have hot water brought to us in such a place by these very queer kind of housemaids, but so it was. The Pongo, I may add, were, like the Zulus, very clean in their persons, though whether they all used hot water, I cannot say. At any rate, it was provided for us.

Half an hour later they returned with breakfast, consisting chiefly of a roasted kid, of which, as it was whole, and therefore unmistakable, we partook thankfully. A little later the Majestic Komba appeared.

After many compliments and inquiries as to our general health, he asked whether we were ready to start on our visit to the *Motombo* who, he added, was expecting us with much eagerness. I inquired how he knew that, since we had only arranged to call on him late on the previous night, and I understood that he lived a day's journey away. But Komba put the matter by with a smile and a wave of his hand.

So in due course off we went, taking with us all our baggage, which now that it had been lightened by the delivery of the presents, was of no great weight.

Five minutes' walk along the wide, main street led us to the northern gate of Rica Town. Here we found the *Kalubi* himself with an escort of thirty men armed with spears; I noted that unlike the Mazitu they had no bows and arrows. He announced in a loud voice that he proposed to do us the special honour of conducting us to the sanctuary of the Holy One, by which we understood him to mean the *Motombo*. When we politely begged him not to trouble, being in an irritable mood, or assuming it, he told us rudely to mind our own business. Indeed, I think this irritability was real enough, which, in the circumstances known to the reader, was not strange. At any rate, an hour or so later it declared itself in an act of great cruelty which showed us how absolute was this man's power in all temporal matters.

Passing through a little clump of bush we came to some gardens surrounded by a light fence through which a number of cattle of a small and delicate breed—they were not unlike Jerseys in appearance—had broken to enjoy themselves by devouring the crops. This garden, it appeared, belonged to the *Kalubi* for the time being, who was furious at the destruction of its produce by the cattle which also belonged to him.

"Where is the herd?" he shouted.

A hunt began—and presently the poor fellow—he was no more than a lad, was discovered asleep behind a bush. When he was dragged before him the *Kalubi* pointed, first to the cattle, then to the broken fence and the devastated garden. The lad began to mutter excuses and pray for mercy.

"Kill him!" said the *Kalubi*, whereon the herd flung himself to the ground, and clutching him by the ankles, began to kiss his feet, crying out that he was afraid to die. The *Kalubi* tried to kick himself free, and failing in this, lifted his big spear and made an end of the poor boy's prayers and life at a single stroke.

The escort clapped their hands in salute or approval, after which four of them, at a sign, took up the body and started with it at a trot for Rica Town, where probably that night it appeared upon the grid. Brother John saw, and his big white beard bristled with indignation like the hair on the back of an angry cat, while Stephen spluttered something beginning with "You brute," and lifted his fist as though to knock the *Kalubi* down. This, had I not caught hold of him, I have no doubt he would have done.

"O *Kalubi*!" gasped Brother John, "do you not know that blood calls for blood? In the hour of your own death remember this death."

"Would you bewitch me, white man?" said the *Kalubi*, glaring at him angrily. "If so——" and once more he lifted the spear, but as John never stirred, held it poised irresolutely. Komba thrust himself between them, crying:

"Back, Dogeetah, who dare to meddle with our customs! Is not the *Kalubi* Lord of life and death?"

Brother John was about to answer, but I called to him in English:

"For Heaven's sake be silent, unless you want to follow the boy. We are in these men's power."

Then he remembered and walked away, and presently we marched forward as though nothing had happened. Only from that moment I do not think that any of us worried ourselves about the *Kalubi* and what might befall him. Still, looking back on the thing, I think that there was this excuse to be made for the man. He was mad with the fear of death and knew not what he did.

All that day we travelled on through a rich, flat country that, as we could tell from various indications, had once been widely cultivated. Now the fields were few and far between, and bush, for the most part a kind of bamboo scrub, was reoccupying the land. About midday we halted by a water-pool to eat and rest, for the sun was hot, and here the four men who had carried off the boy's body rejoined us and made some report. Then we went forward once more towards what seemed to be a curious and precipitous wall of black cliff, beyond which the volcanic-looking mountain towered in stately grandeur. By three o'clock we were near enough to this cliff, which ran east and west as far as the eye could reach, to see a hole in it, apparently where the road terminated, that appeared to be the mouth of a cave.

The *Kalubi* came up to us, and in a shy kind of way tried to make conversation. I think that the sight of this mountain, drawing ever nearer, vividly recalled his terrors and caused him to desire to efface the bad impression he knew he had made on us, to whom he looked for safety. Among other things he told us that the hole we saw was the door of the House of the *Motombo*.

I nodded my head, but did not answer, for the presence of this murderous king made me feel sick. So he went away again, looking at us in a humble and deprecatory manner.

Nothing further happened until we reached the remarkable wall of rock that I have mentioned, which I suppose is composed of some very hard stone that remained when the softer rock in which it lay was disintegrated by millions of years of weather or washings by the water of the lake. Or perhaps its substance was thrown out of the bowels of the volcano when this was active. I am no geologist, and cannot say, especially as I lacked time to examine the place. At any rate there it was, and there in it appeared the mouth of a great cave that I presume was natural, having once formed a kind of drain through which the lake overflowed when Pongo-land was under water.

We halted, staring dubiously at this darksome hole, which no doubt was the same that Babemba had explored in his youth. Then the *Kalubi* gave an order, and some of the soldiers went to huts that were built near the mouth of the cave, where I suppose guardians or attendants lived, though of these we saw nothing. Presently they returned with a number of lighted torches that were distributed among us. This done, we plunged, shivering (at least, I shivered), into the gloomy recesses of that great cavern, the *Kalubi* going before us with half of our escort, and Komba following behind us with the remainder.

The floor of the place was made quite smooth, doubtless by the action of water, as were the walls and roof, so far as we could see them, for it was very wide and lofty. It did not run straight, but curved about in the thickness of the cliff. At the first turn the Pongo soldiers set up a low and eerie chant which they continued during its whole length, that according to my pacings was something over three hundred yards. On we wound, the torches making stars of light in the intense blackness, till at length we rounded a last corner where a great curtain of woven grass, now drawn, was stretched across the cave. Here we saw a very strange sight.

On either side of it, near to the walls, burned a large wood fire that gave light to the place. Also more light flowed into it from its further mouth that was not more than twenty paces from the fires. Beyond the mouth was water which seemed to be about two hundred yards wide, and beyond the water rose the slopes of the mountain that was covered with huge trees. Moreover, a little bay penetrated into the cavern, the point of which bay ended between the two fires. Here the water, which was not more than six or eight feet wide, and shallow, formed the berthing place of a good-sized canoe that lay there. The walls of the cavern, from the turn to the point of the tongue of water, were pierced with four doorways, two on either side, which led, I presume, to chambers hewn in the rock. At each of these doorways stood a tall woman clothed in white, who held in her hand a burning torch. I concluded that these were attendants set there to guide and welcome us, for after we had passed, they vanished into the chambers.

But this was not all. Set across the little bay of water just above the canoe that floated there was a wooden platform, eight feet or so square, on either side of which stood an enormous elephant's tusk, bigger indeed than any I have seen in all my experience, which tusks seemed to be black with age. Between the tusks, squatted upon rugs of some kind of rich fur, was what from its shape and attitude I at first took to be a huge toad. In truth, it had all the appearance of a very bloated toad. There was the rough corrugated skin, there the prominent backbone (for its back was towards us), and there were the thin, splayed-out legs.

We stared at this strange object for quite a long while, unable to make it out in that uncertain light, for so long indeed, that I grew nervous and was about to ask the *Kalubi* what it might be. As my lips opened, however, it stirred, and with a slow, groping, circular movement turned itself towards us very slowly. At length it was round, and as the head came in view all the Pongo from the *Kalubi* down ceased their low, weird chant and flung themselves upon their faces, those who had torches still holding them up in their right hands.

Oh! what a thing appeared! It was not a toad, but a man that moved upon all fours. The large, bald head was sunk deep between the shoulders, either through deformity or from age, for this creature was undoubtedly very old. Looking at it, I wondered how old, but could form no answer in my mind. The great, broad face was sunken and withered, like to leather dried in the sun; the lower lip hung pendulously upon the prominent and bony jaw. Two yellow, tusk-like teeth projected one at each corner of the great mouth; all the rest were gone, and from time to time it licked the white gums with a red-pointed tongue as a snake might do. But the chief wonder of the Thing lay in its eyes that were large and round, perhaps because the flesh had shrunk away from them, which gave them the appearance of being set in the hollow orbits of a skull. These eyes literally shone like fire; indeed, at times they seemed positively to blaze, as I have seen a lion's eyes do in the dark. I confess that the aspect of the creature terrified and for a while paralysed me; to think that it was human was awful.

I glanced at the others and saw that they, too, were frightened. Stephen turned very white. I thought that he was going to be sick again, as he was after he drank the coffee out of the wrong bowl on the day we entered Mazitu-land. Brother John stroked his white beard and muttered some invocation to Heaven to protect him. Hans exclaimed in his abominable Dutch:

"Oh! keek, Baas, da is je lelicher oud deel!" ("Oh! look, Baas, there is the ugly old devil himself!")

Jerry went flat on his face among the Pongo, muttering that he saw Death before him. Only Mavovo stood firm; perhaps because as a witch-doctor of repute he felt that it did not become him to show the white feather in the presence of an evil spirit.

The toad-like creature on the platform swayed its great head slowly as a tortoise does, and contemplated us with its flaming eyes. At length it spoke in a thick, guttural voice, using the tongue that seemed to be common to this part of Africa and indeed to that branch of the Bantu people to which the Zulus belong, but, as I thought, with a foreign accent.

"So *you* are the white men come back," it said slowly. "Let me count!" and lifting one skinny hand from the ground, it pointed with the forefinger and counted. "One. Tall, with a white beard. Yes, that is right. Two. Short, nimble like a monkey, with hair that wants no comb; clever, too, like a father of monkeys. Yes, that is right. Three. Smooth-faced, young and stupid, like a fat baby that laughs at the sky because he is full of milk, and thinks that the sky is laughing at him. Yes, that is right. All three of you are just the same as you used to be. Do you remember, White Beard, how, while we killed you, you said prayers to One Who sits above the world, and held up a cross of bone to which a man was tied who wore a cap of thorns? Do you remember how you kissed the man with the cap of thorns as the spear went into you? You shake your head—oh! you are a clever liar, but I will show you that you are a liar, for I have the thing yet," and snatching up a horn which lay on the *kaross* beneath him, he blew.

As the peculiar, wailing note that the horn made died away, a woman dashed out of one of the doorways that I have described and flung herself on her knees before him. He muttered something to her and she dashed back again to re-appear in an instant holding in her hand a yellow ivory crucifix.

"Here it is, here it is," he said. "Take it, White Beard, and kiss it once more, perhaps for the last time," and he threw the crucifix to Brother John, who caught it and stared at it amazed. "And do you remember, Fat

Baby, how we caught you? You fought well, very well, but we killed you at last, and you were good, very good; we got much strength from you.

"And do you remember, Father of Monkeys, how you escaped from us by your cleverness? I wonder where you went to and how you died. I shall not forget you, for you gave me this," and he pointed to a big white scar upon his shoulder. "You would have killed me, but the stuff in that iron tube of yours burned slowly when you held the fire to it, so that I had time to jump aside and the iron ball did not strike me in the heart as you meant that it should. Yet, it is still here; oh! yes, I carry it with me to this day, and now that I have grown thin I can feel it with my finger."

I listened astonished to this harangue, which if it meant anything, meant that we had all met before, in Africa at some time when men used matchlocks that were fired with a fuse—that is to say, about the year 1700, or earlier. Reflection, however, showed me the interpretation of this nonsense. Obviously this old priest's forefather, or, if one put him at a hundred and twenty years of age, and I am sure that he was not a day less, perhaps his father, as a young man, was mixed up with some of the first Europeans who penetrated to the interior of Africa. Probably these were Portuguese, of whom one may have been a priest and the other two an elderly man and his son, or young brother, or companion. The manner of the deaths of these people and of what happened to them generally would of course be remembered by the descendants of the chief or head medicine-man of the tribe.

"Where did we meet, and when, O *Motombo*?" I asked.

"Not in this land, not in this land, Father of Monkeys," he replied in his low rumbling voice, "but far, far away towards the west where the sun sinks in the water; and not in this day, but long, long ago. Twenty *Kalubis* have ruled the Pongo since that day; some have ruled for many years and some have ruled for a few years—that depends upon the will of my brother, the god yonder," and he chuckled horribly and jerked his thumb backwards over his shoulder towards the forest on the mountain. "Yes, twenty have ruled, some for thirty years and none for less than four."

"Well, you *are* a large old liar," I thought to myself, for, taking the average rule of the *Kalubis* at ten years, this would mean that we met him two centuries ago at least.

"You were clothed otherwise then," he went on, "and two of you wore hats of iron on the head, but that of White Beard was shaven. I caused a picture of you to be beaten by the master-smith upon a plate of copper. I have it yet."

Again he blew upon his horn; again a woman darted out, to whom he whispered; again she went to one of the chambers and returned bearing an object which he cast to us.

We looked at it. It was a copper or bronze plaque, black, apparently with age, which once had been nailed on something for there were the holes. It represented a tall man with a long beard and a tonsured head who held a cross in his hand; and two other men, both short, who wore round metal caps and were dressed in queer-looking garments and boots with square toes. These man carried big and heavy matchlocks, and in the hand of one of them was a smoking fuse. That was all we could make out of the thing.

"Why did you leave the far country and come to this land, O *Motombo*?" I asked.

"Because we were afraid that other white men would follow on your steps and avenge you. The *Kalubi* of that day ordered it, though I said No, who knew that none can escape by flight from what must come when it must come. So we travelled and travelled till we found this place, and here we have dwelt from generation to generation. The gods came with us also; my brother that dwells in the forest came, though we never saw him on the journey, yet he was here before us. The Holy Flower came too, and the white Mother of the Flower—she was the wife of one of you, I know not which."

"Your brother the god?" I said. "If the god is an ape as we have heard, how can he be the brother of a man?"

"Oh! you white men do not understand, but we black people understand. In the beginning the ape killed my brother who was *Kalubi*, and his spirit entered into the ape, making him as a god, and so he kills every other *Kalubi* and their spirits enter also into him. Is it not so, O *Kalubi* of today, you without a finger?" and he laughed mockingly.

The *Kalubi*, who was lying on his stomach, groaned and trembled, but made no other answer.

"So all has come about as I foresaw," went on the toad-like creature. "You have returned, as I knew you would, and now we shall learn whether White Beard yonder spoke true words when he said that his god would be avenged upon our god. You shall go to be avenged on him if you can, and then we shall learn. But this time you have none of your iron tubes which alone we fear. For did not the god declare to us through me that when the white men came back with an iron tube, then he, the god, would die, and I, the *Motombo*, the god's Mouth, would die, and the Holy Flower would be torn up, and the Mother of the Flower would pass away, and the people of the Pongo would be dispersed and become wanderers and slaves? And did he not declare that if the white men came again without their iron tubes, then certain secret things would happen—oh! ask them not, in time they shall be known to you, and the people of the Pongo who were dwindling would again become fruitful and very great? And that is why we welcome you, white men, who arise again from the land of ghosts, because through you we, the Pongo, shall become fruitful and very great."

Of a sudden he ceased his rumbling talk, his head sank back between his shoulders and he sat silent for a long while, his fierce, sparkling eyes playing on us as though he would read our very thoughts. If he succeeded, I hope that mine pleased him. To tell the truth, I was filled with mixed fear, fury and loathing. Although, of course, I did not believe a word of all the rubbish he had been saying, which was akin to much that is evolved by these black-hearted African wizards, I hated the creature whom I felt to be only half-human. My whole nature sickened at his aspect and talk. And yet I was dreadfully afraid of him. I felt as a man might who wakes up to find himself alone with some peculiarly disgusting Christmas-story kind of ghost. Moreover I was quite sure that he meant us ill, fearful and imminent ill. Suddenly he spoke again:

"Who is that little yellow one," he said, "that old one with a face like a skull," and he pointed to Hans, who had kept as much out of sight as possible behind Mavovo, "that wizened, snub-nosed one who might be a child of my brother the god, if ever he had a child? And why, being so small, does he need so large a staff?" Here he pointed again to Hans's big bamboo stick. "I think he is as full of guile as a new-filled gourd with water. The big black one," and he looked at Mavovo, "I do not fear, for his magic is less than my magic," (he seemed to recognise a brother doctor in Mavovo) "but the little yellow one with the big stick and the pack upon his back, I fear him. I think he should be killed."

He paused and we trembled, for if he chose to kill the poor Hottentot, how could we prevent him? But Hans, who saw the great danger, called his cunning to his aid.

"O *Motombo*," he squeaked, "you must not kill me for I am the servant of an ambassador. You know well that all the gods of every land hate and will be revenged upon those who touch ambassadors or their servants, whom they, the gods, alone may harm. If you kill me I shall haunt you. Yes, I shall sit on your shoulder at night and jibber into your ear so that you cannot sleep, until you die. For though you are old you must die at last, *Motombo*."

"It is true," said the *Motombo*. "Did I not tell you that he was full of cunning? All the gods will be avenged upon those who kill ambassadors or their servants. That"—here he laughed again in his dreadful way—"is the rights of the gods alone. Let the gods of the Pongo settle it."

I uttered a sigh of relief, and he went on in a new voice, a dull, business-like voice if I may so describe it:

"Say, O *Kalubi*, on what matter have you brought these white men to speak with me, the Mouth of the god? Did I dream that it was a matter of a treaty with the King of the Mazitu? Rise and speak."

So the *Kalubi* rose and with a humble air set out briefly and clearly the reason of our visit to Pongo-land as the envoys of Bausi and the heads of the treaty that had been arranged subject to the approval of the *Motombo* and Bausi. We noted that the affair did not seem to interest the *Motombo* at all. Indeed, he appeared to go to sleep while the speech was being delivered, perhaps because he was exhausted with the invention of his outrageous falsehoods, or perhaps for other reasons. When it was finished he opened his eyes and pointed to Komba, saying:

"Arise, *Kalubi*-that-is-to-be."

So Komba rose, and in his cold, precise voice narrated his share in the transaction, telling how he had visited Bausi, and all that had happened in connection with the embassy. Again the *Motombo* appeared to go to sleep, only opening his eyes once as Komba described how we had been searched for firearms, whereon he nodded his great head in approval and licked his lips with his thin red tongue. When Komba had done, he said:

"The gods tell me that the plan is wise and good, since without new blood the people of the Pongo will die, but of the end of the matter the god knows alone, if even he can read the future."

He paused, then asked sharply:

"Have you anything more to say, O *Kalubi*-that-is-to-be? Now of a sudden the god puts it into my mouth to ask if you have anything more to say?"

"Something, O *Motombo*. Many moons ago the god bit *off* the finger of our High Lord, the *Kalubi*. The *Kalubi*, having heard that a white man skilled in medicine who could cut off limbs with knives, was in the country of the Mazitu and camped on the borders of the great lake, took a canoe and rowed to where the white man was camped, he with the beard, who is named Dogeetah, and who stands before you. I followed him in another canoe, because I wished to know what he was doing, also to see a white man. I hid my canoe and those who went with me in the reeds far from the *Kalubi's* canoe. I waded through the shallow water and concealed myself in some thick reeds quite near to the white man's linen house. I saw the white man cut off the *Kalubi's* finger and I heard the *Kalubi* pray the white man to come to our country with the iron tubes that smoke, and to kill the god of whom he was afraid."

Now from all the company went up a great gasp, and the *Kalubi* fell down upon his face again, and lay still. Only the *Motombo* seemed to show no surprise, perhaps because he already knew the story.

"Is that all?" he asked.

"No, O Mouth of the god. Last night, after the council of which you have heard, the *Kalubi* wrapped himself up like a corpse and visited the white men in their hut. I thought that he would do so, and had made ready. With a sharp spear I bored a hole in the wall of the hut, working from outside the fence. Then I thrust a reed through from the fence across the passage between the fence and the wall, and through the hole in the hut, and setting my ear to the end of the reed, I listened."

"Oh! clever, clever!" muttered Hans in involuntary admiration, "and to think that I looked and looked too low, beneath the reed. Oh! Hans, though you are old, you have much to learn."

"Among much else I heard this," went on Komba in sentences so clear and cold that they reminded me of the tinkle of falling ice, "which I think is enough, though I can tell you the rest if you wish, O Mouth. I heard," he said, in the midst of a silence that was positively awful, "our lord, the *Kalubi*, whose name is Child of the god, agree with the white men that they should kill the god—how I do not know, for it was not said—and that in return they should receive the persons of the Mother of the Holy Flower and of her daughter, the Mother-that-is-to-be, and should dig up the Holy Flower itself by the roots and take it away across the water, together with the Mother and the Mother-that-is-to-be. That is all, O *Motombo*."

Still in the midst of an intense silence, the *Motombo* glared at the prostrate figure of the *Kalubi*. For a long while he glared. Then the silence was broken, for the wretched *Kalubi* sprang from the floor, seized a spear and tried to kill himself. Before the blade touched him it was snatched from his hand, so that he remained standing, but weaponless.

Again there was silence and again it was broken, this time by the *Motombo*, who rose from his seat before which he stood, a huge, bloated object, and roared aloud in his rage. Yes, he roared like a wounded buffalo. Never would I have believed that such a vast volume of sound could have proceeded from the lungs of a single aged man. For fully a minute his furious bellowings echoed down that great cave, while all the Pongo soldiers, rising from their recumbent position, pointed their hands, in some of which torches still burned, at the miserable *Kalubi* on whom their wrath seemed to be concentrated, rather than on us, and hissed like snakes.

Really it might have been a scene in hell with the *Motombo* playing the part of Satan. Indeed, his swollen, diabolical figure supported on the thin, toad-like legs, the great fires burning on either side, the lurid lights of evening reflected from the still water beyond and glowering among the tree tops of the mountain, the white-robed forms of the tall Pongo, bending, every one of them, towards the wretched culprit and hissing like so many fierce serpents, all suggested some uttermost deep in the infernal regions as one might conceive them in a nightmare.

It went on for some time, I don't know how long, till at length the *Motombo* picked up his fantastically shaped horn and blew. Thereon the women darted from the various doorways, but seeing that they were not wanted, checked themselves in their stride and remained standing so, in the very attitude of runners about to start upon a race. As the blast of the horn died away the turmoil was suddenly succeeded by an utter stillness, broken only by the crackling of the fires whose flames, of all the living things in that place, alone seemed heedless of the tragedy which was being played.

"All up now, old fellow!" whispered Stephen to me in a shaky voice.

"Yes," I answered, "all up high as heaven, where I hope we are going. Now back to back, and let's make the best fight we can. We've got the spears."

While we were closing in the *Motombo* began to speak.

"So you plotted to kill the god, *Kalubi*-who-*was*," he screamed, "with these white ones whom you would pay with the Holy Flower and her who guards it. Good! You shall go, all of you, and talk with the god. And I, watching here, will learn who dies—you or the god. Away with them!"

Chapter 16
The Gods

With a roar the Pongo soldiers leapt on us. I think that Mavovo managed to get his spear up and kill a man, for I saw one of them fall backwards and lie still. But they were too quick for the rest of us. In half a minute we were seized, the spears were wrenched from our hands and we were thrown headlong into the canoe, all six of us, or rather seven including the *Kalubi.* A number of the soldiers, including Komba, who acted as steersman, also sprang into the canoe that was instantly pushed out from beneath the bridge or platform on which the *Motombo* sat and down the little creek into the still water of the canal or estuary, or whatever it may be, that separates the wall of rock which the cave pierces from the base of the mountain.

As we floated out of the mouth of the cave the toad-like *Motombo*, who had wheeled round upon his stool, shouted an order to Komba.

"O *Kalubi*," he said, "set the *Kalubi-who-was* and the three white men and their three servants on the borders of the forest that is named House-of-the-god and leave them there. Then return and depart, for here I would watch alone. When all is finished I will summon you."

Komba bowed his handsome head and at a sign two of the men got out paddles, for more were not needed, and with slow and gentle strokes rowed us across the water. The first thing I noted about this water at the time was that its blackness was inky, owing, I suppose, to its depth and the shadows of the towering cliff on one side and of the tall trees on the other. Also I observed—for in this emergency, or perhaps because of it, I managed to keep my wits about me—that its banks on either side were the home of great numbers of crocodiles which lay there like logs. I saw, further, that a little lower down where the water seemed to narrow, jagged boughs projected from its surface as though great trees had fallen, or been thrown into it. I recalled in a numb sort of way that old Babemba had told us that when he was a boy he had escaped in a canoe down this estuary, and reflected that it would not be possible for him to do so now because of those snags. Unless, indeed, he had floated over them in a time of great flood.

A couple of minutes or so of paddling brought us to the further shore which, as I think I have said, was only about two hundred yards from the mouth of the cave. The bow of the canoe grated on the bank, disturbing a huge crocodile that vanished into the depths with an angry plunge.

"Land, white lords, land," said Komba with the utmost politeness, "and go, visit the god who doubtless is waiting for you. And now, as we shall meet no more—farewell. You are wise and I am foolish, yet hearken to my counsel. If ever you should return to the Earth again, be advised by me. Cling to your own god if you have one, and do not meddle with those of other peoples. Again farewell."

The advice was excellent, but at that moment I felt a hate for Komba which was really superhuman. To me even the *Motombo* seemed an angel of light as compared with him. If wishes could have killed, our farewell would indeed have been complete.

Then, admonished by the spear points of the Pongo, we landed in the slimy mud. Brother John went first with a smile upon his handsome countenance that I thought idiotic under the circumstances, though doubtless he knew best when he ought to smile, and the wretched *Kalubi* came last. Indeed, so great was his shrinking from that ominous shore, that I believe he was ultimately propelled from the boat by his successor in power, Komba. Once he had trodden it, however, a spark of spirit returned to him, for he wheeled round and said to Komba,

"Remember, O *Kalubi*, that my fate today will be yours also in a day to come. The god wearies of his priests. This year, next year, or the year after; he always wearies of his priests."

"Then, O *Kalubi*-that-was," answered Komba in a mocking voice as the canoe was pushed off, "pray to the god for me, that it may be the year after; pray it as your bones break in his embrace."

While we watched that craft depart there came into my mind the memory of a picture in an old Latin book of my father's, which represented the souls of the dead being paddled by a person named Charon across a river called the Styx. The scene before us bore a great resemblance to that picture. There was Charon's boat floating on the dreadful Styx. Yonder glowed the lights of the world, here was the gloomy, unknown shore. And we, we were the souls of the dead awaiting the last destruction at the teeth and claws of some unknown monster, such as that which haunts the recesses of the Egyptian hell. Oh! the parallel was painfully exact. And yet, what do you think was the remark of that irrepressible young man Stephen?

"Here we are at last, Allan, my boy," he said, "and after all without any trouble on our own part. I call it downright providential. Oh! isn't it jolly! *Hip, hip, hooray!*"

Yes, he danced about in that filthy mud, threw up his cap and cheered!

I withered, or rather tried to wither him with a look, muttering the single word: "Lunatic."

Providential! Jolly! Well, it's fortunate that some people's madness takes a cheerful turn. Then I asked the *Kalubi* where the god was.

"Everywhere," he replied, waving his trembling hand at the illimitable forest. "Perhaps behind this tree, perhaps behind that, perhaps a long way off. Before morning we shall know."

"What are you going to do?" I inquired savagely.

"Die," he answered.

"Look here, fool," I exclaimed, shaking him, "you can die if you like, but we don't mean to. Take us to some place where we shall be safe from this god."

"One is never safe from the god, lord, especially in his own House," and he shook his silly head and went on, "How can we be safe when there is nowhere to go and even the trees are too big to climb?"

I looked at them, it was true. They were huge and ran up for fifty or sixty feet without a bough. Moreover, it was probable that the god climbed better than we could. The *Kalubi* began to move inland in an indeterminate fashion, and I asked him where he was going.

"To the burying-place," he answered. "There are spears yonder with the bones."

I pricked up my ears at this—for when one has nothing but some clasp knives, spears are not to be despised—and ordered him to lead on. In another minute we were walking uphill through the awful wood where the gloom at this hour of approaching night was that of an English fog.

Three or four hundred paces brought us to a kind of clearing, where I suppose some of the monster trees had fallen down in past years and never been allowed to grow up again. Here, placed upon the ground, were a number of boxes made of imperishable ironwood, and on the top of each box sat, or rather lay, a mouldering and broken skull.

"*Kalubi*-that-were!" murmured our guide in explanation. "Look, Komba has made my box ready," and he pointed to a new case with the lid off.

"How thoughtful of him!" I said. "But show us the spears before it gets quite dark." He went to one of the newer coffins and intimated that we should lift off the lid as he was afraid to do so.

I shoved it aside. There within lay the bones, each of them separate and wrapped up in something, except of course the skull. With these were some pots filled apparently with gold dust, and alongside of the pots two good spears that, being made of copper, had not rusted much. We went on to other coffins and extracted from them more of these weapons that were laid there for the dead man to use upon his journey through the Shades, until we had enough. The shafts of most of them were somewhat rotten from the damp, but luckily they were furnished with copper sockets from two and a half to three feet long, into which the wood of the shaft fitted, so that they were still serviceable.

"Poor things these to fight a devil with," I said.

"Yes, Baas," said Hans in a cheerful voice, "very poor. It is lucky that I have got a better."

I stared at him; we all stared at him.

"What do you mean, Spotted Snake?" asked Mavovo.

"What do you mean, child of a hundred idiots? Is this a time to jest? Is not one joker enough among us?" I asked, and looked at Stephen.

"Mean, Baas? Don't you know that I have the little rifle with me, that which is called *Intombi*, that with which you shot the vultures at Dingaan's *kraal*? I never told you because I was sure you knew; also because if you didn't know it was better that you should not know, for if *you* had known, those Pongo *skellums* (that is, vicious ones) might have come to know also. And if *they* had known——"

"Mad!" interrupted Brother John, tapping his forehead, "quite mad, poor fellow! Well, in these depressing circumstances it is not wonderful."

I inspected Hans again, for I agreed with John. Yet he did not look mad, only rather more cunning than usual.

"Hans," I said, "tell us where this rifle is, or I will knock you down and Mavovo shall flog you."

"Where, Baas! Why, cannot you see it when it is before your eyes?"

"You are right, John," I said, "he's off it"; but Stephen sprang at Hans and began to shake him.

"Leave go, Baas," he said, "or you may hurt the rifle."

Stephen obeyed in sheer astonishment. Then, oh! then Hans did something to the end of his great bamboo stick, turned it gently upside down and out of it slid the barrel of a rifle neatly tied round with greased cloth and stoppered at the muzzle with a piece of tow!

I could have kissed him. Yes, such was my joy that I could have kissed that hideous, smelly old Hottentot.

"The stock?" I panted. "The barrel isn't any use without the stock, Hans."

"Oh! Baas," he answered, grinning, "do you think that I have shot with you all these years without knowing that a rifle must have a stock to hold it by?"

Then he slipped off the bundle from his back, undid the lashings of the blanket, revealing the great yellow head of tobacco that had excited my own and Komba's interest on the shores of the lake. This head he tore apart and produced the stock of the rifle nicely cleaned, a cap set ready on the nipple, on to which the hammer was let down, with a little piece of wad between to prevent the cap from being fired by any sudden jar.

"Hans," I exclaimed, "Hans, you are a hero and worth your weight in gold!"

"Yes, Baas, though you never told me so before. Oh! I made up my mind that I wouldn't go to sleep in the face of the Old Man (death). Oh! which of you ought to sleep now upon that bed that Bausi sent me?" he asked as he put the gun together. "*You*, I think, you great stupid Mavovo. *You* never brought a gun. If you were a wizard worth the name you would have sent the rifles on and had them ready to meet us here. Oh! will you laugh at me any more, you thick-head of a Zulu?"

"No," answered Mavovo candidly. "I will give you *sibonga*. Yes, I will make for you titles of praise, O clever Spotted Snake."

"And yet," went on Hans, "I am not all a hero; I am worth but half my weight in gold. For, Baas, although I have plenty of powder and bullets in my pocket, I lost the caps out of a hole in my waistcoat. You remember, Baas, I told you it was charms I lost. But three remain; no, four, for there is one on the nipple. There, Baas, there is *Intombi* all ready and loaded. And now when the white devil comes you can shoot him in the eye, as you how to do up to a hundred yards, and send him to the other devils down in hell. Oh! won't your holy father the Predikant be glad to see him there."

Then with a self-satisfied smirk he half-cocked the rifle and handed it to me ready for action.

"I thank God!" said Brother John solemnly, "who has taught this poor Hottentot how to save us."

"No, Baas John, God never taught me, I taught myself. But, see, it grows dark. Had we not better light a fire," and forgetting the rifle he began to look about for wood.

"Hans," called Stephen after him, "if ever we get out of this, I will give you £500, or at least my father will, which is the same thing."

"Thank you, Baas, thank you, though just now I'd rather have a drop of brandy and—I don't see any wood."

He was right. Outside of the graveyard clearing lay, it is true, some huge fallen boughs. But these were too big for us to move or cut. Moreover, they were so soaked with damp, like everything in this forest, that it would be impossible to fire them.

The darkness closed in. It was not absolute blackness, because presently the moon rose, but the sky was rainy and obscured it; moreover, the huge trees all about seemed to suck up whatever light there was. We crouched ourselves upon the ground back to back as near as possible to the centre of the place, unrolled such blankets as we had to protect us from the damp and cold, and ate some biltong or dried game flesh and parched corn, of which fortunately the boy Jerry carried a bagful that had remained upon his shoulders when he was thrown into the canoe. Luckily I had thought of bringing this food with us; also a flask of spirits.

Then it was that the first thing happened. Far away in the forest resounded a most awful roar, followed by a drumming noise, such a roar as none of us had ever heard before, for it was quite unlike that of a lion or any other beast.

"What is that?" I asked.

"The god," groaned the *Kalubi*, "the god praying to the moon with which he always rises."

I said nothing, for I was reflecting that four shots, which was all we had, was not many, and that nothing should tempt me to waste one of them. Oh! why had Hans put on that rotten old waistcoat instead of the new one I gave him in Durban?

Since we heard no more roars Brother John began to question the *Kalubi* as to where the Mother of the Flower lived.

"Lord," answered the man in a distracted way, "there, towards the East. You walk for a quarter of the sun's journey up the hill, following a path that is marked by notches cut upon the trees, till beyond the garden of the god at the top of the mountain more water is found surrounding an island. There on the banks of the water a canoe is hidden in the bushes, by which the water may be crossed to the island, where dwells the Mother of the Holy Flower."

Brother John did not seem to be quite satisfied with the information, and remarked that he, the *Kalubi*, would be able to show us the road on the morrow.

"I do not think that I shall ever show you the road," groaned the shivering wretch.

At that moment the god roared again much nearer. Now the *Kalubi's* nerve gave out altogether, and quickened by some presentiment, he began to question Brother John, whom he had learned was a priest of an unknown sort, as to the possibility of another life after death.

Brother John, who, be it remembered, was a very earnest missionary by calling, proceeded to administer some compressed religious consolations, when, quite near to us, the god began to beat upon some kind of very large and deep drum. He didn't roar this time, he only worked away at a massed-band military drum. At least that is what it sounded like, and very unpleasant it was to hear in that awful forest with skulls arranged on boxes all round us, I can assure you, my reader.

The drumming ceased, and pulling himself together, Brother John continued his pious demonstrations. Also just at that time a thick rain-cloud quite obscured the moon, so that the darkness grew dense. I heard John explaining to the *Kalubi* that he was not really a *Kalubi*, but an immortal soul (I wonder whether he understood him). Then I became aware of a horrible shadow—I cannot describe it in any other way—that was blacker than the blackness, which advanced towards us at extraordinary speed from the edge of the clearing.

Next second there was a kind of scuffle a few feet from me, followed by a stifled yell, and I saw the shadow retreating in the direction from which it had come.

"What's the matter?" I asked.

"Strike a match," answered Brother John; "I think something has happened."

I struck a match, which burnt up very well, for the air was quite still. In the light of it I saw first the anxious faces of our party—how ghastly they looked!—and next the *Kalubi* who had risen and was waving his right arm in the air, a right arm that was bloody and *lacked the hand.*

"The god has visited me and taken away my hand!" he moaned in a wailing voice.

I don't think anybody spoke; the thing was beyond words, but we tried to bind the poor fellow's arm up by the light of matches. Then we sat down again and watched.

The darkness grew still denser as the thick of the cloud passed over the moon, and for a while the silence, that utter silence of the tropical forest at night, was broken only by the sound of our breathing, the buzz of a few mosquitoes, the distant splash of a plunging crocodile and the stifled groans of the mutilated man.

Again I saw, or thought I saw—this may have been half an hour later—that black shadow dart towards us, as a pike darts at a fish in a pond. There was another scuffle, just to my left—Hans sat between me and the *Kalubi*—followed by a single prolonged wail.

"The king-man has gone," whispered Hans. "I felt him go as though a wind had blown him away. Where he was there is nothing but a hole."

Of a sudden the moon shone out from behind the clouds. In its sickly light about half-way between us and the edge of the clearing, say thirty yards off, I saw—oh! what did I see! The devil destroying a lost soul. At least, that is what it looked like. A huge, grey-black creature, grotesquely human in its shape, had the thin *Kalubi* in its grip. The *Kalubi's* head had vanished in its maw and its vast black arms seemed to be employed in breaking him to pieces.

Apparently he was already dead, though his feet, that were lifted off the ground, still moved feebly.

I sprang up and covered the beast with the rifle which was cocked, getting full on to its head which showed the clearest, though this was rather guesswork, since I could not see distinctly the fore-sight. I pulled, but either the cap or the powder had got a little damp on the journey and hung fire for the fraction of a second. In that infinitesimal time the devil—it is the best name I can give the thing—saw me, or perhaps it only saw the light gleaming on the barrel. At any rate it dropped the *Kalubi*, and as though some intelligence warned it what to expect, threw up its massive right arm—I remember how extraordinarily long the limb seemed and that it looked thick as a man's thigh—in such a fashion as to cover its head.

Then the rifle exploded and I heard the bullet strike. By the light of the flash I saw the great arm tumble down in a dead, helpless kind of way, and next instant the whole forest began to echo with peal upon peal of those awful roarings that I have described, each of which ended with a dog-like *yowp* of pain.

"You have hit him, Baas," said Hans, "and he isn't a ghost, for he doesn't like it. But he's still very lively."

"Close up," I answered, "and hold out the spears while I reload."

My fear was that the brute would rush on us. But it did not. For all that dreadful night we saw or heard it no more. Indeed, I began to hope that after all the bullet had reached some mortal part and that the great ape was dead.

At length, it seemed to be weeks afterwards, the dawn broke and revealed us sitting white and shivering in the grey mist; that is, all except Stephen, who had gone comfortably to sleep with his head resting on Mavovo's shoulder. He is a man so equably minded and so devoid of nerves, that I feel sure he will be one of the last to be disturbed by the trump of the archangel. At least, so I told him indignantly when at length we roused him from his indecent slumbers.

"You should judge things by results, Allan," he said with a yawn. "I'm as fresh as a pippin while you all look as though you had been to a ball with twelve extras. Have you retrieved the *Kalubi* yet?"

Shortly afterwards, when the mist lifted a little, we went out in a line to "retrieve the *Kalubi*," and found—well, I won't describe what we found. He was a cruel wretch, as the incident of the herd-boy had told us, but I felt sorry for him. Still, his terrors were over, or at least I hope so.

We deposited him in the box that Komba had kindly provided in preparation for this inevitable event, and Brother John said a prayer over his miscellaneous remains. Then, after consultation and in the very worst of spirits, we set out to seek the way to the home of the Mother of the Flower. The start was easy enough, for a distinct, though very faint path led from the clearing up the slope of the hill. Afterwards it became more difficult for the denser forest began. Fortunately very few creepers grew in this forest, but the flat tops of the huge trees meeting high above entirely shut out the sky, so that the gloom was great, in places almost that of night.

Oh! it was a melancholy journey as, filled with fears, we stole, a pallid throng, from trunk to trunk, searching them for the notches that indicated our road, and speaking only in whispers, lest the sound of our voices should attract the notice of the dreadful god. After a mile or two of this we became aware that its notice was attracted despite our precautions, for at times we caught glimpses of some huge grey thing slipping along parallel to us between the boles of the trees. Hans wanted me to try a shot, but I would not, knowing that the chances of hitting it were small indeed. With only three charges, or rather three caps left, it was necessary to be saving.

We halted and held a consultation, as a result of which we decided that there was no more danger in going on than in standing still or attempting to return. So we went on, keeping close together. To me, as I was the only one with a rifle, was accorded what I did not at all appreciate, the honour of heading the procession.

Another half-mile and again we heard that strange rolling sound which was produced, I believe, by the great brute beating upon its breast, but noted that it was not so continuous as on the previous night.

"Ha!" said Hans, "he can only strike his drum with one stick now. Your bullet broke the other, Baas."

A little farther and the god roared quite close, so loudly that the air seemed to tremble.

"The drum is all right, whatever may have happened to the sticks," I said.

A hundred yards or so more and the catastrophe occurred. We had reached a spot in the forest where one of the great trees had fallen down, letting in a little light. I can see it to this hour. There lay the enormous tree, its bark covered with grey mosses and clumps of a giant species of maidenhair fern. On our side of it was the open space which may have measured forty feet across, where the light fell in a perpendicular ray, as it does through the smoke-hole of a hut. Looking at this prostrate trunk, I saw first two lurid and fiery eyes that glowed red in the shadow; and then, almost in the same instant, made out what looked like the head of a fiend enclosed in a wreath of the delicate green ferns. I can't describe it, I can only repeat that it looked like the head of a very large fiend with a pallid face, huge overhanging eyebrows and great yellow *tushes* on either side of the mouth.

Before I had even time to get the rifle up, with one terrific roar the brute was on us. I saw its enormous grey shape on the top of the trunk, I saw it pass me like a flash, running upright as a man does, but with the head held forward, and noted that the arm nearest to me was swinging as though broken. Then as I turned I heard a scream of terror and perceived that it had gripped the poor Mazitu, Jerry, who walked last but one of our line which was ended by Mavovo. Yes, it had gripped him and was carrying him off, clasped to its breast with its sound arm. When I say that Jerry, although a full-grown man and rather inclined to stoutness, looked like a child in that fell embrace, it will give some idea of the creature's size.

Mavovo, who had the courage of a buffalo, charged at it and drove the copper spear he carried into its side. They all charged like berserkers, except myself, for even then, thank Heaven! I knew a trick worth two of that. In three seconds there was a struggling mass in the centre of the clearing. Brother John, Stephen, Mavovo and Hans were all stabbing at the enormous gorilla, for it was a gorilla, although their blows seemed to do it no more harm than pinpricks. Fortunately for them, for its part, the beast would not let go of Jerry, and having only one sound arm, could but snap at its assailants, for if it had lifted a foot to rend them, its top-heavy bulk would have caused it to tumble over.

At length it seemed to realise this, and hurled Jerry away, knocking down Brother John and Hans with his body. Then it leapt on Mavovo, who, seeing it come, placed the copper socket of the spear against his own breast, with the result that when the gorilla tried to crush him, the point of the spear was driven into its carcase. Feeling the pain, it unwound its arm from about Mavovo, knocking Stephen over with the backward sweep. Then it raised its great hand to crush Mavovo with a blow, as I believe gorillas are wont to do.

This was the chance for which I was waiting. Up till that moment I had not dared to fire, fearing lest I should kill one of my companions. Now for an instant it was clear of them all, and steadying myself, I aimed at the huge head and let drive. The smoke thinned, and through it I saw the gigantic ape standing quite still, like a creature lost in meditation.

Then it threw up its sound arm, turned its fierce eyes to the sky, and uttering one pitiful and hideous howl, sank down dead. The bullet had entered just behind the ear and buried itself in the brain.

The great silence of the forest flowed in over us, as it were; for quite a while no one did or said anything. Then from somewhere down amidst the mosses I heard a thin voice, the sound of which reminded me of air being squeezed out of an India-rubber cushion.

"Very good shot, Baas," it piped up, "as good as that which killed the king-vulture at Dingaan's *kraal*, and more difficult. But if the Baas could pull the god off me I should say—Thank you."

The "thank you" was almost inaudible, and no wonder, for poor Hans had fainted. There he lay under the huge bulk of the gorilla, just his nose and mouth appearing between the brute's body and its arm. Had it not been for the soft cushion of wet moss in which he reclined, I think that he would have been crushed flat.

We rolled the creature off him somehow and poured a little brandy down his throat, which had a wonderful effect, for in less than a minute he sat up, grasping like a dying fish, and asked for more.

Leaving Brother John to examine Hans to see if he was really injured, I bethought me of poor Jerry and went to look at him. One glance was enough. He was quite dead. Indeed, he seemed to be crushed out of shape like a buck that has been enveloped in the coils of a boa-constrictor. Brother John told me afterwards that both his arms and nearly all his ribs had been broken in that terrible embrace. Even his spine was dislocated.

I have often wondered why the gorilla ran down the line without touching me or the others, to vent his rage upon Jerry. I can only suggest that it was because the unlucky Mazitu had sat next to the *Kalubi* on the previous night, which may have caused the brute to identify him by smell with the priest whom he had learned to hate and killed.

It is true that Hans had sat on the other side of the *Kalubi*, but perhaps the odour of the Pongo had not clung to him so much, or perhaps it meant to deal with him after it had done with Jerry.

When we knew that the Mazitu was past human help and had discovered to our joy that, save for a few bruises, no one else was really hurt, although Stephen's clothes were half-torn off him, we made an examination of the dead god. Truly it was a fearful creature.

What its exact weight or size may have been we had no means of ascertaining, but I never saw or heard of such an enormous ape, if a gorilla is really an ape. It needed the united strength of the five of us to lift the carcase with a great effort off the fainting Hans and even to roll it from side to side when subsequently we removed the skin. I would never have believed that so ancient an animal of its stature, which could not have been more than seven feet when it stood erect, could have been so heavy. For ancient undoubtedly it was. The long, yellow, canine tusks were worn half-away with use; the eyes were sunken far into the skull; the hair of the head, which I am told is generally red or brown, was quite white, and even the bare breast, which should be black, was grey in hue. Of course, it was impossible to say, but one might easily have imagined that this creature was two hundred years or more old, as the *Motombo* had declared it to be.

Stephen suggested that it should be skinned, and although I saw little prospect of our being able to carry away the hide, I assented and helped in the operation on the mere chance of saving so great a curiosity. Also, although Brother John was restless and murmured something about wasting time, I thought it necessary that we should have a rest after our fearful anxieties and still more fearful encounter with this consecrated monster. So we set to work, and as a result of more than an hour's toil, dragged off the hide, which was so tough and thick that, as we found, the copper spears had scarcely penetrated to the flesh. The bullet that I had put into it on the previous night struck, we discovered, upon the bone of the upper arm, which it shattered sufficiently to render that limb useless, if it did not break it altogether. This, indeed, was fortunate for us, for had the creature retained both its arms uninjured, it would certainly have killed more of us in its attack. We were saved only by the fact that when it was hugging Jerry it had no limb left with which it could strike, and luckily did not succeed in its attempts to get hold with its tremendous jaws that had nipped off the *Kalubi's* hand as easily as a pair of scissors severs the stalk of a flower.

When the skin was removed, except that of the hands, which we did not attempt to touch, we pegged it out, raw side uppermost, to dry in the centre of the open place where the sun struck. Then, having buried poor Jerry in the hollow trunk of the great fallen tree, we washed ourselves with the wet mosses and ate some of the food that remained to us.

After this we started forward again in much better spirits. Jerry, it was true, was dead, but so was the god, leaving us happily still alive and practically untouched. Never more would the *Kalubis* of Pongo-land shiver out their lives at the feet of this dreadful divinity who soon or late must become their executioner, for I believe, with the exception of two who committed suicide through fear, that no *Kalubi* was ever known to have died except by the hand—or teeth—of the god.

What would I not give to know that brute's history? Could it possibly, as the *Motombo* said, have accompanied the Pongo people from their home in Western or Central Africa, or perhaps have been brought here by them in a state of captivity? I am unable to answer the question, but it should be noted that none of the Mazitu or other natives had ever heard of the existence of more true gorillas in this part of Africa. The creature, if it had its origin in the locality, must either have been solitary in its habits or driven away from its fellows, as sometimes happens to old elephants, which then, like this gorilla, become fearfully ferocious.

That is all I can say about the brute, though of course the Pongo had their own story. According to them it was an evil spirit in the shape of an ape, which evil spirit had once inhabited the body of an early *Kalubi*, and had been annexed by the ape when it killed the said *Kalubi*. Also they declared that the reason the creature put all the *Kalubis* to death, as well as a number of other people who were offered up to it, was that it needed "to refresh itself with the spirits of men," by which means it was enabled to avoid the effects of age. It will be remembered that the *Motombo* referred to this belief, of which afterwards I heard in more detail from Babemba. But if this god had anything supernatural about it, at least its magic was no shield against a bullet from a Purdey rifle.

Only a little way from the fallen tree we came suddenly upon a large clearing, which we guessed at once must be that "Garden of the god" where twice a year the unfortunate *Kalubis* were doomed to scatter the "sacred seed." It was a large garden, several acres of it, lying on a shelf, as it were, of the mountain and watered by a stream. Maize grew in it, also other sorts of corn, while all round was a thick belt of plantain trees. Of course these crops had formed the food of the god who, whenever it was hungry, came to this place and helped itself, as we could see by many signs. The garden was well kept and comparatively free from weeds. At first we wondered how this could be, till I remembered that the *Kalubi*, or someone, had told me that it was tended by the servants of the Mother of the Flower, who were generally albinos or mutes.

We crossed it and pushed on rapidly up the mountain, once more following an easy and well-beaten path, for now we saw that we were approaching what we thought must be the edge of a crater. Indeed, our excitement was so extreme that we did not speak, only scrambled forward, Brother John, notwithstanding his lame leg, leading at a greater pace than we could equal. He was the first to reach our goal, closely followed by Stephen. Watching, I saw him sink down as though in a swoon. Stephen also appeared astonished, for he threw up his hands.

I rushed to them, and this was what I saw. Beneath us was a steep slope quite bare of forest, which ceased at its crest. This slope stretched downwards for half a mile or more to the lip of a beautiful lake, of which the area was perhaps two hundred acres. Set in the centre of the deep blue water of this lake, which we discovered afterwards to be unfathomable, was an island not more than five and twenty or thirty acres in extent, that seemed to be cultivated, for on it we could see fields, palms and other fruit-bearing trees. In the middle of the island stood a small, near house thatched after the fashion of the country, but civilized in its appearance, for it was oblong, not round, and encircled by a veranda and a reed fence. At a distance from this house were a number of native huts, and in front of it a small enclosure surrounded by a high wall, on the top of which mats were fixed on poles as though to screen something from wind or sun.

"The Holy Flower lives there, you bet," gasped Stephen excitedly—he could think of nothing but that confounded orchid. "Look, the mats are up on the sunny side to prevent its scorching, and those palms arc planted round to give it shade."

"The Mother of the Flower lives there," whispered Brother John, pointing to the house. "Who is she? Who is she? Suppose I should be mistaken after all. God, let me not be mistaken, for it would be more than I can bear."

"We had better try to find out," I remarked practically, though I am sure I sympathised with his suspense, and started down the slope at a run.

In five minutes or less we reached the foot of it, and, breathless and perspiring though we were, began to search amongst the reeds and bushes growing at the edge of the lake for the canoe of which we had been told by the *Kalubi*. What if there were none? How could we cross that wide stretch of deep water? Presently Hans, who, following certain indications which caught his practised eye, had cast away to the left, held up his hand and whistled. We ran to him.

"Here it is, Baas," he said, and pointed to something in a tiny bush-fringed inlet, that at first sight looked like a heap of dead reeds. We tore away at the reeds, and there, sure enough, was a canoe of sufficient size to hold twelve or fourteen people, and in it a number of paddles.

Another two minutes and we were rowing across that lake.

We came safely to the other side, where we found a little landing-stage made of poles sunk into the lake. We tied up the canoe, or rather I did, for nobody else remembered to take that precaution, and presently were on a path which led through the cultivated fields to the house. Here I insisted upon going first with the rifle, in case we should be suddenly attacked. The silence and the absence of any human beings suggested to me that this might very well happen, since it would be strange if we had not been seen crossing the lake.

Afterwards I discovered why the place seemed so deserted. It was owing to two reasons. First, it was now noontime, an hour at which these poor slaves retired to their huts to eat and sleep through the heat of the day. Secondly, although the Watcher, as she was called, had seen the canoe on the water, she concluded that the *Kalubi* was visiting the Mother of the Flower and, according to practice on these occasions, withdrew herself and everybody else, since the rare meetings of the *Kalubi* and the Mother of the Flower partook of the nature of a religious ceremony and must be held in private.

First we came to the little enclosure that was planted about with palms and, as I have described, screened with mats. Stephen ran at it and, scrambling up the wall, peeped over the top.

Next instant he was sitting on the ground, having descended from the wall with the rapidity of one shot through the head.

"Oh! by Jingo!" he ejaculated, "oh! by Jingo!" and that was all I could get out of him, though it is true I did not try very hard at the time.

Not five paces from this enclosure stood a tall reed fence that surrounded the house. It had a gate also of reeds, which was a little ajar. Creeping up to it very cautiously, for I thought I heard a voice within, I peeped through the half-opened gate. Four or five feet away was the veranda from which a doorway led into one of the rooms of the house where stood a table on which was food.

Kneeling on mats upon this veranda were—*two white women*—

clothed in garments of the purest white adorned with a purple fringe, and wearing bracelets and other ornaments of red native gold. One of these appeared to be about forty years of age. She was rather stout, fair in colouring, with blue eyes and golden hair that hung down her back. The other might have been about twenty. She also was fair, but her eyes were grey and her long hair was of a chestnut hue. I saw at once that she was tall and very beautiful. The elder woman was praying, while the other, who knelt by her side, listened and looked up vacantly at the sky.

"O God," prayed the woman, "for Christ's sake look in pity upon us two poor captives, and if it be possible, send us deliverance from this savage land. We thank Thee Who hast protected us unharmed and in health for so many years, and we put our trust in Thy mercy, for Thou alone canst help us. Grant, O God, that our dear husband and father may still live, and that in Thy good time we may be reunited to him. Or if he be dead and there is no hope for us upon the earth, grant that we, too, may die and find him in Thy Heaven."

Thus she prayed in a clear, deliberate voice, and I noticed that as she did so the tears ran down her cheeks. "Amen," she said at last, and the girl by her side, speaking with a strange little accent, echoed the "Amen."

I looked round at Brother John. He had heard something and was utterly overcome. Fortunately enough he could not move or even speak.

"Hold him," I whispered to Stephen and Mavovo, "while I go in and talk to these ladies."

Then, handing the rifle to Hans, I took off my hat, pushed the gate a little wider open, slipped through it and called attention to my presence by coughing.

The two women, who had risen from their knees, stared at me as though they saw a ghost.

"Ladies," I said, bowing, "pray do not be alarmed. You see God Almighty sometimes answers prayers. In short, I am one of—a party—of white people who, with some trouble, have succeeded in getting to this place and—and—would you allow us to call on you?"

Still they stared. At length the elder woman opened her lips.

"Here I am called the Mother of the Holy Flower, and for a stranger to speak with the Mother is death. Also if you are a man, how did you reach us alive?"

"That's a long story," I answered cheerfully. "May we come in? We will take the risks, we are accustomed to them and hope to be able to do you a service. I should explain that three of us are white men, two English and one—American."

"American!" she gasped, "American! What is he like, and how is he named?"

"Oh!" I replied, for my nerve was giving out and I grew confused, "he is oldish, with a white beard, rather like Father Christmas in short, and his Christian name (I didn't dare to give it all at once) is—er—John, Brother John, we call him. Now I think of it," I added, "he has some resemblance to your companion there."

I thought that the lady was going to die, and cursed myself for my awkwardness. She flung her arm about the girl to save herself from falling—a poor prop, for she, too, looked as though she were going to die, having understood some, if not all, of my talk. It must be remembered that this poor young thing had never even seen a white man before.

"Madam, madam," I expostulated, "I pray you to bear up. After living through so much sorrow it would be foolish to decease of—joy. May I call in Brother John? He is a clergyman and might be able to say something appropriate, which I, who am only a hunter, cannot do."

She gathered herself together, opened her eyes and whispered:

"Send him here."

I pushed open the gate behind which the others were clustered. Catching Brother John, who by now had recovered somewhat, by the arm, I dragged him forward. The two stood staring at each other, and the young lady also looked with wide eyes and open mouth.

"Elizabeth!" said John.

She uttered a faint scream, then with a cry of *"Husband!"* flung herself upon his breast.

I slipped through the gate and shut it fast.

* * * * * * * *

"I say, Allan," said Stephen, when we had retreated to a little distance, "did you see her?"

"Her? Who? Which?" I asked.

"The young lady in the white clothes. She is lovely."

"Hold your tongue, you donkey!" I answered. "Is this a time to talk of female looks?"

Then I went away behind the wall and literally wept for joy. It was one of the happiest moments of my life, for how seldom things happen as they should!

Also I wanted to put up a little prayer of my own, a prayer of thankfulness and for strength and wit to overcome the many dangers that yet awaited us.

Chapter 17

The Home of the Holy Flower

Half an hour or so passed, during which I was engaged alternately in thinking over our position and in listening to Stephen's rhapsodies. First he dilated on the loveliness of the Holy Flower that he had caught a glimpse of when he climbed the wall, and secondly, on the beauty of the eyes of the young lady in white. Only by telling him that he might offend her did I persuade him not to attempt to break into the sacred enclosure where the orchid grew. As we were discussing the point, the gate opened and she appeared.

"Sirs," she said, with a reverential bow, speaking slowly and in the drollest halting English, "the mother and the father—yes, the father—ask, will you feed?"

We intimated that we would "feed" with much pleasure, and she led the way to the house, saying:

"Be not astonished at them, for they are very happy too, and please forgive our unleavened bread."

Then in the politest way possible she took me by the hand, and followed by Stephen, we entered the house, leaving Mavovo and Hans to watch outside.

It consisted of but two rooms, one for living and one for sleeping. In the former we found Brother John and his wife seated on a kind of couch gazing at each other in a rapt way. I noted that they both looked as though they had been crying—with happiness, I suppose.

"Elizabeth," said John as we entered, "this is Mr. Allan Quatermain, through whose resource and courage we have come together again, and this young gentleman is his companion, Mr. Stephen Somers."

She bowed, for she seemed unable to speak, and held out her hand, which we shook.

"What be 'resource and courage'?" I heard her daughter whisper to Stephen, "and why have you none, O Stephen Somers?"

"It would take a long time to explain," he said with his jolly laugh, after which I listened to no more of their nonsense.

Then we sat down to the meal, which consisted of vegetables and a large bowl of hard-boiled ducks' eggs, of which eatables an ample supply was carried out to Hans and Mavovo by Stephen and Hope. This, it seemed, was the name that her mother had given to the girl when she was born in the hour of her black despair.

It was an extraordinary story that Mrs. Eversley had to tell, and yet a short one.

She *had* escaped from Hassan-ben-Mohammed and the slave-traders, as the rescued slave told her husband at Zanzibar before he died, and, after days of wandering, been captured by some of the Pongo who were scouring the country upon dark business of their own, probably in search of captives. They brought her across the lake to Pongo-land and, the former Mother of the Flower, an albino, having died at a great age, installed her in the office on this island, which from that day she had never left. Hither she was led by the *Kalubi* of the time and some others who had "passed the god." This brute, however, she had never seen, although once she heard him roar, for it did not molest them or even appear upon their journey.

Shortly after her arrival on the island her daughter was born, on which occasion some of the women "servants of the Flower" nursed her. From that moment both she and the child were treated with the utmost care and veneration, since the Mother of the Flower and the Flower itself being in some strange way looked upon as embodiments of the natural forces of fertility, this birth was held to be the best of omens for the dwindling Pongo race. Also it was hoped that in due course the "Child of the Flower" would succeed the Mother in her office. So here they dwelt absolutely helpless and alone, occupying themselves with superintending the agriculture of the island. Most fortunately also when she was captured, Mrs. Eversley had a small *Bible* in her possession which she had never lost. From this she was able to teach her child to read and all that is to be learned in the pages of Holy Writ.

Often I have thought that if I were doomed to solitary confinement for life and allowed but one book, I would choose the *Bible*, since, in addition to all its history and the splendour of its language, it contains the record of the hope of man, and therefore should be sufficient for him. So at least it had proved to be in this case.

Oddly enough, as she told us, like her husband, Mrs. Eversley during all those endless years had never lost some kind of belief that she would one day be saved otherwise than by death.

"I always thought that you still lived and that we should meet again, John," I heard her say to him.

Also her own and her daughter's spirits were mysteriously supported, for after the first shock and disturbance of our arrival we found them cheerful people; indeed, Miss Hope was quite a merry soul. But then she had never known any other life, and human nature is very adaptable. Further, if I may say so, she had grown up a lady in the true sense of the word. After all, why should she not, seeing that her mother, the *Bible* and Nature had been her only associates and sources of information, if we except the poor slaves who waited on them, most of whom were mutes.

When Mrs. Eversley's story was done, we told ours, in a compressed form. It was strange to see the wonder with which these two ladies listened to its outlines, but on that I need not dwell. When it was finished I heard Miss Hope say:

"So it would seem, O Stephen Somers, that it is you who are saviour to us."

"Certainly," answered Stephen, "but why?"

"Because you see the dry Holy Flower far away in England, and you say, 'I must be Holy Father to that Flower.' Then you pay down shekels (here her *Bible* reading came in) for the cost of journey and hire brave hunter to kill devil-god and bring my old white-head parent with you. Oh yes, you are saviour," and she nodded her head at him very prettily.

"Of course," replied Stephen with enthusiasm; "that is, not exactly, but it is all the same thing, as I will explain later. But, Miss Hope, meanwhile could you show us the Flower?"

"Oh! Holy Mother must do that. If you look without her, you die."

"Really!" said Stephen, without alluding to his little feat of wall climbing.

Well, the end of it was that after a good deal of hesitation, the Holy Mother obliged, saying that as the god was dead she supposed nothing else mattered. First, however, she went to the back of the house and clapped her hands, whereon an old woman, a mute and a very perfect specimen of an albino native, appeared and stared at us wonderingly. To her Mrs. Eversley talked upon her fingers, so rapidly that I could scarcely follow her movements. The woman bowed till her forehead nearly touched the ground, then rose and ran towards the water.

"I have sent her to fetch the paddles from the canoe," said Mrs. Eversley, "and to put my mark upon it. Now none will dare to use it to cross the lake."

"That is very wise," I replied, "as we don't want news of our whereabouts to get to the *Motombo*."

Next we went to the enclosure, where Mrs. Eversley with a native knife cut a string of palm fibres that was sealed with clay on to the door and one of its uprights in such a fashion that none could enter without breaking the string. The impression was made with a rude seal that she wore round her neck as a badge of office. It was a very curious object fashioned of gold and having deeply cut upon its face a rough image of an ape holding a flower in its right paw. As it was also ancient, this seemed to show that the monkey god and the orchid had been from the beginning jointly worshipped by the Pongo.

When she had opened the door, there appeared, growing in the centre of the enclosure, the most lovely plant, I should imagine, that man ever saw. It measured some eight feet across, and the leaves were dark green, long and narrow. From its various crowns rose the scapes of bloom. And oh! those blooms, of which there were about twelve, expanded now in the flowering season. The measurements made from the dried specimen I have given already, so I need not repeat them. I may say here, however, that the Pongo augured the fertility or otherwise of each succeeding year from the number of the blooms on the Holy Flower. If these were many the season would prove very fruitful; if few, less so; while if, as sometimes happened, the plant failed to flower, draught and famine were always said to follow. Truly those were glorious blossoms, standing as high as a man, with their back sheaths of vivid white barred with black, their great pouches of burnished gold and their wide wings also of gold. Then in the centre of each pouch appeared the ink-mark that did indeed exactly resemble the head of a monkey. But if this orchid astonished me, its effect upon Stephen, with whom this class of flower was a mania, may be imagined. Really he went almost mad. For a long while he glared at the plant, and finally flung himself upon his knees, causing Miss Hope to exclaim:

"What, O Stephen Somers! do you also make sacrifice to the Holy Flower?"

"Rather," he answered; "I'd—I'd—die for it!"

"You are likely to before all is done," I remarked with energy, for I hate to see a grown man make a fool of himself. There's only one thing in the world which justifies *that*, and it isn't a flower.

Mavovo and Hans had followed us into the enclosure, and I overheard a conversation between them which amused me. The gist of it was that Hans explained to Mavovo that the white people admired this weed—he called it a weed—because it was like gold, which was the god they really worshipped, although that god was known among them by many names. Mavovo, who was not at all interested in the affair, replied with a shrug that it might be so, though for his part he believed the true reason to be that the plant produced some medicine which gave courage or strength. Zulus, I may say, do not care for flowers unless they bear a fruit that is good to eat.

When I had satisfied myself with the splendour of these magnificent blooms, I asked Mrs. Eversley what certain little mounds might be that were dotted about the enclosure, beyond the circle of cultivated peaty soil which surrounded the orchid's roots.

"They are the graves of the Mothers of the Holy Flower," she answered. "There are twelve of them, and here is the spot chosen for the thirteenth, which was to have been mine."

To change the subject I asked another question, namely: If there were more such orchids growing in the country?

"No," she replied, "or at least I never heard of any. Indeed, I have always been told that this one was brought from far away generations ago. Also, under an ancient law, it is never allowed to increase. Any shoots it sends up beyond this ring must be cut off by me and destroyed with certain ceremonies. You see that seed-pod which has been left to grow on the stalk of one of last year's blooms. It is now ripe, and on the night of the next new moon, when the *Kalubi* comes to visit me, I must with much ritual burn it in his presence, unless it has burst before he arrives, in which case I must burn any seedlings that may spring up with almost the same ritual."

"I don't think the *Kalubi* will come any more; at least, not while you are here. Indeed, I am sure of it," I said.

As we were leaving the place, acting on my general principle of making sure of anything of value when I get the chance, I broke off that ripe seed-pod, which was of the size of an orange. No one was looking at the time, and as it went straight into my pocket, no one missed it.

Then, leaving Stephen and the young lady to admire this *Cypripedium*—or each other—in the enclosure, we three elders returned to the house to discuss matters.

"John and Mrs. Eversley," I said, "by Heaven's mercy you are reunited after a terrible separation of over twenty years. But what is to be done now? The god, it is true, is dead, and therefore the passage of the forest will be easy. But beyond it is the water which we have no means of crossing and beyond the water that old wizard, the *Motombo*, sits in the mouth of his cave watching like a spider in its web. And beyond the *Motombo* and his cave are Komba, the new *Kalubi* and his tribe of cannibals——"

"Cannibals!" interrupted Mrs. Eversley, "I never knew that they were cannibals. Indeed, I know little about the Pongo, whom I scarcely ever see."

"Then, madam, you must take my word for it that they are; also, as I believe, that they have every expectation of eating *us*. Now, as I presume that you do not wish to spend the rest of your lives, which would probably be short, upon this island, I want to ask how you propose to escape safely out of the Pongo country?"

They shook their heads, which were evidently empty of ideas. Only John stroked his white beard, and inquired mildly:

"What have you arranged, Allan? My dear wife and I are quite willing to leave the matter to you, who are so resourceful."

"Arranged!" I stuttered. "Really, John, under any other circumstances——" Then after a moment's reflection I called to Hans and Mavovo, who came and squatted down upon the veranda.

"Now," I said, after I had put the case to them, "what have *you* arranged?" Being devoid of any feasible suggestions, I wished to pass on that intolerable responsibility.

"My father makes a mock of us," said Mavovo solemnly. "Can a rat in a pit arrange how it is to get out with the dog that is waiting at the top? So far we have come in safety, as the rat does into the pit. Now I see nothing but death."

"That's cheerful," I said. "Your turn, Hans."

"Oh! Baas," replied the Hottentot, "for a while I grew clever again when I thought of putting the gun *Intombi* into the bamboo. But now my head is like a rotten egg, and when I try to shake wisdom out of it my brain melts and washes from side to side like the stuff in the rotten egg. Yet, yet, I have a thought—let us ask the Missie. Her brain is young and not tired, it may hit on something: to ask the Baas Stephen is no good, for already he is lost in other things," and Hans grinned feebly.

More to give myself time than for any other reason I called to Miss Hope, who had just emerged from the sacred enclosure with Stephen, and put the riddle to her, speaking very slowly and clearly, so that she might understand me. To my surprise she answered at once.

"What is a god, O Mr. Allen? Is it not more than man? Can a god be bound in a pit for a thousand years, like Satan in *Bible*? If a god want to move, see new country and so on, who can say no?"

"I don't quite understand," I said, to draw her out further, although, in fact, I had more than a glimmering of what she meant.

"O Allan, Holy Flower there a god, and my mother priestess. If

Holy Flower tired of this land, and want to grow somewhere else, why priestess not carry it and go too?"

"Capital idea," I said, "but you see, Miss Hope, there are, or were, two gods, one of which cannot travel."

"Oh! that very easy, too. Put skin of god of the woods on to this man," and she pointed to Hans, "and who know difference? They like as two brothers already, only he smaller."

"She's got it! By Jingo, she's got it!" exclaimed Stephen in admiration.

"What Missie say?" asked Hans, suspiciously.

I told him.

"Oh! Baas," exclaimed Hans, "think of the smell inside of that god's skin when the sun shines on it. Also the god was a very big god, and I am small."

Then he turned and made a proposal to Mavovo, explaining that his stature was much better suited to the job.

"First will I die," answered the great Zulu. "Am I, who have high blood in my veins and who am a warrior, to defile myself by wrapping the skin of a dead brute about me and appear as an ape before men? Propose it to me again, Spotted Snake, and we shall quarrel."

"See here, Hans," I said. "Mavovo is right. He is a soldier and very strong in battle. You also are very strong in your wits, and by doing this you will make fools of all the Pongo. Also, Hans, it is better that you should wear the skin of a gorilla for a few hours than that I, your master, and all these should be killed."

"Yes, Baas, it is true, Baas; though for myself I almost think that, like Mavovo, I would rather die. Yet it would be sweet to deceive those Pongo once again, and, Baas, I won't see you killed just to save myself another bad smell or two. So, if you wish it, I will become a god."

Thus through the self-sacrifice of that good fellow, Hans, who is the real hero of this history, that matter was settled, if anything could be looked on as settled in our circumstances. Then we arranged that we would start upon our desperate adventure at dawn on the following morning.

Meanwhile, much remained to be done. First, Mrs. Eversley summoned her attendants, who, to the number of twelve, soon appeared in front of the veranda. It was very sad to see these poor women, all of whom were albinos and unpleasant to look on, while quite half appeared to be deaf and dumb. To these, speaking as a priestess, she explained that the god who dwelt in the woods was dead, and that therefore she must take the Holy Flower, which was called Wife of the God, and make report to the *Motombo* of this dreadful catastrophe. Meanwhile, they must remain on the island and continue to cultivate the fields.

This order threw the poor creatures, who were evidently much attached to their mistress and her daughter, into a great state of consternation. The eldest of them all, a tall, thin old lady with white wool and pink eyes who looked, as Stephen said, like an Angora rabbit, prostrated herself and kissing the Mother's foot, asked when she would return, since she and the "Daughter of the Flower" were all they had to love, and without them they would die of grief.

Suppressing her evident emotion as best she could, the Mother replied that she did not know; it depended on the will of Heaven and the *Motombo*. Then to prevent further argument she bade them bring their picks with which they worked the land; also poles, mats, and palm-string, and help to dig up the Holy Flower. This was done under the superintendence of Stephen, who here was thoroughly in his element, although the job proved far from easy. Also it was sad, for all these women wept as they worked, while some of them who were not dumb, wailed aloud.

Even Miss Hope cried, and I could see that her mother was affected with a kind of awe. For twenty years she had been guardian of this plant, which I think she had at last not unnaturally come to look upon with some of the same veneration that was felt for it by the whole Pongo people.

"I fear," she said, "lest this sacrilege should bring misfortune upon us."

But Brother John, who held very definite views upon African superstitions, quoted the second commandment to her, and she became silent.

We got the thing up at last, or most of it, with a sufficiency of earth to keep it alive, injuring the roots as little as possible in the process. Underneath it, at a depth of about three feet, we found several things. One of these was an ancient stone fetish that was rudely shaped to the likeness of a monkey and wore a gold crown. This object, which was small, I still have. Another was a bed of charcoal, and amongst the charcoal were some partially burnt bones, including a skull that was very little injured. This may have belonged to a woman of a low type, perhaps the first Mother of the Flower, but its general appearance reminded me of that of a gorilla. I regret that there was neither time nor light to enable me to make a proper examination of these remains, which we found it impossible to bring away.

Mrs. Eversley told me afterwards, however, that the *Kalubis* had a tradition that the god once possessed a wife which died before the Pongo migrated to their present home. If so, these may have been the bones of that wife. When it was finally clear of the ground on which it had grown for so many generations, the great plant was lifted on to a large mat, and after it had been packed with wet moss by Stephen in a most skilful way, for he was a perfect artist at this kind of work, the mat was bound round the roots in such a fashion that none of the contents could escape. Also each flower *scape* was lashed to a thin bamboo so as to prevent it from breaking on the journey. Then the whole bundle was lifted on to a kind of bamboo stretcher that we made and firmly secured to it with palm-fibre ropes.

By this time it was growing dark and all of us were tired.

"Baas," said Hans to me, as we were returning to the house, "would it not be well that Mavovo and I should take some food and go sleep in the canoe? These women will not hurt us there, but if we do not, I, who have been watching them, fear lest in the night they should make paddles of sticks and row across the lake to warn the Pongo."

Although I did not like separating our small party, I thought the idea so good that I consented to it, and presently Hans and Mavovo, armed with spears and carrying an ample supply of food, departed to the lake side. One more incident has impressed itself upon my memory in connection with that night. It was the formal baptism of Hope by her father. I never saw a more touching ceremony, but it is one that I need not describe.

Stephen and I slept in the enclosure by the packed flower, which he would not leave out of his sight. It was as well that we did so, since about twelve o'clock by the light of the moon I saw the door in the wall open gently and the heads of some of the albino women appear through the aperture. Doubtless, they had come to steal away the holy plant they worshipped. I sat up, coughed, and lifted the rifle, whereon they fled and returned no more.

Long before dawn Brother John, his wife and daughter were up and making preparations for the march, packing a supply of food and so forth. Indeed, we breakfasted by moonlight, and at the first break of day, after Brother John had first offered up a prayer for protection, departed on our journey.

It was a strange out-setting, and I noted that both Mrs. Eversley and her daughter seemed sad at bidding good-bye to the spot where they had dwelt in utter solitude and peace for so many years; where one of them, indeed, had been born and grown up to womanhood. However, I kept on talking to distract their thoughts, and at last we were off.

I arranged that, although it was heavy for them, the two ladies, whose white robes were covered with curious cloaks made of soft prepared bark, should carry the plant as far as the canoe, thinking it was better that the Holy Flower should appear to depart in charge of its consecrated guardians. I went ahead with the rifle, then came the stretcher and the flower, while Brother John and Stephen, carrying the paddles, brought up the rear. We reached the canoe without accident, and to our great relief found Mavovo and Hans awaiting us. I learned, however, that it was fortunate they had slept in the boat, since during the night the albino women arrived with the evident object of possessing themselves of it, and only ran away when they saw that it was guarded. As we were making ready the canoe those unhappy slaves appeared in a body and throwing themselves upon their faces with piteous words, or those of them who could not speak, by signs, implored the Mother not to desert them, till both she and Hope began to cry. But there was no help for it, so we pushed off as quickly as we could, leaving the albinos weeping and wailing upon the bank.

I confess that I, too, felt compunction at abandoning them thus, but what could we do? I only trust that no harm came to them, but of course we never heard anything as to their fate.

On the further side of the lake we hid away the canoe in the bushes where we had found it, and began our march. Stephen and Mavovo, being the two strongest among us, now carried the plant, and although Stephen never murmured at its weight, how the Zulu did swear after the first few hours! I could fill a page with his objurgations at what he considered an act of insanity, and if I had space, should like to do so, for really some of them were most amusing. Had it not been for his friendship for Stephen I think that he would have thrown it down.

We crossed the Garden of the god, where Mrs. Eversley told me the *Kalubi* must scatter the sacred seed twice a year, thus confirming the story that we had heard. It seems that it was then, as he made his long journey through the forest, that the treacherous and horrid brute which we had killed, would attack the priest of whom it had grown weary. But, and this shows the animal's cunning, the onslaught always took place *after* he had sown the seed which would in due season produce the food it ate. Our *Kalubi*, it is true, was killed before we had reached the Garden, which seems an exception to the rule. Perhaps, however, the gorilla knew that his object in visiting it was not to provide for its needs. Or perhaps our presence excited it to immediate action.

Who can analyse the motives of a gorilla?

These attacks were generally spread over a year and a half. On the first occasion the god which always accompanied the priest to the garden and back again, would show animosity by roaring at him. On the second he would seize his hand and bite off one of the fingers, as happened to our *Kalubi*, a wound that generally caused death from blood poisoning. If, however, the priest survived, on the third visit it killed him, for the most part by crushing his head in its mighty jaws. When making these visits the *Kalubi* was accompanied by certain dedicated youths, some of whom the god always put to death. Those who had made the journey six times without molestation were selected for further special trials, until at last only two remained who were declared to have "passed" or "been accepted by" the god. These youths were treated with great honour, as in the instance of Komba and on the destruction of the *Kalubi*, one of them took his office, which he generally filled without much accident, for a minimum of ten years, and perhaps much longer.

Mrs. Eversley knew nothing of the sacramental eating of the remains of the *Kalubi*, or of the final burial of his bones in the wooden coffins that we had seen, for such things, although they undoubtedly happened, were kept from her. She added, that each of the three *Kalubis* whom she had known, ultimately went almost mad through terror at his approaching end, especially after the preliminary roarings and the biting off of the finger. In truth uneasy lay the head that wore a crown in Pongo-land, a crown that, mind you, might not be refused upon pain of death by torture. Personally, I can imagine nothing more terrible than the haunted existence of these poor kings whose pomp and power must terminate in such a fashion.

I asked her whether the *Motombo* ever visited the god. She answered, Yes, once in every five years. Then after many mystic ceremonies he spent a week in the forest at a time of full moon. One of the *Kalubis* had told her that on this occasion he had seen the *Motombo* and the god sitting together under a tree, each with his arm round the other's neck and apparently talking "like brothers." With the exception of certain tales of its almost supernatural cunning, this was all that I could learn about the god of the Pongos which I have sometimes been tempted to believe was really a devil hid in the body of a huge and ancient ape.

No, there was one more thing which I quote because it bears out Babemba's story. It seems that captives from other tribes were sometimes turned into the forest that the god might amuse itself by killing them. This, indeed, was the fate to which we ourselves had been doomed in accordance with the hateful Pongo custom.

Certainly, thought I to myself when she had done, I did a good deed in sending that monster to whatever dim region it was destined to inhabit, where I sincerely trust it found all the dead *Kalubis* and its other victims ready to give it an appropriate welcome.

****

After crossing the god's garden, we came to the clearing of the Fallen Tree, and found the brute's skin pegged out as we had left it, though shrunken in size. Only it had evidently been visited by a horde of the forest ants which, fortunately for Hans, had eaten away every particle of flesh, while leaving the hide itself absolutely untouched, I suppose because it was too tough for them. I never saw a neater job. Moreover, these industrious little creatures had devoured the beast itself. Nothing remained of it except the clean, white bones lying in the exact position in which we had left the carcase. Atom by atom that marching myriad army had eaten all and departed on its way into the depths of the forest, leaving this sign of their passage.

How I wished that we could carry off the huge skeleton to add to my collection of trophies, but this was impossible. As Brother John said, any museum would have been glad to purchase it for hundreds of pounds, for I do not suppose that its like exists in the world. But it was too heavy; all I could do was to impress its peculiarities upon my mind by a close study of the mighty bones. Also I picked out of the upper right arm, and kept the bullet I had fired when it carried off the *Kalubi*. This I found had sunk into and shattered the bone, but without absolutely breaking it.

On we went again bearing with us the god's skin, having first stuffed the head, hands and feet (these, I mean the hands and feet, had been cleaned out by the ants) with wet moss in order to preserve their shape. It was no light burden, at least so declared Brother John and Hans, who bore it between them upon a dead bough from the fallen tree.

Of the rest of our journey to the water's edge there is nothing to tell, except that notwithstanding our loads, we found it easier to walk down that steep mountain side than it had been to ascend the same. Still our progress was but slow, and when at length we reached the burying-place only about an hour remained to sunset. There we sat down to rest and eat, also to discuss the situation.

What was to be done? The arm of stagnant water lay near to us, but we had no boat with which to cross to the further shore. And what was that shore? A cave where a creature who seemed to be but half-human, sat watching like a spider in its web. Do not let it be supposed that this question of escape had been absent from our minds. On the contrary, we had even thought of trying to drag the canoe in which we crossed to and from the island of the Flower through the forest. The idea was abandoned, however, because we found that being hollowed from a single log with a bottom four or five inches thick, it was impossible for us to carry it so much as fifty yards. What then could we do without a boat? Swimming seemed to be out of the question because of the crocodiles. Also on inquiry I discovered that of the whole party Stephen and I alone could swim. Further there was no wood of which to make a raft.

I called to Hans and leaving the rest in the graveyard where we knew that they were safe, we went down to the edge of the water to study the situation, being careful to keep ourselves hidden behind the reeds and bushes of the mangrove tribe with which it was fringed. Not that there was much fear of our being seen, for the day, which had been very hot, was closing in and a great storm, heralded by black and bellying clouds, was gathering fast, conditions which must render us practically invisible at a distance.

We looked at the dark, slimy water—also at the crocodiles which sat upon its edge in dozens waiting, eternally waiting, for what, I wondered. We looked at the sheer opposing cliff, but save where a black hole marked the cave mouth, far as the eye could see, the water came up against it, as that of a moat does against the wall of a castle. Obviously, therefore, the only line of escape ran through this cave, for, as I have explained, the channel by which I presume Babemba reached the open lake, was now impracticable. Lastly, we searched to see if there was any fallen log upon which we could possibly propel ourselves to the other side, and found—nothing that could be made to serve, no, nor, as I have said, any dry reeds or brushwood out of which we might fashion a raft.

"Unless we can get a boat, here we must stay," I remarked to Hans, who was seated with me behind a screen of rushes at the water's edge.

He made no answer, and as I thought, in a sort of subconscious way, I engaged myself in watching a certain tragedy of the insect world. Between two stout reeds a forest spider of the very largest sort had spun a web as big as a lady's open parasol. There in the midst of this web of which the bottom strands almost touched the water, sat the spider waiting for its prey, as the crocodiles were waiting on the banks, as the great ape had waited for the *Kalubis*, as Death waits for Life, as the *Motombo* was waiting for God knows what.

It rather resembled the *Motombo* in his cave, did that huge, black spider with just a little patch of white upon its head, or so I thought fancifully enough. Then came the tragedy. A great, white moth of the Hawk species began to dart to and fro between the reeds, and presently struck the web on its lower side some three inches above the water. Like a flash that spider was upon it. It embraced the victim with its long legs to still its tremendous battlings. Next, descending below, it began to make the body fast, when something happened. From the still surface of the water beneath poked up the mouth of a very large fish which quite quietly closed upon the spider and sank again into the depths, taking with it a portion of the web and thereby setting the big moth free. With a struggle it loosed itself, fell on to a piece of wood and floated away, apparently little the worse for the encounter.

"Did you see that, Baas?" said Hans, pointing to the broken and empty web. "While you were thinking, I was praying to your reverend father the Predikant, who taught me how to do it, and he has sent us a sign from the Place of Fire."

Even then I could not help laughing to myself as I pictured what my dear father's face would be like if he were able to hear his convert's remarks. An analysis of Hans's religious views would be really interesting, and I only regret that I never made one. But sticking to business I merely asked:

"What sign?"

"Baas, this sign: That web is the *Motombo's* cave. The big spider is the *Motombo*. The white moth is us, Baas, who are caught in the web and going to be eaten."

"Very pretty, Hans," I said, "but what is the fish that came up and swallowed the spider so that the moth fell on the wood and floated away?"

"Baas, *you* are the fish, who come up softly, softly out of the water in the dark, and shoot the *Motombo* with the little rifle, and then the rest of us, who are the moth, fall into the canoe and float away. There is a storm about to break, Baas, and who will see you swim the stream in the storm and the night?"

"The crocodiles," I suggested.

"Baas, I didn't see a crocodile eat the fish. I think the fish is laughing down there with the fat spider in its stomach. Also when there is a storm crocodiles go to bed because they are afraid lest the lightning should kill them for their sins."

Now I remembered that I had often heard, and indeed to some extent noted, that these great reptiles do vanish in disturbed weather, probably because their food hides away. However that might be, in an instant I made up my mind.

As soon as it was quite dark I would swim the water, holding the little rifle, *Intombi*, above my head, and try to steal the canoe. If the old wizard was watching, which I hoped might not be the case, well, I must deal with him as best I could. I knew the desperate nature of the expedient, but there was no other way. If we could not get a boat we must remain in that foodless forest until we starved. Or if we returned to the island of the Flower, there ere long we should certainly be attacked and destroyed by Komba and the Pongos when they came to look for our bodies.

"I'll try it, Hans," I said.

"Yes, Baas, I thought you would. I'd come, too, only I can't swim and when I was drowning I might make a noise, because one forgets oneself then, Baas. But it will be all right, for if it were otherwise I am sure that your reverend father would have shown us so in the sign. The moth floated off quite comfortably on the wood, and just now I saw it spread its wings and fly away. And the fish, ah! how he laughs with that fat old spider in his stomach!"

Chapter 18

Fate Stabs

We went back to the others whom we found crouched on the ground among the coffins, looking distinctly depressed. No wonder; night was closing in, the thunder was beginning to growl and echo through the forest and rain to fall in big drops. In short, although Stephen remarked that every cloud has a silver lining, a proverb which, as I told him, I seemed to have heard before, in no sense could the outlook be considered bright.

"Well, Allan, what have you arranged?" asked Brother John, with a faint attempt at cheerfulness as he let go of his wife's hand. In those days he always seemed to be holding his wife's hand.

"Oh!" I answered, "I am going to get the canoe so that we can all row over comfortably."

They stared at me, and Miss Hope, who was seated by Stephen, asked in her usual Biblical language:

"Have you the wings of a dove that you can fly, O Mr. Allan?"

"No," I answered, "but I have the fins of a fish, or something like them, and I can swim."

Now there arose a chorus of expostulation.

"You shan't risk it," said Stephen, "I can swim as well as you and I'm younger. I'll go, I want a bath."

"That you will have, O Stephen," interrupted Miss Hope, as I thought in some alarm. "The latter rain from heaven will make you clean." (By now it was pouring.)

"Yes, Stephen, you can swim," I said, "but you will forgive me for saying that you are not particularly deadly with a rifle, and clean shooting may be the essence of this business. Now listen to me, all of you. I am going. I hope that I shall succeed, but if I fail it does not so very much matter, for you will be no worse off than you were before. There are three pairs of you. John and his wife; Stephen and Miss Hope; Mavovo and Hans. If the odd man of the party comes to grief, you will have to choose a new captain, that is all, but while I lead I mean to be obeyed."

Then Mavovo, to whom Hans had been talking, spoke.

"My father Macumazana is a brave man. If he lives he will have done his duty. If he dies he will have done his duty still better, and, on the earth or in the under-world among the spirits of our fathers, his name shall be great for ever; yes, his name shall be a song."

When Brother John had translated these words, which I thought fine, there was silence.

"Now," I said, "come with me to the water's edge, all of you. You will be in less danger from the lightning there, where are no tall trees. And while I am gone, do you ladies dress up Hans in that gorilla-skin as best you can, lacing it on to him with some of that palm-fibre string which we brought with us, and filling out the hollows and the head with leaves or reeds. I want him to be ready when I come back with the canoe.

Hans groaned audibly, but made no objection and we started with our impedimenta down to the edge of the estuary where we hid behind a clump of mangrove bushes and tall, feathery reeds. Then I took off some of my clothes, stripping in fact to my flannel shirt and the cotton pants I wore, both of which were grey in colour and therefore almost invisible at night.

Now I was ready and Hans handed me the little rifle.

"It is at full cock, Baas, with the catch on," he said, "and carefully loaded. Also I have wrapped the lining of my hat, which is very full of grease, for the hair makes grease especially in hot weather, Baas, round the lock to keep away the wet from the cap and powder. It is not tied, Baas, only twisted. Give the rifle a shake and it will fall off."

"I understand," I said, and gripped the gun with my left hand by the tongue just forward of the hammer, in such a fashion that the horrid greased rag from Hans's hat was held tight over the lock and cap. Then I shook hands with the others and when I came to Miss Hope I am proud to add that she spontaneously and of her own accord imprinted a kiss upon my mediaeval brow. I felt inclined to return it, but did not.

"It is the kiss of peace, O Allan," she said. "May you go and return in peace."

"Thank you," I said, "but get on with dressing Hans in his new clothes."

Stephen muttered something about feeling ashamed of himself. Brother John put up a vigorous and well-directed prayer. Mavovo saluted with the copper assegai and began to give me *sibonga* or Zulu titles of praise beneath his breath, and Mrs. Eversley said:

"Oh! I thank God that I have lived to see a brave English gentleman again," which I thought a great compliment to my nation and myself, though when I afterwards discovered that she herself was English by birth, it took off some of the polish.

Next, just after a vivid flash of lightning, for the storm had broken in earnest now, I ran swiftly to the water's edge, accompanied by Hans, who was determined to see the last of me.

"Get back, Hans, before the lightning shows you," I said, as I slid gently from a mangrove-root into that filthy stream, "and tell them to keep my coat and trousers dry if they can."

"Good-bye, Baas," he murmured, and I heard that he was sobbing. "Keep a good heart, O Baas of Baases. After all, this is nothing to the vultures of the Hill of Slaughter. *Intombi* pulled us through then, and so she will again, for she knows who can hold her straight!"

That was the last I heard of Hans, for if he said any more, the hiss of the torrential rain smothered his words.

Oh! I had tried to "keep a good heart" before the others, but it is beyond my powers to describe the deadly fright I felt, perhaps the worst of all my life, which is saying a great deal. Here I was starting on one of the maddest ventures that was ever undertaken by man. I needn't put its points again, but that which appealed to me most at the moment was the crocodiles. I have always hated crocodiles since—well, never mind—and the place was as full of them as the ponds at Ascension are of turtles.

Still I swam on. The estuary was perhaps two hundred yards wide, not more, no great distance for a good swimmer as I was in those days. But then I had to hold the rifle above the water with my left hand at all cost, for if once it went beneath it would be useless. Also I was desperately afraid of being seen in the lightning flashes, although to minimise this risk I had kept my dark-coloured cloth hat upon my head. Lastly there was the lightning itself to fear, for it was fearful and continuous and seemed to be striking along the water. It was a fact that a fire-ball or something of the sort hit the surface within a few yards of me, as though it had aimed at the rifle-barrel and just missed. Or so I thought, though it may have been a crocodile rising at the moment.

In one way, or rather, in two, however, I was lucky. The first was the complete absence of wind which must have raised waves that might have swamped me and would at any rate have wetted the rifle. The second was that there was no fear of my losing my path for in the mouth of the cave I could see the glow of the fires which burned on either side of the *Motombo*'s seat. They served the same purpose to me as did the lamp of the lady called Hero to her lover Leander when he swam the Hellespont to pay her clandestine visits at night. But he had something pleasant to look forward to, whereas I——! Still, there was another point in common between us. Hero, if I remember right, was a priestess of the Greek goddess of love, whereas the party who waited me was also in a religious line of business. Only, as I firmly believe, he was a priest of the devil.

I suppose that swim took me about a quarter-of-an-hour, for I went slowly to save my strength, although the crocodiles suggested haste. But thank Heaven they never appeared to complicate matters. Now I was quite near the cave, and now I was beneath the overhanging roof and in the shallow water of the little bay that formed a harbour for the canoe. I stood upon my feet on the rock bottom, the water coming up to my breast, and peered about me, while I rested and worked my left arm, stiff with the up-holding of the gun, to and fro. The fires had burnt somewhat low and until my eyes were freed from the raindrops and grew accustomed to the light of the place I could not see clearly.

I took the rag from round the lock of the rifle, wiped the wet off the barrel with it and let it fall. Then I loosed the catch and by touching a certain mechanism, made the rifle hair-triggered. Now I looked again and began to make out things. There was the platform and there, alas! on it sat the toad-like *Motombo*. But his back was to me; he was gazing not towards the water, but down the cave. I hesitated for one fateful moment. Perhaps the priest was asleep, perhaps I could get the canoe away without shooting. I did not like the job; moreover, his head was held forward and invisible, and how was I to make certain of killing him with a shot in the back? Lastly, if possible, I wished to avoid firing because of the report.

At that instant the *Motombo* wheeled round. Some instinct must have warned him of my presence, for the silence was gravelike save for the soft splash of the rain without. As he turned the lightning blazed and he saw me.

"It is the white man," he muttered to himself in his hissing whisper, while I waited through the following darkness with the rifle at my shoulder, "the white man who shot me long, long ago, and again he has a gun! Oh! Fate stabs, doubtless the god is dead and I too must die!"

Then as if some doubt struck him he lifted the horn to summon help.

Again the lightning flashed and was accompanied by a fearful crack of thunder. With a prayer for skill, I covered his head and fired by the glare of it just as the trumpet touched his lips. It fell from his hand. He seemed to shrink together, and moved no more.

Oh! thank God, thank God! in this supreme moment of trial the art of which I am a master had not failed me. If my hand had shaken ever so little, if my nerves, strained to breaking point, had played me false in the least degree, if the rag from Hans's hat had not sufficed to keep away the damp from the cap and powder! Well, this history would never have been written and there would have been some more bones in the graveyard of the *Kalubis*, that is all!

For a moment I waited, expecting to see the women attendants dart from the doorways in the sides of the cave, and to hear them sound a shrill alarm. None appeared, and I guessed that the rattle of the thunder had swallowed up the crack of the rifle, a noise, be it remembered, that none of them had ever heard. For an unknown number of years this ancient creature, I suppose, had squatted day and night upon that platform, whence, I daresay, it was difficult for him to move. So after they had wrapped his furs round him at sunset and made up the fires to keep him warm, why should his women come to disturb him unless he called them with his horn? Probably it was not even lawful that they should do so.

Somewhat reassured I waded forward a few paces and loosed the canoe which was tied by the prow. Then I scrambled into it, and laying down the rifle, took one of the paddles and began to push out of the creek. Just then the lightning flared once more, and by it I caught sight of the *Motombo's* face that was now within a few feet of my own. It seemed to be resting almost on his knees, and its appearance was dreadful. In the centre of the forehead was a blue mark where the bullet had entered, for I had made no mistake in that matter. The deep-set round eyes were open and, all their fire gone, seemed to stare at me from beneath the overhanging brows. The massive jaw had fallen and the red tongue hung out upon the pendulous lip. The leather-like skin of the bloated cheeks had assumed an ashen hue still streaked and mottled with brown.

Oh! the thing was horrible, and sometimes when I am out of sorts, it haunts me to this day. Yet that creature's blood does not lie heavy on my mind, of it my conscience is not afraid. His end was necessary to save the innocent and I am sure that it was well deserved. For he was a devil, akin to the great god ape I had slain in the forest, to whom, by the way, he bore a most remarkable resemblance in death. Indeed if their heads had been laid side by side at a little distance, it would not have been too easy to tell them apart with their projecting brows, beardless, retreating chins and yellow *tushes* at the corners of the mouth.

Presently I was clear of the cave. Still for a while I lay to at one side of it against the towering cliff, both to listen in case what I had done should be discovered, and for fear lest the lightning which was still bright, although the storm centre was rapidly passing away, should reveal me to any watchers.

For quite ten minutes I hid thus, and then, determining to risk it, paddled softly towards the opposite bank keeping, however, a little to the west of the cave and taking my line by a certain very tall tree which, as I had noted, towered up against the sky at the back of the graveyard.

As it happened my calculations were accurate and in the end I directed the bow of the canoe into the rushes behind which I had left my companions. Just then the moon began to struggle out through the thinning rain-clouds, and by its light they saw me, and I saw what for a moment I took to be the gorilla-god himself waddling forward to seize the boat. There was the dreadful brute exactly as he had appeared in the forest, except that it seemed a little smaller.

Then I remembered and laughed and that laugh did me a world of good.

"Is that you, Baas?" said a muffled voice, speaking apparently from the middle of the gorilla. "Are you safe, Baas?"

"Of course," I answered, "or how should I be here?" adding cheerfully, "Are you comfortable in that nice warm skin on this wet night, Hans?"

"Oh! Baas," answered the voice, "tell me what happened. Even in this stink I burn to know."

"Death happened to the *Motombo*, Hans. Here, Stephen, give me your hand and my clothes, and, Mavovo, hold the rifle and the canoe while I put them on."

Then I landed and stepping into the reeds, pulled off my wet shirt and pants, which I stuffed away into the big pockets of my shooting coat, for I did not want to lose them, and put on the dry things that, although scratchy, were quite good enough clothing in that warm climate. After this I treated myself to a good sup of brandy from the flask, and ate some food which I seemed to require. Then I told them the story, and cutting short their demonstrations of wonder and admiration, bade them place the Holy Flower in the canoe and get in themselves. Next with the help of Hans who poked out his fingers through the skin of the gorilla's arms, I carefully re-loaded the rifle, setting the last cap on the nipple. This done, I joined them in the canoe, taking my seat in the prow and bidding Brother John and Stephen paddle.

Making a circuit to avoid observation as before, in a very short time we reached the mouth of the cave. I leant forward and peeped round the western wall of rock. Nobody seemed to be stirring. There the fires burned dimly, there the huddled shape of the *Motombo* still crouched upon the platform. Silently, silently we disembarked, and I formed our procession while the others looked askance at the horrible face of the dead *Motombo*.

I headed it, then came the Mother of the Flower, followed by Hans, playing his part of the god of the forest; then Brother John and Stephen carrying the Holy Flower. After it walked Hope, while Mavovo brought up the rear. Near to one of the fires, as I had noted on our first passage of the cave, lay a pile of the torches which I have already mentioned. We lit some of them, and at a sign from me, Mavovo dragged the canoe back into its little dock and tied the cord to its post. Its appearance there, apparently undisturbed, might, I thought, make our crossing of the water seem even more mysterious. All this while I watched the doors in the sides of the cave, expecting every moment to see the women rush out. But none came. Perhaps they slept, or perhaps they were absent; I do not know to this day.

We started, and in solemn silence threaded our way down the windings of the cave, extinguishing our torches as soon as we saw light at its inland outlet. At a few paces from its mouth stood a sentry. His back was towards the cave, and in the uncertain gleams of the moon, struggling with the clouds, for a thin rain still fell, he never noted us till we were right on to him. Then he turned and saw, and at the awful sight of this procession of the gods of his land, threw up his arms, and without a word fell senseless. Although I never asked, I think that Mavovo took measures to prevent his awakening. At any rate when I looked back later on, I observed that he was carrying a big Pongo spear with a long shaft, instead of the copper weapon which he had taken from one of the coffins.

On we marched towards Rica Town, following the easy path by which we had come. As I have said, the country was very deserted and the inhabitants of such huts as we passed were evidently fast asleep. Also there were no dogs in this land to awake them with their barking. Between the cave and Rica we were not, I think, seen by a single soul.

Through that long night we pushed on as fast was we could travel, only stopping now and again for a few minutes to rest the bearers of the Holy Flower. Indeed at times Mrs. Eversley relieved her husband at this task, but Stephen, being very strong, carried his end of the stretcher throughout the whole journey.

Hans, of course, was much oppressed by the great weight of the gorilla skin, which, although it had shrunk a good deal, remained as heavy as ever. But he was a tough old fellow, and on the whole got on better than might have been expected, though by the time we reached the town he was sometimes obliged to follow the example of the god itself and help himself forward with his hands, going on all fours, as a gorilla generally does.

We reached the broad, long street of Rica about half an hour before dawn, and proceeded down it till we were past the Feast-house still quite unobserved, for as yet none were stirring on that wet morning. Indeed it was not until we were within a hundred yards of the harbour that a woman possessed of the virtue, or vice, of early rising, who had come from a hut to work in her garden, saw us and raised an awful, piercing scream.

"The gods!" she screamed. "The gods are leaving the land and taking the white men with them."

Instantly there arose a hubbub in the houses. Heads were thrust out of the doors and people ran into the gardens, every one of whom began to yell till one might have thought that a massacre was in progress. But as yet no one came near us, for they were afraid.

"Push on," I cried, "or all is lost."

They answered nobly. Hans struggled forward on all fours, for he was nearly done and his hideous garment was choking him, while Stephen and Brother John, exhausted though they were with the weight of the great plant, actually broke into a feeble trot. We came to the harbour and there, tied to the wharf, was the same canoe in which we had crossed to Pongo-land. We sprang into it and cut the fastenings with my knife, having no time to untie them, and pushed off from the wharf.

By now hundreds of people, among them many soldiers were hard upon and indeed around us, but still they seemed too frightened to do anything. So far the inspiration of Hans' disguise had saved us. In the midst of them, by the light of the rising sun, I recognised Komba, who ran up, a great spear in his hand, and for a moment halted amazed.

Then it was that the catastrophe happened which nearly cost us all our lives.

Hans, who was in the stern of the canoe, began to faint from exhaustion, and in his efforts to obtain air, for the heat and stench of the skin were overpowering him, thrust his head out through the lacings of the hide beneath the reed-stuffed mask of the gorilla, which fell over languidly upon his shoulder. Komba saw his ugly little face and knew it again.

"It is a trick!" he roared. "These white devils have killed the god and stolen the Holy Flower and its priestess. The yellow man is wrapped in the skin of the god. To the boats! To the boats!"

"Paddle," I shouted to Brother John and Stephen, "paddle for your lives! Mavovo, help me get up the sail."

As it chanced on that stormy morning the wind was blowing strongly towards the mainland.

We laboured at the mast, shipped it and hauled up the mat sail, but slowly for we were awkward at the business. By the time that it began to draw the paddles had propelled us about four hundred yards from the wharf, whence many canoes, with their sails already set, were starting in pursuit. Standing in the prow of the first of these, and roaring curses and vengeance at us, was Komba, the new *Kalubi*, who shook a great spear above his head.

An idea occurred to me, who knew that unless something were done we must be overtaken and killed by these skilled boatmen. Leaving Mavovo to attend to the sail, I scrambled aft, and thrusting aside the fainting Hans, knelt down in the stern of the canoe. There was still one charge, or rather one cap, left, and I meant to use it. I put up the largest flap-sight, lifted the little rifle and covered Komba, aiming at the point of his chin. *Intombi* was not sighted for or meant to use at this great distance, and only by this means of allowing for the drop of the bullet, could I hope to hit the man in the body.

The sail was drawing well now and steadied the boat, also, being still under the shelter of the land, the water was smooth as that of a pond, so really I had a very good firing platform. Moreover, weary though I was, my vital forces rose to the emergency and I felt myself grow rigid as a statue. Lastly, the light was good, for the sun rose behind me, its level rays shining full on to my mark. I held my breath and touched the trigger. The charge exploded sweetly and almost at the instant; as the smoke drifted to one side, I saw Komba throw up his arms and fall backwards into the canoe. Then, quite a long while afterwards, or so it seemed, the breeze brought the faint sound of the thud of that fateful bullet to our ears.

Though perhaps I ought not to say so, it was really a wonderful shot in all the circumstances, for, as I learned afterwards, the ball struck just where I hoped that it might, in the centre of the breast, piercing the heart. Indeed, taking everything into consideration, I think that those four shots which I fired in Pongo-land are the real record of my career as a marksman. The first at night broke the arm of the gorilla god and would have killed him had not the charge hung fire and given him time to protect his head. The second did kill him in the midst of a great scrimmage when everything was moving. The third, fired by the glare of lightning after a long swim, slew the *Motombo*, and the fourth, loosed at this great distance from a moving boat, was the bane of that cold-blooded and treacherous man, Komba, who thought that he had trapped us to Pongo-land to be murdered and eaten as a sacrifice. Lastly there was always the consciousness that no mistake must be made, since with but four percussion caps it could not be retrieved.

I am sure that I could not have done so well with any other rifle, however modern and accurate it might be. But to this little Purdey weapon I had been accustomed from my youth, and that, as any marksman will know, means a great deal. I seemed to know it and it seemed to know me. It hangs on my wall to this day, although of course I never use it now in our breech-loading era. Unfortunately, however, a local gunsmith to whom I sent it to have the lock cleaned, re-browned it and scraped and varnished the stock, etc., without authority, making it look almost new again. I preferred it in its worn and scratched condition.

To return: the sound of the shot, like that of John Peel's horn, aroused Hans from his sleep. He thrust his head between my legs and saw Komba fall.

"Oh! beautiful, Baas, beautiful!" he said faintly. "I am sure that the ghost of your reverend father cannot kill his enemies more nicely down there among the Fires. Beautiful!" and the silly old fellow fell to kissing my boots, or what remained of them, after which I gave him the last of the brandy.

This quite brought him to himself again, especially when he was free from that filthy skin and had washed his head and hands.

The effect of the death of Komba upon the Pongos was very strange. All the other canoes clustered round that in which he lay. Then, after a hurried consultation, they hauled down their sails and paddled back to the wharf. Why they did this I cannot tell. Perhaps they thought that he was bewitched, or only wounded and required the attentions of a medicine-man. Perhaps it was not lawful for them to proceed except under the guidance of some reserve *Kalubi* who had "passed the god" and who was on shore. Perhaps it was necessary, according to their rites, that the body of their chief should be landed with certain ceremonies. I do not know. It is impossible to be sure as to the mysterious motives that actuate many of these remote African tribes.

At any rate the result was that it gave us a great start and a chance of life, who must otherwise have died upon the spot. Outside the bay the breeze blew merrily, taking us across the lake at a spanking pace, until about midday when it began to fall. Fortunately, however, it did not altogether drop till three o'clock by which time the coast of Mazitu-land was comparatively near; we could even distinguish a speck against the skyline which we knew was the Union Jack that Stephen had set upon the crest of a little hill.

During those hours of peace we ate the food that remained to us, washed ourselves as thoroughly as we could and rested. Well was it, in view of what followed, that we had this time of repose. For just as the breeze was failing I looked aft and there, coming up behind us, still holding the wind, was the whole fleet of Pongo canoes, thirty or forty of them perhaps, each carrying an average of about twenty men. We sailed on for as long as we could, for though our progress was but slow, it was quicker than what we could have made by paddling. Also it was necessary that we should save our strength for the last trial.

I remember that hour very well, for in the nervous excitement of it every little thing impressed itself upon my mind. I remember even the shape of the clouds that floated over us, remnants of the storm of the previous night. One was like a castle with a broken-down turret showing a staircase within; another had a fantastic resemblance to a wrecked ship with a hole in her starboard bow, two of her masts broken and one standing with some fragments of sails flapping from it, and so forth.

Then there was the general aspect of the great lake, especially at a spot where two currents met, causing little waves which seemed to fight with each other and fall backwards in curious curves. Also there were shoals of small fish, something like chub in shape, with round mouths and very white stomachs, which suddenly appeared upon the surface, jumping at invisible flies. These attracted a number of birds that resembled gulls of a light build. They had coal-black heads, white backs, greyish wings, and slightly webbed feet, pink as coral, with which they seized the small fish, uttering as they did so, a peculiar and plaintive cry that ended in a long-drawn *e-e-é*. The father of the flock, whose head seemed to be white like his back, perhaps from age, hung above them, not troubling to fish himself, but from time to time forcing one of the company to drop what he had caught, which he retrieved before it reached the water. Such are some of the small things that come back to me, though there were others too numerous and trivial to mention.

When the breeze failed us at last we were perhaps something over three miles from the shore, or rather from the great bed of reeds which at this spot grow in the shallows off the Mazitu coast to a breadth of seven or eight hundred yards, where the water becomes too deep for them. The Pongos were then about a mile and a half behind. But as the wind favoured them for a few minutes more and, having plenty of hands, they could help themselves on by paddling, when at last it died to a complete calm, the distance between us was not more than one mile. This meant that they must cover four miles of water, while we covered three.

Letting down our now useless sail and throwing it and the mast overboard to lighten the canoe, since the sky showed us that there was no more hope of wind, we began to paddle as hard as we could. Fortunately the two ladies were able to take their share in this exercise, since they had learned it upon the Lake of the Flower, where it seemed they kept a private canoe upon the other side of the island which was used for fishing. Hans, who was still weak, we set to steer with a paddle aft, which he did in a somewhat erratic fashion.

A stern chase is proverbially a long chase, but still the enemy with their skilled rowers came up fast. When we were a mile from the reeds they were within half a mile of us, and as we tired the proportion of distance lessened. When we were two hundred yards from the reeds they were not more than fifty or sixty yards behind, and then the real struggle began.

It was short but terrible. We threw everything we could overboard, including the ballast stones at the bottom of the canoe and the heavy hide of the gorilla. This, as it proved, was fortunate, since the thing sank but slowly and the foremost Pongo boats halted a minute to recover so precious a relic, checking the others behind them, a circumstance that helped us by twenty or thirty yards.

"Over with the plant!" I said.

But Stephen, looking quite old from exhaustion and with the sweat streaming from him as he laboured at his unaccustomed paddle, gasped:

"For Heaven's sake, no, after all we have gone through to get it."

So I didn't insist; indeed there was neither time nor breath for argument.

Now we were in the reeds, for thanks to the flag which guided us, we had struck the big hippopotamus lane exactly, and the Pongos, paddling like demons, were about thirty yards behind. Thankful was I that those interesting people had never learned the use of bows and arrows, and that their spears were too heavy to throw. By now, or rather some time before, old Babemba and the Mazitu had seen us, as had our Zulu hunters. Crowds of them were wading through the shallows towards us, yelling encouragements as they came. The Zulus, too, opened a rather wild fire, with the result that one of the bullets struck our canoe and another touched the brim of my hat. A third, however, killed a Pongo, which caused some confusion in the ranks of Tusculum.

But we were done and they came on remorselessly. When their leading boat was not more than ten yards from us and we were perhaps two hundred from the shore, I drove my paddle downwards and finding that the water was less than four feet deep, shouted:

"Overboard, all, and wade. It's our last chance!"

We scrambled out of that canoe the prow of which, as I left it the last, I pushed round across the water-lane to obstruct those of the Pongo. Now I think all would have gone well had it not been for Stephen, who after he had floundered forward a few paces in the mud, bethought him of his beloved orchid. Not only did he return to try to rescue it, he also actually persuaded his friend Mavovo to accompany him. They got back to the boat and began to lift the plant out when the Pongo fell upon them, striking at them with their spears over the width of our canoe. Mavovo struck back with the weapon he had taken from the Pongo sentry at the cave mouth, and killed or wounded one of them. Then some one hurled a ballast stone at him which caught him on the side of the head and knocked him down into the water, whence he rose and reeled back, almost senseless, till some of our people got hold of him and dragged him to the shore.

So Stephen was left alone, dragging at the great orchid, till a Pongo reaching over the canoe drove a spear through his shoulder. He let go of the orchid because he must and tried to retreat. Too late! Half a dozen or more of the Pongo pushed themselves between the stern or bow of our canoe and the reeds, and waded forward to kill him. I could not help, for to tell the truth at the moment I was stuck in a mud-hole made by the hoof of a hippopotamus, while the Zulu hunters and the Mazitu were as yet too far off. Surely he must have died had it not been for the courage of the girl Hope, who, while wading shorewards a little in front of me, had turned and seen his plight. Back she came, literally bounding through the water like a leopard whose cubs are in danger.

Reaching Stephen before the Pongo she thrust herself between him and them and proceeded to address them with the utmost vigour in their own language, which of course she had learned from those of the albinos who were not mutes.

What she said I could not exactly catch because of the shouts of the advancing Mazitu. I gathered, however, that she was anathematizing them in the words of some old and potent curse that was only used by the guardians of the Holy Flower, which consigned them, body and spirit, to a dreadful doom. The effect of this malediction, which by the way neither the young lady nor her mother would repeat to me afterwards, was certainly remarkable. Those men who heard it, among them the would-be slayers of Stephen, stayed their hands and even inclined their heads towards the young priestess, as though in reverence or deprecation, and thus remained for sufficient time for her to lead the wounded Stephen out of danger. This she did wading backwards by his side and keeping her eyes fixed full upon the Pongo. It was perhaps the most curious rescue that I ever saw.

The Holy Flower, I should add, they recaptured and carried off, for I saw it departing in one of their canoes. That was the end of my orchid hunt and of the money which I hoped to make by the sale of this floral treasure. I wonder what became of it. I have good reason to believe that it was never replanted on the Island of the Flower, so perhaps it was borne back to the dim and unknown land in the depths of Africa whence the Pongo are supposed to have brought it when they migrated.

After this incident of the wounding and the rescue of Stephen by the intrepid Miss Hope, whose interest in him was already strong enough to induce her to risk her life upon his behalf, all we fugitives were dragged ashore somehow by our friends. Here, Hans, I and the ladies collapsed exhausted, though Brother John still found sufficient strength to do what he could for the injured Stephen and Mavovo.

Then the Battle of the Reeds began, and a fierce fray it was. The Pongos who were about equal in numbers to our people, came on furiously, for they were mad at the death of their god with his priest, the *Motombo*, of which I think news had reached them and at the carrying off of the Mother of the Flower. Springing from their canoes because the waterway was too narrow for more than one of these to travel at a time, they plunged into the reeds with the intention of wading ashore. Here their hereditary enemies, the Mazitu, attacked them under the command of old Babemba. The struggle that ensued partook more of the nature of a series of hand-to-hand fights than of a set battle. It was extraordinary to see the heads of the combatants moving among the reeds as they stabbed at each other with the great spears, till one went down. There were few wounded in that fray, for those who fell sank in the mud and water and were drowned.

On the whole the Pongo, who were operating in what was almost their native element, were getting the best of it, and driving the Mazitu back. But what decided the day against them were the guns of our

Zulu hunters. Although I could not lift a rifle myself I managed to collect these men round me and to direct their fire, which proved so terrifying to the Pongos that after ten or a dozen of them had been knocked over, they began to give back sullenly and were helped into their canoes by those men who were left in charge of them.

Then at length at a signal they got out their paddles, and, still shouting curses and defiance at us, rowed away till they became but specks upon the bosom of the great lake and vanished.

Two of the canoes we captured, however, and with them six or seven Pongos. These the Mazitu wished to put to death, but at the bidding of Brother John, whose orders, it will be remembered, had the same authority in Mazitu-land as those of the king, they bound their arms and made them prisoners instead.

In about half an hour it was all over, but of the rest of that day I cannot write, as I think I fainted from utter exhaustion, which was not, perhaps, wonderful, considering all that we had undergone in the four and a half days that had elapsed since we first embarked upon the Great Lake. For constant strain, physical and mental, I recall no such four days during the whole of my adventurous life. It was indeed wonderful that we came through them alive.

The last thing I remember was the appearance of Sammy, looking very smart, in his blue cotton smock, who, now that the fighting was over, emerged like a butterfly when the sun shines after rain.

"Oh! Mr. Quatermain," he said, "I welcome you home again after arduous exertions and looking into the eyes of bloody war. All the days of absence, and a good part of the nights, too, while the mosquitoes hunted slumber, I prayed for your safety like one o'clock, and perhaps, Mr. Quatermain, that helped to do the trick, for what says poet? Those who serve and wait are almost as good as those who cook dinner."

Such were the words which reached and, oddly enough, impressed themselves upon my darkening brain. Or rather they were part of the words, excerpts from a long speech that there is no doubt Sammy had carefully prepared during our absence.

CHAPTER 19

The True Holy Flower

When I came to myself again it was to find that I had slept fifteen or sixteen hours, for the sun of a new day was high in the heavens. I was lying in a little shelter of boughs at the foot of that mound on which we flew the flag that guided us back over the waters of the Lake Kirua. Near by was Hans consuming a gigantic meal of meat which he had cooked over a neighbouring fire. With him, to my delight, I saw Mavovo, his head bound up, though otherwise but little the worse. The stone, which probably would have killed a thin-skulled white man, had done no more than knock him stupid and break the skin of his scalp, perhaps because the force of it was lessened by the gum man's-ring which, like most Zulus of a certain age or dignity, he wore woven in his hair.

The two tents we had brought with us to the lake were pitched not far away and looked quite pretty and peaceful there in the sunlight.

Hans, who was watching me out of the corner of his eye, ran to me with a large pannikin of hot coffee which Sammy had made ready against my awakening; for they knew that my sleep was, or had become of a natural order. I drank it to the last drop, and in all my life never did I enjoy anything more. Then while I began upon some pieces of the toasted meat, I asked him what had happened.

"Not much, Baas," he answered, "except that we are alive, who should be dead. The Maam and the Missie are still asleep in that tent, or at least the Maam is, for the Missie is helping Dogeetah, her father, to nurse Baas Stephen, who has an ugly wound. The Pongos have gone and I think will not return, for they have had enough of the white man's guns. The Mazitu have buried those of their dead whom they could recover, and have sent their wounded, of whom there were only six, back to Beza Town on litters. That is all, Baas."

Then while I washed, and never did I need a bath more, and put on my underclothes, in which I had swum on the night of the killing of the *Motombo*, that Hans had wrung out and dried in the sun, I asked that worthy how he was after his adventures.

"Oh! well enough, Baas," he answered, "now that my stomach is full, except that my hands and wrists are sore with crawling along the ground like a *babyan* (baboon), and that I cannot get the stink of that god's skin out of my nose. Oh! you don't know what it was: if I had been a white man it would have killed me. But, Baas, perhaps you did well to take drunken old Hans with you on this journey after all, for I was clever about the little gun, wasn't I? Also about your swimming of the Crocodile Water, though it is true that the sign of the spider and the moth which your reverend father sent, taught me that. And now we have got back safe, except for the Mazitu, Jerry, who doesn't matter, for there are plenty more like him, and the wound in Baas Stephen's shoulder, and that heavy flower which he thought better than brandy."

"Yes, Hans," I said, "I did well to take you and you are clever, for had it not been for you, we should now be cooked and eaten in Pongo-land. I thank you for your help, old friend. But, Hans, another time please sew up the holes in your waistcoat pocket. Four caps wasn't much, Hans."

"No, Baas, but it was enough; as they were all good ones. If there had been forty you could not have done much more. Oh! your reverend father knew all that" (my departed parent had become a kind of patron saint to Hans) "and did not wish this poor old Hottentot to have more to carry than was needed. He knew you wouldn't miss, Baas, and that there were only one god, one devil, and one man waiting to be killed."

I laughed, for Hans's way of putting things was certainly original, and having got on my coat, went to see Stephen. At the door of the tent I met Brother John, whose shoulder was dreadfully sore from the rubbing of the orchid stretcher, as were his hands with paddling, but who otherwise was well enough and of course supremely happy.

He told me that he had cleansed and sewn up Stephen's wound, which appeared to be doing well, although the spear had pierced right through the shoulder, luckily without cutting any artery. So I went in to see the patient and found him cheerful enough, though weak from weariness and loss of blood, with Miss Hope feeding him with broth from a wooden native spoon. I didn't stop very long, especially after he got on to the subject of the lost orchid, about which he began to show signs of excitement. This I allayed as well as I could by telling him that I had preserved a pod of the seed, news at which he was delighted.

"There!" he said. "To think that you, Allan, should have remembered to take that precaution when I, an orchidist, forgot all about it!"

"Ah! my boy," I answered, "I have lived long enough to learn never to leave anything behind that I can possibly carry away. Also, although not an orchidist, it occurred to me that there are more ways of propagating a plant than from the original root, which generally won't go into one's pocket."

Then he began to give me elaborate instructions as to the preservation of the seed-pod in a perfectly dry and air-tight tin box, etc., at which point Miss Hope unceremoniously bundled me out of the tent.

That afternoon we held a conference at which it was agreed that we should begin our return journey to Beza Town at once, as the place where we were camped was very malarious and there was always a risk of the Pongo paying us another visit.

So a litter was made with a mat stretched over it in which Stephen could be carried, since fortunately there were plenty of bearers, and our other simple preparations were quickly completed. Mrs. Eversley and Hope were mounted on the two donkeys; Brother John, whose hurt leg showed signs of renewed weakness, rode his white ox, which was now quite fat again; the wounded hero, Stephen, as I have said, was carried; and I walked, comparing notes with old Babemba on the Pongo, their manners, which I am bound to say were good, and their customs, that, as the saying goes, were "simply beastly."

How delighted that ancient warrior was to hear again about the sacred cave, the Crocodile Water, the Mountain Forest and its terrible god, of the death of which and of the *Motombo* he made me tell him the story three times over. At the conclusion of the third recital he said quietly:

"My lord Macumazana, you are a great man, and I am glad to have lived if only to know you. No one else could have done these deeds."

Of course I was complimented, but felt bound to point out Hans's share in our joint achievement.

"Yes, yes," he answered, "the Spotted Snake, Inhlatu, has the cunning to scheme, but you have the power to do, and what is the use of a brain to plot without the arm to strike? The two do not go together because the plotter is not a striker. His mind is different. If the snake had the strength and brain of the elephant, and the fierce courage of the buffalo, soon there would be but one creature left in the world. But the Maker of all things knew this and kept them separate, my lord Macumazana."

I thought, and still think, that there was a great deal of wisdom in this remark, simple as it seems. Oh! surely many of these savages whom we white men despise, are no fools.

After about an hour's march we camped till the moon rose which it did at ten o'clock, when we went on again till near dawn, as it was thought better that Stephen should travel in the cool of the night. I remember that our cavalcade, escorted before, behind and on either flank by the Mazitu troops with their tall spears, looked picturesque and even imposing as it wound over those wide downs in the lovely and peaceful light of the moon.

There is no need for me to set out the details of the rest of our journey, which was not marked by any incident of importance.

Stephen bore it very well, and Brother John, who was one of the best doctors I ever met, gave good reports of him, but I noted that he did not seem to get any stronger, although he ate plenty of food. Also, Miss Hope, who nursed him, for her mother seemed to have no taste that way, informed me that he slept but little, as indeed I found out for myself.

"O Allan," she said, just before we reached Beza Town, "Stephen, your son" (she used to call him my son, I don't know why) "is sick. The father says it is only the spear-hurt, but I tell you it is more than the spear-hurt. He is sick in himself," and the tears that filled her grey eyes showed me that she spoke what she believed. As a matter of fact she was right, for on the night after we reached the town, Stephen was seized with an attack of some bad form of African fever, which in his weak state nearly cost him his life, contracted, no doubt, at that unhealthy Crocodile Water.

Our reception at Beza was most imposing, for the whole population, headed by old Bausi himself, came out to meet us with loud shouts of welcome, from which we had to ask them to desist for Stephen's sake.

So in the end we got back to our huts with gratitude of heart. Indeed, we should have been very happy there for a while, had it not been for our anxiety about Stephen. But it is always thus in the world; who was ever allowed to eat his pot of honey without finding a fly or perhaps a cockroach in his mouth?

In all, Stephen was really ill for about a month. On the tenth day after our arrival at Beza, according to my diary, which, having little else to do, I entered up fully at this time, we thought that he would surely die. Even Brother John, who attended him with the most constant skill, and who had ample quinine and other drugs at his command, for these we had brought with us from Durban in plenty, gave up the case. Day and night the poor fellow raved and always about that confounded orchid, the loss of which seemed to weigh upon his mind as though it were a whole sackful of unrepented crimes.

I really think that he owed his life to a subterfuge, or rather to a bold invention of Hope's. One evening, when he was at his very worst and going on like a mad creature about the lost plant—I was present in the hut at the time alone with him and her—she took his hand and pointing to a perfectly open space on the floor, said:

"Look, O Stephen, the flower has been brought back."

He stared and stared, and then to my amazement answered:

"By Jove, so it has! But those beggars have broken off all the blooms except one."

"Yes," she echoed, "but one remains and it is the finest of them all."

After this he went quietly to sleep and slept for twelve hours, then took some food and slept again and, what is more, his temperature went down to, or a little below, normal. When he finally woke up, as it chanced, I was again present in the hut with Hope, who was standing on the spot which she had persuaded him was occupied by the orchid. He stared at this spot and he stared at her—me he could not see, for I was behind him—then said in a weak voice:

"Didn't you tell me, Miss Hope, that the plant was where you are and that the most beautiful of the flowers was left?"

I wondered what on earth her answer would be. However, she rose to the occasion.

"O Stephen," she replied, in her soft voice and speaking in a way so natural that it freed her words from any boldness, "it is here, for am I not its child"—her native appellation, it will be remembered, was Child of the Flower. "And the fairest of the flowers is here, too, for I am that Flower which you found in the island of the lake. O Stephen, I pray you to trouble no more about a lost plant of which you have seed in plenty, but make thanks that you still live and that through you my mother and I still live, who, if you had died, would weep our eyes away."

"Through me," he answered. "You mean through Allan and Hans. Also it was you who saved my life there in the water. Oh! I remember it all now. You are right, Hope; although I didn't know it, you are the true Holy Flower that I saw."

She ran to him and kneeling by his side, gave him her hand, which he pressed to his pale lips.

Then I sneaked out of that hut and left them to discuss the lost flower that was found again. It was a pretty scene, and one that to my mind gave a sort of spiritual meaning to the whole of an otherwise rather insane quest. He sought an ideal flower, he found—the love of his life.

After this, Stephen recovered rapidly, for such love is the best of medicines—if it be returned.

I don't know what passed between the pair and Brother John and his wife, for I never asked. But I noted that from this day forward they began to treat him as a son. The new relationship between Stephen and Hope seemed to be tacitly accepted without discussion. Even the natives accepted it, for old Mavovo asked me when they were going to be married and how many cows Stephen had promised to pay Brother John for such a beautiful wife. "It ought to be a large herd," he said, "and of a big breed of cattle."

Sammy, too, alluded to the young lady in conversation with me, as "Mr. Somers's affianced spouse." Only Hans said nothing. Such a trivial matter as marrying and giving in marriage did not interest him. Or, perhaps, he looked upon the affair as a foregone conclusion and therefore unworthy of comment.

We stayed at Bausi's *kraal* for a full month longer whilst Stephen recovered his strength. I grew thoroughly bored with the place and so did Mavovo and the Zulus, but Brother John and his wife did not seem to mind. Mrs. Eversley was a passive creature, quite content to take things as they came and after so long an absence from civilization, to bide a little longer among savages. Also she had her beloved John, at whom she would sit and gaze by the hour like a cat sometimes does at a person to whom it is attached. Indeed, when she spoke to him, her voice seemed to me to resemble a kind of blissful purr. I think it made the old boy rather fidgety sometimes, for after an hour or two of it he would rise and go to hunt for butterflies.

To tell the truth, the situation got a little on my nerves at last, for wherever I looked I seemed to see there Stephen and Hope making love to each other, or Brother John and his wife admiring each other, which didn't leave me much spare conversation. Evidently they thought that Mavovo, Hans, Sammy, Bausi, Babemba and Co. were enough for me—that is, if they reflected on the matter at all. So they were, in a sense, for the Zulu hunters began to get out of hand in the midst of this idleness and plenty, eating too much, drinking too much native beer, smoking too much of the intoxicating *dakka*, a mischievous kind of help, and making too much love to the Mazitu women, which of course resulted in the usual rows that I had to settle.

At last I struck and said that we must move on as Stephen was now fit to travel.

"Quite so," said Brother John, mildly. "What have you arranged, Allan?"

With some irritation, for I hated that sentence of Brother John's, I replied that I had arranged nothing, but that as none of them seemed to have any suggestions to make, I would go out and talk the matter over with Hans and Mavovo, which I did.

I need not chronicle the results of our conference since other arrangements were being made for us at which I little guessed.

It all came very suddenly, as great things in the lives of men and nations sometimes do. Although the Mazitu were of the Zulu family, their military organization had none of the Zulu thoroughness. For instance, when I remonstrated with Bausi and old Babemba as to their not keeping up a proper system of outposts and intelligence, they laughed at me and answered that they never had been attacked and now that the Pongo had learnt a lesson, were never likely to be.

By the way, I see that I have not yet mentioned that at Brother John's request those Pongos who had been taken prisoners at the Battle of the Reeds were conducted to the shores of the lake, given one of the captured canoes and told that they might return to their own happy land. To our astonishment about three weeks later they reappeared at Beza Town with this story.

They said that they had crossed the lake and found Rica still standing, but utterly deserted. They then wandered through the country and even explored the *Motombo's* cave. There they discovered the remains of the *Motombo*, still crouched upon his platform, but nothing more. In one hut of a distant village, however, they came across an old and dying woman who informed them with her last breath that the Pongos, frightened by the iron tubes that vomited death and in obedience to some prophecy, had all *gone back whence they came in the beginning*, taking with them the recaptured Holy Flower. She had been left with a supply of food because she was too weak to travel. So, perhaps, that flower grows again in some unknown place in Africa, but its worshippers will have to provide themselves with another god of the forest, another Mother of the Flower, and another high-priest to fill the office of the late *Motombo*.

These Pongo prisoners, having now no home, and not knowing where their people had gone except that it was "towards the north," asked for leave to settle among the Mazitu, which was granted them. Their story confirmed me in my opinion that Pongo-land is not really an island, but is connected on the further side with the continent by some ridge or swamp. If we had been obliged to stop much longer among the Mazitu, I would have satisfied myself as to this matter by going to look. But that chance never came to me until some years later when, under curious circumstances, I was again destined to visit this part of Africa.

To return to my story. On the day following this discussion as to our departure we all breakfasted very early as there was a great deal to be done. There was a dense mist that morning such as in these Mazitu uplands often precedes high, hot wind from the north at this season of the year, so dense indeed that it was impossible to see for more than a few yards. I suppose that this mist comes up from the great lake in certain conditions of the weather. We had just finished our breakfast and rather languidly, for the thick, sultry air left me unenergetic, I told one of the Zulus to see that the two donkeys and the white ox which I had caused to be brought into the town in view of our near departure and tied up by our huts, were properly fed. Then I went to inspect all the rifles and ammunition, which Hans had got out to be checked and overhauled. It was at this moment that I heard a far-away and unaccustomed sound, and asked Hans what he thought it was.

"A gun, Baas," he answered anxiously.

Well might he be anxious, for as we both knew, no one in the neighbourhood had guns except ourselves, and all ours were accounted for. It is true that we had promised to give the majority of those we had taken from the slavers to Bausi when we went away, and that I had been instructing some of his best soldiers in the use of them, but not one of these had as yet been left in their possession.

I stepped to a gate in the fence and ordered the sentry there to run to Bausi and Babemba and make report and inquiries, also to pray them to summon all the soldiers, of whom, as it happened, there were at the time not more than three hundred in the town. As perfect peace prevailed, the rest, according to their custom, had been allowed to go to their villages and attend to their crops. Then, possessed by a rather undefined nervousness, at which the others were inclined to laugh, I caused the Zulus to arm and generally make a few arrangements to meet any unforeseen crisis. This done I sat down to reflect what would be the best course to take if we should happen to be attacked by a large force in that straggling native town, of which I had often studied all the strategic possibilities. When I had come to my own conclusion I asked Hans and Mavovo what they thought, and found that they agreed with me that the only defensible place was outside the town where the road to the south gate ran down to a rocky wooded ridge with somewhat steep flanks. It may be remembered that it was by this road and over this ridge that Brother John had appeared on his white ox when we were about to be shot to death with arrows at the posts in the market-place.

Whilst we were still talking two of the Mazitu captains appeared, running hard and dragging between them a wounded herdsman, who had evidently been hit in the arm by a bullet.

This was his story. That he and two other boys were out herding the king's cattle about half a mile to the north of the town, when suddenly there appeared a great number of men dressed in white robes, all of whom were armed with guns. These men, of whom he thought there must be three or four hundred, began to take the cattle and seeing the three herds, fired on them, wounding him and killing his two companions. He then ran for his life and brought the news. He added that one of the men had called after him to tell the white people that they had come to kill them and the Mazitu who were their friends and to take away the white women.

"Hassan-ben-Mohammed and his slavers!" I said, as Babemba appeared at the head of a number of soldiers, crying out:

"The slave-dealing Arabs are here, lord Macumazana. They have crept on us through the mist. A herald of theirs has come to the north gate demanding that we should give up you white people and your servants, and with you a hundred young men and a hundred young women to be sold as slaves. If we do not do this they say that they will kill all of us save the unmarried boys and girls, and that you white people they will take and put to death by burning, keeping only the two women alive. One Hassan sends this message."

"Indeed," I answered quietly, for in this fix I grew quite cool as was usual with me. "And does Bausi mean to give us up?"

"How can Bausi give up Dogeetah who is his blood brother, and you, his friend?" exclaimed the old general, indignantly. "Bausi sends me to his brother Dogeetah that he may receive the orders of the white man's wisdom, spoken through your mouth, lord Macumazana."

"Then there's a good spirit in Bausi," I replied, "and these are Dogeetah's orders spoken through my mouth. Go to Hassan's messengers and ask him whether he remembers a certain letter which two white men left for him outside their camp in a cleft stick. Tell him that the time has now come for those white men to fulfil the promise they made in that letter and that before tomorrow he will be hanging on a tree. Then, Babemba, gather your soldiers and hold the north gate of the town for as long as you can, defending it with bows and arrows. Afterwards retreat through the town, joining us among the trees on the rocky slope that is opposite the south gate. Bid some of your men clear the town of all the aged and women and children and let them pass though the south gate and take refuge in the wooded country beyond the slope. Let them not tarry. Let them go at once. Do you understand?"

"I understand everything, lord Macumazana. The words of Dogeetah shall be obeyed. Oh! would that we had listened to you and kept a better watch!"

He rushed off, running like a young man and shouting orders as he went.

"Now," I said, "we must be moving."

We collected all the rifles and ammunition, with some other things, I am sure I forget what they were, and with the help of a few guards whom Babemba had left outside our gate started through the town, leading with us the two donkeys and the white ox. I remember by an afterthought, telling Sammy, who was looking very uncomfortable, to return to the huts and fetch some blankets and a couple of iron cooking-pots which might become necessities to us.

"Oh! Mr. Quatermain," he answered, "I will obey you, though with fear and trembling."

He went and when a few hours afterwards I noted that he had never reappeared, I came to the conclusion, with a sigh, for I was very fond of Sammy in a way, that he had fallen into trouble and been killed. Probably, I thought, "his fear and trembling" had overcome his reason and caused him to run in the wrong direction with the cooking-pots.

The first part of our march through the town was easy enough, but after we had crossed the market-place and emerged into the narrow way that ran between many lines of huts to the south gate it became more difficult, since this path was already crowded with hundreds of terrified fugitives, old people, sick being carried, little boys, girls, and women with infants at the breast. It was impossible to control these poor folk; all we could do was to fight our way through them. However, we got out at last and climbing the slope, took up the best position we could on and just beneath its crest where the trees and scattered boulders gave us very fair cover, which we improved upon in every way feasible in the time at our disposal, by building little breastworks of stone and so forth. The fugitives who had accompanied us, and those who followed, a multitude in all, did not stop here, but flowed on along the road and vanished into the wooded country behind.

I suggested to Brother John that he should take his wife and daughter and the three beasts and go with them. He seemed inclined to accept the idea, needless to say for their sakes, not for his own, for he was a very fearless old fellow. But the two ladies utterly refused to budge. Hope said that she would stop with Stephen, and her mother declared that she had every confidence in me and preferred to remain where she was. Then I suggested that Stephen should go too, but at this he grew so angry that I dropped the subject.

So in the end we established them in a pleasant little hollow by a spring just over the crest of the rise, where unless our flank were turned or we were rushed, they would be out of the reach of bullets. Moreover, without saying anything more we gave to each of them a double-barrelled and loaded pistol.

Chapter 20

The Battle of the Gate

By now heavy firing had begun at the north gate of the town, accompanied by much shouting. The mist was still too thick to enable us to see anything at first. But shortly after the commencement of the firing a strong, hot wind, which always followed these mists, got up and gradually gathered to a gale, blowing away the vapours. Then from the top of the crest, Hans, who had climbed a tree there, reported that the Arabs were advancing on the north gate, firing as they came, and that the Mazitu were replying with their bows and arrows from behind the palisade that surrounded the town. This palisade, I should state, consisted of an earthen bank on the top of which tree trunks were set close together. Many of these had struck in that fertile soil, so that in general appearance this protective work resembled a huge live fence, on the outer and inner side of which grew great masses of prickly pear and tall, finger-like cacti. A while afterwards Hans reported that the Mazitu were retreating and a few minutes later they began to arrive through the south gate, bringing several wounded with them. Their captain said that they could not stand against the fire of the guns and had determined to abandon the town and make the best fight they could upon the ridge.

A little later the rest of the Mazitu came, driving before them all the non-combatants who remained in the town. With these was King Bausi, in a terrible state of excitement.

"Was I not wise, Macumazana," he shouted, "to fear the slave-traders and their guns? Now they have come to kill those who are old and to take the young away in their gangs to sell them."

"Yes, King," I could not help answering, "you were wise. But if you had done what I said and kept a better look-out Hassan could not have crept on you like a leopard on a goat."

"It is true," he groaned; "but who knows the taste of a fruit till he has bitten it?"

Then he went to see to the disposal of his soldiers along the ridge, placing, by my advice, the most of them at each end of the line to frustrate any attempt to out-flank us. We, for our part, busied ourselves in serving out those guns which we had taken in the first fight with the slavers to the thirty or forty picked men whom I had been instructing in the use of firearms. If they did not do much damage, at least, I thought, they could make a noise and impress the enemy with the idea that we were well armed.

Ten minutes or so later Babemba arrived with about fifty men, all the Mazitu soldiers who were left in the town. He reported that he had held the north gate as long as he could in order to gain time, and that the Arabs were breaking it in. I begged him to order the soldiers to pile up stones as a defence against the bullets and to lie down behind them. This he went to do.

Then, after a pause, we saw a large body of the Arabs who had effected an entry, advancing down the central street towards us. Some of them had spears as well as guns, on which they carried a dozen or so of human heads cut from the Mazitus who had been killed, waving them aloft and shouting in triumph. It was a sickening sight, and one that made me grind my teeth with rage. Also I could not help reflecting that ere long our heads might be upon those spears. Well, if the worst came to the worst I was determined that I would not be taken alive to be burned in a slow fire or pinned over an ant-heap, a point upon which the others agreed with me, though poor Brother John had scruples as to suicide, even in despair.

It was just then that I missed Hans and asked where he had gone. Somebody said that he thought he had seen him running away, whereon Mavovo, who was growing excited, called out:

"Ah! Spotted Snake has sought his hole. Snakes hiss, but they do not charge."

"No, but sometimes they bite," I answered, for I could not believe that Hans had showed the white feather. However, he was gone and clearly we were in no state to send to look for him.

Now our hope was that the slavers, flushed with victory, would advance across the open ground of the market-place, which we could sweep with our fire from our position on the ridge. This, indeed, they began to do, whereon, without orders, the Mazitu to whom we had given the guns, to my fury and dismay, commenced to blaze away at a range of about four hundred yards, and after a good deal of firing managed to kill or wound two or three men. Then the Arabs, seeing their danger, retreated and, after a pause, renewed their advance in two bodies. This time, however, they followed the streets of huts that were built thickly between the outer palisade of the town and the market-place, which, as it had been designed to hold cattle in time of need, was also surrounded with a wooden fence strong enough to resist the rush of horned beasts. On that day, I should add, as the Mazitu never dreamed of being attacked, all their stock were grazing on some distant veldt. In this space between the two fences were many hundreds of huts, wattle and grass built, but for the most part roofed with palm leaves, for here, in their separate quarters, dwelt the great majority of the inhabitants of Beza Town, of which the northern part was occupied by the king, the nobles and the captains. This ring of huts, which entirely surrounded the market-place except at the two gateways, may have been about a hundred and twenty yards in width.

Down the paths between these huts, both on the eastern and the western side, advanced the Arabs and half-breeds, of whom there appeared to be about four hundred, all armed with guns and doubtless trained to fighting. It was a terrible force for us to face, seeing that although we may have had nearly as many men, our guns did not total more than fifty, and most of those who held them were quite unused to the management of firearms.

Soon the Arabs began to open fire on us from behind the huts, and a very accurate fire it was, as our casualties quickly showed, notwithstanding the stone *schanzes* we had constructed. The worst feature of the thing also was that we could not reply with any effect, as our assailants, who gradually worked nearer, were effectively screened by the huts, and we had not enough guns to attempt organised volley firing. Although I tried to keep a cheerful countenance I confess that I began to fear the worst and even to wonder if we could possibly attempt to retreat. This idea was abandoned, however, since the Arabs would certainly overtake and shoot us down.

One thing I did. I persuaded Babemba to send about fifty men to build up the southern gate, which was made of trunks of trees and opened outwards, with earth and the big stones that lay about in plenty. While this was being done quickly, for the Mazitu soldiers worked at the task like demons and, being sheltered by the palisade, could not be shot, all of a sudden I caught sight of four or five wisps of smoke that arose in quick succession at the north end of the town and were instantly followed by as many bursts of flame which leapt towards us in the strong wind.

Someone was firing Beza Town! In less than an hour the flames, driven by the gale through hundreds of huts made dry as tinder by the heat, would reduce Beza to a heap of ashes. It was inevitable, nothing could save the place! For an instant I thought that the Arabs must have done this thing. Then, seeing that new fires continually arose in different places, I understood that no Arabs, but a friend or friends were at work, who had conceived the idea of *destroying the Arabs with fire.*

My mind flew to Sammy. Without doubt Sammy had stayed behind to carry out this terrible and masterly scheme, of which I am sure none of the Mazitu would have thought, since it involved the absolute destruction of their homes and property. Sammy, at whom we had always mocked, was, after all, a great man, prepared to perish in the flames in order to save his friends!

Babemba rushed up, pointing with a spear to the rising fire. Now my inspiration came.

"Take all your men," I said, "except those who are armed with guns. Divide them, encircle the town, guard the north gate, though I think none can win back through the flames, and if any of the Arabs succeed in breaking through the palisade, kill them."

"It shall be done," shouted Babemba, "but oh! for the town of Beza where I was born! Oh! for the town of Beza!"

"Drat the town of Beza!" I shouted after him, or rather its native equivalent. "It is of all our lives that I'm thinking."

Three minutes later the Mazitu, divided into two bodies, were running like hares to encircle the town, and though a few were shot as they descended the slope, the most of them gained the shelter of the palisade in safety, and there at intervals halted by sections, for Babemba managed the matter very well.

Now only we white people, with the Zulu hunters under Mavovo, of whom there were twelve in all, and the Mazitu armed with guns, numbering about thirty, were left upon the slope.

For a little while the Arabs did not seem to realise what had happened, but engaged themselves in peppering at the Mazitu, who, I think, they concluded were in full flight. Presently, however, they either heard or saw.

Oh! what a hubbub ensued. All the four hundred of them began to shout at once. Some of them ran to the palisade and began to climb it, but as they reached the top of the fence were pinned by the Mazitu arrows and fell backwards, while a few who got over became entangled in the prickly pears on the further side and were promptly speared. Giving up this attempt, they rushed back along the lane with the intention of escaping at the north-gate. But before ever they reached the head of the market-place the roaring, wind-swept flames, leaping from hut to hut, had barred their path. They could not face that awful furnace.

Now they took another counsel and in a great confused body charged down the market-place to break out at the south gate, and our turn came. How we raked them as they sped across the open, an easy mark! I know that I fired as fast as I could using two rifles, swearing the while at Hans because he was not there to load for me. Stephen was better off in this respect, for, looking round, to my astonishment I saw Hope, who had left her mother on the other side of the hill, in the act of capping his second gun. I should explain that during our stay in Beza Town we had taught her how to use a rifle.

I called to him to send her away, but again she would not go, even after a bullet had pierced her dress.

Still, all our shooting could not stop that rush of men, made desperate by the fear of a fiery death. Leaving many stretched out behind them, the first of the Arabs drew near to the south gate.

"My father," said Mavovo in my ear, "now the real fighting is going to begin. The gate will soon be down. *We* must be the gate."

I nodded, for if the Arabs once got through, there were enough of them left to wipe us out five times over. Indeed, I do not suppose that up to this time they had actually lost more than forty men. A few words explained the situation to Stephen and Brother John, whom I told to take his daughter to her mother and wait there with them. The Mazitu I ordered to throw down their guns, for if they kept these I was sure they would shoot some of us, and to accompany us, bringing their spears only.

Then we rushed down the slope and took up our position in a little open space in front of the gate, that now was tottering to its fall beneath the blows and draggings of the Arabs. At this time the sight was terrible and magnificent, for the flames had got hold of the two half-circles of huts that embraced the market-place, and, fanned by the blast, were rushing towards us like a thing alive. Above us swept a great pall of smoke in which floated flakes of fire, so thick that it hid the sky, though fortunately the wind did not suffer it to sink and choke us. The sounds also were almost inconceivable, for to the crackling roar of the conflagration as it devoured hut after hut, were added the coarse, yelling voices of the half-bred Arabs, as in mingled rage and terror they tore at the gateway or each other, and the reports of the guns which many of them were still firing, half at hazard.

We formed up before the gate, the Zulus with Stephen and myself in front and the thirty picked Mazitu, commanded by no less a person than Bausi, the king, behind. We had not long to wait, for presently down the thing came and over it and the mound of earth and stones we had built beyond, began to pour a mob of white-robed and turbaned men whose mixed and tumultuous exit somehow reminded me of the pips and pulp being squeezed out of a grenadilla fruit.

I gave the word, and we fired into that packed mass with terrible effect. Really I think that each bullet must have brought down two or three of them. Then, at a command from Mavovo, the Zulus threw down their guns and charged with their broad spears. Stephen, who had got hold of an assegai somehow, went with them, firing a Colt's revolver as he ran, while at their backs came Bausi and his thirty tall Mazitu.

I will confess at once that I did not join in this terrific onslaught. I felt that I had not weight enough for a scrimmage of the sort, also that I should perhaps be better employed using my wits outside and watching for a chance to be of service, like a half-back in a football field, than in getting my brains knocked out in a general row. Or mayhap my heart failed me and I was afraid. I dare say, for I have never pretended to great courage. At any rate, I stopped outside and shot whenever I got the chance, not without effect, filling a humble but perhaps a useful part.

It was really magnificent, that fray. How those Zulus did go in. For quite a long while they held the narrow gateway and the mound against all the howling, thrusting mob, much as the Roman called Horatius and his two friends held the entrance to some bridge or other long ago at Rome against a great force of I forget whom. They shouted their Zulu battle-cry of *Laba! Laba!* that of their regiment, I suppose, for most of them were men of about the same age, and stabbed and fought and struggled and went down one by one.

Back the rest of them were swept; then, led by Mavovo, Stephen and Bausi, charged again, reinforced with the thirty Mazitu. Now the tongues of flame met almost over them, the growing fence of prickly pear and cacti withered and crackled, and still they fought on beneath that arch of fire.

Back they were driven again by the mere weight of numbers. I saw Mavovo stab a man and go down. He rose and stabbed another, then fell again for he was hard hit.

Two Arabs rushed to kill him. I shot them both with a right and left, for fortunately my rifle was just reloaded. He rose once more and killed a third man. Stephen came to his support and grappling with an

Arab, dashed his head against the gate-post so that he fell. Old Bausi, panting like a grampus, plunged in with his remaining Mazitu and the combatants became so confused in the dark gloom of the overhanging smoke that I could scarcely tell one from the other. Yet the maddened Arabs were winning, as they must, for how could our small and ever-lessening company stand against their rush?

We were in a little circle now of which somehow I found myself the centre, and they were attacking us on all sides. Stephen got a knock on the head from the butt end of a gun, and tumbled against me, nearly upsetting me. As I recovered myself I looked round in despair.

Now it was that I saw a very welcome sight, namely Hans, yes, the lost Hans himself, with his filthy hat whereof I noticed even then the frayed ostrich feathers were smouldering, hanging by a leather strap at the back of his head. He was shambling along in a sly and silent sort of way, but at a great rate with his mouth open, beckoning over his shoulder, and behind him came about one hundred and fifty Mazitu.

Those Mazitu soon put another complexion upon the affair, for charging with a roar, they drove back the Arabs, who had no space to develop their line, straight into the jaws of that burning hell. A little later the rest of the Mazitu returned with Babemba and finished the job. Only quite a few of the Arabs got out and were captured after they had thrown down their guns. The rest retreated into the centre of the market-place, whither our people followed them. In this crisis the blood of these Mazitu told, and they stuck to the enemy as Zulus themselves would certainly have done.

It was over! Great Heaven! it was over, and we began to count our losses. Four of the Zulus were dead and two others were badly wounded—no, three, including Mavovo. They brought him to me leaning on the shoulder of Babemba and another Mazitu captain. He was a shocking sight, for he was shot in three places, and badly cut and battered as well. He looked at me a little while, breathing heavily, then spoke.

"It was a very good fight, my father," he said. "Of all that I have fought I can remember none better, although I have been in far greater battles, which is well as it is my last. I foreknew it, my father, for though I never told it you, the first death lot that I drew down yonder in Durban was my own. Take back the gun you gave me, my father. You did but lend it me for a little while, as I said to you. Now I go to the Underworld to join the spirits of my ancestors and of those who have fallen at my side in many wars, and of those women who bore my children. I shall have a tale to tell them there, my father, and together we will wait for you—till you, too, die in war!"

Then he lifted up his arm from the neck of Babemba, and saluted me with a loud cry of *Baba! Inkosi!* giving me certain great titles which I will not set down, and having done so sank to the earth.

I sent one of the Mazitu to fetch Brother John, who arrived presently with his wife and daughter. He examined Mavovo and told him straight out that nothing could help him except prayer.

"Make no prayers for me, Dogeetah," said the old heathen; "I have followed my star," (i.e. lived according to my lights) "and am ready to eat the fruit that I have planted. Or if the tree prove barren, then to drink of its sap and sleep."

Waving Brother John aside he beckoned to Stephen.

"O Wazela!" he said, "you fought very well in that fight; if you go on as you have begun in time you will make a warrior of whom the Daughter of the Flower and her children will sing songs after you have come to join me, your friend. Meanwhile, farewell! Take this assegai of mine and clean it not, that the red rust thereon may put you in mind of Mavovo, the old Zulu doctor and captain with whom you stood side by side in the Battle of the Gate, when, as though they were winter grass, the fire burnt up the white-robed thieves of men who could not pass our spears."

Then he waved his hand again, and Stephen stepped aside muttering something, for he and Mavovo had been very intimate and his voice choked in his throat with grief. Now the old Zulu's glazing eye fell upon Hans, who was sneaking about, I think with a view of finding an opportunity of bidding him a last good-bye.

"Ah! Spotted Snake," he cried, "so you have come out of your hole now that the fire has passed it, to eat the burnt frogs in the cinders. It is a pity that you who are so clever should be a coward, since our lord Macumazana needed one to load for him on the hill and would have killed more of the hyenas had you been there."

"Yes, Spotted Snake, it is so," echoed an indignant chorus of the other Zulus, while Stephen and I and even the mild Brother John looked at him reproachfully.

Now Hans, who generally was as patient under affront as a Jew, for once lost his temper. He dashed his hat upon the ground, and danced on it; he spat towards the surviving Zulu hunters; he even vituperated the dying Mavovo.

"O son of a fool!" he said, "you pretend that you can see what is hid from other men, but I tell you that there is a lying spirit in your lips. You called me a coward because I am not big and strong as you were, and cannot hold an ox by the horns, but at least there is more brain in my stomach than in all your head. Where would all of you be now had it not been for poor Spotted Snake the 'coward,' who twice this day has saved every one of you, except those whom the Baas's father, the reverend Predikant, has marked upon the forehead to come and join him in a place that is even hotter and brighter than that burning town?"

Now we looked at Hans, wondering what he meant about saving us twice, and Mavovo said:

"Speak on quickly, O Spotted Snake, for I would hear the end of your story. How did you help us in your hole?"

Hans began to grub about in his pockets, from which finally he produced a match-box wherein there remained but one match.

"With this," he said. "Oh! could none of you see that the men of Hassan had all walked into a trap? Did none of you know that fire burns thatched houses, and that a strong wind drives it fast and far? While you sat there upon the hill with your heads together, like sheep waiting to be killed, I crept away among the bushes and went about my business. I said nothing to any of you, not even to the Baas, lest he should answer me, 'No, Hans, there may be an old woman sick in one of those huts and therefore you must not fire them.' In such matters who does not know that white people are fools, even the best of them, and in fact there were several old women, for I saw them running for the gateway. Well, I crept up by the green fence which I knew would not burn and I came to the north gate. There was an Arab sentry left there to watch.

"He fired at me, look! Well for Hans his mother bore him short"; and he pointed to a hole in the filthy hat. "Then before that Arab could load again, poor coward Hans got his knife into him from behind. Look!" and he produced a big blade, which was such as butchers use, from his belt and showed it to us. "After that it was easy, since fire is a wonderful thing. You make it small and it grows big of itself, like a child, and never gets tired, and is always hungry, and runs fast as a horse. I lit six of them where they would burn quickest. Then I saved the last match, since we have few left, and came through the gate before the fire ate me up; me, its father, me the Sower of the Red Seed!"

We stared at the old Hottentot in admiration, even Mavovo lifted his dying head and stared. But Hans, whose annoyance had now evaporated, went on in a jog-trot mechanical voice:

"As I was returning to find the Baas, if he still lived, the heat of the fire forced me to the high ground to the west of the fence, so that I saw what was happening at the south gate, and that the Arab men must break through there because you who held it were so few. So I ran down to Babemba and the other captains very quickly, telling them there was no need to guard the fence any more, and that they must get to the south gate and help you, since otherwise you would all be killed, and they, too, would be killed afterwards. Babemba listened to me and started sending out messengers to collect the others and we got here just in time. Such is the hole I hid in during the Battle of the Gate, O Mavovo. That is all the story which I pray that you will tell to the Baas's reverend father, the Predikant, presently, for I am sure that it will please him to learn that he did not teach me to be wise and help all men and always to look after the Baas Allan, to no purpose. Still, I am sorry that I wasted so many matches, for where shall we get any more now that the camp is burnt?" and he gazed ruefully at the all but empty box.

Mavovo spoke once more in a slow, gasping voice.

"Never again," he said, addressing Hans, "shall you be called Spotted Snake, O little yellow man who are so great and white of heart. Behold! I give you a new name, by which you shall be known with honour from generation to generation. It is 'Light in Darkness.' It is 'Lord of the Fire.'"

Then he closed his eyes and fell back insensible. Within a few minutes he was dead. But those high names with which he christened Hans with his dying breath, clung to the old Hottentot for all his days. Indeed from that day forward no native would ever have ventured to call him by any other. Among them, far and wide, they became his titles of honour.

The roar of the flames grew less and the tumult within their fiery circle died away. For now the Mazitu were returning from the last fight in the market-place, if fight it could be called, bearing in their arms great bundles of the guns which they had collected from the dead Arabs, most of whom had thrown down their weapons in a last wild effort to escape. But between the spears of the infuriated savages on the one hand and the devouring fire on the other what escape was there for them? The blood-stained wretches who remained in the camps and towns of the slave-traders, along the eastern coast of Africa, or in the Isle of Madagascar, alone could tell how many were lost, since of those who went out from them to make war upon the Mazitu and their white friends, none returned again with the long lines of expected captives. They had gone to their own place, of which sometimes that flaming African city has seemed to me a symbol. They were wicked men indeed, devils stalking the earth in human form, without pity, without shame. Yet I could not help feeling sorry for them at the last, for truly their end was awful.

They brought the prisoners up to us, and among them, his white robe half-burnt off him, I recognised the hideous pock-marked Hassan-ben-Mohammed.

"I received your letter, written a while ago, in which you promised to make us die by fire, and, this morning, I received your message, Hassan," I said, "brought by the wounded lad who escaped from you when you murdered his companions, and to both I sent you an answer. If none reached you, look around, for there is one written large in a tongue that all can read."

The monster, for he was no less, flung himself upon the ground, praying for mercy. Indeed, seeing Mrs. Eversley, he crawled to her and catching hold of her white robe, begged her to intercede for him.

"You made a slave of me after I had nursed you in the spotted sickness," she answered, "and tried to kill my husband for no fault. Through you, Hassan, I have spent all the best years of my life among savages, alone and in despair. Still, for my part, I forgive you, but oh! may I never see your face again."

Then she wrenched herself free from his grasp and went away with her daughter.

"I, too, forgive you, although you murdered my people and for twenty years made my time a torment," said Brother John, who was one of the truest Christians I have ever known. "May God forgive you also"; and he followed his wife and daughter.

Then the old king, Bausi, who had come through that battle with a slight wound, spoke, saying:

"I am glad, Red Thief, that these white people have granted you what you asked—namely, their forgiveness—since the deed is greatly to their honour and causes me and my people to think them even nobler than we did before. But, O murderer of men and woman and trafficker in children, I am judge here, not the white people. Look on your work!" and he pointed first to the lines of Zulu and Mazitu dead, and then to his burning town. "Look and remember the fate you promised to us who have never harmed you. Look! Look! Look! O Hyena of a man!"

At this point I too went away, nor did I ever ask what became of Hassan and his fellow-captives. Moreover, whenever any of the natives or Hans tried to inform me, I bade them hold their tongues.

Epilogue

I have little more to add to this record, which I fear has grown into quite a long book. Or, at any rate, although the setting of it down has amused me during the afternoons and evenings of this endless English winter, now that the spring is come again I seem to have grown weary of writing. Therefore I shall leave what remains untold to the imagination of anyone who chances to read these pages.

* * * * * * * *

We were victorious, and had indeed much cause for gratitude who still lived to look upon the sun. Yet the night that followed the Battle of the Gate was a sad one, at least for me, who felt the death of my friend the foresighted hero, Mavovo, of the bombastic but faithful Sammy, and of my brave hunters more than I can say. Also the old Zulu's prophecy concerning me, that I too should die in battle, weighed upon me, who seemed to have seen enough of such ends in recent days and to desire one more tranquil.

Living here in peaceful England as I do now, with no present prospect of leaving it, it does not appear likely that it will be fulfilled. Yet, after my experience of the divining powers of Mavovo's "Snake"—well, those words of his make me feel uncomfortable. For when all is said and done, who can know the future? Moreover, it is the improbable that generally happens.[1]

Further, the climatic conditions were not conducive to cheerfulness, for shortly after sunset it began to rain and poured for most of the night, which, as we had little shelter, was inconvenient both to us and to all the hundreds of the homeless Mazitu.

---

1. As the readers of *Allan Quatermain* will be aware, this prophecy of the dying Zulu was fulfilled. Mr. Quatermain died at Zuvendis as a result of the wound he received in the battle between the armies of the rival Queens.—*Editor*

However, the rain ceased in due time, and on the following morning the welcome sun shone out of a clear sky. When we had dried and warmed ourselves a little in its rays, someone suggested that we should visit the burned-out town where, except for some smouldering heaps that had been huts, the fire was extinguished by the heavy rain. More from curiosity than for any other reason I consented and accompanied by Bausi, Babemba and many of the Mazitu, all of us, except Brother John, who remained behind to attend to the wounded, climbed over the debris of the south gate and walked through the black ruins of the huts, across the market-place that was strewn with dead, to what had been our own quarters.

These were a melancholy sight, a mere heap of sodden and still smoking ashes. I could have wept when I looked at them, thinking of all the trade goods and stores that were consumed beneath, necessities for the most part, the destruction of which must make our return journey one of great hardship.

Well, there was nothing to be said or done, so after a few minutes of contemplation we turned to continue our walk through what had been the royal quarters to the north gate. Hans, who, I noted, had been ferreting about in his furtive way as though he were looking for something, and I were the last to leave. Suddenly he laid his hand upon my arm and said:

"Baas, listen! I hear a ghost. I think it is the ghost of Sammy asking us to bury him."

"Bosh!" I answered, and then listened as hard as I could.

Now I also seemed to hear something coming from I knew not where, words which were frequently repeated and which seemed to be:

"O Mr. Quatermain, I beg you to be so good as to open the door of this oven."

For a while I thought I must be cracked. However, I called back the others and we all listened. Of a sudden Hans made a pounce, like a terrier does at the run of a mole that he hears working underground, and began to drag, or rather to shovel, at a heap of ashes in front of us, using a bit of wood as they were still too hot for his hands. Then we listened again and this time heard the voice quite clearly coming from the ground.

"Baas," said Hans, "it is Sammy in the corn-pit!"

Now I remembered that such a pit existed in front of the huts which, although empty at the time, was, as is common among the Bantu natives, used to preserve corn that would not immediately be needed. Once I myself went through a very tragic experience in one of these pits, as any who may read the history of my first wife, that I have called *Marie*, can see for themselves.

Soon we cleared the place and had lifted the stone, with ventilating holes in it—well was it for Sammy that those ventilating holes existed; also that the stone did not fit tight. Beneath was a bottle-shaped and cemented structure about ten feet deep by, say, eight wide. Instantly through the mouth of this structure appeared the head of Sammy with his mouth wide open like that of a fish gasping for air. We pulled him out, a process that caused him to howl, for the heat had made his skin very tender, and gave him water which one of the Mazitu fetched from a spring. Then I asked him indignantly what he was doing in that hole, while we wasted our tears, thinking that he was dead.

"Oh! Mr. Quatermain," he said, "I am a victim of too faithful service. To abandon all these valuable possessions of yours to a rapacious enemy was more than I could bear. So I put every one of them in the pit, and then, as I thought I heard someone coming, got in myself and pulled down the stone. But, Mr. Quatermain, soon afterwards the enemy added arson to murder and pillage, and the whole place began to blaze. I could hear the fire roaring above and a little later the ashes covered the exit so that I could no longer lift the stone, which indeed grew too hot to touch. Here, then, I sat all night in the most suffocating heat, very much afraid, Mr. Quatermain, lest the two kegs of gunpowder that were with me should explode, till at last, just as I had abandoned hope and prepared to die like a tortoise baked alive by a bushman, I heard your welcome voice. And Mr. Quatermain, if there is any soothing ointment to spare, I shall be much obliged, for I am scorched all over."

"Ah! Sammy, Sammy," I said, "you see what comes of cowardice? On the hill with us you would not have been scorched, and it is only by the merest chance of owing to Hans's quick hearing that you were not left to perish miserably in that hole."

"That is so, Mr. Quatermain. I plead guilty to the hot impeachment. But on the hill I might have been shot, which is worse than being scorched. Also you gave me charge of your goods and I determined to preserve them even at the risk of personal comfort. Lastly, the angel who watches me brought you here in time before I was quite cooked through. So all's well that ends well, Mr. Quatermain, though it is true that for my part I have had enough of bloody war, and if I live to regain civilized regions I propose henceforth to follow the art of food-dressing in the safe kitchen of an hotel; that is, if I cannot obtain a berth as an instructor in the English tongue!"

"Yes," I answered, "all's well that ends well, Sammy my boy, and at any rate you have saved the stores, for which we should be thankful to you. So go along with Mr. Stephen and get doctored while we haul them out of that grain-pit."

Three days later we bid farewell to old Bausi, who almost wept at parting with us, and the Mazitu, who were already engaged in the re-building of their town. Mavovo and the other Zulus who died in the Battle of the Gate, we buried on the ridge opposite to it, raising a mound of earth over them that thereby they might be remembered in generations to come, and laying around them the Mazitu who had fallen in the fight. As we passed that mound on our homeward journey, the Zulus who remained alive, including two wounded men who were carried in litters, stopped and saluted solemnly, praising the dead with loud songs. We white people too saluted, but in silence, by raising our hats.

By the why, I should add that in this matter also Mavovo's "Snake" did not lie. He had said that six of his company would be killed upon our expedition, and six were killed, neither more nor less.

After much consulting we determined to take the overland route back to Natal, first because it was always possible that the slave-trading fraternity, hearing of their terrible losses, might try to attack us again on the coast, and secondly for the reason that even if they did not, months or perhaps years might pass before we found a ship at Kilwa, then a port of ill repute, to carry us to any civilized place. Moreover, Brother John, who had travelled it, knew the inland road well and had established friendly relations with the tribes through whose country we must pass, till we reached the brothers of Zululand, where I was always welcome. So as the Mazitu furnished us with an escort and plenty of bearers for the first part of the road and, thanks to Sammy's stewardship in the corn-pit, we had ample trade goods left to hire others later on, we made up our minds to risk the longer journey.

As it turned out this was a wise conclusion, since although it took four weary months, in the end we accomplished it without any accident whatsoever, if I except a slight attack of fever from which both Miss Hope and I suffered for a while. Also we got some good shooting on the road. My only regret was that this change of plan obliged us to abandon the tusks of ivory we had captured from the slavers and buried where we alone could find them.

Still, it was a dull time for me, who, for obvious reasons, of which I have already spoken, was literally a fifth wheel to the coach. Hans was an excellent fellow, and, as the reader knows, quite a genius in his own way, but night after night in Hans's society began to pall on me at last, while even his conversation about my "reverend father," who seemed positively to haunt him, acquired a certain sameness. Of course, we had other subjects in common, especially those connected with Retief's massacre, whereof we were the only two survivors, but of these I seldom cared to speak. They were and still remain too painful.

Therefore, for my part I was thankful when at last, in Zululand, we fell in with some traders whom I knew, who hired us one of their wagons. In this vehicle, abandoning the worn-out donkeys and the white ox, which we presented to a chief of my acquaintance, Brother John and the ladies proceeded to Durban, Stephen attending them on a horse that we had bought, while I, with Hans, attached myself to the traders.

At Durban a surprise awaited us since, as we trekked into the town, which at that time was still a small place, whom should we meet but Sir Alexander Somers, who, hearing that wagons were coming from Zululand, had ridden out in the hope of obtaining news of us. It seemed that the choleric old gentleman's anxiety concerning his son had so weighed on his mind that at length he made up his mind to proceed to Africa to hunt for him. So there he was. The meeting between the two was affectionate but peculiar.

"Hullo, dad!" said Stephen. "Whoever would have thought of seeing you here?"

"Hullo, Stephen," said his father. "Whoever would have expected to find you alive and looking well—yes, very well? It is more than you deserve, you young ass, and I hope you won't do it again."

Having delivered himself thus, the old boy seized Stephen by the hair and solemnly kissed him on the brow.

"No, dad," answered his son, "I don't mean to do it again, but thanks to Allan there we've come through all right. And, by the way, let me introduce you to the lady I am going to marry, also to her father and mother."

Well, all the rest may be imagined. They were married a fortnight later in Durban and a very pleasant affair it was, since Sir Alexander, who by the way, treated me most handsomely from a business point of view, literally entertained the whole town on that festive occasion. Immediately afterwards Stephen, accompanied by Mr. and Mrs. Eversley and his father, took his wife home "to be educated," though what that process consisted of I never heard. Hans and I saw them off at the Point and our parting was rather sad, although Hans went back the richer by the £500 which Stephen had promised him. He bought a farm with the money, and on the strength of his exploits, established himself as a kind of little chief. Of whom more later—as they say in the pedigree books.

Sammy, too, was set up as the proprietor of a small hotel, where he spent most of his time in the bar dilating to the customers in magnificent sentences that reminded me of the style of a poem called "The Essay on Man" (which I once tried to read and couldn't), about his feats as a warrior among the wild Mazitu and the man-eating, devil-worshipping Pongo tribes.

Two years or less afterwards I received a letter, from which I must quote a passage:

"As I told you, my father has given a living which he owns to Mr. Eversley, a pretty little place where there isn't much for a parson to do. I think it rather bores my respected parents-in-law. At any rate, Dogeetah spends a lot of his time wandering about the New Forest, which is near by, with a butterfly-net and trying to imagine that he is back in Africa. The Mother of the Flower (who, after a long course of boot-kissing mutes, doesn't get on with English servants) has another amusement. There is a small lake in the Rectory grounds in which is a little island. Here she has put up a reed fence round a laurustinus bush which flowers at the same time of year as did the Holy Flower, and within this reed fence she sits whenever the weather will allow, as I believe going through 'the rites of the Flower.' At least when I called upon her there one day, in a boat, I found her wearing a white robe and singing some mystical native song."

Many years have gone by since then. Both Brother John and his wife have departed to their rest and their strange story, the strangest almost of all stories, is practically forgotten. Stephen, whose father has also departed, is a prosperous baronet and rather heavy member of Parliament and magistrate, the father of many fine children, for the Miss Hope of old days has proved as fruitful as a daughter of the Goddess of Fertility, for that was the "Mother's" real office, ought to be.

"Sometimes," she said to me one day with a laugh, as she surveyed a large (and noisy) selection of her numerous offspring, "sometimes, O Allan"—she still retains that trick of speech—"I wish that I were back in the peace of the Home of the Flower. Ah!" she added with something of a thrill in her voice, "never can I forget the blue of the sacred lake or the sight of those skies at dawn. Do you think that I shall see them again when I die, O Allan?"

At the time I thought it rather ungrateful of her to speak thus, but after all human nature is a queer thing and we are all of us attached to the scenes of our childhood and long at times again to breathe our natal air.

I went to see Sir Stephen the other day, and in his splendid greenhouses the head gardener, Woodden, an old man now, showed me three noble, long-leaved plants which sprang from the seed of the Holy Flower that I had saved in my pocket.

But they have not yet bloomed.

Somehow I wonder what will happen when they do. It seems to me as though when once more the glory of that golden bloom is seen of the eyes of men, the ghosts of the terrible god of the Forest, of the hellish and mysterious *Motombo*, and perhaps of the Mother of the Flower herself, will be there to do it reverence. If so, what gifts will they bring to those who stole and reared the sacred seed?

> P.S.—I shall know ere long, for just as I laid down my pen a triumphant epistle from Stephen was handed to me in which he writes excitedly that at length two of the three plants are *showing for flower.*
>
> *Allan Quatermain*

ALSO FROM LEONAUR

AVAILABLE IN SOFTCOVER OR HARDCOVER WITH DUST JACKET

TROS OF SAMOTHRACE 1: WOLVES OF THE TIBER *by Talbot Mundy*—When his ship is taken and his crew slaughtered Tros of Samothrace is captured by Imperial Rome.

TROS OF SAMOTHRACE 2: DRAGONS OF THE NORTH *by Talbot Mundy*—Tros of Samothrace burns for vengeance and has declared himself the implacable enemy of Rome.

TROS OF SAMOTHRACE 3: SERPENT OF THE WAVES *by Talbot Mundy*—Tros, his allies and the forces of Rome have drawn apart to prepare for the conflict to come.

TROS OF SAMOTHRACE 4: CITY OF THE EAGLES *by Talbot Mundy*—As Tros of Samothrace continues in his attempts to confound Caesar's plans for the invasion of Britain, he journeys to the Eternal City to seek the aid of its great leaders—and Caesar's opponents—Cato, Pompey and the Vestal Virgins themselves!

TROS OF SAMOTHRACE 5: CLEOPATRA *by Talbot Mundy*—Cleopatra—Queen of Egypt—is a formidable character ever ready to play the game of intrigue, betrayal and shifting loyalties to suit her own objectives. Blood will surely be spilt and once again Tros finds himself inexorably caught up in monumental events that threaten his life and those he loves.

TROS OF SAMOTHRACE 6: THE PURPLE PIRATE *by Talbot Mundy*—The epic saga of the ancient world—Tros of Samothrace—draws to a conclusion in this sixth—and final—volume. Julius Caesar has been assassinated and Queen Cleopatra of Egypt finds herself in a perilous position and desperate for allies to secure her power.

THE ILLUSTRATED & COMPLETE BRIGADIER GERARD *by Sir Arthur Conan Doyle*—These are the adventures of Conan Doyle's incomparable French hero-the finest swordsman in the Light Cavalry-Etienne Gerard. Arranged for the first time in historical chronological order, his many enthusiasts can now properly appreciate his colourful career as he fights, loves and blunders his way through the Napoleonic epoch-from his earliest adventure as a young blade determined to reach his lady love despite the unwelcome attention of her fathers bull-through many campaigns and special missions-to the bloody field of Waterloo, the downfall of his beloved Emperor and beyond. This is the complete collection of these classic stories. What makes this edition exceptional is the inclusion of nearly 140 illustrations-mostly by the famed military artist William Barnes Wollen-which accurately portray the spirit of the stories and the uniforms and scenes of the events they portray.

AVAILABLE ONLINE AT
www.leonaur.com
AND OTHER GOOD BOOK STORES

www.ingramcontent.com/pod-product-compliance
Lightning Source LLC
LaVergne TN
LVHW050912080826
845145LV00001B/62